JANUS

RETICERE SERIES
BOOK 3

LAUREN LOGAN

COPYRIGHT

Artwork: Zack Simpson
Instagram @Zachariah.C.Sampson
Front Cover Design: Allen Wahlström
Instagram @Bafacoach.W
www.asenzathletic.myportfolio.com

Editor: Beth Sullivan
BSullivanEdPro@gmail.com

Writing Assistant: Kathy Hunter

Change is coming.

LATIN

TRANSLATIONS BY AMANDA FOX

This work includes Latin dialog which is written within quotations and formatted in *italics*. Any Latin dialog will be directly followed or preceded by the English translation.

Please note: Long dialog segments written in Latin will only include the first and last sentence to avoid pulling readers from the story.

CONTENT WARNING

Trigger and content warnings for Janus are listed on
www.authorlaurenlogan.com

Janus is strictly from mature readers of 18+

Please protect your mental health.

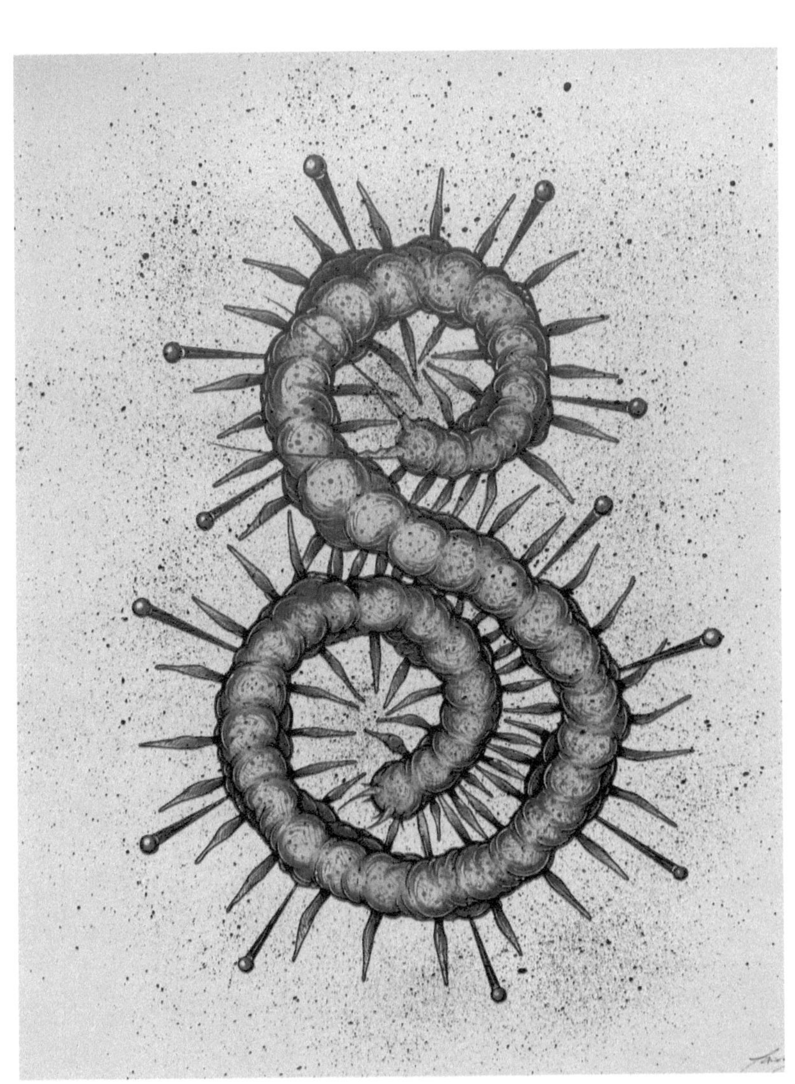

"*Tressa!*" the old woman demanded from the back bedroom of the tiny apartment.

Her voice sounded like the motorbikes the couriers use, and Tressa could hear the wet smack of the old woman's toothless mouth as she tried to swallow. The scent of the sizzling sausage hit her nose, and she inhaled the delicious aroma. She had already eaten her rations for the day, so she ignored her aching stomach. It was only grandmother's breakfast cooking in a dented pan over one of the two burners they had on the stove. Only three people could even stand in the kitchen. The apartment wasn't much roomier. She rolled her hazel eyes and, with feigned effort, hollered back, I'll be right there! I'm making your breakfast. If I walk away, it will burn, and we can't afford to replace it. *"Ero ibi! Ientaculum tuum facio. Si desero, uret et res nostri non suppetit ad repositum."*

Tressa could hear the cheap scratchy covers shifting around on the bed when she poked her head around the corner to check on her grandmother. The sound made her cringe. They were the same covers they'd had for the last twenty years. She hated them. When Nan did not answer, Tressa leaned back toward the burners to check the sausage.

After grumbling something incoherent, Nan croaked, Liar! You little bitch. You're in there stealing. *"Mendax! Tu canicula. Surripes ibi."*

Staring at the empty shelf in the open cabinet with crumbs along the edge, Tressa yelled back, If I were going to steal, I would go where they had food in their box! *"Si ut surripeam, iero ubi cibum habuerunt in cellam penariam."* Under her breath, Tressa fumed, That woman is going to make me snap. When I do? I'm sure I'll end up on the daily patrol arrest lists. I'm also sure my ass will end up shipped off to the prison planet. *"Illa femina itum est facere insolentem. Et quando? Scio evadabo in cotidie prehensiones numeros. Etiam scio asinum evadabo mitterendum est ad planetam carceris."* Sometimes talking to herself was the only way she could make it through the days with Nan.

Fuck you! *"Futue te ipsum!"* Nan cried out as something fell off the nightstand while she rustled around in the bed.

Tressa knew the routine. Nan was glaring at the covers and sneering as she yanked at them. The woman was a raging bitch. Not one day in her long life had that woman ever been kind. Many years ago, her Nan's father dumped her on Emendo with her guard, who also happened to be their grandfather. Her grandmother was the daughter of a rich man on Melior. When she fell for what her father called the *wrong man,* a member of the guard and not a member of their social circle, he was beyond upset. After the birth of Tressa's mother when her grandmother was only seventeen, he was furious and disowned her.

Her grandfather, Pop, was mostly silent as Nan would

have her rampages. They were often and usually unprovoked. Pop loved her though, no matter what.

Other than her Nan's anger problems, her grandparents worked hard and created a decent life with their mom. Pop passed away when a transport hit him. He died instantly, but no one ever notified them. Her mom saw a video clip of the incident on a news screen inside the market. She recognized her father, and it took years before she could sleep again.

When Tressa's mother had fallen pregnant for the first time at eighteen, Nan was disappointed, raged, but eventually understood. Cinnis, Tressa's older sibling, was Nan's favorite. When their mom found out she was expecting a year later with Tressa, that was when Nan turned truly bitter. She had never been kind, but when Tressa was born, she was not sure her Nan ever smiled again.

Tressa looked down at her own protruding belly smashed up against the counter and wondered about the little shit inside of her who would be handed off to a rich couple wanting a custom baby. She didn't care and tried to ignore it. She dumped the overcooked sausage onto a plate and slid the egg onto the other side. The yolk ripped as it slid on the plate, and she hoped she could slip out of the apartment before Nan noticed it. When Tressa sat the plate down, it clinked against the cheap plastic table. Pale yellow yolk pooled from under the egg.

"*Audio te! Noli abdere ab me!*" I hear you! You can't hide from me! Nan seethed and coughed from the over-exertion. Tressa closed her eyes and took a slow breath. Visions of clouds and a bright star filled her mind. She was soaring through the sky as the cool air slid across her skin. She was free. Nan's hacking trailed off as Tressa's daydream crashed back to reality. She had never lashed out at Nan, and she would not start now.

The light poured into the small room from the tiny window from the large video screen on the opposite building, and she could already tell the Empress was making an announcement. Her videos were always too bright.

At that moment, she missed her mother. Tressa and Cinis's mother died of cancer many years before when Tressa was only six. It was caught early, but they couldn't afford the necessary treatment. Nan even sought out to her father who was still alive. He wouldn't even respond to the distress message.

Everyone on Emendo knew several people who had cancer at any given time. Very few affordable treatments existed. An aristocratic map collector from Melior owned forever patents for a number of functional cures, but she regulated the price of the infusions. It was a single dose treatment working in a matter of days for not only cancer, but there were also many other formulas to treat diseases of the immune system. No one had ever hacked the pharmaceutical company's computer system and lived long enough to disperse the formula.

Wringing her aching hands, she walked back to retrieve her furious Nan. She dreaded this part.

"Canicula. Pono tuum sordidum siculam est ingens andronis nunc," Little bitch. I bet your dirty cock trap is the size of a hallway by now, she prodded as Tressa tossed back the covers and reached her hands out, ignoring what Nan said. Her self-esteem would be crushed underfoot in the street if she ever listened to her Nan. She forced herself to ignore the abuse, but it wasn't always easy.

After a moment of blinding pain in her hands, she

guided her Nan to her wheelchair. With her now seated, Tressa wearily took the handles, wheeled her down the hall, and parked her at the table. The moment she lifted her hands she ran into the kitchen to run them under cool water. They were throbbing. Something was wrong with her. Sometimes it was her hands, sometimes her feet. Sighing, she pushed the pain aside and spoke over her shoulder to her Nan, I need to pick up some things at the market on the street. "*Volo tollere aliquas res ad macellum in viam.*"

"*Extendesne pedes tui iam. Esne tamen gravidum?*" Oh, going to spread your legs already? Aren't you still pregnant? Nan simmered as she narrowed her beady green eyes. Tressa sighed and wondered if her Nan understood what a surrogate was and didn't care, or if she really thought she had gotten herself pregnant over and over on accident. Either way, no one should be shaming her.

She could hear Nan belch like she had a giant Vidar tree frog inside of her and complained, These eggs taste like shit. You broke the yolk. How hard is it not to break the yolk? "*Hi ovi faecam sunt. Franges vitellum. Quomodo est difficile factu non franget vitellum?*"

Sinking her head with her eyes squeezed shut, she shook it off and headed to the door. Looking back, she apologized, Sorry, Nan. I'll be back in a few minutes. "*Ignosce, Nan. Ero retro aliquot memento temporis.*"

Closing the door and locking it behind her, she walked down the long hallway to the lift. The smell of vomit enveloped the hallway, so she held her breath and ran by where the floor looked wet. Once inside the lift she took a deep breath and gagged at the hint of the scent still lingering in the air. She hoped they weren't sick with some kind of virus. She had already used up most of her medical allowance for the year, and she couldn't get pregnant again for six more months. If she became sick, she would have to tough it out.

Looking down at her growing belly, she sighed and shuddered thinking about the delivery. She could feel all the scars from previous surgeries running across her belly and hoped this birth wouldn't leave a new one. The lift door opened leading to the front doors, and she walked around to the side of the building.

The wall shifted and a form emerged from nothingness. A blue and grey skinned Vultus and his gyroscopic eyes focused on her as he slid his tongue out and snatched a water bug from the sidewalk next to her foot. She shivered as she passed by, watching him winding his tail up as he swallowed the bug. As he neared her, he stopped and leaned his body to the side, pivoting on his ankles. When his head was finally close to hers, he cleared his throat softly. The price went up on pasta. Lady two spots down on the right doesn't know it yet. Hurry over. *"Pretium collyrae subivit. Femina duo de maculae in dextra nescit adhuc. Matura,"* he offered quietly to her under his breath, far too close for comfort. As soon as she saw him shift his weight, he disappeared. He must have changed his colors.

The Vultus had been brought to Emendo when they were told about the insect problem. They have color adaptive skin, long sticky tongues, and can crawl on the sides of buildings to reach some of the nesting bugs. They have no desire to do anything else. They were also, as an entire species, the biggest gossipers she had ever encountered. The Vultus would seemingly appear out of nowhere and lean in to repeat a bit of gossip. She was just glad they only mated interspecies, for she had heard horror stories about what was happening in their pants.

Shivering, she headed to the second table to the right and sure enough, the pasta was underpriced. After grabbing a bag of long, thin noodles, she leaned into whisper to the lady her prices were too low but Tressa halted when she saw the Vultus man shift color behind the vendor. He was glaring at her.

Snapping her mouth shut, she paid and cowered. She wasn't doing that again. Who knew what the guy would do if she told his gossip to the very subject of the juicy information. She heard about the Vultus war with the Corvus and the Iris. She wanted nothing to do with one of their people. Anything which could best an Iris or a Corvus was a hard no in her book.

Heading to another table, she picked a few other things and headed back to her apartment. As she turned the corner, she landed in the dark tan hairy chest of a large Resper man. He fluttered his wings and hissed at her before he looked down to see she was pregnant. He was towering with short black hair and seemingly solid onyx irises. His striking face was eerie as he leaned in towards her. His species, the Resper, had vertical ridges under their ears as well as above a slightly upturned nose. His tall, pointed ears twitched, and she watched him carefully as he shifted his weight. He stopped and widened his eyes at her. He sniffed the air and smiled softly as he crooned, Why hello, beautiful. You smell delightful. *"Cur salve pulcher. Oles suaviter."*

She ran as quickly as she could for the doors, the sounds of her beating heart pounding in her ears, but still, she could still feel his eyes following her.

1

PLANET PORTUM - UTC COMMAND MISSION

"Looks like we have company," Zoe wearily announced as she studied the sonar image on the holo-screen from her position in the captain's seat of the watercraft. Reaching down, she gripped the throttle and eyed the controls, calculating her next move. Amelia and Oz simultaneously turned their attention to the underwater radar. They rose from their seats to see what Zoe's definition of company was.

"Company?!" All Oz could fathom was, *run*.

Deep under the water, and approaching rapidly, was a massive form that couldn't be identified on the three-dimensional sonar. Tentacles massive enough their boats could fit in side-by-side swiftly slid by the screen. From the look of it, it was swimming toward the surface. With her hands a blur, Zoe selected a few options on the screen and slammed the throttle down. The boat launched forward and continued to pick up speed, but the creature was closing in on them. The tip of the tentacle jutted out on the side of the sonar screen as it ascended from the deep, revealing its position as it grew nearer. It was not far from the surface, and it had only been a matter of seconds.

Oz turned to face the team and forced his voice to carry over the churning sea. "Helmet's on; we might get a little shook up."

Jael and Aurelia looked to one another nervously before they each slipped on their sleek-black helmets. Amelia had just pulled hers over her head when the arm of the octopus came from the depths of the sea and wrapped around the boat's shields. The milky white underside of the arm was wide enough to wrap around the bubble of the shields. They watched in horror as the suction cups pulsed all around, desperate to take purchase. The rusty color of the top of the tentacle shifted in the light to lavender spots and grey flesh. It forced the boat partially under the surface, but the buoyancy sent it flying back up. The jarring action sent everyone in the boat tumbling into one another. No one had a chance, even those holding on.

When it happened again, the force was so great, the boat within the surrounding shields dunked completely under the surface of the water. It went soaring up from under the massive arm lined with suckers, sending everyone careening into the air. Still tangled together, they all grunted as their bodies hammered into the deck of the vessel on their descent. Three-foot-wide suckers tried to grasp onto the boat's shields above them, but its efforts were fruitless. Each time, the gargantuan arm went sliding back into the depths without the meal it was seeking.

After a small window of reprieve, Jael climbed off Mercy, who had landed on top of Carter. Amelia was tangled in a heap with Zoe and Oz. Aurelia and Lark had grasped one another and were pinned under Dion and Wynn, two younger men from the mountains. Everyone groaned and scrambled to grab the handles mounted on the sides of the boat. When Oz leaped over the chaos to reach the steering wheel, he checked the sonar. With distress behind his voice, he yelled, "Oh fuck!" as he slammed his hand down on the throttle. Zoe latched onto Oz's arm and hoisted herself up as Amelia jumped to the side of the boat, seeking a handle.

The octopus arm came from below, and the boat went soaring much farther from its grasp. It landed with a massive splash. They were all lucky someone had thought of stabilizers in the boat's design phase, or it would have been a painfully short mission. This time, Oz had planted his hands on the wheel and didn't let go as the boat was jolted forward. When he landed on his feet, he cried out, "Hang on!" He checked back to make sure everyone had held on and then slammed the throttle all the way down.

The enclosed hover-engines propelled the boat at breakneck speeds, gliding over the top of the wave from inside the shields. Everyone in the boat lifted in the air as the boat flew, but no one let go of their handles this time. The force made it nearly impossible to hang on, but they knew it was hang on or risk injury or death.

Jael strained her neck and looked to the front of the boat and saw Hazel and Harlen, siblings, with their arms wrapped around one another along and their team member Thorn, who must have been knocked out in the chaos. She wasn't sure of the names of the three soldiers, but they each had ahold of their handles and were frantically searching the area, trying to see who needed help. If they were pummeled again, they could easily lose grip of all of them. One more hit to the head for Thorn, and his brain could be too far gone for his body to repair.

Zoe took back the wheel, and Oz stepped over and grabbed the closest handle to him. He sighed in relief looking down at the sonar depth and gauges noting they were in much more shallow water. He hoped they had escaped the giant octopus. Fortunately, checking the sonar screen just in time, Oz screamed, "HOLD ON!"

The octopus had not given up and had two colossal arms already outstretched over them. The arms slammed down onto the boat in a great crash. The shields held strong, which caused the boat to be squeezed up between the two closing arms of the beast, sending it flying forward far too fast. The boat launched onward into shallow water, and everyone slammed into one another again. Groans echoed in response.

Zoe fought to keep control of the helm. When they landed, she braced her feet and slapped the throttle back. The last thing she wanted to do is burn up a good boat engine by grounding it too far inland, even if they were ditching it. She was sure Carter or Jacob had some plan for it to be retrieved and reused later.

Oz stood up and looked back. The disturbing sensation of a predator turned prey dissipated as he scanned the water for the creature. He saw nothing but calm waters behind them as they glided over the sea toward the snow-covered mountains. Taking a deep breath, he slipped his helmet off and watched as the octopus took one last angry slap at the water. It was too far off to do anything but send a few promising waves their way, and everyone on the boat hesitantly began pulling off their helmets.

Aurelia leaned over to Carter in a panic and asked, What the fuck was that? *"Futus est ille?"*

Carter chuckled as he answered, We have some interesting things living on this world. *"Habemus res iucundos habitant in mundo."*

Eyes nearly bulging out of their sockets, she raved, That was a lot more than just interesting. I had no idea this trip would include sea monsters. The last time I heard such things was when I was a child in tales of epic odyssey and adventure, to make us behave. Now that I know they're real, I may never sleep again. *"Ille fuit plus quam iucundos... Nunc scio veros sunt, non dormiebam rursus."*

Oz slid a bit of hair behind his ear and offered, I'm sure we will meet a few more monsters in the mountains. Who knows what vile things live there? *"Ego certus conveniam paucos plus monstra in monte. Quis scit quem vilem res habitant illuc?"*

Jael gave Oz an odd look, and he translated, "We are talking about the giant octopus and mountain monsters."

"Ah, thank you for that. I wish I could learn Latin. I feel like it will take forever. I wish I could just download it like you can," Jael spoke louder than usual, and she checked to see if Amelia was listening.

Amelia was busy with her four-square breathing and trying to regain her wits as Mercy held her hand seeming to be fairly distressed as well. She wasn't sure which one of the two was more rattled. Jael would revisit the language issue later, for now she needed to support her friends. The fact that she made it through the octopus incident without being rattled was not lost on her though. Who knew a near death experience with a giant octopi wouldn't freak her out.

They eventually reached the shore, and Zoe ran the boat up into just a few feet of water. She beached it as close to the sand as she could without completely grounding. Pike told her not to do that but didn't elaborate. The sand was different, darker, from the beach they left behind, a shimmery charcoal when dry and shiny onyx when it was wet. Under the hue of the Aura's above, it gleamed where the water had touched it.

"Is this far enough, or should I keep going? How far do you think the tidal wave will reach?" Zoe threw over her shoulder at Oz.

"This is fine. I think Pike may have a plan to move it back to base," he replied, busy evaluating the ship and his team for damages.

"Everyone get ready for the drop. I'm turning off the airtight shields," Zoe announced as she pushed the button and grabbed the helm for balance.

The boat dropped about a foot and then rocked a few times side to side before it came to a stop. As it rocked back and forth, the sides of the metal boat ground against the sand under the shallow water. The air smelled of salt and rotting fish or something else putrid.

They all slowly and wearily climbed out of the shining silver boat, splashing as their boots searched for the sand under the water. Thorn was last to climb out since he had lost consciousness during the octopus attack. Harlen and Hazel supported either side of him. Amelia walked over and checked his eyes before muttering something about a lucky bastard when they discussed him hitting his head on the side of the boat. He hadn't put his helmet on in time. Thankfully Harlen had plucked it from the air and slipped it on his unconscious body. He looked to have a large lump forming on his forehead and still seemed unsteady.

As her legs felt the current of the sea water wash in and out, Jael grabbed her backpack from Oz and slipped it on.

With his usual poise, he hoisted his up and tightened the straps. Once everyone in the group was ready, they started walking towards the middle of two giant mountains. Jael had never seen the Rocky Mountains but assumed these were about that size, if not bigger. She reached up and lay her fingers over the tip of her chilly nose. She looked over at Oz and complained, "I hope the armor is warm enough. My nose is already numb." Sliding one arm out of the straps, he pulled his pack over to one side and reached around for a pocket. Slipping his hand in and pulling out two thick hats, he passed her one. She grinned as she took it from him, "You even thought of warm hats." She patted the outside of the cozy hat with her hands after tucking her hair in the sides.

"I hate the cold," Oz whispered back, his breathe now forming a cloud in the frigid air.

It had dropped several degrees in temperature since they had left the base and crossed the sea. The chill was just beginning to settle in, and the Iungo all seemed to be a little agitated, all except Mercy. She seemed to have a motor deep within, one burning tirelessly. It was rare to find a moment where she wasn't moving. She sauntered up in her sassy Mercy way to stand next to Jael and leaned in, "I think the tents sleep five. Do you and Oz want to share with Amelia and me? I think Lark wants to stay with us as well."

Oz turned and smiled as he replied, "Sure, Mercy, I think that works great."

Jael grinned at her with pride. After losing August and Luna, she didn't know how Mercy would be able to function. She lost her best friend and the man she loved all at once. There was still a twinkle of pain behind her eyes, but she was trying.

Mercy was doing her best to stay positive, but the relationship with August was now a forever *what if.* She never had a chance to tell him how she felt. She didn't ever learn how he felt. It was over before it really began. The first few days she unconvincingly told herself it was all just a trick and he would be back any minute, fighting his way back to her, against all odds. She wasn't sure what her mind or heart would make up next. Dread filled her knowing where her grief inevitably led her. However, reality sunk in, and the longer she waited to face the truth, the worse she felt. A whisper of anger began as her mind echoed the words, *August is gone, and he isn't coming back.*

He had been sent to a hell planet in Aurelia's home system. It could be years before she may see him again if she ever did. She hadn't heard any more than hell planet about Aduro, but she could imagine what it was like. Emendo sounded worse than her own planet before her people had reclaimed it. Silence was true hell from her perspective, but forced labor for inferior lodging and minimal rations was far worse. She cringed thinking of what he could be living through while she stewed over how badly she missed him.

Her people helped one another. No one ever went hungry or without a home. There was another side though, one she loathed with all her being. What a clear picture pain paints. Her customs were beginning to make a lot more sense. The anguish of her loss didn't change, but she now understood why her people moved on so quickly, with unbearable certainty. According to their customs, she was no longer in a relationship. It ended the moment he was taken. She guessed this was a practice dated back since the beginning of her people disappearing. They had to make themselves move on without delay when someone was ripped away. No matter how deep the cut is, as a people, they had to learn how to sew themselves back up before the cut festered.

They had to build new relationships and friendships when someone was taken. There was a need for the ability to build meaningful relationships quickly. In their skewed perception, it was critical to their survival as a species. Their numbers would dwindle if they didn't. They would lose hope too deeply, allow it to change them. Learned hopelessness meant the end for all, so everything had to be done to fight it. None of her people ever had many friends or serious relationships. It was just too hard to have lots of friends when they had to hide how they communicated. They always felt so far away, no matter how close they were, and the risk of a broken heart was just more than most wanted to bear.

Mercy peered over at Amelia, to see concern in her gaze. She must have had an odd look on her face while she found herself lost in thought. Mercy gave her a small smile, but it quickly faded when she heard a crunch under her boot. She lifted her sandy boot to see what she stepped on, and it was a massive snail. The tendrils of the goo lengthened as she raised her foot. Looking closely at her sole, she noticed a sizzle and a bit of steam wafting up on the edge where the slime trail had made contact with it. She leaned in and discovered the scent was horrendous. She gagged and tiptoed away from the smashed snail.

Amelia surveyed the ground all around, realizing what Mercy had stepped on, and warned the group, "Watch out for all the snails. They are covering the ground up to the edge of the snow ahead. Don't step on the snail trail. It's corrosive and smells like burned chemicals."

Jael heard Amelia right as she stepped on one. The snail

crunched under her foot, and the snail's insides trailed behind her for a few steps with a piece stuck to her boot. Since she hadn't avoided the slime trail either, her sole was sizzling. She stomped her boots against the packed sand, and the burning rubber scented steam eventually stopped wafting up.

As Oz noticed the snails were all moving in one direction along the beach, he slipped his tablet out of his bag and dialed Jacob. Not wasting any time, Oz asked, "Jacob, can you check the shore where we landed and see why the hell all these snails are going in a similar direction along the beach?"

"Uh, sure," Jacob answered as he clicked on a few options on his viewscreen, which was just out of sight. Jacob snarled his lip but didn't look up as he explained, "Looks like something dead just washed up on the shore. It resembles a lobster from Jael's world, but much smaller limbs and a slimmer tail fin. It's at least seventy, maybe a hundred feet long, with a chunk out of its side missing. I'm sure the snails are heading to the body. Just hope the wind doesn't pick up, because if it does, I'm sure you will be able to smell it."

Oz deadpanned him, "I'm glad we have the helmets."

"I don't envy you and this journey," Jacob replied with little emotion in his eyes.

Smiling sarcastically with his eyes narrowed and lip snarled, Oz snapped, "Thanks asshole." Laughing, Jacob hung up the holo-call. Oz put his tablet back in his bag, slipping it in a side pocket. They carried on, avoiding the snails as their boots crunched against the ground which had become more of a thin gravel as they moved further inland. It transitioned into patches of mixed dirt and snow. When they reached the line of solid snow, and since none of them had ever seen the substance before, none stepped foot into it right away except for Jael.

She turned around to the team and asked, "Well? What are you waiting for?" She quickly swooped up a handful, formed a snowball, and launched it at Oz. In shock, he didn't immediately respond, just stared at the frozen mess on his chest before he made his own snowball. Snowballs filled the air as the team members shouted and laughed.

2

PLANET ADURO – MINE 03

Jerking up in a sweat-slicked fright, August sucked in a deep breath of hot-dry air. After wiping the sleep from his eyes, he blinked until the blur faded and he could make out more than just dark looming forms. In front of him were several of his kind, all dressed in ragged clothes, dirty, barefoot, and clearly malnourished. His gut twisted, and he filled with sorrow. How had this nightmare been going on for thousands of years?

He ran his hand over his unbraided hair, which had been tied back with a small band. The clothes he woke in were itchy and uncomfortable - unlike the clothes he wore back in his old village before Jael's arrival. The magnitude of the situation weighed heavily on him as he took in the harsh conditions of the room before looking back at the small, gathered group. They were all staring at him incredulously.

Why were they looking at him like that?

He looked around swiftly and found he was in a large cavern with ruddy stone walls. Hundreds of rusty metal bunk beds filled the room in organized rows. Their slightly bent shapes made him wonder how old they were.

How long had he been out?

As he looked down, he cringed as he saw his fingertips. The black char was flaking off where his filed claws once were. His nail beds had all been cauterized, on his hands and his feet. August wiggled his aching toes in the dirt under his bare feet, and he quietly mourned, missing his old boots. His ankles were still dark with bruising so he couldn't have been out for too long. A few days at the most.

He rubbed his wrists where the straps had ripped his skin. His red skin was black with scabs where he had fought the restraints. His breath quickened and his heart pounded. He clenched his jaw as he could feel the cold touch of that venomous human as she leaned on the table while she slipped the cauterizing device over his hand. Her icy blue eyes were carved into his memory. He shook as he boiled with rage, fists clenched.

Blinking and realizing he still had an audience, he took a deep breath and grabbed the side of the bed. He needed answers. Now. He reached out and tried to grasp the hand of a light beige woman, but she threw her hand up and bounced back. They all acted like he had committed some heinous crime. They all leaned away, each one taking a step backward. He couldn't help but wonder why no one would connect with him and tell him what was going on. It wasn't like the guards would know what they were doing, or would they?

As his head cleared, he noticed his increasingly dry mouth. Noting everyone else's crusted mouths, he decided he better get used to it. He ran his dry, rough tongue along his now smoothed teeth. He wished he could rid himself of the memory of them grinding down his fangs. The nauseating grinding sound rang in his ears before he could stop the memory from surfacing. He snapped his eyes shut and felt for the solidity of the ground with his feet. He begged his body and mind to calm. The sound of the grinder slowly faded.

He was afraid those memories would take him to a dark place no matter what he did about it. He missed his sharp fangs. He looked behind him and peered at his clipped tail. Touching the black-charred cauterized end, he hissed. It was still as raw as the memory.

He had never felt so defenseless.

Defenseless and alone.

Standing up and walking through the parting crowd which had formed, he slowly and carefully walked from one end of the cavern to the other. He felt pulled down, like he was wearing heavy armor. The gravity must be more of a force here than at home. When he approached the entry, where the only door was found, he looked around then walked through. The light metallic color of the newer doors was stark against the red tone of the rock. He guessed this room had been carved out from a natural cave. Upon closer inspection, small cracks filled the walls and ceilings. As he went through the doors, and he wasn't sure he knew what to expect. What he saw, he wasn't prepared for at all.

Before him was a vast, round tunnel, dug deep into the reddish rock at a forty-five-degree angle. The hole was the size of one of those skyscrapers on Jael's world. It had flimsy iron scaffolding mounted all along its spiraling walls. The metal creaked as the workers moved. The tunnel reached so far, the end seemed a minute point in the darkness. The deeper cavern was lit by hundreds of four-foot-long glowing worms hanging all throughout the tunnel. The worms had clear, bubbly slime dripping from them, likely to catch bugs he thought as he swatted at a flying bug buzzing near his eyes.

Every so often, there were a series of foot long lights, all mounted along a cord running along the top of the scaffolding. Streams of light shown from under the iron walkways as workers, August's people, moved around. They wore reflective hard hats of neon yellow or fire red. He squinted as someone looked over at him, sending the reflected light into his eyes. They were each filling one large white bucket with rock they were excavating from the wall with small metal picks and hammers.

A dark-haired woman wearing a slim fitting black military uniform approached August. Her uniform was one solid piece but seemed to have thicker armored areas. The heat in the air and her lack of sweat told him those suits were probably breathable and comfortable, maybe even self-cooling. Her uniform seemed much more comfortable than the itchy clothes he woke up in. He shivered when he realized someone had dressed him in his sleep. He hoped it wasn't this small human woman. She looked like she had calloused hands. She shoved him with her long staff before pointing while saying, You have been asleep for too long. Go put a hard hat on and get to work. *"Pone petasum durum et labora!"* Staring at him, she trailed off to herself, Your kind is not supposed to need sleep anyway. *"Tuus genus non dormit quoquomodo."* Pointing her staff to the hard hats, she mimed how to put it on.

August turned around swiftly, intending to say something back, but the woman's eyes flared with his action.

Feeling a small delicate hand slip into his, he looked

down before he made a mistake and offered a rebuttal. A young boy, hardly nine, looked up at him. He had sandy brown hair and a verdant green skin tone with tan eyes. He was a brighter, more saturated green than Oz. The guard walked away with August's shift in attention, and he held the boy's hand as the child gently guided him to the stacks of hard hats.

August slipped one on and afterward the child slipped on his own. He knew kids back home worked in the garden as young as six, but this was something else. No child had any business being here. He didn't think children this young were taken, and thought the boy might not have been born on his own home world. He took August's hand again and led him down a path toward the spiraling scaffolding. The aging metal creaked under their feet, threatening to break with every step. On the descent, he passed over a hundred of his people of all ages, each one blinding him with their turn in his direction, each one unable to resist seeing who the newcomer was.

The boy continued to pull him along until they reached a space in the wall where no one was chipping away. Setting his bucket down, the boy pointed to the ground where August could set his. He watched the boy as he raised the pick and hit it with his hammer. The action loosened a chunk of rock which seemed to have a sparkling glow to it under the dim light from the reflector on his hard hat. August watched as the child expertly held his head so the light would hit the space, removed a large rock with his hammer, and set it in his bucket after it fell loose. He looked up at him and nodded his head toward the vacant area so August would work on his own area of the stone.

August surveyed the spot and found a stone that seemed

like it was out of place with the rest of the wall, so he took his pick and wedged it in around what looked to be the edge and hit it softly with his hammer. The rock popped free, and when he retrieved it, he could feel warmth emanating from within. Something inside of him screamed to drop it. A rock that produced its own heat could never be a good thing. He forced his hands to drop it in the bucket, which caused a crashing sound. The echo sent streams of light from all around in his direction as each person swung their head at a different angle to catch the light. He flinched in response and turned to the boy, who was already staring at him.

With no expression, the boy turned around and returned to work. August cowered inside as his mind spun over why the rock was warm. *Was it radioactive? Did it have some kind of caustic chemical or was the rock itself the chemical?* Bile rose in his throat as his new reality sunk in, no more talking, no more friends and family, and no more Mercy. If he said a single word here, it would surely be his death. He wouldn't stay quiet to maintain a sliver of control; he would only refrain to spare his life.

It was all gone. It was over. He did not know what happened to everyone else, but he assumed they were taken over and all their friends at the base were hauled off to different locations in the galaxy to be sold. They had to have failed. Despair scratched at his heart, wiggling its way in. His hope was strangled with every thought of home.

He couldn't remember what happened after his and Mercy's date. Everything was so fuzzy. He remembered tasting her and reveling in it, and then nothing. Nothing until he woke up strapped to that sadistic doctor's table, where they burned his fingernails and toenails before they clipped his tail. They ground down his fangs while his head was in a vise. That's what it took after they clipped his tail. He had nearly broken free of his restraints. If he had, everyone in that torture chamber would have died. The primal need to rip them open coursed through him. Huffing, he settled as the boy's gaze fell on him.

One thing he didn't understand is how he had been sleeping. He sleeps every night like clockwork, and he could not stand it. He dreamed, and he hated that the most. They were always filled with Mercy and Mazarin. Good or bad, the dreams always happened. The nightmares filled him with misery. Slumbering terrors of Mercy behind a glass wall, unable to reach her. Shouting inside to warn to her, knowing she was in danger, and being completely restrained from helping save her.

The boy tapped his arm, drawing him out of his thoughts of Mercy, and looked toward the entrance of the long spiraling tunnel. A guard walked to the end of the top balcony, and called out, Rest time begins now. Get in line for your rations. *"Tempus dormire incipit nunc. Assenti in linea demenso tuo."*

The boy again took August's hand, pointed to their filled buckets, picking his up, and pulling August along. August reached for the boy's bucket halfway through their walk, but the boy batted his hand away. He looked back to find the boy guarding his bucket with both arms. August smiled at him and waved his hands to explain he wasn't trying to steal it, just carry it. The boy shook his head no and gave August a look like he should know better. He just faced forward and when it was his turn to weigh his rocks, he walked up and dumped them in the chute like the person before him did and then placed the emptied bucket in a stack next to the hard hats.

They arrived in the meal line together, and August looked back at the boy as he tried to see what they were being served. August knew better than to be excited about what he was about to have to eat. He just prayed to the creator it wasn't so awful to make him gag. He had been so spoiled by good food at home. His mouth watered remembering Mercy's neighbor's flatbread. He neared to find what looked to be some kind of dried chips, but they were a strange shape and one kind of mush. They handed him two dried chips, and he took a bowl from the next person as he walked on. The boy didn't hesitate and dug in and had half his bowl eaten by the time they sat on August's bunk together.

August gazed down at the dried chip, and his stomach turned sour when he realized it was a large flat grub worm which had been smashed and dried. Its guts were dried to its side in a splatter shape. Just when it hit him it was a dried bug, he heard the crunch of the boy devouring it next to him. He tipped up the bowl and drank the mush in a few gulps before handing the grub worm chips to the boy.

The boy greedily ate them and smiled at August with a few teeth missing around the front of his mouth. He was still too young to even have all his teeth, and August's heart broke for the boy. He had clearly been there for a while, and his dirty body had many scars, especially his legs. They were covered in fine scratch line scarring. His hands and feet showed no sign of ever having any nails or toenails. Had this child truly been here since birth?

August's eyes became too heavy to keep open, and he dreaded the next part. He would drift off to sleep and be vulnerable, unconscious. It terrified him. A deep, involuntary sigh forced its way up as he felt overwhelmed with the desire to slumber. The boy gave him a reassuring smile, and August scooted back on his bunk, making enough room for the boy if he wanted to lie down. The boy grinned as wide as he could and curled up next to August's back. This boy could be alone, or *was* alone, he thought as he looked down at him. Unable to help it, August lay back and slipped off into the dreaded darkness after two slow breaths.

A crack against the iron bed caused August to bolt onto the floor from his peaceful rest on the bed. As soon as he could pry his eyes open, he looked around frantically for the boy. Not seeing him anywhere, he instead saw a tall brown skinned woman. From his place, lying at her feet, his gaze glided up to her face. Her stunning eyes were as blue as the sea, and her head was shaved clean. The lights hung on cords around the room shone off her head creating a gleaming crown. A goddess of life and death stood over him. The next breath he took, moved through him like his first taste of air.

3

PLANET PORTUM - IUNGO BASE

"There is something brewing in the UTC soldier camp. It looks like they're moving a massive piece of equipment. I think it's a weapon," Pike threw over his shoulder to Jacob who stood a couple of feet away.

Jacob approached Pike, "Zoom in on this area here," as Jacob pointed to the holo-screen.

After brushing a tuft of his freshly cut, shoulder length black hair off his neck, Pike zoomed in, and they watched as six people leaned full tilt pushing a large rail gun on wheels across the camp. Lines of painfully straight tents with a security fence surrounding them filled the screen as he zoomed back out so he could see the camp as a whole. Steam billowed from some of the tents, likely used for cooking and laundering. What looked to be the tent with showers always had a massive line wrapped around it. Humans bustled through the wide rows of tents working on various tasks. They watched for a brief time as they moved along the screen in small groups.

"Do you ever just want to take care of this the easy but

fucked way?" Pike leaned his head to the side with his eyes narrowed as he stared back at Jacob.

"All the time. There is a hell of a difference between carrying out the act and the contemplation of it, so we chose to be better than them. We will win the right way. With the least number of deaths possible," Jacob offered in a hushed tone as he remained steadfast on the screen. Clearing his throat, he continued, "I'll send Oz a message about this. Will you clip some images and send them to my tablet so I can forward them to him?"

Pike went back to work, agreeing "Sure thing."

Jacob moved through the bright hall where the space bustled with their people. It was almost time to visit the prisoners, and he was less than enthusiastic about it. He just hoped he wasn't peed on. Best-case scenario, someone would actually offer to talk.

He was glad he had the rest of the day to himself to spend with Callum and plan their trip to the other side of the mountain. They had failed over and over to spread the gift among the other villages with travelers. Some of them never returned at all, and he had an uneasy feeling. He knew how important it was to build as strong of a resistance as they could at the base, as quickly as possible. The mountain town, they had named Serene, was well on their way to rebuilding. They would have plenty more recruits from there soon. It wasn't enough, but it was something.

He passed by glass being installed in the open-air windows, gleaming in the bright lights of the hallway. He was glad he didn't have to listen to any more of the racket coming from the training room. He was just across the hall and heard nothing but grunts and groans all day from his office. The rather dirty sounds were immensely distracting, and he ended up wearing earplugs when he was in his office. Thankfully his lab had at least been made soundproof. According to Oz, it was a necessary addition after all the explosions. He walked in his apartment and found Callum stretching on the floor with headphones on and his eyes closed. His body was stretched out face down and all he had on was a pair of workout shorts. The muscles in his back gleamed with sweat. Leaning against the wall, Jacob slipped his boots off and tip toed over. Inching up, he leaned his foot in and pinched Callum on the side, right below his ribs with his toes. Callum screeched as he shot up and tackled Jacob to the ground.

Pinning him to the floor, Callum jabbed his elbow in Jacob's back as he straddled his body. Once he was in position, he flipped Jacob on his side and rolled him between his legs. Callum quickly locked his feet together and had him in a chokehold before he could even react. Callum prevailed, pinning a laughing Jacob between his legs. Even without air, Jacob heaved with laughter and tears poured down his face. He couldn't fight back at all, and his body had become a limp sandbag.

Tapping Callum's leg in surrender, he released his faux chokehold enough that he could move a bit. Still unable to contain his laughter, Jacob struggled to say, "Okay. I give up!" He released Jacob and rolled over.

Swinging around and off the floor, Callum stood up and took off his headphones, "What the *fuck* is up with the toe pinch as a greeting?! Is that a thing Earth people do? Why? I don't like it. Let's not add that one to the greeting list." He looked down at his skin where Jacob had pinched him and rubbed it softly before adding, "You're a prick." Jacob was still on his back, laughing, so Callum walked up to kick him in the side before he went in the kitchen to fill a plate with avocado and flatbread.

Callum sat down to eat, and once Jacob calmed down, he joined him at the table. Jacob's chair creaked as he sat, then the wood table groaned as he shifted his weight to his elbows. "We have our trip soon. Are you ready?" Jacob asked, as he nonchalantly slipped his hand over to Callum's plate, intent on stealing one of his pieces of flatbread. The scent was more than he could manage, and his mouth was watering.

Callum slapped at his hand and snatched the bread away, then threw it at him. Jacob caught it and took a bite of the fluffy sweet bread before smiling at him pompously.

"Yes, I'm always ready. I can't wait to see the other side of the mountain. I saw a memory once of the giant mushrooms growing in the marshes of the village to the south. I can't wait to see them in person. They look like something out of a fantasy story from Jael's world. In some places, they even build homes out of them, and I would do just about *anything* to see inside one." Callum's eyes were distant with the images rolling through his mind.

"I heard some of them are big enough to carve out and make into a two-story home. Some are businesses. My great aunt traveled by there once, but her vision was awful, so you can't see much," Jacob said, further inspiring Callum's imagination.

"When we get back, can we start on our new home? If we have time?" Callum hoped, worried about the answer.

Jacob beamed, "We can start building it as soon as we reclaim the planet. Oz's team will reach the UTC command in time. I hope."

"Do you think Pike can handle the base?" Callum asked with a dark blue brow raised.

Jacob tilted his head in thought and with his brown eyes narrowed, he asked, "Have you met him? I think he's got it. Plus, Vida is also in command, and she can do anything *except* stay in an airtight suit for over ten minutes." Stopping to take a bite, Jacob bit off an enormous piece, smearing avocado on his face.

"They will be fine without us. We are taking two guards though, I don't know who they are yet. I'll grab two people living in the base who have had training," Jacob explained as he licked some avocado off the edge of his lip. The last thing he wanted was to take resources from the base, but they needed more than just him and Callum if something happened. Their world was far too dangerous for just the two of them to venture out on a journey.

"We get separate tents, right?" Callum teased, curiosity in his growing grin.

Jacob smiled through his answer, "Yes, we will have separate tents."

With his shoulders falling back into place, Callum rose from his chair with the corners of his mouth tipped up and went off to clean his plate in the kitchen. He hummed to himself the entire way.

Remembering he needed to call Oz and check on how they were doing after the eerie snail situation on the beach, Jacob hopped up. "I need to go check on the team heading north. I'll be right back," Jacob grabbed his tablet and headed outside to the stairs to sit. While dialing Oz, Jacob stretched his legs out.

With his face in a grimace, Oz answered, "Yes."

Rearing back a bit, Jacob asked, "That bad, huh?"

"My nuts are trying to climb inside of my body for warmth Jacob. What do you want?" Oz queried with obvious irritation.

Jacob smiled deviously, "Callum and I are heading off to the other side of the mountain tomorrow - Where it's nice and warm."

Oz slowly shifted his now murderous gaze back to Jacob and snapped, "Fuck you. Fuck you, your shorts sleeves, *and* your warm, floppy nuts." Jacob howled and nearly dropped his tablet. All the while, Oz glared at him with fury in his eyes.

After he pull himself together, Jacob asked, "Pike and Vida will have the base for around two to three weeks or so. We are taking the hover bikes. How are Aurelia and Jael faring in the cold?"

"They're a hell of a lot better than the rest of us. I can't feel my feet, and I think the tip of my tail is frostbitten. We are stopping for a rest soon. I'll check back with you later," Oz growled as he hung up.

Jacob leaned his head back still laughing before he stood and went back inside his apartment. This journey was vital, and he just hoped it all went according to plan. In just a few short weeks, they could have new recruits heading to the base for training.

4

PLANET PORTUM - UTC COMMAND MISSION

Shivering and clenching his jaw so his teeth wouldn't chatter, Oz slipped his tablet back in his pack, and he pulled up the options for his armor found on his forearm holo-screen. With a flip of his finger, he turned the heat up and sighed when he felt his body begin to warm. The heat moved through the suit, sliding from the center out to his extremities.

"Are you turning it up again?" Jael asked. She couldn't help it.

Oz gave her a stern look. "I'm not even half-way to the maximum. You're going to be really sad if my dick freezes off, so hush. This helps us both."

Jael giggled as she trudged through the drifts. Her eyes widened at her own thoughts as it struck her how glad she was for participating in the amount of training she did back at the base. The cardio Oz put her through after their months of hiking was like salt in the wound, but it did the trick. After a few weeks, she was desensitized to the memories of their travels, and she could push herself again. If she hadn't, she would be in real trouble trying to keep up with Oz's exceptionally athletic people. They were taller than humans on average, so their legs were all much longer than hers. Heaving, she struggled to keep up. Peering up at the mountains they were crossing between, she remembered the map Jacob had drawn them with the best route. She hoped the route he had planned included any major obstacles considering they were solely working off satellite imagery. "Did anyone send drones down these paths to make sure we didn't miss something the satellites can't see?" Jael fixed her focus on the grand mountain ahead of them.

"Even drones can't find every obstacle. If we pass a deep fissure in the rock when we get higher up the mountain, we might end up finding it the hard way. That's why part of the training was to practice building your intuition. Remember, having to go through the course blindfolded?" Zoe explained.

Exempt from trying out had not meant she was exempt from to attending training. At first she wondered why the hell they had made her work out with a blindfold on a few times, and it all made sense. She could still feel the pain in her cheek when she slammed into the oak tree on her first blind course. She will never forget the sound Zoe made as she held in a laugh. The bark had left an imprint on her face. She needed to be able to trust her senses in this terrain, and she first felt like a freshly blinded child. By the end of just a week, she was much more vigilant and nearly running. Her last session of her brief training ended with Oz slicing through all the targets, dancing like a graceful predator. Fluid and powerful, his balletic movements were etched in her memories.

The terrain sloped upward at a steeper angle through a

small pass. The thicker pine trees were still another day's walk away, so the unbroken wind blistered their faces. The siblings, Hazel and Harlen, wore their helmets because they had had enough of the cold stinging their cheeks.

After a day of traveling through the snowdrifts, Oz turned to the group, and with weariness in his gaze, announced, "I'm feeling frost burned. Let's set up camp here." Oz's pack slipped from his back, and it hit the snow with a crunch. After he had a necessary stretch, he helped Jael with her pack. She stood in a daze and seemed to snap out of it when her pack landed on the pillowy snow. As he headed over to help set up tents, Oz watched as Jael made her way toward Amelia, who stood next to Mercy and Aurelia.

"I have to pee. Who is coming with me?" Mercy blurted out as she shimmied out of the straps over her arms.

"Me too," Jael breathed. She, Amelia, and Mercy took off with Aurelia to find somewhere to relieve themselves. While stripping down to their under lining in the bitter breeze, Jael trembled as she watched Mercy, Amelia, and Aurelia speak in Latin, frustrated to only catch a few words. She had no idea what they chatted about. Quietly huffing to herself about having difficulty learning the language, she thought again about Oz just transferring it to her through their connection. The idea had been burning in her mind for some time and desperation was settling in. Once Jael pulled back up the warm, skintight armor, she approached Amelia and nervously asked, "Do you think Oz could transfer Latin to me through the connection? He can send memories and even his senses, why couldn't it work for language?"

"That's a good question. Was it uncomfortable to receive his memories? Did you experience any kind of headache or after effect? Dizziness?" Amelia hadn't thought much on this.

"I sometimes feel dizzy, so he makes me lay down. Other than that, it wasn't bad," Jael answered as she slid her heated gloves back on, groaning softly as the warmth eased her stinging fingers. A particularly cold wind kissed their faces and Jael shivered. She slid her hands up to warm her cheeks as she waited for the answer.

Amelia considered Jael for a moment before saying, "I don't know. It's a lot of information, much more than just a memory clip. It would be like an entire year of memories being passed over. Our neurons weigh substantially more than a human's. Each neuron has three axons instead of one, meaning three neuron cells are found in a space where there should be only one. They are like little conjoined triplets with the number of connections your brain would need to make in such a short time. I'm concerned; it might inflict some damage to your nervous system. It might be painful as well; in fact, it may be agonizing. I think it could be possible though."

"I want to try. I'm struggling trying to learn Latin, and I must know it fluently if I'm going to be any help when we move against to the UTC command," Jael admitted, intense self-disappointment evident in her gaze. A prepared spy proficient in the language is a spy who lives.

"Let's talk to Oz, but he will not like this idea at all," Amelia warned with her laser focus on Jael.

Jael gave Amelia an admitting grin and replied, "That's why I asked you first."

Rolling her big blue eyes, Amelia quipped, "Oh, thanks. Make me the bad guy."

Jael grinned gleefully as they all trekked through the

deep snow toward the camp. The two approached Oz as he was sliding a folding pole into the loops of their tent. As she and Amelia neared, Oz checked to see who was coming up behind him. "I already don't like this," Oz muttered as he turned around to face Jael and Amelia.

Jael gave him a half grimace, half grin, as Amelia offered, "You're probably right, but it's something we need to consider. I think you should try to pass Jael Latin through connection. I think if you use the connection at the base of her skull, it will work. She might have some side effects, but I think it's worth it. We were just speaking Latin with Aurelia, and Jael hasn't picked it up enough to even understand basic conversations yet. She needs to be fluent, and you know our plan won't work if she's not."

"I'm more than willing to try. We only have about two weeks left. After all my lessons, I still haven't picked up nearly enough to even pass for basic understanding." Jael thoroughly disliked reminding everyone of her short-comings.

Oz closed his eyes in defeat, and his voice broke. "I've been thinking the same thing since she suggested it. Amelia, if anything happens to her, I don't know if I can cope."

Amelia put her hand on Oz's arm assuring him, "I know. We all know, but it's a risk we need to take."

Closing his eyes, he stood stoically as he desperately tried to come to terms with it. When his eyes flew open again, Jael could see his turmoil. Muscles in his face were twitching, and he seemed far too quiet. "Fine. Let me finish setting up camp, and I need to start some stew over a fire. I guess can try," Oz folded with sorrow in his voice. When he finally said it aloud, his stomach twisted, and his belly ached with dread.

Jael walked over and put her arms around him. "I'll be ok, I promise. I know it will work."

Oz side eyed Jael as she embraced him. He wasn't sure anything could help his nerves at this point. His mind spun. Defeated, he walked off to finish the tent and start the fire for the stew. Jael waited with Amelia in the tent and watched Oz as he worked. The tent opening flapped in the gentle, chilly wind. "I'm going to hook up my monitoring equipment while we wait," Amelia quietly said from behind her, so Jael nodded as she sat on the cot. Without turning around, Amelia asked, "Can you please take your shirt off?" After Jael removed her armor lining and was in just a sports bra, Amelia began putting wireless round sticky white circles on her temples and her chest in various places. Just as Amelia was finishing up with the prep on her tablet, Oz ducked down as he walked into the tent.

"Let's get this over with, but I want to make something clear. I do not like this at all. I am only going along with it because I know Jael learning Latin is pivotal for the mission," Oz's was face stern and cold as he tucked his black hair behind his ears. The depth of the emotion behind his eyes reminded Jael he had spent fifteen years alone. The possible loss terrified him.

"I understand. I can do this," Jael assured him with the little confidence left in her voice. She was scared out of her mind, but she knew this was necessary. She had to learn Latin. That was the common language in the galaxy. If she couldn't learn it, all their plans would have to be remade, and this mission would be for nothing. She needed to be able to report back what shea heard and learned after she crossed over into enemy territory.

Oz knelt next to her cot as she lay back. Amelia sat on

the cot next to hers. Amelia nodded to Oz she was ready, and he brought his hand up to Jael's neck.

The first thing Jael noticed was how much his hand was shaking. Her heart broke as he found the place in her neck. It took everything she had not to cave and tell him to stop, but she knew she couldn't. The pad of his finger found the perfect place on her neck, and he paused a moment, giving her a chance to back out. She didn't move or say a word. When the spine pierced her skin, it was a small shock since it had been a while since they had needed to communicate in this way.

She took a calming breath and focused on Oz and into the connection promised, "I swear I will be alright. We have to try."

"You don't know that." He paused then told her, "Thank you for everything you do for my people. You are always so quick to give so much. I love you. Don't you dare fucking die," Oz demanded, before he opened the flood gates of his mind and poured the electrochemical imprint of language down their connection and into Jael's network of neurons.

At first, she could feel her core heating, but when she began to tremble uncontrollably, distress rose in her gut. Pressure built behind her eyes and led to twinges of pain. *Was it over yet? How much longer? This may have been a mistake.* She rasped for deep breaths and closed her eyes tightly, and then the transfer was complete, and Oz ended the connection. Her head ached. The ache became deeper by the moment morphing into a migraine and sweat poured from her body. The heat and sweat concentrated around her spine and inside her head. Frantic, Oz snapped, "I don't like this. What's happening?"

"I think she may have a migraine," Amelia explained as she walked over and opened the flap to the tent, allowing the frigid air to cool Jael off. Her skin turned a deep cherry right above her nerves, showing up on her skin like a network. Her face flushed with intense heat. Jael groaned and clutched her head. The headache was drilling, and nausea rolled around in her belly. "Shit, she's going to be sick. Give me that bucket!" Amelia ordered Oz, and he leapt to grab and toss the bucket to her from the corner of the tent. Amelia snatched it from the air and turned Jael's head just in time for her to spew vomit into the bucket. She continued to vomit, and Oz stood over her with his hands grasping his head in despair.

Oz voice broke, "What the fuck did I do?"

Shooting her eyes up, Amelia snapped, "That's enough of the panicking! Focus. I need your help. Go get some snow and pack around her. Her temperature is rising again; she's at a hundred and six now." Shaking his head, Oz exhaled a rigid breath and passed Amelia a bewildered look as he replied, "Yeah, yeah. Okay." He rushed out and packed a sack full of snow. He poured it over Jael, Amelia nodded, and Oz went back for more.

Amelia peeled open Jael's eyelids to look for pupil changes signifying brain damage, but all she saw were fully dilated eyes. Jael was unresponsive but had a steady heartbeat and her blood pressure was holding in normal ranges. The first and biggest issue was lowering her temperature. With the snowpack, Jael's temperature began to slowly drop nearing one hundred and three again. Sighing in relief, Amelia looked back down at Jael, and Jael was looking straight up at her, fully aware. Amelia startled and reared back. Jael's pupils glowed gold, and a trickle of blood fell from her nose and eyes. Amelia gasped and checked her tablet readings and looked back to Jael.

"I'm alright," was all Jael could mutter in a soft breathy tone, clearly using every bit of her strength to stay aware. Jael turned her head to face up, and Amelia saw another drop of blood flow from her ear. Finding Oz, her heart pounded as he fearfully observed her. He had seen the droplet of blood fall from her ear. With a shaking soft voice, tears of desperate hope gathered in Amelia's eyes as she asked, "Jael, you swear to me you're still all there?"

Jael reached her arm from the snow packed around her and grabbed Oz's hand, so he leaned over. She whispered softly, It worked, you fucking doubter. Worth it. *"Solvet. Tu futues dubium. Dignitas."*

Neither Jael nor Amelia had ever heard Oz make such a noise as he made at the sound Jael's words. His cry was a heavy mix of desperation, anger, love, and pure gratitude. "God damn it Jael! You fucking scared me to death. We are not trying any more of your ideas," Oz seethed in the most loving way he could, with his brow creased and bright yellow eyes glaring at her.

Jael smiled wide with blood from her nose, dribbling down, staining her perfect teeth as she snapped back, I know I'm going to have to sneak into UTC command with Aurelia. It just makes sense. How the fuck else am I going to get all of you inside, protect myself, and collect information? I know you've been avoiding that plan, but it's the only way. Why else would we be crossing through the mountains? *"Scio correpam in UTC iusso cum Aurelia. Est facet prudentiam... Cur ut transibamus per montes?"*

With that, Oz leaned over to grab his coat. He slipped his boots on and left the tent in silence. Oz walked over the hill and over another. He walked until his face was numb and he thought his nose would truly fall off from frostbite. He didn't care as he stood in the icy air, looking toward the mountains. How could he send the woman he loved into UTC command so they could get inside? No, they had to find another plan. He couldn't do it. This could make him go mad. Oz turned and looked over his shoulder, toward the campsite. The smoke was billowing up, and he sighed, slowly heading back. His brief excursion did nothing to clear his head and only made him colder.

Back at the campsite, Jael was sitting up and drinking some water when Oz climbed back into the tent. She seemed fine, and Amelia nodded to him as she took off the wireless sensors. "How do you feel?" Oz asked, clearly burying his true feelings.

Jael smiled as she answered, "I have a headache, but it's tolerable. At first, it was so bad it felt like my brain was being torn in half, but that was just for a few minutes. I blacked out for a moment, but when I woke up, I could think in Latin. It worked exactly like I hoped it would."

"You are never doing anything that risky again. You will not sneak into the UTC- base not happening. We will find another way. That's not negotiable," Oz demanded, an air of absolute authority to his tone. Not wanting to piss him off, Jael just solemnly nodded her head and looked over at Amelia. Amelia had a look of concern as Oz left the tent and headed over to where the stew was cooking.

Amelia moved close and whispered, "He panicked when you blacked out. I had to help him snap out of it. I don't think it's a good idea to press him on the plan he just trashed, especially right now. We are not packing up, so that might just be words, or he thinks he can come up with another plan. He doesn't trust Aurelia enough yet and likely won't for some time. I agree with that, and so do Jacob and Zoe. He's making his choice right now on emotion, and we need to let it run its course."

"You're right. I'm not going to say anything else about it. Maybe we will be able to come up with another plan when we are closer," Jael agreed as she watched Oz stir the big pot outside. He was stirring unnervingly slowly.

Mercy came in the tent to plop on her cot, "What just happened in here and why does Oz look like someone just died?"

Pushing her cot toward the door of the tent, Jael brushed the snow off it then changed out of her melted snow-soaked clothes. Jael answered, Oz gave me Latin through the connection and there were a few hiccups. I passed out, and bled out of all my holes, but I do know Latin now, so I would say it's worth it. *"Oz dedit me linguam latinam per coniunctionem et sunt pauci singultus. Eog dormiens et sanguinem fundo de omnium foramenium, sed scio linguam latinam nunc, ut dicam dignitas."*

Mercy's jaw may as well have dropped to the ground as she stopped in the middle of stripping off her armor. "You did what, to who now? Did you just say he gave Latin to you via the connection?" she asked as she sat and pulled off her boots. She was itching and wiggling to peel off the rest of her tight armor. The top half was flattering, but her favorite part was how it made her butt look, if she was being honest with herself. She had designed it after all.

Amelia answered, "Jael didn't have long enough to learn Latin the human way, so Oz transferred it to her through the connection. She developed a high fever with a terrible headache, but she lived, and it worked. It's probably a good idea *not* to bring it up around Oz."

Mercy sat and stared at them both blankly before asking, "How did you know if it was possible or not? That could have killed you. Even with all the conversation we've been having around you, it hasn't helped?"

"No. It didn't kill me, and now I know Latin, so it's done," Jael stared down at her hands. She squeezed the rag she used to wipe the blood off her face and ears. The fresh blood was still gathered on the surface of the silk, and it had become a deep red where it was saturated. She couldn't take her eyes away as the crimson blood slowly filtering through the fibers of the silk.

Lark climbed in with a bowl of stew, "I have never had stew I liked, but this is really good. I'm so glad Oz knows how to cook."

Mercy asked doubtfully, "It's good? Really? I was avoiding it because I hate veggie stew."

Lark stared at her like she was a talking tree before replying, "It's great! You should all try some."

They all filed out after putting their gear back on and grabbed bowls of stew before returning to the tent, thankful for Oz's culinary skills. However, Oz was nowhere to be found.

5

PLANET ADURO – MINE 03

A pair of soft, full lips parted and a contrasting, threatening voice broke the spell that had fallen over him. The towering regal woman used hang gestures while she commanded, Get the fuck up. Why do you sleep and none of the others do? Are you defective? Did you not hear the bell to get back to work? *"Perite! Cur dormis et nemo aliqui facent? Esne vitiosus? Non audis campanam favere labori?"* Distracted by her stunning beauty, August just stared at her unable to process her words. He was too busy wondering why this guard had to be so perfect. It was hard to hate someone he was entranced by. Her dewy brown skin glowed under the lights in the cavern and her bright blue, piercing gaze oozed power. She tilted her head to the side and supposed, I swear sometimes I think you understand more than you lead on. *"Iuro interdum cogito intelleges plus qum tu duces."* Much louder and with a tip of her head toward the door and a pointed finger, she demanded, Let's go, you're going to the palace physician. We need to figure out what's wrong with you. Hopefully that sandy bitch didn't give us a defective gift. The king will take that as a great insult. *"Imus, corripes ad medicum regiam... Rex accipiet hunc contumeliam magnam."*

The guard next to her, a tall man with pale peach skin, red hair the color of the cave walls, and freckles all over his face offered, You know she did. She just showed up out of nowhere with a gift for King Claudius. It was suspicious from the start. *"Scis eam facet. Ea apparuit ex nusquam cum domum regi Claudius. Fuit suspicacem ab initii."*

"Trudamus eum ad regiam ut oblitteremus ex specu calido." Let's hustle him to the palace so we can get out of this hot cave, the woman tugged at her armor that was quite different from the man's. Her armor had gold lined elements and no one else's armor had anything near that level of decorum. She must be their leader August supposed.

The man stepped over to August and wrenched him up from the floor. The red-haired guard walked in front of him and the woman followed behind. August trailed after the man out of the bunk room and down a long, dusty hallway. When he decided the hallway was never going to end, they finally reached a set of double doors. The red-haired man opened the door, and August was temporarily blinded from the flood of light.

August threw his arm up to shield his eyes. There was a large system star in the sky, and he could not look anywhere near its direction. The star's rays were so radiant he could see it through his eyelids. It took several minutes of blinking with his hands up protecting him from the glare to be able to see. He inhaled the hot dry air, and it parched his throat with the first gulp. The guard behind him guided his steps with taps from her staff.

They reached a small round flying vehicle August

deduced as he ducked under one of the six round open circles which lined the top of the egg-shaped body. Jacob and August had been working on the design for one with him before he was taken. The door slid open, and August was shoved inside the back as the woman took the pilot's seat. He squinted as they settled but was able to open his eyes all the way again after the door had been shut for several seconds. He looked over to evaluate the man and saw his irises turn from a black color and fade into a light green. Those eyes were electronic. The male guard shifted his gaze over to August and scowled before he righted himself and kept his focus forward.

When August looked out of the tinted windows of the transport, for the first time he saw a star. He swore it looked enormous outside. Behind the glass it was much smaller. Its light rays must have made the actual size an illusion. From his current view it was the size of a small orange and hung halfway up in the sky. It seemed to be frozen in time. The white light beaming from it was mesmerizing. He was locked in its brilliant embrace.

The guard hit him on the shoulder. He turned to look at the guard as the man jeered, Stop staring into the sun, you dumb sandflea! You will go blind without the iris shades. Livia, I don't know why I try to talk to them. They don't know what I'm saying anyway. Do you ever wonder what goes on in those empty heads of theirs? *"Mora stupes in solem tuum stultum pulicem! Esne miraris quid facet in capitem vacuum illos?"*

With a sigh, Livia answered, Sometimes I think they understand much more than they lead on. There is a gangster on Emendo with seventeen of their women. I heard he freed and married them. *"Interdum cogito intellegent plus quam ducent. Est grassator in Emendo cum septendecim femi-nae. Audivi liberavit et nupsit eas."*

"Audisne rumorem ut Rex Sarto futuerit cimicem caeruleum donatus est? Audivi consobrinum mei in custodiae privatae is etiam pugnavit regnum quando apparuit capere cimicem caeruleum retro," Did you hear the rumor that King Sarto was fucking a blue bug he had been gifted? I heard from my cousin on his personal guard he even fought the Empress when she showed up to take the blue one back, the man gossiped, a smirk on his face.

Livia responded, I don't know King Sarto, but I don't believe that. Your cousin has said some unbelievable things. *"Non scio regem Sarto, sed dubito illum. Tu consobrinus dictus est iniquos res."*

The man leaned over toward the front seat where Livia sat and stared at August as he asked, Why would someone want to fuck one of them when they're engineered without the ability to speak? They're people shaped bugs, just like the advertisements always explain. That's like screwing a giant Vidarian beetle. I guess there are people who are into that. *"Cur aliquis vollo futuere illum quando creati sunt sine poteste dicere?... Puto homines qui amat."*

It took everything in August's power to not tell these two guards that not only could he speak, but he understood everything they were saying. He kept his cool and pretended he couldn't understand, even when the topic arose about a blue woman of his kind. He knew Mazarin was out there somewhere.

Knowing the average patron of Venus was open to dating other species, Livia argued, I don't know Felix, I know of human's who live in the Venus District who like to have sex with those blood sucking, winged Resper. They pay for sex with their own blood. Emendo has a brothel filled with them. I heard they were taken from the prison planet during a rescue mission of a downed UTC transport. I don't think any of it was legal. I bet they don't bust them because it just helps the UTC secure it as their prison planet. I've heard rumors about that place for years, and it personally brings a tinge of fear, thinking of it. "*Non scio Felix, scio homines qui vivunt in regione Veni qui vollo futuere cum illos vespertiliones alatos Resper... Audivi rumores circa illum locum in anni, et timeo.*"

"*Illuc locus non timeo me sed amo homines. Nollo mira, non caudae et non alae,*" That doesn't bother me as much, but I like human men and women. I don't want strange, no tails and no wings, Felix declared as he scowled at August.

Beginning to bend the metal of the seat under his straining hands, August trained his breath as best as he could amid his raging anger. The insults from this human were going to send him off the edge. He understood why his people never spoke a word after being sold off. Who he was inside was all he had left. He would protect it with his life.

They all sat quietly for the remainder of the trip, and August leaned forward, searching for a better view as he saw a dome in the distance, perched atop of a mountain. The gleam of the transparent glass against the falling system star behind them reflected a colorful light of oranges, yellows, and deep reds. They landed on a flat dusty slab, and Livia shut off the engines. Dirt clouds wafted up around them, but Felix didn't wait, and when his door opened, he was pelted.

The side door of the transport was flung to the side by Livia, and Felix shoved August out. He landed face down on the hard, sooty ground. Livia hit Felix on the shoulder when he stepped out, and she shot him a disdainful look. He just shrugged as August pushed up off the ground and stood tall to glare at him. Livia demanded, Let's go, you overgrown lab experiment. "*Imus, obistum experimentum.*"

August pulled his shoulder away as she placed her hand on it to guide him. She could fuck off too, even if she was a goddess of a woman. She glared at him as he went toward the entry doors to the dome.

A tall oval arc over a set of rounded doors led into a lush and humid garden. In some places, condensation dripped down the massive dome of glass in small streams. The moisture filled his lungs, and he felt it was the finest full breath he had taken since his capture. The garden seemed to stretch along the perimeter of the dome. In the center, a massive building made up of sharp jutting points like pieces of black glass cut into impossibly sharp pyramids reached the top of the dome in seven places. The rest of the peaks jutted at random heights. Lights in different areas told him people either lived or worked there, maybe both. He bet a small mountain would fit in this dome and wondered how many people lived in this palace made of glass.

They seemed to be the only ones in the vast gardens. August recognized many of the plants from his world but also saw variations of the plants from Jael's. Palm trees with bananas stretched like long fingers toward the top of the dome and below them were all kinds of flowering bushes. Some of the flowers he knew and one in particular, a bird of paradise, had been one of Jael's favorites. He wanted to reach out and touch it, but he didn't dare.

They followed the path to a door leading into the building. He was awestruck by the grandeur inside and decided it must be the royal palace. Gleaming spiraling silver sculptures reached to the ceiling from the center of an enormous room. The ceiling looked like slices of cream-colored natural shaped crystals in a random pattern above the hallway floor. Light shown from behind the crystals, and August was entranced by the aesthetic of it all.

They passed through the room and into an irregular hallway, long and bent in several angles. When they finally arrived at a door at the end of the hallway and went inside, they walked in to find an older man standing by an exam table. He pointed to the table, and August shook his head no. There was no way in hell he was going back on an exam table willfully.

A staff cracked on his shin, and he did everything he could to keep from falling to the floor in pain. He glared back at Livia before slowly climbing onto the table.

The physician took care to approach him carefully.

The white curly haired, tan skinned doctor took August's hand and attached a small blinking device before saying, This is going to prick your skin. It will hurt but only for a moment. *"Punget cutem tui. Nocebit sed paulisper."*

Felix looked to Livia and rolled his eyes over the doctor's warning. Felix scoffed, Doc they're engineered bugs. They can't understand you. *"Doc sunt cimices machinatores. Non intellegunt te."*

August looked over at the physician and was surprised by his warm, kind eyes. He relaxed a little, and when the blinking device on his hand pricked his skin, he was ready for it. It turned out to be almost nothing. The white-haired man walked over and retrieved the small metal instrument. He sat it on a flat panel on his desk and furrowed his brow. *"Hic non rectus est,"* This can't be right, the old physician mumbled.

He rose from his seat and adjusted his overlapping grey tunic before he made his way over to August with a small limp as he walked. He looked in August's eyes and ears before tapping his jaw for him to open his mouth. He complied, and the doctor looked back at Livia and explained, Tell your father someone altered his genes from the usual. I don't know why they would have turned on a dormant gene, but they did. This one will need sleep. "*Dice patrem tui aliquis mutavit gentes eius ab solito. Non scio cur excitaret gentem residem sed facent. Hic dormietur.*"

"*Capio eum ad regem. Nec mirum hic fuit donum fortuitum. Is vitiosus est,*" I'll take him straight to the king. No wonder this one was a random gift. He's defective, Livia replied as she nodded her head for August to move off the table.

He plopped his feet down on the floor, and when he did his pants slipped down a bit. As he lifted his tunic and pulled up his loose pants, he found Livia, studying him. What the fuck was she looking at? Hadn't she just hit him with her staff?

A thought rolled over him, and something the doctor said registered, but must not have heard them right. There was something wrong with his genetics, *and* he was standing before a king's daughter. *No wonder she had an air of royalty about her*, he thought to himself as he passed by her to enter the hallway. She smelled like elegance and power, smoke and roses.

They backtracked a few yards down the hall then entered an inconspicuous set of doors. Entering the room, the grand architecture again struck August. The tall ceiling reached to the top of the glass dome in three places inside this room with the same large spiraling sculptures connecting at the low points of the spires. He looked around spotting where they were headed.

A tall dais stood at the end of the room, and the chair atop it matched the neoteric, yet aging palace's aesthetic. The black spires pointing from the back looked to be made from some kind of dark crystal. A man with salt and pepper hair, well in his seventies, if August had to guess, sat atop the luxuriously cushioned chair with a scowl. His porcelain pale skin emphasized his piercing midnight eyes. August had a snaking feeling in his belly that his own death was near.

They approached the king, and Livia bowed her head before announcing, Father, this one is defective. Someone altered his genes from the normal product we order, so now he sleeps. "*Pater, est vitiosus. Aliquis mutavit gentes eius ab solito ope imperamus, sic nunc dormit.*"

"*Immo, quid vult me facere? Alicui caput perfringere. Is fuit liber quoquomodo.*" Well, what do you want me to do about it? Call the Empress and tell her the gift she sent is dead, and we want a replacement. Just bash him over the head. He was free anyway, the king ground out, his brow furrowed and angry.

Holding himself still, he was already preparing for what might happen next. August tried to calm his raging heart, but he heard every word.

Livia wearily nodded to her father, and August heard her lift her staff from the floor. It sliced through the air as she swung it in an arc, aiming for August's head. He instinctively ducked, and Livia grunted as she braced her feet from the miss. The king threw his head back and laughed as August spun around and crouched, ready for the next attack. He wasn't being taken out without a fight.

"*O gaudium! Amo bonam pugnam! Non ivit ad ludos*

Emendo in anni. O da me spectaculum Liviola," Oh joy! I love a good fight! I haven't been to the Emendo games in years. Oh, do give me a show my dear Livia, he roared as he clapped.

"My dear Livia?" The only time he ever showed me a minuscule amount of affection was when I am fighting, she might as well have said the words aloud though they echoed in her head. Clearing her mind, Livia prepared herself for a fight. She had a feeling this man was going to give her hell, and she intended on dishing out the hell right back. She would not lose. She never lost. She was one of her father's highest ranked generals, and she led his Aduro planetary military. Just not his *galactic* military.

Livia looked back at Felix who was standing at attention with his staff gripped in his hand. She commanded, Stay there. *"Detine."* August couldn't help a smile as she leaped in attack. Her face changed from stone hard battle ready to confusion as she swung her staff at his head. He ducked again, but this time he rolled by her and sat up behind her with just enough time to kick her in the back. She went sliding across the shining floor as August braced himself once again. Livia popped up, enraged with death in her stare and blood running down her rosy lip.

August's eyes widened, and he backed up. She charged for him with her staff spinning above her head as she descended on August. He blocked her staff with his forearm, which made a crack and shot his blue blood in a streak across the otherwise pristine floor. Livia struck out with a kick to his thigh, and August grabbed her foot and yanked. She landed on her back with her foot still in his grasp. She swiftly kicked him in the gut with her free foot. The kick elicited a grunt from August before he landed on top of her.

He wrapped his hand around her throat, and she retaliated by pressing her thumbs into his eyes. August decided this was over, and he pinched the artery in her neck, cutting the blood supply to her brain. She slumped over and lost consciousness. He hoped they wouldn't catch on to what he just did. He knew human anatomy quite well.

August stood up and walked back a few steps, ready for the next opponent.

The king cheered and hollered as he stood on his dark, carved crystal throne. Livia shook her head as she awoke and looked around the room in dismay. Her hand went to her neck, and she glared at August with fury. "*Is est bonus, Livia! Non vidi pugnatorem illum. Pulsat te!*" He is good Livia! I've never seen a fighter like that. He bested *you*! The king goaded with a broad grin, his perfect teeth shining in glee. Livia, unable to find words through her anger and shame, just stood and stared at her father's feet. There was only one person who had ever bested her before.

"*Vollo pugnare cum hoc, Livia... Plus aspicet unum Pluto daemoni cum capillo et cute rubro. Amo.*" I want you to spar with this one, Livia. For your weight, you are the best in ten systems, if not more than that. You cost a fortune, yet this insect beat you. I want you to learn until you can take him down. Kill him when you've learned all you can, when you can kill him fairly in a fight that is. He is too talented to dispose of for now. Plus, he looks like one of Pluto's demons with his red skin and hair. I like it, King Claudius said, his eyes bright with excitement and a devious smile on his lips.

August loosed a pent-up breath, his imminent demise now postponed. His fiery orange eyes slid down to Livia, her piercing gaze *murderous.*

6

PLANET PORTUM - IUNGO BASE

Jacob's dreaded meeting with the prisoners went exactly nowhere, which was to be expected. He looked down at his clean boots, thankful no one peed this time. He hated the entire idea of forcing a connection for information. It went against their unspoken cultural laws, and more importantly, it went against his morals.

The only one of the captives who cooperated at all so far was Aurelia. He suspected some heavy brainwashing was involved in their training as many of the soldiers maintained a spiteful disgust of the Iungo People, of his people. When all are desperate and hungry, it is easy to convince them of anything as long as it comes from the mouths of the rich. Someone who they themself wished to be. They all used the same derogatory words and took the same angle of attack that the Iungo were so low as beings they didn't deserve to exist as anything other than mindless servants. The more decent humans believed they were helping by giving the Iungo purpose. No matter how much tech they developed, or how many of Jacob's people could now speak two languages, the humans never changed. The only reason they behaved at all was from fear and fear alone. His tail curled at his back and thought it interesting they were more afraid of the connection than they were of their venom.

He wondered about the Iungo the humans had encountered. How would he have perceived the experience of being taken before he had been given the gift? How would he have acted? The answer was simple, and he realized why he kept hearing none of his people ever spoke. Even after they learned the language, none ever said a word. Everyone believed them to be incapable of speech. Silence was the only thing they could still control after they were taken. He would have done the same.

If they had learned to speak, would they have ever gained rights? Not likely, he decided. From what he was hearing, the Galactic Center was not a forgiving place. They would have just come up with another reason to maintain their iron grasp.

Thinking of unsafe places, he was dreading their first stop, no matter how warm it was there. His mind went through the possible outcomes as he headed back to his apartment. The closer he came, the worse he felt about teasing Oz. This was supposed to be a *light and fun* trip. The thought left a sour taste in his mouth.

When he arrived at his apartment, he found Callum waiting with their bags. It was time to go. He had knots in his gut about the trip and was rightfully worried of what may happen when they reached the southernmost village across the mountain, the one with the giant mushroom fields and marshes. They were the only village to eat seafood, and they sent boats out on the water to catch lobsters and octopus. He wondered if they were riddled with parasites and how those parasites would impact their behaviors. He had heard rumors the infections caused cannibalism, but he told himself it couldn't be real.

He had to stop thinking about it, or he would have to explain to Oz why they never left. It was probably nothing to be concerned about anyway. The instance of parasites could still be low. He knew plenty of people went through the village just fine.

He shifted his mind to facts first, something solid. With Sarah's help they finally named their own village, Aranea after the Latin word for spider. They named their village in honor of the tarantula silk farms. He used to love to sneak into the woods and lay in the fresh spider silks suspended in the trees. It had a unique fresh scent of the woods after a rain. Memories flooded his mind of when he finally was too big, and he fell out of the silk hammock onto a massive tarantula. It had bucked him off, and he had rolled into a fresh mix of mud and likely some spider poop. His dread faded to the back of his mind as he chuckled from the pleasant memory and ran up the stairs.

Callum had just opened the door wearing his sleek black armor. Smiling at Callum, Jacob said, "The hover bikes are outside and ready for us. We are taking two guards named Adrian and Juni. Pike told me they're the best trained. They're both from Serene. He did warn me Adrian is usually an asshole so don't try to chat it up with him." He walked by Callum and headed to the bedroom to gather his things.

Crossing his arms, Callum scoffed, "Typical of Pike to send us with a dick. Put your armor on so we can go."

Reaching down to grab his armor off the bed, Jacob said, "I guess you're right. He couldn't care less about anyone's personality. I don't think that man knows what fun means."

Jacob pulled his armor up and grabbed his bag, heading toward the door. "That's a hell of an insult coming from you, Mr. Vice President of squares," Callum pushed by Jacob with his pack on his back.

Standing there processing what Callum said, Jacob scowled, "I'm not that bad."

Callum threw his head back and laughed, "Right. You talk about your engineering projects at every party."

"But I'm *at* the party, doesn't that account for something?" Jacob rebutted as he put his hands on his hips.

Callum faced Jacob, "Even Pike goes to the base parties."

Rolling his eyes, Jacob followed Callum through the base and out of the large base door. The whoosh and click of the new doors were still something Callum was becoming accustomed to. They strolled down the lava tube and took the newly built stairs up to the surface. The wood was solid enough it didn't make so much as a creak as they walked over them. When they approached their hover bikes, Callum had a thrill shoot through him about being able to take the bikes. He had been waiting to ride on them and let loose, but he didn't dare say anything. He knew what his reserved lover would have to say if he even mentioned flying fast on them. They were sleek and long, tapered to a point at either end. Perfectly balanced and floating in front of him, ready to bolt through the woods. The handles and glass were rounded like the rest of the bike. He loved how they looked. He had seen them before, but now that he was up close, his heart rushed with excitement.

He mounted his bag on the back and heard the hum as the coated magnets electrified slightly to adhere it to the surface. He looked down into the helmet and wondered if he remembered to upload his music. Surely, he had remembered. They turned when they heard leaves crunching behind them. A sandy salmon colored man and a small brown skinned woman approached them with travel bags.

The first thing Callum noticed was the man's obvious RBF. He loved discovering resting bitch face in Jael's memories. It was the highlight of his day three weeks ago. Weeks, days, hours, the concepts were finally registering for him. Time was starting to settle for him, even though he hated the idea of clocks at first. After months of it, he understood the importance of it, in a way. It wasn't his favorite thing in the world, but he had let it sit with him for a long while. He accepted it as a decent reference to segment his day, so he let his frustration with it go.

When everyone had climbed onto the bikes with their gear, Jacob explained, "I have sent the plotted course to your hover bikes' navigation systems. If you need to stop, just signal on the map so the rest of us know." They all nodded before sliding their helmets on and taking off on their bikes.

Callum weaved between the trees and was bursting at the seams to hold back a whoop of excitement. These hover-bikes were by far his new favorite thing. They would be going on bike trips more often after this. "Jacob, we need some of these for us. Can we keep these?" Callum asked into the comms as he steered around a tightly packed group of trees. He did his best not to sound as thrilled as he was. A scream of delight bubbled in his throat, begging to overflow.

Smiling to himself, Jacob replied, "I'll build some when we get back and those can be ours. Are you already wanting to plan more trips?"

"We are going to the beach the moment this is all over with," Callum revved the engine and soared through the massive oak trees.

He let off the throttle and slowed down for the rest of the group to catch up. While waiting, he watched as a massive wild tarantula climbed up a tree nearby. They were always docile, wild or domesticated. He looked down and saw the little red markers showing where Jacob and the rest of the group were. He took off right as they began their approach. Jacob zipped past him, and Callum gunned it to catch up. When they were riding side by side, Callum felt an elation he had not in a long time.

They had traveled in a tight group for around four hours when Jacob signaled on the holo-map they should stop. They all pulled over, and Adrian hopped off, pulling his suit down to relieve himself next to his bike, utterly uncaring if anyone saw him. It was fairly typical for his people. Callum, however, ignored Adrian and walked off to find a tree he and Jacob could walk behind for a bit of privacy. A rustling came from deep in the woods, but no one could see anything. It was too far off to tell what it could be. "Are we going to risk it?" Callum asked as he held the collar of his armor in his hand. Jacob stood with his hands at his collar as well and thought for a moment before agreeing while peeling off the armor. Callum followed, stripping down just as their forest guest made its appearance.

A sixty foot long, reddish-black millipede skittered by a few yards away as Jacob and Callum took care of their business. Callum was just happy it wasn't something that could eat them, or worse. Its legs clicked as it scuttled through the leaves on the ground. "I've never noticed the pattern their legs move in. It's like little waves of legs," Callum noted as he watched it disappear into the woods. He guessed Jacob knew it was a giant millipede, but he would not ask how. He honestly wasn't sure how he could still hear or smell anything after all the lab explosions.

They went back around to the bikes, and Jacob could hear his tablet loudly alerting him of an important message, so he jogged over to grab it.

Oz:

> I transferred Latin to Jael through the connection, and we almost lost her. We need a new plan. I can't send her into the UTC.

The dread Jacob had just brushed off came rushing back and he slowly blew out a long breath, replying:

> I'll be thinking about it. Message Pike and put him on it, too. He is good with strategy, and he has been following the movements of the UTC up north. How is everything else going? I see on the satellite you're packing up camp.

Oz:

> We've rested for ten hours. It's time to move on. There is a harsh storm coming, and I want to get as far as possible before it hits.

Jacob zoomed out the satellite image and saw the approaching blizzard. His heart sank for Oz and their team. He hoped the armor would keep them warm enough. He felt a pang of guilt in his chest for teasing Oz about the cold he hoped he wouldn't regret his words. As his eyes followed the storm, the memory of his words already stung.

Putting up his tablet, Jacob climbed back on his bike and peered around at the small group waiting for him. He took off into the woods, and they followed behind closely. A few more hours later, Callum signaled they would stop. Jacob wondered if everyone else's ass hurt as much as his did from all the sitting. While it was smooth ride, not rough at all, comfortable actually, he didn't think he had ever sat that long before. Well, maybe once, but it wasn't by choice. A memory of his leg wound flashed in his head, and he moved on from that memory quickly.

Callum pulled into a clearing, and everyone dismounted their bikes. After they all had a much-needed a stretch, Jacob lifted his helmet from his head and pulled his bag free of the magnets holding it to the bike. Callum had the bag with their tent and the water jug, and Jacob helped him move it to the ground to begin setting up.

Once camp was ready, they sat on their cots in their tent and shared some dried fruit. "Did you say three days of travel to get around the mountain?" Callum asked after he had taken a drink of water.

Jacob nodded, "Yes, after today it will be two more nights before we will make camp outside of the village. We need to change into our old clothes to blend in. We have to be careful in the south village because they are heavily rooted in our old ways. I heard their leader may be visually impaired in her old age, and I'm told she never developed her color as a child. Someone said you can see her veins and muscles under her milky-clear skin. I'm not going to lie. I am not excited about meeting her. We've all heard the rumors about people who have wound up missing around the area."

Callum protested, "You're just now telling me this? How the fuck are we supposed to spread the gift and recruit people? What if I believe the rumor? Why are people disappearing?"

"I don't know yet. We will have to go and see to make a case with her," Jacob sighed, not meeting Callum's bright blue eyes.

Heat emanated from Callum's face. He grimaced and asked, "How? By hand signals and grunts? What happens when no one lets us connect with them?"

Grumbling, Jacob looked away, "I have no idea. I'm good at engineering and design, not people."

Narrowing his eyes, Callum slowly asked, "Is that your ulterior motive for having me here?"

"No," Jacob replied flatly as he reached over and took Callum's hand.

Jacob looked back up at Callum, "I brought you because I wanted to travel with you. It sounded nice to do it together. The other villages will be easier. Carter and Amelia told me who to find in their old villages. We just don't have an in when we visit the first one. Okay, maybe a little of why I invited you was also to help with the southern village."

"Why didn't we start with the northern villages?" Callum asked with a hand palm up.

Jacob smiled softly and admitted, "It's colder up there, and I hate it. I wanted to start somewhere warm."

Nodding as Callum closed his eyes, "Fine. Good call. Plus, it's a bit warmer knowing Oz probably has frostbitten toes, or, hopefully, worse."

Huffing, Jacob asked, "Have you ever hated someone more than you hate Oz? They have a storm they're trying to move out ahead of."

"Oh, that's awful for everyone except Oz. To answer your first question, oh yes, I've hated plenty of people more than him. The top of my most hated list of all the people I have ever encountered was when I was friends with a yellow-haired girl my age when I was younger. She connected with a girl who I liked and shared how I had been looking at the girl often. Yellow Hair even revealed some of my secret feelings about my crush to her. I'm still pissed about that. My crush got embarrassed and avoided me. I think the yellow-haired girl was taken when she was thirteen for making symbols in the dirt behind her house," Callum revealed.

With a shocked expression Jacob tilted his head and asked, "You are still pissed at her? Who was the girl you liked?"

"I had about twenty years of silence to think about it. What do you think? How do you not have past anger about anything? My crush was Penny, who lives all the way down the path from my parent's old house. I think she works in the medical lab. It's still awkward."

Looking around at anything but Callum, Jacob admitted, "My parents. I'm angry about my parents."

Squeezing Jacob's hand, Callum held back a gasp at Jacob bringing up his parent's. He never talked about them. Sarah had been a mother to him just like she had been one for Mercy. His parents had been taken when he was a boy, around nine, and he lived with his aunt next door from then on. His rather cold, elder aunt died around the same time Callum's parents passed away.

He had never brought his parents up before. They had been so warm and loving, full of exploration and wonder, and his mother was always tinkering with something. His father was a carpenter, and his work was known for being exceptional. He had no question as to why they had been taken. They left a hole in his heart so great that he had no choice but to pretend like they didn't exist for much of his childhood. As an adult, the idea they were out there somewhere broke his heart. The idea was unbearable.

Callum chose his next words carefully, "I'm sorry Jacob. You were robbed of your time with your parents. I know they were young, so maybe they're out there somewhere."

Jacob winced and finally met Callum's gaze as he whispered, "I hope they're dead."

7

PLANET PORTUM - UTC COMMAND MISSION

Jael was asleep when Oz slipped into the tent. He pushed his cot next to hers and wrapped himself around her warmth. She emitted her usual blistering heat, and he savored every moment of it.

He was fully aware the only reason he now enjoyed the time when she slept was because of the mouth guard he created for her. Memories of her snore floated through his mind. The drool wasn't gone entirely, but the mouthguard helped that, too. Her body was often damp from sweating in her sleep, but he didn't mind, especially not now. He pulled her into him and spent the rest of the time she was sleeping in deep thought. He had to make logical decisions as president, and his love for Jael was interfering with his responsibility to his people. This is why he never wanted to be president. If he had to pick between his people and Jael, he would choose her every time. He would give up everything for her, and she would *hate* him for it.

After Jael woke many hours later, they packed up camp and headed on. The powdery snow was beautiful, but lifting their legs up in the deeper snow to trek through was something none of them ever wanted to do again. A day of frigid travel through the snow-covered rocky terrain past by and they were again making camp, but this time they were amid the more compact trees in the higher elevations.

Thorn was helping Jael set up her tent since she was still supposed to be resting after her Latin language transfer. "Is it okay here, or do you want it pointed in a different direction?" Thorn asked, trying to determine the direction of the wind to set up the tent base.

Jael smiled, answering, "It's perfect right there. Thank you!"

Thorn spread out her sleeping bag and carefully fluffed her pillow before folding up the rest of her pack and sliding it under the cot. He shot Jael a kind smile before he headed back to his tent with the twins, Carter and Aurelia.

The third tent had Dion, Wynn, Sands, and Costel. Jael finally learned their names by eaves dropping since she hadn't been paying attention the first time they introduced themselves. They were all kind, and she wondered if all of the other villages were nice people. She hoped that was the case since Jacob and Callum were heading toward one of the southernmost towns for recruitment.

As Jael lay back on her cot, Mercy came into their tent, "We need some firewood before the blizzard roles in. All the surrounding trees are alive, so I'm going to go further out and see if I can find some branches on the ground I can cut up and bring back. It looks like everyone else is going to be busy setting up their tents for a while."

"It's that bad now? I can go with you," Amelia asked before she jumped up to slip on her armor. It took her less than a minute to shimmy into it and grab her helmet.

Mercy slid her helmet back on and they took off into the snow drifts between the trees. Mercy was shivering, so she pulled up the controls on her armor, slowing down as she adjusted the heat setting.

Amelia asked, "Are you ready to talk about August?"

Turning her head to look over at Amelia, Mercy flatly replied, "He's gone. I'll probably never see him again."

"So, that's what you've decided?" she asked, treading lightly.

Mercy flipped up the visor on her helmet. "Yeah, that's what I've decided. I still miss him, but eventually I'll move on. I'm nowhere near ready yet, but maybe one day."

They keep walking, and Amelia flipped her visor up, before losing her nerve said, "I need to tell you something-something about August."

Mercy stopped and looked behind Amelia. Amelia followed her line of sight to see what she was focused on. There was a cave a few yards away behind a snowdrift, so Mercy reluctantly offered, "Let's go in there and talk." They walked over to the cave and went just inside the entrance. With the windbreak in the cave, it was noticeably warmer. Mercy pulled her helmet off and shook her two fishtail braids out.

After pulling her helmet off and running her hand through her short hair, Amelia admitted, "Vida sent me a message. They had to access August's tablet so they could find and extract his work notes. He had been tracking data one of the science teams were using in Jacob's lab."

Mercy scowled as if she already knew where this conversation was going. Amelia should have known this would not go well. "What does that mean?" Mercy demanded as she stared back at Amelia, her helmet wedged under one arm and her other hand on her other hip.

Amelia looked down and cleared her throat. "Things that might change the way you feel. He was using a shared work notes file for a daily journal where the files they needed were found. Vida found some things he said in there, private things about you."

"What did those private things he put in a public place say?" Mercy asked, a deeper scowl growing on her face.

A pit of dread was forming deep in Mercy's belly. This was the last conversation she wanted to have right now. Desire for him to return her affection became sludge in her lungs, heavy and wet. Every breath became a sea of longing, one she was drowning in.

Amelia's heart broke as she softly answered, "Merc, he was going to end things with you the day after your date in the woods."

When she focused on the woman before her, Mercy met her gaze. Stunned with sparkling tears gathering in her golden eyes, Mercy hissed, "You're lying. You're fucking lying."

Sorrow filling her, Amelia breathed back, "If you need proof, I'll show you the messages. Vida hid the tablet and has made sure she was the only one to see it."

Tears erupted from Mercy, and she went to slip her helmet on, but Amelia wrapped her hand around Mercy's arm and gently offered, "I'm sorry Mercy. You deserved to know the truth."

"Why, so you can finally make your move Amelia? Don't think I haven't seen the way you look at me. You're fucked up!" Mercy yanked her arm out of Amelia's grasp and stormed out of the cave. Her boots crunched under her feet as she took off into the snow drifts. Running into the woods, she slipped her helmet on and didn't look back.

"Mercy!" Amelia yelled after her as she ran toward the mouth of the cave. Fucking venom, Amelia thought. She had made a terrible mistake. This part of learning language was hard. What to say and when to say it. Who to say it. Maybe Vida should have told Mercy. How the fuck did she notice her interest? Amelia had worked so hard to hide it. It killed her when Mercy was with August, but she never dared to say anything. She would never interfere with their relationship. She was not capable of doing something like that.

Mercy had been a beam of light the first time Amelia saw her. So much so, Amelia had lost her breath. Mercy emitted much more than just her stunning beauty. The moment when Amelia had looked up at her from her place, resting in the entry way of the base, was the moment her life had changed forever.

August didn't see who Mercy was at all, and didn't appreciate her unique nature. He just saw Mercy, the pretty girl, and Mercy, the friend. Mercy was the most unconditionally caring person she had ever met. She was perfect. Her passion for life and creative energy was addictive. She was a hopeful aura in a dark sea of misery. Amelia roughly swallowed, for her throat had developed a knot.

How was she going to fix this? She had hurt the woman she loved and probably ruined their friendship all at the same time. Amelia dropped her head and closed the visor on her helmet. One thing she was not going to do, was let her go, especially in this frigid snowstorm. "Where is Mercy?" she asked the helmet. A little red dot appeared on a map and Amelia wondered for a split second if she should follow the dot or go return to camp.

She followed the dot. Amelia couldn't help but follow her. Mercy was everything to her.

The wind picked up, and the snowfall fell from the sky in sheets. Drudging through the heavy drifts, Amelia followed the little red dot on the map for over a mile. By the time she was able to start catching up to Mercy, they were in the midst of the blizzard. Mercy was tracking Amelia as well in her helmet, always staying just ahead, so Amelia knew she wouldn't reach her.

The wind howled, and the temperature dropped a degree every five minutes.

"Mercy, it's going to be twenty below zero in about an hour. We need to find shelter. If we turn around, we can make it back to the cave. I know you are furious with me, but I can't let you freeze to death. The team needs you; our people need you," Amelia pleaded into the helmet's comm. Hearing no response, she checked the map again and saw Mercy had stopped walking. Taking the opportunity, she ran as quickly as she could through the piling snow, stumbling through the fresh drifts, and falling over big rocks in her path. She finally found Mercy, leaned against a pine tree. She was absolutely still. The snow was at their thighs now, and it was quickly rising.

Amelia approached Mercy from behind, pulling her away from the tree before Amelia wrapped her arms around her as she begged, "I'm sorry." Mercy stayed still. She didn't respond and didn't move.

"Merc, we have to go back to the cave. We will die out here. The armor can't keep up with the cold. Mine is on the highest setting, and I'm freezing my ass off. I know you are too. *Please*." Amelia pleaded as she squeezed her arms around Mercy.

Sinking her head further, Mercy nodded but wrenched herself out of Amelia's grip. Filled with guilt and anguish, Amelia followed her through the snowdrifts. They followed the map in their helmets back to the cave through the blinding blizzard. The wind was screaming like a banshee between the trees. The mountain groaned with the temperature drop and Amelia begged the creator if they could just make it back to the cave, she would do *anything*. She would give *anything*.

Just as they began losing all feeling in their hands and feet, they breached the entrance of the cave. Still without a word, they turned on their helmet lights to explore further back. Toward the back of the cave, lines of what looked to be insect eggs clung along the ceiling. The floor was littered with the shells of snails and a few dead beetles, but otherwise, it was empty. A pile of rock protruding from the side of the chamber was positioned halfway between the entrance and the back of the cave, so they sat down on the other side of it. Mercy sat down a few feet away from Amelia. The partial barrier broke the wind, and the feeling began returning to their hands and feet, but the true cold was the chilling distance emanating from Mercy.

Amelia's heart was in a vise. They say there is no such thing as cold, only an absence of heat. She understood that fact now better than ever. Losing Mercy's warmth was the coldest she had ever felt. How had she been so stupid? This language thing seemed so easy at first, but the more social interaction they all had, the more she experienced how nuanced communication really was. She would much rather solve a medical mystery than have to figure out how to fix this relationship error she made with Mercy. She scooted closer to Mercy. Mercy moved away. Frustration overwhelmed her, and Amelia slammed her head back into the cave wall, closing her eyes. A few rocks broke free and fell over her shoulders. Mercy ignored her and leaned over to curl up on the ground. "Mercy, please. It's freezing. I know you hate me, but it's cold as fuck. We need each other if we are going to make it through this storm." Amelia's desperation was mounting.

Shivering in a ball on the ground, her tail curled tighter around her body before Mercy spoke finally, "I would rather freeze to death than touch you right now."

Searing fire laced through Amelia at Mercy's words. It burned a hole in her frozen exterior. "You deserved to know the *truth*. I'm sorry it hurt you, but I am not sorry that I said it. I didn't want to see you mourning a man who didn't love you the way you deserve" Amelia revealed, letting the truth slip out in the bitter cold. Mercy leaned her head up and peered at Amelia briefly before crashing her head back down on the ground and curling into a tighter ball. Amelia couldn't hear anything through the comms, but inside the privacy of her helmet, tears poured down Mercy's face. A little salt pool gathered on the inner edge of her visor. She didn't care about the cold. She didn't care about anything. Her heart was shattered into a million pieces. She watched as frost formed on the outside of her visor and steadily spread across. She didn't care enough to turn the glass warmer on. Nothing mattered anymore.

Unable to hide her sorrow, her breaths became uneven, and Amelia noticed the change. Mercy could no longer hide her sorrow. Amelia crawled over and slid her arm under Mercy to pull her up and between Amelia's legs. She hoisted her up and slid her legs around Mercy's. Wrapping her arms around her and holding her close, Mercy let it all loose as her body shook with each sob. Amelia squeezed her eyes shut and held Mercy as she grieved. It was not just the loss of August, but the finality of the loss of her relationship with him, that it would have been over either way. It was the grief of not knowing why and trying not to care. It was pretending not to care. It was her desire to scream at August for leading her on, but the pain of it all, the worst was in knowing he's probably being worked to death in a radioactive mine on Aduro.

Looking back, she saw all the signs. She and August weren't compatible, knowledge which made her sob a river. She had wasted so much time and effort trying to prove something that should have never been. The embarrassment of knowing he humored her in her pursuit and her looks were probably the reason he caved, was obvious now. He did it because he was her friend. He was probably just trying to be a good friend in his odd August way, and all of it made her sick.

"Stop with the catastrophic thoughts, Mercy. I know what you're doing. You haven't calmed down in thirty minutes. Please breathe and talk to me. You're going to burn all of the energy you need to stay warm," Amelia counseled as she gave Mercy a squeeze and rubbed her arms.

Mercy sniffed and replied, "I feel like such a fool. I convinced him to give me a chance. I forced it. How could I be so stupid?"

Amelia leaned her helmet against Mercy's and replied, "You can't think that way. He was out of his mind for not seeing *you*, the real you. You're perfect how you are, and he did not understand or appreciate you for you." Amelia squeezed Mercy closer as she repeated in a whisper, "You're perfect."

Mercy sobbed again, but this time didn't tell the helmet to mute the sound. She let Amelia hear her emotions and slid her hands up to grasp the strong arms around her. Letting her feelings flow from her as her tears fell, she pulled her legs up to her chest, and Amelia pulled her legs up and around Mercy tighter.

Several hours passed, and the snow built up so high on the cave entrance that the wind stopped blowing and the cavern wasn't nearly as cold. Hours of shivering and dumping out her boiling emotions made Mercy lethargic and empty. Her body was a vast hollow vessel. Her thoughts seemed to be whispers coming from the depths of a crevasse. Her hopes and dreams fell off great cliffs and crashed into pieces at the bottom, falling onto rocks and jutting points of crystal. How had she been so oblivious to it all? Mercy racked her brain trying to answer impossibilities and conundrums that spun like little dirt devils over the vast lands empty of her mind. From the outside, she was utterly still and formless, but on the inside, she was battling a raging war of self.

Who she was would need to be rebuilt, but what would she rebuild on? Now she had nothing- no foundation. It all crumbled away. She would have to start from square one. Mercy had to figure out who she was, aside from August. He had been part of her life for far longer than they had been together. He had always been there. After years, she finally had what she wanted, to be with him. Then it was all gone, plus now the added pain of knowing he was planning to reject her. August had been so much of her identity. He had consumed her life. Now that he was gone, she realized there wasn't much left over inside of her. She had given her all, everything she was, to him, and now she had nothing left for herself. He had scooped out her identity and taken it with him.

Mercy's hip began to hurt, so she moved to stretch. She pried off her helmet and wiped out the inside corner of her visor where her pool of tears had dried. Amelia removed her helmet slowly from her head.

"Mercy?" Amelia asked, trying not to say the words. *Are you Okay?*

Shaking her head, Mercy met Amelia's blue eyes, "I'm not, but I'm going to work on it. I'm sorry I said such mean things to you. I didn't..."

Amelia cut Mercy off by grabbing her in a hug. She knew Mercy wasn't ready yet. Amelia desperately wanted to crash her lips against Mercy's but knew it wasn't right. Her desire burned her inside and out, yet she had to wait until she knew Mercy wanted it as well. Having Mercy in her arm's was devouring her, but she wouldn't want it any other way. If this was how she would die, she would die happy. Just as long as Mercy survives, that was all that matters.

8

PLANET ADURO - CLAUDIUS ROYAL PALACE

After she had shoved him in the holding cell, Livia slammed the barred door shut. The metal slamming echoed through the training area behind her. As she strode off, she ordered the guard to bring him food once a day and to beat him if he acted up. She leaned in close to the guard and whispered her commands, but August could hear everything she was saying.

His thoughts shifted to Mercy while he closed his eyes. He wondered how she was doing- if she had moved on yet. He knew that was their way. He was stupid for waiting so long for Mazarin. He wondered where she was as his mind continued its usual rotation of thoughts. He hoped Mercy and Mazarin were safe and happy. He hoped Mazarin didn't end up in a place like he did, this hellscape of a planet. His mind shifted to the boy in the cave. He prayed to the creator the boy was okay. He couldn't stop worrying about him.

Then the lingering scent of Livia slipped by his nose, and her face made its way into his mind. Damn that woman with no hair on her head, the king's daughter. After he knew she was long gone, he opened his eyes and adjusted his body on the thin mattress in the cell's corner. The cell was small, but he had a toilet and sink. It was at least better than the mine.

Sucking in a deep breath of air, he was glad it didn't dry his throat with every gulp. The humidity balanced air inside the palace dome was a stark difference from the arid conditions outside.

Why could he not stop her face from creeping into his thoughts? Why was her presence so heavy? Another whiff of her delicate perfume crossed his nose, likely flowers he had never heard of or seen before mixed with the natural scent of her skin. The way she sauntered, never simply walking, she filled any space she found herself, and her words dripped with power. He closed his eyes once again, and the world faded away.

A cracking noise rang in his ear, and he shot up from the cot from a deep sleep. He didn't understand when he slipped off into the land of dreams, or for how long, but he was awake now and staring at a sour Livia. She threw a set of clothes at him, and they landed on the other side of the bowl of food near the bars at the front of the cell. They were athletic clothes, a stretchy, fitted grey sleeveless shirt and shorts. He guessed they would fight today.

He stood and faced her. She stared at him from the other side of the bars of the cell. August noticed the room was empty save her. He tilted his head at her and smirked before he dipped down and took the clothes from the floor. She didn't look away, so neither did he. He pulled his tunic off and tossed it to the ground, and she didn't bat an eye. He knew exactly how good his body looked, and he was going to use it to his advantage. She remained stoic as he slipped his loose pants off. He made sure not to hide his nudity from her as he slid on the snug pair of shorts. When he looked back up at her, she was now glaring at him.

He smirked again and slipped the fitted sleeveless shirt over his head. Livia was wearing something similar, and he watched as she slowly unlocked his cell door.

"*Exercemus hodie,*" We're practicing today, Livia ordered sharply as she opened the cell door.

He strolled through the door as he held his sights on her. He was close enough to notice a black bruise on her brown skin. It was on the side of her neck, the skin there raised. She must spar a lot because he did not grip her neck with enough force to bruise it, he thought. Why did this woman make him feel so odd? It was a stirring inside, something unsettled, and he didn't like it. The sentiment had been previously undecided, but in that moment, he truly wanted to hate her.

She gestured to the open doorway, and August walked toward it. When he crossed the threshold, he found a giant room the size of the cave back home, before they had finished it out. The walls were a smoky grey toned opaque glass. The ceiling flowed in a ripple pattern from the center as if it was moving with waves of crystal, just like the hallways.

They were the only two in the vast room, and Livia jabbed him in the back of the shoulder with her staff for moving too slowly. Fury burst from the depths of his soul. That was the last time *that woman* was going to touch him with *that stick.* Yes, he hated her. He glowered and side-stepped her. In a blink, he leapt toward her to grab her staff, yanking it from her hands.

With anger radiating from her like a raging flame, Livia

yelled, Fuck you, damned, *"Futue te ipsum, damnate..."* He smiled and tossed the staff at her, cutting off her words. She caught it, but before she could react, he had already dropped down to kick at her knees and knock her down. She leapt up to dodge his kick and tossed her staff behind her. It clattered to the ground, and August looked over at it. His eyes shifted back to her, but it was too late. *Well, that was a mistake*, he watched her weight shift from one foot to the other.

She leapt forward like a cat, twisting in the air and then slamming her fist into his shoulder. He fell back, and she pulled on his outstretched arm using the momentum. Still holding his arm, she careened forward and struck again by kneeing him in the side. He didn't have time to block either attack and had to refrain from reacting aloud. *That knee fucking hurt*!

He decided quickly this woman was highly skilled and possibly as smart as he was. No, she was smarter. He wheezed as he fought for a breath. The recovery after this sparing session was going to be brutal. His wince didn't go unnoticed, and she pounced.

They fought for three hours, and August only managed to pin her four times.

The only reason he was able to do it at all was because of all the practice with Oz when they were young. She fought exactly like Oz, brilliant and strategic. She was half his weight, which by weight class, she was easily about a hundred times better than him relatively speaking. He wasn't sure how he felt about that. With the right technology, this woman would be unstoppable. The thought of that truly frightened him.

She stood heaving in front of him, maintaining her regal poise at all times. They were both drenched in sweat, and

August made a motion for something to drink. Livia nodded consent, and they headed into the room with his cell. He went inside, and she closed and locked the door as he leaned over and drank from the sink in the corner.

She nodded to him without making eye contact and walked out. A few moments later the younger male guard came in the room from the hallway and slid a thin mattress pad and towel through the bars of the cell.

He smirked at the guard as he took his position by the door. August looked at the inch wide pad before he lay over on his mattress and wondered if his little show earlier earned him that minute inch of comfort. He doubted it was anything, but he would keep trying. Maybe he could at least convince Livia to respect him enough not to kill him. Maybe he could be sent back to the mine, anything but being killed and thrown away like trash.

Livia came back through the door just as August was comfortable and slid a bowl under the bars of his door. She looked over at the guard as she slipped a cup next to the bowl. With a grunt, August stood and picked them up. The bowl was the typical mush, but the cup had something other than water in it.

He leaned over and sniffed it as Livia walked out, excitement burst when he realized it was fruit juice. He was winning her over after all. He smiled as he guzzled it greedily. It was the best damn fruit juice he had ever had although he had no idea what kind of fruit it was. The juice was pink and had a fresh, lightly sweet flavor. He gulped down the mush and smiled at his extra meal. Even the mush was better after the juice.

He peered around the small room after his meal and changed back into his loose clothing. He didn't hide himself when he changed, and he was not completely unaware of the guard at the door who didn't look away. He assumed a guard would have to be rotated several hours later, and he hoped the next one wasn't an asshole. Pondering the rotation schedule, he dosed off.

Just as he had fallen asleep, or so it felt, he heard a hiss. He opened his eye a sliver realizing the lights in the room had been dimmed. Livia stood in some loose night clothes with her hands on her hips. Her deep blue eyes were hard with distress, and her shoulders sat high. Something was wrong.

"Cur rursus cogito intelleges me... Cur es sic differentia?" Why do I keep thinking you understand me? Why the fuck do you seem like you can truly communicate? You are nothing like any of them I have ever seen. Why are you so different? Livia asked in a hushed tone.

August couldn't help it and cracked a small smile to himself as he laid his head back down and ignored her. She had taken a couple cheap shots when they fought, so he was going to drag this out. Noticing his smirk, she stared at him with her mouth parted slightly, waiting. When she didn't make a move to leave, August finally opened both of his eyes and leaned up to look at her. When their eyes met, his heart raged in his body. He wasn't sure if he hated her or wanted her. One thing he did know was he desperately wanted to say something but didn't dare. He knew it would mean immediate death. He was not stupid. This could be a trap. She had just tried to kill him the day before.

He dropped his eyes down to look beyond her to the room behind her where they had trained all day, where he felt her damned soft skin on his. Livia tilted her head where the guard usually stood and softly asked, There's no guard, no cameras, and no microphones. This is the training room.

If you understand me, can you give me a sign? I have to know. Please. *"Sunt non custodiae, photomachinulae microphonique. Volo scire. Grate."* August slowly licked his cracked dry lips and brought his eyes back up to hers. Did she just say please? He didn't know what else to do, so he slowly winked and gave her a closed lip smile before he rolled over to go to sleep.

With a hand on her chest, she gripped her nightshirt in a wad as she gasped, I fucking knew that rumor was true. I *knew* you were different too. What the fuck did the empress do to you? How did they make you smarter? *"Futuo scio illum rumorem est verum... Quomodo fecierunt te callidum?"* At that, August glared at Livia. If there was one way to piss him off, it was to imply he was altered to be more intelligent. His people were reticent, not stupid and not created.

Her eyes went wide and her mouth slowly fell open. Heavy breaths passed through her lips for several moments before she swallowed roughly. She whispered, Are there more like you? If the Empress didn't do this, did you *evolve?* *"Suntne magis te? Si regna non facit, esne progressus?"* August lifted an eyebrow as he gave her a long look before he nodded twice, almost imperceptibly.

With an exhaustive huff, Livia crashed to the floor with her legs crossed and put her head in her hands. Grasping her face, she toiled inside about what this meant. This so-called insect was smart, fully sentient, not an overgrown brainless pest like the First Humans had always claimed they had created.

They were simply *uncommunicative*, not unintelligent. Her family bought them for such a painfully long time to work in the mines. She had to do something. This was immeasurably wrong. It was *always* wrong in her opinion, but fully sentient beings who evolved naturally on their home world had rights in the Galactic Center. This smelled of typical First Human rot.

Without looking up, she spoke, I have spent a lot of time on guard rounds in the mine. I long suspected your people were smarter than they led on. I'll make sure you are sent back to the mine after we train enough that my father is satisfied. It doesn't feel right to kill you. I'm not a politician; I'm a warrior. Killing for no reason is not honorable. None of this is acceptable. *"Impenderam multum tempi in custodia in fodina... Interfectu nihil causae est non honestus. Nihil sunt accepti."*

Livia rose and stalked out of the room just as the guard came back from the hallway. August still didn't trust her, not an inch.

9

PLANET PORTUM – RECRUIT MISSION

Jacob had just emerged from his tent to complete some work when his tablet pinged with a message from Oz:

> Mercy and Amelia were caught in the storm. I think they're in a cave, but my tablet is not loading the satellite images. Track their location and update me.

Heart sinking to his feet, Jacob quickly pulled up the satellite images, but they also weren't loading. He called Pike in a panic.

"Yes," Pike answered in an exasperated tone as his face materialized over the holo-tablet.

Jacob quickly asked, "What's going on with the satellite images?"

"Look up in the sky. It's a radiation burst from the black hole. Our satellites are going to be blurry for hours. Have you not noticed the Auras? Our sky is quite a bit brighter today," Pike explained, his exasperation even more obvious.

Looking up, Jacob noticed the Auras were far more intense than usual and nodded his head in agreement. "Mercy and Amelia are stranded out in the snowstorm up north. Track them the moment you're able to," Jacob instructed.

Pike nodded in understanding, "I'll see what I can do."

Ending the holo-call with a shaking hand, Jacob turned to a concerned Callum.

"I heard everything. Jacob, they must find Mercy. She's my best friend. We *just* lost Luna, and we can't lose her, too." Callum rambled, his voice cracking and tears welling in his eyes.

Jacob walked over to put his arms around Callum and assured him, "They will find her. I know she's wearing her armor and has her helmet. She wouldn't have walked off without it. Plus, Amelia is with her. She will be okay."

After the brief embrace, Callum walked to the edge of the woods and did his best to gather his thoughts. He wasn't going to be any help anytime soon, so Jacob began tearing down the tent and the cots inside. Once camp was packed up and loaded, they climbed on their hover-bikes. Callum zoomed ahead of everyone while Jacob did his best to stay caught up as Juni and Adrian stayed together a little way behind. They had heard the conversation between Jacob and Oz and were giving Callum some space.

Only one more stop before they had to find a way to convince the south town to accept the gift. Pike had sent Jacob a message earlier in the day reporting three more groups of people from Serene had arrived. They needed much more help and Jacob hoped he could have more recruits headed to the base soon. That's if everything went well. If it didn't, he didn't want to think about that. Thinking about work again, Jacob wondered if they were close to needing to build more accommodations for the waves of new recruits showing up or not. He would send Vida a message. Keeping his mind off Mercy and Amelia was proving to be difficult as he tried to continue thinking about anything else. He itched to be able to pull up the satellite images despite knowing they wouldn't load. Keeping one eye on the Auras, he made sure to watch for when they dimmed back to normal.

One of his best team members back at the base, Thorn, had thought to not only line all their electrical components with copper, but also include a layer of the jade sap. It obviously wasn't enough for the radiation bursts, but in normal conditions, all the components worked perfectly. In testing the satellites they had built, he had been right to suggest it as the hardened sap was an exceptional barrier for most EM radiation. He was a brilliant addition to their team and had been one of Sarah's best recruits. He hoped they were all staying as warm as possible considering the blizzard.

Jacob's mind wandered as they steered the bikes through the mix of oak and the palm trees which were now beginning to pop up. The flower types were changing too, he saw more hibiscus and jasmine. When they saw a towering orange tree, they stopped to eat.

Pulling their bikes over, Jacob relayed into the comms, "Don't park directly under the tree, we don't want our equipment filled with caterpillars and poop when we want to leave."

Kicking a melon sized beetle away from his boot, Callum admitted, "I've never seen so many damn bugs in one place."

Jacob picked a foot long bright orange and yellow centipede off his thigh and tossed it away saying, "They're all attracted to the scent of the rotting fruit on the ground. I'm actually surprised there aren't more."

Adrian was in the tree and bellowed down, "Catch!"

Throwing her head back, Juni took one large step to the left and caught a sack full of oranges. She walked over and connected the bag's magnets to the one on the bike, securing it. The bag snapped into place with a click, now streamlined against the side.

Adrian dropped from the tree and landed on his feet. After shaking his body and flinging bugs everywhere, he pulled off his helmet. The man had a cutting glare. He grumbled something under his breath and walked briskly over to his hover bike to mount it, making it clear he was ready to move on. Callum frowned after him and leaned over to Jacob to whisper, "He really is a prick." Jacob nodded as he took a bite of an orange slice, he had just peeled. They both looked over to find him staring at them, fury in his eyes. Callum softly squeaked as he twisted around to face Jacob, who gladly let him be a shield to the shower of eye daggers.

After a few more bites, while avoiding Adrian's seething eyes, Jacob reluctantly approached and announced, "We're going to travel another few hours and stop for the day. We will reach the south village tomorrow on foot, and I want us all rested."

Juni and Callum nodded as they mounted their bikes while Adrian just stared ahead. The surrounding air seemed to simmer with irritation. Everyone was wondering if ungrateful was just part of Adrian's personality or if there was a more personal resentment.

Jacob scowled in thought and mounted his bike, sliding his helmet over his head. Inside the safety of the helmet, he said, "Open comms to Callum." He waited a moment and asked, "Is it just me or does Adrian *radiate* shitty mood?"

Putting his hand on top of his helmet to keep it from bobbling as Callum laughed, "No, it's not just you. He acts like he has a stick up his ass. Where the fuck did he come from again?"

"Callum, remember? They both came from Serene. Choir sent them." Jacob wondered if they had sent him because they wanted rid of him and his moodiness. Juni was a kind, as well as innovative person, and her pleasant agreeable nature was a stark contrast to Adrian's. Jacob considered himself somewhat average for his people and Adrian to be the outlier.

Callum stopped a moment and offered, "I wonder if he's angry because of what his town went through, or maybe he lost someone."

"That's a good point. Maybe we should cut the guy some slack," Jacob replied as he scrunched his nose from an itch. He wondered if he should have installed a scratching arm inside the helmet. The idea formed in his head, along with a little smile at the thought of a scratcher.

Just as Jacob refocused on the terrain, Callum yelped. They all heard it and subsequently leaned to the left to bypass a massive termite's nest in the middle of their path. He was thankful for the warning because he may have launched himself right off the top of that termite mound. He eyed the mound sourly as he passed by.

They continued for several hours before reaching their final campsite. Next to a small pool of water with water trickling from a small natural wall of rock, it looked like a washed-out ancient canyon. There were palm trees and a variety of fruit all around. Adrian scaled one he found with bananas and brought them a large bunch. Juni walked around and found a few avocado trees. She had a sack of them over her shoulder when she returned. The green flesh of the avocados she had scarfed down while gathering was smeared on her face when she walked up.

Callum discretely motioned with his hand for her to wipe her mouth. Stopping and staring at him, she slowly brought her hand up to her mouth and ran her fingers lightly against the side of her face. Upon seeing green fingertips, she gasped and looked around for something to clean her face. Grabbing a large flat leaf from a small banana tree, she scraped off her face before rubbing the rest off with the back of her hand.

After they made camp, Jacob wearily checked the satellites, fearing the worst. To his relief, he saw the video feed had cleared up some. He zoomed until Mercy's and Amelia's red dots showed up. They seemed to be inside of a small cave, and the suits showed their hearts were beating. Relief flooded him. He went straight into his messaging app to send Oz a message.

Jacob:

> Looks like Amelia and Mercy found a cave to hide in. I picked up two strong heartbeats just now.

His tablet pinged, with a response from Oz:

> My tablet still won't load the satellite feed. Thank you for the update. We've been worried about them. We have all thought the worst. I'm sending a rescue group now.

Setting down his tablet he crawled over to Callum's cot, straddling his waist as he leaned over and whispered in his ear, "Mercy is alive, and Oz has their location. Let's go for a walk and stretch our legs before we rest." Jacob strung a line of kisses down Callum's bare neck, and he groaned.

"Fine, but if I get bit in the ass by a bug I'm going home. By home, I mean the base. I will march back to my bike and drive straight home," Callum grumbled but a smile grew on his face.

While sliding his hands down Callum's muscular back, Jacob doubted him, "Whatever. Liar. You won't leave me."

Jacob swung his right leg over the cot and found his footing but remained leaned over Callum. Taking one hand and snaking it over his thighs, Jacob grabbed him under his right leg and sat up, lifting Callum up by the leg at the same time. It was to force Callum to flip over but his body went sailing to the ground at Jacob's feet as the cot tipped instead. The metal legs of the cot hit the fabric of the tent, causing it to have a shaking fit.

"What the fuck was that for?" Callum asked as he angled his head back.

After licking his lips, Jacob's voice oozed lust as he replied, "You're taking too damn long."

Jacob blinked a few times, urges he didn't understand were pulsing inside of him. His iris's fought his pupils for control as the tan of his eyes receded along with his civility. Callum's jaw dropped as he wondered what was sparking

Jacob's desire. Whatever it was, he liked it. No, he loved it. After a quick sniff of the air in the tent, Callum realized Jacob may have been affected by their time in the woods. The air smelled of ferocious, primal need.

He was going to climb out of this tent and run. He just wanted to see what would happen. *Research.* Research. Jacob pulled him up from the ground, and Callum used the momentum to launch himself out of the tent into a run. The air sang as he cut through it. His body flew through the trees around the camp. He could hear Jacob's feet pounding the ground behind him, and a thrill of the pursuit chased up his spine at the sound. Not daring to look, Callum's heart raced, knowing Jacob's long stride would catch up to him soon. The anticipation was too much. Not to wait until he was caught, Callum started ripping at the top of his armor.

The breath was knocked out of him as Jacob took him to the ground. When Jacob's hard body slammed into his, they rolled together over the sandy ground. Their limbs already intertwined. When they came to a stop, Jacob had Callum pinned to the ground. As he looked into his eyes, Callum quaked with fright and desire. The tan of Jacob's eyes was gone, replaced with the ebony of lust, and he was growling over him. "God damn, where have you been all my life?" Callum breathed as he reached up and loosened the neck of his armor to release the magnets. As Jacob peeled away Callum's suit, his hands shook.

Watching his face, Callum realized he was shaking because the suit was resisting him. Callum yanked at it to force the magnets to release. The suit loosened, and it was peeled off Callum so quickly Jacob had nearly flipped him over in the process. With a hand in the center of his chest, he shoved Callum down and took his bared length in his left hand. As he stared Callum hungrily, he thoroughly licked his pointer finger on his right hand.

"Jacob, what are you?" Callum started to say, before he was abruptly cut off - in the very best way. Jacob's mouth descended on the tip of Callum's length as he slid his finger deep inside of him. Callum leaned his head back and let out a half singing, half moan as Jacob found that delicate spot inside. He couldn't form words as Jacob had his way with him. His long tongue curled up and down his length in a synchronized rhythm. Pressing into that place inside, the little knot of nerves, Callum's breath quickened. Thoughts could not form in his mind as Jacob stroked him inside and out. The deep clicks in his throat erupted from him, and he curled upward with the impending explosion of pleasure. He faintly heard the clicks in Jacob's throat as the sounds of the wind through the palm trees faded into the background of his mind.

Callum was not prepared for the ecstatic end as he reached up and grabbed his own wind-blown fishtail braids on either side of his head. He had to have something to grab onto, anything would do. When he exploded, time seemed to come to a standstill. Stars fills his eyes, and he struggled to suck in air as his body curled. He whimpered so loud he swore they probably heard him back at camp. Falling back onto the ground, Callum was paralyzed and struggling to take in a full breath. Jacob lay next to him, equally still. "Jacob, what the fuck was that? Where did that come from?" Callum gasped, swallowing roughly.

Leaning his face over toward Callum, Jacob replied, "Something about staying in the woods. I think it has brought back some animalistic feelings. I just had this screaming urge to fuck you. I can't explain other than that. I can't explain anything I just did."

"We need to go camping a lot more often. A lot. I need to return the favor. That was a whole new experience," Callum's blue eyes were wide and voice low and lusty. Callum dropped his head back down onto the dirt in exhaustion, sweat beading on his brow as he felt a pinch on his nude rear end. Leaning over to Jacob, he complained, "That's not funny." Realizing he could see both of Jacob's hands, he screamed as his body flailed. He leapt up and saw a small solid white spider on the ground where he had been lying, eliciting another scream of fury out of Callum.

10

PLANET PORTUM - UTC COMMAND MISSION

Once the embrace melted into a rest of tangled limbs, Mercy lay curled up with Amelia for several more hours trying to stay warm before Thorn and Harlen burst through the snow. With clearing skies, the rescue team finally made their way to the cave. The relief they both felt when the powdery snow at the mouth of the cave poured inside as their rescuers pushed their way through was indescribable. They peeled their slumped bodies off the floor and prepared themselves for the hike back to camp.

Hazel crafted some snowshoes from strips of wood Harlen had cut from a tree next to the campsite, making the hike even possible. Harlen announced as he handed the shoes over, "When you don't sleep and you're worried about your friends, you stay up all night weaving wooden snowshoes. Hazel made them for everyone."

After a good stretch, Mercy and Amelia strapped on their sets of snowshoes and were not surprised at all when they easily traversed through the snow. They could remain on the top of the snow instead of sink to their knees with each step. They somberly followed Harlen and Thorn's path back to the campsite. The gleam of the auras on the snow turned the white powder into a bright array of colors. Their helmets visors provided necessary glare protection and let them enjoy the snowy view.

With things at least partially resolved with Mercy, Amelia felt a veil removed from her psyche. Thoughts about the auras flooded her mind.

She knew auras on Jael's world were just at the poles and wondered if her own planet had a different shaped core causing the electromagnetic shields on their world to produce the pole from the middle of the planet. Could their planet's axis shift, and they were on their side?

That had to be it. She had thought about it for months, to no avail, but this to be the answer. Something someone said in the main dining room about the plant life had stuck with her. The group at the next table had been having an intense conversation about how the robust plant life on their world survived with only auras for light. They thought the auras themselves were creating light for the plants to absorb, but it occurred to Amelia enough ultraviolet radiation from the black hole must be reaching the plants. Just not any visible light would explain the intense auras. The color of their plants was probably dictated long ago by their world's original star.

When they reached the camp site, she shared her thoughts with Oz. "An idea hit me on our walk back from the cave. I think the planet was tipped on its side at some point when our former system star fell into the black hole. I think the planet's north pole is pointing towards the black hole's accretion disc. That's why we only have auras over the middle of one side of the planet. I think enough of the ultra-violet radiation from the black hole is still able to seep through, which explains the intensity of the auras and our lush plant life."

"We tried several times to make a compass back at the base and failed. I think it's because the black hole is pulling our molten core toward the surface of the planet facing it, and it's scrambling the magnetic direction. It's the closest to the surface just south of where Aranea is. That's what Pike's geology team said anyway. I'll pass along what you explained about our northern pole being tipped toward the black hole. That does make sense. Do we need to be concerned with humans on the planet taking radiation medication?" he asked, concern in his voice.

"No, I do not believe so. The UV radiation might be slightly more here than Earth but not much more than Earth ranges. Maybe we can talk about it after I've had some rest." After Oz nodded, Amelia went inside her tent and crashed onto her cot.

Mercy followed and pulled her cot up next to Amelia's. The metal legs scraped the ground as she pulled. Both settled in desperate for some real rest after shaking and shivering for half of a day.

Jael was relieved to see the two had returned when she awoke from her ordered rest. She wanted to speak to Mercy but didn't dare as she watched her move closer to Amelia. With her mind reeling, she had to know what happened. She wondered if Oz had any idea. She softly slipped out of the tent to not disturb her friends, she approached Oz and asked, "I'm so glad they're alright, but I can't help wondering what happened?"

"I'm not going to ask. I followed the journey of their red

dots, and it looked like a disagreement may have happened. We are leaving that one alone," Oz stated pointedly as he walked over to fill his bowl with hot stew.

Jael hadn't ever seen him eat this much. He had been eating twice a day and stuffing his face every time. She wondered if it was the cold making him so hungry. She yawned from all the shivering; it was making her tired again. She watched as everyone began lining up and realized the line of hungry Iungo before her answered her question. Every one of them inhaled their stew like they hadn't eaten in days.

She plopped down on a log next to Oz and leaned her head over onto his shoulder. The wind had all but completely died down, and they were able to go without their helmets. Jael noticed her hair liked to cling to the charged exterior of the armor. It stole her attention when the tips of her braids would begin crawling along the suit and spreading out. It was silly, but it kept her from becoming too bored and finding herself seeking some kind of nonsense.

Maybe she should try to rest her eyes, even if she wasn't tired. With her head resting on Oz's shoulder, Jael closed her eyes briefly, but they flew back open when a scream erupted from somewhere in the pine trees. It was one of their people.

Oz sprinted to their tent, grabbed his plasma sword, and slipped his helmet on as Harlen and Hazel did the same. With the helmet on, Oz asked, "Who is screaming? Where are they?" The blinking red dot on the screen showed the name *Thorn* next to it. All three bolted into the woods toward Thorn's blinking red dot on their holo-screens and his echoing screams.

The sounds of his screams stopped, and Oz had a sinking feeling as they ran toward him, fighting the snow drifts. His cries of pain didn't just stop; they faded. Oz spotted his body through the trees in a clearing. Thorn lay convulsing on the ground. Throwing his arm out in front of Hazel and Harlen to stop them, Oz saw Thorn's body still, and Oz knew he was gone.

"Zoom in on Thorn's face," Oz demanded the helmet. The camera moved to focus on Thorn's face. There was something long, brown, and furry emerging from his nose. Oz cringed as he watched another one slide into Thorn's mouth and disappear. Blood began seeping from his ears. Pure terror filled Oz as his heart raced.

Nausea flooded his gut at the sight, and he commanded, "We need to move out of here, NOW. Pack the tents and move out!"

He turned to run, and something plopped onto his helmet. His heart wanted to pound right out of his body as a long, furry-brown caterpillar slid over his face shield and landed in the snow below him. It was easily ten inches long and with the fluffy brown hair, it seemed to be over an inch wide. He knew the brown hair was an illusion, and the creature underneath was much thinner - thin enough to wiggle into Thorn's nose.

Unable to hold in his mounting terror, he let out a high-pitched scream in his helmet and leapt over the small hairy creature. Oz ran for his fucking life. Hazel and Harlen were not far behind as more of the caterpillars-from-hell dive bombed from the trees. Every time one fell on one of them, screams would tear from their throats, and they would run faster. They were soaring over the snowdrifts like they were running hurdles.

When they reached about a quarter of the way back to the tents, Oz's mind finally cleared, and he started hollering into to his comms repeating his earlier orders, "Pack up now! Throw everything together and leave what we have to, Thorn is dead! Don't fucking touch the hairy brown caterpillars! They ate him! They crawled inside his goddamn face!"

Carter wheezed as he responded, "I'm on it."

Once Oz reached the camp, it was already more than half packed up. Everyone was in armor and had helmets on. No matter how sealed their armor was, they were not safe here. There was no telling what those dammed things could bite through.

When Oz looked over at Jael, she had her back to the woods on the other side of the camp and was forcefully shoving her things into her pack. He ran to her and as he neared, his heart raced wildly. There was a hairy brown caterpillar on the side of her back, crawling up her shoulder blade toward her neck. Oz screeched in his helmet as he batted it off her back. *This was his worst nightmare.*

Everyone scrambled, protecting the gear from the caterpillars. They were in a small clearing, so Oz hoped they could pack everything and relocate quickly enough to escape from whatever caterpillar nest in the area had just hatched. They were going to run until they couldn't anymore. He desperately hoped they could cover enough ground and escape from those damned bugs.

Carter offered, "Let's electrify the gear when it's packed up. It's all fireproof. If we run a current through it, we can kill anything alive in it."

Frantically, Oz cried out, "Before you put the packs on, send a current through the suit and fry anything living in it. Mercy did it in the woods to kill that giant wasp. It has to work. Send a command through your helmets."

Nodding, Carter leaned down and instructed his armor to shock his bag. Something inside caught fire, and they saw a little stream of smoke coming from deep inside. He looked over at Oz before pulling a bag out of the pack with a long, charred hairy caterpillar stuck to it.

Everyone stopped to watch before doing the same. A few more packs had smoke seep out, but most of them did not. They rapidly slipped on the packs after they were finished. In his comm, Oz commanded in the helmet, "Computer, I need an override setting until further notice. Keep a small charge on all the suits in this group and alert them if they have any unwanted guests crawling on them."

Oz shivered again at the thought as he heard something sizzle and shot his eyes to Mercy's ankle where a caterpillar was trying to hitch a ride. It fell off, and Mercy jumped away.

Amelia threw her hands up and yelled, "The fucking egg sacks in the cave! They were all over the ceiling. This is fucked! We need to run! There were thousands!"

"Go!" Oz cried out with a leap as they all took off running.

Oz and Carter stayed at the back behind Jael and Aurelia, who were lagging while the rest of the group moved ahead. Amelia was at the front with Mercy. All had on their snowshoes, which made traveling in the snow less of a headache, but it was still difficult. At one point, Oz decided they were not putting enough distance between them and the flesh-eating caterpillars, and he contemplated putting Jael on his back.

Hours later, when they were so high the trees on the mountain thinned out from the higher atmosphere, Oz stopped the group for a brief rest before crossing over the highest point of the summit. Turning around, they could see across the land to the sea. It was clear all the way to the continent they lived on and even the peaks of the mountains in the center. After the day they had, they all needed a reminder of why they were there, and this was a powerful one. Standing on the edge of their world was breathtaking. One side filled with light, the other filled with darkness, and all of it should, and could, belong to them.

Zapping and sparks filled their resting spot as they sent a charge through their bags one more time for good measure. Setting their gear in a pile together, they took turns relieving themselves behind a large boulder. They guzzled plenty of water before slipping back on their helmets and trekking on.

Unanimously, they agreed to walk until they physically could not anymore. Oz was positive Jael or Aurelia would tire first, but he was wrong. Hazel was the first to call it quits when she landed face first in a snowdrift. Everyone waited for her to stand up, but she just stayed there. Amelia looked down at her and asked, "Hazel, are you okay?"

The computer in the helmet responded with opening the comms into Hazel's helmet where she could hear Hazel mumble, "Must rest."

Looking up at Oz, Amelia shook her head no. They would not continue until everyone had some rest. Oz shrugged and offered, "We made it a long way from the last campsite. Be careful when you unpack. Turn on your helmet lights so you can see what you're doing. Go through everything and make sure none of hell's hitchhikers escaped the electric shock."

Everyone dumped everything out of all the packs and sorted it all, finding nothing but charred remains of the furry caterpillars. A tentative relief spread through the group, all except Oz, who was still rattled. He wasn't sure he wanted to rest with his helmet off.

The image of the caterpillar crawling from Thorn's mouth and nose would not leave his mind. The inability to forget anything, cursed him, especially the worst memories. Those seem to like to bury themselves deeper than any of the others.

Jael slipped in her mouth guard and was asleep as her head hit the pillow on her cot. Oz curled up next to her as everyone else found their places on their cots. They had lost Thorn but were lucky they were able to save the rest of their people and the gear. Oz hoped going down the dark side of the mountain they wouldn't have any more unwanted surprises. They couldn't afford to lose anyone else.

11

ADURO - CLAUDIUS ROYAL PALACE

Standing in the middle of the training room, August heaved from his strenuous workout. He had run about three miles, he guessed. Livia let him out to train alone for the second morning in a row. The guard still stood at the door, but Livia wasn't there. It was the guard who had not looked away when he changed. He had caught him peeking around the corner three times. The truth was, he was never going to pass up an opportunity to be the center of attention. He also knew precisely how good he looked, and besides, the guard was kind enough. He could look all he wanted.

August spent some more time running and used the weights he found. He only knew how to use them because of the memories from Jael in high school gym class, not from her workouts though. Who knew what the hell she was doing with that squat machine? Was she even working out?

He didn't learn from her workouts. Instead, it was the memories of other teenagers in her gym he paid attention to. He studied the football team on the weight machines and using free weights intently to learn. He often wondered why she, too, paid such close attention to them working out. When a set of peering eyes from the next room met his once more, he realized her fascination, and August bit his lips together to hold in a laugh.

Curling his biceps with the weights and using them for squats was giving him a much-needed push in his workout. He could tell after the first time lifting what a difference they made. He had used almost all the free lift equipment in the gym until his body ached. He didn't dare touch the complicated equipment though. There were a few things he had never seen before. One machine looked like two trees with bungee cords drooping down from both of them. There were a few harnesses hanging on the wall, and he wondered if it was a device for a kind of people he hadn't seen yet. Just because he hadn't seen anything but his species and humans, it didn't mean they didn't exist. Finding out what else was out there was on his list of things to do.

He tired, so he stopped to admire himself in the mirror. A tall, wall mirror stretched the length of the mats and weights. He had never truly seen himself with his own eyes before. He had a glimpse of his reflection in the med room glass a few times but seeing what other people see for the first time was life changing. He *knew* what he looked like now. He had not realized how much it would do for his identity. They never had mirrors back home. His mother once showed him her memory of him being caught breaking the rules or doing something she thought was humorous, but that was as a child. As he peered at himself in the mirror, he could see he was already a big man, but he quickly decided he could be larger. He continued to flex his muscles in the reflection and revere himself for long enough he lost track of time.

Standing in the stillness, he wondered why Livia would work him out. She had been kind to him a few times but was still ruthless when they practiced together. She had not bested him yet, but she had come damn close twice.

She is not a normal human, he thought, *she is much more on my skill level*. Even at her best, with an equal amount of training, he knew Jael could never do what this woman does on her worst day. *She has to be over fifty pounds heavier than she looked, at least.*

He also discovered she had a mind so complicated it was as if she had some kind of otherworldly presence within. In battle, she was creative, deliberate, and cunning. She was graceful and gentle, but ruthless and fierce, all at the same time. She was filled with kindness, but she did her best to hide it. He had a good guess kindness was frowned upon in her father's court of horrors.

It helped, too, she was exhilaratingly beautiful. He couldn't believe he was allowing these thoughts to be loose in his mind. When had his thoughts shifted? He was enamored with her.

August's skin reacted to her touch like it was to feel heaven itself. He was struggling to concentrate when they fought. She was a delicate and tender soul in the body of a warrior, the body of a goddess.

The entry door crashed open against the wall, and someone with small quick feet padded inside. It was Livia; he could tell before her scent ever reached his nose. He heard boots shuffling as the guard went out, and the door shut behind him. According to the clock on the wall, it was nowhere near time for their sparing. She stood in the doorway, panting and looking around. She seemed to look for somewhere to hide in the sparse room.

He looked at her with his head tilted to the side, and she shook her head *no* as if to say to back off and don't bother her. Her eyes were pleading.

She swiftly spotted the weights and put her hands on the end of the rack for balance while she caught her breath. The door opened in the entry, and she turned her head around toward the open archway leading directly to her. The defensive shift in her posture caused a foul sensation to roll down August's spine, a spark of protection mixed with preparing for a threat.

A large man, around August's size, came strolling in and asked flatly, My wife, what do you think you are doing? You *are* aware I called for you? "*Mi uxor, quid enim? Scisne ad se vocare te?*"

She didn't change the cold, emotionless glare on her face as she answered, I'm busy right now. "*Ego sum occupatus nunc.*"

"*Scis illum non operae sunt... Tempus est te accomonodas id.*" You know that's not how this works. Get your fucking ass upstairs to our room. I just got home from a long scouting mission. You will obey, or I will make you. You are mine and have been for five years. It's time you get used to it, the dark-haired, green-eyed man was agonizingly calm, with a cruel sneer on his mouth.

His tan skin was scarred on his arms, and he had a scar on his face where half of his eyebrow would no longer grow. The hair on his face, his beard, was well groomed, and August stared at him, debating whether it was worth his life to kill this overgrown toe-sucker now, or wait for the near future. He was absolutely positive this man sucked his own big toe at night when he missed his mommy. One thing for certain, green eyed, toe-breath just became number one on August's hit list.

His fist clenched so tightly his knuckles ached. He would taste of her first and kill that fucker second. He was determined to make her his.

The man stalked over to Livia and slid his hand over her shoulder, but she cowered away from his touch. He forcefully guided her out of the room, and she turned her head to August with a demanding flare. She was threatening him not to act. The man didn't move but tilted his head and furrowed his brow at Livia before she set her eyes forward again.

That toe licker had not even acknowledged August. Rude. And his wife? Livia was his *wife*? Nausea filled August. *How could she have married someone like that? Had it been her choice?*

He fought the desire to follow and rip that fuck's hands off her. Actually, he wanted to rip his hands off completely. He imagined poking out his eyes and feeding him his own prick after ripping it off too. August wanted to see him choke to death. He wanted to watch the life slip away from him. He fantasized about the many tortures and deaths he would inflict on Livia's husband as he let out his anger on the workout equipment. He found a jump rope and back-flipped between jumps with it as he stewed.

Hours later, as August lay in the middle of the training room floor, his tail stretched out straight between his legs, Livia returned. This time, she was dressed for their fight. He was exhausted, but he sat up and jogged to meet her near the door.

"*Circa praecocem, mei consobrinus est crudelis podex.*

Pater mei impepulit nos nubere partes sequi luas matri famil-iae. Sunt alius stemma regni familiae Claudii." About earlier- my cousin is a cold-hearted asshole. My father forced us to marry to align with Lucas's mother's side of the family. They are another branch of the Claudius royal family, Livia explained as she rubbed her sore neck. Unable to help himself, he went up to her and slid his hands around her jaw, gently tilting it to the side. He caressed his thumb down her throat softly, and she winced, but she did not pull away and reject his touch.

He growled, and she responded, I'm fine. Back away from me. My father tortured me for years before Lucas took up the practice. It's what happens to all the women in this fucking royal family. It's how I lost my mother. Now enough of that. It's time to fight. *"Ego bene. Refuge ab me... Tempus est pugnare."*

That walking dead man strangled her? Did she just admit her father, or Lucas, killed her mother? He began shouting out questions in his mind. The only hand that should ever be around her throat was *his*. August saw nothing but red, and Livia could see it in his stare.

"Seda de fututo... Non est via in Pluto inferorum intelle-garis." Calm the fuck down. There's not a gods' damn thing you could do. Only Jupiter himself could intervene. My own mother tried, and now she's dead. No one jeopardizes General Lucas's place in line to the throne. He is my father's pick of successor and already holds the Claudius name of succession. I don't know why the fuck I am explaining all of this to you. There's no way in Pluto's hell you could possibly understand, Livia scoffed as she rolled her eyes.

August widened his eyes and looked at the floor. He wasn't sure how much longer he could keep his mouth shut. He more than understood her, and he also understood what that corpse-to-be of a cousin she was married to did and what he would one day do about that wormy prick.

He looked back up at her and lifted his eyebrows in a searing concern. Livia narrowed her eyes and whispered, I swear you *do* look like you caught every word. It's not possible though. *"Iuro aspices ut intellegas omnem verbum. Non possible est."* She shook her head as they walked toward the center of the training room. They turned and faced one another. Livia attacked first and launched herself at August, leaping and landing on him. Her legs wrapped around his waist, and she grabbed his head with her arms, sending him careening backward. He hit the mat, and she wrestled his arms down with her deceptive frame.

August was overtired, and she was much heavier than she looked. He leaned up as best he could, but he quickly gave up. He didn't mind at all that she was straddling him. She leaned over his lips and she hissed, Get the fuck up and fight me. What is wrong with you demon? *"Futue sursum et pugna me. Quid est daemon?"*

Why haven't you killed them? *"Cur es non interfecisti ea?"* August whispered to her, in his husky, gritty voice.

Livia's eye's widened with shock, and he could feel her body tremble.

"In templis omni dei, iuro cogito audivi dicas aliquid," On the temples of all the gods, I swear I thought I heard you say something, Livia gasped, their faces inches from one another.

August glared and quietly seethed, "I did fucking say something, Livia! I'm not a god damned idiot. You heard what I asked. Why haven't you killed them? *"Futuo dico aliq-*

uid, Livia! Ego non deodamnatus stultus. Audis quid rogavi. Cur es non interfecisti ea?"

After her moment of shock subsided, she took a deep breath and prepared herself for her own answer. *"Quia....quia strangulavit me ad mortem et mei pater permisit! Is bis est magnitudo mei et is habet idem gentem mihi sum. Ubi ibo? Submissus est aut mori. Insculpo faces tibi nunciam dicens, tu deodamnate daemone."* Because...because he would strangle me to death and my father would let him! He's twice my size, and he has the same genetic alterations I do. Where would I go? It's submit or die. I should slit your throat right now for speaking, you damned demon, Livia seethed, moving closer to August's face.

"Sed non fuero. Non narras aliquem pugnas me hodie quoque. Ut tantem frui daemonem, habeo nomen est Augustus." But you won't. You won't tell anyone you beat me today either. As much as I enjoy *demon*, I have a name. It's August, he said quietly, his face neutral and trying.

Her lips were dangerously close to his.

Livia scoffed, and August pushed her off him. He strolled straight to his cell and shut the door. He lay down on his mattress with desire and frustration exhausting him. Livia approached and went to lock the door but stopped and put the key back in her pocket. The guard walked in and stood by the door as Livia stepped out at a painfully slow pace.

A few moments later, she returned with an extra meal for August, setting it at the edge of the bars. He couldn't resist seeing what she had brought him. He knew she could hear him get up, but she didn't turn around as she stepped back out.

Again, she included juice to drink. The meal was

different this time too. It was a mix of fruits and vegetables, not the nasty gruel he had to force himself to swallow.

When the door clicked, and he knew she was gone, he released an anxious breath. He wondered if she would tell anyone he could speak, or if she would protect him like he hoped. He couldn't have kept his mouth shut any longer. He had to say something.

The cell was quiet, but August's words rattled loudly in his mind, *General Lucas Claudius and King Claudius. Both are on my list. They will both die, I don't know how or when. But I will find a way. You fuckers will suffer.* He scarfed down the food and slid the plate and cup over for the guard to take.

Why did she not lock my cell? August wondered. He could easily overtake this kind faced guard. He was a younger man with wide, concerned eyes, full of innocence. *It is a test. It must be. She wants to see how much she can trust me. She knows I won't hurt anyone who doesn't deserve it.*

He sat back down on his mattress. His thoughts ricocheted from topic to topic. He really wanted to ask the guard how old he was. He guessed about twenty-five to thirty. As it often did now, his mind slid to the little boy in the mine and decided that he needed to go back down there to check on him. He would ask Livia to send him back as soon as possible. *This must be what it's like to be a parent.* His chest hurt thinking of leaving Livia in this palace with that piece of shit husband, but that boy was in even more danger. He had to find a way to fix this for the boy. Livia had become just as important though, he needed to find a way to save both and himself.

12

PLANET PORTUM – RECRUITMENT MISSION – SEASIDE VILLAGE

His palms were sweaty. Callum pinched his traditional tunic pulling it from his sticky chest and waved it trying to cool off. His nerves were rattled. This part of their trip scared him more than anything. This was the ocean side village, none of the other villages were anywhere close to the sea. There wasn't much to eat other than octopus, squid, and crabs. He shivered at the thought of the possibility of parasites. No one really understood why they didn't just grow more tropical fruit instead of eating those saltwater creatures.

His mind went straight back to his time as a child playing in the woods when he found a large dead snail. He had only been maybe four earth years old when it happened. After a few pokes with a stick, a white parasitic worm pierced the side of the visible part of the snail and began crawling toward him. It was followed by a yellow one. He never questioned his parents' rules about what he could and could not eat after that.

They came around a dense section of trees and saw the

first of many giant round cap mushrooms. The mushrooms were much wider than the giant oak trees back home. The rounded tawny and creamy yellow caps spread out wide, giving the home plenty of shade and rain protection. Some had doors and open-air windows with thick storm shutters. It looked like a fairy tale from Jael's memories where caterpillars smoked atop giant mushrooms, and pink cats perching in trees disappear into thin air.

Jacob knew Callum wanted to connect and tell him all about the natural setting of buildings he was designing so that they blended in with the environment. He knew how hard it was for him to remain silent. He hoped over his excitement about the buildings, he could still maintain his composure.

They could not be caught speaking aloud under any circumstances. That mistake would end their mission before it began.

Slowly entering what Jacob assumed was the center of the village, an old ochre-haired woman came walking out of her mushroom home with a deep green-haired child in tow. The home had a dainty garden in the front yard and a rain collector on the side of the mushroom. Lush foliage from the garden spilled over onto all the walking paths. They had clearly not developed indoor running water, but at least they ate something other than the parasite filled seafood.

Callum squeezed Jacob's hand as the old woman lifted her head enough to see them walking. She startled, and the child ran to the next home and pounded on the door. At the sound of the distressed knock, several people came out of their homes. Adrian surveyed the expressions of the people, which were filled with disdain and heading toward disgust. This was a bad sign, a terrible one.

Jacob's breath caught in his throat as he noticed a small crowd of large-framed people creeping toward them. This situation was turning sour enough that Jacob could taste it. Adrian swung around as someone tried to put a rope around his hand. They noticed too late that they had been surrounded by several large villagers. Ropes flew all around, and before they had a chance to fight, they were all restrained. Callum's eyes were filled with fury as he watched a tall olive-green man with black hair walk up to Jacob and knock him out clean with one punch to the side of the head. Jacob hit the ground with a thud, and Callum's chance to react was cut short when he was struck next.

Blinking away the dancing spots of pain, Callum already knew they were fucked feeling the cold dirt under him. He opened his eyes to find they were all piled up inside a dark room. Their hands were bound behind their backs, and so far, he was the only one conscious. Trying to move his legs, he found them to be tied too. He kicked at Jacob with his bound feet, and Jacob shook his head. Adrian and Junie were still out. He was facing the wall, so Callum moved down where they would be able to connect by interlacing hands.

"What the fuck happened?" Callum asked in Jacob's mind.

Jacob sighed and asked, "How the hell should I know what's going on? We obviously pissed someone off with our presence."

Callum shook his head and asked, "What are we going to do? What are they going to do to us? What if they slit our throats? Or worse? What if we have to have sex with old women who have bad breath! Jacob, what if they eat us?!"

Ignoring Callum's stupid jokes, frustration and anger

soared through the connection as Jacob filled with guilt at his lack of preparation and observation of the town. He had no idea what to do. Scared out of his mind, he was desperately holding back from spilling too much over into the connection. He didn't want Callum to know how terrified he was. He knew exactly how bad his people could be. They could all be looking at their deaths, and Jacob had waltzed them toward their doom on a bright warm day. He had caressed his love's hand as he led him to his end. Bile rose in his throat, and Jacob kicked Adrian's leg.

In his panic, Jacob conveyed his plan in the connection, "We need to wake them up. Maybe Adrian knows what to do." Adrian and Juni roused and peered around the dark room. The cold dirt floor told Jacob they were in some kind of barn or storage building. It was wood and not a mushroom like the houses with empty shelves lining one wall. The door swung open before he could assess further, and soft light from the auras spilled into the room. A hulking figure loomed in the doorway, and Jacob drew back. No one was coming to save them. He was going to have to figure this out on his own.

A giant man with white hair and dirty, beige skin pulled Jacob to his feet and untied his legs so he could walk. He looked back one last time at Callum before the man shut the door. The large man had a broken tail which had never been fixed for the end hung at an awkward angle. Knowing what it took to break their bones, Jacob cringed as he looked at it. He had only known a few people in his life to break a bone.

The man led him to a tall mushroom house. It had a second story window shining with the light of a flame inside. He was aggressively shoved through the door and landed face first on the wood floor. Jacob groaned as the big man with dirty, beige skin pulled him up and forced him to his feet again. In front of him, he saw a milky clear skinned woman. The muscles in her face were visible, and he thought he could see all her veins. This was not albinism. He had seen that before in his people. Albino Iungo were white with red or blue toned eyes, and their complexions manifested in a spectrum like many of their other skin tones.

This, however, was like nothing he had ever seen before. She was a genetic anomaly.

She was exceedingly elderly and smelled like she had been incontinent for years. The odors of feces and urine assaulted his nose. Someone was not caring for her, and irritation over her conditions took root in his heart.

With slow careful movements, Jacob inched forward until the man at his back shoved him. He took one large step to prevent falling on his face. He stood in front of the old woman noting she had no hair and her white, eyes were blind. Her skin hung from her face. Another scent overcame her body odors and he nearly vomited from disgust. The stench of rotting sea life filled the room, and he was conflicted by a desire to help her and horror at his situation.

The man behind Jacob cut his bindings free, and his hands dropped to his sides. Bringing them together, he rubbed his wrists. The woman slowly tilted her face up at Jacob and grabbed his hand in a vice-like grip. She connected with him and conveyed a fire-filled anger, searing Jacob down the connection.

Panic set in. *We are definitely going to die! What am I going to do? How can I reason with her?* He needed to help her somehow. *Could I force the gift on her? Would it work?* It was a risk, a huge one. She might kill him on the spot, or worse.

He had to try something, maybe after the language, she would understand. Already assuming he was going to be killed by her, he took the chance and forced the gift down the connection. He shoved it past her locked flood gates.

Her eyes went wide, and she shoved Jacob backward. He had been able to transfer the entire gift, so he knew she could speak now. He even included their takeover of the planet and how Oz and their team were planning to defeat the humans in the north.

Before he could do anything else, he was face down on the ground, and his wrists were bound again. He grunted as he was hauled to his feet and shoved out of the door. He landed face down in the dirt and could feel his chest bruising from the repeated impacts. Someone else was there. He could hear more than one person breathing above him.

The big green man with black hair lifted him up and slammed him down on his feet. Jacob winced as he felt something pop. He was shoved into the-decrepit shed to the side of the old woman's mushroom house where he landed on top of Adrian.

Jacob made an involuntary squeak as he slid off Adrian's back. He landed on his side on the ground and tried not to groan at the impact. The door slammed, leaving them in darkness. Callum scooted toward him and when they were back-to-back, they connected.

Sarcasm filled Callum's words, "I'm guessing that went well."

Jacob sent him the memory of the events and Callum replied, "Wow, Jacob. Could you have possibly screwed us any worse? I don't think so. If we weren't dying before, we sure are now. We might even end up on the fucking menu now."

Jacob sighed, "Don't say that. I took a chance, and it was a bad call, but it was all I could think of to do. I have no idea what they're going to do now."

They ended up in the dark shed for over a day before someone finally opened the door and took them all outside so they could use the restroom. One at a time, they were fed some kind of grain mush and had their wrists rebound afterward. The longer they sat in the shed, the more filled with alarm they became. *What were they being kept alive for?*

Jacob thought two days passed when they were finally all hauled up and forced outside again. They looked up to find a crowd of people standing silently around the shed. A chill crawled down Jacob's spine, and Callum took a step over, so his shoulder touched Jacob's. They looked at one another wondering if this was it if they were about to be killed.

The crowd surveyed them, but they were unable to determine their mood or intentions. An elderly woman walked up with a knife, and Callum winced as she approached him. Looking him up and down, she nodded. His eyes went wide with fear of her possible plan. She turned to Callum and cut the bindings on his wrists and grabbed his hand. Her hand was calloused and cold, and he wanted to let go of it so desperately his arm tingled. He turned what he feared was his last look at Jacob and saw the villagers were surveying the rest of the group.

The woman led him away from the crowd off to a smaller mushroom house on the right side of the two-story home near the shed. They passed through the door, and the old woman looked up at Callum before connecting with him. She showed him a rotting octopus she was preparing to eat then showed him Jacob, Adrian, and Juni. The woman passed along sinister feelings of *hunger*. She showed Callum an image of himself followed by warm feelings. They wanted to spare him, but not the rest of the group. *Does she want to eat everyone else?!*

Panic spread through him, and he sent love and admiration down the connection, along with images of him and Jacob. He showed parts of the trip without showing the modern equipment. He showed Adrian and Juni as their helpers, strong and resourceful. *Adrian better be nice after this*, Callum thought to himself as he sent her as much positivity about his friends as he could muster.

The old woman nodded, and she patted her long bench before hobbling back out of her home. He looked out the window and saw Jacob, Adrian, and Juni being shoved into the shed and the door slammed shut again. Relief poured over him, and he could have cried tears of joy if the woman hadn't come waddling in again. He felt increasingly unsafe as she went to her kitchen and pulled a long knife free.

She began chopping some kind of octopus, and Callum did everything in his power not to gag. The smell entered his nose and thoroughly assaulted his nostrils with its rank stench. The pile of arms had to have decayed in open air for over a day or two by the rankness.

Was she going to make him eat rotted meat? As the words bounced around in his mind, bile filled his throat, and he choked it down, gagging as he did. He knew this village ate from the sea, and he wondered if they all had brain worms and other parasites from the infected marine life. Internally screaming, Callum watched as the woman teetered over with a pan filled with old octopus slices and set it next to her stone hearth. He was going to die of brain worms and Jacob would have his throat slit. This was *not* how he imagined this trip going. They were supposed to be lounging on the beach with drinks!

After the ancient woman warmed the stinking octopus, she shuffled her feet along the ground as she went back toward her kitchen. The heated sea creature's flesh smelled worse than the scent of shit in this woman's pants. She dumped the cooked octopus onto two plates before slowly making her way over to Callum. Images of brain parasites crawling around in his head made him sweat. Dreading this, he felt he was stepping toward his own death. Was he, though? How was he going to swallow it?

In the shed, they had fed them some kind of mushroom chunks and grain mush, and he asked himself, *why couldn't he have that?* Panic set in as she put the plate in front of him, and he had to take it from her frail old hands. She shook handing it over, and he almost dropped the plate. The smell of the hot, rancid octopus meat wafted up to his nose, and he fought retching with everything in his soul. *How did we get into this situation? I just wanted to go on a vacation with Jacob.* Now he was having to fight back the aggressive bile rising in his throat, which stung like salt in a wound. He really might throw up. The old woman sat down and devoured her steaming meal.

Yes, this was definitely a severe case of brain worms, he decided, as he did his best to pretend to eat. He brought the round piece of grotesque meat to his mouth and took a bite, noticing something was inside of the meat as his teeth sunk in. He brought his hand down and saw half of a worm in the center of the bite he had just taken. Slipping his hand up, he inconspicuously spit the bite into it and tossed it under the bench.

He looked up, and the old woman had thankfully not

noticed. He gagged as he watched her scrape her plate. She looked over and saw he had not eaten much so she grabbed his plate, dumping more of his onto her own plate before handing it back. He watched as she ate every bit, and she let out a belch to rival one of August's father's. Blown away by sheer disgust, Callum nearly began shedding tears.

He was terrified to his bones. One way or another, they were going to die. He hoped his fate wasn't in the hands of the parasitic worms he may have just ingested. He didn't know if it just took getting it in his mouth or if he actually had to swallow it. He knew he was already exposed. Saliva fell from the corner of his mouth in his desperation not to swallow.

The people in this town acted like his people did thousands of years ago, like time never touched this place. Pure dread filled Callum as the old woman handed him a metal file and propped her cracked and gnarled foot on the bench. She gingerly tapped one of her claws, which had grown sideways. His hand shook as he reached over and took her filth encrusted, scaly, gnarled foot in his hand, grimacing as he began to saw away at her long, crooked toe-claw. Despair and disgust filled his soul.

13

PLANET PORTUM - UTC COMMAND MISSION

Two days of cold travel over the mountain finally plunged them into darkness, and they were able to see the brown dwarf behind their planet. It was so close and it seemed belittled by Portum. The red glow was faint. Jael thought it was a little less than a night on Earth with a full moon. The brown dwarf seemed rather bright for being a brown dwarf, but maybe it just seemed brighter because it was close. As her mind wandered, her eyes passed over Amelia and Mercy who had hardly said two words to one another in days as they sat on the ground staring off into the trees.

They were stopped at the second campsite since they were almost dinner to the furry caterpillars, and Oz was not okay. Jael knowing he had seen what the caterpillars did to Thorn, and she felt terrible for what his heart experienced. Any down time he spent absently staring off into the woods like Amelia and Mercy kept doing. She gained his attention by putting her hand on his shoulder. He startled and faced her.

"Sorry. Why would evolution on our planet spawn such disturbing things? Why are we so different than everything else here? It makes me wonder if we really are genetically altered. We... we are peaceful people." Oz looked back at his tail, to his open palm, and to Jael.

She took a moment to organize her thoughts, then she asked, "Vida is running your people's DNA against the scorpions, right? They are close enough genetically for a cure from the fungus, so that would be proof, right? Have you been receiving results from her and her team?"

He took in the area to look and make sure no one was listening. "She has been sending me the results. We only have part of their DNA. We should share almost all of it. I haven't wanted to share the results yet. They're running more tests. It doesn't look good. We might be doing all of this for nothing," Oz answered, his eyes increasingly distant.

Jael shook her head, not accepting his response and replied, "There is no way your kind was created in a lab. I don't believe it."

"You don't have to believe it for it to still be a fact. We are a mix of other animals and plants which make us exceptionally resistant to radiation. The scorpions are resistant, but they don't have a mix of genes like we do. They just seem to hold more damaged DNA codes if anything. If we can't prove another living thing on our planet is close enough to our DNA, we will have to accept the truth." Oz's pain filled gaze found Jael's.

She shook her head again and offered, "What about your ancient history? There must be evidence of your kind in other places. Bones you can carbon date? Other creatures that branched off?"

"Do you know how many resources that would take? How many people? The time it would require? Where would we even start looking? I wish your options were easily viable, but they're not, and yet we might have to try as a last resort." Oz acknowledged as he stared back into the pine trees.

She was quiet as she rolled through what he said.

Trying to change the subject, Oz leaned in close to Jael's ear and whispered, "I think Aurelia and Carter hooked up a few hours ago out in the woods. You were asleep. They were *not* quiet."

Slapping a hand over her mouth she searched the camp and saw how close Aurelia and Carter were sitting. She turned back around to Oz, mouth gaping with her eyes wide. "I didn't see that one coming at all."

Grinning slyly, Oz whispered, "I hope for Carter's sake that she really is on our side."

Tilting her head to the side she asked, "Why don't she and Carter connect, and he can find out?"

Oz faced her to reply, "That's a good idea, but she's probably terrified of the connection. I'll say something, anyway. Sex while connected is on another level. It's a good enough reason for them to try it."

Amelia, who overheard, tapped Jael on the shoulder and interrupted, "Excuse me I am sneaking in on the conversation you two are having, so *not* quietly over here. Did you just say you've had sex while *connected*? Why has no one shared this information, and why did we not know about this until now? That seems like something we should have figured out a long time ago!"

Oz grinned and shrugged his shoulders. "Jael and I tested

that one out for the first time when it was just the two of us at the treehouse. It was her idea."

With her big blue eyes wide in thought, Amelia walked off mumbling something incoherent. She headed for the stew and made a bowl.

"What are you mumbling about?" Mercy asked as Amelia sat down on the ground next to her with a bowl from the stew Oz made. He had gladly become the campsite cook, which Mercy loved because she knew everything would be delicious, or at the very least, edible. He hated vegetables as much as she did, so his stews were tasty. Mercy cringed thinking of the stew if Amelia was cooking.

Mercy looked over at her, then joined her on the ground. "I am so glad you are not cooking the stew." Mercy admitted to Amelia, her brows raised.

Throwing her head back, Amelia laughed, "Oh hush, my stew is not that bad."

"Bullshit. *You* gave Risk that recipe then tricked us all into eating it. It was so bad I wanted to cry. I made him admit the truth," Mercy snapped with her eyes narrowed on Amelia.

Amelia lost it. Her beanie slipped off as she laughed, and she spilled the remainder of her stew on the snow. She *had* slipped Risk the recipe.

Amelia balled up some snow and chunked it at Mercy. Mercy cried out and threw some snow back, but Amelia was too quick with her long legs and had already taken off into the woods. Mercy ran to catch up to her, balling up snow in her hands on the way. When she finally saw her, she threw the snowball and nailed Amelia in the back of the head. Snow covered her deep blue short hair, and she shook her head upside-down before it melted on her scalp. She collected more snow while she was bent over. She howled, laughing, turning, and tossed a snowball at Mercy. The first snowball missed, but she threw the other one she had ready.

Mercy loosed another volley, and one hit Amelia in the face. When it did, she charged for Mercy. With her heart soaring, Mercy took off in the woods as Amelia chased her. Mercy was rounding a tree right as Amelia grabbed her around her waist and pushed her against the trunk. Face to face, they were so close they could feel each other's radiating body heat. Mercy darted her tongue out, licking the tip of Amelia's nose. With a frantic gasp, the blue of Amelia's eyes began to deepen until they were black.

Amelia slammed her mouth down on Mercy's, and the kiss was echoed with roaming, desperate hands. The heat overwhelmed the cold air, and their mingling breath created a frozen cloud swirling around them. Something about the woods made them feel feral and wild. It had been brewing among all of them but mixed with the loneliness and despair in Amelia, it was an overwhelming combination. She pulled out of the embrace to study Mercy's face and demanded, "I can't fucking wait any longer. I tried. Take your God damn armor off. Now."

Mercy froze. Amelia was inches from her face, her blue eyes smoldering, demanding. She knew the truth. Amelia had waited a long time for her. She knew if she put her hand at her collar and pulled it down, she and Amelia would be together and that would be it for them. Amelia wanted forever. Is this what she wanted?

Looking back at Amelia, she made her choice.

Hungrily, as if she was going to devour Amelia's very soul, Mercy drifted her hand up to her collar and pulled, releasing the magnet's hold and causing the front to drop.

She kept pulling, freeing her breasts into the frigid air. Sighing with anticipation of pleasure, Amelia put both of her hands on Mercy's ample chest and squeezed them as she breathed, "Fucking perfect." She leaned into Mercy against the tree and kissed down her throat never releasing her breasts. Mercy was stunned at how right it felt. Amelia's touch, soft and demanding, was more than she could ever want. Her skin sang with the possessive contact.

Amelia took a golden-brown peak into her mouth, and Mercy moaned softly as she flicked the tip with her tongue. Mercy peeled her armor down further, not caring in the slightest about the bitter cold. She shimmied it down over her hips as far as she could after she pulled her arms free.

Taking over, Amelia pulled her armor down to her ankles to reach between Mercy's thighs. With Mercy's knees bent, Amelia placed one hand between her breasts to hold her against the tree, and she knelt to slip her tongue in between her thick thighs. Tasting her thoroughly first, she took her time as she found her delicate point of pleasure. Amelia twirled her tongue around her bud, causing Mercy's parted thighs to tremble.

The auras above shifted and shined its purple and pink light on them reflecting their passion. Mercy's hips couldn't remain still as Amelia feasted. She gripped what she could of the tree behind her, hands sliding down the rough bark. The contrast of the pain of the rough bark against her back and the pleasure of Amelia's hot mouth was exquisite. She was held up by Amelia's hand between her breasts, her thumb stroking the underside of her breast while her other thumb held a rhythm between her thighs. Leaning her head back, the deep clicks in her throat sounded right before the fire building inside engulfed her. The concession ripped through her body, and she cried out softly. The sound echoing in the small cove of trees.

She had never had an explosive finale quite like that before.

Despite the cold, sweat dripped down her face as she found her breath. Amelia began pulling up Mercy's armor to help her redress. The cold air caused her to shiver from the sheen of sweat on her body. Still kneeling in front of Mercy with her hand between her breasts, Amelia looked up and admitted, "You are perfect in every way. I've wanted you since you walked into the base. The day I formally met you, I lost my breath and could hardly utter a word. Becoming your friend after that was a delightful torture."

When Mercy and August entered the door at the base that day, and she looked down at Amelia, she should've known in that moment what they were meant to be. She remembered what she had seen behind Amelia's eyes. The light there that had shone for her, and only her.

Mercy had assumed Amelia had wanted her for a while but hadn't been fully aware of exactly how long. All the signs had been there. She was so wrong to think Amelia had just developed her feelings over the last few months, and she couldn't believe she didn't see that she had cared for her since that first day. Something moved inside of Mercy, a feeling of solidarity. She knew how that felt. To care for someone, someone who seemed so beyond reach.

Leaning down she smiled, pulled Amelia up and kissed her lips. Against them Mercy declared, "Screw waiting. I'm more than ready to have you." Mercy shoved Amelia into the snow and kissed her deeply. "I want you now. Lean up against the tree and pull your armor off," Mercy demanded as she looked into Amelia's blue eyes.

A grin spread on Amelia's face as she backed to the tree and slipped down her armor. It rolled to her thighs and Mercy took her time running her hands down Amelia's fit body. It was nothing like her curves and softness. Amelia was hard and powerful, strapped with muscle and a beautiful face of sharp angles.

Mercy ran her hands down the muscle of Amelia's stomach and between her thighs. Running her hand all the way down she found Amelia soaked for her. Mercy leaned up and kissed Amelia on the forehead. She kissed her on the lips and right above her collarbone on her neck. She kissed her softly on both nipples, taking a navy-blue peak into her mouth and drawing a gasp from Amelia.

Mercy kissed Amelia down her hard abs and slowly slipped her tongue between the depths of her thighs. Finding Amelia's bud, she pressed her hands down to hold her shaking hips as she explored. The sensuous moans Amelia made as she ran her hands over Mercy's fishtail braids and grabbed them on either side made her smile as she continued. She would draw this out. This stunning woman deserved to be feasted upon. She wanted her pleasure to linger as long as she could.

Pressing her face between her thighs, she devoured her. Mercy gently stroked up and down the center of Amelia's cut abs, her body quivering under the touch. The way she reacted to her touch thrilled Mercy, and she couldn't keep her hands off her. She wanted to explore every inch of her body.

Pressing down on her lower belly, Mercy flicked her bud relentlessly until Amelia threw her head back and made clicks deep in her throat. With her muscles tight, she shook as her pleasure crested, and she cried out when the climax overtook her.

When Mercy lifted her eyes, Amelia's body was a furnace, steaming in the freezing air. The power swirling between them surpassed anything either of them could have anticipated, assuring Mercy of the choice she made, and both knew this was a fire that could not be extinguished.

14

PLANET ADURO - CLAUDIUS ROYAL PALACE

Lucas worked out for many hours and slammed the doors on the way out. He didn't acknowledge August in the slightest, which was for the best. He was in his cell, locked this time. Livia must have been concerned he would do something stupid and attack Lucas during his workout. While tempting, he was not that dumb. She must have locked it when he was asleep. He hated having to sleep, being so vulnerable.

It had been hours cooped up, and he had no idea when Livia would show up to let him out, but he was bored and increasingly tired of waiting. Quite a while past the time she usually came, she burst through the doors in her usual tight fitting workout clothing. She also had a face full of makeup like she had been at a fancy ball. He noticed heavier makeup on her neck.

The blue blood in his veins simmered as she approached his cell, her eyes on the ground. She brought her bright blue eyes to meet the fire in his and something sparked inside of August, something full of anger and heat. Livia was going to be his. He didn't know how, but he would make it happen. His mind was void of all other desires when he looked at her. He walked out of his cell, and she left the door open as he headed into the training room and toward the center of the padded mat for their sparing matches.

Following behind August, Livia said, You're going back tomorrow. Lucas thinks something is going on. He hasn't said anything, but I know it's coming. He suspects *someone* but not you. Even with you being what you are, he might figure it out. He is leaving next week for his next mission, but he's claimed he is leaving someone in command to watch me. This is our last fight. "*Revertis cras. Lucas cogitat aliquid eundum. Relinquit hebdomadem proximum nam eius mox missio, sed postulavit is relinquit aliquem in iusso spectare me. Hic est nobis pugnam postremam.*"

He went over her words again and his insides became a whirlwind. He struggled to comprehend what she had just said. After a moment of thought, August turned around and softly replied, Well, I guess we will just have to make it count then. "*Immo, conicio faciemus summam tum.*"

Giving her no warning, August pounced on Livia. Grabbing her waist and lifting her above his head, he spun her around. She wrapped her legs around his arm and squeezed them together, causing August to lose his balance from the shift in weight. They fell over, and Livia had him in a headlock with her legs. He tapped her thigh, but slammed her down when she let him go and crawled over her from between her legs.

"*Quid facies?*" What are you doing? Livia asked.

August licked his lips and replied, If this is my last day, I'm shooting my shot. "*Si hic est postremus diurnus mihi, conicio mei coniecturam.*"

Livia grabbed his face before he could land a kiss on her painted red lips and whispered, Not a fucking chance. Maybe on another planet, in another universe, but not here and not today. If I go back and my makeup is smeared, I'm dead. "*Non fututus est casus. Fortasse in alia planeta, in alia universite, sed non hic et non hodie. Si reverto, et mei compositio oblinevit, sum mortuus.*"

August growled and rolled her shirt up along with the strip of fabric she had covering her breasts, and he descended on her. He twirled his tongue over each one of her taut nipples, causing her to arch and gasp. She tasted like salt and honey.

"*Siste. Nessese est sistis.*" Stop. You must stop. Livia groaned, while begging him inside her mind never to stop at all. She wanted him to continue, so badly she ached. He met her eyes, and she shook her head with a sorrowful no. Her eyes, in contrast, were pleading for him to keep going. He leaned over and gently kissed the tip of her peak before he rolled her shirt back down. She slammed her bald head back on the mat and growled as she grasped each side of her face. "*Dices sistere.*" You said to stop. August grumbled at her, his tone thick with suppressed frustration.

Livia seethed, I know, you fucking demon. I have to go. I shouldn't have ever come down here. I'm risking us both. I'm sending you back to the mines tomorrow morning. Felix and your cell guard will take you. Don't do anything stupid. "*Scio, futuo daemone... Non face aliquem stultum.*" With that, she easily wrapped her legs around August and flipped him off her. He landed face down on the mat with a grunt. The scent of her thick need fell over him, and he squeezed his eyes shut.

Livia sprinted to the door, slamming it on the way out.

August slowly made his way to his cell and closed the door. Fully aware she had left it unlocked, he stretched out to be comfortable. If this was his last night here, he should appreciate it while he could. The guard came back in and stood at his post. He stood staring at the wall next to August's cell. Not daring to be caught looking him in the eye but always peeking when he thought August was preoccupied.

His mind went straight back to Livia once he relaxed. He licked his lips. Her skin tasted like heaven. The way she squirmed under him was like nothing he had ever experienced. She was divine, and he knew that the waste of oxygen she was with would never satisfy her like he could, not a chance. August slid off to sleep and dreamed of the perfect set of breasts he had just tasted. The rest of the woman was just as perfect and filled his dreams.

The room darkened as the guard's shift ended. The night guards always strolled along the halls but never stood post in the training room like the day guard. There seemed to be no need with the cell locked, and August asleep.

August felt warm, sweet breath over his lips, and he drifted from wondering what was real and what was a dream. His eyes flew open to find a dark feminine scented being hovering over him. He knew that scent. He grabbed Livia's hips and pulled her form down on his growing excitement. She leaned into him, her lips met August's.

Her lips were soft and warm. He twirled her tongue with his and slid his hand to cup her breast under her loose sleep shirt. His other hand aimed to slide between her legs, and he couldn't resist as he found his way under her waistband. August cupped her center then twirled and caressed her heat with his finger, causing her to gasp into his lips.

He grabbed her hips and flipped them both over, so he

was on top of her, and she began running her hands under his shirt. He pulled her loose pants off and dove between her thighs. He buried his face in her little deep brown curls, with sharp breaths, Livia's leg's shook as he explored every inch of her and settled on her most sensitive place. He twirled and nipped her swollen bud as he snaked one of his hands up her body to play with her peaks. He found one of her hands already on her breast and wondered if she was forced to take care of herself to find pleasure. He batted her hand away so he could take over, and she let out a sweet sound, one he would do anything to hear again.

His heart pounded at the thought of her having to pleasure herself, and he took her to the edge repeatedly before he intentionally kept a rhythm which caused her legs to begin squeezing his head like a vise. Her hips rocked, and he grabbed them with force as he ran his tongue up and down her swollen and sensitive bud. She slapped a hand to her mouth as she shattered and rocked. Her body was overwhelmed as August wrung out every ounce of pleasure. She had never fallen apart like that. No one had ever given her what she wanted before, not like that. It was too perfect. He was too perfect.

This was a mistake. Covered in sweat, she frantically searched the dark for her pants, *I have to go. I'm sorry.* "*Debeo ire, miser ego.*"

"No. You're not going anywhere," August demanded, as he grabbed her hips and waited to thrust into her from behind.

Unable to resist, she leaned up and grabbed his hips in a crushing grip, pulling him to her as he lined himself up to pound into her flesh. He wadded her pants up and shoved them into her mouth as he leaned over to grab her shoulders.

He slammed into her, and she cried out into her gag. Pushing her down onto the mattress, he pressed into her from behind, and she pushed back. He slid his length into her over and over until the deep clicks sounded in his throat. He spilled into her and shook with the desire to cry out. He held her hips in bruising hold as he finished filling her. He bit his lips and moaned.

That was far too fast for her to have found her pleasure too. Annoyed with his body for being as excited as a young boy, he began preparing for round two. Livia slid off him and turned around to kiss him. Her searing, swollen lips found his.

The next thing he knew, the area was cold, and he was alone in the locked cell. Her scent still thick in the air.

What had just happened? Did I just have thirty second sex with a woman I just met days ago? Did I accidentally speak English to her? Damn. It all seemed like a wet dream. His face became hot with a hint of shame as he chuckled to himself.

August couldn't return to sleep as he stared into the darkness of the room and his mind raced. He had sex when he wanted to seal a relationship. He always did plenty of other things in lieu of sex if he was just casually dating some-one. He had sex with Livia without thought. In his entire life, he had only had sex with one other woman. He walked over to the small sink and cleaned himself before he laid back down to sleep. He didn't know how, but he had to find a way back to Livia. Somehow.

There was a creak as the doors opened, and Felix came through as August opened his eyes from a deep sleep. He signaled to the guard who handed him the key to the cell. August looked at Felix's red hair and then his own. The colors were different than one another. August's was much deeper and saturated. Felix had freckles like Jael but a lot more of them. They were not as nice looking on Felix as they were on Jael. Felix was a rather unsavory looking fellow, to him anyway.

When Felix opened the door of the cell, and August strolled out with his hands at his side. Felix adjusted for August to move out down the hall. Following the guard and with Felix behind him, they made their way down the long hall with the ceiling mosaic of crystals and through the doors at the end, they emerged in the gardens, and August looked around like he had before.

This time his eyes fell on Livia and Lucas arguing by the edge of the gardens on the other side of the room from him. Lucas struck her in the face with his open palm, and she was forced over with the violent slap. August vibrated with anger and clenched his fists.

Felix noticed at his change in stance and snapped, Cool it, demon. "*Alge, daemone.*"

Either they couldn't see what just happened or didn't care. August didn't know. He just needed to beat that big sack of toe sucking rot into a pulp, but if he moved from the direction he was going, the two guards he was with would have to die too. He didn't know if he could take all three and get Livia out. One guard he didn't particularly want to kill, and he knew of no safe destination. There were too many holes in his possible plans. There was no way out of this one yet. He would have to figure something else out.

They forced him outside, over to a transport, and he was thankful the system star was not up yet. It was hot enough, and he began sweating. The dry air sapped all moisture the instant the sweat beaded on his skin. He missed the cool, somewhat humid air in the palace. He ducked down and found his seat in the small transport.

Once they completed the uneventful ride, August was led back into the mines. He ran and grabbed a bucket, wanting to find the boy. August hiked down the ramp for a quarter mile before he realized he forgot his helmet with the reflector and had to return to the top of the mine.

When August turned around, a glob of mucus from one of the glowing worms hanging above dropped onto his face. He shook it off in disgust and wiped the rest with his shirt. He was not aware the disgusting creature did that, and he would never forget his helmet again. It took everything in his being to not yell yuck. The goo all over his face smelled like feces.

On his way again, with his helmet on his head, he sprinted down the twisting ramps all the way to where he hoped the boy would be. As he neared the area he was working in last, August didn't see him and his heart sank, but then he felt a tap on his arm and he turned, to find the boy standing next to him. The knot in his gut untied at the sight of the little boy. He silently walked over and resumed his place chipping away at the rock.

August sighed and found his place next to him. He picked his chisel up and struck the end with his hammer. Flat hammerheads crashing against the walls echoed throughout the enormous mine. As he listened, they created a unique music. Each person had their own beat, but together they produced a soul moving drum line. The music of his people resonated in his mind, and he decided in that moment what he was going to do, what he had to do.

His people were naturally gifted beyond reason, and he could not believe they could hide it for so long. As he looked around the cavern at all the blinking reflectors on the top of his people's helmets, an idea struck him. It was a long shot with his stubborn people, but it may work. He just needed to find someone to connect with him - someone who trusted him completely. That someone was the little boy he had befriended.

First, he would give the boy the gift.

Next, he would begin assembling a silent army.

This war would be won.

15

PLANET PORTUM – RECRUITMENT MISSION – SEASIDE VILLAGE

Long, thin strips of seaweed were draped over suspended tree branches which hung from the ceiling with twine. Some were dry, and others were so fresh they dripped. Small clusters of mushrooms would sprout in damp areas, making the walls and floor seem diseased.

Callum's stomach growled, and he begged it to stop. He had been trapped in her home for days. In the time he had been a hostage, his worry for Jacob had worn on him. The air was so thick with repulsive scents he could taste it. He truly did logically not believe the situation he was in could get any worse, yet he feared it would. He leaned up and looked out of the window noticing the overcast sky and the gathering darkness.

He knew he didn't actually *need* to eat, but he sure would have liked something not half rotten. He just hoped the old woman didn't hear his empty stomach growling, or she would try to give him more octopus. Why was his stomach rumbling so often? It had to be the nauseous smells. He was running out of hiding places for the food, and the tiny red, brown, and blue crabs running wildly around the floor were not eating his dropped pieces quickly enough to hide the evidence of his distaste. The little piles were beginning to grow behind the bench legs, and he did his best not to knock them over when he moved. Maybe it would be better if he could scatter the noxious bites around for the crabs to collect. He peered around the room and glowered at the angry old woman where she slept.

If he had to file on her rank claws anymore, he would vomit. Her feet smelled of putrid sea and rotten octopus. There was sand and pieces of kelp under her claws, like she was using them to dig. *Was she wading in the ocean and snatching these octopuses out of the water with her gnarly toes?* Callum shivered in disgust. He looked over at her again, lying there with her eyes closed, so peaceful, yet utterly repulsive.

He couldn't take it anymore. He understood why Jacob did it now. He stood over and grabbed her hand to connect. Waking, she looked at him strangely, but she didn't pull away. Her eyes widened, and her mouth dropped open as the gift flowed into her. She pulled her hand away and looked around the room as if the walls were on fire. Callum could smell her breath if he came too close, so he backed up to spare himself.

Everyone else in this village was just as low from the looks in their eyes. *How could a being become so crude?* His parents had never been this disgusting as they aged. They were elderly yet exceptionally clean people while this old woman was abhorrent. Callum gagged as the scent of her open mouth hit him. He hadn't backed up enough. Queasiness was obvious on his face, and he did everything he could not to tell this woman out loud exactly how grotesque she was. The dried dead creatures hanging all over her kitchen gave her home a complex and layered scent of fish and death under the fresh rot, and neither were pleasant. Callum fear dying in this deceptively cute yet horrifically filthy house. How quickly dreams can become nightmares!

Panic began to set in as he desperately backed away from the creepy old woman. His tail bumped the wall, and he sat down on the bench under him. He was trapped in hell, a backwoods, disgusting hell, where his love Jacob was still tied up in the shed along with Adrian and Juni.

The old woman walked up and sat next to him, grabbing his hand to connect. "Our leader is twin sister. She out first when birth. She make rules. You can go but other stay," she relayed into the connection.

"Jacob is my love, my person, my everything. You can't ask me to leave him here," Callum pleaded to her.

Nodding she replied, "Maybe you take. I talk sister."

"What about the other two?" Callum asked, sending extreme worry through the connection.

"Oh, we will keep them until octopus stop washing up, then we eat them." She explained, absolutely matter of fact as if this course of action wasn't something out of Callum's nightmares.

A feeling of hunger like he had never known ripped through him, straight from the connection, and he nearly vomited with the sensation. He knew she was thinking about how good his friends would taste. Bile rose in his throat, and he pressed the back of his hand to his mouth. "No, no, you can't! They are our friends. They're not food! You can't eat them." Callum pleaded as he held back the gag.

How had the rest of their world been unaware these people were cannibals? Why did no one warn them?

She laughed and, in the connection, said, "Take it back. We eat all. You leave."

"What if we offered you something?" Callum asked, desperate beyond measure.

"What you have I want?" she asked, sure of herself and sure he had nothing she wanted.

Callum thought long and hard before he replied, "Our doctors have medicine which can kill your brain worms."

She abruptly pulled the connection away and slapped Callum hard across the face. His heart sunk, and he was afraid he had just creeped back up onto the dinner menu. The skin on his face stung where she struck him. He put his hand to his cheek and glared at her. She angrily hobbled off to the kitchen where she poked around a bit aimlessly and came back. She sat down next to him and held her hand out for him to connect, "You think that's what wrong all us? You think got worms in head?"

Callum couldn't tell if she was serious or not, so he just answered truthfully, "Yes, I think you're getting parasites from the octopus, crabs, and anything else you eat that's living in the sea. These parasites are strong."

"Does eating our own kind give you parasites?" she asked, sincerely her eyes wide with wonder.

Callum's eyes went wide as well, and he quickly drummed up some additional disgust to his tone, "Oh, so many, lots of parasites, the worst kind, they um, they make nipples and legs fall off." Praying to the creator, Callum begged with every fiber of his being this old woman believed him. Nipples and legs? Was that really the best he could come up with?

She looked at him with narrowed eyes, reached up with her free hand and grasped the end of her long breast, thinking. She nodded and conceded, "Oh. Well, better do." He held his breath. Scrunching her brow, she asked, "How do medicines?"

"I don't know, but I can have them here in a couple days if you just let us go," he begged with truth in every single word.

Nodding, she relented, "OK, I let friends go, but I want brain worm things, or I will hunt down, and I will have friends supper."

Callum swallowed down his fright and acknowledged her, "Yes, ma'am. I believe you."

She waddled over to the door and went through it, heading toward the shed. Callum's heart leapt uncontrollably as they approached. As they walked up, she opened the door and shoved Callum inside. She locked the door back behind her and walked off. Callum looked around the cracks of the door wildly as he tried to figure out what the fuck just happened. His confusion cleared when he realized he was not tied up. She had thrown him in the shed with a way to untie his friends.

He kicked all of their legs to make sure they were awake, and his movements were frantic as he showed them his free hands. Juni's eyes hadn't adjusted, so he took her face in his hands, and she noticed right away, gasping. Jacob shoved his bound hands in Callum's face.

He worked as fast as he could, untying Jacob's hands first and Adrian's next. When he was done with Adrian's, Jacob had already untied Juni's hands. They all searched the back of the shed, and Adrian slowly pulled at the first loose board he found. It hardly made a sound as it slid free from the wall. They all looked at each other as they slid the next board away then another. They soon had enough free they could all crawl out of the back.

One by one, they squirmed out of the small hole and into the space beyond the shed. Adrian was the only one who struggled because of his enormous size, but once they were all in line behind the shed, they surveyed the area and Jacob signal a point in the woods at the edge of the village, and they took off. They sprinted through the woods until Adrian barreled into someone. The mix of oak trees in palm trees were thick, and it was impossible to see with the lush canopy above in combination with the cloudy day. Adrian righted himself and swung his fists. They continued to swing fists until Adrian finally took out the villager with a punch to the head, and they landed on the ground with a thump. Callum helped Adrian off the ground while Jacob made sure the villager was knocked out. Even if he was just in the wrong place at the wrong time, they wouldn't let him tell the others where they were headed.

The group continued, heading back toward their camp-site. They needed to move before they were caught again. Their bare feet crunched on the leaves all over the forest floor. Different fungus, in an array of pastel colors, grew out of all the surrounding trees. As they ran, they knocked into some of them hanging low in the spaces between the trees. Their caps exploded with spores at the impact creating eerie arial bombs.

As soon as they reached the clearing, they scrambled to pack up and rapidly threw everything together onto their bikes. None of them put on their armor and just slung it over their packs. The magnets would hold it to the bike.

They had just slid their helmets on as two huge men

with their tails extended over their shoulders came jetting from the woods. Distress exploded in them as the men leaped toward their hover-bikes. Slamming on the throttles, the four hover-bikes shot out of the clearing and away from the two hulking men, who continued to charge after them, seeming to be even more enraged at the side of technology.

Callum was on the verge of tears as he cried into the helmet comms, "They were going to eat all of you. They weren't going to eat me, but they were planning to eat the rest of you. I couldn't let them do it."

Jacob turned his head slowly toward Callum before righting it again as he replied, "You just had to mention that they didn't want to eat *you* though. Thanks for throwing that extra tad bit in there, Callum."

Shivering from a nearing storm's cold wind whipping his body, and from the thoughts of those backwoods cannibals, Jacob hit the throttle again. He was so glad he had only found out about the cannibal part now. If he had found out in that shed before they had escaped, he might have been the first Iungo to have ever experienced a natural cardiac arrest.

They were going to travel for as long as possible before stopping.

Next time, they were doing more reconnaissance, and they were not *ever* just strolling into a village as a group again.

16

PLANET PORTUM - UTC COMMAND MISSION

Mercy and Jael strolled under the red light of the failed star while searching the snow for branches and twigs tumbled down from the mountainside. The snow looked pink under the rosy sky. This side of the mountain didn't have many trees besides at the top where the light of the auras arched across. Jael spotted a branch and picked it up, adding it to the rest under her arm. To look out from the other side of the mountain was to look on a wasteland, there was nothing but snow and rock. After the mountains, stretched miles of flat desert.

They were running out of firewood as it was even colder here than it was on the other side. The lack of solar energy on the temperature was astounding. The cold on this side of the mountain sunk deep into their bones and rattled them.

The walk had been quiet so far and she didn't want to break the silence, but Jael couldn't wait any longer. "Is everything okay? You have been distant lately."

"Oh, sorry, I haven't meant to be that way. I just have a

lot on my mind," Mercy replied as she leaned down to grab a tiny stick and add it to her bundle.

Side eyeing her, Jael pushed, "Spill it. Something is going on."

"I may have fucked Amelia," Mercy stopped and stared at Jael with her golden eyes wide.

Jael's mouth fell open, and she asked, "Wait, what? Really? That is not what I thought happened. I mean, I didn't know, I just didn't think it would be that. It all happened so fast."

"We don't typically hide our feelings or wait. We also tend to be a little more outgoing than humans are. That's my opinion. I was different in the way I waited for August for so long. He ended up being taken from me. You can't wait, not ever. I should have let him go before I ever had him," Mercy's words were clipped and her voice cracked.

"I just thought you might wait for August since you waited so long before," Jael admitted.

Pain laced through Mercy at her words. She didn't want anyone to know he had been planning to end things with her. Her heart broke all over again, and she did her best to keep her face from showing her pain. She held so still. She still had a long road of healing ahead. Her time with Amelia helped, but it was going to take time to mend herself.

Jael noticed her change in composure and apologized, "I shouldn't have said that. I'm sorry. Let's finish collecting these bundles of twigs and head back."

"It's okay. It wasn't really what you said," Mercy replied quietly.

Mercy nodded blankly at Jael when she was ready, and they grabbed the last few sticks before heading back to camp. Her feet were worn out, she was hungry, and she couldn't wait to eat some stew. She could smell the flatbread Oz was making on a large stone next to the fire. Her stomach howled at the scent. She was ecstatic, so she skipped the rest of the way back.

She wondered if they were possibly drawing attention to themselves with the fire but decided there wasn't much that could be done. They couldn't cook without it, and she was not eating raw vegetables. They didn't have nearly enough dried fruit to last, so that wasn't an option either. The fire was small and mostly hidden by stones anyway, and it was too dark to see any smoke.

As she and Jael sat eating their stew, Amelia joined them. "So, Jael, I've been reviewing some of your old memories from Earth and some of the specific linguistics of different Earth languages. Are you aware you are pronouncing your name incorrectly?" Amelia asked.

Jael slowly turned and looked at her in confusion, "I am doing what now?"

Before turning to face them, Mercy slowly slid a hand over her mouth. Amelia realized she may have just made a social goof, and she carefully explained, "You pronounce your name *jail*, like a prison, but in the language your name is from, you would pronounce your name *Yale*."

Jael stared at Amelia blankly and asked, "Are you telling me I've been mispronouncing my name this whole time?" Behind Jael, Mercy's eyes were blazing and pleading at Amelia to shut up.

Amelia, trying to make things better, explaining, "I'm sure where you're from in Texas it is common for people to make such linguistic mistakes. All of us have a little of your twang because we have your memories."

With her mouth gaping, Jael replied, "That does NOT

help. In fact, I think that makes it worse. I really gave an entire race of humanoid beings a country twang? I don't think that's something I'm ever going to get over. I haven't felt like this much of a backwards country girl in a long time. I'm going to need a minute."

Behind Jael, Mercy continued glaring at Amelia. When Jael stood up to clean her bowl, Mercy leaned over to Amelia and snapped, "You just had to say that, didn't you?"

Amelia slowly slid her eyes down into her bowl and finished it quietly. As she dipped her flat bread in her stew, she thought about how she really needed to work on her social skills. These emotional connections were trickier than battle strategy.

After an uneventful break, they packed up and headed down the mountain. The trip down was much easier than the trip up, even with the bitter cold pushing them to the brink. This side of the mountain was littered with boulders and obstacles, making their trip more of a random zigzag than a straight path. When they reached the bottom at the edge of the ice, Carter stopped and stared at the open dirt in front of them. An odd scent filled the air, a scent one would consider curiously alluring.

The stationary red glow from above cast permanent shadows on rocks spread over the land, each one with little ice patches in the darkness. No one took a step forward as Oz looked over at Carter for an answer, but Carter remained still and quiet. Looking out into the crimson cast land, he shifted his weight and tilted his head but stayed silent. Oz walked over to him and leaned in softly, "What's going on? Are you okay?"

He shook his head and admitted, "Something about this

ground is not right. I don't trust it. I sense suspiciously attractive pheromones in the air."

With a worrisome look in her eye, Aurelia spoke up, There is supposed to be something out here, something that steals soldiers. We are told to stay close to the camps so we are not targeted. We were never told what was out there. "*Est opinari aliquem ex hoc, aliquis surripet milites. Narratus sumus detinere propa ad castra ut non scopus sumus. Numquam narramus quid fuit foris ibi.*"

Internally groaning, Oz wondered if they would encounter this *something* or not, but he stayed on high alert for a monster of an unknown kind. He was really tired of all the hungry creatures who wanted to eat him for dinner. Everything from the trees to the creatures wanted a bite. In the back of his head, worry whispered, *You're not like anything else on this planet Oz... you aren't really from here.*

Lies, he told himself, and Oz took one step forward onto the sandy soil.

Carter said, "Wait." Dion stood next to Carter, his blonde hair pulled back in a single knot at his nape. His light beige skin was pink in the glow of the brown dwarf. He looked over at Carter and asked, "Do you think there's something under the sand?"

Carter nodded, "My intuition rarely lies. Watch every step. If the sand moves, run."

Dion, Wynn, and Sands all went first, then Mercy and Amelia behind them. Carter and Aurelia were next, and he grabbed her hand before taking a step. Hazel and Harlen held hands while they moved forward in line. Zoe, Lark, and Costel followed behind Oz and Jael.

In pairs with Zoe at the end, they slowly crossed the sand. There were little black succulents scattered in the dirt.

Some had little open mouths lined with spikes like fly traps. The immature jade trees crossed Oz's mind, and he cringed. This would be the perfect environment for carnivorous plants. Roughly exhaling, he asked, "Does this place receive rain? Or it is a desert?"

"I think it's a dark desert," Carter replied, his steps still soft and light.

They reached a large flat stone after a slow day's walk and stopped for a rest. It was cold but not nearly as bitter as it was on the mountain. They had all been able to turn their armor's heat setting halfway down. Without solar energy to recharge from the auras, they needed to conserve when possible.

Carter stood at the edge of the stone and kept his eyes out to the west toward the mountain to their left. The entire journey through the pass and down the mountain dread filled him. It built with each step. The huge form of the brown dwarf looming in the sky, transfixed in one place glared down on them like an angry eye. He shifted and faced it. Nothing here felt right.

Curious, Amelia walked up to Carter and asked, "You came in for a checkup right before the base was attacked. Have you had a similar feeling since?"

Looking to the left first, Carter turned and caught Amelia's eye before softly saying, "There's something out there."

She took that as a *yes* and nodded her head. Amelia approached Oz and waited until he was finished talking to Jael before she butted in, "Carter had a feeling like this before the base was attacked. I don't know if it's exactly the same or not. He keeps saying there's something out there, and I think we need to listen. I think he has a deeper sensory perception which we are not able to process. I don't think he is supernaturally gifted; I think his intellect is twenty steps ahead of the rest of us," Everything inside of Amelia screamed to believe him.

"What do you want to do? Go in that direction?" Oz asked, hoping that's not what Amelia meant.

Nodding Amelia replied, "That's exactly what I think we should do. Instead of running, we should face it. I think we should go left."

"What happens when we all die and the whole mission is ruined? Our people will be enslaved again, probably forever this time," Oz said emphatically.

Amelia considered her idea and offered, "But what if Carter is right, and we are walking into a trap? Or what if some horrible creature is hunting us? We might be facing an enemy on both sides."

Oz closed his eyes and leaned his head back. *Why did she have to be right?* He grumbled about getting fucking eaten and walked over to Zoe.

He leaned over toward her to quietly speak, "Amelia wants to go the other way and find out if something has been following us, all based on Carter's intuition or spicy magical sense. I think I agree."

"I believe Carter because he is smarter than all of us. Magic is not real," Zoe answered flatly.

Rolling his eyes, Oz replied, "You know what I mean. He did predict the base raid. He has some kind of ability we don't."

Making a guttural sound of annoyance Zoe replied, "Oh yeah. That sounds great. Let's go into the dark desert for a deadly fucking adventure. Good plan. Why did I sign up for this again?"

"Uh, saving the world and such." There was an air of smugness to Oz's voice.

Zoe glared at him and replied, "Right, so tell me again why we are heading the opposite way that we need to go, in order to fight a monster we know nothing about. I feel like we are a bunch of moths, heading straight for a flame, and when we arrive, ZAP!"

"Listen. All good points, but I think we're going for it." Oz stood confidently with his hands on his hips.

Squeezing her eyes shut, Zoe grumbled, "This is really going to bite. I just hope not literally."

Zoe, Amelia, Mercy, Dion, Sands, Oz, and Costel all suited up with their plasma swords. They slipped their helmets on and headed out onto the sandy ground. Oz called Jacob from the helmet and was shocked to see Jacob looking so distant and quiet, not at all like himself.

"Are you okay?"

Shaking his head Jacob rambled, "We were taken. The south village is off limits, no one goes there. Never again. NEVER. Callum got us out. He had to file some nasty old woman's dirty toe claws or something to get on her good side. He said he traded medicine being dropped off for our release, so I have the base on it.

"Oz, I think that whole village is full of people with brain parasites. There was something wrong with all of them. It was like the commercials of horror movies from Jael's memories, except it was real. I thought we were all going to die. We were tied up in a shed for days. Turns out, after all of that, they wanted to eat us! *Eat us*, Oz!"

Oz stopped moving as he asked, "Whoa! How do you know they wanted to eat you?"

"Because Callum gave one of the old women the gift.

Well, technically I gave her sister the gift first, but she got mad, umm, well anyway, she told Callum her sister was going to eat us when the octopus stopped washing up!" Jacob's words came out in a jumble.

As shock ran through him, Oz's eyebrows shot up, "You're being serious? That's fucked up. Have Pike outfit a drone and send the medicine right away."

"That's what I'm doing. I have to have them drop some off to Callum, too. He was forced to eat the octopus. He's in the tent right now, groaning about a stomachache. I haven't broken it to him yet, but that means the parasites have hatched, and they're already burrowing through his intestine walls," Jacob explained, trying to calm down but also not actually calming at all.

Disgusted, yet trying not to show it, Oz changed the subject, "We are taking a detour because Carter had a feeling."

"Wait, what? Carter had a feeling? That's all you're going on? I knew we shouldn't have sent you to lead the mission," Jacob admitted, his brow furrowed.

Oz smiled as he started walking again. The group was several yards ahead now. "Amelia agreed, and we talked Zoe into checking out what it is. I'm sure we can take care of it," Oz replied, suddenly not feeling so confident.

Jacob grumbled something and hung up, his face dematerializing into nothing. A gleam of light hit the corner of Oz's eye, drawing his attention. He stared at the footprints in the sand and noticed something odd. There was a small piece of metal. It was bent, and one part was melted on the edge. He scrutinized it with narrowed eyes and wondered what the hell could have caused a piece of metal to land all the way out here. He looked around and noticed several mounds. They were small and seemed to blend in with the scenery. Something about the mounds was enticingly strange, and Oz couldn't break his eyes from them. Something wasn't right. Shifting his focus to the head of the group, he noticed some mounds were in their path, right where Dion was walking. He had Zoe right behind him. Oz stopped and loudly warned, "Be careful up there. The mounds look suspicious."

With no warning, Dion screamed and thrashed on the ground sending sand flying. He was being dragged into the den of a giant trap-door spider. The beast was the size of one of their hover bikes. Snapping into action, Zoe reached out and grabbed Dion, kicking the spider in the face repeatedly. They all watched as the spider sunk its fangs into Dion's leg, causing him to lean his head back and scream. Beginning to lose consciousness, Dion slumped over, and the spider started dragging a furious Zoe into its den. Costel, who was closest, dove for Zoe and Dion while Oz ran for them from behind.

As Oz neared, he leapt and pulled out his plasma sword, plunging it into the head of the massive spider. It slumped over dead, releasing Dion, and they fell forward in a pile.

Dragging Dion away from the dead monster, removing his helmet, Zoe began assessing him for injuries starting by putting her hand near his face to feel for breath. He was breathing, barely.

Amelia checked the bite for bleeding and venom reaction. Oz felt guilty because he consented to this random excursion and asked, "Is he going to make it?"

Amelia had her hand at his wrist, "I don't know. It might take a few days to see what the venom does. He's in bad shape. We need to move him somewhere safer."

Leaning his head back momentarily, Oz cleared his throat and reevaluated the situation. "Let's haul him back to camp. These damn tunnel spiders must have been what Carter was worried about. We should have fucking stayed where we were."

Shaking his head, he watched as they picked up Dion. Zoe had him under his arms and Amelia had his feet. His head lolled back lifelessly. They hadn't taken more than three steps when a noise came from about a mile away. The sound was a strange oscillating pattern, and Oz instantly filled with dread.

What had they gotten themselves into? Had he led them into a trap? Panic set in as the sound of the engine grew. His team began looking around for the origin of the sound. "Run!" Oz cried out, and they all began sprinting from the sound. Oz ran up and grabbed one of Dion's arms and Costel grabbed his other leg. He hung between them, suspended, dangling, and swinging wildly as they ran. When Oz checked behind them, there was a single point of light, and it was growing closer.

"Fuck! Run! Faster!" Oz yelled as the group did their best to increase their speed, but it was no use with Dion unconscious.

Just as the camp came into view, the machine caught up. The egg-shaped transport swung in front of them and a large sliding door swung open and banged on its hinges. A tiny old human woman with curly white hair, wearing some kind of night vision goggles and clad in leather, tottered around the corner, and cried out, Hop in, bitches! Get in if you want him to live! *"Sali caniculae! Intrate si vis eum vivare!"*

Stunned too much to speak, Oz just froze and stared up at the woman. Dressed in a dusty military style leather uniform, she was missing one of her front teeth and wore a strap of thick fabric over her body with various loops each filled with tools and weapons. The skin on her face was deeply wrinkled and a pale pink in the red light of the brown dwarf. Her outfit was topped off with a tattered dark green beanie on her fuzzy white hair.

Oz was not getting in that flying egg.

In a gravelly tone only a lifetime smoker could have, the woman croaked, I know you're not stupid. Look at what you're wearing. I'm on your side. Just get in the transport so we can get your friend some medicine. That spider's bite will liquify his insides over the next four days. "*Scio to non es stultus... Ille aranae ictus liquefaciet eius viscera super deinde quattor dies.*"

Tilting his head to the side as he slipped off his helmet, Oz asked, Who are you? "*Quis es?*"

Flipping up her night vision goggles, she glared at him.

"*Aliquis Regna vult assare in ramulo. Venisne aut non?*" Someone the empress wants to roast on a skewer. Are you coming or not? she demanded, her patience overtly running thin as she tapped the door of the transport.

17

PLANET ADURO - CLAUDIUS ROYAL PALACE

Nude and dripping wet, Livia balanced on the narrow lip of her bathtub. The gleaming wall of windows reached from the floor to the ceiling and reflected her battered body and the bruised emotions flashing across her face. She had sent him back. The demon. She had never been with anyone when she married Lucas. It wasn't possible. Her father had been strict about where she went and what she did. It was rare a guard wasn't close by. Her demon was the only other man she had ever been with besides her wretched husband.

Her father could have named her to succeed him. His mother was the crowned queen of Aduro. *Why couldn't he see I would have made a better ruler than Lucas?* It was always about submission. Her grandmother was beat within an inch of her life over decisions the king didn't approve of. It was her voice which was law, but she still forcibly submitted to her husband. Her mother's death was from abuse. It was the unfortunate way of the Claudius royal family - *A result of only ordering male children with low empathy, perhaps.*

There was no question, something was deeply wrong with the Claudius' males. She dreaded the inevitable day of her father's death, the day Lucas came home and stayed home. She looked down at her bruised wrists, the dark purple visible on the slightly paler brown skin of the inside of her wrist, the deep, green tinged black, splotches on the palms of her hands. Would she survive him, or die like her mother? She knew Lucas caused her mother's death. She couldn't prove it, but she knew he was in her room that day. She had pulled the door sensor log. His neural codes were not on the list, but there was evidence the codes had been tampered with, edited. Only he and her father had the royal clearance to alter it. Her broken body had Lucas's signature abuse all over it. She knew her father had consented to it, probably even the rape.

She will never forget her mother's light bronze skin in the bright starlight as she danced in the atrium palace just a few days before her death. She glowed in the warm light streaming through and her joy in the music and her movement was radiant. She wished she had known it would be the last time she would see her mother.

As she stood, still balancing on the rim of the tub, the water dripped from her wet body and ran over the edge to form a pool on the floor. The drips were the only sound in the room besides her breath. She searched the desert view through the window and found the little shimmering metal pole at the end of the transport landing pad. It was her point of reference to find the mine from the palace, where *he* was held. The one living person in the universe she cared about, the one who had so quickly stolen a piece of her heart, was at the same time her father's prisoner.

Only one of Pluto's demons could have melted her bitter heart so quickly.

Mine 03

Sweat dripped down August's face as he chipped away at the stone. It was almost time for their rest period. When he heard the chime of the bell, he followed the boy to the top to turn in his bucket and gear. He followed him to the food line, and they both headed together to the same bunk as before. The scent of the air was thick with sorrow and dry sweat. The bed creaked as he sat. The boy sat right next to him and lay his head on his shoulder. The love emanating from him was overwhelming.

August did not know why this child took to him so swiftly. When they finished eating, the kid took their bowls, and he lay down on the cot. When the boy returned, August pulled one blanket over the mattress first. The boy curled up next to August's side, like a kitten, as August took the second blanket and tucked it over the child.

He needed to send this gift of language around the people somehow. He didn't have a choice, and this little boy was the only one who trusted him. On a hunch, he suspected the kind and open hearts of his people would never deny communicating with a child.

August reached behind his back, gently nudged the child, and signaled to him he needed to convey something. The boy moved quickly, sitting up facing away from August.

He held his hand between them to initiate a neural connection. Back-to-back, they stayed vigilant.

The boy conveyed trepidation, but also great familiarity with August. He had been born on the factory planet, Sclavus Six. He saw long industrial apartment buildings where the boy's people lived. The work camps spread out over hundreds of miles. They were being used for refining, and all of them had a band around one of their extremities of various colors. He showed August his father, and the boy's father could have been August's twin. They looked almost identical. No wonder the boy took to him so deeply. Significant pain came after the memories, and August almost didn't want to know what happened to the boy's family.

The boy conveyed total trust in him, and he knew it was time.

August decided since he had the boy's attention, he would share the gift right then. He passed it over, and he could hear the boy pull in a sharp breath after a few moments. The boy turned his head over to August with wide eyes and spoke through the connection, "We are not supposed to connect! If anyone of our people found out, they would push us into the depths of the mine, thousands of feet down. The connection is sacred. They won't care I'm a kid. The cave worms' acidic saliva would dissolve us into nothing but bones in just a few weeks. I don't want to die like that!"

"I understand, but I need your help. I need to pass the gift to anyone who will listen. Will anyone else talk with you?" August asked while transmitting feelings of desperation.

The boy shook his head no and broke the connection. He didn't run off, so August wasn't feeling like a complete failure, yet. Maybe he could still convince him to help. He hoped. The rough blanket under him made his skin itch. He missed the mattress of the cell inside the palace. This one under him stunk of sweat and piss.

After he fell asleep, the boy stayed next to him. He had never dreamed he would find someone who looked so much like his father. He knew it wasn't really his father, but something inside of him felt comforted, anyway. He let the language August had given him sink in while he rested. The world Jael lived in was so much more than he had ever experienced. His world was so tiny by comparison. Overwhelmed, he silently wept before he sorted through it. He never knew his thoughts could be organized, much less symbols could have so much meaning. August asked him for help, and he had answered no. He felt so bad. He signaled to his father "no," and that's when he lost him. It had been his fault, but not this time. This time he would do the right thing. He squeezed his eyes shut, trying to force away the memory of his father being dragged away. He knew he shouldn't have been so close to the edge of the canyon. His father had just whistled. That was all. They took his father away for whistling at him so he wouldn't fall.

He slipped down from his spot as August twitched in his sleep. The boy cringed, feeling troubled for August's need to sleep. The idea of sleep, and its helplessness, scared him. A bed nearby creaked, and he absently shifted his attention. He studied the two in the bunk, glancing to one another. Sorrow consumed them both.

A name, he wanted his name to be Chris. There were superheroes on Jael's world named Chris. It seemed like a good one. He knew they were just movies, but he didn't care. He made his way over to the woman's bunk where he usually hung around and sat on it with her. He was usually at the end in a ball, so this was a little different. He had never tried to connect with anyone before, so he took her beige colored hand slowly.

She yanked it away and glared at him, but he persisted. She finally relented when she realized he wasn't taking no for an answer. He set his hand against hers and connected with her. Her hand was warm, but rough from years of work in the mines.

He passed her the gift, and her eyes went wide with consideration. The memories and knowledge soared by her consciousness as they settled in her mind. It was as if someone had struck her with a staff of understanding. Her head ached as her thoughts shifted, and she broke the connection with Chris.

There was a message at the end of the gift from August. In a soft kind voice, he explained, "I want to take over this planet like my people did on our home world. If we did it there, we can do it here." The woman scoffed. She had thought about rebellion before. That's what sent her into this sandy hell in the first place.

She hissed at a guard on Sclavus Six. Twice. She was hit over the head and then sent to Aduro. She only knew what it was called because the guards had said it many times. It had taken her a month, but she picked up their language. In Earth years that was over twenty years ago.

She had only been about thirty when it happened. She had been so stupid to be torn away from your family for simply hissing. She missed her husband and her children desperately. They would be grown by now. It had been so many lonely years.

Maybe the one who sleeps, August, is right. Maybe they

should form a resistance. It was reckless, but what else were they going to do with their lives? Just work them away until they die? She had watched hundreds of elderly become too old to work. They were just pushed off into the center of the mine, to hit the bottom and rot in the saliva of the glowing worms.

They all just meekly stood by and cowered when one of their own was shoved in, never doing anything to stop any of it. All of them were too fearful, too desperate to hold onto what little life they're allowed to have. Their captors truly believed her people were on the same level as an insect she thought as her blood began to boil. They had numbers, but so many of them were docile and meek. They were a soft and gentle people, not hard, never harsh.

The bed beneath her creaked as she stretched her legs out echoing the screams in her heart. Her mind twirled, and she decided she needed a name. She knew it was uncommon, but she liked Dragon. It seemed like if she had a strong and formidable name, maybe it would empower her to be more than just an obedient, subservient worker who drudged through each day until death. She would play along in her daily duties, but she would help August in his endeavor. She took Chris's hand and connected with him saying, "I'm in, but no more connecting like this. Either our own people or the guards will catch on."

Feeling Chris's embarrassment flutter through the connection, she said, "My name is Dragon. I see you picked Chris. Good choice. Let's be careful, okay? I could see how a child can get away with making the guards think you're wanting to hold someone's hand. Don't. Get. Caught."

The boy agreed, "Okay, I know exactly who I am going to tell next."

He slid off Dragon's bunk and went back to August, who was breathing heavily as he lay there dreaming. As usual, he had attracted a crowd, and Chris pushed through all the people entertained by watching him sleep. One woman leaned in fascinated by his eyes move under his eyelids. Chris sat in front of August and glowered at everyone standing around. They all backed off and went back to their own bunks.

Chris made himself comfortable and started forming a plan on how he could connect with the big blue man. The blue man was tall and would be a good person to help August. He had been kind and had shared his grub chips with him before. He had no idea why August would not eat those. They were delicious, so much better than some of the slop he had to eat back home. After the blue man, who else could he connect with?

When the bell dinged for them to start work, Chris leapt up and ran for the front of the room. He saw the tall blue man and dove onto the ground at his feet, pretending to fall down. He made the situation a little bit too real and accidentally skidded to a halt. When he looked down, he could already see a bit of blue blood on his loose tan pants. He grabbed his skinned knee, and the navy blue-haired man knelt down to help him back up. As their hands met, Chris connected with him and sent him the gift. The entire act took less than ten seconds. It worked exactly how he had planned it out. He looked down at his dusty clothes and began brushing them off. Dust flew everywhere. His shirt and pants were now stained the color of the floor.

After coughing from all the dust, the blue-haired man slowly stood and peered down at Chris. He tilted his head to the side and glared at him sharply. Chris peered around, looking to see if anyone was paying attention. It seemed like they did it! The man was still scowling, but now it was in a thinking way and not an angry way. The entire interaction between their hands had only taken ten seconds. Chris's developing mind had already come up with several ways he could make one of his kind hold his hand, and he just needed ten seconds.

He found his place in line next to August and nodded his head at him. August tilted his head to the side, not understanding. A glow worm glob fell between them, landing in a sizzling pile they both grimaced at as they passed. Chris bit his lips and hid a smile. He had a great surprise for August when they could speak next. As they walked, he began formulating more plans and different ways he could spread the gift. He was determined to help this time. He wasn't going to make the same mistake he made before.

18

PLANET PORTUM – RECRUITMENT MISSION – AMELIA'S VILLAGE

"I am so glad we don't sleep and dream. After the bullshit we just went through, I know we would have nightmares. I find it interesting humans on Jael's world invest in dreams like they do fortunetelling. I wonder if the other humans we're fighting are superstitious," Callum speculated as he side eyed Jacob, trying not to make it obvious he was staring.

He would do anything to take his mind off his aching gut. There was a little natural spring bubbling from under a rock, and Jacob stood in the freezing cold water washing himself. Each splash made him cringe and suck in sharp breaths. Shivering from the cold and from the memories of their last stop, he closed his eyes and willed the thoughts away. Peering down, he wondered if his balls were ever going to emerge from hiding. He was not made for cold! "Do you think it was a mistake to give them language? What if they use it for their own benefit and come after us?" Jacob asked, fright spawning into dread in his gut. His stomach groaned.

He nervously looked around the woods and back to

Callum who was propped up under the trees at the edge of the spring. Callum responded, "Maybe after the parasite medicine they will be able to think more clearly. You know since the brain worms will be dead."

Registering the literal holes in Callum's positive suggestion, he just stood and appreciated his love's constant attempts to ease his anxiety. "They will just have holes where the brain worms used to be. I don't think it's going to help anything." Jacob cringed as he toweled off.

"Speaking of, when are my meds supposed to be dropped off?" Callum asked, as his stomach cramped in distress.

He groaned and leaned over, resting his head on his knees. The pains all over his stomach were increasing in frequency and duration. He felt like they were burrowing through his intestines, and they probably were. That thought grossed him out so badly that he just avoided the whole subject all together. He knew what was happening medically, but facing it was another matter.

After toweling off, Jacob pulled his armor up, "Today, sometime. I'll get an alert on my tablet."

"What are we doing today? Just scouting? No strolling into a village full of backwoods cannibals, right?" Callum leaned back on a tree and curled his arms around his middle, thankful the medicine was on its way.

Jacob tossed him the bag with soap, "Wash your stinky ass before you attract something that wants to eat us. I've had enough of being on the menu for a lifetime. Also, yes, we're just scouting today and the next day. We are scouting until we know for a fact we aren't walking into a trap."

"No wonder the UTC never takes people from that creepy village. Ick. How did we miss that?" Callum asked no one in particular as he stood up and stripped off his armor.

Wading in the tiny frigid stream, Callum shivered as he washed up. Splashing into the water, he had to hold back a yelp. It was rough enough as his feet submerged in the freezing water. The slick rocks mocked him as he stepped carefully, hoping he would not fall in.

Once he was clean, he jogged to his armor and quickly slid it on, not waiting until he was completely dry. He had no time for that. He just wanted to be warm so his blood could flow again. Spinning his finger on the dial, he turned the temperature up and waited for the heat to thaw him.

A terribly odd sound erupted from somewhere around him. The unexpected noise startled him but he quickly realized what it was as he felt a brief flutter at his neck. As the armor heated, more steam begun erupting from Callum's armor. The suit had a moisture removal feature in case they sweat. The only reason Callum knew was because he helped design the suits. The sound was similar to a particularly gravely, breathy voice, and Jacob searched the area trying to locate the source. Biting his lips together, Callum hid a grin as the suit let off more steam, causing Jacob to panic, desperately seeking the surrounding area for the source of the eerie noise.

Reaching the campsite, Callum couldn't hold in his amusement as an enormous bubble of steam worked its way up the suit and sounded like a giant had exhaled roughly nearby. Callum's lips parted in a howling laugh. Jacob glared at Callum when he looked up and another burst of laughter exploded from of him. "I didn't dry off enough. The armor warmers and air circulation in the suit are making the armor release steam from the seal around my neck," Callum explained with a sly grin. If he was going to have to deal with this wretched stomachache, he could at least be amused at Jacob's expense. Jacob scowled at him and stalked in the tent to rest a bit before it was their turn to scout. As the pain in his gut returned, Callum went inside and lay down too.

After a few hours, Adrian and Juni came back, and Juni in her sweet voice asked, "This village looks safer than the last. I think this one is Amelia's, right?"

"Yes, it's Amelia's former village. She said to walk along the outside of the rows of connected homes until we find the split tree. The house of the healer she worked for is in the building you can see from between the trees," Jacob replied as he brushed his braid off his shoulder.

Adrian spoke up saying, "I saw a split tree. It was a couple miles from here. I'll give you the memory when you're ready." Jacob didn't like connecting with anyone but a few people. Connecting was so personal. He cringed inside but forced a nod. It was the thing he hated the most about their old ways. All their communication had been memory clips spliced together mixed with feelings pushed through. Speaking was so much better for him now that he could.

Adrian strode to his tent, and Jacob didn't hesitate to leave without the directions. He would rather wander around aimlessly for two hours than deal with Adrian's asshole mood.

Dread set in as he headed to his hover-bike. Approaching this next village would take everything he had in him. He was terrified. This trip was one nightmare after another for him. He had no idea how sheltered he and his people were until he had to travel somewhere new. He was hopelessly traumatized on the first go around.

Going in unprepared was the dumbest thing he had ever

done. With all these brain cells firing in his head and not one said, *Jacob, this is probably not a good idea*. Intelligence alone is not everything he decided as he slipped his helmet on his cot and dressed in their people's normal clothes. His love had a lot more common sense than he did. Wisdom, he decided, was much more important than raw intelligence.

they headed off together into the thick oak trees with fruit trees mixed in. There were lots of apple and orange trees with avocado trees too. Callum furrowed his brow at the trees and asked, "Those don't grow anywhere near one another on Jael's world. Did this village plant all of this?"

"Yes, this is where most of our tree fruit comes from. We sometimes get tropical fruit but that's only when the cart comes south around the mountain. I see now why he rarely goes that way. We should probably stop talking before we are heard by anyone," Jacob said flatly.

Approaching the small house Jacob had spotted between a split tree, he couldn't erase Adrian's connection offer out of his head. He hoped Adrian didn't think anything of it when he just walked by his tent instead of connecting for the memory. He just didn't want to connect and really didn't want to explain why. Boundaries were something rather new he had had to explore in the last few months. He decided connecting with anyone but Cal, or their future children, was on his hard no list. Avoiding was always the easiest option.

As they neared the door of the pleasant house, it smelled of roses, rosemary, and cinnamon. Foliage grew on either side of the door, a willow on the left and on the right were little vines with simple oval leaves and red berries. Jacob stared at the vines as he knocked softly on the door.

Realization dawned on hi. He was looking at a coca

plant. He knew Amelia had explored it and guessed this was the healer she learned from and where the idea had come from in the first place. It had been critical in multiple topical pain medications they were now using regularly.

An elderly man with brown skin and black hair answered the door and opened it wide, signaling an invitation to come inside. His bright shining brown eyes were warm and kind. He seemed to be well over the age of one hundred. Callum gave Jacob a wide-eyed look before heading inside. Following Callum, Jacob pulled his broad shoulders in and tried not to knock off the drying herbs all over the walls. The home smelled strongly of herbs and spices they didn't recognize, and the air was so dry it was hard to swallow.

The old man shuffled through the room as the floorboards creaked under his feet and patted a bench for them to sit. Jacob complied although everything in his body was telling him to run and save himself while he still could. A grunt left the old man as he sat down. The old man turned and put his hand out for Jacob to connect with him, and Jacob cringed as he held his hand out. He connected with the elder anyway, and was surprised to find his hand to be warm and soft, filled with kindness.

Jacob showed him Amelia, and the man expressed great love for her. Jacob felt a surge of relief and sent the old healer the gift, along with a slew of memories of Amelia and what she had done for them. He also included where she was on the planet right then, and how he could speak to her if he chose. The elderly man pulled his hand away and stared at Jacob, his eyes filled with stars and tears. He didn't know whether the man was going to be angry or happy. He just did his best to be patient.

Inside, his instinct yelled warnings to run away and hide. *This old man was going to eat him.* He knew this was unlikely, really what were the odds that two villages in a row would be parasite infected cannibals, but he couldn't help it. His fear was overwhelming him.

As the little old man absorbed the change, a smile slowly grew on his face. Relief washed over them as they watched him roll the new language over, settling in his mind. Clearing his throat, to speak for the first time, he confidently asked aloud, "You mean I don't have to be quiet anymore? Amelia is her name? It is beautiful. She is my daughter. I miss her dearly. She was taken, and your people saved her. No one has ever come back."

Jacob tried not to look stunned and didn't dare look at Callum. Amelia had not ever talked about her parents before. She was private about her prior life. "Her father was taken when she was a baby then her mother died when a great wasp took her. Her poor mother likely died a slow death filled with misery and pain. Amelia understood the implications of her capture, and she often cried for her mother. She was just a young girl, so I raised her as my own after that. I loved her like my own. She was a gifted healer, and her empathy was unparalleled. She could calm even the unruliest soul.

"She was taken, and your president retrieved her? They are all on a mission together to take over the planet? I am dying of something strange. There are lumps all over my body and my bowels are blood. You just made the last days of a dying man beautiful. Thank you." His tears flowed freely now. The elderly man had cancer. Jacob's mouth was open for so long his tongue and throat felt like cement had formed. He dropped his hands into his bag and pulled out his tablet to call Amelia. He scrolled and found the contact number to her helmet, pressing the holo-call option. Her face materialized, and she gave Jacob a strange look, but said nothing. He didn't know what to say. Shaking his head, Jacob quickly twisted the holo-screen to face the old man, and he had a wide smile on his face, ready to go. Amelia's mouth dropped open and tears welled in her eyes.

The old man slowly started, "My darling Amelia, I have missed you so. I am so proud of all that you've done. I knew you were a storm ready to pour your life-giving rain to the world, even when you were a small girl."

"I never thought I would be able to see you again. I am so relieved you accepted the gift, and we can speak. I miss you so much. How are you?" Amelia asked, trying her best not to scream in delight.

He smiled as wide as he could and replied, "I am doing fantastic. Better than I have in years. Even better now that I've been able to see you. Be safe on your journey. I love you."

She smiled back, "I'll come visit you as soon as this mission is over. I can't wait to see you. I love you too."

He nodded to Jacob, who ended the call.

"Why did you lie to her?" Callum asked softly, confusion in his tone.

The old man smiled, "She has great things to do. Amelia doesn't need me to hold her back. If she knew, she would probably want to find a way to come say goodbye. I don't want her conflicted."

"She's going to skin us alive when she finds out we lied to her about this. Do you remember what she did when you and Oz sent Luna to take the samples during the fungal attack?" Callum asked in a hurried tone, this time not quietly as he glared at Jacob.

Jacob's eyes went wide, admitting, "That *is* a day I will never forget."

The man laughed, then coughed a bit, before he assured, "She will forgive you. That tall, blue-haired girl was the pride of my life. Just make sure she receives these memories eventually." They both nodded, and the old man continued, "I'll go meet with the elders and our leaders. You leave the gift giving to me. Everyone knows I'm dying, so I'll use that to make a connection and pass it along. After all, who can tell the dying man 'No'?"

Jacob smiled at the man's plan, and unable to handle the kindness and selflessness of this man, Jacob nodded and just replied, "We will head back to camp. I'll leave a tablet here for you. Contact us when you return, and we will come back. Be sure to choose a name." He wasn't sure what else there was to say.

The old man shuffled them out of the door with a grin and grabbed his own bag on the way out. Walking stick in hand, he took off into town.

As Jacob and Callum hiked back to camp, they took a longer way around. Strolling through the trees, they watch a few foot-tall snails, making their way across the fallen leaves. The ground behind the snails sizzled where their slime left in a little trail. Their movement was so lethargic, they hardly seemed to move at all, but the trail made it clear they were slowly advancing on their path.

Although they smelled terrible, Callum noticed a bit of warmth growing deep inside after encountering the snails. It wasn't a typical sensation, and it caused something in him to want to run. Confusion overrode, and he brushed it off.

After several hours of waiting back at camp, the old man sent a message to Jacob's tablet telling them he was ready for them to return. The responses of the people he chose went well.

They returned to the town, this time in their armor and carrying several bags of various electronics, a signal booster, and multiple tablets for communication. They brought everything they were supposed to give to the first town too, so it was several bags. The walk to the door was different this time as they could sense, something was wrong.

Jacob looked over at Callum and narrowed his eyes in concern. Callum reached up and softly tapped on the door. A beige woman with jet black hair answered the door. When it swung open to let them inside, a dark green man stood on the other side of the short hallway. The tall forest-green man nodded, "Welcome back. A lot has happened in the last few hours. The village healer decided his name is Ellis. I chose Henry, and my sister here chose Etta. We are both the leaders of the village. We named our village Nemus for our fruit groves."

"It is nice to formally meet all of you," Jacob strode into the little home, worry sprouting deep in his gut. He found Ellis lying on the bench. Ellis looked as though his illness had progressed significantly since they had last seen him a few hours ago. Walking around the town spreading the gift had consumed the last of his energy.

Peering up, Ellis croaked, "It looks like you arrived just in time. This seems to be my end." Beginning to slump and roll off the bench, Jacob dove to catch Ellis under his arms to ease him to the floor. Guilt laced through Jacob as he put his arms around the elderly man. Everyone gathered around as Jacob held his head in his lap.

As his gaze took in the caring faces, Ellis grinned, "What a wonderful end. Oh, you must win, you and your friends. Tell Amelia her mother would have been so proud of her. Tell her I am proud of her. Let her know her butterflies came back, the little orange ones."

"We will tell her everything," Callum sobbed.

Jacob nodded to Henry when their eyes met, and together they carried Ellis to his bed. Once the old man was comfortably tucked in, they returned to the living room where they could all speak in private.

"I suspect he has a few days at best. Are you going to stay or do you need to head on to the next village?" Henry asked Jacob, sadness in every word.

Callum interrupted Jacob, "Oh, we are staying. You couldn't pay me all the money in the universe to not visit that sweet old man all day every day until he passes. We will be back until the end. We can move on after that."

Jacob didn't disagree, and Henry nodded, a look of relief on his face. They needed to move on, but this old man deserved to be honored at his end. They all knew what he was giving up.

19

PLANET PORTUM - UTC COMMAND MISSION

"Who was that?" Oz asked as Amelia pulled off her helmet and wiped her eyes.

Clearing her throat, Amelia replied, "Someone from my old village, someone dear to me, the man who raised me. I guess he would be my father."

Nodding, Oz gave her some space sensing she needed to process this unexpected moment. He moved away from her over the cold metal floor. His boots clinked loudly in the rounded room. They were inside the remains of a spaceship that had crashed landed there after being attacked by the UTC. The fallen ship had been converted into a dwelling. It was metal and cold, but it was out of the elements. That was all the woman was willing to explain yet. They had to gain her trust before she would say more. She had made that abundantly clear.

"*Kagne, quid debemus te nam servas Dionem?*" Kagnus, what do we owe you for saving Dion? he asked as he approached her.

After giving Dion some kind of multi-use anti-venom

serum from a UTC lab, she had hobbled straight over to her projects and promptly ignored them. She was sitting at a work bench with hundreds of trinkets and metal forms, tinkering was all she really seemed to be doing. She completely ignored his question and just made a grimace as she lit a cigar and poured herself a glass of a golden liquor. She held the amber glass up, We were posing as a transport. We bought all the dried food and liquor as a cover. Lucky break. "*Statum sumeremus ut vecturam. Emimus omnem cibum aridum et temetum ut tegmentum. Intercapedo felix.*" She downed the glass of liquor, slamming it down onto the metal workbench. The sound echoed in the small metal room.

Oz studied the room with a few rusted edges on the wall panels and asked, Does anyone else live here with you? "*Aliquisne vivit hunc cum te?*"

Just as he spoke, a woman came from the back, one of his kind. She had a navy-blue band around her neck. Her skin was deep red, and her eyes were neon yellow. She had a thin but fit figure. Her long maroon hair was simply pulled back at her nape.

She nodded her head, Yes, I live here too. My name is Mira. She might be too ornery and prideful to speak about it, but I am not. I went too long silent to keep my mouth shut now. We were on a mission from an underground resistance sect, but we were shot down by the UTC rail guns. They bombed this entire area for a while and finally left us alone a few years ago. I guess they think they killed us all. They killed most of us. Our leader was a Sarter woman, but she was killed on impact when we crashed. We had a crew of ten, but everyone else died when the bombs fell. Well, except for Troy. He was eaten by a sand spider during the raid. "*Ita, vivo hunc quoque. Mihi nomen est Mira... Esserat a aranea harena inter incursionem."*

"Respondisti quaestionem habui circa esse primus gentis dicere." You just answered a question I had about being the first of our kind to speak, Oz crossed his arms, deep in thought.

"Sumus dicere nam multum mille anni... Cogito multum hominum intellegent, etiam si diximus, non faciet differentiam ad situm nobis. Sumus uti in multis vis." We've been able to speak for many thousands of years. We likely even had a language before the humans first arrived here. All the rest of us are so full of fear, and generally so passive, we let these things happen to us and do nothing about it. I was the only one of our kind to speak I know of. I mean, I'm sure there were others, but I don't know of any. We have become so comfortable in our silence that when plucked from it, we hang onto it like it's a lifeline. It is the one thing we can control, so we do. I think many of our people realize, even if we spoke, it wouldn't make a difference to our situation. We would just be used in more ways, Mira explained as she sadly shook her head.

"Cur habes illum collarem?" Why do you still have that collar on? Oz asked, a sense of disgust toward it.

Mira scowled and rubbed the dark blue fabric around her neck before she replied, I can't take it off without triggering it. I don't want to be strangled to death while being injected with my venom, so I leave it alone. There is a pleasure house on Emendo in district seven, region ten, and it is owned by a big hairy Makros man with smelly breath. He is the only one with the codes to remove it. He probably wants to serve me as a live dinner to his Haculae slaves, so I'll just leave it on. I should really ask you why you still wear those braids. "*Non detraho sine facesset... Probabiliter vult servare me ut cenam vivam ad servos Haculae, sed relinquet in. Rogabo te cur geres rursus illas spiras.*"

Braids? What about their braids? Oz cringed at her words, trying to recall the different creatures she was naming, and catching her meaning perfectly. They used her own venom in her collar. That thought made his blood turn to fire in his veins. *What kind of sick fucks were they heading into war with?* "*Multum stellarum exercet ab UTC bene? Estne locus tu describes communem prep stellarum aut estne locus terribilis?*" Most of the galaxy is run by the UTC, right? Is the place you're describing common for the galaxy, or is it a terrible place? Oz asked, wanting a different perspective from Aurelia.

Mira's eyebrows raised, and she looked over at Oz and explained, "Emendo is one of the best places to live, especially for indentured servants and the owned populations. It's one giant city in a ring around the planet, with a vast open wasteland on either side. Sure, there is crime and life is hard, but it is not as bad as an outer planet. The UTC pushes the idea people who are owned are so different, so underneath the so-called *free humans*. The reality is on Emendo, every poor person living on that planet is a *slave*, whether they realize it. It's often better to be a registered servant or even sell yourself. Those who are owned are fed by law while the homeless starve. In answer, in a galaxy where food is king, Emendo is a paradise. Once a true paradise, Emendo had a great forest on either side of the city. When the First Humans and the Sarters battled for the system, all the massive trees the Sarters had planted to terraform the planet burned. Much of the oxygen went with it. The fires were to force off the rest of the Sarter people living on the planet's surface. The UTC knew they needed more room for the humans. They didn't want to share the freshly planned out Melior with the poor, so they burned it all down. The planet had to buy and transport in new terraforming carbon dioxide scrubbers from the First Humans which bankrupt the economy. The war cost had been heavy enough, and the added need for oxygen set them over the edge. The planet is still paying off the loans they borrowed from the UTC with heavy taxes. They likely will pay it off for the next hundred thousand years, you know, because of interest and such. That's also why Emendo does not have any kind of royal leader. No one wants to rule the debt-ridden planet. Sure, people own the surface, but the planet itself and the resources below the surface are basically worthless. The resources will never outweigh the debt. The city itself is the only reason it hasn't been abandoned yet. That, and I don't think the first human scouts have found another available system to terraform and move to yet. Most of the other planets in the galaxy are extremely poor. They are planets with little natural resources compared to the first humans, who flew around for a million years and mined thousands of worlds for their own profits. Who knows what else they did while they were running around out there? They have massive stockpiles of precious metals and rare elements, as well as secret maps of hard to find low light systems they've discovered and not yet exploited. It's only a matter of time before they overrun those systems as well. *"Emendo est uni optimi loci habitare, praecipue nam famuli et proprii multitudes... Solum res tempi ante percurrunt illas rationes quoque."*

Mira stopped as Oz asked, What happens to the planets? *"Quid accident ad planetas?"*

There are once priceless worlds in this galaxy floating around with nothing but a hollow shell left inside and the remnants of their interior rock floating around them in a ring. Some eventually collapse in on themselves and become a moon sized lump of uneven rock, all of it because of the first humans. One of the first human royal families owns a planet in my system named Aduro, and King Claudius is in the processing of mining it. They will eventually strip it to a shell and move on to the next planet. The environment is toxic, and the rock is extremely radioactive, so all the people there are genetically altered humans, or they are our people. *"Semel inaestimabilies mundi in stellaris fluitant circum cum nihil sed concha cava relinquit intus et relinqui earum interior saxum fluitat circum eas in anulo... Circumiecta venenum est et saxum summe radiatio est, sic omens homines ea sunt simulationes homines aut ea sunt homines nobis."*

Disgusts rolled in Oz's gut as he thought over her words. He knew the cave in which they built the base was rich in natural resources. What about this planet? Have the first humans mined it too? *"Quid est hae planeta? Habentne primi homines effoderunt quoque?"* Oz asked.

She considered it for a moment and answered, There are surely a few pockets of metals and rare elements but not enough for them to pay it any mind. With the UTC keeping it under wraps, it's in no danger of being stripped. Our people don't reproduce much outside of our home planet. *"Certe sunt pauci sacculi de metallo et elemento raro sed non satis nam ea solvere ullum animum cum UTC tenet sub amictibus, non in periculo spoliatus est. Nobis homines non multum regenerant extra planetam domi."*

Oz couldn't help but ask, "Why do you speak, but no one else does? *"Cur dices sed nemo facient?"*

The Makros who owned me forced me to learn several languages because it added to the intrigue of illegally fucking me. Eventually he found a translation implant, but they are hard to come by on Emendo, so I learned the first few languages the hard way. When I would suddenly speak in the middle of performing, the customer would be so shocked they would sometimes stop and applaud. I made him a fortune. *"Markos qui tenuerant me, impepulerunt me discere linguas multas quia id addidit ad clandestinum de futuit contra legem me.*

We are not supposed to be used for sex. It's technically against the law. They look the other way about it. If you are kidnapped, you are on your own. Trafficking everything from sentient beings to food is almost completely overlooked. Those are just some of the laws the UTC ignores, along with the fair treatment of servants and laborers. They look the other way for anyone willing to pay off the local authorities which are more like unorganized militias with rogue bounty hunters than police. *"Vident ullam viam nam aliqui vult solvere auctoritates loci quas plus ut militiae auctorices cum furciferi largitates venatrices quam vigiles."*

What laws do the UTC enforce then? *"Quid leges UTC exercent tum."* Oz asked, curiosity overruling his logic.

Mira considered him a moment and explained, Well, for one, most adoption and abortion is illegal, and they will put you to death over either if you're caught. They control all the genetically perfect designer embryos and all the orphanages. The orphanages are set up to snare the children into forced enlistment. Once adults, they owe the UTC for their own care as children, and it's an impossible debt to work off. By outlawing adoption and abortion, the UTC can keep the orphanages filled and have a pathway to enlistment. There is an anonymous baby drop off on the side of every orphanage. They all claim to be saving children's lives, but all they're doing is filling up their military and mines. The designer embryos are for anyone who can afford the UTC's high price. This means all the rich are perfect humans, while all the poor are riddled with disease and cancer from unregulated polluting and industrial practices. Most of the rich use surrogates and none of their own genetics. They are always offering things like usable body part sales offers, mostly egg and sperm donation, but some people regularly donate plasma. Anyone can opt to grow a second organ and may sell to receive a profit from that. There are not a lot of options for education, so unless you're talented, pretty, or want to grow extra body parts, you're probably going to go hungry. They love to issue heavy citations and taxes onto the poor knowing they can't pay, just to keep them poor. The UTC will kill anyone who tells any of their secrets, true or not. One time in particular, I witnessed the UTC's wrath. Their soldiers burned a home with a family of seven inside because the parents were caught with an illegal water pipe connected to one of the city lines. They had been stealing water they need to live, and they all burned to death for it. Their screams could be heard all the way down my street. Meanwhile, the UTC has looping advertisements on video screens all over Emendo. All of them with the same message of community and loyalty, of protection and love. I could hear the video loop across from my room say the "United Trust's and Colonies assures that you're not alone." They were always watching, always finding new ways to ensure our safety, but all I could hear were the children's screams. *"Immo nam unus, plurima adoptia et abortus est illicitus, et ponent te ad mortem supra si cepisti... Sunt semper observant, semper inveniunt ullas vias confirmare salutes nobis, sed audio erunt vagitus liberorum.”*

Stunned and nauseated from all the disturbing information, Oz just stared at Mira. How could the rest of the galaxy be in such dark disarray? The rich First Humans set it all up to stay rich and powerful while the poor just continue to become poorer. They were trapped in their small lives with no hope of conquering the evil controlling them. Oz had a good idea the First Humans had been doing things this way since the beginning. When they first left their home world was it because they had destroyed it like they did Emendo in a war, or did they strip it like Aduro? Just another question he wanted an answer to but doubted he ever would know the truth.

Mira walked into the next room, and Oz noticed the end of her tail had been clipped. He shook his head and sat down with Amelia on the bench mounted on the wall. She was sitting sideways to accommodate her tail. “Sounds like the entire galaxy is fucked, and there’s no group that’s big or strong enough to face off with the UTC and the First Humans. What did we get ourselves into?” Amelia asked as she watched Dion take deep slow breaths, his eyes beginning to flutter.

Watching Dion as he moved his head, Oz groaned, “It seems we are closer to a mosquito than a scorpion in this fight. Eventually we will gather enough mosquitos together so that we can drain some blood from the UTC and the First Humans. We can’t beat them alone though. I think we need to head to the Sarter’s planet first. We need some friends, and it sounds like they may have an old grudge.”

Amelia nodded, “I spoke to Jael. They’re all doing well. She said they will have everything packed and ready for the

Kagnus to come in the transport to pick them up in a few hours when it's finished charging."

"Thank you. We can gather here, and with Kagnus's help, we can form a plan. I'm curious to find out what secrets she has hidden up in this downed ship. I have a feeling she will have some helpful insight along with Aurelia if we can earn her trust."

20

PLANET ADURO – MINE 03

Over thirty people at the mine had the gift, and it was spreading like wildfire. They created diversions in the front of the mine so they could connect further down where it was dark, so the guards would never see. August's plea for help had not faded; in fact, multiple others had tacked on their own pleas afterward.

August leaned over and put his hand out as he struck the wall absently.

Dragon took his hand and connected with him, "Our numbers are increasing. We need a plan."

"We need to watch the guards and log their rounds. The mine has a full staff of guards, so we need to watch them and keep track of any who might pose a real threat. If we can spread the gift to everyone down here, we would have about two hundred people. We would outnumber the humans six to one or more. I didn't see many people at the palace either. We need to make sure we utilize our numbers. That's the only real plan I have so far," August explained.

"How do we know we can keep the planet once we take it over?" Dragon asked concern flowing down the connection.

August didn't know how to answer her question. He didn't know if they could. The UTC might very well send reinforcements to the royal family and kill them all. He shook his head, "We can't think about that. We need to take this planet, and we can't wait for anything. I've spent so much of my life waiting, I'm not waiting anymore." Dragon nodded, and she pulled her hand away, breaking the connection.

They finished their shift of hammering hot sparkling rocks from the wall and headed up to the bunks. August noticed several people doubling up in the beds, many more than usual, and he held in a cringe. He hoped the guards didn't notice. His people needed to be much more discrete about connecting. He found Chris, and they stood in line together for rations. August gagged as he looked at the dried, flattened bugs. The boy smiled, knowing he would soon have August's bugs. August thought about Mercy's neighbor's flatbread when Chris tapped him to move forward. He would give just about anything for a bite of that flatbread.

Trying to hold back a groan, he took his portions. They found a seat on his bunk and ate. After they finished, he handed his bowl to Chris, and the boy scurried off to put it away.

August's eyes met Livia's at the end of the room, and he guessed she was the guard for the night. Unable to help himself, he strolled by her and shot her a look as he passed. She scowled at him as he headed toward the bathrooms.

He thought for sure she would find a way to talk to him, but when he passed by again, she remained standing stoically at her post. He gave up and lay down again, but there was no sign of Chris. Hopefully, he was off fake tripping and spreading the gift. August chuckled when he found out that was his most effective method.

No matter how far his mind wandered, it always found its way back to Livia. Unable to keep his gaze from where Livia stood watch, he found her eyes already on him. She quickly darted them away. He had to figure out a way to talk to her. He wouldn't tell her his plan to take over. He wanted something else entirely, a need burned inside of him to make sure she was, and Lucas had gone back to wherever he whatever hell he crawled out from. He just needed a creative diversion.

There was a water station behind the wall where they stored their ration bowls. He wondered if he crossed a few wires, could he start a fire? He walked over to the panel and saw a crack in one side, so he worked it up with his finger. The end of his finger slid easily into the groove. It felt odd with no nail there. The end of his finger was soft and round, and he had no claws at all. He missed the ritual of filing them down, the feel of the sanding stone in his hand, the ache of his fingers afterward. What a strange thing to miss.

He pulled two wires free and a third, and then a fourth. He traded off crossing them until the two sparked, and he twisted them as they sizzled against one another. The panel blinked and in seconds, flames erupted from around the edges of the waterspout. August smiled and causally walked away.

He sat back on his bunk just as one of Livia's guards alerted, I smell smoke. *"Olfacio fumum."*

Well, figure it out, *"Immo, puta id foris."* Livia demanded, an air of authority to her tone. She was royalty, and August needed to not forget that. August watched as the only other guards in the room moved away from her and toward the back of the room. He made his way by her and back to the bathroom, giving a wink as he passed. The scowl on her face would have alarmed a giant scorpion, he thought as he rubbed his dry hands together.

He was almost at the door when someone shoved him behind the wall and into a small room he didn't realize was there. From the look of it, it was a meeting room that had gone completely unused. By the level of dust, no one had been in the room for many years. Scenting the air, August knew exactly who was behind him. He turned to find Livia with an angry frown. He grabbed her face and kissed her, but she hardly responded.

What? I had to see you. How else was I going to pull it off? "*Quid? Volo videre te. Quomodo pervictus sum procul?*" August asked with a smirk.

Fury in her eyes, Livia hissed, I had a feeling the waterspout didn't catch fire on its own. You're fucked when they scrub it for DNA. "*Sensi os non ignem in proprio. Futuisti ubi detergent id nam DNA.*"

Are you okay? Did that sack of shit leave yet? "*Tu es bene? Estne caput sterocoris relinquet?*" August asked, ignoring her warning.

Biting her lip at the fact that he had done what he did just to ask her if she was safe, Livia finally responded, Yes, he left, but he will be back in two weeks. "*Ita, relinquit, sed reveniet in hebdomadibus duos.*"

Kissing her again, August leaned them both back against the wall and whispered, Watch for me through the windows of your grand palace. One of these days, I'll set the desert on fire and set us free. "*Specta ad me per fenestras de regia grande tui. Unus dies, accendiet deserta in ignem et liberabo nos librum.*"

"*Tu non scis me. Cur tu sic certus non dico aliquem? Tu es sic certus credo te?*" You don't even know me. Why are you so sure I won't say something? Are you so certain I'm on your side? Livia asked, her fierce eyes trained on August's.

Giving Livia his best smug grin, August answered, "The sounds you made when I tasted your wet pussy told me I'm the only man who ever brought you pleasure. You're mine; you just haven't caught up yet."

"*Qua lingua est?*" What language is that? Livia asked, not understanding a word he said.

August answered saying, English. That's the language of my first teacher. I learned your language afterward. "*Anglicus. Est lingua de primae magistrae. Didici tui linguam postea.*"

Livia narrowed her eyes and brushed the dust off her tunic. August marveled at how similar their tunics were to the ones his people wore in the village. All the attire was strikingly similar.

He wondered if his people adapting these styles back on his planet meant even more of their evolution was warped. It had been manipulated down to the way they dressed. He wondered what the common homes looked like. He bet they looked exactly the same as their village. The fury at that revelation made something inside of him break.

It sounds like one of the forbidden languages. I have heard it before in a news clip from a station on Emendo. Anyone caught speaking it would be put to death, "*Somus ut unus de linguae odiosae. Audivi ante in acta diurna ab statione in Emendo. Aliquis cepit dicens id interiectus est,*" she whispered as the meaning behind him knowing this language sank in.

Nodding in understanding, August said, Doesn't surprise me. I bet the planet Jael was from is a secret of the First Humans. It's a planet full of humans. *"Non miratio me. Pono planeta Jael vivit est secretum de Primi Hominum est planeta plena de hominum."*

What's the planet's name? *"Quid est nomen planetae?"* Livia asked, wonder in her eyes.

"Vocant Tellus." They call it Earth, August replied.

Livia stopped and stared at him and admitted, That probably is one of the First Humans sacred origin planets. I only know because I snuck in my father's office when I was needing a plan reviewed and found documents on a meeting with the empress' seal on it. Something about voting on regular visits to make sure they don't discover light-speed or some other mode of faster than light transportation and sneak up on us. How in Pluto's hell did one of their people end up with your people? Wherever you're from. *"Probabiliter unus de Primi Hominum sacrarum originum planetarum... Quomodo in Pluto infenis fecit unum homines evenit cum hominibus? Ubicumque es habitas."*

My home planet is next to the black hole in the center of the galaxy. It's tidally locked, and I hear it's another UTC secret. We are trying to prove we were not genetically created by the First Humans. Jael, from Earth, built a machine called an electromagnetic drive and accidentally transported herself to my planet. My best friend found her in the woods, and they fell in love. She taught him English, and after that, he taught the rest of us. *"Planeta domi mei proximus foramene ateri in medio stellarum. Obseravit ab aestu et audio aliquem UTC secretum.*

"*Ceperam recte ante capti erimus planetam retro.*" We fought back or tried to. I was taken right before we were going to take the planet back, August explained.

"You what? You should see your kind's genetics. You're not a naturally evolved species. Your people were planning on fighting the UTC for your planet? The UTC hasn't had a system wide rebellion in thousands of years. The last one was by the Sarters. Their overthrow gave us Aduro. My family was gifted the planet by the empire, but we didn't discover the deeper ore pockets until a few thousand years ago. The planet was gifted in a bundle of several worlds to my ancestors, but in the fine print, was a binding agreement. When the planets were signed over, they included a clause about mining and natural resources. My family has been trapped in a contract with the UTC even before we moved here and were forced to start ordering designer babies from them. The radiation sterilizes humans, so the royal family consists completely of all made to order children now. That's why it was possible for my cousin to be picked as heir; direct kinship doesn't matter. I'm just trying to explain, you can't win. You will be taken back over. If not by my soldiers, then by the First Humans. This planet, and almost everything else in the galactic center, belongs to them, and we can't do anything about that, "*Tu quid?... Illa planeta, et paene omnes in medio stellarum, esse eis et non faciemus aliquis circum,*" Livia explained.

Completely ignoring her warnings, August tipped his lip up in a small half smile as he looked into Livia's eyes that weren't her own. The electronic orbs moved seamlessly like real eyes. The blue lenses over her mechanical irises seemed to shimmer in the dim light. He thought about what hers looked like before she swapped them out for these high-tech eyes. August paused and asked, *"Quis partes fueris si cepi planetam nam mei et homines mihi?"* Who's side would you be on if I took this planet for myself and my people?

Livia was silent as she stared back into August's gaze of fire. Flashes of her childhood sparkled in her eyes. Innocent, sweet little dreams of liberating the oppressed and saving the galaxy, forgotten hopes that died the day her father chose Lucas. How dare he give her such tender hope in a galaxy filled with such vitriol and violence.

She took his face and kissed him long and hard before she kneed him in the balls. She shoved him against the wall and strolled out of the room, slamming the door behind her. August slumped against the wall, the scent of her still surrounding him while he groaned and leaned on the cold stone behind him.

He breathed in the dusty dry air and leaned up from the wall, meaning to walk out of the room, but a faint blinking light drew his attention. He walked over to a panel, and it lit up. It was a computer. August flipped through the menu as he rubbed his aching balls through his pants and found a file labeled "Radiation levels" in Latin.

He clicked on the file, and it opened a data sheet with millions of readings from the first several thousand years when they started the mine. He expanded the graph and saw the radiation levels were extremely high when they began the mine; however, as they harvested the radioactive rock, the levels dropped. That was all of it.

He let out a frustrated huff at the dead end and went to the next menu item. The next item read, "Manifest." He clicked on it, and it was filled with files with years listed. The first years showed about two hundred humans. The next list showed one hundred and seventy-five, and by list seven and eight, all the remaining original people were missing teeth and hair. August cringed as he scrolled through the photos of the ill people. He became especially disgusted when he noticed most of the humans had the same names. They were whole families who lived and died here. Every one of their contracts ended the same.

Deceased.

He cringed and wondered how many humans died before they started using his kind. Knowing the value of the ore, he didn't understand why they didn't just build robots. He guessed when he took over the planet, he could decide that sort of thing. He would find a way to memorialize everyone lost in the mines. Those humans didn't have much choice by the sound of it. It didn't look like this computer had much more information, so he decided to head back to his bunk.

He looked both ways before running across to the bathroom. Opening and shutting the bathroom door, he pretended to come from there as he rounded the corner and found Livia standing with two guards. They had the burnt and melted waterspout device in their hand. She glared at him as he passed by, and he could feel her electronic blue eyes penetrate him like tiny daggers.

There's no way they could know it was him, so he headed to his bunk and made himself as comfortable as possible in this hell hole. She said he would be caught by his DNA, but it was burned to a crisp; thus, no DNA. Chris sat down next to him at his back, and August just started to slip into dreamland when Chris grabbed his hand.

Into his mind, Chris said, "We will have the gift spread to everyone in the mine by the end of our next rest."

21

PLANET PORTUM – RECRUITMENT MISSION – AMELIA'S VILLAGE

Jacob made everyone a meal of fruit over toasted seeds with honey and chopped nuts. They had been there for hours, and Callum had just finished bathing Ellis and changing all the soiled bedsheets, giving him a clean place to rest. They knew he was aware, balancing on the line between life and the unknown.

Callum peered around the room and looked closely at all the rows of dried herbs and spices hanging upside down to dry. Many of them looked like they had been there for years. Most of the home was clean, other than the taller areas which he was positive the old man could not reach any longer. He was far too old to be balancing on a stool. He bet the high spots were Amelia's job when she lived here. She was easily six inches taller than the old man.

Jacob had inquired to Vida at the base about a concoction to ease his pain. She replied with a long list of things he could give Ellis, along with descriptions and instructions for each mixture. What she did not ask was why he needed to know, and he was thankful. Vida and Amelia were good friends. He could easily find all the ingredients to make some powerful painkillers, and they seemed to be effective. The time had come to ensure his comfort.

Ellis was no longer eating, but they were still making meals for everyone and filling the home with the scent of fresh food. They were hoping he would rouse for a bite but knew deep down a recovery would not happen. Cancer of some kind had invaded the man's body to the point he had large painful lumps visible under his skin. They were surprised Ellis had been walking at all when they met him, alone able to have shared the gift as he did.

Despite all the jostling, cleaning, and moving his body around, he had yet to open his eyes during this visit. His heart ached thinking of Amelia and how they were having to keep this important secret from her. Hoping she didn't call to check in, Jacob kept his tablet on its silent setting. That was one conversation he was petrified to have right now. He would rather just completely ignore everything and every-one. He was a terrible liar, and everyone always knew it. Amelia was an exceptional person. The last thing he wanted to do was hurt her. He had known for some time she had some previous trauma surrounding her family because she never spoke of it, just like him. This was going to be so hard to explain, he may just give her the memories. He wasn't sure he could bear hurting her.

Jacob walked in and handed Callum his dinner plate. Callum peered up and smiled at him as he took the warm dish in his hands. Callum pulled up another stool for Jacob, and they ate in silence as Ellis's breathing became increas-ingly labored. His chapped lips mumbling incoherence as he slowly slipped further into the afterlife.

They quickly finished their meals, and Jacob collected

the plates to clean them. When Jacob returned and sat down, Callum took Ellis's hand, "I think we are nearing the end; his lungs are beginning to rattle."

Jacob stopped and listened closely, they sounded deep and damp.

Confirming he heard the declination in Ellis's breathing, he stood saying, "I'll go get Henry and Etta."

Callum stayed and held Ellis's hand as Jacob went for the two town leaders. Moments after Jacob's swift departure, Ellis began mumbling. As they sat alone in the quiet home, the man's words rattled him.

Swallowing roughly, Callum leaned in closer to listen as he thought he could hear Ellis mumble softly, "Sheeez doctor now, saves worlds." Some incoherent nonsense followed, and then he clearly whispered, "Stars and flowing rivers, disease and metal cures, sand, and rotten bones. Scales, feathers, and crimson. It blazes to vast nothingness, they find the truth."

What the hell did that mean? Callum wondered as he leaned over, listening, close enough to the old man's face to hear every word. He heard the door swing open, and he sat up abruptly. Jacob walked in, but he didn't hear any footsteps behind him.

In a rush, before anyone walked in, Callum grabbed Jacob's hand and connected with him. He showed him what Ellis had said. When the memory had been reviewed, he looked at him with curious eyes and a furrowed brow.

"What does that last part mean?" Jacob queried as if Callum had all the answers.

He responded unsurprisingly, "How the hell am I supposed to know what any of it means? Do you believe there is more after this?"

Pulling his hand away, Jacob pursed his lips and replied, "Yes. There has to be."

"Do you think we should tell Oz what he said?" Callum wondered, as he looked back over at the kind, dying old man.

Ellis's labored breathing slowed, and they could hear the chatter outside of Henry and Etta approaching the house. From what he could see, it looked like they had bedding in hand prepared to stay.

"Yeah, we probably should. They seemed interested in what Jael said during one of her mushroom trips, so I would think they would want to know about this, too," Jacob agreed as he shifted his eyes to the old man, who was struggling to breathe.

Callum swung his head around and looked at Jacob with realization pouring over him right as the front door shut.

Callum spoke quickly, "Jael mentioned something about August seeing a bright star soon; it was right before he was taken."

Halting the previous conversation in its tracks, Henry and Etta appeared in the doorway, looking grim. They sat their bedding down in the living room next to the bench.

"Doesn't look like he has much longer based on his breathing. I wish Amelia could be here for him he dearly loves her.

"Would you like for us to bring additional bedding over or are you two returning to camp tonight? I'm not sure he will make it through the night," Etta offered as she looked Ellis over and felt his pulse.

His already gargled breathing worsened, and Jacob knew he only had a few hours at the most; for that matter, he may only have minutes. It was hard to tell exactly when someone's end would be. That last breath can be as unpredictable as the first ever taken.

"We will stay, but we don't need bedding," Jacob agreed with a nodding Callum.

Nodding Etta pulled up a stool, "I'll sit a while and give you two a break. Why don't you step outside and get some fresh air."

Callum rose up for Henry to take his seat on the stool, and he and Jacob walked outside, the floorboards under their feet creaked as they strode across them.

Once the front door shut and they were a little way from the house, they both began to loosen their shoulders from the heavy weight of death and sorrow. As they strolled through the middle of the village, Jacob asked, "Do you honestly think Jael had a mushroom induced vision about what was going to happen? August did end up on a planet with a star." Some villagers gave them fearful looks because they were speaking aloud, but frankly neither cared. They had dealt with enough emotional trauma over the last few days, so perturbed looks weren't going to matter in the slightest. Hopefully, soon, the villagers would find silence unusual.

"Maybe? I don't know. It's just too much of a coincidence. If Oz hadn't already explored her whole mind, I would have thought she was a spy." Callum scoffed, as the reality of his own statement sank in, and he cringed. What a terrible mistake rejecting Jael could've been. Not knowing the circumstances of how Oz and Jael were able to first connect, something told him their chance to learn this language had been pure luck, or maybe it was the universe returning the balance.

The wind blew a bit of hair across his face, and Jacob

brushed at it as he asked, "Has she had any other dreams or anything else she may have told you but no one else?"

"No, Jael is still pretty reserved. I can call and ask her, but she might feel more comfortable sharing it with Oz," Callum hoped Jacob understood and could read between the lines.

Jacob needed to ask Oz, and Oz needed to ask Jael. Some of the memories or visions may be disturbing or were hard to talk about.

It must have been time to harvest; the streets were bustling with people carrying baskets back-and-forth from the massive wall of grapevines which ran around the center of the village. Villagers were cutting bunches of the dark blue globes setting them gently in the basket woven from the vines.

Within the fence line made of grapevines, there was a large grove filled with fruit trees spliced with multiple different kinds of fruit. Some of the stone fruit trees had different varieties of mango, apricot, and cherries sprouted on every branch. Jael would find this biological engineering fascinating. The sounds of children playing and laughing in the center was delightful.

A bright blue boy of around twelve bumped into them and quietly apologized, "Excuse me."

In astonishment, they stopped walking and looked around, noticing some of the people quietly speaking to one another. Conversation softly traveled up and down the grape vines.

Callum reached for Jacob's hand, "That was fast. Didn't we just get some nasty looks for speaking aloud two blocks away? I hope the next village is this easy."

Pondering a moment Jacob looked back at the boy and

then to Callum, "A thought just occurred to me. Someone just gave a little boy some very adult memories. That may not have been the best idea. We may need a filtered version for children."

Callum chuckled to himself remembering his years as a preteen. He would've loved Jael's memories back then, yet he could also see why it was highly inappropriate. He hoped the little boy's parents only passed along her language and not the rest of her memories.

Sighing, he peered over at a two-story apartment building with clothes hanging on the balconies and flapping in the breeze. The wind seemed to pick up, and he noticed the breeze had a bit of a chill to it. A crack of thunder sounded in the distance, and Callum looped his arm into Jacob's. "Let's walk back. That storm will be here in about twenty minutes," Callum noted.

Jacob narrowed his eyes. "You hated time in the beginning. What made you change your mind?"

Callum reluctantly answered, "I understand the value of it now. It makes the descriptions of many things much easier and more precise. I stopped counting the moons a while ago. I can't believe we accurately kept an account of passing time that way."

Leaves stirred in the streets. The wind gusted as they approached Ellis's home, and big droplets of water fell right when they stepped in his front door. The sound of the large droplets of rain hitting the ground filled the space around them as the sky opened up.

Henry was there to greet them at the door. "He is passing now. I was just heading out to find you." The three of them quietly joined Etta around the bed. Ellis was taking his last shallow breaths as she held his hand. Callum, Jacob, and Henry surrounded his bed as Etta whispered sweet words gently in Ellis's ear. He relaxed and released one last powerful breath before his chest rose no more.

Etta stood, and they all put their fists to their chests in silence.

Henry's tears welled in his eyes. "He sewed my side up when I injured myself as a child. He was so gentle and kind. I think he has mended each person in the village at least once. He will be dearly missed."

"It's heartbreaking to lose one so precious to a community." Callum admitted as he looked down on the man, eyes burning.

Etta smiled sadly, "Oh, he assisted many families in the village by donations. He has contributed to over fifteen live births during his long life. For a while, he was quite popular. He certainly left behind a slew of his genetics, and every one of them looks like him. He will still be a part of this village for a long time. We plan to spread his ashes with the families he assisted."

Callum raised his eyebrows and held back a chuckle, "Ah, well, good for him."

Jacob and Callum turned to face Henry and Etta as Jacob explained, "It's time we head to camp and rest before we head to the next town. Thank you for everything you've done for us while we've been here. Your kindness was appreciated more than you'll ever know."

Thunder further away cracked after a lightning strike, letting them know the storm had passed with the time between the strikes. The small home groaned as the rain slowed soaking the ground.

"Good luck. They're not too welcoming of outsiders. They might be worse than the village to our south," Henry replied as they rounded the corner and walked down the hallway.

Henry opened the door to allow Jacob and Callum outside as Jacob responded, "Nothing could be worse than the cannibals to the south."

Henry shut the door behind them as they headed off into the woods. The drips of water from the trees all around were soothing after the sorrow they had just experienced. Their hearts would be in a vise over Ellis for quite some time. They would still have to tell Amelia. When they arrived in camp, the ground was wet, but the rain clouds had passed by, allowing the auras to light the ground.

"Do you want to take an extra day and rest, or should we leave in the morning?" Callum asked as he walked over to take a bag off one of the hover bikes.

Jacob squeezed his eyes shut before he replied, "I think we should go right away. I want this over with. I am not looking forward to visiting Carter's old village. He already warned me when we go, attempt to connect with his neighbor first; otherwise, we might not be welcome."

Callum stalled, "But, no filing gnarly toenails this time right? I can't go through that again."

22

PLANET PORTUM - UTC COMMAND MISSION

Why the fuck do you have that UTC cunt with you? *"Cur futuens habes UTC caniculam cum te?"* Kagnus seethed as Aurelia stepped inside. Her eyes widened with the insult, but her instant air of acceptance spoke volumes of the people she once associated herself with.

Oz put his hands up and asked, *"Quomodo narras? Ea commutavit turmas, ita? Culpasne eam?"* How can you tell? She switched teams, alright? She's with us now. You know how horrible it is on Emendo. Can you blame her?

Kagnus whipped around and scowled at him, She walks and stands like a UTC soldier, and how the fuck do you know that you overgrown green bean? Have you poked around in her skull yet? Did you put her through a little torture, or did you just let that old friend of yours over there fuck her a bit? Figure her out that way? The UTC uses electric shock as their go-to punishment for minor infractions. They put chemicals in their recruits' rations when they condition them in training. They never defect. *"Ambulat et*

Stat ut UTC milites, et quomodo futuo scis te obsite faba viride?... Numquam deficent."

Narrowing his eyes, Oz turned to Mira and asked, "*Scit Kagnus circa coniunctionem cerebri homines nobis habent?*" Does Kagnus know about the neural connection our people have?

Shocked, Mira put her hand to her chest and looked at Kagnus before hissing, I will not speak about it. That is sacred! How *dare* you. "*Non dico circa id. Sacrum est. quomodo fueras.*"

Oz sighed roughly and rubbed his forehead. "*Facio necesse est vincere illum bellum... Facile pectet per omnes secretos altissimos et obscurissomos, et non abdet solum res aut faciet aliquem circum id.*" I'll do what is necessary to win this war. I figured out how to establish a neural connection with humans. Carter can connect with her, and he can assure everyone she is on our side. Humans don't have a shield in their minds to protect their memories and thoughts like we do. He can easily rifle through all of her deepest, darkest secrets, and she can't hide a single thing or do anything about it.

Kagnus scowled before she scrunched her nose and explained, I'll say nothing until I know for certain she's not working for the enemy. Plenty of ex-UTC went through the small rebellion I was part of, but after we tortured them a bit, their true colors would come out. They were always spies. "*Dico nihil usque ad scio sane non laborat ad hostem. Sunt semper speculatores.*"

Aurelia paled as Oz turned to her and Carter. Heart pounding in her chest, her eyes slid to Carter, and he looked back at her wearily. She was terrified of the connection, and they had not discussed the two of them connecting yet. He slid his arm around her waist, and she trembled as he pulled her close.

Carter explained softly, "*Non facio ullam perpetuam iniuriam ad te. Coniunctio concedit mihi partire memorias mei vitae ante convivi te.*" I will not cause any permanent harm to you. It will be extremely painful, but I swear you will be safe. The connection is how my people secretly communicated for thousands of years. The connection allows me to be able to share the memories of my life before I met you."

Aurelia looked to the floor and solemnly nodded with her eyes pinched shut. They sat down on the bench attached to the metal wall of the ship, and Carter brushed his tail against the cold dusty metal of the wall. He missed the warm, protection of his armor and shivered. He gently took Aurelia's shaking hand. I am going to have to hold on to your arm while I connect with your wrist. "*Volo tenere de bracchio tibi dum connecto cum primore manu.*"

Jael walked up and set her hand on Aurelia's shoulder, "*Non facio mentiri ad te. Malum est primus tempus, sed post haec est doloris expers.*" I am not going to lie to you. It's bad the first time, but after that it's almost painless." She showed her the scar on her wrist where she and Oz connect, and Aurelia brushed her finger over the spot. She peered down to where Carter firmly held her hand. She nodded and sniffled as tears welled in her eyes.

Knowing the act that was about to occur would be far more painful than Jael described, she looked around for something to put in between Aurelia's teeth. Grabbing a small empty silk sack, Jael rolled it up and offered it to her right before Carter plunged his spine into her flesh.

Unable to help it, Aurelia screamed, shook, and fought

Carter as he held her arm in his iron grasp. Sweat beaded on her brow as her screams became whimpers, and she panted around the roll protruding her clenched teeth. Jael grabbed her other hand and tears poured down both women's cheeks.

Aurelia abruptly stopped shaking, and her pupils dilated as the connection was made. The absolute stillness of her body made Jael pause as she remembered the moment before the connection was made the first time, the moment when she too was paralyzed, unsure of what would happen next. She took a deep breath to calm herself. It was not the time for those traumatic memories. She needed to focus on the connection between Aurelia and Carter and what it could mean to their mission.

Softly releasing Aurelia's hand, Jael backed away to give them some privacy. She remembered exactly how it felt to connect once she could hear Oz's voice. It was something she would never forget, the joy of knowing she could finally hear his thoughts, to be able to feel someone else's feelings, to sense their needs, wants, or wishes, to be able to look into the past to see the people that they loved. She knew everyone called the language she passed on a gift, but she considered the connection itself to be a much more precious thing. Language provided oral communication, but it could be deceptive. Connections did not allow for lies.

It was bittersweet that such a beautiful thing had such an intense trauma tied to it. The relationship was more than worth the initial trauma, but the mind doesn't like to forget. It likes to resurrect recurrent fears at the worst possible moment. It likes to knock on the door in the middle of the night and loves to shout pain and secrets from the rooftops in the middle of the day.

Looking over to check on Aurelia, she was relieved to find them both calm.

In Aurelia's mind Carter spoke, I see you were honest about everything. I care for you very much. Would you like to experience how I feel? *"Video probum est circum omnes. Visne experiri quomodo sentio?"*

Excitement filled her and Aurelia responded, *"Ita vero."* Of course.

Carter passed over his feelings for her as he took his time reviewing her mind. He found her prior life to be filled with despair and great hunger. They were starving for so much more than just food. The hopelessness of the people from her home planet stunned him. His planet and people had hardships, but they didn't suffer from hunger, emotional or physical.

His feelings for her poured in, and she gasped. *"Non scio sentis valde circum aliquos, nedum circum me... Scio te multum tibi sub reservationem."* I did not know you felt so strongly about anything, much less about me. You are always filled with such beautiful calm. Your inner world is so vast. I knew you had more to you under all that reservation," Aurelia was inundated with Carter's warmth for her.

She reciprocated his feelings as he finished up searching around in her mind to indisputably verify who she was. Taking a deep breath and grinning at her, he nodded briefly, and she braced herself. He pulled his spine from her wrist, and she hissed in pain as it retracted. A drop of blood formed on her wrist, and Carter led her over to the counter where a med kit was laid out. He was exceptionally caring as he mended her wound.

Aurelia was relieved to have found the experience incredible rather than terrifying. She oddly found herself unable to wait until the next time they could connect. To think she had been so afraid of something so beautiful! She and Carter looked back to Oz, and Carter nodded to Oz in confirmation.

Are you satisfied? *"Satis es?"* Oz asked as he peered over at Kagnus.

Nodding, she scowled and, facing Mira, demanding, *"Volumus dicere circum quomodo facies omnes tempos et non curas narrare aliquos?... Si ego fuit in Emendo, cogitabo vendens asine futue!"* Are we going to talk about how you could do that this whole time and didn't care to tell anyone? Sacred or not, do you understand the information on the UTC we missed out on because this wasn't explored? If we were on Emendo, I would contemplate selling your fucking ass!

Mira, go get the damn translation implants we plucked from that Melior transport. And a scalpel. Oh, and grab my star chart. It's rolled up in my cabin under the desk. The one to the left. Then pick up the rest of their group out on the flat rock. Don't fucking talk to me when you come back. *"Mira, I damnatos inseros elegimus ab vecturis Meliore. Non futue dicere ad me dum venisti retro."* Mira didn't so much as blink as she made her way down the dark hallway leading to the cabins. She came back with a two-foot-long roll of what looked like clear plastic, a large med kit, and a small shiny metal box in the shape of a perfect square.

Mira placed the metal box next to the med kit and leaned the roll of plastic material up against the workbench where Kagnus was sitting. She walked out the door of the ship and shut it with a firm click before Kagnus patted the spot next to her on the bench.

Oz walked over and sat down, helping her prepare the

surgical kit. Kagnus disinfected her hands and opened the metal box with her thumb pressing a code on the side facing her. The lid split into four corners, and each side slid down into the bottom of the box. A red glow emanated from the inside, and Kagnus put her hand up for Oz to hand her the scalpel.

She angled her body toward Oz and growled, *"Erit dolere."* This is going to hurt. Giving no further warning, she immediately brought the scalpel to Oz's ear and sliced him right under it, making a half inch cut. Oz hissed, and she reached up again to slide in the tiny bean sized device.

Oz felt it come alive and send its tendrils searching for his ear canal. He grabbed his head and groaned as the device wriggled around inside his head. Wrapping itself around his ear canal, it settled itself in. Oz took a breath of relief, thinking it was over, yet the real surprise came when it pierced his eardrum. Shaking his head from the nauseating sensation, he snapped, What does this do exactly? *"Quid facit accurate?"*

Tilt your head up, *"Prafige caputem tibi supra."* Kagnus demanded.

Oz narrowed his eyes at her. He slowly did as she said. He wished he would have asked what she was going to do because he felt a stinging slice next to his vocal cords. Next was searing, mind scrambling pain. He was in too much agony to utter a sound as the device wrapped itself around his vocal cords. Unable to move his head from the face up position, he shook until his neck muscles became impossibly tense. Just when he thought the muscles in his neck couldn't be pushed any further, he felt the tendrils of the device pierce his vocal cords. Searing hot pain enveloped his throat. Oz coughed and grabbed his neck as he tried to catch his breath. He wondered if it was similar to what Jael felt when they connected that first time. He shuttered with the memory. The screams. He hoped she could one day forget that pain, and he could forget this.

Glaring at Kagnus, Oz gasped for air as she rose from the bench and asked cheerfully in, Who is next? "*Quis proxime?*"

Kagnus spent the next two hours installing the translation implants on everyone, and once all the torment was over, there was no more need for anyone to think about languages. "The translators work in two ways, in the ear and in the throat. The ear implant can filter and translate any word spoken in ear shot. The throat implant can alter the sound emitting from the person's vocal cords, making it seem as if the person is fluent in any language detected by the ear implant. It can even learn a new language if it's spoken a few times around you," she explained as she cleaned up her implements.

Sitting next to Oz, Jael rubbed her neck and asked, "Is there a place to sleep here?"

Hearing her, Mira approached, "Absolutely, this ship was designed for a crew of thirty. It has ten rooms and lots of beds."

"You need to delay your plans, green bean. Your lot is not ready, not by a long shot. Get your woman to bed and meet me in my cabin so I can review these star charts with you," Kagnus barked at Oz.

He didn't argue, but he was not rolling over so easily. He took Jael by the hand and led her out as he followed Mira. They walked down the dark hall, and Mira pushed on one of the first doors. It slid backward an inch then disappeared into the floor.

The room was sparsely furnished, but there was a nice

large bed, and Jael ran for it, landing face down and collapsing in the grey covers. They smelled like the ship, old and musty, but they were comfortable. Oz walked over and slapped her on the ass before saying, "I'm going to go back and speak with Kagnus. Get some sleep. I have a feeling these next few days are not going to be fun for any of us."

Jael leaned up and kissed him. "Go ahead. I'll have no issue sleeping."

"You never do." Oz smiled at her and reluctantly headed to the door.

When he stepped out, the door shut behind him with a whoosh. The rush of air gave him a chill up his spine. He made his way to the open door up the hallway and found Kagnus standing next to her kitchen table. The star charts lay open and glowing with visualizations of star systems. The rolled-up pieces of plastic ended up being far more interactive than at first impression.

"How exactly are you planning to break into UTC command? I see only one way in," Kagnus asked, her beady eyes searing holes into Oz's.

Trying to hold back his anger, Oz feigned calm, "I'm not sending her in."

"Then go home because this doesn't work otherwise. They won't give Aurelia the crown of laurel leaves for bringing me in. If they bring you in, they'll kill you and send the video to the empress. They will be handsomely commended for their noble actions to aid the empire against a dangerous terrorist who threatened them all. I can hear the rolling video announcements already. You're a dumbass if you think you can do this any other way.

"She's the only way in. We need to get her ready. You can't win wars without sacrifice. Wars in this galaxy are won by strategy and power, and you barely have a strategy. You sure don't have power. You only have one ticket inside. That's her. They will not kill her. If she is really from the planet you say she's from, they will want to save her so they can use her as an example of human progress. I bet the empress already has a ship on route to her world. The empress will be looking for proof she designed the device which transported her. If so, the Empress will have the galactic center law behind her to make first contact with Jael's world. If this happens, her former people will be doomed to be imprisoned by the greedy and their fertile lands stripped bare. They have been waiting thousands and thousands of years for a new human planet to become ripe to add to their poor gene pool. They will destroy it like they do to every habitable world. Just as the Genil descendants," Kagnus lectured.

Her words rolled through him, and before he reluctantly accepted the truth in them, he enjoyed his last moment of peace. Once he allowed the thoughts through, he knew the pain inside would be unbearable. He loved this woman with every fiber of his being and sending Jael into an enemy base with a turned enemy soldier was a fucking nightmare, a knife in his gut hollowing him out, sawing back-and-forth. His breath became short, and he struggled to remain calm.

Oz stared at her with his jaw clenched and sighed in defeat, "How do we prepare her?"

23

PLANET ADURO – MINE 03

Standing in line for his bowl of grey mush and dried bug chips, August looked up and found himself caught in the line of sight of a large cerulean man wearing a dirty tunic with a torn sleeve. The man winked sensually and slightly tipped his chin up at him.

He froze. His focus had been on his throbbing thumb from smashing it with the hammer the day before. He hoped it was just a bruise and not actually broken. He was staring off into nothingness right before the tall man walked into his line of sight.

Why is he winking again? Is that man hitting on me?

Chris nudged August with his elbow, and when their eyes met, Chris tipped his head to the blue man and touched his fingers together at the tips.

Was the man winking because of the gift or because he was on board? This is the kind of bullshit that happens when you can't freely talk aloud.

He had no idea if Livia would tell if there were microphones in the bathroom or not. There were none in the barracks or mine he could find. He wondered if there any here at all.

It was a day full of questions with so few answers. He was just relieved he knew the gigantic blue man was not hitting on him. He was not August's type, at all. He was attracted to a balance of strength and grace. That man seemed more of the good looking, full of himself, brute type.

Wait. That wasn't what he was, was it? The full of himself, brute type?

Pausing for a moment, he sighed at how thoroughly he had just called himself out. He sat there, soaking in the fact he had managed to hurt his own feelings after rejecting a come on which never existed. *Am I always this dramatic? Shit.*

Comments made about him and his mother being just alike crossed his mind, and he smiled, thinking about her. She was loved, but she had a flare for the dramatics. If he was anything like her, he wasn't doing too badly after all. He dearly missed his mother; she had an unending thoughtfulness to her. Under her watch, no child in the village ever went hungry or went to sleep without a bed. *He should work on being more like her, but maybe with less drama.*

As he walked back to his bunk and people all around began sitting on their mattresses, the sounds of the old springs flexing within the rusty bed frames filled the room. The crunching and grumbles of food being eaten began, filling the room with even more odd sounds he had yet to adjust to. The mush and worm chips looked disgusting as usual, and he cringed as he thought about Chris crunching them every day. He wondered if the mush was also some kind of worms and decided not to go there. The slop was his only food, and it was better to not know.

Crunch, crunch, slurp... the sounds echoed around the room. While he missed talking, there were times he wished the noise would stop. August closed his eyes and leaned his head back, praying he didn't dream about eating worms, or worms eating him, when he slept. His nightmares already were filled with that evil bitch grinding down his fangs while they flew around in the winds of a tornado. He didn't need any fresh horrors.

The cavern groaned suspiciously, and August felt uneasy. He listened as one of the guards comm's made a ding from his belt. The guard pulled his shoulders back and eyes wide. He released the communication device from his belt and looked at it warily before flipping it open. The voice on the other end crackled, The seasonal rains have begun. Halt all mining and have the laborers wait it out in their bunks. There is supposed to be heavy rains this year. Expect some flooding in the cave. Use the pumps if you need them. *"Anni temporis pluviae inceperant... Uti ose si neccesse es."*

The man answered, but August couldn't make out what he said before he disconnected. Even before the call ended, his people began heading toward their bunks. The guard had an uneasy look about him as he watched everyone moving before he announced the rains were beginning.

After the announcement, Chris finally made his way over to August's bunk, and they sat in silence next to one another. After looking around and sure no one was watching, Chris slipped his hand into August's and initiated the connection.

"Are you fucking the General?" Chris asked.

Whipping his head around, August shot his eyes down to the boy's and asked, "Why would you ask me that?"

"You are not a good actor. I already know the answer.

I'm nine, and you gave me an adult's memories. What did you think was going to happen?" Chris asked sincerely.

Closing his eyes and realizing what a mistake he had made as some of the more *adult* memories he had sent to the boy spun in his mind. He had really fucked up. He had sent that little boy information that was far too old for him. Guilt shot through his gut. How could he have done something so stupid? He let ambition override his common sense, and now this little boy had lost a piece of his innocence because of his carelessness.

"I'm a mine worker; I was already fucked," he admitted with wide eyes focused on him.

August narrowed his eyes down at the boy and through the connection scolded, "Cut it with the bad words."

Chris rolled his eyes and watched as a drop of water from the ceiling hit the floor. Everyone was in bunks, but no one was on the top bunks this time. Confusion filled August as he pulled his hand back. He broke the connection so Chris could get comfortable for the evening. He would never admit it to the little boy, but August normally could only sleep well stretched out. For Chris though, he'd manage.

Large drips from the ceiling began hitting the dirt floor, creating little puffs of red dust. Drops became trickles and soon small waterfalls cascaded down and formed little muddy rivers flowing toward the door and mine below.

August wondered what the storm looked like outside as he listened to the rushing water under his bunk. Even under all the sand and solid rock, it sounded like a full-blown hurricane. He knew the destructive power of the cyclones, but after reviewing Jael's memories of bad weather, he couldn't wait to see one for himself. The power of untamable nature would be impressive.

The murky water rose higher, and he noticed everyone climbing to the top bunks. He assumed the bunks would fall over as they climbed, but they stayed steady. They must be bolted the floor. He realized he hadn't noticed that before and needed to improve his observation skills.

The water was still pouring from the cracks in the ceiling and raining down over the bunks, but it was better than sitting in the cold rushing water. He and Chris threw a blanket over themselves, but it quickly soaked through. Under their saturated blanket tent, they watched as the water rose so high it rushed out of the door leading to the mine. Studying the door, he wondered where the hell the guards were. He guessed no one wanted to be swept into the mine, so they didn't really need guards at the moment. Curiosity to find out where they went and hid nearly had him debating if it was worth it to brave the waters.

Watching the raining ceiling, he thought about the guard numbers during a normal day. Only ten guards were visible at any time, so the numbers were good we're over-taking them. Leaving the mine and crossing the desert would be the true obstacle. They would need to eliminate the guards, cross the stretch of sand dunes, and then breach the palace without destroying it. He had only seen one tiny hallway and a few rooms but knew it was bigger than his entire village and the tarantula silk farms combined. Maybe even bigger than the mountain town, he guessed.

A droplet of water hit him in the eye, and it burned. As he rubbed his eye, he sniffed and realized water had a slight sulfur scent. Dissolved chemicals must be flowing through the desert sands; he cringed and was thankful his body was resistant to radiation. He hoped it was also resistant to all the chemicals that he was pretty sure were being absorbed through his skin in this chemical shower.

He noticed a difference since being in the mine though, and not just the slight increase in gravity. He felt sluggish and uncomfortable, his hair shed more, and their water sometimes burned as he swallowed. Just because their genetics were resistant to the radiation, didn't mean it was not affecting the cells in their bodies. The thought made him nauseous. He wondered what the life expectancy of people in the mine was. He bet it didn't compare to what it was on their home planet. He personally knew elderly people from his village much older than one hundred and twenty.

August missed home desperately. Droplets stung his scalp and trickled down under his tied hair to slide down his back. The water dripped in his eyes continuing to sting. The small cut on the thumb he had slammed with the hammer came in contact with the water now seared with pain. Maddening, he decided. This situation was enough to drive someone out of their wits.

He watched Chris who sat peacefully with his knees pulled up and his arms wrapped around them. This was obviously not his first time though the cave flooding. The boy had fully retreated into his own mind, ignoring the entire external world. August could really take a hint from the kid.

The water dripping down and swirling under them was becoming colder, and he worried the temperature would keep dropping. He was already shivering, and so was Chris. They scooted to the middle of the bed and sat shoulder to shoulder as August wrapped them in the soaked blanket. Everyone else was doing it, so he followed suit. A small amount of warmth collected under the wet blanket, and he was able to stop them both from shaking as badly. He was exhausted and wanted to sleep but was afraid of what would happen if he dozed off. Chris saw his eyes drooping and took his hand to connect.

"If you need to sleep, go ahead. I'll wake you up if anything happens. The flooding only occurs a few times a year. It will get really cold at the end so you might want to sleep now. They will come by after that with dry bedding and blankets so we don't get skin rot," Chris explained, trying not to shiver.

"What about you?" he asked.

Chris replied, "Remember, I don't have to sleep: that's just you. I'll just lie down behind you like always. I'll only be cold for a couple of hours. Once we have dry bedding, we will all be fine."

"If you get too cold, wake me up," He demanded though he wondered what he could do about it.

August broke the connection and nodded before he moved around, and water sloshed off of the top of the bunk. He lay under his half of the sopping cover and noticed the water from the ceiling had slowed. The draining seemed to be catching up, and he sighed with relief. The newest scourge was almost over. He wondered what the storm was like from the palace, and he hoped Livia was watching. Maybe one day he could connect with her, and she could show him the memory.

The next thing he knew, he was being shoved on his shoulder by a little hand. Through blurry vision, he found Chris staring at him. He blinked the sting from his eyes and slid his groggy gaze around the area. His eyes landed on a familiar face.

Livia stood next to the bunk beds with a stack of fresh

blankets, and she had a dry thick mattress, compressed, and rolled up under her arm. Her returning gaze brimmed with contrition. She knew her role in this misery and wanted to make up however she could.

Was she truly upset that he had to sit through the rain pouring from the cracks in the ceiling? He sat up, and Chris jumped off, pulling the wet mattress off the bottom bunk as August slid off and pulled the top mattress down. Water gushed and sloshed everywhere as August and Chris shivered. Livia tossed the fresh bedding on the mostly dried bottom bunk and turned to help the guards pass out the rest of the dry bedding.

August stepped into Livia's path and held her there with his gaze while he took in her scent. He debated if his life was worth putting his hands on her in public. Her big blue eyes flared wide telling him to move. Reluctantly, August stepped to the side but never took his eyes off her. The lights above made her skin shimmer as she walked away and he wanted to feel the heat of her glow.

Chris punched August on the arm, and he looked down to find a little boy with a hell of a scowl trying to unfold the dry mattress. His eyes widened at his mistake, and he grabbed one side of the foam mattress to help straighten it out. It had popped open, and Chris had been fighting with it on the other side of the bunk. August leaned on the frame and found it was sturdy. He gave it a good shove, and the metal groaned but didn't move. It was somehow attached to the floor and attached well he discovered. He looked at where it was connected to the floor yet didn't find any bolts. He wondered if the posts themselves were embedded in the rock. He straightened the dry mattress on the top bunk and tossed a blanket up there.

His palm ached from shoving the iron bar, and as he checked it, his vision blurred. He was still so tired he could hardly take a full breath as he climbed up and lay down again. Chris walked around to move bedding on the top bunk as August tried to go back to sleep. He heard Chris give up after walking a few steps and felt him settle near August's feet, curled up at the end of the bunk

As August thawed under his warm blanket, he noticed a bulge in the mattress as he sunk down on it. His first reaction was one of irritation that not even a dry mattress was comfortable, but then again, Livia brought it over personally. His mind reeled with the possibilities. Pulling the side of the covers away, he felt the top of the mattress, and there was a small slit cut in the foam. He wiggled his hand in and felt a small fabric bag. He slid his hand out and peered inside the brown bag. There was a small assortment of dried and candied fruit. He leaned down and nudged Chris. His little head popped up from under the blanket where he rested with a look of curiosity. August tilted his head over to the side once and reached his hand out toward the boy. Chris extended his hand and accepted August's offering.

The instant ankle grab almost launched August into a laughing fit. Chris had a deathly firm grip on his ankle and within seconds sat next to him. He didn't ask; he just slid his hand into the bag and devoured a handful of dried fruit. The soft sounds he was making as he chewed raised memories of home and his mother giving him snacks of sweet, dried fruits.

Feeling guilty the boy might not even know what most fruits taste like, August slid the bag over. Chris's eyes met his, and he saw tears form. Smiling at him, August shook his head no to being emotional over it and signaled to dry his tears. His little friend smiled as wide as his cheeks allowed, wiped his face, and the bag was devoured in a matter of minutes. August knew he had just made a best friend for life. After all the treats were enjoyed, he had a cheerful kid staring at him. Chris deserved so much more, and more was something he was working on for Chris and the rest of his people.

He wanted to sleep, but sleep never came because he kept feeling someone staring. The little tingles on the back of his neck became too much, and he turned his head to find Livia looking at him through the rows of bunk beds. He could see her blue eyes, like little star sapphires, shining in the sea of rusty dirt. Huffing a bit, he rose from the bed and made his way to the bathroom. He noticed Livia was the only one standing guard at the door, so he headed straight into the small, unused office space across from the bathroom. The door blended in with the cracks in the wall so well it was hardly noticeable. August pushed it open but misjudged his entry and almost knocked both of his shoulders on the narrow door frame. Tucking in his wide shoulders at the last moment, he avoided making any noise.

Before he even had a chance to turn around, Livia knocked him to the ground. The door shut behind them, and his eyes adjusted in time to see Livia standing over him with her staff pointed to his throat. She demanded, *"Quid futue facies?... Egeo responsos."* What the fuck are you doing? The guards are talking. Something is going on with your people here. They don't act like your kind we have in the other mines anymore. I need answers.

Focusing his eyes on the end of her staff and smiling at her with all his teeth, August replied, I've taught them everything I know. *"Didici omnes scio."* Then with realization, he asked, "*Quid est ullas fodinas?*" What do you mean other mines?

Did you think this is the only mine we have on Aduro? King Claudius has hundreds of your people, almost a thousand, in different mines all over the planet. You can't possibly think you can take over this mine and just usurp the planet. My father will bomb this mine into dust the moment he hears a whisper of rebellion. How could you have taught them all you know? You haven't even been here a month, and you can't speak aloud?! "*Scisne solam fodinam habemus on Aduro?... Tu non habes hic mensem et tu non dices clare?!*" Livia fumed, her face set with fury and her eyes ablaze.

Grinning back at her, August offered, "*Monstrabo secretum mei si tu iverit me in regiam ut interficiam tui patrem et maritum.*" I'll show you my secret *if* you can get me into the palace so I can kill your father and husband.

Good try. There is another person you would need to kill before you could take the planet from the royal line. Me. "*Bene conari... Me.*" Livia seethed with anger. Her hardened expression faded, "What do you mean a secret? "*Que... secretos?*"

Tilting his head to the side at her words, August replied, "*Habeo multos secretos. Est punctum.*" I have lots of secrets. What do you mean kill you? You would make a great King. That's the point.

Finally pulling her staff away from his throat in understanding, Livia dropped to the ground at August's feet, and he sat up and crossed his legs, adjusting his tail behind him. She set her staff down next to her and rubbed her eyes.

"They itch sometimes. I know my biological eyes are not there anymore, but I can still feel them. They are like little ghosts in my eye sockets. I miss them. I know I can see just as well with these new eyes, but I don't trust them. I have had them longer than my real eyes, yet I feel that I haven't had them long enough, *"Pruriunt aliquando... Habueram longium ut oculos veros, tamen sentio ut non haberim longum tempum."* Livia explained while she held her fingers over her eyelids. Livia eventually looked up at August and sighed, I don't even trust my own mechanical eyes, so I don't know why I believe you. Why I believe *in* you. *"Non fideo mi mechanicis oculis, sed non scio cur credo te. Cur credo in te."*

Heirs were picked for their strength and ruthlessness alone. I am number three in line, which is dead last. I am too much like my mother to ever have been considered a first or second in line to be heir. She started off strong, but my father eventually broke her. By the time my siblings had come and gone, she was already a shell of a person. Being raised by a hollow being, but being shown love, was my undoing, I guess. *"Heres elegerunt nam eis viribus et immisericoridibus solum. Sublatus est ab cavo homine, sed fudiendo amorem, faciet me conico."* She paused as memories of her mother filled her heart, but when the image of her beaten body appeared, her tone and body hardened again.

I've wanted to kill Lucas for a long time, and I've wanted to kill my father for even longer. I hate almost all my cousins. They're all just as evil as Lucas and my father. I'll find a way to get you in the palace. I'll play your game, demon. What's your secret? *"Vollo interficere Lucas ad longum tempum et vollo interficere mei patrem ad etiam longium... Quid est tui secretum?"*

"Debeo monstrare te. Scio dolens, sic para ipso." I'll have to show you. I give you my word it won't kill or damage you. I'm sure it hurts, so prepare yourself, August rubbed Livia's ankle in reassurance.

She nodded consent, and he moved toward her. Sliding his body as close to her as he could, he took her wrist where Oz always connected with Jael. He recalled the anatomy books Jael had read and determined the best place on her wrist before his spine shot out and searched for her nerve.

Her eyes widened she shook with the pain. She had not fully believed his warning. The mist sweat sparkling on her brow grew into droplets while August desperately searched. When he found it, his specialized neural spine dove into her nerve, and she crushed her cries into her balled up fist as the agony ripped through her.

A gasp escaped from her lips as August's voice became clear inside her head, through the connection, for the first time.

She could hear him explain, *"Sumus non muti aut nimis humilis dicere. Quid est mei homines facient in fodina degere circum scientiam et linguam."* We are not mute or too lowly to speak. We were forced into silence. Our bodies and minds searched desperately for a way to communicate, and this is the result. We can pass memories and feelings this way. This is what my people in the mine are doing to pass around the knowledge and language.

Livia's thoughts were restrained as if she was afraid of what August might see. She tried to speak, and some of her thoughts spilled over- dark and sinister times of misery and pain, of emotional torture, hers and her mother's, and the king behind all of it. The rage inside of August was at a tipping point when he received another small release of devastating thoughts. Memories flew threw his mind of Livia being pummeled with a staff while chained to a post, being struck in the face while bound to a chair, and still forced to succumb to her husband's cruel desires. The ripping of her flesh as the vile monster took what he wanted from her echoed in his head. August could feel the tears in her body and the scars in her mind. First, she was abused by her whimsically sadistic father, next it was her brutal training, and finally she was handed over to a savage Lucas was doing so much more than physically abusing her. He was a constant reminder of her lost mother. For their crimes, her mind raged for vengeance, but under it all, there was a softness, an indescribable desire to make things right. Anger was not what drove her. It was justice. Behind great walls, armored down to the teeth, he found carefully hidden grace in a heart belonging to a hopeful little brown eyed girl.

It took August several minutes to calm himself. He didn't want Livia to see or feel his fury. She didn't deserve his wrath; her soon-to-be dead father and cousin did. He would find her instructors, and they would pay as well. Swallowing his rage, he regained his focus and demanded, *"Iuva me capet supra planetam et libera homines mei. Fieri Regnem."* Help me take over this planet and free my people. Help me fight. Do it for yourself. *Become the King.*

24

PLANET PORTUM – RECRUITMENT MISSION – NORTH VILLAGE

Callum pinched his nose as a foul smell twirled around his nostrils. Curling his lips into a snarl, he turned to Jacob who intently watched the bustling village far below. A warmth blossomed inside as he admired Jacob's profile, and he adjusted his position on the branch. This was no time for such a delightful distraction. The wretched scent found him again. He recognized it, but couldn't place it. *Did Jacob not smell that?!*

They were on day one of their stake out, perched together on a tall tree branch like two love birds. The odor wafted by his nose again, and he scowled at Jacob, poking his leg with his finger to draw his attention. Facing Callum, Jacob's eyes met his. Callum shot his eyebrows up with his hand out to let Jacob know he wanted to speak to him. Now.

Reaching his hand out, Jacob connected with Callum and sharply asked, "What?"

"What do you mean, *what?!* You don't smell that? It smells like something rotting. You know that cannot possibly mean anything good," Callum replied as he sniffed the air again.

Through the connection, he could tell Jacob was frustrated. Wait, frustrated but not from what he said. Was it something more? Was he feeling something warm stirring inside too? Shit!

Jacob pulled his hand back and sat up from his crouched position. Surveying the area, he looked back at Callum once more and put his hands up in confusion.

Jacob froze and his eyes widened as he finally smelled it. It was a sharp stench of decay, but under the initial rot was an acidic sulphury scent. Closing his eyes to concentrate better, he sniffed the air and turned to look at Callum shaking his head and shrugging his shoulders. He smelled it strongly now, but didn't recognize the source either.

Closing his eyes momentarily to center his hearing to locate at source, Callum picked up a soft crunching sound then narrowed his eyes in concentration at it. Waiting. Jacob shifted, and Callum shot his hand out to grab his ankle firmly, causing Jacob to still. There was a distinct scrape, and they angled their focus to the ground.

Callum's mouth dropped open just as the first of many giant snails became visible. He stood on the branch to see better and gasped when what he saw were hundreds of slowly sliding snails, rippling their way through the woods. All of them were varied sizes, and some of their antennae were tall enough to reach the branch where he crouched.

Their skin was mottled in color, but it seemed reflect light from its smooth texture. The largest of them had vertically wrinkled skin with loose gullets gently swaying as they moved their heads, gathering foliage to munch on as they progressed.

Making his way along the branch, Jacob grabbed the one above to steady himself, he inched over to Callum's side. It looked like they would be here for a while with the ground filling with snails, so he put his arm around his love and leaned into him. They stood on the branch and watched as all the snails made their way by, leaving slick, wet trails of goo behind in their paths.

As they passed by, the variety in color increased. Some toward the back of the slimy caravan had shells of violet rounded with swirls to the center and others had cerulean pointed shells. Some were a plain brown or cream color with little speckles dotting their shells. Their soft bodies were a mix of yellows, pinks, and whites, but some were blue, and others were a deep red. They were all sizes and shapes; some were so small they seemed lost under the larger ones. They blanketed the ground like a living multicolored quilt. One particularly towering snail slunk by and gave them a deep stare through one of its big, round eyes at the tip of its antenna. The long appendage, with an eyeball at the end, studied them both up and down thoroughly, coming uncomfortably close. The head the curious eye was attached to seemed to be disconnected from what the eye wanted. The mammoth mollusk continued its slow path below, the eye stretching impossibly long for a last look up and down before it pulled away. The sizzling sound of their slime trails filled the trees and more of the putrid scent followed. The leaves trapped in the slime bubbled and disintegrated before their eyes.

With all of his intentions still focused, Callum had stars in his eyes from the rout of massive snails moving through the woods by the village. Their gargantuan shells swayed back and forth as they disappeared between the trees, and even Jacob had been entranced for a few moments. They were quite beneficial creatures aside from the horrendous smell. He knew they migrated through this area, but he was unaware the wave came so close to the village.

Jacob tilted his head to the side and looked long and hard at the corrosive goo. He evaluated the surrounding tree limbs and sighed in relief. They would be plenty strong enough to jump on. He would hate to have to climb through acidic slime, doubting they would survive it.

Smiling at Jacob, Callum knew it was time to head back. He nodded and watched as Jacob leaped from the branch they were on to land on a tree branch nearby. Callum followed, hoping they didn't make too much noise. The trees rustled as they bounded from tree to tree until Jacob stopped and looked over at Callum, clearly worried.

"What?" Callum asked softly after he landed on the branch next to Jacob.

Pursing his full lips, Jacob nodded to the space in front of them. Callum didn't understand until he looked down and saw the clearing where their gear and hover-bikes had been. A thick layer of slime buried their tents and their hover-bikes were scratched up and hovering over by a tree several yards from where they had left them. The sides of the bikes were covered in slime. The campsite was dissolving.

The branch shook and Callum looked over to find Adrian perched in a crouch with his mouth hanging open. "What the fuck happened?"

Adrian looked over at Callum, his brow creasing and anger beginning to simmer.

"Don't look at me like it's my fault. It's called snails, big guy," Callum retorted.

Giving Callum a look of promised fury, Adrian asked,

"Where the fuck are we going to rest when it rains? How do we get this shit off everything, or do we just leave it?"

The branch shook slightly with her graceful landing, and Juni spoke with reason, "Adrian, calm your stinger. The corrosive slime will dissolve everything in a few days. We don't want any of it on us. It will keep eating through your body tissue down to the bone, and it will eventually liquify your bones too. There is nothing we can do until after it rains.

"Water breaks down whatever chemical is in the slime that keeps it held together so it will easily dissolve into the ground. I was obsessed with snails as a child. They were the subjects in my play kingdoms. After I grew up, I was still fascinated and eventually found a surprise after their slime breaks down everything. The organic material left over is some of the best fertilizer I've ever used."

Looking down at the current situation, she was happy she knew so much about the snails. Childhood memories of her raw, burned fingers and a cup of water she kept close by to extinguish the slime, flashed in her mind. Fond memories filled her mind of her mother standing over her shaking her head at the mess she always made behind their home. She continued by asking, "We're going to be stuck in the trees with just our armor. Did anyone have a helmet with them? Or is everything, down there?"

Callum faced Adrian, who was still scowling. Looking past him, he met Juni's eyes as he asked, "I don't think any of us have a helmet. Is the goo eating up the paneling on our hover bikes too? Can it eat metal?"

Juni looked over at the bikes, "If it's in contact long enough it probably could eat through metal. They should be OK, but we will need a lot of water to clean them off and need to do it right away. It looks like they're pretty heavily slimed up from here."

Selecting her holo-screen on her forearm, Juni scrolled through and pulled up the weather updates from the base. Concern crossed her face as she read, Callum focused in on her expression.

Juni peered up at him, "Good news is the signal boosters in the bikes are still working well, so we still have comms in our suits. Bad news is it will be about two days until it rains, so we're stuck for a little while. That should be plenty of time to wash the bikes before it eats through the metal though. We are going to need shelter, so I'm going to look for a cave we can camp in. They should have plenty of caves and lava tubes on this side of the dead volcanos."

Relieved, Callum said, "That's probably a good idea."

Growling in frustration, Adrian leapt off the branch and left the other three watching him spring away.

Juni shook her head, "He is such an ass. He complains the entire time we do surveillance."

"Thank you for planning everything out, Juni. There's no reason to contact the base about the equipment. We should be able to finish this part of the mission without helmet replacements or any extra gear. Since we should only be here for a week, hopefully no longer. We can have the base drop off tech when we contact the village."

"I'll say something to Adrian about his mood when he comes back *if* he comes back," Jacob scoffed.

Juni smiled at the holo-screen on her arm, "I found a perfect spot where we can wait for the rain and rest while we keep doing surveillance. We can signal a route for the bikes and have them meet us at the cave. I'll do that now." Juni selected some options on her holo-screen before it vaporized into nothing. She looked over as the bikes took off toward the cave.

"Follow the direction of the bikes on your forearm controls. I don't want anyone off track. After you," Jacob said with his hand stretched out for Juni to lead the way.

Nodding, Juni leapt away, and Callum looked over at Jacob before he jumped and asked, "Are we going to tell Adrian about the cave or nah?"

Laughing, Jacob landed on the next branch by Callum and replied, "We are definitely not telling him. He can figure it out."

"Speaking of figuring things out, do you have any idea why the fuck I have been so goddamn horny since we've been in the woods? I think that snail scent has something to do with it, or maybe the woods?" Callum asked, his eyes full of desire.

Unable to help himself, Jacob smiled as he looked down at his forearm where he could see Junie vaulting across the canopy toward the cave. The heat had done nothing but grow, and he, too, was consumed with desire. Grabbing Callum by the arm he shoved him against the tree.

With his eyes wide, Callum started tearing at the neck of his suit asking, "Right here? Right now?"

With a demanding gaze, Jacob growled, "Now."

"Shit. You too? Oh fuck, yes!" Callum grabbed the branch above him as Jacob pulled his armor down his legs.

Gripping the branch that was a little too high above him, he balanced on his toes and watched as Jacob lay his armor over the branch behind him.

Facing Callum, Jacob took his length in his hand as Callum leaned back and pressed his back against the bark, barely able to speak as he breathed, "Can we just live in the woods?"

Stroking him, he gave Callum a devilish smile before he slid down his body and wrapped his tongue around his length. While he leaned his head back at the sensuous touch, Jacob lightly stroked Callum up his inner thigh and then wrapped his hand around his softness underneath. Groaning and rolling his hips, he did his best to hang on and restrain his passion.

Unable to hold back, Callum tipped his head to the side, voicing deep clicks in his throat. Within moments he erupted, and Jacob positioned his mouth right at the tip, collecting every viscous drop. After swallowing it down, he kissed up Callum's body, all the way to his lips.

With molten fire in his blazing blue eyes, Callum demanded, "Lean back."

Jacob's hands gently shook as he pulled his armor down, taking Callum's arm for balance. While his armor off and laid on the branch behind him, he gripped the branch as Callum leaned forward and kissed down his chest.

Painfully erect, Jacob nearly came undone when Callum took his pebbled nipple into his mouth, twirling his tongue and making Jacob squirm. Callum took his time kissing Jacob down his ripped abs and gently licking, following the arrow of his muscles down the valley leading between his legs. He kissed his way down and back up his thigh and descended on his sensitive length. Jacob made a deep, breathy moan as Callum wrapped his long tongue down his length and spun it up over his tip like he was pulling the string to begin a twirling top.

Jacob bucked against the branch as he tried to hold on. His hips rocked desperate for more, and the branch shook with their passion. After Jacob's reaction, Callum did it again, this time slower. Leaning his head back and releasing a deeper, slower moan, the clicks following not far behind. He could see the aura swirling in the sky above them as Callum grazed a gentle circle around his back entrance with his finger, causing his pleasure to overflow.

With a few deep breaths, they sat close together enjoying their all to brief moment of pleasure. Callum reached back trying to grab the arm of his suit. Just as he did Juni's face popped up on the hollow screen. The arm of his suit was laid over the branch at just the right angle for her to see them both, in all their glory.

The moment she realized they were both nude, her eyes went wide. There was a startled "Oh!" and her face disappeared as quickly as it had appeared.

Staring at one another, trying to think the situation through, there was an uncomfortable silence until Jacob awkwardly suggested, "We should probably give her a minute."

Callum howled with laughter.

25

PLANET PORTUM - UTC COMMAND MISSION

Their hearts slamming, Aurelia and Jael cautiously approached the metal fence surrounding the legion camp. Dust kicked up with every step. It took every ounce of willpower Jael had to resist the screaming urge to run.

With a rail gun pointed at Jael, Aurelia held her by the arm and Jael's hands were bound with rope behind her back. Their faces were smeared with dirt. Jael was wearing a tattered uniform which had belonged to one of the dead soldiers who had stormed the Iungo base. It still had his dried blood on it. The wardrobe and situation may be fake, but the exhaustion written on their faces was real. Swallowing down their dread, they moved forward cautiously.

Oz wanted to alter the plan after the connection-language incident with Jael, but they had always known this was the only way inside, and she prayed it worked. With Aurelia's maps of the camps, along with Oz's and Kagnus's planning, they had formed what they all hoped would be a viable way to bring the rest of the team inside. There was no other way to penetrate the base defenses without a massive battle with heavy casualties, and there was no possibility their small squad could win in something horrendous like that- not when they could simply send her in. Jael repeated the plan in her mind, reminding herself to stay focused on the mission and not let her fear override the logic.

Clearing her throat, Jael thought about the device in her ear and neck and how nice it was to not have to worry about what language to use. The cuts healed in hours with a bit of salve Mira had saved for such an occasion, but either the devices or the surrounding tissues itched like hell. That better be temporary, or it was coming out after this was over.

She would need to pay very close attention to who did and who did not have a translation device. She knew how to override it and only use English to speak, thanks to Kagnus and her repeated and direct instructions. Leaning close to her, Aurelia whispered, "Don't look anyone in the eye and look at me when someone asks you a question. Remember to flinch a bit when I look back at you." Jael nodded her head in agreement as they stopped before the gated compound. They had been over the routine about twenty times, and she knew what to do.

With a rough exhale, Aurelia yelled, "Hey! Hey you! Hey! Go have the tower guard open the gate. I have a wanted prisoner and no comms!"

A uniformed person with long brown hair waved and ran toward the guard tower. As they approached, Jael looked up to find a two-foot-long rail gun pointed at her and found it moved on its own, tracking her every movement. She shivered, but not from the cold, and Aurelia squeezed her arm in reassurance. When they reached the gate, a tall brown haired human man with a beard opened it and narrowed his eyes at the two. He spit an olive pit on the ground as he popped another olive in his mouth. Titling his head at Jael but still chewing, he spoke to Aurelia. With his hand on his communicator, the gruff man asked, "What is this here? Who have you captured and brought? How did you arrive undetected?"

Responding, Aurelia deceptively smiled, "I was in the ground unit tasked to attack the enemy cave. I am Aurelia Cestus, officer number 836-355-839. This is wanted human Ariel Summer Green being presented for questioning demanded by the empress as stated in the mission briefing."

Sensing his skepticism, she continued, "I escaped the bug cave with provisions and found her knocked out in the woods as I made my way back to command. I stripped a dead soldier and dressed her in his uniform so she could survive the journey on foot. We had to travel a hell of a distance to get here. I'm fucking starving, and I'm freezing my ass off. What's the hold up? Send for a wheeled transport to take us in."

Still chewing and giving Aurelia a gaze of distrust, the man read her ID patch and read into his comms, "This is tower seven, Aurelia Cestus legion officer number..." He squinted and continued, "836-355-839-076, just showed up at my gate with wanted human Ariel Summer Green. She's alive...." He took a short pause as they responded, and he surveyed Jael with a scowl then acknowledged, "Sure, thing I'll have them brought right in." He slammed the coms down onto the table, but he didn't break his stare. "A truck will be here in a few minutes," he growled and walked back inside, the door to the guard tower crashed against the door frame. Dust fell from the sides of the building as it shook from the unnecessarily rough action.

Leaning her head over to Jael and pretending to look in the distance, Aurelia whispered, "Count to five after the last gate, right before we pull into the garage to start the coughing fit. I need to toss the jammer just inside the bay door. They should take us directly to the top where the empress's office is. It is where the UTC legion commander Dolion will be. I don't know if they'll take me up there with you or not. *Don't* be alone with Dolion. Good luck."

The open top truck came into view in a cloud of dust stirred up from the dirt road. The eerie red glow of the brown dwarf with the dirt billowing in the air made it impossible to see. A plain-looking younger woman pulled up firmly gripping the wheel. Aurelia guided Jael to the truck and shoved her down in the back first. She stepped in behind her and grabbed a hold of her arm as if Jael would run away.

The interior of the truck looked almost identical to the ATV they had burned. It had grey fabric down the center of the black cloth seats. They were just a scratchy as the ones in the ATV at the campsite as Jael shifted her rear on the seat.

That was the day they found out their enemy was humans, the day she became truly ashamed to be the species she was. Humans had proved they could be so treacherous over tens of thousands of light years of space and for such unfathomable lengths of time. Humans, no matter where they originated, were driven to control at any cost. Realizing the greatest enemy was her own people, she feared down to the depths of her soul about what they would find within the enemy base.

The woman took off with a heavy foot and kicked dirt everywhere behind her. With a set scowl, she drove Aurelia and Jael across the camp and toward the looming base. From the angle Jael was watching, there was a curved wall of glass, and a small corner of the building jutted out. The building looked as if it had been a rectangle, but someone had taken a big bite out of one corner. There were two gleaming imperial ships parked there, fitting perfectly within the curve.

Aurelia followed Jael's line of sight and kicked her foot. She looked over at her and Aurelia made her eyebrows bounce once before she set her gaze at the end and top of the building where there seemed to be a room of heavier tinted glass. From there someone would be able to monitor a large area from a single point. She guessed this was the empress's office.

The shocks on the truck groaned as they traveled over the rough terrain. The truck hit a bump, and they all flew about three inches off their seats. The young, uniformed woman never took her eyes off the road as she headed toward the closed garage door around the side of the building. It didn't seem as though the door would ever open, and Jael tensed as they neared. At the last moment, the door flew open allowing them to pass through, and she roughly exhaled. Her heart had been in her throat.

Aurelia stomped on Jael's foot, and she remembered she was supposed to be coughing. Jael began a wailing, coughing fit as Aurelia tossed the small disc from her pocket onto the ground, right inside the garage door as they drove past. Their eyes met, and Aurelia released a tense breath. She had almost been too late. Aurelia gave a stern glare to remind her to focus on the mission.

The young woman brought the transport to a screeching halt, and Jael's face and upper body hit the seat in front of her. Aurelia grabbed her arm and yanked her out of the truck just as the woman threw it into reverse. The wheels screeched as she backed up in the mostly empty garage.

Seeing only a few trucks were parked in the center, they hoped the lack of vehicles meant a smaller opposition. Aurelia expected guards to meet her, but she guessed they believed her story. That, or they were both walking into a trap.

She let go of Jael's arm as they approached the lift, stepping in cautiously after the large metal doors opened, effortlessly sliding into the dark recess on either side of the door. Jael made her way into the lift, and when she turned around, she found a long list of options on the right. The print was so small she couldn't read it, so Aurelia chose the top one without looking at the writing. It lit up with a white light behind it when the option had been selected. The doors slid shut slowly, but within seconds the doors were opening again, and Aurelia tightened her hand around Jael's arm. It had hardly felt like they even moved at all.

The air was humid and thick, almost too warm. The sound of her heart pounding in her ears was overwhelming. Something was wrong. Jael could feel something dragging its sharp claws down the inside of her bones. The palms of her hands began to sweat. She tried rubbing them together but because of the bindings, it was useless.

They passed through a lush garden, and Jael gaped as her eyes fell upon the corrugated decorative pillars holding up the balcony at the end of the vast room. They looked suspiciously like Roman architecture, adding to the many questions Jael had. *Latin language and then Roman architecture?* Ice slid down her spine and her brow creased. She didn't understand why these people had such a connection with Ancient Romans on Earth. *Had they been there? And if so, who had influenced whom?*

Nausea wrapped around her gut as they walked through

the winding path. The garden was filled with giant fruit trees and flowers Jael had never seen before. They passed by some flowers two feet across with bright yellow feathery petals jutting out in all directions. They smelled like citrus and honey. One flower bed was filled with miniature lilies, in a vibrant pink, but unlike Earth lilies, they shook when the two passed. All of these flowers were likely from different worlds, Jael suspected, as Aurelia pulled her by her arm toward the doors of another elevator. This one was much nicer, and Jael watched as Aurelia pressed the only button on the panel, then the doors slid shut.

Aurelia's face was ice, but her sweaty, trembling grip told another story. At least her reaction to being brought in would be realistic. Releasing a pent-up breath, Aurelia gave Jael a small smile right before the door slid open with a whoosh. They emerged onto the balcony and tread along the glossy floor toward a doorway to their left. Aurelia found a tall, sandy haired guard on the other side, standing at attention. He startled her, but she managed to maintain her composure.

The two made their way by him and down a winding path to the darkened door of the glass office. More unrecognizable plants and flowers decorated the path. The flowers were round and indigo with white edges, resembling little cauldrons. The flowers called to her; they begged her to come experience their delicate scents. They were mesmerizing, and Jael was surprised to see such beauty in such a wretched place.

The glass door made a *ting* as it opened. Aurelia's gaze met the commander's sitting behind a desk, and he motioned his arm for them to enter. He wore the First Human's formal battle uniform, complete with his command ranking on his sash. This man wanted it acknowledged he was a First Human commander above any UTC position he may carry. Aurelia saluted with her hand, palm faced out and raised to her shoulder, and stood at attention until the commander acknowledged her. When he did, she led Jael to the chair facing his desk, and pushed her down. Aurelia stood at ease, but still seeming to guard her prisoner. The commander placed his tablet on the glass desk. He stared at her with his piercing brown eyes and brusquely asked, "It seems you have brought us, Ariel. How did you do it?"

Aurelia nodded deferring to the dark-haired man, "Commander Dolion, I waited until they trusted me. I used sex and revealed selective secrets, just like we are taught in prisoner training. It was easy after that. They really are easily fooled as we were taught. I escaped their base with travel gear and found Ariel in the woods. I knew exactly who she was from the information packets we received before we went on the mission. I knew she was valuable." Give me your boot," the commander demanded in his low, grumbling voice.

Not understanding why, Aurelia decided against asking him and slid her boot off. When she had it slipped off, she handed it over to him, and he lifted a small measuring stick from a drawer. The light from the brown dwarf mixed with the ambient lighting in the room seemed to make his unusually pale skin glow a ghostly pallor.

He held the measure to the sole of the boot and agreed, "This measures up to the wear and tear on a new pair of boots after the long journey you claim to have made. Although it is an unbelievable story, your prior valor and this evidence say it is true. You truly dragged this wanted person back here for us? That sort of loyalty does not go unnoticed."

Aurelia smiled with false compliance, "I will do anything for the sake of the betterment of the empire."

With his brows lifted, the man handed her boot back and asked, "What will your prize be, Aurelia? Will it be riches or perhaps a promotion? I have a lieutenant commander position open here at the UTC S-7 Command Center. This would be a big move up to the First Humans regime. Very few makes it this far. It's yours with just a signature here."

He slid his tablet over to Aurelia as a guard they hadn't noticed in the corner stalked up and pulled Jael from her seat. Aurelia quickly looked over at Jael as she took the tablet from the glass desk.

"What happens to the prisoner?" Aurelia asked as she pretended to read the form. She felt nausea building inside and tried to allay it.

With a saccharin smile, Dolion replied, "That's for commanders, not Lieutenant-Commanders, to know."

"Yes, sir," she acknowledged humbly lowering her eyes. With the tip of her finger, she signed her name on the line and set the tablet down. Rising to salute the Commander, she stood at attention until he told her to report to the officer outside and dismissed her. She obediently turned and left the room.

With Jael firmly in the guard's grasp, the Commander faced Jael and asked flatly, "What do you have to say for yourself, you insect loving whore? Or do we have it wrong? Were you fucking him, or was he raping you?"

With a twirl of Dolion's finger, the guard behind her sliced through the binding rope around her wrists.

Squeezing her eyes shut Jael pinched her lips together. She had no idea what to do other than meet his eye, stare dumbly, and keep her mouth shut.

"Not going to talk, eh? Do you even know our fucking language? Or just the language you brought from Earth. I know all about your little planet of primitive humans. Thankfully that's for other commanders to worry about. I am much more interested in you," the commander reached down and took one of her hands into his. His skin was cold and calloused. She jerked her hand away, and he half laughed before returning to the chair behind his desk. After he sat a moment, he leaned back in his chair, "The empress wants you alive, but she never said in what condition. I want to make sure you being dropped in my lap isn't a trap. You have awfully pretty hands. I think I'll keep one as a trophy, if you will."

Terror careening down Jael's spine, she forgot everything Kagnus had taught her as she replied, "Fuck you. You're not taking my fucking hand!"

Grinning wide enough to show all his perfect white teeth, the commander simply nodded to the guard, and Jael was hauled toward the door. "I saw the little translator scar on your neck. I'm going to let them know to question you about it. I bet when they get you to the prison around Emendo, they will love to open up your neck and pry it from your vocal cords while you scream. Too bad I'll have to miss that. I'll likely be offered some extra vacation time for finding you. I may even collect some additional souvenirs while I'm at it. They all have lovely hands and feet on Teresk." Clearing his throat, the commander followed the guard to the door saying, "Make sure you cauterize both sides thoroughly. She needs to live, and the hand needs to be ready to be flash frozen so I can have Pleren preserve it. I'll want to have it added to my collection when I visit my home on Melior later this year."

With stars dancing in her vision and heavy breaths caught in her lungs, the guard pulled her to the lift and through the garden. His iron grip on her was bruising. He was such a large man there was no way she could break away from him, and he seemed pleased with his power over her.

They reached the second lift that led down into the base, and Jael's heart began pounding in her ears. It was all she could hear as the doors opened. They were going to cut her fucking hand off, and there was nothing she could do. She flexed her hands in front of her on instinct as she fought the grip of the hand around her arm. Tears threatened to stream down her face as she strode toward hell. She prayed Oz succeeded before this monster's assistant took her hand from her.

A scream bubbled in her throat, and before she could even think twice or release her terror, the lift door opened. The bright lights of the lab blinded her as she was dragged. She stumbled along in a daze, unable to think about anything but the sound of her own heart, threatening to pound right out of her chest.

In the center of the room stood foggy chambers with tall beings inside, their hands slid down the glass. Pounding and scratching, though their efforts muted.

She screamed, trying to pull away, to escape this monster's lab.

The enormous guard picked her fighting body up and lay her on the table as if she hadn't been kicking and thrashing. He began strapping her down, and she cried out as he secured her. He shoved a leather strap over her mouth as a gag and tied it behind her head, muting her. Narrowing his eyes at her, he yanked her arm down and secured the strap onto her arm, leaving only her wrist and hand dangling free.

With visions of Oz and their love dancing in her mind, she desperately searched for the happiest places she could send her mind - anything to survive the pain she was about to experience. Tears poured down her eyes as she continued to fight, trying to free herself.

The buzz of the tool was a distant song as the pain in her wrist exploded through her nerves. She screamed through the strap over her mouth as the guard slowly sliced through her wrist with a searing laser beam. All she could understand was agony. Deep and soul wrenching suffering consumed her.

A shout sounded somewhere in the distance, but Jael was too busy blinking the terror from her eyes and trying to take a full breath around her gag to register what was happening. Another shout rang out as she convulsed with the shock of the trauma. Her body trembled uncontrollably.

She continued to blink frantically trying to see anything through her blurred vision. She could hear the scratching and pounding on the glass of the thrashing creatures. Deranged people, manipulated into something else, something hungry. Trying to take a deep breath around the gag, she frantically looked around the room finding herself alone and still not understanding what was happening. Lights faded in and out. Her vision blurred and cleared once more, but yet her thoughts did not. Where was everyone? So much time had passed, too much time. Was this it? Had they detonated the bomb yet? Did the diversion work? Are they coming?

The searing anguish in her arm consumed her, and she

felt like she had been strapped to that table for an eternity. Continuing to shiver, she pleaded for someone to help her; however, nothing but gargled cries left her lips. Her world faded into nothingness, a heavy darkness consuming her.

A warm hand landed on her right arm and frantically worked at the strap. The warm, soft hand moved and loosened other straps. "Oz, get over here now," Amelia demanded as she found Oz staring at the glass chambers, each with multiple compartments. Every compartment held one of his people, right at the point of madness. All were infected with the cerebral fungus. Turning and making his way over, Oz froze in horror when he saw it was Jael on the table.

"What the fuck happened?" Oz yelled as he rushed over to her.

As Amelia finished releasing Jael and was helping her sit up, Oz shouted back at Aurelia, "What the fuck? She was just with you! Did you know this would happen?" Oz wrapped his arms around Jael, and she released a quiet sob before collapsing into him.

Aurelia stood with her hand over her mouth and tears in her eyes, crying "No, I was told it was not my business. They made me leave. Jael, I am so sorry."

Blinking her eyes and catching her breath, refusing to look at her maimed wrist, Jael murmured, "Not your fault, Aurelia. It's not your fault. Oz, please."

Amelia nodded to Mercy, who went over to help Jael sit back on the table. Amelia searched the cabinets in the lab for something to give her for the pain but only came up with a mild pain reliever. She looked at Oz and shook her head no. There would be no heavy pain medication, only something to take the edge off. She had no nano-bots in her body to help. Amelia handed Jael some water and the anti-inflammatory.

Jael's severed hand had landed on the ground next to the table, and Oz went to pick it up. Approaching Amelia, he asked her something, but she cut him off, "I can't reattach it if that's what you want to know. I wouldn't even know where to start."

Stopping and dropping the hand where he stood, he sighed and walked over to Jael. He met her eyes and kissed her on her forehead.

"We have to finish the mission. We are here. Let's get this done." Jael slid off the table and winced as her arm was jostled. Nausea bubbled in her gut with the pain, and she vomited bile. Amelia grabbed a roll of bandages and wrapped Jael's arm. She flinched and tremors rocked her slight frame as the fabric was tucked around her forearm and over her wrist. Once she was bandaged up, she again tried to stand and only two steps before her knees gave out.

Oz looked at Amelia with doubt, and she shook her head no.

"Jael, we need to go on without you," Amelia reluctantly admitted as she searched the room for a place where she could hide her friend.

Aurelia stood by the storage room door and opened it before she offered, "In here. She can hide in here while we shimmy down the air vents."

"No, I want her out of here. She's done enough," Oz demanded.

Zoe faced Oz and reminded him flatly, "We are lucky we even made it inside. We cannot risk sending her out. We do not know if Kagnus has made it back around the building after planting the bomb. She could've been caught, and Jael would walk straight into a trap. They have not pulled the intruder alarm yet, so we still have a chance to take the base."

One of their deranged people behind the glass in the center of the room could be heard growling softly. Other scratched frantically; their fingers squealing and screeching on the glass. Oz flinched at the sound.

Jael peered up at Oz. "I'm OK. I'll wait here in the storage closet. You don't have the time or resources to get me out right now. I'll be safe in there. Go. Save us all." Furrowing his brow, Oz reluctantly conceded, though and everyone in the room could feel his anxiety.

Jael found a place far behind the air vent in a hole she barely fit through and curled up on the floor. Her arm throbbed, and she was fighting for consciousness. The last thing she heard was Oz whisper *I love you* into the darkness before she passed out from exhaustion and pain.

Closing and barricading the door behind him, Oz prayed to the creator they could pull this off. If not, they would all pay dearly. Following Aurelia, one by one, everyone crawled into the narrow air vent.

26

PLANET ADURO – MINE 03

The Dream

The crumbling, desolate city had been abandoned long ago. Putrid clouds floated in the sky as he passed through the empty streets, if that's what they were called, streets. They looked more like train tracks to August. Two long lines of metal alloy with smooth concrete ran down the center. Several rows of the tracks headed into the city. He slid his gaze down to his wrist and found he was wearing the armor Mercy designed, the armor his people made. He'd know that hexagonal pattern anywhere.

Was he not on Aduro anymore? Had his people won their freedom?

He began running toward a tall white building made of marble. The top of the entry way was etched with an intricate carving. The marble foliage and fruit seemed to spill down from the eve of the flat roof. Long elegant columns and the wall behind the columns were decorated with scenes of lush verdant gardens and joy. There were humans in the scenes; all *were jovial and full of life. The designs of the people seemed to be carved deep into the stone as if something above was erased or removed. The paintings were different somehow. They stuck out and didn't belong.*

He passed through a large set of open doors, and after he did, they slammed shut behind him. Inside he found a temple, one with a massive statue of a human in the middle. August approached cautiously as he felt a twinge of fear in this room. Candles burned in random assortments along the perimeter of the room. Were the candles even real? Were they holograms? They didn't smell like real candles. Nothing smelled like anything now that he focused. He put his finger in the flame and felt the heat on the other side of his protective gloves, penetrating through.

It seemed real enough, then he sensed it- he might not be alone.

Someone or something was clearly here with him or had been here recently. Who lit the candles? A shiver slithered down his spine like a snake of ice.

He walked up to a digital plaque, but he couldn't read the writing. It seemed to be blurred. Why couldn't he read it? He huffed and continued on. Reaching the back of the temple he swung open a small door, the top only inches from the top of his head. Why was it so small? Why did he feel like it was becoming smaller? He rushed through feeling he didn't have enough time to make it inside.

Frozen in his tracks, he stared out into another dark room. Glowing tanks filled with a liquid, contained a suspended human fetus. Each fetus was in a different stage of growth. He warily inched up to one of the tanks and stared at a fully formed fetus. It had a full head of hair, and its plump body glowed with health.

The baby opened its bright green eyes and focused on August. It began to cry, raising its little hands to reach for August. The cries intensified, and August could hear the baby splashing through the glass wall of the tank. Frantic, he rushed around to an instrument panel, but the words were blurred, and he couldn't read anything. Panic set in as the infant began to thrash, seeming to be in agony. In distress, wailing and trying to scream, it shook within the viscous liquid it was suspended in.

Deciding he must act, August leapt on top of the tank and opened the hatch, jumping inside with a splash. Reaching for the child, he lifted it up out of the water. Pulling a clear mask from over the infant's mouth, the tubing slowly slipped free from it's throat. The baby let out a blood curdling scream, and August saw the child's face begin to take on a grey hue. Peering down at its tiny body, he watched as the grey spread. A dark inky force began leaking out of the baby's mouth as it continued a single unending scream.

The flesh decayed and seemed to disappear, revealing a skeleton underneath, one of both metal and bone, pieced together and fused into one.

August dropped the ever-screaming skeleton of the infant and scrambled out of the tank, but he found the tank sealed at the top. Pounding on the glass, he could see a figure standing in the doorway, unmoving. The water began to rise, and he knew his death was near. They should've never come here. This was a warning.

He felt a sharp shock of pain as something wrenched deep in his shoulder, and he was ripped out of his bunk. Three guards were stood over him with their long staffs, the ends crackling with electricity as rings of current rolled down the staff.

The tallest guard kicked him in the ribs and demanded, Get the fuck up. You are the stupid insect who broke the water pump. "*Perite! Tu es stultissimum cimicem qui fregit osem.*"

August raised his eyes and saw Livia at the door, looking somber. A heavy sadness weighed in her eyes. He had been caught, and he knew his punishment would be brutal.

And Livia wasn't going to be able to do a thing.

He rose to his feet, and the guard behind him swiftly hit his shin to make him to walk faster. He followed the leading guard out of the bunk room and down the long red rock hallway. Livia kept her eyes on his until he rounded the corner.

Without a clue of what was about to happen, August did his best to swallow down his alarm. He had not believed they would investigate into who broke the water pump this thoroughly. Livia warned him, but he didn't listen. Once they reached the landing pad outside, they marched August over to a post on the dusty hot pavement. It was early in the morning, and the system star was less than a quarter of the way over the horizon. The ground below his feet was searing hot, and the post was shining in the bright light of the star.

The tallest guard picked up a cord connected to metal cuffs and slipped them onto August's hands. They tightened the moment they were slipped on. His arms jerked up above his head pulling him towards the post. A sharp pain lashed across his back, and he collapsed against the wide post. It happened again, and this time he distinctly felt the electricity flow through him. It happened a third time, and August warily shifted his eyes around to see just as one of the guards raised his staff and brought it down onto the back of August's leg. He groaned with the impact. After a few more blunt hits, he hoped it was over. He tried to catch his breath while he turned to look back at the door.

A coldness in her gaze, Livia stood in the doorway, unmoving. She held her staff close as she forced herself to stay, to watch August's electrocution. He wondered if she knew this was coming, if she had tried to stop it. He knew she couldn't have done anything. He kept his eyes on her even when they resumed their assault. They were more interested in electrocuting him than anything else, and he began to smell his own flesh as it burned.

When the guards finished, August's body was charred, broken, and bleeding. The guards congratulated each other on a job well done then went back inside, and Livia followed, the door screeching as it was slammed shut.

Leaning forward against the post, August closed his eyes and slid to his knees. His arms were wrenched up, and he found he was inches from being able to sit on the ground. This punishment was far from over as he felt the searing heat building on his raw back from the sun. Blinking in the bright light, he peered down at his bronze flesh, and he wondered how long it would remain intact in the heat. The surrounding sand dunes seem to grow in height as the crushing weight of his situation spiraled in on him. The wind picked up, and the sand blasted against his skin, removing layer after layer. He wondered if he would survive this punishment.

A few hours later, he was hanging from the post by his arms trying to give his legs a rest when a shadow appeared over his outstretched leg. He looked up, but couldn't make out anything through the blinding light of the star. His eyes weren't meant to see with a bright star in the sky.

Livia whispered, "I told you they would search the

pump to find out who did it. They thought I would give them an accommodation for finding the one who broke it. You should've seen their beaming faces when they showed me the evidence. We are reassigning a lot of your friends here. They're being moved on my recommendation to keep the unrest down that has sprouted in this mine. The guards noticed and brought up the issue to the king. I had to do my job. I know you think you can take this planet, but you're wrong. All you're going to do is get yourself and your people killed. *"Dico te investigaverant osem invenire qui faciet... Omnes facies ipsum et tui homines interfeciunt."*

August leaned his head to rest on the searing post. *"Non facio si credes facio aut non. Habeo prandium aut illic est?"* I don't care if you believe I can do it or not. If you hold up your end of our bargain, I'll hold up mine. I'm glad you're sending my people around and mixing everyone up. They will spread the plan to the rest of my people in the other mines. Is this my new home? Attached to this post? Do I get a lunch break or is this it?

Snarling and showing him her teeth, Livia hissed, *"Iocaris sed tui punitio incepit... Iam narravi custodias ero serum quia gressus cum medico."* You joke, but your punishment just began. This was my idea to save your fucking life, you damn demon. They wanted to kill you. I said it would be more fun to torture you and put you back to work. You're lucky they bought it. You have two more days, and your body already looks like you've been attacked by a hungry Haculae with a blowtorch. I brought something I can spray on your skin, but it only lasts a few hours. It's a mineral compound we use to prevent burns. It's going to sting, but it will help prevent you from scarring. I'll come back tomorrow morning and spray it on you again. I already told the guards I'll be late because of a meeting with the doctor.

Nodding, August gritted his teeth and prepared for the sting. Livia pulled the bottle from her hip bag and flipped up the cap. As she sprayed and the droplets touched his open wounds, he crashed his forehead into the metal post and grasped at the manacles with bruising strength. The searing sting lasted for over a minute.

Drink this, *"Bibe hunc."* Livia demanded as she shoved the end of a tube into August's mouth. August sucked and found it was a sweetened juice watered down. He gulped until it was gone, and Livia slid the tube from his mouth. *"Aequipa. Modo aequipa."* Stay alive. Just *stay alive*, Livia growled before she walked toward the doors.

Walking through the entrance, the cool rush of the air from the cavern caressed Livia, and she took one last look back at August before closing the door behind her. She headed toward the guards, and they all had an odd look at them. She hoped they hadn't seen her attending to August, but when she approached, she realized it was something else entirely. The tablet on the table was blinking with a message from the palace:

> Livia's presence is requested. Direct her to her personal rooms.

An oily weight settled in her gut. *Is Lucas home?* Dread sprouted, and she swallowed roughly before she set the tablet down. She hoped it was just her father wanting something from her. She prayed to Juno to tell her what was going to happen, to warn her. She needed the goddess's protection.

She made her way back to the landing pad and climbed

aboard a transport. The engine whirred to life as she slid her eyes over her shoulder to her fire eyed demon. She found his gaze was already on her. *How have I fallen for him? How has August ensnared me so thoroughly?* All she ever thought of was his hands on her and his mouth on hers. His idea was out of the question. It could never work. His kind had been created in a lab thousands of years ago, and she had little hope they would prove origin status. They were insects turned into people. She had seen their DNA firsthand. Livia doubted very much they were natural to their supposed home world. August was probably just different. That had to be it. Nothing ever changed. One of the cornerstones of the first humans' culture was to prohibit change. Once something works, set it in stone. By adapting elements of many other cultures, they developed an air of creativity, when really there was none to be found. The First Humans were nothing but thieves, greedy thieves and assimilators.

She thought back to the ancient people, the humans her family line descended from, the Genil. They were not part of the same group as the First Humans although they had many of the same tendencies. Humans seem to really love destroying home worlds for their benefit, and her people loved to destroy other people for theirs.

Her transport landed unusually roughly with her lack of attention and shot nerves. She hopped down, and tossed her helmet into the seat, and made her way to the palace doors. She padded in and peered around, but nothing seemed out of place. She calmed herself before she went down the hallway to the lifts. Making her way to her rooms, she planned to stop there first to wash up before facing the king. As she walked down the hall, she caught a whiff of Lucas's sharp cologne and stopped dead in her tracks. Her skin tightened with apprehension. He wasn't supposed to be back for another week.

Shaking off her suspicions, she tried to convince herself there was no way he was back yet. He wouldn't have missed a chance to take out a common pirating space hub, Sinex Station, a few systems over. The UTC called General Lucas to threaten the station with magnetic missiles after a transport was discovered heading from there with a loading bay filled with illegally obtained pharmaceuticals. He would never pass up the opportunity to kill others by blowing them up.

She cringed thinking about those magnetic missiles. They were designed to attach to a metal hull with a powerful magnet. When they detonate, a charge is sent through the magnet. The charge causes the magnet's power to grow exponentially, resulting in a massive chunk of the ship compacting into a tiny space. They designed it to work similar to a black hole just on a much smaller scale and controlled. Anything and everything in the way was crushed and massive holes ripped through the hull. A ship could be destroyed in seconds with just one of the sinister devices. There was no explosion, only the thump of the bomb attaching. Lucas *loved* them.

Approaching her door with wariness, Livia prayed her rooms would be empty. She turned toward the facial scanner, and her door opened with a swoosh, splitting in the middle, and disappearing into the door frame. She took one step into her door and felt a hard hand wrap around her neck, a hand she knew all too well. Terror filled her body. She had just made a horrible mistake.

Good. You received the message, *"Bene. Accepisti nuntium."* Lucas ground out in her ear before he slammed her to her knees on the ground. The door behind her sealed with a suctioning sound. Livia kept her eyes to the ground as Lucas strode around the room. She knew what came next. It was what always came after he returned from a mission.

She could hear his anger in his steps as he approached, and she submissively put her arms up. He grabbed her wrists and pulled her up by her arms. Keeping her eyes to the floor, she followed him to their room where he forced her to remain facing the wall. She didn't have to be told to know he wanted to rip her uniform off. She didn't dare touch it. It was his routine.

Moving close to her, Lucas let out a feral growl as he ripped her tunic off. He reached around and removed her utility belt. Throwing it against the wall, her emergency communicator burst into pieces. Her breath trembled as she watched his shadow approach from behind her. He hooked a finger in her leggings and ripped them off as well.

The bombing must have gone wrong. Livia could tell what he wanted this time. He didn't want his usual rough rutting. He wants to see her blood.

Taking his staff, he ran it down the length of her bare back stopping at the scar on the middle of her back where the word sponsa was scarred onto her flesh. It was her wedding gift from him, or that's what he had called it. He spit on the ground near her feet and with a simple press of his thumb, turned the electric current on at the end of his staff.

Livia's head shot back, and she shook violently with the current racing through her. When Lucas finally pulled the end of his staff away, her body slammed into the cold wall, and she panted for breath. With her face pressed against the wall she could see behind the small banana tree next to the window. Her view stretched across the desert, and she searched for that little point of light.

She could hear Lucas picking up something from the bed before dropping it on the floor, but she couldn't focus on that. Not with all the willpower in the world could she care about what he was doing behind her. She had done treacherous things in her life. They all had. They all deserved to be beat, to be electrocuted right to the end of their wits for what they had put others through.

After he picked up his favorite metal rod from his collection, she heard him turn back and his steps neared. He cracked the rod against the floor between her feet.

Something changed in that moment. She realized she wasn't the princess on the throne like she had always told herself, like she had sworn to herself in the back of her mind. That was always what she had said to calm herself, the reason why she didn't retaliate when her mother was murdered, or now as she leaned nude against the cold wall about to have her body willfully broken. Shortly after, he would take her however he wanted. She would let him.

This time she was not visiting the doctor for skin grafts or repairs. This time, if he etched into her skin, she would leave it. For this, this would be the last time.

Her former Claudius house loyalty disgusted her. She might as well be tied to the pole with August in the desert. *Why did I let this go on for so long?* All she could fully comprehend was the twinkle she could see at the end of the landing pad next to the mine, the little sparkle of the light from their brilliant star bouncing off the post. *August.* All she could hear were August's words as the electric rod came down on her, scorching her skin.

If you hold up your end of our bargain, I'll hold up mine.

27

PLANET PORTUM – RECRUITMENT MISSION – NORTH VILLAGE

A creaking sound close by took Jacob's attention across the clearing where he found Juni, who had just landed on a branch. He brought his finger up to his pursed lips and scowled at her to be quiet. The last thing they needed was to be discovered. A flight of butterflies flew by Jacob headed north, and as they haphazardly bumped into him, he narrowed his eyes.

Callum was watching intently and chuckled under his breath. Jacob aimed his wide eyes to Callum to be quiet as Jacob heard a crunch in the leaves below. The north parts of the woods were covered in slime from the snails, so they stayed to the south of the village. The snails made him think about the massive beast on the shore just south of where Oz's team landed. The creature seemed like it was prehistoric. Jacob's mind wandered, and he began pondering what the most efficient equipment for archaeological mapping would be. What could they use to penetrate the ground and see what's underneath to avoid having to do so much senseless digging? Jacob had been scanning Jael's memories and did his best to find some type of evidence the humans were using high-tech tools in archaeology. Unfortunately, he found she did very little study in archaeology back on Earth. They needed a computer program which could isolate the most probable places on their world to search for good dig sites. Would that work? Would they have enough raw data about their world to put into a computer program? Wouldn't they need geological history? Did they even have enough people to spare to send to a dig site? That *was* the whole reason he was sitting in a tree at the moment, wasn't it? He was sure it was on Oz's list of things to eventually do, to map their animal kingdom and find where their people fell on it. That should be easy, though. They were related to the scorpions.

Amelia had used the scorpions to make a cure. They must be closely related to them. Right? That area of science was absolutely not his realm. Biology confused the hell out of him.

He had become fairly accurate at predicting what Oz would say or do, though. He made a little game of it when they were stuck at the base together. He told himself it was a fun game, but it was really to keep him sane.

Ideas popped up and fizzled quickly. He was bored. Jacob released a frustrated breath. Jael had so many helpful memories in physics and technology, but she had little information about geologic history and animal kingdoms. *I bet she fell asleep in those classes.*

A few butterflies landed on the branch next to him, and he watched as their black wings fluttered. They had little baby blue bodies, and they twitched their antennae when he shifted his weight on the branch. Their wings made them look like the stealth jets on Jael's world. The butterflies moved quickly, and the entire group disappeared within a second. Their speed and beauty were mesmerizing.

At first, Jacob hated all this waiting. He changed his view with the realization he could do a lot of thinking while he was sitting in the trees. It turned out okay, but better when he actually found a conclusion.

Surveillance felt like spying, and he was not too big of a fan of that part. He couldn't wait until it was over, and they could finally talk to the people of the town and finish this mission. All he wanted was just to go home. He didn't care if it was in a cave. It was his home, and that was all that mattered. The bathroom at home had a door. It had a toilet to sit on. Jacob didn't want to admit it to anyone, but he absolutely hated going to the restroom in the woods, despised it. The restrooms in the base spoiled him more than he cared to admit.

He rolled his eyes at himself and thought back to the problem of proving they were a species which evolved on this planet, this secret planet. He wondered if Oz would find evidence of it when he took over the UTC base, or if they would find out otherwise. *What would we do if he found no evidence at all? Would we truly have to start digging in the dirt and searching through nature to find their genetic relatives?* He just knew that would be Oz's backup plan. He guessed it was their only option.

Knowing what Oz was doing while they sat in trees with pretty butterflies made guilt blossom. He then remembered the first village's cannibals and decided to call it even. He shivered at the thought of that horrific place. He wouldn't wish what they went through on his worst enemy.

Wait, yes, he would. He shook his head at his own tendency to show mercy, knowing it was an engrained trait from thousands of years of tainted evolution. Their collective subservience was achieved through a long process of plucking out the most daring and inquisitive of all their people, leaving the rest to be a population of people who only produce pushovers. The most kind and gentle of people were left over, the people who remained quiet.

Bile rose in his throat, and his mission shifted in this new light. He needed his head back in his work. He had been so caught up over their capture, he had kept his mind on their time in that old shed and not on the matters at hand. He would not remain silent about their future.

Callum inched over and whispered, "I'm going to the bathroom. Be right back."

Jacob nodded as Callum inched away and climbed upward. It was easier to see the branches higher in the trees so he could jump over to the next tree. Callum leaped a few trees over and made his way down. The bark bit into his hands, but he hardly made a rustle as his feet landed on each of the branches. Once he made it to the ground, he went off a few yards away and did his business. When he was finished and heading back toward the tree he climbed down, he heard a small crunch. He did his best to keep panic from flooding his system, but it was too late. His heart was already pounding, and he was scared out of his mind. He was going to need therapy after this damn trip.

Freezing in his place, Callum adjusted his armor. He felt around on his waist for his plasma sword but remembered it had been a casualty of the acid slime. Alarm laced through him, wrapping its tendrils around his heart, and he closed his eyes trying to calm down. He felt the pressure in the air change as something swooped down from above, crashing into him.

A cloth was pushed into his mouth creating a gag, and he was shoved to the ground. Terror and pain filled him as someone began kicking him in the side, repeatedly. He felt someone else drop to the ground but didn't hear a sound. Dread took root and blossomed into terror as more footsteps neared.

Callum curled in a ball with his arms over his head for protection as a hulking figure slammed their foot down into Callum's face. He groaned with the sharp pain, and the attackers quickly responded to the sound with more kicks. He heard a third person drop to the ground and did his best to hold back his screams when yet another foot joined in on the kicking. He felt them kick his ribs and cried out when one grabbed his tail and bent it sideways. He heard a crunch and by the blinding pain was certain his tail was broken. He begged inside for Jacob to sense something was wrong, to run and save himself. He prayed Juni could escape.

The gag slipped from his mouth, and the beating stopped. He tried to catch his breath, desperate for air. Tears slid down his face, and he brushed them away. He looked down at his blue hand and found dark blue blood smeared on it. He felt all over his face and couldn't find where it was coming from when he finally tasted the copper in his mouth. The blood was coming from inside of him.

Callum gasped and tried to take a deep breath. He coughed and a stream of blue blood came from inside his lungs and poured out onto the ground. He struggled to breath and wondered if this was it. *Am I going to die? Please let Jacob be far from here.*

Lying in the dirt in a pool of his own blood, he heard someone move in the leaves surrounding him and cringed before he opened his eyes. When he mustered the courage to open them, he found it was Jacob, and he didn't know if he should be happy or devastated. *Are the people still there? Would they be back? Am I the bait?*

A large forest green man with black hair landed on top of Jacob right before he could reach Callum. Watching from the ground, Callum could do nothing as Jacob was beat just like he was. His love was succumbing to the same fate, and he was too broken to even look away, much less do anything. Tears poured down his bloody face, and he softly said "Jacob" over and over as Jacob was kicked repeatedly. More people fell to the ground and joined in, beating Jacob for several minutes. Callum couldn't scream, crawl, or do anything, so he prayed, He prayed so vehemently he could feel a blood vessel burst in his eye.

They eventually stopped, and Jacob was left, a broken shell on the ground, not making a sound. With his heart beating erratically, Callum whimpered as he tried to stand. Unable to, he pulled his elbow up and brought it down a little farther from him. He pulled with all his might to force his other elbow to crawl even further. Trying to be as quiet as possible, he slowly and painfully made his way over to the man he loved.

After what seemed like an eternity, Callum finally reached Jacob and found him unconscious. Callum grabbed Jacob's hand as best as he could. He found Jacob's first finger and initiated the connection. Callum screamed down the connection for Jacob to wake up and found nothing. He didn't know what else to do, so he pushed down through the connection, through their bond. He compelled some of his life force into those little nerves at the tip of Jacob's finger. Callum began to sweat as he gave up his last, little bit of strength to see Jacob's eyes open.

Taking one long, deep breath, Jacob opened his eyes and flopped his head over toward Callum. Callum slowly closed his eyes and dropped his head down on the ground next to Jacob.

What happened? Jacob thought as he heard someone land on the ground from the tree branches. His heart pounded. *Was someone else here to finish beating them to death?*

Juni dropped down and looked over Jacob's and Callum's broken bodies and bruised, bleeding faces with alarm in her eyes. She had no more than mouthed, "What the fuck?," just as someone slipped a gag over her mouth, and Jacob winced when he heard her body hit the ground with a thud.

Jacob tried to look away as they whaled on Juni and prayed she survived. He wondered where Adrian was and had his answer when he heard the leaves rustle nearby. Adrian made a loud grunt as he was beaten like the rest of them had been. Leaning his head back to see, Jacob wished he hadn't because he watched Juni get a swift kick to the stomach and her lunch shot from her mouth.

Jacob turned his head and found someone dragging Adrian into their pile of despair. Blinking tears and blood away, Jacob watched as they dumped Juni's limp body into the pile. One of the townspeople stalked up and grabbed Jacob's hand roughly. The man initiated the connection and showed a man tied to a pole with fire all around him. They wanted nothing to do with a plan which could lead to a torturous end. It was a warning to leave them alone, one Jacob would respect.

The cruel villager kicked dirt into Jacob's battered face as he and the other townspeople went back toward town. Jacob closed his eyes and for many hours they all lay in the grass until the scavenger bugs came for a bite. Callum regained consciousness as Junie groaned next to him. Adrian was the first to leap up when a beetle bit him between the thighs, eliciting a faint yelp. No one was sure exactly where he was bitten, but they all knew it was close to his plumbing by the way he acted.

Staggering to stand, they helped each other to their feet as best they could and hobbled their way to the little cave where they had been sleeping. Each step was worse than the last, but they finally made it and collapsed in a broken line on the dusty cave floor. Rain poured down, eventually creating a water curtain at the cave opening. Pain forced them to rest, one full of groans and misery, but it gave them time to begin healing. As the rain ended, they began waking, and painfully with moans ate emergency rations Junie had stored in the cave before the attack.

While she mindlessly dug in the dirt, Juni made a gruesome discovery. The cave was the nest for a giant wasp. The bones of multiple people were right under the top layer of soil and some were so new, they still wore their clothes. Callum shivered in disgust and sorrow for all the people who met their end in such a torturous way, eaten alive by a parasitic larva. Shaking his head, Callum did his best to rid himself of that thought. They needed out of this cave and away from this violent village. "Are we going to get a small creature to heal, or do it the hard way?" Adrian asked gruffly. They all gave him a disgusted look, and he responded, "Fine, you could have just said no." Leaning over, Jacob stretched, and Adrian had a direct view of the area beyond the clearing. Adrian gasped before he whispered, "Oh, shit." They turned in their places and saw the villagers with long sticks and rope approaching.

In pure panic, Callum yelled, "Run!"

They all scrambled and leapt onto their slightly rusted, hover-bikes right outside of the cave. Their bikes now had small rust spots because of the snail slime, but they were partially cleaned from the rain. Callum landed on his sideways and didn't right himself before a woman with a long stick was already upon him, and he had to slap his hand on the throttle to avoid another pummeling. He screeched at the near miss and zoomed away, trying to right himself. He passed Jacob, who was wide eyed and leaping onto his hover bike. Adrian and Juni both zoomed by, but Adrian had an unwelcome hitchhiker who was attempting to pull him from the bike.

Callum watched in horror as Adrian slammed himself against a massive tree and his unwanted bike mate slid off the back. He finally through his leg over the hover-bike the right way, and they all pushed their throttles to the limit.

A slew of curse words fell from Callum as he rubbed a crushed fly off his face. He grimaced when he found the guts of the bug smeared on his hand. Shivering in disgust, Callum swung his hand around and the slime from the smashed bug flew off into the woods. Opening his mouth to gag, Callum wished he hadn't. Another flying bug flew down his throat, and he grasped his throat with his hand, thrashing back and forth. He coughed and did his best to dislodge it, but in the end, he was forced to swallow it. *Is it not enough I was beaten to hell? Was it not enough I was forced to eat seafood with parasites? No? When will this living hell end!* This was the end of Callum's rope.

He brought his bike to a halt and leaned forward to grab

his throat as he tried to swallow the bug down. Unable to hold it back, he screamed as the bug fluttered its wings and kicked its legs as it made its way down his esophagus. By the time he swallowed it all the way down, he was hollering so loud the other three stopped. Callum jumped off his bike and shrieked at the top of his lungs, "Fuck this! Fuck it all! I am so done!"

He searched wildly for Jacob in the clearing and when he found him, Callum snarled, "I ate a God damned bug. I don't want to hear a thing from any of you. I just need a minute. It was big, and it had wings. Don't open your mouth while you're moving." Callum grabbed his stomach and gagged a few more times before he mounted his bike and grimaced. He motion to the rest of the group he was ready to go.

Jacob almost said, *well, a few more and you'll heal faster,* but thought better of it, only nodding back solemnly, but when Callum and Adrian zoomed away, he smiled at Juni, and they both began laughing as they followed their team-mates home.

28

PLANET PORTUM - UTC COMMAND MISSION

After securely attaching the rope to a metal hook near the top of the air duct, they belayed down the dark duct one by one. Before Oz climbed in, he whispered, "I love you," into the dark where he left Jael to hide. She hadn't replied. He hoped she was still alive. With the rope attached to rigging at his waist, he and the rest of the team carefully made their way down.

They had Aurelia's memories of the base, but even with her high clearance, she had only been through the ground level lab down to level two. Level one was still unknown territory just as the ground floor lab had been.

Even deep inside the air duct, he could still hear the infected people in the lab scratching down the glass and banging against it.

Were the clear cages with their deranged people meant to strike fear? No. That couldn't be it because no one he had connected with to that point had seen inside. He cringed. It didn't make sense. What else were these scientists doing with his people? Why were they keeping it all a secret? After this was over, they would have to find a way to put down the infected test subjects humanely.

Inside the confines of his helmet, Oz refocused as best as he could. This mission had already become too much for him to bear. To the computer in the helmet he said, "Use the sensors to detect if this air shaft takes us low enough to reach the last level." The helmet computer took a few moments to send its sensors out and take readings. Hopefully it would give him a solid idea what hid below them in the shaft.

A visual representation of the base came up on his holo-screen, and he studied it a moment. Something didn't seem right, so he commanded, "Stop. We might have a problem. I don't think this air duct reaches all the way down to the bottom floor where the main power is. The scanners on the suit are missing a few floors that should be there Zoe, what do you think?"

"One of us needs to drop down through the vent at each level after Hazel and Mercy drop at level nine. The rest of the team needs to head to main power. I know it wasn't the original plan for only one person to drop per level, but we don't have another choice at this point. We don't know if there are additional floors before the level with main power. When we drop, they will throw the base into lockdown. Once the blast doors fall, we're trapped in here. Their first line of defense is to suck out all the oxygen. Just a reminder, that means we'll survive for a time in our suits, but the people in the lower levels, including our people, will not. We must reach main power in the lowest level, unlock the system, and turn the power back on. There are no telling how many of our people, as well as base guards and UTC command personnel are here. We need to assume everyone is dangerous," Zoe instructed with a flare of authority.

"Zoe is right. One person per air duct. I know we hoped for two, but it's not going to happen. Let's move," Oz agreed as he continued down, nearly knocking his boot against Aurelia's helmet under him.

Just as Zoe instructed, they broke off one by one into the main vents for each floor. First Hazel and Mercy, then Harlen and Lark went down the dark air ducts as they passed them. Carter, Amelia, Dion, Wynn, all paired off and followed into the dark spaces.

"Crawl to the end, and on my mark we will drop down. I have no idea what you'll find. You could be up against anything. Remember, taking this base means taking our planet. Good luck." Oz carefully made his way down the last vent on level two. He was behind Aurelia with Costel, Sands, and Zoe following.

Everyone except for Oz made their way to the other side of the vent and waited. Aurelia positioned herself in the lead. Once Oz saw Aurelia had reached the vent cover, he ordered, "Aurelia, Costel, and Zoe, first we need to take out the guards and rush to level one. Sands, you secure level two behind us Go on three" Each of them readied themselves as they waited for Oz to count down, "One, two, three."

Aurelia kicked at the vent cover, and it popped open and swung down. Her body flew through the square hole, and Oz followed, landing next to her. They both charged the guard station, finding two wide eyed guards – too stunned to speak or move. Hearing shouts to their left, Oz pivoted to find a group of five guards, who had just entered the room, with railguns pointed in their direction. *Fuck.*

Moving like lightning, Oz spun to catch the rounds and watched as the molten rail gun rounds bolted over the top layer of his electrified suit. It was almost too instantaneous to see, leaving only a long metallic trail in its wake. He found his first target and zeroed in, his helmet's aiming system triangulated to his pupils as it locked on. He swung his arm up just like he practiced. The rounds flew from the top of his outstretched wrist, his hand pointed down. He hit one of the guards in the chest, a second round hitting another of them in the leg.

Oz tried to contain his thrill as realization fell over guards. The armor was shooting their own rounds back at them. With a devious smile, Oz threw his arms out in a taunt, and they foolishly opened fire. He twisted his body into the molten bullets, catching and seamlessly returning the shots. With two more down, there was now only one remaining guard who turned to run. Oz couldn't let him escape. They needed the stairs to access level one. The last thing he wanted was to have to cut through a barricaded door. He tackled the guard and snapped his neck right before he escaped through the door.

Screams erupted from behind him as Costel and Sands breached the guard station behind Aurelia. Sands had climbed over the instrument panel to leap on a guard who was hard at work plugging something in his computer. Aurelia held the other guard at bay while Costel took him out with a plasma sword through the gut. The alarm blared above their heads and a feminine voice began counting down from five. Oz knew that meant they were seconds from being sealed inside the base.

Sands growled and leaped on the man who sounded the intruder alarm and put his hands around the man's neck to strangle him. Costel turned and skewered the guard with his sword. As he climbed over of the dead man, Sands nodded appreciatively at Costel's help. Peering around the room, they found it filled with their wide eyed Iungo people.

"Level five is secure," Amelia reported into her helmet, panting heavily.

A bit of relief went through Oz as he, Zoe, Aurelia, and Costel all ran for the stairs. They hurdled over the dead guards, and Oz held the door open as they all filed in the stairwell. The red emergency lights began shining as they heard several shaking blasts from above.

The base was plunged into a crimson bath as the main power was severed.

Zoe and Oz met railgun fire from guards down at the first level. They rotated into the gunfire and caught the rounds, returning them into the dark hall indiscriminately with screams following in their wake.

"I can't tell if it's clear. I'm heading down!" Zoe yelled as she fearlessly darted down the stairs.

The team climbed over the bloody bodies littering the stairwell as Zoe pushed on the door, but it wouldn't budge. One of the downed guards reached up and grabbed Costel by the leg causing him to yelp, and he stomped on the man's arm. He swung his plasma sword from its place at his belt and plunged it into the man's chest. Lifting a commanding hand for everyone to back up, Zoe pulled her plasma sword from her belt, and it buzzed to life in her hand.

"Level six is secure," Carter reported with heavy breaths over the helmet comms.

Zoe pushed the plasma sword through the center of the door, leaning into it to cut down the middle. Excruciatingly long minutes passed before she cut through. She kicked at the metal creating a crash as the double doors hit the walls. The fallen doors revealed seven soldiers, ready with guns raised. The team crouched and braced themselves for the onslaught.

When the humans opened fire, Oz, Zoe, and Costel moved like cyclones as they caught the rounds and returned them. The gunfire peppered the trio until the last soldier fell, revealing two more guards standing at the station, both shaking with their arms raised in surrender.

The two fell to their knees, and the woman pleaded, "Please don't kill us. Please have mercy."

Taking adrenalin filled strides, Zoe reached down and smashed their heads together, knocking them both out and snapped, "Shut up, I'm trying to think." Costel bound the two guards after Zoe signaled him to take care of it.

Surveying the concrete room, Oz found a tall stack of old files in boxes to his far left. Before him, was the main power console, a monstrosity of a circuit board enclosed in glass in the middle of the room. Behind it looked to be a console to search electronic files. He made his way over and lay his hand on the machine as it sank in that they were about to finish taking the base.

Wait, something isn't right. That was far too easy.

Dread blossomed in him, and he searched the room again as if he would find the answers there.

"Level seven is secure." Lark reported on the comms.

This time, the update seemed like the ticking of a clock, one counting down to their demise. "Something is wrong," Oz announced as he stared at Zoe.

She faced him abruptly and demanded, "What the fuck does that mean?"

"It means this was too easy, *way* too easy," Oz shook his head as he fought a powerful urge to run. His legs begged him to move, to save himself.

The room fell silent.

"Level four is secure," Dion reported over the comms.

The silence grew into an ominous, thick presence, filling their lungs with every breath, their hearts fluttering with a heavy warning. It grew with every passing moment, snaking around each of them where they stood.

"You're fucking right. Damn it. What did we miss?" Zoe asked, her words hurried as she approached the main computer.

"*Something is coming,*" Carter breathed into his comms directly to Oz, his voice hoarse, strained.

Replying just to him, Oz whispered, "I know. We feel it too."

"Level three is secure," Wynn reported into the comms.

They were just waiting on level eight and nine.

"Level nine is secure, but I hear something above us. Something is happening up there." Hazel relayed into her comms as she lifted her visor.

In the background, Mercy dealt with a guard who had barricaded themselves in a back room. There was a crash, yelping, groaning, and finally, the sound of a body hitting the floor. It was followed by Mercy's approaching footsteps.

Hazel looked over at the lone base employee they had spared, Cinis, and they shivered as they explained, "I think it's the lab. Up there, they have some of your people they do experiments on. I heard there are twelve of them at all times. They keep them in glass cages."

Hazel focused on Cinis and with sadness in her eyes asked, "Do they keep our people like that in all the bases?" She would have given anything in that moment to be back in the med bay even if it meant she had to wear one of those inflated suits.

Concern fell over Cinis as they faced Hazel and replied, "I don't think so. In every UTC base there is a lab like it, but I don't know if most have your people or not. I only know about it because I pay attention to whispers around the base. Why? What is going on?"

Mercy grabbed Hazel by the arm, giving her a narrowed gaze as they all heard the echo of metal banging against metal coming from the stairwell.

"Barricade the doors! It's the Iungo test subjects. I think they are getting out. They will be coming down the stairwell," Hazel warned into the comms for everyone to hear.

"Wait, what? What's wrong with them?" Cinis frantically asked.

Hazel's heart broke when she heard Oz's pain filled scream into his comms before the helmet cut the sound. Jael was up there. Alone. What about her brother? She hadn't heard anything from him yet. Dread like never before settled in knowing he had not announced his level was clear. Had they gotten it wrong? Had they sent him in alone to the packed barrack level when she and Mercy dropped into the nearly empty command area?

Cinis and Mercy sprinted toward the door to hold it shut. Climbing over the dead guards, Cinis offered, "Go get a bed frame. I think we can wedge it in this hallway and block the door from opening."

Huffing with exhaustion and anxiety, Hazel agreed, "Great idea." Hazel sprinted into the room just as she heard a crash from above. Tremors racked her body as she tossed the mattress off and shoved the bunk bed frame out of the bedroom door. Lifting the frame up, she made her way to the door where Mercy braced herself. Hazel tripped over the body of one of the dead guards and almost smashed Cinis into the door with the bed frame.

Hazel and Mercy efficiently wedged the bed frame into the doorway as a heavy body slammed into the door. The door and frame shook violently with the impact, but held

A sinister growl followed by chittering told Hazel exactly what was looming just outside. She grabbed Cinis's and Mercy's hands, and they stood together in the mess of dead bodies, all horrified by the near dead outside of their door. They stood silently, and she closed her eyes to concentrate as best she could on the sounds outside.

Hazel's visor was open, and she began whispering into her helmet comms, "The infected people are out. They are on level nine heading down. There are possibly twelve of them. Harlen, they're coming!"

As Harlen watched the door from where he crouched, he knew his time was up. He had failed to secure his level. It had been filled with first human command soldiers planning their invasion, but there was no way anyone could have known that. He huddled in front of the cafeteria cabinets, and the doors to the hallway were right in front of him. He had nothing between him and what would soon be barreling down the hallway One of the rounds the soldiers shot at him was aimed low, and he had been struck in the foot. He looked down at the blue blood trickling out of his boot and pooling onto the ground underneath him. He prayed his sister had her level barricaded, and she lived through this day. He feared she would not be seeing him again.

As the doors shook violently with the impact of the deranged people, he opened a comm channel to his sister. "I love you Hazel. Promise me you'll make it to tomorrow," Harlen said, love in every word. Not waiting for an answer, he took his helmet off and set it down. As if the levy had broken open, infected Iungo people poured through the door. Just as the first fungus fueled Iungo reached him, he turned his plasma sword on and it slid through his own head in one swift motion, killing himself instantly, moments before his body was ripped apart.

Hearing his last words, Hazel leaned onto Cinis. Mercy's voice cracked as she spoke into the comms. "Harlen is down. Level eight has been overrun."

Cinis and Mercy wrapped their arms around Hazel as tears poured down her cheeks. The crashing sounds and blood curdling screaming of humans being torn to shreds and eaten alive echoed down the hall. It continued for several agonizing minutes until their cries faded.

A silent period stretched for a few seconds before the comms opened up and banging could be heard. "Fuck! They're strong! They're pounding on the door on level seven. We are holding with the help of some of our freed people," Lark yelled into the comms.

"They are on level six now, too, Oz. They are being funneled down to you at the bottom. How can you lot take on all twelve?" Carter frantically asked as he looked over at a horrified Iungo woman holding the door with him. Her face was a picture of confusion as she watched him speak.

"Don't let them through any of the upper levels," Oz demanded into the comms. He spoke with strength, but inside he was broken.

"I can hear some of them outside of level three. They are moving fast!" Wynn cried into the helmet comms, his voice high pitched and pleading.

Oz ordered, "Hold it together team," then Oz cursed under his breath as he, Zoe, Aurelia, and Costel all stood in a line with their plasma swords drawn. He flexed his hands around the handle of his sword and begged his heart to stop screaming at him to find Jael. If she was gone, he... He had to clear his mind, or they could all die.

Trembling, Sands choked out, "They are on level two."

Shaking her head, Zoe yelled, "Fuck!" as she planted her feet firm onto the ground. Rattling on the other side of the door stole their attention.

Oz turned, "They're here."

The doors swung open, and the infected Iungo streamed through the hallway and began sprinting toward them.

Swinging his sword, Oz intercepted them and took the head off the first one. Zoe leapt next to him and cut down one about to take a bite out of his shoulder. He turned to see one vault onto Aurelia, so he took two long strides and stabbed the snapping creature in the head.

Zoe cut down two just as more of them rushed through the door. Costel ran toward one to slice it down, and it attacked him. It knocked his sword out of his hand and began pulling his helmet off. Costel screeched as the growling man bit into his face and ripped away the flesh. Blue bloods sprayed from the wound. Several of the infected swarmed onto him as if he was raw meat dropped in a tank of piranhas. He cried out in agony as they ripped his body apart.

Enraged, Zoe swung her plasma sword through the group of the infected devouring Costel, forcing her sword into the mass of frantically shredding limbs. She stabbed and sliced, cutting down four of them in a matter of seconds as Oz skewered another.

Frantically, Oz counted nine of the infected sprawled dead on the ground. That meant there were still three more somewhere in the base. His thoughts slid to Jael, and his heart ripped in half all over again. *I left her in the room with them.* His breath caught as he tried to find his words. "There are three still missing. We need to start working on the main power, or none of us are getting out of here. The sensors are registering oxygen levels are dropping rapidly," Oz reported to Zoe and Aurelia.

Zoe pulled her helmet off and ran over to the main power monitor, a large rectangular machine with a simple keyboard. After setting her helmet down, she pressed a few buttons and tipped her head to the side, glaring at it in irritation. "This tech is ancient but advanced, still it's nothing like I expected," Zoe explained as she searched through file after file.

After removing his helmet, Oz leaned on the machine and asked, "Well, can you, do it?"

"Yes, but it's going to take longer than I thought. I think I can do it. I'm going to need to enter a sequence of codes in a timed order open these encrypted files, so if we have company, I'm going to need you to watch my back. If I stop, I could be locked out permanently, and we all die," Zoe stated as she clicked away on the instrument panel.

She raised her arm up to the monitor, allowing the suit to detect what the frequency required to connect to this machine. Once the connection was made and their computers back at the base ran the detection software, the holoscreen on her forearm emerged with the sequences of codes for her to enter.

Oz looked over at Aurelia, and she was visibly trembling. She pulled off her helmet and tossed it to the side before she adjusted her grip on her sword. "Does the general population know the UTC weaponized the fungal infection?" Oz asked Aurelia as he kicked the leg of one of the dead infected Iungo.

"Not specifically, but they weaponize everything. I don't know why you even asked that," Aurelia ground out.

Oz could hear chittering and froze. They made it up the stairwell. He prayed it was all three. The idea of Jael alone with any one of them was far too much for him to bear.

The machine behind him beeped, and he turned to Zoe for hope. When he faced forward again, there were three infected Iungo standing in the doorway. Red blood dripped from their mouths, and it ran down their nude bodies in trickling rivers. Furry exploded in him as the three charged toward them.

He was able to swing his sword and gut one of them, but as he did, another one landed on top of Aurelia, violently slamming her head against the ground. He knew she wasn't getting back up. He vaulted over and took out the infected man on her by cutting into his side. When he brought his eyes back up, it was too late to react to the third. He was already being slammed into the wall, and his sword was knocked from his hand and rolled away.

Aurelia was out cold and with Zoe entering the codes, he knew he was on his own. He grappled with the woman, but in her diseased state, she was much stronger. Terror filled him as she leaned in close to take a bite, her mouth opening wide to reveal a dark void of jagged, broken teeth. His hands were firmly around her neck, but it was no use. Oz cried out in pain as the Iungo woman bit onto the skin of his neck, tearing his flesh. As he strained holding her steady to keep her from taking a deeper bite, he fiercely kicked his legs trying to dislodge her.

Zoe quickly checked over her shoulder, finding Oz

pinned. "Fuck!" Zoe yelled as the next prompt popped up asking for the next code sequence, she had to be close to the end. The oxygen readings on her holoscreen were still dropping.

Gathering all of his strength, Oz forced her diseased, torn face up away from his neck and rolled over her. The infected woman pushed him off like he weighed nothing and pinned him again. She leaned down to Oz's face and showed her ravaged teeth, again releasing a breathy growl.

Time seemed to stop as recognition hit him like a bomb. When he peered into her hungry eyes, he saw a nightmare, his nightmare. It was her, the woman who was taken from him, the woman he loved so long ago, the one he was banished for. This was the same woman who was now hovering over him and growling, preparing to devour him. His blood coated her broken teeth. "Not you, *anyone* but you," Oz cried out as his heart broke again. This woman he once loved dearly was infected and had him trapped. She inched closer to his face, and he could clearly see the beautiful green eyes he yearned to see again for years.

For this to be his end? For it to be hers? That they would meet again in this way, after so long?

His warm blood streamed down his neck from where she ripped his flesh away. Oz closed his eyes and braced for a gruesome death by the gnashing teeth of a woman he once loved. He begged the creator that Zoe would be able to finish, and he had bought her enough time. His eyes opened one last time, and he found the woman had paused to look at him. Her head was cocked to the side, and her mouth was slightly parted, the way it always was when she used to be deep in thought. For a brief moment in time, he knew she saw him. She remembered him. Something inside of her still knew him, even if it was for just that one moment.

A familiar buzz came from somewhere far off in the distance, and he watched as a light shined behind her, illuminating her as she held her gaze. She remained still, with her face hovering over his, as a plasma sword plunged through her side. Blue blood fell in a river from her lips as she slumped to the ground.

Blinking until his unfocused, tear filled vision cleared, he found Jael standing over him with his plasma sword in her shuddering hand. She was panting, and her face was dripping with sweat. His plasma sword was in her right hand with a stream of red blood dripping from under the handle. She had a grease and soot stained bandage over her wrist on her left arm. Oz's mouth opened in a gasp as Jael dropped his plasma sword, and it shut off as it rolled away. The loss of light from the plasma sword sent the room back into a blood toned darkness. He sat up and slapped a hand over the open wound on his neck.

Oz slowly reached up and slid his free hand around Jael's right wrist, pulling her into his lap. When she was inches from his face, "Spots? How?" was all he could think to ask.

Clearing her throat, she showed him her bloody, blistered hand as she rasped, "Amelia couldn't find the device for administering painkillers because it was hiding behind the air vent. The screen lit up when I picked it up, and it was easy to understand, so I selected a single dose. I climbed... well *slid*, down the lift emergency support cords after I heard the infected Iungo escape the lab. They woke me up when they tried to open the closet. I couldn't just lie there and hope you made it. I had to do something."

Shifting his eyes around the room, he saw the lift shaft

maintenance door cracked open behind the tall stacks of files. Grabbing her face and kissing her, Oz once again was overwhelmed by his little alien.

"You two love bugs cut it out. I just unlocked the computer to access the main power. Get over here, Oz," Zoe ordered.

Oz rose to his feet and helped Jael up. They walked over to the main power console as Zoe clicked away at the keyboard. The blinking red alarm lights shut off, and the bright white overhead lights came on. They surveyed the damage, and Aurelia groaned as she began waking up.

"Oh, shit, look at this," Zoe breathed.

Oz looked down at the old screen and watched the surveillance footage from the UTC base commander office as the bomb Kagnus had planted shook the base. The commander stood from his desk and entered a code into his computer. The desk became a lump of smoldering liquid glass, melting from the top. He quickly headed to a cabinet and took out a bag, slinging it over his shoulder. The commander jogged down the garden path to his imperial ship. He boarded and took off, not giving the base a second glance. The base alarm sounded right as his ship left port.

Oz shook his head. "He left in a hurry."

Zoe nodded, "I'm going to pull up the footage of the camps. I wonder if they will stick around or take off just as fast?"

She switched the feed to show the camps, and they were already scrambling to fill their legion transports to evacuate the planet. She scoffed as she read the list of armaments they now had access to. No wonder they were running. This base could blow off the back half of the planet. Oz and Zoe watched as they switched the feed again, this time to the garage door where Kagnus and Mira waited to be let inside after they had detonated the diversion bomb.

Zoe poked around in the base functions to find the command code to open the door and watched the feed as Kagnus and Mira walked inside the base.

"So, who gets to call home and tell Jacob we won?" Oz asked Zoe and Jael, his blue blood leaking between his fingers where he held pressure on his neck.

29

PLANET ADURO - CLAUDIUS ROYAL PALACE

Her breathing trained and controlled, Livia took one step inside of her father's private rooms, that lying sand devil. There was no alarm like he always boisterously claimed. She had no plan if the alarms had gone off. Thankfully, with her father, being a liar was a sure thing. It was typical of him to have lied about having something expensive installed that he didn't want to pay for. He never even took her imprint off the doors of the king's rooms after her mother died. She had just walked up, scanned, and the doors opened.

If this little plan of hers had failed, she would have had to kill one of the humans with access to the rooms in order to steal their mechanical eyes. She would've had to remove her own mechanical eyes to replace them. That process was tedious and a highly uncomfortable experience. The port was deep in her head, and she cringed thinking about having the eyes installed in the first place. She remembered it like it was yesterday. Fading sounds of drills and her own heartbeat echoed in her ears as she surveyed the room, making sure she was alone.

He had no idea she watched him leave from his private launchpad earlier that morning. One of her best kept secrets was an old king's perch, high inside one of the tall glass supports. She had found it as a child before her father constructed his private pad right under the view of the perch. She often went to the hiding spot to escape Lucas, just like today. When he had flown off planet unexpectedly, she knew this was her chance.

She slowly made her way over to his office, carefully sliding her body through the partially opened door. He had an uncanny talent at knowing if someone had been in his rooms, so she was careful not to disturb anything. She tiptoed over to the desk where she remembered seeing a specific box, one she needed. She slid open the top right drawer and lightly pressed on the wood at the back. A tiny door opened with a faint click.

The little box sat exactly where she remembered. She opened the little metallic lid, the red glow of the light inside mesmerizing. Her thoughtless father had failed to even set a lock code on the box. After taking out the four tiny devices, she slid them in a small bag at her hip and returned the empty box to its hiding place, closed the door, and slowly shut the drawer. Exiting the room, she hissed as she grazed her back against the door frame. Groaning at the pain in her back, she made her way to the front door and slipped out.

As she turned the corner, her heart stopped as a woman from the cleaning staff stood in front of her. She was one of August's people, tall with an elegance to her. Sometimes the females arrive pregnant, so she was born here and lived with the doctor after her mother died in a mine accident. When she was born, the doctor begged the king to allow her to stay in the palace. He offered to take her and raise her until she was old enough to work. She had worked cleaning the palace ever since, but she still lived in the doctor's spare rooms. She stood staring at Livia, unmoving, no change in her expression. Livia froze terrified. She had been caught in the act. There was no reason she should have been in this hallway at all.

Sliding her eyes up and down the hall, the woman nodded at Livia then simply went around her like Livia didn't exist.

Livia nearly fell to the ground with relief. Her usually diamond strong knees buckled, and she braced herself against the wall. The firm texture of the wall scraped against her hand, the pain refocusing her. Once she regained her bearings, she moved quickly. Running down the hall, she swerved from her typical path and took the servants' route. Stair after stair her feet flew as she descended the tower and ran all the way around the perimeter of the palace in the gardens to avoid seeing anyone or being seen. She made it look like she was going for an early morning run should anyone stop her or ask.

It was hours before her shift, so hopefully she could park her transport out in the desert and make it back before anyone knew she was gone. She ran to her transport, climbed into the pilot's seat, and after pressing a few buttons, her blades were spinning, and she was in the air.

Soaring at speeds much faster than normal, Livia made it to the mine faster than she had ever before. As she approached, she saw August was somehow asleep while he hung from the post. His legs were folded under him on either side of the pole with his body pressed into it. The way his arms were hanging, she could not imagine how sore his shoulders must be. Nearing, she discovered it was worse. She could plainly see his shoulders were both dislocated from their sockets. She winced. Gently putting her hand on his raw arm, he tensed as he woke from his semi-conscious state. He softly groaned as he peeled his face from the pole and turned his head to the side, trying to stretch the stiffness out of it.

With a dry cracking voice, August gave her a broken smile, "*Cogito amo hunc somnium.*" I think I like this dream.

Livia put her hand on the back of the pole and the manacles opened, releasing August's wrists. He leaned back on his rear, and his arms fell uselessly to his sides as Livia took a step forward and put her hand out.

He sat still as she took his elbow in one hand and pressed on the top of his shoulder. Closing his eyes, she shoved his arm back into the socket with a pop. He winced as she moved to repeat the process with his other arm. Once his shoulders were back in their sockets, she slid her hands under his arms to grip him by the ribs as she helped him rise with a whimper. He stood a moment, rolling his shoulders tentatively. He swallowed roughly and met her eyes as she tipped her head toward her transport.

He followed her but groaned when he needed to stop to stretch after only a few steps. With hesitant steps they reached her transport, and she slid open the door, revealing the back of the large vehicle. August slowly crawled inside, and she followed, shutting the door behind her.

I brought something for you. We got them in years ago but my father is full of conspiracy fears and never gave them to any of the royal family who still lived here. He claims a royal once told him the translation devices were a way for the

First Humans faction to eavesdrop. The manufactured discourse was based on absolute hearsay, but he never accepted the truth. The translation devices were not even created by the UTC or the First Humans. They're translation implants made on Melior by an Iris company. I'm bringing you back to the palace as soon as I can, and I want you to listen in from your cell in the training room. My father has some royalty coming in from Melior, but they are not human, and I don't know what language they speak. I think I overheard it's the Iris Queen, but we will see. I know their guards love to use the training room. *"Attuli aliquid tibi... Scio custodias amant uti conclavem institutionem."* Livia explained, as she opened her hip bag.

August nodded, and Livia pulled out the box along with a scalpel, a syringe, and some wound glue. He gulped as she brought the sharp tool to his throat but held still, knowing Livia would not harm him. She made a small cut at his neck and slipped in the device. The mechanical arms slithered out and wrapped around his vocal cords causing him to fall back against the seat and thrash. He threw his hands up, but all his hands could do were shake.

Damn, I didn't know this was going to hurt that bad. I'm next if it makes you feel any better, *"Damnate, non scio hunc doluit male. Sum proxime si faciat sentis melior."* Livia explained as August glared at her, his hands now wrapped around his neck protectively.

He slowly leaned up, and she finished by sliding the scalpel against his skin by his ear and inserting the earpiece. Grasping his head, he wheezed as the device wrapped around his ear canal. When he finally peered up at her, he grabbed the scalpel from Livia's hand with a nasty look in his eye.

He quickly repeated the process on her, and she didn't

take it much better. Rubbing her throat after the process was over, she took the scalpel from August and put it back in the med kit. "The doctor will notice it's missing," she whispered as she closed her bag.

Taking her eyes from her bag and bringing them back up to August, her heart broke. His face was rough from burns and his lips were cracked.

"This injection will speed your healing," she said as she slid the needle into his thigh and pressed down the plunger. From the side of her bag, she pulled out a jar of ointment. Slowly unscrewing the top, she raised her eyes to August. She twirled her finger for him to turn around. He did as she asked, and she knelt behind him. Taking half of the jar's contents on her fingers, she slathered it in her hands as she surveyed his back. He wasn't as injured as she anticipated. He had blisters, but no open bleeding wounds. "Do your people heal fast?" Livia asked, curiosity blazing in her.

August nodded, "Yes. If I had some kind of creature from my world, I could take its life energy and heal myself much faster. That's only if we're dying. My injuries now are not that severe, though. "

"Through that connection of yours?" Livia asked intently.

"Yes, through our connection," August replied as he rolled his shoulders again.

His shoulders radiated with pain at the salves initial contact, but August forced himself to remain still and calm. He had to remind himself that what she was doing would end up feeling better in the end, even if it hurt like hell right then. He was just glad he had not been nude since they had only removed his tunic. He cringed as she touched a particularly sensitive place. The burns weren't so bad after the ointment. She worked the slick salve into his muscles, and he began melting into her touch. It was fire and a cool breeze all in one.

"Turn around," Livia commanded.

August slowly turned around, and she started on the front of his shoulders, rubbing in the ointment as she went, unaware of his eyes following her every move. He watched her electronic eyes twirl inside of the stunning blue lenses. She was perfect in every way.

Rubbing down his abs, she stopped and looked up at him. Entranced by her gaze, August couldn't tear his eyes from her. Unable to help himself, he leaned in to kiss her. She shot a finger up and rubbed a bit of salve on his cracked lips. He watched her eyes move back and forth as she smeared the salve on, so focused. He slid his hands up her arms. She was trembling. August pulled her into his lap and asked, "What's wrong?"

"Realization has run deep, that in choosing you, I am now the biggest threat our line of succession has ever had. In thousands of years, the succession has never been broken. If Lucas does not inherit the throne, the line will end with him. I'm trembling because I know I will have to slaughter the family's heirs for one blood red demon with a tail. Nearly everyone in the royal guard is a relative in some regard. Thank Jupiter no one has children right now because this will probably end in blood," Livia whispered as she looked down at her own hands, now in her lap. "This only works if most of the guards die, so that no one can contest my reign." She could already see the blood of her family dripping from her fingers.

Pulling her in close to him, August conceded, "You don't have to do this, Livia. You can walk away and clean your hands of all of it. I will go back to my place at the pole, and you can go back to your life like none of this ever happened."

With a burning intensity, her eyes met his as she took his face into her hands. She softly pressed her lips against his. She slid her tongue past his broken lips to meet his tongue, dancing and intertwining. They made love with their mouths until August could no longer wait. He pulled her tunic up over her head and tossed it away. He found her lips again and kissed her deeply as he slipped her pants down her hips. Her pants slumped to the floor and a small cloud of dust danced into the air. She was bare underneath, and he growled at her lips as his hands found the curls between her legs without a barrier. He took her by the hips and gently laid her down. As he did, he kept his eyes fixed on her.

She flinched as her back made contact with the floor. He froze. He pulled his face away abruptly, and she knew he had felt her reaction. She shook her head no. Her eyes pleaded with him not to ask.

"Livia, turn over," August demanded.

She sucked her bottom lip into her mouth as she closed her eyes and turned her body over, complying to his demand. All he could do was blink as he surveyed the deep sprawling damage to her skin, all surrounding a scar spelling 'sponsa' carved across her lower back.

"Wife," August read it aloud. His heart tore in half. He knew who had done this. "I want to kill him, but I will give his kill to you. You deserve it," August whispered as he hovered his finger across the word etched into her flesh.

"I don't want it. He doesn't deserve the honor of my blade at his throat. He deserves to be mutilated by a powerful, crimson demon," Livia countered as she warily peered over her shoulder at August.

August held his hand over her lower back, "It would be my pleasure, my king." Gently, he kissed over her shoulder and down her arm. He hovered over her and kissed down her side as he pulled her hips up, angling her rear in the air. Carefully lifting her legs, he set them on his aching, blistered shoulders, whispering "Perfection," before he buried his face between her legs.

Giving him what she knew he wanted, she wrapped her thighs around his head and squeezed. Livia shook with pleasure as he licked and flicked her relentlessly. She had never imagined such wickedly perfect sensations. She had heard it existed, but never thought it was something that happened in real life, and never for her.

As he firmly grasped her thighs, the points of pleasure within her built like nothing before. She intended to fully surrender to her demon, and so she let herself go. With her apprehension and barriers gone, her pleasure spilled over, and she groaned. Pressing her face against the cold floor of the transport, she rocked her hips and shook with her release.

August set her down, and her legs twitched against the cold bite of the metal. He slid his hands up her body and turned her around, setting her up on the floor. Careful of her back, he pulled her curvy body onto his massive frame and settled her over the top of his length. "You're more than a king; you are a goddess," August breathed into her ear as he slowly slid her onto him.

She gasped as he filled her. He slowly pulled in and out as he rolled his hips under her. Locking his gaze with hers, he kissed her softly. Livia had never had such affection and attention, so much care and dare she say, love. The tenderness of his touch was her undoing. August had swept her away as if she was a speck of sand in a spinning cyclone, carving out canyons in the desert. This red demon dropped into her life, and he turned it upside down.

She felt the waves grow inside her again as he continued his slow and gentle thrusts. A sweet sound of ecstasy fell from her lips as he filled her. She broke into a million pieces and threw her head back in a breathy scream. After watching as the look of found pleasure melted her gaze, he leaned his head back to release the deep clicks in his throat. Taking her face into his hands, August groaned against her forehead with his own ecstasy.

Even with her eyes closed, her electronic eyes read the increased solar radiation, and Livia knew their time was short. She gently rubbed his arms as she climbed off him. "Are you going to put me back on the post?" he asked as he stared out the window of the transport toward the sand dunes stretching out into the distance. Their tracks were gone, erased by the wind.

"You know the answer to that question," Livia sighed as she slipped on her pants.

August did know the answer.

After Livia finished cleaning up, she opened the sliding door of the transport. She stood in the open doorway long enough for her calculating eyes to take an imprint of the light in the sky. Very little of her optical information was purely visual. It was mostly radiation waves and shapes.

The night sky on Aduro through her eyes was breathtaking. She could see a plethora of colors where during the day there was none. She would never admit it, but sometimes she liked her eye implants better than her old eyes, even though the implants still itched sometimes.

Her mind was wandering, taking her away from the task at hand. She dreaded leading August over to the post and reattaching the manacles. He closed in behind her, and she felt his warm breath on the back of her neck. He rested his head on her shoulder and saw the pole begin to shine with the first hints of dawn. "It's time, Livia," August pushed by her and trekked up the dune to the post.

Livia followed, her eyes whirling as she looked to the sky. She and August would be free of this soon. For the first time in her life she was choosing freedom, and the task felt perilous but liberating They may die trying, but it would be better than living like this.

Her feet sank in the sand as they made their way up the dune. They solemnly strode to the pole, and once they reached the transport launch pad, August knelt with his legs straddling the pole. He lifted his arms into position, and Livia was filled with guilt and dread as she made her way around.

"Am I going to die tied to this pole?" August asked her sincerely as she put the manacles around his wrists.

Livia peered down into his eyes of firelight, "No, my beautiful demon, you will not die yet. We have work to do first. When I arrive at my post today, I'm going to tell the other guards that I have had a bad day and I want to enjoy a few rounds of beating your ass in the palace training room to work out my anger." Livia grimaced as the metal tightened around his wrists. With his legs folded under him, he relaxed his arms, taking pressure off his shoulders.

August leaned his face against the post, and quietly joked, "Your solitary confinement sleeping arrangements are sub-par. I'm not sure if you're aware. Maybe I should file a complaint with management."

Leaning toward his face pressed against the pole, Livia smiled into his lips. "I told you they would catch you. When I'm king, you're going to be by my side and quite comfortable, so, don't do anything stupid and get yourself killed before then."

"I am not promising anything, but I'll do my best," August replied as he leaned forward and kissed her goodbye.

As she headed toward the mine door, she heard metal clinking behind her. It took everything she had not to run back.

30

PLANET PORTUM – IUNGO BASE

Face down on his bed, Callum grumbled, "I hate everything and everyone."

"I told you I would get you a bug," Jacob groaned as he turned over to look at him.

In the dimmed light of their room, they were trying to recover from their journey. He moved closer as Callum turned to face him.

"Ewe, fuck no. Why would you ask that?" his lip curled in disgust, "I've had enough run-ins with bugs to last a lifetime." Callum asked.

Smirking, Jacob leaned his head in and replied, "You offered when I cut my leg. I figured I would return the favor."

Glaring at Jacob, Callum rolled over and pulled the covers tightly around himself. Jacob chuckled and closed his eyes. His body melted into the sheets, and the warmth surrounded him. He wanted to stay in this soft bed forever.

Their moment of peace and comfort was disrupted when his tablet lit up next to him, and a ding followed.

Rolling his eyes as hard as he could, Jacob flopped around like a fish in protest. After a sigh of acceptance, he angled his tablet off the side table to see what the message was.

Oz:

> We took the UTC S-7 base. We lost two, Costel and Harlen. They sealed us in and attacked us with lungo who had been infected with the cerebral fungus. They weaponize everything they can get their hands on.

Jacob:

> That's unsettling. I'll let Pike know. I guess that confirms the fungal breakouts in the mountain town and our village were planted from dead test subjects. I'm not sure any of us questioned that in the first place, but now we have confirmation.

Oz:

> How did your mission go?

Jacob:

> We got our asses beat by the people in the northern village.

Upon receiving that last message, Oz dialed him, and Jacob accidentally accepted the call. He scowled at the tablet, cursing, "Shit," under his breath as Oz's face materialized on the holo-screen. Jacob dropped his jaw and snapped, "I'm in bed you fucker."

"I do not care in the slightest. You got your ass beat? By the people in the north village? Oh, shit you do look bad. What happened?" Oz queried, his eyes wide and blue blood still smeared on his face. The nano-bot's in his body were hard at work repairing his neck, and Jacob could see the metallic sheen from them moving around where Oz's skin was missing.

Leaning back against his pillow, Jacob closed his eyes as he explained, "They jumped us and kicked us until we bled from all of our holes. All four of us got it. I guess they think we have endangered our people by taking the planet back. It still beats the cannibal village though."

Callum groaned, "I don't know. I think it's still a tie at this point."

Moving slowly, Jacob wiggled his cold feet through the covers and put them on Callum's leg, causing him to jolt and flail his legs in protest.

"That's easy for you to say. They didn't want to eat *you*. Remember, you made that perfectly clear while we were escaping," Jacob reminded, trying not to chuckle at the furious blue eyes burning holes in his head.

Oz did his best to hold back a grin then his mouth fell into a serious line before he said, "We need you to send a drone for a pickup. You'll need a translation implant in case we have to go up to the UTC Council Chamber on Melior. They are excruciating to install, but do it anyway. Kagnus has a few more I'll send to you. That brings me to my next task for you. The comparative scorpion DNA results Vida has been sharing with me have not been promising. I gave her as much time as I could, but time is ticking, and we can't just keep testing random creatures. We need you to put everything you have into finding proof of our existence on this planet before the first humans found us."

"Ok, I'll get up. I'm on it," Jacob conceded as Oz's face disappeared.

"Damn it. I can't even recover for five minutes. Why does everything have to go wrong all the time? I can't believe I was ever excited to take this position, stupid fucking idea. I have to go." Jacob's annoyance was written under every word.

Callum slowly leaned toward Jacob noting, "I am right here. I know you're leaving. I heard you two talking mere inches away from my face. You really need to work on your people skills, my love."

With his mouth twisted to the side, Jacob held back his response as he got up and dressed in his casual tunic and loose pants. Without another word, he kissed Callum's forehead and left to find Pike.

He strolled in the door of the systems control room to find Pike zeroed in on his holo-screen as usual. The glow of colorful screens in the darkened room took some adjusting for his tired eyes. "Oz just called. We need to put together several geology teams. Vida is not finding the comparative DNA percentages we need," Jacob explained as Pike begrudgingly paused his work. "Okay, I'll put something together. Juni is perfect to lead a team, and once Adrian is better, he can run a team as well. We can start with caves and a few of the areas with ancient settlements we know of. I think the satellites have detected some ancient centipede dens you can check, too. Those caves might actually be more promising if you want my opinion. We can put the tech team to work on something to aid the search." Pike slid his hands over his keyboard, lightly tapping his pointer finger on a key in thought.

Jacob closed the door behind him and headed off to find Juni. He passed door after door down the long hallway of apartments and knocked on the door he thought was hers. The door creaked as Adrian swung it open. He stood in the doorway, his usual sneer on his face. Dread filled Jacob, the man who towered over him defined rotten mood.

"What do you want?" Adrian growled as one of his eyes twitched, the other was still swollen shut. He vigorously scratched his between his legs, and Jacob had to bite his cheek to keep from grinning. The sour fellow probably deserved those itchy balls. It must have been those little parasitic bugs that came out after a rain. They bite and leave little welts which itch so badly people have been known to scratch their own skin off.

"Oh, sorry, I'm just looking for Juni's apartment." Jacob apologized softly, smiling politely and doing his best not to laugh. Adrian grunted and pointed to the apartment next door to his. The extreme irritation on his face was enough to make Jacob gulp. "If I hear you laugh, I will fuck you up. I don't give a damn that you're the vice president." Adrian threatened before slamming the door in Jacob's face.

Slapping a firm hand over his mouth, he bolted to Juni's apartment a few yards away and pounded on the door. When she answered, he pushed by her, flinging the door shut behind him. Jacob muffled his laugh with his hand until tears sprouted in his eyes. Juni just stood and stared at him, unable to understand what was so funny.

"Adrian has an itchy crotch and just told me he would fuck me up if I laughed. It was too much," Jacob squeaked between muffled laughter, still fearing Adrian but unable to hold back any longer. Giggling, Juni said in her smooth voice, "I've been in here laughing every time he goes into a cussing fit about it. I can hear him through the wall. He got into them at some point on our journey home. I think it was when he went off too far on our last rest stop. He kept wiggling in his seat after that. Do you have news on Oz and the team yet?"

"Yes, Oz's team secured the base, but we lost Costel and Harlen. I know you are friends with Hazel, I'm sure she could use a kind message. "Giving her a minute to process the news, he continued. "We need you to pack again. You're leading an archeology team and Adrian is too, when he recovers. The base has already scouted archeological sites missions, so we have a few places to check out."

With a nod, Juni replied, "That's something I'm interested in anyway. I'll stop by the med room and collect the genetic sample kits after I message Hazel. She must be devastated. They were close."

"I can grab the long-distance drones from my lab. I need to send one off to Oz up north, anyway."

Over her shoulder, Juni said, "Give me twenty," as she disappeared in her bedroom, and Jacob left to collect his gear.

After taking several folded drones, he went by the med lab and handed one to Vida. "Can you send this to Oz's location with a med box attachment? He needs to send us some translation implants."

She met his eyes as she took the device. Concern radiated from her, but she didn't respond as she turned to go inside. He was not ready in the slightest for this journey but knew it was necessary. The walk back to his apartment seemed to drag on forever, and once he arrived, he set the drones outside of his front door.

He found Callum inside tossing things from their shelves next to his bag on the bed. Jacob's bag was open on the bed and his clothes were already packed. Jacob sat on the end of the bed with a sigh, and Callum sat down next to him.

Callum nestled his head against Jacob's neck and sniffed a few times before sweetly saying, "Baby, you need another bath. You still smell like a hot and spicy butthole."

Turning slowly to meet his eyes, Jacob made sure Callum was looking at him before he smirked, "You would still lick it, and you know it."

Falling back on the bed, Callum roared with laughter as Jacob made his way to the bathroom for a shower. While Jacob showered, Callum filled him in on Adrian's itchy crotch, and they both enjoyed a much needed laugh.

Once he was clad in his tactical gear, his gaze fell on Callum, leaning against the wall by the door as he distractedly inspected his neatly filed claws. A spark of need bolted through Jacob, and he pinned Callum to the wall whispering in his ear, "I already can't wait to be back home."

"We haven't left yet," Callum breathed as Jacob wrapped his arms around him.

Jacob leaned in sliding the tip of his tongue against Callum's parting lips. "We might as well have."

Regretfully breaking the kiss, Jacob continued, "I think we're going somewhere to the south first to look at a cave. Pike thinks the ancient centipede dens are a good place to start, and I agree. The giant centipedes have always preyed on our people."

"We don't have time for a weekend getaway yet, do we?"

Callum joked as he untucked Jacob's shirt and slid his hand up his rock-hard abs.

With pleading eyes, Jacob said, "Listen, if we find proof we were here before the First Humans, we can take as many vacations as you want."

Callum half smiled, and melded his lips to Jacob's. The two bound themselves together for a few more moments before Jacob reached behind his back and opened their front door. They pulled their packs on as they strolled out of their apartment.

Upon reaching the big metal door to the command room, Jacob stopped with his fingers wrapped around the handle and studied the open area Callum set his hand on Jacob's shoulder in encouragement, and he reluctantly opened the door to the hallway. The base bustled with people heading to the mess hall to check the excavating team lists Pike had just posted.

After weaving through the crowd and exiting the base, they found Juni mounting a holo-bike with six more lined up waiting for their riders. "I have a surprise for you Jacob," Juni said with a sly grin. "It was something your team put together. They just finished the project an hour ago. Head on towards the launch bay doors. You'll see it."

They attached their bags to the hover-bikes, slipped on their helmets, and took off for the bay doors. As they neared, Jacob's excitement grew. He had a feeling he knew exactly what his team had built.

Parking haphazardly, Jacob tossed his helmet to the ground and leapt off his hover-bike, overjoyed. His team had constructed the large transport he had designed. It held twelve people and used their hover tech, but it could climb high in the atmosphere. Delighted, he searched the transport, studying all the features. Callum popped his head inside to check it out.

"This is going to be fun to fly," Callum said absently as he peered around inside the sleek interior.

Jacob leaped out of the doorway and looked at the back, where he found two distinct concave shapes. Two spots for hover-bikes to fit perfectly. They had built it exactly like he designed, and he could not have been prouder. He pulled his tablet from his bag and sent his team a message thanking them for their exceptional work and informing them that they would all be rewarded.

"Your team is bad ass, Jacob," Callum praised as his hand ran over the sleek controls, "This transport looks just like your drawings and plans."

Jacob grinned and admitted, "I'm starting to feel a lot better about this mission. I was worried it would end up like our last one, but I think things are looking up."

"Scorpion nuts, Jacob! Don't say that!" Callum glared sharply.

"Say what?" Jacob thoughtlessly asked.

Miming him, Callum said, "*I think things are looking up. Are you trying to screw us?* No more of that. We planned a couple fun nights to go along with work last time, and you saw where that got us."

In unison, they said, "Cannibals."

"What?! Where?" Behind them Juni screeched.

Callum nervously chuckled under his breath, "Oh no, I was just telling Jacob to stop saying we are going to have a good trip. We did that last time and..."

Wide eyed, Juni interrupted saying, "Jacob, don't you dare say those words. I am not down for cannibals today. I am not ever down for cannibals. Let's just not talk about cannibals at all, shall we?"

She pushed past the two and loaded her things into the back of the transport. She secured them before sending her hover-bike back to the base. As the remainder of the geological team entered the clearing wearing their armor, she climbed in and buckled up. They all secured their bags and found a seat.

Jacob and Callum slid their hover-bikes in the docking bays under the back of the transport and climbed in the front seats. The seats were all U shaped to comfortably accommodate their tails.

Pike approached as Jacob was buckling himself in and asked, "You like it?"

Jacob's grin grew as he asked, "Is it fast?"

Laughing, Pike asked, "Why do you think everyone in the back is wearing armor?"

Knowing he was wearing his tactical clothing, he slid his eyes to Pike who held two helmets and two sets of armor. "You're going to want your helmet on even if you're not taking it to high speeds. Some of the controls are synchronized with the holo-screen in your helmet. If you plan to fly with the door open, you'll want your helmet on for comms," Pike explained.

Jacob and Callum unbuckled the seat harnesses and climbed out to change. Stripping down next to their doors, they tossed their tactical clothes to the person in the back of the transport for them to pack the clothes into one of the bags. Once in their armor and helmets were synced with the transport, Jacob started the engine of the transport and was surprised at the silence. He felt a vibration, but there was nothing else indicating the engine was running. The back sliding doors on either side closed, and the last safety checks were completed. Jacob lifted off and raised above the tree level before testing out the engines of the transport.

"I'm going to test the limits of the transport. Brace yourselves." Jacob said, a little too excitedly for Callum's comfort. Callum turned toward Jacob before he refocused forward, pressing back into his seat, and checking his safety harness one more time.

When they were at the correct altitude, Jacob gripped the throttle as he pushed it forward, and they all sank into their seats. Screaming with delight, Jacob flew the transport in multiple loops before taking it to max speeds all while Callum screamed in terror beside him.

31

PLANET PORTUM - UTC COMMAND

The bright lights glared again, illuminating the carnage all around. The blue blood smeared and sprayed over the room intermingled with crimson blood from the mutilated human's creating pools of violet. Aurelia found a box of folded white sheets and covered Costel's mangled, bloody body. She quietly walked around and lay sheets on the Iungo and human soldiers' bodies. The two soldiers who had surrendered lay mutilated near the entryway, blood pooling under them. In the chaos, they tried to run but didn't make it past the diseased Iungo. "Looks like the base is clear, main power is back on, and I have shifted command codes and control to you. The M-code was a no-go so far. It didn't fit any of the encrypted files. We will keep searching. There are hundreds of more files to sift through," Zoe noted as she clicked away on the server keyboard. She shifted her attention back down at the holo-screen on her arm, guiding her through Iungo base computer aided encryption codes and began entering another code.

Oz nodded, acknowledging her work. "Thank you, please have Amelia come down to comb the data you're unlocking in this block of a server. I'm sure more than a few secrets can be found in the files. Make sure someone finds the star charts for the Sarter's home planet or main military base, somewhere we can contact a representative. It's not in any of the databases. Aurelia said they have as many systems as the UTC and are possibly just as ancient as the first humans, but they were erased from the UTC history books. The UTC and Sarters have a boundary line neither ruling party has crossed in thousands of years. It's going to take some digging. Jael, let's tour the imperial ship upstairs."

Jael hobbled over, and he hooked his arm under hers before helping her over the bodies in the hallway and up the stairs. The maintenance hub for the lift went all the way into the basement, but the lift track ended before that on level two. They passed Amelia in the hallway, and she had a ghostly presence to her, so they nodded and said nothing.

Once they reached the second floor, Oz met Sand's exhausted gaze, and he returned a grim expression. He was hard at work sharing the gift to all their people who had been held at the base. There had been six levels of their people in holding cells. Now, all of them had cautious smiles and optimistic, curious eyes.

She felt their uncertain gazes as she passed, her humanity making her seem a threat. Arm aching, Jael smiled anyway as they passed by. She was arm in arm with Oz, and all the Iungo flattened their expressions as their eyes fell on her. She knew who had not received the gift for their eyes went wild, and they all shifted nervously. She understood. How could their president have a human on his arm? This was exactly what she feared.

Oz pulled her closer as they approached the command lift and kept his eyes on the line of people. He wasn't chancing anything with the way Jacob and Callum had been treated in the northern village. He didn't know where these people had been taken from. The lift doors opened, and he led Jael on.

Looking at the panel, Oz pressed the button. He could hear Jael's breath become erratic behind him. She leaned into Oz for comfort, and when her grip became bruising, he turned to face her.

"Are you okay?" Oz's concern focused on Jael.

Hesitating, then blowing out a slow breath, Jael answered, "I just need a moment. I rode in this lift down from the top right before they took my hand." Her voice broke with the last three words. She looked down at her new form and held onto him for support. She wouldn't allow this injury to define her, but for right now it hurt like hell, and she felt depleted.

Oz held her close to him as the Roman numerals on the elevator rose.

They reached the top, and Jael released another slow breath from her pursed lips as the door slid open. The beautiful garden was untouched, and they crossed the path to the elevator leading them to the dock of the imperial ship.

They stepped onto the balcony, and Jael looked out at the rows of tents. Soldiers stood in one long line down the center boarding their transport ships. She saw how different the UTC military transports were from the Imperial vessels as she neared the glass. They seemed in disrepair, but simultaneously new. It was clear they weren't constructed well, shoddy at best with exterior panels missing or warped. The command vessels on the other hand were beautiful, sleek machines clearly hundreds of times the cost of the military transports. They gleamed even in the ruddy glow of the brown dwarf.

"Do we just have this one ship?" Jael asked as she turned where Oz was focused on something out of the window to her right.

Oz just turned to her and smirked. He hooked a finger at her, and she made her way over. Jael saw one more of the Imperial command vessels in a hanger next to the base, as well as a small fleet of electric vehicles, and something she thought was a cross between a drone and a helicopter.

"Let's look inside the ship." Oz kept his eyes on the small fleet outside the window. Once they faced the airlock door of the ship, Oz held his face up to the sensor and it scanned him.

A feminine voice acknowledged, "Command access granted. Welcome, President Green."

Oz slowly twisted his head around to Jael, and her face burned with heat as he asked, "Was that your idea?"

Unable to help herself, she burst into laughter. "No! I swear I had nothing to do with that."

"Zoe better have done that because your last name is Green. I am going to have to have a talk with her about this. She's worse than August sometimes," Oz grumbled as the door slid open and he took a step inside the soft white rounded hallway.

"To be fair, I think she did ask you at some point back at the base what you wanted your last name to be. I'm pretty sure you ignored her." Jael responded as the airlock opened with a cooling whoosh of air. He narrowed his eyes back at her, completely ignoring her response as he held out a hand for her as she stepped onto the ship's airlock ledge. He knew she was right, he *had* ignored Zoe's question about a last name.

"Do you know where you're going?" Jael asked.

Not turning to look at her Oz answered, "Nope. We are looking for the bridge."

The computer voice sounded above, and Oz pointed his attention to the ceiling in search of the source of the sound, "Follow the lights on the wall to the bridge."

Jael chuckled a bit under her breath, and Oz shot her a look before he began following the white lights crawling along the wall. They trailed the light down a curve in the hallway and stopped at a door. Oz took a step forward unsure of how it worked. The door sunk into the floor, and he stepped into a well-lit room with three elevated stations for people to stand and one captain chair in the middle.

Oz had a look in his eye Jael had never seen, one of passion and success. Jael was enamored with this shift in his posturing. The mesmerized look in his eye continued as he surveyed the room. With his eyes burning holes in the seat in the center, he approached it slowly. It seemed to emerge from the floor and was made of a metallic material frozen in place rather than solid. Once he sat in the seat, a small glass screen slid up from the arm as the computer said, "All systems normal."

Jael, she smiled and asked, "What kind of engine does this ship have?"

"Good question. Let's find out." Oz stared at the glass screen intently. He scrolled through the options for a moment before he found the files. "They have general thrusters, a light-speed engine, and they create some kind of singularity. By the look of it, they send out some type of solid carbon projectile in the path of where they want to open the wormhole. It has an atomically unstable acidic liquid chemical that when triggered empties out in the center of the ball of carbon and causes a domino effect, collapsing the carbon infinitely. The ship has a resonant radiation harmonics sensor to find and match the collapse radiation signature. The electromagnetic projection cannon inundates the collapsing carbon with the matched signature of radiation, which shifts the aim of the collapse energy away from the singularity point and opens up a bridge. So basically, it rips a hole in space and time by a resonated targeted radiation burst from the projection cannon. The momentous energy occurs when the particles which fall into the center of the ball of carbon are harnessed as a doorway and bridge, used to move the ship on its plotted course.

"Is this a sales information file they used as the engine description? There is a whole paragraph here on where and when to buy the next upgrade. Okay, now back to how it works. "Just kidding, it's more sales information. According to flight records, the distance they travel when they pass through the wormhole doesn't register as distance at all. Wormholes are interesting, but I thought they would have come up with an engine design like yours by now. If they do, it's not on this ship. We will need to integrate one of ours."

Lifting his arm and accessing the holo-screen on his forearm Oz dialed Carter, his face materialized, and Carter asked, "May I help you?"

"We need the Imperial, er, the new Iungo command ships outfitted with an engine like Jael's design. They only have light-speed and a resonate-singularity wormhole method," Oz requested as he eyed the information files.

With a wide smile, Carter beamed as he explained, "Before we left, Jacob put his team in charge of building several rocket sized jump engines. I bet we can transport and integrate two of them, and that should be plenty to travel across the galaxy if we need it. I'll call Pike and have him up there with the engines by the end of today. Upload the ship files and please have them sent to the base so my team can review their method of transportation."

"How fast can the engineering team install them?" Oz asked, the urgency to keep moving was eating at him.

Shifting his gaze around as he thought, Carter said, "With several trained people from Jacob's best team, I will say a few days. Not long. The med crew are using Jacob's lab for overflow on bone dating, so his teams want out of there anyway."

"Perfect. Let's make that priority. I want you, Amelia, Mercy, Lark, Zoe, and Aurelia on the mission to the Sarter's planet. Make sure you, Lark, and Zoe are well versed on the workings of this ship before we head out," Oz ordered.

"It will be done." Carter confirmed.

Oz nodded and turned off the holo-screen. Carter's face dissolved into nothing.

Oz turned to face Jael, "We might as well get comfortable. This is our new home for a little while. Computer, show me the ship plans."

The ship computer complied and pulled up an image of the four different floors of the ship. The bottom level held the engine room and engineering. The second level was made up of crew rooms and a mess hall, as well as infirmary where they could find painkillers and antibiotics for Jael. Level three was the captain's room and three other rooms of almost an equal size. Oz studied the top level and tilted his head to the side in thought. There was a weapons storage room down the hall, and he wanted to see what they were holding.

The door slid into the floor, and Oz walked into a room full of blinking lights. The wall was sectioned into a grid and each grid held some kind of missile. He felt the air move as Jael came in behind him. "Explain how the missiles work," Oz asked the computer.

A dim light came on in the room's corner and a voice spoke, "This is the weapons armament. Each light magnetic missile can incapacitate a vessel of imperial size. Each heavy magnetic missile can incapacitate any currently produced vessel or structure."

Oz furrowed his brow and asked, "How does it incapacitate?"

A video screen lit up, and they walked over. A training video was what he guessed it to be, so Oz let it play out. A missile was shot from an imperial ship onto a ship of equal size. He took in a sharp breath as he realized it wasn't a training video at all. It was the last time one missile had been used by the ship they were on.

The missile struck the ship. The other ship seemed to be some kind of pirate vessel; however, instead of exploding, it landed on the hull and attached itself. Oz cocked his head to the side as he watched intently. In an instant, half of the ship was crushed into the small space of the missile.

Jael gasped, and Oz's mouth dropped open.

"What the fuck?" Oz shook his head and put his arm around Jael. He turned her around and led her out of the room as fast as he could move.

Looking around, Oz quickly changed the subject saying, "Let's go find our room."

"Yeah, that's a good idea. I think I have had enough disturbing surprises for one day."

Making their way to the center of the ship where the lift was found, Oz asked, "Do you want Amelia to look into growing you a new hand or some kind of prosthetic?"

"I'm at peace with it. I know it just happened, but what's done is done. A prosthetic will work eventually. Maybe Carter can make me a cool high-tech one. I'm more upset the bastard got away," Jael admitted as she looked up at Oz.

"Maybe there are some good pain killers in the infirmary." Oz offered as he tried to give her a genuine a smile.

The grin on his face faded as Jael said, "That would be great. It was so bad I thought my heart was going to give out. It doesn't hurt so bad now, but when..."

Oz interrupted her as he pulled her to him. Tears spilled from her eyes as she shook and sobbed. Her tears were not for her lost hand, or the pain, they were from the trauma, helpless and restrained. Oz held her tighter as she tremored, then he leaned down and picked her up. Moving to the lift, he held her close and kissed her on the head, murmuring words of love and calm. His attentiveness alone kept Jael from drowning in her torrent of tears. The lift shut its door with a swoosh, and Oz selected the glowing numeral three on the wall as Jael held on to him.

The lift door swished open and found themselves in a common room in the center of four large cabins. He noticed one door was slightly taller than the rest. Reaching the largest door, Oz turned to the side and swung his foot by the bottom of the door to activate it.

The displaced air cooled her face as the door disappeared

into the floor. Jael found herself in awe of the decadence of these humans. The sleek, silver-metallic space was filled with intricate sculptures of gold and abstract paintings which seemed to move. All the furniture and cabinetry subtly glowed underneath and behind it. The overly ethereal feel extended to the central seating part of the ship as it could emerge and disappear from the floor with a simple command. She noticed a full kitchen and dining area as well as what seemed like a work desk in a small nook off to the side. There were few corners and even fewer edges.

Motioning to let her down, Jael made her way over to the door leading to the bedroom and stepped in as the door disappeared into the floor. She found the same type of furniture seeming to extend from the ship's floor. The bed was large and rounded, and it had an odd looking headboard Jael thought. Two lumps to either side of the bed caught her attention, as well as the lack of pillows. The white sheets were stark against the dim tone of the room. She made her way into the bathroom and had to squint as the bright lights automatically illuminated the space.

When her eyes eventually adjusted, she peered around and found floor to ceiling mirrors and one long sink with several spouts. There was a large shower wet area with a bathtub inside of it. What Jael was really looking for was a place to relieve herself.

"Where is the toilet? I need to use the bathroom," Jael asked aloud.

"Please rephrase," The ship replied.

Rolling her eyes, Jael rambled, "I need to pee, tee tee, urinate."

There was a dinging tone, and the room dimmed as one area lit up.

To her left, Jael found a small white glowing line around

an area in the wall. As she neared, she discovered something uncomfortably different from her version of a toilet. A couple of tubes with what seemed to be suction cups at the tiny ends came out from the wall.

"You have to be kidding!" Jael narrowed her eyes down at the tubes.

Oz coming up behind her asked, "What's going on?"

"I said I needed to use the bathroom, and it presented me with *tubes*. I am about to squat in the shower. I am not seeing how this is going to work. Sticking a tiny cup with a tube up to my urethra every time I need to pee just sounds like a disaster waiting to happen." Jael explained.

"That cannot be how they use the bathroom. How are those of us with penises supposed to use it?" Oz asked Jael with confusion on his face, as if she had any of the answers. "How do the relieving facilities work, exactly?" Oz asked aloud toward the ceiling, in an attempt to access the computer.

A video popped up on the wall. Thankfully this time it was an animation and not real people. It showed a person bending over, and the tubes lining up on their own. Jael stared wide eyed at Oz by the time the video ended. The person was clearly having their excrement sucked down a tube. She was not sure about this *at all*.

"We have to try it," Oz said with a grin.

The odd space toilet seemed to taunt her, and she cringed. She hoped it didn't actually touch her labia, but she didn't have much of a choice. It was that, or pee in her pants.

Oz's armor on the bed dinged, and he went into the next room to answer the holo-call.

It was Amelia.

Standing at the data server, Amelia said, "I found an

ancient file with our DNA research, and it doesn't look good. I have compared it to the logs of DNA of our people who went through this facility, and they all have a strange code attached to their DNA in the center. It looks like a long series of lines. I think this is some kind of virus that attaches itself to the double helix. I am not sure what the lines are for just yet, but I'm working on it. There is something else I found. It's about Jael. I ran her DNA in their database. She was part of a project when she was, um, born. Without her DNA, we wouldn't have even been able to access this specific file information."

Confused Oz checked back at the bathroom to make sure Jael couldn't overhear them, and heard her squeak, so he quietly asked, "What are you saying?"

"I'm saying, Jael was engineered by a group of the first humans. It doesn't say what the group was for exactly, but they were searching for some type of rare human genes. It says they abducted over a thousand people for the project, many of them from Earth. They all came from the First Humans sacred planets. The DNA was taken, spliced, and randomized, and over a thousand embryos were brought to term with surrogates. They were kept for different amounts of time, though for what, it doesn't say. After that, the children were planted on various human worlds up until age four. I scrolled through, and it just says the *study ended* at the bottom."

Aurelia walked up and lay her hand on Amelia's shoulder before she explained, "When they end a study, they end the subjects too. Sometimes the researchers are killed as well. It just depends on what the research was about. Often, researchers go into certain projects knowing they will be sacrificed at the end. They do it for money for their families.

Some even trade a free ticket to Melior for a sick loved one. They were likely looking for natural immunity genes. The First Humans are always on a mission to figure out why humans immune systems don't allow them to live as long as all the other origin species. With the First Humans, I'm sure they were conditioning the children before depositing them back on the various human worlds."

Oz already knew Jael's earliest memories were blank until the morning she was found. He had always thought human's didn't remember that far back. He may have been wrong. *What if her memory had been altered somehow? And what about all the left over children?*

"Do you mean they murdered all the remaining children? Her scientific siblings?" Oz asked, disgust boiling inside.

"Yes, that's what I mean. Any left over were likely killed. This is common practice with the FH," Aurelia softly explained as her heart broke for a countless time. Grief was a constant. It ate at her for all the people she had watched the First Humans and UTC murder.

Amelia narrowed her eyes at Aurelia in disbelief, "But there were over a hundred children left over. They couldn't..."

Aurelia just lowered her gaze, interrupting, "You're not from Emendo or one of the other poor planets, so you don't understand. This is our life. It's full of death, pain, hunger, and hardship. It may have been a mercy they were killed. It's better than some of the alternatives. The galactic center is a pitiless, harsh place and you must be ready for that when you go out in it. Your president is not going to like what he finds when we leave here."

"We will address this as soon as possible. I'm going to

sign off for a little while. Jael needs my full attention. This is not going to be an easy conversation," Oz admitted as she could see him staring in the distance.

Amelia nodded and replied, "I'll collect as much information as I can and send it to you later."

His face disappeared from above her forearm as the crossing, concentrated light points making up the hologram faded to nothing. She heard a ding a moment later, and it was a map from Oz, showing her the way to what he named the physician's lodging.

She figured it would be hers and Mercy's room. Looking up at the screen she scrolled through the information for a while before coming to a file labeled Code Data Virus. Curious, she opened it and read the contents.

The Iungo held here were exposed to a virus causing a common cold with a cough and fever and one hundred percent symptom rates. She become more suspicious by the second. Scrolling on, she found the virus was given to every one of them to imprint them with what the first humans called a barcode. *So what did that really mean?* Amelia thought as she focused on the screen.

Then it hit her a literal barcode on their DNA, those little mysterious lines, all the lines on their double helix were the scannable code. The UTC had put a barcode on their DNA so they could be cataloged by a scanner. The scanner could detect a code from DNA sourced anywhere on the body. It could also detect any type of DNA evidence by just scanning an area.

This was a sinister level of tracking and absolute invasion of privacy. This type of coding could be detected from miles, possibly even from space if it presented a radiation signature. Her heart raged. The UTC had created a full proof way to keep their Iungo people from ever becoming anything other than property to sell. They could never run away. No one owing that so-called life debt would be spared if this continued.

Turning around and taking a deep breath, Amelia swallowed down bile that had made its way up her throat. She looked back once more and narrowed her eyes at the brightly lit devastating news. With an almost involuntary motion, she turned it off. That was enough for the moment. Carter could download all the data, and she could review it in her room.

Emerging from her deep focus and surveying her surroundings, she found everyone had vacated the room, and she was alone. As she wondered where everyone went, she peered over at the pile of storage file boxes. Her attention was drawn to a blinking light shining on the wall at the back. Curiosity wiggled its way inside her, and she huffed at her own lack of willpower to ignore it.

Muttering something about stupid moths to a flame, and she peeked around the corner. She found a component and device printer with thousands of chemical compounds, circuits, sensors, and materials to choose from. Amelia stood and smiled at the machine. "Just when I thought today was going to have a rotten end. I think I'll turn the evening into an exciting one," Amelia's face lit up deviously as she plugged away at the screen.

In just a few moments she had completed her designs, and the lights on the machine alternated solids and flashes as it buzzed and whirred. The two devices she designed took a few minutes to finish, and when they were cooled off, she slipped them into a bag she grabbed from behind the guard station.

Mercy was in for a hell of a surprise later. After they had connected a few times, she knew a little bit more about Mercy's desires. With the little toys, she just made, Mercy would have exactly what she wanted.

A thrill she could hardly contain zipped through her as she slung the bag behind her back, heading up from the bottom of the base with her mind reeling. Imaging how her evening could play out, Amelia rode the lift up to the top level, then up the second lift to the balcony. She heard Mercy talking as the door slid open, and she searched around the corner to see Mercy focused on something out of the window with Lark, Zoe, Aurelia, Mira, and Carter. They were watching, in the distance, the UTC soldier ships were still being loaded. It seemed like they were taking a long time to evacuate.

Smiling at Amelia's arrival, Mercy asked, "I was wondering where you went. Did you see all the ships in the hanger?"

"Not yet. Do you want to see our room?" Amelia asked, Mercy's answering smile causing a thrill to thunder down her spine.

Carter spoke up, "Aurelia, we should follow and find our room. Oz sent everyone directions." Smiling softly, Aurelia reached out and took Carter's hand. They moved toward the ship dock as Mercy walked over and slipped her arm in Amelia's.

Amelia held back a sly smile as she led Mercy to the airlock. The door slid down for Carter and Aurelia, and they all filed inside. Lark, Zoe, and Mira followed behind, searching their own maps from Oz.

Carter and Aurelia zoomed away on the lift, and Mercy's eyes went wide at the small pad that seemed to disappear.

They stepped onto the pad, and it whisked them away after Amelia selected level three.

They reached the common room, and Amelia took Mercy's hand as she led her to their door. Their room's door opened as Amelia's attention was stolen for a moment as the lift stopped at their floor and Zoe emerged. She found her own door to the right of Amelia and Mercy's room and headed toward it, clearly tired.

Turning back to face her own room, she found Mercy gasping as she surveyed the sleek space complete with a kitchen and dining area. It had a couch protruding from the floor and lounge area in the living room as well as twirling abstract sculptures. Amelia skipped exploring the living areas and headed straight for the bedroom.

Feeling around the headboard she found exactly what she was searching for. There was a rounded area with a specialized device for holding the sheets on the bed. As the round device opened, she smiled at what she found inside. "I don't know what this is for, but it is surely an opportunity for me," she whispered with a grin on her face.

Mercy entered the bedroom, "I need a shower. I'm going to check out the bathroom. You should join me after, well, when you finish whatever, you're doing..." Amelia nodded as she trailed off and gave her a smile as Mercy padded into the bathroom.

Pleased with herself, she set her bag down next to the end of the bed and shimmied out of her armor, leaving it in a pile on the floor. Heart fluttering, but fatigued from the day, Amelia tripped over the corner of the bed. Laughing at herself, she righted her body and peered up at the bathroom door. She regained her balance, stripped off the clothing under her armor and made her way to the bathroom, finding the room filled with steam. In the shower she found the most beautiful sight she had ever seen. Mercy was rinsing her hair in the stream and her plump breasts were bouncing with her scrubbing. She had a toe pointed and Amelia wanted nothing more than to kiss up that leg, but knew it wasn't time for that yet. Yet.

Turning on the shower next to Mercy, Amelia cleaned herself thoroughly and watched as Mercy grabbed a towel and started to head out of the bathroom.

"Don't get dressed," Amelia commanded, an air of authority in her voice.

Mercy twisted her head around, her wet hair arched in a fan around her.

"You heard me," Amelia said as she maintained eye contact.

Biting her smile, Mercy nodded and tiptoed into the bedroom to look around. Turning off the water, Amelia quickly toweled off and tucked it around herself before following Mercy into the bedroom. She found her with her head tilted to the side at the odd headboard. She pursed her lips, and Amelia knew Mercy was staring at the rounded lumps on either side.

"Do you trust me?" Amelia asked quietly. Mercy slowly turned to her and nodded.

"I need you to answer me," Amelia demanded.

"I trust you with my life," Mercy replied as she looked back at her.

"Do you trust me with your body?" Amelia asked as she took a step closer.

Mercy nodded, "I trust you with my life, body, and soul."

Amelia leaned in close to her ear and softly whispered, "Lay on the bed in the middle."

Complying, a nude Mercy found her place in the center of the bed, and Amelia crawled on top of her. Taking each of her hands Amelia held them up, and Mercy was compliant, allowing Amelia to do as she pleased. Flipping open the small round lump on the side of the headboard. Amelia pulled a wriggling string from inside of it. Yanking it down, she wrapped it around Mercy's wrist and her eyes flew open.

Smiling down at Mercy, Amelia whispered, "Trust me." Releasing a tense breath, Mercy nodded and let Amelia take her other hand. Crawling down her body, Amelia couldn't help but give Mercy's right peak a taste. Mercy's body squirmed, and she gasped with thoughts of what was coming.

She crawled down to Mercy's feet and placed a kiss on her ankle as she reached under the bed for the slithering ropes. They made their way around Mercy's ankle, and she shivered as it caressed and grasped her skin.

"Amelia, what?" Mercy whispered.

Once she was secured to the bed, Amelia reached into her bag and set the two devices she had made on the bed between Mercy's legs. She made her way up Mercy's body, kissing up her leg all the way to between her breasts. Whispering into Mercy's ear, Amelia breathed, "I want to be the first to penetrate you, to make you mine. I want you all to myself."

"I am all yours."

Smiling against Mercy's cheek, Amelia turned Mercy's face and kissed her. Slipping her tongue in her mouth, she teased her mouth before licking her lip. Amelia kissed down her neck and down to a breast, taking her nipple into her mouth and twirling her tongue. Mercy arched into the sensation and leaned her head back. With Mercy's movement underneath her, Amelia found her body unbearably perfect. She kissed along the swell of her belly and headed further down. Amelia buried her face into the apex of Mercy's shaking thighs and devoured her. Mercy's legs pulled against the restraints with pleasure, and she whimpered with Amelia's twirls and nips.

Amelia licked Mercy to the edge and pulled her back. Over and over, she took her right there but didn't keep going. Mercy trembled as a bead of sweat trickled from between her breasts up to her collarbone as Amelia lifted her.

A breathy plea came from Mercy as Amelia edged her again, "Please let me come."

"Not yet. You're going to come when I'm inside of you," Amelia demanded as she grabbed one of the two devices she had.

The first one she pressed the button on and slipped inside of herself. The sensation made her squirm, and she couldn't wait to see what the beauty tied to her bed thought. Mercy heard the hum as Amelia turned on the device, and her head leaned up to find the source. "What...?" Mercy started to ask as Amelia slid the device over Mercy's sensitive bud.

Just like Amelia designed, it stayed in place with a gripping material. When it made contact, Mercy's right leg began shaking so hard the bed began to creak. Amelia kissed her up her shaking right leg before settling on top of her. Leaning down and kissing her, Amelia shifted her body and slid her tail around to Mercy's entrance.

Amelia knew she needed to tease her thoroughly at her entrance before she dared go further. Once her tail was dripping wet, she lined up to her entrance. Mercy stole a sharp breath as Amelia gently pushed her tail inside of her. She paused for a moment until she felt Mercy relax. Then Amelia rocked as her tail slid in and out. Throwing her head back, Mercy shook and groaned with pleasure. The clicks deep in her throat sounded and moments later, Amelia's sounded as well.

A mere moment later, Mercy didn't shatter, she exploded with a scream. The pleasure from the device buzzing at her bud and Amelia's tail had taken her breath away after her cry. Amelia leaned back and watched as Mercy arched and fought her restraints. Her hips swinging back and forth, desperate for somewhere to go. Amelia grabbed her own lower belly as her pleasure ripped through her, causing her to release a high pitch sound from the back of her throat.

"Amelia, oh please, I think. It's happening again, oh gods!" Mercy cried out and the clicks sounded jumbled in her throat as she had a second explosive pleasure wave rocked through her. Mercy thrashed, unable to make a sound.

Reaching up, Amelia pressed down on Mercy's belly so she could pull the vibrating device off her. Mercy's body crashed against the bed, and Amelia reached up to put her hand against her entrance. The sensual pulses of energy flowed through her hand from inside of Mercy's body. Amelia loved to sense the soft beat of the waves. It was the rhythm of life.

32

PLANET ADURO – MINE 03

A few hours after Livia returned to the palace, August heard the humming sounds of the transports heading toward the landing pad for the guard shift change. He hoped they were coming to take him to the palace like Livia said, but when they landed, they strolled right by him. When they passed by him, he gave their backs a cheery smile and middle finger.

The pole had been his home for days. Now that he required sleep, he felt himself losing a grip on reality without much of it. Sanity was slipping away like moisture from his skin on this scorched world. In the sky, he swore he could see the whisps of water vapor leaving the atmosphere and floating off toward the big star in the center of the system. His mind drifted to the cities he glimpsed of in Livia's memories. They were so grand they wrapped around worlds like one of their gods had slipped a claiming ring over the middle of the planet, forever declaring the world had been conquered in the name of their God's followers. He had heard the god's name Jupiter on the quiet lips of the guards in the cave. They had mentioned others too, Juno, Mars, and Venus, but he knew there were more. They spoke of them as if there were many entities with a multitude of powers.

August leaned his face against the hot metal of the pole and wondered how the hell he would survive the beating Livia would give him after she found out he stole some of her memories. She might even skin him alive. He would let her.

He loved that woman more than life. How had he fallen so deeply, so quickly, when he hadn't been on this world for long?

Guilt flooded him when his thoughts slid to Mercy. *Why did I let her think we could be together?* He had been taken before he could even form a way to end their relationship. His stomach groaned as the regret churned. He had been disgraceful; she deserved so much better than him. She was so soft and kind, such a gentle person; he was so hard and rough. He should have known he would hurt her. Maybe he deserved this hell planet. He hated many of their customs, but the practice of moving on right away made sense. Life was far too short to sit around and wait. It was too short to put anything important off. He had been so foolish waiting for as long as he did after Mazarin.

He once swore to Mercy he would conquer worlds to return home. At first, his own words echoed in his head, but now they screamed at him. If it took until the end of his life, he would do everything he could to find Mercy and beg forgiveness and atone for what he did. He knew Mercy was now free to find love that would be returned. He prayed she found it. This also meant he was free to love this human woman, Livia, his future king. He felt like a steaming lump of shit. None of those thoughts made him feel any better.

August chuckled aloud, "Only I would find some way to hurt my own feelings while tied to a pole in a blistering desert."

The wind relentlessly whipped his hair in his eyes, forcing him to leave them closed, so he kept his ear trained on the door. When something stirred in the sand, his eyes flew open and zeroed in on the movement. Small ripples told him something was slithering under the surface. Livia hadn't told him there were living things in the sand!

Someone needed to come release him *immediately*.

He stood in a panic and frantically hopped high enough to look at the top of the pole. It was flat. He decided he could *unquestionably* perch on the top of it. More movement in the sand a few feet away had his eyes bulging and his arms moving to grip the pole. When he reached the top, he had a moment of panic where he wasn't sure how he could balance on the top.

Catching his eye again, the movement in the sand was faster, flitting sand into the air. His stomach lurched to his throat as he scrambled to find a way up. Even a few toes would work. Balancing on his stomach, he inched his body over the pole and pulled his legs up as he pivoted his torso up and forward.

Shaking as he gripped either side of the pole, August peered down and saw some kind of long, thin creature with a metallic sheen pass so close to the surface the skin shone in the sunlight. His feet were still not on the top of the pole. His heart exploded with terror, pounding hard enough he saw stars dance in his eyes. The manacles clinked against the pole, bringing him out of the fear induced delirium.

As a scream swelled in his throat, he felt his toe graze the lip of the metal under him. He grasped the edges with his toes and slowly let go with his hands and carefully stood up. The manacles on his wrist rubbed his raw skin, but the manacles cable was just long enough to let him almost fully extend his legs. Relief washed over him like a soft shower as he surveyed the area. He was satisfied he was safe, for the moment. He had never been more thankful for all the time he and Oz had spent playing games in the trees as children.

The door to the mine slammed, and August brought his gaze to find two guards with their heads cocked to the side, eying him as if he had lost his mind. He shrugged and pointed to the sand. The manacles attached to his wrists, grated against the pole under him with the movement. The two guards faced one another in confusion and hesitated He waved his hands at them to alert them of the danger, but when he checked, there was nothing there. He's squinted his eyes in the direction of the guards as they approached.

Did I hallucinate the entire thing? Dropping his shoulders, he realized how he must look perched on the pole pointing to the sand, so he swung down just as the guards reached the pole.

"What the fuck are you doing? Trying to be an acrobat? I don't know why they call you golden. You're not worth shit, possibly the dumbest species in the galaxy. They could get better work paying unaltered humans to come and die in the mines." The guard was so close August could feel his nasty breath on his face.

August pinched his eyes shut and secretly hoped his imaginary sand creature would come eat this fucker. He stood as still as he could. The other guard stepped around and loosened the manacles. August pulled his hands free and rubbed his wrists.

"Why does Livia always want to train with it?" the one behind him asked.

The other guard stared at him, "You saw him on top of the pole. I'm sure he is good training. After seeing that, I wouldn't mind a round myself."

"I think it's weird as fuck," the guard spat as he hit August on the shin with his staff.

They led him over to a transport and shoved him inside. He fell forward but was too exhausted to steady his balance. His head hit the floor first, and they laughed as he groaned on the ground. He memorized their laughs, their voices. These two, he would target himself if he could.

They kicked his legs and forced him the rest of the way inside. One of the guards took a seat next to him in the back. The journey was much like the other times he had flown to the palace, long, hot, and boring. This time to keep him company, he had the lovely stench of his own body odor and the foul feet of the guard next to him.

He couldn't wait to be thrown into his cell so he could take a cloth bath. Was that awful stench really his own body? He couldn't believe Livia had sex with him smelling like this. His eyes looked around the transport and slowly leaned his head to the side to sniff his own body, discreetly. It wasn't all him, his eyes found the pair of boots on the other side of his head. Nearly gagging, he wished he hadn't searched for the smell. *How* had he not noticed how awful it was until now. He almost gagged but managed to keep his lips shut. With that, he sat up and crawled into a seat. When the raw skin on his back touched the fabric, he cringed.

They arrived on the palace landing pad and made their way inside the giant glass dome. The palace seemed exactly like it had the first time he saw it, pristine with tall pointy towers of glass. It was beautiful, despite the evil which built it. It reminded him of the crystals in the caves on his home planet. The tall spires glistened in the sun, their shimmering light nearly blinding him before being led inside the palace.

He was led down the hall toward the training room. They forced him into his cell and shoved him inside, snickering when he slammed against the wall. He wanted to turn around and tell them how delectable their future king's pussy tastes, but he decided he better not. They might beat him and chain him back to that pole for saying such a thing, or just kill him because he spoke aloud. He rolled his eyes.

Remaining silent was driving him mad. He wasn't sure if he could have remained quiet much longer if Livia hadn't been on board. Words would have eventually slipped out, and he would have been beat to death or thrown out into the sand to rot. Maybe the sand worms would have shown him a mercy and eaten him before his skin burned off in the desert if what he saw was real. If not maybe he'd become a dehydrated corpse.

He wasn't sure how decay worked on a hell planet. He wondered if the radiation levels would change the process somehow. It probably killed most of the microbes he decided, so desiccation it was. *Just like good ol' fungal Fred,* he shook his head, trying to dislodge the image of that nasty corpse from his mind. How did he end up on that subject anyway? *Damn, I need some sleep.*

The lock on the door clanged, and the guards walked off, nodding to the training room guard on duty. It was still the smaller built younger man. The square shape of his jaw and the angle of his lips enthralled August. He always looked as though he was frowning, but his eyes told another story. Without giving any kind of warning, he pulled his drawstring to drop his pants, and the man gasped. He smiled to himself and wondered about this guard. He took his cloth and began washing his shoulders. Sliding his eyes over, he found the guard with his gaze focused on the wall ahead of him and beads of sweat forming on his brow.

As he thought, the kind, handsome guard liked him.

August knew they needed as many friends as they could on the inside, but more than a friend would work too. He made sure to flex his legs as he bent over to wash them, and as he did, the brown-haired guard cleared his throat roughly. Turning to wash his torso, he found him openly staring at August. A small tuft of hair hung over his right eye, but he didn't seem to care. He had clearly lost all ability to control himself, so August smirked at him. The guard's complexion shifted, red bloomed on his cheeks.

Whatever he was unsure about before, he had no doubts now. August took the cloth down his body and washed his length, keeping his smoldering, fiery eyes on the guard.

The man wheezed and fell through the doors trying to run. The moment the doors shut with a click, August leaped onto the small mattress and made himself comfortable, all with an enormous smile. He hoped the guy had a fun time in the bathroom. His eyes found his own erect length and groaned as he ignored it. He would have to take care of that later.

A few moments passed before the guard returned with his face flushed and his brow hair and face dripping with water. August could smell his freshly washed hands. All the guards used the same soap with a light floral scent. He rolled over on his mattress with his bare ass pointed to the door, and he could hear the brown-haired guard clap a hand over his mouth to keep from groaning. August had hardly kissed a male before, but he decided he could certainly give this man a chance if the occasion ever arose. After a bit of unstructured thought, he decided he certainly had to have kissed a boy at some point during his younger days. With that thought, he fell into an exhausted sleep.

Several hours later, August awoke to a loud commotion outside, and the young guard's voice cracked as he softly warned, "The Iris guards are due to be here soon. As much as it pains me to say this, you might want to put your pants back on."

Dare he say, did the pouty lipped guard *like* him? August flashed him a pearly smile and the man's knees buckled. He wished he knew his name.

The brown-haired guard whispered under his breath unaware August had superior hearing, and could make out every word, "You understand everything I say. I knew it. I knew it was a fucking lie like everything else here."

August leaned up and kept his orange eyes on the man as he slipped his pants on. Flashing him another smile as he turned over to rest more, he heard the guard bang his head on the wall. The sound echoed through the room. Unable to help it this time, he shook with a chuckle he was desperate to keep down. He understood exactly how the guy felt as he adjusted himself in his pants.

The door flew open and slammed against the walls as two male and one female Iris waltzed in. They wore tunics and loose pants similar to his people's traditional clothing, which he found increasingly odd. They fluttered their colorful wings as they approached August's cell where all three sneered and hissed at him. They had sharp pointy teeth, and all had bright colorful hair matching the color patterns in their wings. Their hair was oddly lightweight and seemed to defy gravity. It was almost floating around their heads. Their skin tones in this group ranged from light beige, to tan, to dark brown.

One strand of the colorful hair fell off one of the Iris, the air draft from their sweeping wings sending it twirling into the cell. August reached out and took it from the floor. He looked closely at the strand and saw their shiny, voluminous hair was actually tiny, long feathers. It was impossibly soft and the center quill shone like a diamond in the light.

They were stunning people, but August wasn't a fan of their mouth full of sharp teeth. They were built like warriors, and the feminine one had a curvy body of dreams. She slid her loose pants down to reveal workout attire underneath, and her two accompanying guards did as well. They were all clearly familiar with the gym.

"Yix, are you going to club Venus for the show next week?" one of them hissed in a deep tone through his dreadfully sharp teeth.

Yix cocked her head to the side and asked, "Why do you care?"

Furrowing his brow he answered, "I want to see the blood Resper they caught in the Mars district. Someone said they are feeding a criminal Rubus to him. I want to see him rip the Rubus open and feast on its blood. I wonder if they will throw the tail into the crowd like they did last time."

Yix smiled at his boisterous laughter and asked, "A blood Resper? That sounds deliciously entertaining. Before the show, let's go to that restaurant the famous Haculae chef just opened. They have added a secret special to the menu to celebrate the opening. I heard it is the raw, steaming heart of a freshly killed Vultus."

The male Yix was speaking with slammed his practice sword down, and she met it with aggression.

They fought for several minutes before the third Iris spoke. "Are you two on duty for King Claudius's festivities? He's celebrating because he's closing two mines and selling the mine workers. Many were gifts from the empress, so he stands to make a fortune. People all over Melior and the galactic center are coming to the feast to butter up the king so they will move up his offer list. Someone said he might hold an auction."

Yix grinned, "I knew there was a reason all the ships' staff were all lining up at the spaceport clinic for travel radiation inoculations. I hope our Iris Queen will buy some for the arena games. I'll go just to beg her to buy some. I bet we can find insect hormone on Flowers Lane by the old Emendo Janus temple, get them all hyped on fighting hormones and send them out to battle one of the first human's engineered Vistalian raptors. It would be a glorious arena battle."

August leaned against the bars and strained to listen. With his ears focused on the conversation, he blocked everything else out.

"Let's go and fuck with the one they have in a cage. I wonder if they put him here for us," Yix hissed.

August froze and knew he couldn't move, or they would know he was listening. Dread shot through him, and he waited for the first blow. Seconds later, he felt a staff crash against the top of his head. He scrambled to the back of his cell. All three reached in and began to beat him with their staffs. He was fully exposed and had nowhere to go.

The brown-haired guard he shared a moment with caught his eye behind the wings of the Iris. He was frantically yelling something into a communicator, but August couldn't hear anything over the sounds of the Iris hissing and laughing.

One turned on the electric shock on their staff and hit him in the neck with it. He shook as the electricity coursed through him. The searing burn of the rolling current rattled his teeth and the scent of his own singeing flesh filled his nostrils. He kept his eyes sealed shut as the young man at the door cried out, "That's enough! He trains with Livia! She will be angry if you damage him! He is property of King Claudius!"

Relief washed over August as they all turned around to glare at the human guard, but they pulled their staffs out of the cell. He could feel his wounds steaming and groaned inside. Within his mind, he cursed at the ruthless Iris.

After the three Iris left, slamming the doors as they went, the guard carefully approached. He whispered, "Are you alright? Do you need me to call the doctor?" August met his eyes and tried not to make a face as he held the guards kind gaze and lay down on his mattress. His head throbbed from a staff crashing down on it, but his body had fared worse. His skin had already been burnt to boils, and the electrified staffs made it crack and peel away in places.

He rolled over on his side and thought about what the Iris had said. He had a lot to tell Livia, so he hoped she visited him soon. Behind him, he could hear the kind eyed guard quietly contacting the doctor over his communicator.

One thing he learned from the Iris was, they lived lives that were nothing like the one he had growing up. They were nothing like his people. This busy place filled with different species of space faring people all seemed far more cruelly primal than his people had been in thousands of years. They held games of blood and death in giant arenas and kept intelligent beings with some kind of ridiculous justification over genetics and life debts. Money and power ruled this galaxy, not just the Earth Jael came from.

Now he needed to take this planet for much more than just his people. He needed to take it because people all over the system needed a better place to live. He needed to take it for the woman he loves. He and Livia would improve the galactic center, together.

33

PLANET PORTUM – DNA MISSION

Soaring through the light of the swirling auras in pink, blue, and green toward the red dot on the map, Jacob banked to the right and brought the transport down in a clearing. He was astonished at how swift the journey went, just under an hour to reach the southern coast. He may have flown around wildly for most of that hour. He did need to test the aircraft after all. Next to him, Callum scrambled to unbuckle himself and leap out of the door. He ripped his helmet off, sending it flying, and spewed vomit all over the ground.

Cringing, Jacob shut his eyes as he took his own helmet off. When the hacking ended, he saw Juni hand Callum a small towel and a water can. He felt terrible. Maybe he shouldn't have made all those loops right before they landed. Callum slowly turned and glared at him, his piercing sapphire eyes taking Jacob's guilt to a whole new level. "Thanks, you prick-hole," Callum grumbled as he tipped up the water can.

Focused with contrition on Callum, Jacob admitted,

"Sorry, I got a little carried away." Everyone else sluggishly filed out of the sliding doors as Jacob hopped out and scanned the area for the cave they were searching for. Jacob's guilt deepened when yet another person pulled her helmet off and puked.

They were somewhere on the south end of their continent near what would be their equator. It was steaming hot which was just making matters worse. Nearby, Juni altered her suit's temperature settings, and he decided it was probably wise for him to do, too, as a bead of sweat formed on his brow and slid down his nose. Jacob raised the holo-screen on his forearm and selected the option to vent the suit. The rush of air against his clammy skin was refreshing, and he relaxed once he cooled down. A gentle breeze with the scent of the briny ocean water slipped through the woody mix of palm, willow, and oak trees around the clearing.

Resuming his search for the cave, he peered around and finally saw a dark spot on the ground across the clearing. Nearing the cave opening, he could see a small stream running through the saturated floor. Foliage sprouted from the ground and crawled up the sides of the opening, spilling over the top edge. A ring of moss began a few feet inside, just on the other side of the vines and leaves. "Has anyone been inside of this cave yet? Is it the one spotted on the satellite feed?" Jacob asked as he turned to Juni.

Furrowing her brow, she answered, "I am not sure. Why do you ask?"

"There is a water source. That could mean a complicated *ecosystem*," Jacob explained as he began contemplating all of the possibilities of life in this cave system.

"Oh, you mean you're not going to just leap down into the unexplored dark hole without checking it out first?

Really? I thought you loved surprises!" Juni teased. "Don't worry. That's one of the jobs of the drones we brought. Oh, and Jacob? If you bring up the C word again? The one that almost rhymes with animal? I'm going home, and you are on your own then," Juni said cheerily with her eyes burring into Jacob like plasma drills.

As Juni unfolded a drone, Jacob bit the insides of his cheeks knowing he had been seconds from mentioning the Juni-forbidden C-word. She casually tossed the drone into the air as the little machine came to life. The round propellers unfolded as the lights illuminated, and it hovered around the entrance of the cave before it dove inside. The hum quickly faded along with its light as it disappeared in the tunnel.

The bright light of the holo-screen on her arm shone in her eyes as Juni studied the interior of the cave. "I don't see anything. It looks long abandoned. I think we're good to go," she remained focused on the changing imagery as she spoke.

After the drone surveyed more of the cave, she lifted her gaze as the drone raced back by them and landed next to the transport where one of the team members put it away.

Curling her tail up tightly, Juni hopped down a few feet inside of a ledge where the ground began to slope into the cave Jacob followed cautiously. The two looked around inside the cave mouth, and it seemed to be an ancient centipede den just as they had suspected.

Searching the ceiling around the mouth of the cave for any sign of the centipede leg scrapings, Juni seemed satisfied about the safety and turned and absently asked, "Oh, you need to be officially briefed about the mission don't you? You know part of this, but I'll just start from the top.

There should be bone remains starting just inside the cave opening. We think we began the practice of burning sometime after humans arrived, so we suspect before that we had always allowed nature to recover our dead. Hopefully, we will find lots of our ancient peoples' bones in giant centipede caves like this one all over the continent. Larger scavengers tend to pull their meals to their dens, and we are starting here because this area is full of giant centipedes."

Dropping his mouth open, Jacob said, "Excuse me, what now? This area is filled with *giant centipedes*? When the hell was someone going to tell me this?"

Juni slowly backed away, avoiding Jacob's question. She turned abruptly, hopped out of the cave, and power-walked to the transport. Juni was as nonconfrontational as they came, he probably should have phrased his question better. *This was still better than the giant orb spiders up north, right? Or cannibals?* His heart went into overdrive, and he threw an arm out to the cave wall for balance. Thinking about the giant spiders didn't help at all. He had the first round of team leading. This was going to be the longest hours of his life. A bead of sweat dripped from his brow into his eye, and he blinked it away as he leaned up from the wall.

A few team members clambered down and began putting up metal stakes to line out the first dig spot. Several more people jumped down with bags of equipment in hand and began passing out shovels. The first shift of six people began vigorously digging, and within three hours they had discovered more than one seemingly ancient bones of Iungo origin.

After several hours, having an opportunity to leave the dark cave, Jacob leapt out and sprinted over to the transport.

His skin was going to crawl for the rest of the day after being in that unnerving dampness.

Before long, the drones could be heard, flying off toward the base.

"All available drones have been sent with the samples. Hopefully, we should hear something from Vida soon," Juni threw over her shoulder as she climbed in the transport to retrieve her tablet from her bag.

Leaning against the transport, Jacob acknowledged her, "Good. I am going to check on Callum. Have dig team one take a break in a couple hours and switch to team two. Make sure the teams dig until there are no more bones. We need to be as thorough as possible before we move on to the next dig site unless we hear from Vida."

Turning toward his tent, Jacob saw two people struggling to attach the bag to a drone, so he gave them a hand. Peering down into the bag of his peoples' black bones, greyed and cracked from time, his heart leapt with hope. He showed them how to clip the magnets on the bag to the drone, and they quickly caught on. Once the bag was attached, they all watched as it zipped away.

He looked over toward his tent and wondered if Callum was ready to eat something. Heading toward the tent, Jacob grabbed a ration sack and ducked inside. Callum stretched out on his cot facing the side of the flapping tent. Setting his hand on Callum, Jacob asked, "Are you up for something to eat?"

Callum groaned, "Sure. Not what is in that bag though. I want something fresh. When we travel on the transport, try not to spin so much. I would like to keep my lunch inside of me next time."

"I promise I will not test the transport with you aboard

anymore. We have more dig sites to visit this week. If we don't find anything, we will have to put more people on the cave scouting teams. We're already limited, and I don't know how Pike is going to find the people to do it. He's going to have to beg Sarah to help us find more people from the village unless Henry and Etta can come through with some additional help. Pike said the mountain town will be able to spare more people in the next month or so, but they are still rebuilding," Jacob said as he rubbed his burning eyes. The stress of the mission was settling in his bones, and the weight of their situation was heavy on his shoulders. Callum reached up and pulled him down to lie with him on his cot, and Jacob melted into his side.

"I'm sure you will find what you're looking for. Centipedes have used these caves for hundreds of thousands of years. We only need to go back before ten thousand years, right?" Callum asked as he wrapped his arm around Jacob.

Pausing to think, Jacob tapped the tips of his fingers together. He felt like his nerves were eating him alive. His eyes stung, and his head ached. "That's easier to say than to pull off. It could take years to find DNA evidence we were created. Vida confirmed one bone we've sent today has been close to the age we need, and it was still off by over two thousand years. She can process fifty bones samples or more a day, and the medical team has taken over part of my lab to organize all of them," Jacob wrapped his hands around one another and wrung them.

Exhaling roughly, Callum asked, "How about a walk? You seem agitated."

Jacob rose from the cot and reached his hand out for Callum. They both ducked under the edge of the tent and went toward the woods.

"Are you two going for a walk? Can you grab some firewood? Risk sent a cooler with flatbread dough and a pan," Juni shouted across the clearing as she poked her head out of the transport.

Jacob smiled and yelled back, "Sure. We will be back in about twenty minutes."

They turned and continued toward the woods, the soft ground not making a sound underfoot. Jacob slid his arm in Callum's as they passed by a towering palm tree.

"Wait, is that a coconut?" Callum asked, halting Jacob with his arm out.

Grabbing the rolled-up bag on his utility belt, Jacob handed it to Callum as he headed over to pick up the pristine, fibrous fruit a few feet away. Once the coconuts were retrieved, they saw a shady area of trees.

As they neared, Jacob gasped at the sight. Tree after tree of a different types of fruit spread as far as they could see. Cherries the size of Callum's hand had him making a soft squealing sound as he searched the ground for one without a worm hole in the side.

When Callum finally discovered a dark red cherry without a hole, he exclaimed, "Oh bliss," loudly as he dove his face into the fruit. After devouring one side of the cherry and staining his face purple, he and tore off a chunk to hand to Jacob. Jacob groaned at the flavor and ate his piece in seconds as Callum ate the rest. The pit was the size of Callum's palm. "I am keeping this." He whispered to himself as he popped the pit into his bag.

Jacob pulled another bag from his belt and collected firewood from a peach tree as Callum made his way over to an avocado tree. He held up an avocado and laughed as he had to open his bag up all the way to fit it inside. It was just soft enough to squeeze it in. "These avocados are the biggest I've ever seen. Look this one is as big as my head! Why do people not come here for the fruit?!" Callum smiled as he held the giant fruit by his face.

Smiling and beginning to let himself calm down, Jacob chuckled and asked, "Did you see the oranges?" Whipping his head around, Callum scanned the woods for anything orange. He finally spotted them several yards to his left. They were far too big to fit any his bag, so he held one under his arm.

"We should head back soon and send someone from the team out to collect more fruit. The soil here must be excellent," Jacob said trying to figure out what was so different here. This was all *too* perfect.

Looking to the sky, Callum noticed the auras were more intense. The sky seemed much brighter than it was back at the village, and it got Callum thinking. "Do you think maybe the radiation from the black hole is higher in the middle of the planet, and that's why the plants grow bigger fruit here?" Callum asked his eyes still on the aura's above, desperately trying to justify a decent reason, *one not involving centipede excrement.*

Jacob considered his question as he pulled his bag of wood scraps onto his back before saying, "That would make sense. I'll call Pike."

Pressing some buttons on his forearm, Pikes face materialized above Jacob's arm.

"Can you compile a solar radiation map of our planet from our satellites?" Jacob asked.

Pike answered, "Sure, it will take about five seconds once I plug in the parameters. We just ran a study and discovered the reason we have solar radiation and will for millions of years. It is because the black hole that ate our star is bouncing back half of the original solar radiation. It's likely more than we would have received from our original star. I believe Earth humans have something similar they theorized called *hawking radiation*." Moments later, Pike spoke up again, "The image is being sent to your tablet, Jacob. Your armor should be able to download it in a few seconds."

"Thank you, as Vida given any updates?" Jacob asked.

Shaking his head, Pike responded, "No. She's been working non-stop, and I don't think she plans to rest until she finds a bone older than ten thousand years. Do you think the bigger creatures took over the continent about ten thousand years ago *because* the humans took so many of us when they first arrived? There are a million of us on the UTC factory planet. Do you think maybe we haven't found any older bones because they won't be there?"

"Pike, I hope you're wrong because this is the only clue for a dig location we have. I've never heard of any old communities or places we could find ancient evidence of our people. I think I remember someone back at the base said our planet had a series of volcanic eruptions at least a few hundred years before the humans arrived. Maybe it was all buried, and we just resettled on top. That must be where the ancient north land bridge memories come from. Our people would have taken refuge there for a short time during any eruptions. We are just going to have to test every bone we find and hope we can find one old enough. Make sure Vida rests every three days minimum. She becomes delirious if she doesn't rest at least some. Amelia said when they were searching for the fungus cure, on day four, she almost accidentally cut her own finger off. She had to force her to take a rest. You can tell her those are my orders,"

Jacob explained, knowing damn well she wasn't going to listen to Pike.

They would have to tranquilize Vida to force her to sit down, maybe with a tranquilizer gun. He chuckled, thinking about her reaction to something like that. The base would be thrown into chaos, and it would be questionable if there would be any survivors. Hopefully she will see reason.

A hand went under Jacob's rear to cup his firm ass, and it required all of his iron will to not jump. Slowly turning his focus around, he found Callum grinning and making a circle gesture with his pointed finger for Jacob to hang up with Pike.

Jacob brought his attention back to Pike who had a single eyebrow raised in confusion.

"I'll check back later," Jacob said as he hung up. "What are you doing?"

Grinning, Callum explained, "It's fucking hot when you start giving orders. I couldn't help it."

Rolling his eyes, Jacob said, "Let's get back. I'm ready to eat and get some rest."

"Too bad our tent is so close to everyone else's," Callum said suggestively.

Smiling Jacob asked, "When the hell has that ever stopped us? Just because we can speak now doesn't mean we have to get all bashful about sex. In fact, not much really needs to change."

Considering his words, Callum continued strolling through the trees a while before agreeing, "That's a good point. I don't think we should change anything now that we can speak. Our lives were great other than the silence and constant, existential fear."

Jacob scoffed, "Some things are bound to change. I'm

sure there are friendships that were lost and relationships that won't last because of it." His mind went straight to his best friend although his words meant something completely different. He was a lost friend and any form of the concept brought August to the forefront of his mind.

Much had changed since they had fought and gained their ability to speak on their planet, and one of the biggest changes was the loss of his closest friend. Guilt and pain laced through him as he grieved the loss of August. Jacob froze in place as his mind created images of the hell planet where his best friend had been imprisoned flashed through his mind. In his *heart*, the loss of his friend and the deaths of all the humans would never be worth it, but in his *mind*, it was all justified. As a whole he was a dichotomy, heart and mind forever at war.

Sometimes Jacob hated how logical his mind was. His heart never had enough time to heal because his head constantly moved on. When two kindred spirits meet and grow together, friends become siblings and blood ties are born. His head needed to give his heart a break, he decided as he realized August was so much more than a mere friend. He was a brother, and he was gone.

"I miss him too," Callum whispered as he leaned in and reached out for Jacob's hand.

As their hands folded together Jacob replied softly, "Oz will find him. Mercy won't let it go."

"You're right. She won't. Nothing will stop her, and I mean nothing. She sent me a message with some news while I was lying down. I guess she and Amelia are together now. I won't go into all the private details, but she said something about mind blowing sex and being treated like a queen. I'm happy for them. She ended her message saying how no matter how well things go with Amelia, her main goal is still to find August," Callum explained, carefully watching for Jacob's reaction.

Jacob tilted his head to the side and admitted, "I would have never guessed Amelia and Mercy would end up together."

"What? You really are oblivious. I knew Amelia had her eyes on Mercy within a month of her arrival. You should see how Amelia's face changes when Mercy strolls into the room. A light shines in her when Mercy is around, one that was absent before. That woman is in *love* and has been since she met Mercy. She was careful and respectful to her and August, but I could always tell." Callum peered off into the trees, thinking of all the times he watched Amelia perk up when Mercy could be heard approaching.

Furrowing his brow, Jacob said, "I know it's our way, but it seems so soon. I just wonder, could I move on that quickly? I know it's been plenty of time for our people. Didn't your mother move on to your father after just a few days when her first male companion was taken? It just feels like August was here yesterday. I hope we find him in time. The thought of losing him permanently, to never see him again-- ."

"Don't say that. We will find him. I can't promise what condition he will be in, but we will find him. I *know* we will," Callum quietly lied as much for himself as for Jacob.

Remembering Jacob's questions, Callum cleared his throat and answered, "It wasn't a few days later. My mother had my father at her house the same day her first love was discovered to be missing. I don't blame her. I understand it. Sometimes when you lose someone, it leaves such a substantial void in your life that you'll do just about anything to fill it, even if it's just a little. Love can become consuming; it can eat you whole, so when it's stripped away, you're left exposed and empty, desperate to feel something, *anything*."

Noticing Jacob's blank stare into the rustling leaves in the distance, Callum again lied, "We will find him. I swear we will."

As Callum found Jacob's loving eyes, he knew it was a slim chance they would ever see August again, but he would say it anyway. He would lie until his lie became true.

34

PLANET PORTUM - UTC COMMAND

This is odd, Amelia thought as she scrolled through the archive information. Raising her arm to access the holo-screen controls, she set up a connection to the server in her tablet.

Once connected, she began scrolling through the files on her tablet. The line read "Virus-636 dispersion capsule ready for launch," and it showed a long series of numbers. Reading them through a few times, she realized they were coordinates and a date. The more she dug into these files, the more she found integrating the human doctors' knowledge into her brain gave her an edge. She could not imagine how lost she would be had she not taken the information from Oz. The horrors of it still haunted her, but the knowledge was critical. It had been worth it, despite her initial thoughts.

Absently leaning her leg into the side of the table for balance, she asked the base computer, "Show me what happened at these coordinates and this date."

Through her suit's connection to the Iungo base computers, she was aiming for a way to tell the UTC server to find the information she was looking for. With her tablet in her hand, she pointed at the holo-screen with the lines of coordinates and the long date to select and search. A blinking light signaled the search had been completed, and she selected the option to show it on the screen. The row of search results populated on the screen, and she felt a hint of success because there would be no more combing and scanning files.

The screen on the computer server lit up, and it showed a small rocket landing on a rocky asteroid. Little arms extended from the rocket and drilled into the surface anchoring itself, sending dirt floating away from it.

Curiosity ruled and Amelia asked, "Where is this asteroid headed after the rocket was secured?"

No results. *Damnit. Well, that was worth a try*, she cursed. Onto the old fashion way, fast forward. She squinted looking for a way and found a little double arrow. She hesitantly touched the arrows, and the video began moving much faster.

The screen quickly zoomed through what seemed to be hundreds of thousands of years of space travel before the video slowed as the small asteroid neared a rocky planet with abundant water and flourishing plant life. The plants were all a pale indigo, and the atmosphere was a soft pastel peach. The video ended abruptly when the asteroid hit the ground, and she was left with more questions than answers, again.

"What the fuck does that mean? Where is the rest of the video? What the venom did those UTC fucks just do to that planet?" Amelia asked aloud, alone in her cabin on the ship.

A feminine voice from above her spoke, saying, "A First Human's empire level clearance code is needed to access further files on Virus-636."

Amelia knew the virus creating the barcodes on their DNA was not called Virus-636. It was called Virus-9716452. There were too many numbers between those two virus names. Questions burned through her like wildfire. *Why the hell would they have planted a virus and sent it to a planet with life? There are very few scenarios where it meant they were doing something to help that planet,* she thought as a sick feeling began snaking around her gut. She rubbed the side of her head where it was shorn short on the sides and pulled her straight hair from the tie it was in.

She shook her head, trying to clear it, and looked over at the lumps on either side of the bed. Curiosity again ruling her mind, she leaned away from the table and asked, "What are the mechanical ties for on the edges of the bed?

A video began on the wall showing an animation of the ship in space. It showed a human walking over and lying on the bed. They pulled the covers over their head and the tendrils emerged from the round lumps grasping all four corners and securing the sheet over the person. The person seemed to lift off the bed and float under the sheet.

These were anti-gravity beds? Gasping, she jumped up with excitement. She had to try it. Running across the room, she leapt onto the bed and crawled under the sheet. Pulling the corner to the edge of the lump, the tendrils emerged just like the video and grabbed the sheet corner. Once all four corners were secured, she felt herself go weightless. As her body lifted from the bed, she giggled uncontrollably. Her giggle turned into a full-blown laughter under the sheet as she floated weightlessly. She hadn't had much of a real childhood, and this moment was a slice of heaven for her.

"Mercy is going to love this!" she said to herself as she peeked out from the top of the sheet.

A faint knock sounded, stopped, and then sounded again. It was coming from the other side of the wall. It happened again, this time followed by a banging sound. Something was definitely going on next door in Oz's room. Considering everything that had happened recently, she probably needed to check on him. Reluctantly sliding from the zero gravity bed and onto the floor, she rose and grabbed her tablet to dial Oz.

After a few rings his face materialized, and he sharply asked, "What?"

Clearly he was in the shower, but he was also panting.

Amelia's face disappeared as instantly as it had appeared, and Oz chuckled as his gaze slid down to Jael, who had met his eyes with a smile between his legs. He tossed his tablet across the room, and it clattered into the corner.

"Are you sure you are up for this?" Oz asked.

Jael gave him a devious smile, "The pain killers are working great right now," before she opened her mouth to take him in. Closing his eyes, Oz leaned his head back, banging it against the wall as she slowly slid her mouth down. She pumped up and down a few times with her hand wrapped around the base causing a soft groan to fall from his lips. Jael slid her hand down around his softness and continued trailing her fingers further behind. Oz was already squirming and let out a groan as she grazed his back entrance.

"Spot's, uh, what?" is all he had time to ask before she slipped her wet finger in, causing his hips to thrust forward. Jael was fully prepared and moved with him. She had her left arm wrapped around his thigh. With a high pitched sing-song screech, Oz clenched his body as Jael hooked her finger forward and found what she was looking for.

The sound that left Oz was a mix of singing and screaming as Jael pressed her finger into the sensitive bundle of nerves and descended her mouth on him at the same time. His tail began slamming against the wall as his head tipped back as the deep clicks sounded in his throat. He was still making the sounds in his throat when he erupted. His body went stiff, and he couldn't take a breath as the release shot from him. A shaky moan left Oz as Jael finally pulled away, the evidence of his pleasure rolling down her chin.

Oz rolled onto the floor and lay face down in the shower stream as he caught his breath. Leaning over, Jael grabbed the soap to wash her hands. She took a soapy hand and slapped Oz on the rear, expecting him to react as usual.

He lay there motionless.

"Are you alive?" Jael asked as she gingerly poked his thigh with her toe.

"Who the fuck taught you that?" Oz muttered from his place, face down on the shower floor.

Jael sweetly answered, "Don't think for a second I haven't caught your hints about it when we connect."

Oz rolled on his side and groaned, "You didn't answer my question... and I think you emptied my nuts."

Tossing her head back, Jael laughed, "I knew you would like that little surprise."

"Like? Are you, what? I just found a whole new thing. I should have known when you said you were going to try something new earlier. You're not cracking, huh?" Oz asked as he closed his eyes.

Jael leaned over and squinted at the wall where the foggy clock on the bathroom wall was rolling to the next Roman numeral and explained, "We have fifteen minutes."

"Oh good, ten to lie here and five to shower and dress,"

Oz spoke in a serious tone while still face down on the shower floor.

He eventually rolled over onto his back and into the shower stream as Jael soaped up her body. He was in the way, so she reached over and poked his leg with her toe to move over so she could rinse.

He didn't move. Instead, he turned his face and put his hands up over his nose and eyes.

"Are you serious?" Jael asked skeptically.

"I am not moving. I don't think I could if I wanted to," Oz breathed.

Shaking her head, Jael put her foot on the other side of his head and rinsed herself off. All of the soap and suds from her body fell directly onto his face. When she stepped out of the stream, his hands flopped to his sides. He didn't move until she started to towel off.

By the time she was dressed and ready to return to work, Oz was just shuffling out of the shower with a towel around his waist. He dressed slowly and put his boots on even slower. Hanging his head between his legs after he slipped his boots on, he grunted, "We can't do that before I have a shift."

Bursting into laughter, Jael said, "I heard it was like the atomic bomb of orgasms. I guess they were right."

Popping his eyes up to meet hers, he blurted, "It was Callum."

With her eyes wide, Jael asked, "How the hell did you know?!"

"Ever since something about a cockroach and an atom bomb was brought up on our trip to bring Jacob sand, Callum has been referencing it randomly," Oz explained as he closed his eyes and held his head at a strange angle like he was trying to stretch.

"Let's go. I know the people who were trapped in the base want to see you before they travel back to their villages."

Oz nodded absently as he did his best to blink away the fog and rose to his feet. Jael followed as they exited the ship and stepped into the lift to head down to the garden. This time her nerves weren't as frazzled, and she was able to stand tall. When they lift chimed, she was relieved for the doors to open. Maybe with time even the chime won't drum up moments of terror, she hoped as she pushed away the dark thoughts for another time.

A crowd of Iungo who had been captured by the UTC and held at the base were all waiting for Oz and Jael in the garden. As they approached, Zoe joined them. Zoe climbed on top of one of the raised flower beds and loudly announced, "This is our President Oz and Jael."

The crowd watched silently with glittering eyes and faint smiles as Oz and Jael stood in front of them.

Smiling faintly at Jael first, Oz turned and addressed the gathered people, "I know you are eager to return home, but before you board the transport with Zoe, I wanted to speak to you personally. We desperately need volunteers to help us find our ancient ancestors to prove we were not created by the UTC. There are many other jobs needing to be filled in technology and development. If you are willing and able, please let Zoe know for instructions on how to reach our base and join. Our ability to keep our planet and our freedom rests on us. The hard work is far from over." Murmurs sounded among the smaller groups, and Oz was happy to see several nods and some smiles. Taking Jael's hand, Oz waved to the crowd, and they made their way toward the lift on the other side of the room.

Just as the doors opened and they stepped on, Zoe announced, "Group one from the north village line up here. We are working on placement homes, but we have no communication with them, so you're going to the Iungo base first. You won't be leaving until this evening so get comfortable. Anyone going to Serene to assist there, please form a group on the opposite side of the room. I will return and transport you in a few hours. Those going to Nemus to go home, please line up here. We will be leaving in twenty minutes..."

The doors shut before they could hear any more. The soft hum of the lift filled the silence. The doors opened quickly, and they emerged in the parking garage.

Pulling out his tablet, Oz selected a few options and watched the large doors as they opened. The cool air outside of the building caressed Jael's face, and she was reminded of how badly she needed such simple, raw things - fresh air, dirt under foot, and the aura's twirling in the distance along the horizon. The red cast on her face from the failed star was slightly warming, so even it offered comfort from the unnaturally rigid, cold concrete and metal buildings.

They were headed to the shipyard where Carter and Jacob's teams were unloading the jump engines from the back of the Iungo cargo transport. "Oh good, you're here. We've been working out the schematics, and we are ready to install them. We brought four so we can outfit two of the ships right away. The smaller vessel will take much longer so I'm assuming you want the first two engines installed in the bigger ship? I will need it brought over to the first bay in the hanger," Carter explained as he approached.

"I think we can use autopilot." Oz headed over to the first bay in the hanger. Jael followed behind as he neared a control panel and it scanned his face.

"Welcome, President Green," the feminine voice said.

He groaned before saying, "Engage autopilot and bring Iungo ship one to bay two for maintenance."

A tone sounded, and they could hear the walkway detach from the ship docked at the UTC command building behind them. In less than five minutes, the ship was overhead and pulling into the service bay. Oz watched as the ship came to a stop in front of them. The docking arms extended down to brace the ground before it came to a full stop.

Oz's com rang, and he answered it on his forearm. The holo-screen materialized with Amelia's blazing face. Her hair was down around her face, and her feral expression promised pain. "When was someone going to tell me you were moving the ship? I just rolled across my room. Can we also maybe make it a standard procedure to turn on the seatbelt sign before we take off?" Amelia vented with fury dripping from every word.

"I forgot you were in your room working on your tablet. Sorry, Amelia." Oz cringed and then hung up on her. Jael tapped Oz's shoulder as Amelia's face disappeared. He followed where she was pointing to the last of the soldiers boarding a ship to leave the planet. They were almost finished packing up the camps and loading all the soldiers. A corner of Oz's mouth tipped up, but his face melted and a brief, chilling silence fell over him.

"What's wrong?" Jael asked, worry sprouting with his abrupt change in demeanor.

Keeping his eyes on the soldiers leaving, he absently began feeling for the edge of his tablet. He pulled it from under his arm and began scrolling, "This is a *secret* planet. Aurelia had to sign special clearance forms to work here, secrecy agreements. I just had a realization about those UTC soldiers leaving."

"Wait, you don't mean..." Jael paused before finishing and her mouth dropped open. "Oh, Oz. I hope you're wrong," despair filled her eyes.

Pike's face materialized on the tablet as Oz said, "I need you to send a probe out right away. We need to see what's happening to the UTC soldiers when they reach the other end of the wormhole. Send out one of the new probes that can jump and follow the next ship."

"Done. Jacob's team has six they just completed. I'll send one right now and link you to the video with the sensor feed," Pike said right before his face disappeared, and Oz lowered his tablet.

A chime sounded, and he lifted his tablet to see the feed of the probe and they had already lined up at a nearby, small singularity. The round, almost bubble like entry point was just large enough for the ship to fit through. Oz watched as a ship filled with hundreds of soldiers started moving through the entrance point of the wormhole. After jumping, the probe attached itself to the hull of the next ship in line to pass through. The signal blurred briefly before it went black.

Discouraged, Oz looked over at Jael who put her hand on his arm to comfort him. The signal bounced back to life, and Oz lifted his tablet back up to watch. The ships emerged from the wormhole, and there were three imperial vessels waiting, just like the one they were currently fitting with two jump engines.

Oz looked over at Jael, "I guess that drop in signal was just the wormhole."

The probe jumped from the side of soldier transport and the view on the screen shifted. He could see from the angle the imperial ships as the probe latched onto the one in the center. A small vibration was picked up by the sensors, and Oz watched in horror as they attached magnetic missiles on the soldier transports, causing all of them to implode. Within seconds, the large ships containing just under a thousand soldiers were nothing but clumps of floating rubble. Tractor beams pulled the bundles of rubble toward the imperial ships where they concentrated laser beams and heated the remaining clumps of material into a ball of molten metal. Jael gasped and threw her hand over her mouth.

Oz dropped his arm, tapping the tablet on his hip twice as he found his words calling "Carter," as he watched the last transport take off for the wormhole.

His gut twisted as they slowly rose to break the atmosphere to join their fellow soldiers.

Carter approached quickly, "Yes? Is everything alright?"

"The UTC is killing all the soldiers on the other end of the wormhole. Their welcome home is death," Oz softly explained as Jael slid her arm through Oz's.

Carter stood stunned a moment and asked, "All of them?"

Oz lifted his tablet and saw as the second round was beginning. The fourth transport had lined up before the imperial ships as they waited for the last two transports to arrive through the wormhole. Readings showed the wormhole to be taking them to a remote and empty part of space.

Nodding, Oz swallowed the knot in his throat, "It looks like all of them except the commander." He put his tablet under his arm and counted to ninety before he lifted it again.

When he looked, Melior was in full view. The beautiful moon was lush with rivers snaking over the surface. A ring circled the planet shining a bright light on the dark side. It seemed to be absorbing light on the bright side with large fanned out panels, shifting its opened panels to catch more rays as the celestial body moved through space. The glittering lights of the sprawling cities filled the screen as the ship neared the planetary atmosphere.

The ships were heading to dock at a space station when Oz had enough and set his tablet down on a nearby table. He turned around and leaned against the table, running his hands over his face. Disgusted with humanity, Oz remembered an earlier discussion with Jael. "How are you okay after finding out you were created by the UTC? They are truly evil. It gutted me for it to even be a possibility for me to be a human created being, and you just took it in stride. I don't understand," Oz admitted.

She smiled softly and peered down at herself before replying, "I found out the truth. It's not what I wanted to hear, but it's my history, and it's a part of me. Questions I've had for my entire life about who my parents were are now answered. It also explains the odd DNA test I took back on Earth when I was eighteen. It showed an error three times before the company finally said they couldn't sequence my DNA. It was clearly because I wasn't related to anyone. The only thing that bothers me is what happened to me before I was two years old? Did the UTC or first humans do something to the babies who were not part of the report?"

"I don't know if we will ever find out, but we will look for the answers," Oz reassured her. Oz's tablet lit up with a message.

Amelia:

How do I get down from the ship without the dock? We need to head to the lab inside the base.

He shifted his gaze up and saw Amelia waving at him from the open door of the ship where the loading dock had been.

"Just jump!" he shouted with his hands cupped around his mouth.

Amelia rolled her eyes before leaping on top of a large truck parked in the service bay next to the ship. She jumped onto the floor from there. Oz and Jael met her halfway as she was clutching her tablet so hard Jael thought she could see the solid crystal body of the device bending.

"I found something. I think the UTC and the First Humans have a lot more dirty secrets than the one you just found out about. Carter already told me about the soldiers. This may be worse if I'm right, but I need your help to learn more." Oz and Jael quietly followed Amelia as she headed to the lab inside.

When they arrived Amelia turned and creased her brow before she spoke, "There is a virus I'm looking for called 636. It will be in one of these freezers on this wall."

Amelia began opening the freezer doors. Jael and Oz were behind her at the cabinets helping her search all the samples.

"I found it," Oz said as he reached in and plucked the little frosty vial from its place in a small cabinet freezer.

He handed it to Amelia, and she nodded before saying, "They are sending this virus to rocky worlds with life carried by small asteroids or missiles. They might be sending it other ways too. I don't know why yet, but I can't imagine it's good with the UTC or FH being involved."

"Fuck. What the hell did they do?" Oz asked as he watched Amelia put the virus tube in a small hole by the computer screen.

The feminine voice above announced, "Clearance required to access further files on virus."

She scowled as she realized this computer called the clearance and virus something different. This retched place had layers of secrets on top of their secrets. Oz took a step forward and let the computer scan his face. There was a quick green flash, and the computer popped up with a visual of the virus.

"Thank you. I'll update you when I have more details." Amelia already turned to start on the sequencing.

"Get yourself command clearance from Zoe when she is back," Oz instructed as he turned around to find Jael. When he did, she was staring at the table with the straps. She quietly ran her finger down the strap that had held her left arm. When she reached the end of the strap, her fingers wrapped around it one by one, and her knuckles went pale under her grasp.

35

PLANET ADURO - CLAUDIUS ROYAL PALACE

Just when August believed Livia was not coming, she burst through the doors and dismissed the older guard standing at the door with a look dripping with death. He slammed his body backward into the door behind him and scrambled down the hall. He admired her, how she took her pain and hammered it into a fortress instead of allowing it to burn her and charr her heart into something cruel, like many other royals from her world.

She slid her weary eyes around the room and approached the cell, slamming the key in the lock and turning it to let him free. As he walked out, she reached a hand out, and it grazed his arm, giving him a thrill that shot down his spine. This regal woman did things to him he could not explain.

When they reached the mat in the training room, Livia turned to him and began rattling off all she knew since their time could be limited. "Earlier I instructed the guard to stay outside the door so that we can fight privately. He has instructions to bang his staff on the door if we have any company. The doctor called me. Your skin looks healed. I wouldn't have known if he hadn't told me what happened. The Iris Queen brought at least twenty people from her court with her, but most of them stay in the gardens drunk. All of them are gathered there now playing some kind of drunken wing-power wrestling. Idiots. We should have enough time to catch up before I have to take you back. What did you find out?"

"Your father is selling off all of my people in two mines. There is some celebratory ball to welcome all the potential buyers. You should know, since those Iris guards beat and electrocuted me on their way out, I don't know how much training I can do."

She stopped in her tracks and turned away from him and said more to herself, "The king is selling off two whole mines worth of your people? He is closing two mines. Why?" After a moment of silent thought, she continued, "They must be declining in output. He probably thinks he can sustain the UTC demand with the others, but I know they can't add any extra work to their production. Your people would die after just weeks. They are already being pushed to the edge of their ability. We have to act now; we can't wait."

He nodded and replied, "The Iris want to buy us for some kind of games. Are the creatures they speak of a giant lizard beast with wicked teeth and claws?"

Livia's eyes widened, and she gulped before saying, "Yes, and feathers. The Iris love them. They're originally from one of the Sarter's planets, but when the UTC took the system from them, they didn't have time to take all their animals and people. They had to leave too quickly to save them from their fate in the UTC science and technology labs. The Sarter's people were the first to go, many were tortured and worked to death. The rest died in work camps. Most of the animals died off from the brutal scientific testing, but they were more careful with the cunning and calculated raptors. They quickly bred them into crazed bloodthirsty monsters by manipulating their DNA. Eventually they implanted them with control devices so they could be directed. The UTC love to show them off as a sign of their power.

"I've heard rumors the Sarters were devastated when they learned the perverse things done to their people and creatures. Many were said to be truly broken over the loss of the people they were forced to leave behind. They planned to strike against the UTC, but it never materialized. They have been reclusive ever since. They are the only threat the UTC and First Humans have. I don't see them as a threat. I see them as a debt."

"Can we connect soon so you can show me what all these beings look like? I keep hearing all these names, and so far, all I've seen are people who have giant bird wings and mouths full of fangs. I thought mine were bad," August trailed off sounding confused.

Livia finally cracked a smile and asked, "Can I give you more than just memories? Wait, did you say you had fangs?"

"I had four on top and four on the bottom. The physician at the processing center ground them down after they clipped my stinger off my tail and cauterized my claws," he explained as he kept his eyes on hers. "The connection is how I knew your language. I had been given the language from Jacob who got it from Oz, all through our connection."

"I didn't know your people ever had claws or stingers either. I bet the doctor is the only one who knows," she paused a moment to think. "Who are Oz and Jacob?" she finally asked.

"My people's President and Vice President. I was voted to be our General. They're also my closest friends." Guilt flooded him about not being there to help them back at the base on his home planet, and he closed his eyes, desperately hoping they had succeeded. They had been so close.

"You were your people's General?" Livia slowly asked, eyes wide with astonishment.

August met her eyes and asked, "Why is that so surprising?"

"When you were taken, your people were far enough into your rebellion to have elected officials?" Livia asked in clarification.

Nodding, his chest clenched as he told her, "We built rockets with missiles to take out the satellites. We were almost close to launch when I was taken. I had been in the woods and... and I just don't remember. I don't even really know if I was alone or not. I thought Merc..." He paused and squeezed his eyes shut as he tried to hold back his anguish. "I missed all of it. I have done next to nothing for my people. I left my best friends to fight without me, Mercy too. I left her and didn't even tell her the truth about how I felt. I thought I could make it work, but it wasn't right, we weren't right. I fucked everything up. Venom, I hope she wasn't with me when I was taken."

"After we take Aduro we can send a message to them. Do you know a reference point to find your planet?" Livia asked, avoiding asking about Mercy. She wasn't going anywhere near whoever she was.

August stared at her blankly, "I know exactly how to get there. My planet is tidally locked with the black hole in the center of our galaxy."

Livia's mouth dropped open, and she snapped, "There

has been a gamma radiation zone around our galaxy anchor for over a hundred thousand years. You are telling me your planet is *inside* the zone's boundaries? Do you understand what a gamma radiation zone is? How the fuck could anything survive on a planet that close to that pulsar being devoured by our anchor?"

"I don't know if it will help, but I know there is also brown dwarf on the other side of our planet."

Blinking and trying to comprehend how any of what August said was possible, Livia finally spoke after a long pause, "They use the brown dwarf and slingshot themselves to escape the anchor without burning up all their nav fuel. Section four of our spaceflight mock scenarios must have been based on your fucking system. They had it under our damn noses at the training facility. After that they're just opening a standard wormhole to the closest star system. A brown dwarf and a small rocky planet tidally bound to the anchor, they must be inside of the blazing fast orbit of the pulsars. No one is allowed close enough to do research. What if there are no gamma rays in the area at all? I heard a guard once talking about a rebellion sending a vessel to verify the legitimacy of the gamma radiation zone, but I never heard anything else about it. I assumed they probably died. I guess they may have been onto something."

"I don't know anything about that. I just know our sky is lit by auras. We don't have a star for light. I remember Jacob saying something to someone on his team about a massive magnetic field coming from the equator of our planet. There are no stars visible in our sky, so I don't know where any of the other stars are for reference. Oz and I talked about the brown dwarf, but that's all I know." August rubbed his brow as he spoke, his eyes focused on Livia.

Livia shifted her focus to the door, "We can talk more about it all later. Right now, we need to figure out how to disperse staffs to your people. I found several unopened boxes of them in a storage room under the palace. I have enough stashed in my transport for all the mines. I'll need a diversion to pass them out."

Leaning his head to the side and tipping his face down, August asked, "I'm not creating the diversion this time, right?"

"No, I'm sure something will come to me. The only other thing is I need to find out who my father invited to the ball and who is staying at the palace. Some of the guests will want to stay aboard their ships in orbit afterward. I need to find out if any have heavy weaponry. We can lock them out, but I don't want them firing on us or our staffed satellites. Lucas is attending. I don't know how much help I will be until I can drip his drink. I have a lot to do if we are going to make this happen before your people are shipped off."

August could feel her stress radiating towards him, "Take me back to the mine. I know you would rather me be here, but you have too much to do right now."

Livia stared at the floor and rubbed her head before agreeing, "Let's go. I need to load the staffs in my transport before anyone sees them."

August turned, and Livia followed close behind. When they reached the door, she opened it and nodded to the guard. It was the younger man, August's admirer. He opened the door and upon seeing August, he gasped and stumbled a bit before righting himself. Sliding his eyes to Livia, he sighed when she was oblivious and checking the hallway. August noticed how his eyes ran down Livia as she leaned around the corner.

He couldn't help himself and also admired Livia's round backside along with the guard. Before she took off down the hallway, August slid a single finger down the back of the guard's hand. He heard a sharp breath, but he didn't look back as the two briskly headed from the training room and down the long hallway to the transport pad.

As they passed through the garden, August turned his head and spotted several Iris with their wings spread out warming them in the sun. They were all admiring the view of the endless desert. He wondered if all people who evolved from birds were as awful as the Iris, or if it was just them.

One with brilliant emerald wings and canary yellow flowing hair saw August and called out, "Look it's that red one! I wonder if he will be part of the sale? Stop! I want to see this one!"

Livia pretended not to hear them, but whispered, "Hurry the fuck up!"

The two were nearly running by the time they reached the transport and Livia struck her transport controls with her fist once the door sealed shut. August kept his eyes on the spot she struck and could see a clear divot in the middle. He watched her hand, and it didn't have more than a trickle of blood running from it. She was much stronger than she led on.

"I didn't want them to see you again. They took much more of an interest in you than I thought they would. Fucking Yix will not shut up about you. That hissing bitch wants to do disgusting things to you before she sends you off to the games. It took everything not to leap over the table last night and rip her black pointed tongue out of her pretty mouth," Livia spat. She clenched her fist, and August patiently waited to see what she would say or do next, but she simply lay her hand out flat on her controls.

Smiling, August leaned back, "I think the brown-haired guard wants me too. Looks like everyone wants a little August."

Shaking her head in wonder, Livia narrowed her eyes at him. "Only you would make a joke at a time like this. Buckle up. I need to get back, so we need to make this as quick as possible."

Grabbing the harness, August secured himself in the back, and Livia took off like a rocket. He slammed back into his seat and struggling to keep his head up when she landed with a solid thud. She pulled her transport next to another strategically, placing it so that she could make it around the other transport with the box of staffs without being seen.

He reached up and rubbed his neck as Livia hopped out of the front seat. She went around to the back and slid the large box of staffs out. After pulling the heavy box to the storage door on the side, she made her way back to her transport. The side door slid open, and Livia grabbed him by the arm and yanked him out.

"I like it when you're rough," August whispered, and Livia gripped his arm harder.

Two guards snapped to attention by the doors and opened them both for Livia as she neared. She nodded as they passed and continued down the hall. August remembered one of them being the man named Felix, who eyed them suspiciously. When she heard the doors shut at the end of the hall, she held back and watched the two guards make their way up the stairs and out of sight.

Dropping her shoulders, she said, "I think those two are up to something. I have caught Felix watching me a few times in the last week. I don't know if he is onto me or just wants to fuck." August stopped in his tracks. *Over his fucking dead body would Felix fuck her.*

"You stupid demon, did you forget I'm still married, too?" Livia sighed.

"For now," he muttered. Her husband was going to die too, he thought. He rolled his eyes and kept moving as Livia guided him. Searching the hallway, he didn't see anyone. When they approached the door to the old dusty room, August shoved her through the door. She hit the ground stunned and glared up at him. He landed on top of her on the floor as the door slowly shut with a click.

Leaning down, he consumed her lips, kissing her deeply, sliding his tongue by hers, eliciting a soft moan from her. He couldn't hold back any longer at that sound, and he stripped her athletic pants off in one swift motion. He wanted a taste of her more than anything in the world.

Diving between her legs, August devoured her heat. His tongue was desperate to please her the way she deserved, and he licked her thoroughly. She began panting as he twirled his tongue around her most sensitive part and took it into his mouth, sucking and flicking her bud relentlessly before stopping and doing it again. Taking her to the edge over and over, Livia was dripping with sweat, and her shaking legs wrapped around August's head in a vise grip. Overwhelmed, when she finally broke the surface, it took biting her own forearm to keep from screaming in pleasure. The waves rocked her body as he lapped up her core.

Not waiting to catch her breath, Livia rolled over and pushed August back onto the dusty ground. Pulling his pants down while crawling on top of him, she settled over his length and brought herself down onto it. As she fully seated herself, she rocked her hips, and August groaned as he matched her rhythm. Pressing down with every roll of her hips, Livia knew exactly how to move to take August's breath away. Nearing the edge, he leaned his head back, and the deep clicks in his throat sounded before he released himself into her. His body quaked as he filled her.

Leaning down, Livia kissed August from his collarbone to his lips and whispered over them, "Demon, you have crawled under my skin and made yourself a home. You have possessed my body and soul. I belong to no one but you."

He took her face in his hands and kissed her again before they rose and dressed. Livia walked out first and signaled to August it was clear to move into the hall. Running by her, he tapped her behind and jogged off to join his people down in the mine.

Livia turned on her heels and went back to her transport. Just as she put her hand on the door at the end of the hallway, Felix whistled from the top of the stairs. "You seem to be leaving in a rush. What is all the hurry? You've only been here an hour," Felix said as he leaned on the rail, looking down at her.

Clearing her throat she responded, "I have work to do before the celebration tonight."

"I'm sure you do. It can wait a moment though, I need to speak with you, now," he demanded as he began taking the steps down to where she stood. With each step, he shifted his weight around and dropped down onto each stair with a lazy stomp. The sound echoed through the halls.

Her heart began racing right along with her mind. What could Felix possibly want other than to try to fuck her? His stance told her he was not asking for sex. Alarm spread like a wildfire inside of her as he neared.

Time seemed to stretch on forever as he descended the stairs. He tilted his head to her ear and whispered, "Let's speak outside."

Fear blossomed into terror as she walked behind him. He pressed the door open, and the two spilled out onto the landing pad. She had sparred with him before. She knew exactly what this man was capable of. He was almost as good as she was.

When the door clicked shut, Livia forced her eyes to look up at him, and she found him with a devious grin. He had been her close friend in the past, but she knew how cunning he could be. Bile rose in her throat, and she swallowed before she casually asked, "We are outside. What do you need to discuss?"

"You and the red bug seem to be spending a lot of time together. I've been watching you two closely. It almost seems like you enjoy one another's company. Livia, are you fucking him? Are you letting him eat your pussy like an insect eats trash? I can smell him on you. What would Lucas think? What would the king do if he found out? Fucking one of our fellow guards is one thing, but you chose the brainless bug?" Felix sneered at her.

Livia's heart was the only thing she could hear as Felix waited for her to respond. She took a deep breath, trying to think. Her brain spun in her head.

"You are fucking him, and you have nothing to say for yourself. Venus herself should strike you down for this, but she's not here, is she? I am. So, you can answer to me instead." Felix spoke with fury as he glared at her.

"Felix..." Livia started.

Felix cut her off saying, "Felix what? What Livia? What

the fuck could you possibly say for yourself? We are taking a little trip to see the King. Get in your transport."

Livia felt it then, the rail gun pointed at her gut. She would never survive being shot at that range in the belly, so she complied and made her way to her transport. Climbing in, she put her hand flat on the side of the seat by the door and pressed in slightly. It revealed the tip of a raw edge knife peeking out from a hole in the seat cover. As she climbed in, she twisted and slid her thumb to the edge of the seat. The end of the knife easily slid out as she sat down.

With her right hand now on the controls, she reached over with her left hand to shut the door. When she did, she quickly dropped her hand and slid the knife free. As she brought her left hand up to the controls, she slid the knife under her leg.

Felix latched his harness and slammed his door shut. Livia started the engine, and when she did, she flipped a switch with her pinky to turn on the engine fluid flush cycle. The transports all had the custom flushing pumps added to clean the sand out of the combustion chambers. Livia helped install them, so she knew the chemical they used to flush out the sand was corrosive and highly combustible. It skirt the edge of an explosive. She had less than sixty seconds to find a way out of the transport before the engine would become a ball of fire.

Settling her breath, she slid her eyes to Felix as the transport lifted off. As his gaze moved to meet hers, she turned the controls toward the palace. As she turned, she slid her left hand down and grasped the blade of the knife under her leg. In one swift motion, she tossed the knife from her left hand to her right and planted the knife into Felix's shoulder.

She aimed in her periphery and made sure she positioned the strike though the thick strap.

Felix screamed, "Fuck!"

As he reached his hand up to the wound, he cried out with anger and pain. "You stupid bitch!" Felix screeched as he desperately tried to pull the knife out.

Livia had imbedded the jagged knife through the thick harness strap and deep in between his ribs by his shoulder. Felix tore at the knife as the transport autopilot took over, and they slowly began to descend from the low altitude Livia had maintained. She kicked her door open, and smiling at Felix, she yelled over the wind, "I'm going to be king. Too bad you're going to miss it."

Livia leaped from the open door of the transport and hit the sand below with a grunt before rolling down the dune in a wave of sand. She raised her head just in time to see her transport hit the top of the dune and burst into flames.

Counting down from three, Livia put her fingers in her ears and braced for the first of two blasts. The explosion from the pump would have easily heated the inner fuel cell enough to set off the domino process needed to detonate the reserve power cells. She had to be sure Felix would not make it. She put her fingers in her ears for the second blast and shut her eyes. The ground shook with the explosion, and thick smoke barreled into the sky as sand pelted her face.

When the smoke cleared, enormous spires of glass stood splayed out from the sand. It was a snapshot of the explosion. The tall steaming pointed glass flared out around a mangled mess of metal in the center. She tilted her head allowing her eyes to fully scan the scene. It occurred to her the design she was seeing in the sand was the same design of the palace. The palace was the visual copy of what happened when high heat explosives detonate in this radioactive sand. She wondered if her ancestors had replicated it that way on purpose.

Looking back toward the mine, she calculated she was only a few minutes from the transport pad, so she started on her way. By the time she reached the door, three guards were rushing toward it. Sloppily dressed, all three had been off duty and were disoriented from sleep. One was still tucking in his shirt.

"What was that? We were down in the mine. Did you see what happened?" a guard with green eyes asked, obviously lying.

Another guard chimed in, "It sounded like a blast."

Behind them, Livia dusted sand off her shoulder before she explained, "I think the flush pump malfunctioned and engaged during flight. Felix was pinned by a piece of metal from the first blast. He couldn't release his harness in time. He's gone. I barely made it out in time."

The three guards stood stunned as Livia brushed by them and commanded, "I want the accident investigated immediately. I will stand guard, and I want everyone who is still asleep upstairs on it too. I want to make damn sure this was just an accident and someone didn't fuck with my transport."

The guards all shot one another concerned looks before scattering to do as Livia had ordered. With Felix out of the picture, Livia far outranked everyone. As she made her way down the hall slowly and waited until she heard the three run upstairs to tell the rest of the guards on shift what happened. As soon as she heard drawers opening and sinks turn on, she moved quickly. Whipping around, she sprinted for the door and over to the box of staffs. She grasped the edge and opened it. Inside there were bundles of staffs so she pulled out a few and bolted inside.

Once she reached the bunks, she slid the bundle under the first bed and ran back to the door to peek around the corner. The three guards were just leading the other five out the doors and toward the accident. When the door clicked shut, she ran toward the open door of the mine and straight down toward the first person digging.

"I need help passing out staffs. Hurry before the guards return. They are under the first bunk on the right. I need one staff slipped under each occupied mattress. We don't have long," Livia commanded as she neared a woman with golden skin and hair who looked back at her like she had lost her mind.

She didn't see August and had no idea where he went, but there was no time to find him. She looked around, frantically, trying to figure out what to say to make this woman trust her.

Huffing, Livia finally acknowledged the earned distrust, "I need you to trust me. I am working with August. I have staffs I stole from the palace. Please! I need your help passing them out!"

Understanding dawned on the woman, and she signaled to several other people who also heard Livia. She nodded to them and Livia filled with relief as all seven sprinted toward the bunks. As they flew past her to the door, Livia was astonished at their speed. Checking the hallway, Livia found it was clear and waved the group on toward the bunks. They smiled at her shyly or curiously as they ran by.

They went to work quickly and slipped a staff under each bunk as she stood watch. It was finished in a matter of minutes, and Livia kept watch as they all sprinted back into the mine. They resumed their work as the first guard came through the doors at the front of the mine and began heading down the hallway.

He approached Livia who was now leaning casually against the wall, "Other than a piece of melted metal that looks like it was lodged in Felix's shoulder, we couldn't find anything out of the ordinary. He was nothing but charred bones in the middle of cooling metal and a transport frame. There was nothing left of the engine or any of the pump to check for any errors. The computer log melted, and Felix's metal leg is bonded to what's left of the seat."

She had completely forgotten about that metal leg bone. Their doctor was good at hiding scars. It had been nearly invisible when Felix was an adult. Although they were supposed to be genetically resistant to radiation, Felix had bone cancer as a child in training. Instead of fighting the cancer and saving his bone, they simply replaced it with 3-D printed metal bones every year as he grew. A whisp of guilt blew through her as she peered up at the guard in front of her, waiting on an answer.

"I want a detailed report written up right away. Find me a new transport, and have it delivered before the end of my shift," Livia demanded, "You're dismissed."

36

PLANET PORTUM – DNA MISSION

J acob's tablet chimed, and he jogged to the rock it was on. When he picked it up and read the first of the message, he could feel his heart race.

Pike:

> Adrian's team found a site with some promising specimens. The bones at the top seem to be much older than anything you've uncovered with Juni's team. Vida is testing them now.

Jacob:

> I'll head that way.

Pike:

> Bring Juni. Adrian is coming back to the base. He just sent a message saying he is finished being stalked, and he's quitting. I have no idea what he's talking about. Can you ask his team when you get there?

Jacob:

> Sure.

Searching the clearing, Jacob found Callum who was busy eating, and he took a seat next to him on the grass. The moment his eyes met Callum's, his cheery demeanor disappeared. His eyes narrowed as he chewed his bite and swallowed.

"What?" Callum asked sharply.

"We have to go visit the other dig site." Jacob chose his words carefully as he considered scooting away from Callum.

With a look of frustration, Callum asked, "Why?"

"Adrian went back to the base," Jacob admitted flatly.

Glaring at him, pausing before his next bite, Callum asked, "*Why* did Adrian go back to the base?"

"He said something about a stalker..."

"Stop!" Callum threw up a hand.

Jacob closed his gaped mouth, and Callum swallowed before continuing.

"Are you saying we are walking into a potential situation, or did you even ask?" Callum asked before he took another bite.

After a long rough exhale, Jacob said, "Pike asked if we could bring Juni to lead the other team. We also need to investigate what this mysterious stalker is Adrian is talking about."

With his head leaned back, still chewing, Callum squeezed his eyes shut and grumbled, "Great. Here we go. I'm calling it now. There will be fuckery when we arrive." He roughly swallowed and didn't look back at Jacob who was already wondering if he should take Callum back to the base first. "Don't even think about it," Callum demanded as he watched Jacob's expression change.

"What?" Jacob asked, fully aware Callum had no way to know what he had been thinking.

"You are not taking me back to the base. No way in hell. We're trauma bonded, and I am not leaving your side," Callum explained before he shoved the last bite in his mouth.

With confusion written on his face, Jacob asked, "What? Callum, I don't think trauma bonded means what you think it means."

"We have a bond because of our shared trauma. Makes sense to me." Callum said as he wiped his plate off before sliding it back into his bag.

Shaking his head, Jacob explained, "A trauma bond is when an emotional bond arises from reoccurring abuse and reinforcement, oh, never mind."

Callum had already begun walking off toward the tent to gather his things.

"I'll grab your bag and Juni's. Let's get this over with," Callum threw over his shoulder right before he dipped his head to enter their tent.

Jacob turned and found Juni already standing behind him.

"We have to go..." Jacob started, but Juni cut him off.

With her eyes narrowed, Juni snapped, "Can that big grump not deal with this ghost-stalker himself? Why do I always have to pick up for him? Does the stalker even exist? Why does my left little toe get cramps when I cough? Who knows if any of these questions will ever be answered?"

"Um? Alright. You just got promoted. Congratulations!" Jacob said with a beaming smile, hoping it appeased Juni enough to not razz him for the next few days.

With a grin slowly spreading on her kind face, she tipped her head, "Thank you."

Jacob loosed a long breath, and they met Callum who was slipping his helmet on and opening the visor next to the transport.

As Juni climbed in the back and they all strapped in, Juni picked up her tablet and read the message, "Pike said he will send the transport once Adrian arrives in it. The team only has maybe a day left here. They haven't found any bones in hours. Oh, am I supposed to be using our titles? It's Colonel Pike, right?"

"Yes, it's Colonel Pike, and no, please don't call me vice president. Titles are not my favorite. It's too strange without picking last names. It might be weird with last names too. I don't know." Jacob furrowed his brow at the thought.

Callum chimed in, "Maybe we should do that? Pick last names? When we find the evidence, we're looking for, don't we need to bring it to the UTC Science and Technology space station? Anyone going will probably need a full name, right?"

Before slipping his helmet on, Jacob admitted, "Shit, you're right. Who knew naming everything would be so arduous. I know we have far too many people for just first names. Names are much more stressful than I anticipated."

Once everyone secured their helmets, they lifted off, and Jacob leaned over to Callum and offered, "How about you pick our last name? You're better at that sort of thing than I am."

Jacob could tell Callum was beaming as he bashfully accepted, "Okay. I have to be honest though, I'm not sure how you are so smart but can't figure out what to name yourself. I already have one picked out. I like Parker. It's simple and sounds good with our names."

Flying much smoother this time and smiling at Callum's comment, Jacob flew closer to the treetops as they headed to the red dot on the map. The location was in the south on the continent where there were no villages anywhere close. A stone in the pit of his stomach grew as they neared the dig site and by the time he landed, the stone had turned to lead. It weighed heavily on him as he surveyed the locale, and he hoped it was just nerves.

Callum pulled his helmet off and looked around the clearing, people were leaping in and out of the abandoned giant centipede hole as drones were reloaded. Everything seemed perfectly normal.

The breeze blew, warm and calm, too calm. Something was not right. He looked over at Jacob and it was obvious he wasn't the only one feeling unsettled. The mix of pine and palm trees all around towered above them in an ominous circle, seeming to lean in on them.

Cautiously searching between the trees, Juni spoke quietly, "I don't like this either, but we need to get it over with."

After a few more attentive steps, Juni slowly stopped and asked, "Giant centipedes are just scavengers, right?"

Eying Jacob for confirmation, Callum asked, "I think so?"

Jacob did not know, and the two clearly read his uncertainty from his expression. Shaking his head, Callum followed Jacob and Juni to the cave entrance. It was much wider than the last cave, and Callum halted when a foul, yet curious, scent hit his nose. It wrapped around his senses like a lasso. The smell drew up a bubbling sensation. It wasn't good, but something was underneath, another layer. He couldn't place it, but maybe another whiff and he could tell. Was it a flower?

Carefully surveying the area, Callum sniffed the air again. It was coming from his right, somewhere in the woods. He drew in another deep breath and knew he was closer, so he kept going. It was somewhere out here, and he *had* to find it. The scent just kept growing stronger. The sickly sweet odor seeming to draw him in like a fly to honey.

A rush of air blew by Callum as he plummeted into the opening of a different cave. He landed with a small splash followed by the gut wrenching scent of decay. Terror filled him when he found himself knee deep in muck. He knew exactly where he was, and he really fucked up this time. He was in the den of a giant centipede. He should have known they would have luring scents and traps. No wonder so many bones were found in the old tunnels. Telling himself to breathe, he started looking around for a way out.

As his eyes surveyed the thick sludge, they caught on a strange, curled shape. He waded over and slid his finger under it and lifted it up out of the goop. It splashed into the sloppy mess as it slid from Callum's fingers. He looked down in horror.

It was a tail from one of his kind, and blue blood still seeped out. As he moved his leg, he felt something brush against it and froze. Forcing himself to still, he peered up and saw the root of a tree protruding just above his head. With a deep breath, he gritted his teeth and stepped on whatever was floating next to him for good grip on the root.

Once he pulled himself onto the root and over the side of the cavern opening, he searched the water to see what he had used to step on. The freshly dead body of a man floated to the surface with a leg missing and half of his torso torn away. His entrails spilled out of the gaping hole in his side. Callum gagged and scrambled to his feet as he heard the first rustle of leaves from the woods behind him. He knew what the rustle behind him meant, and this was going to be a run for his life. Without another thought, he shot out of the cave.

Sprinting through the woods, Callum's heart pounded as thoughts of death gripped their bony fingers around his throat. He let out a blood-curdling scream as he saw how quickly the bright sunny yellow centipede was gaining on him. Its big black eyes zeroed in while its yellow-orange legs moved seamlessly between the trees. Its body defied understanding as it slithered through narrow passes, keeping up with Callum.

As he pounded the ground desperately, he could see Jacob's face materialize on his forearm, so he released a high pitched, "People eating centipede! It's fucking chasing me!"

Jacob's face disappeared just as Callum could see the edge of the trees. Leaping into the clearing, Callum soared right over two tents just as the massive beast crashed into the campsite. It leaned up and rolled its body around before slamming it back down, causing the ground to quake beneath them.

Three of their people charged the beast with blazing plasma swords as Jacob ran toward Callum to toss him a helmet. Once he was on his feet and his helmet secured, Callum followed suit as Jacob pulled his plasma sword from his belt and rounded on the transport sized centipede. Two of their people had already vaulted onto its head, and one of them was hugging its antennae as the creature tried to shake them off. As its head thrashed back and forth, the other man couldn't find a place to hang on. He was tossed off, only to be gruesomely speared by the centipede's sharp pointed leg. Blue blood sprayed onto the bright yellow leg, turning it a sickly green.

A woman jumped onto its back and plunged her plasma sword into its thick, waxy flesh. It flailed its head around, sending her to the ground in front of its face. In one swoop, the monster bent its head forward with its mouth open and devoured the woman whole. Her plasma sword fell to the ground as she was sucked inside of its mouth. Just as she disappeared, Jacob recognized the way she held her hands out, and he realized who had just been eaten alive.

"Fuck! That was Juni!" Jacob yelled into the helmet comms.

Without a second thought, Callum and Jacob screamed as they both charged with their plasma swords lifted. Three people attacked the other end of the wriggling monster as Jacob and Callum landed on its back near what would be its shoulders.

Over the comms someone in a deep voice yelled, "Get to the first segment! Cut its head off!" The three people who had just landed on its back sprinted and struggled up the body of the beast as it fought to shake them off. One of the three fell to the ground followed by a sickening crunch.

Callum plunged his sword into the back of the beast as he reached for his knife. Jacob understood right away and retrieved his own knife. The knife would come in handy if one of them began to slide off the slick waxy skin. The bucking, swinging, and waves of sword like legs continued as they all slowly made their way to the creature's neck. Another soldier was knocked off as four more vaulted on its back behind Callum and Jacob. A scream erupted from the ground as the one who was knocked off was impaled in the chest by one of the legs.

Jacob clawed up to the first segment, slamming his knife down into the crease to anchor him. The centipede slammed its body onto the ground, forcing its face down, and Jacob lost his balance, crashing straight over its head.

Screaming in his helmet, Callum watched helplessly as it swung its head back up and Jacob was slurped into its awaiting, open mouth.

"OH, HELL NO!" Callum screamed into his helmet as he dove for the first segment of the beast where Jacob had been just seconds before.

The creature swung its head further back as Jacob slid down its throat, giving Callum just enough time to anchor himself with his knife so he wasn't thrown off. As its head came crashing down, Callum planted his feet on its first segment gap. He thrust his plasma sword in and pulled it across the fleshy gap, forcing it down as hard as he could.

The sword sliced through the beast like a hot knife through butter, and Callum used his body weight to continue to force the sword along between the segments of the centipede. He slid off the side and shoved the sword in deeper. By the time his feet hit the ground, the beast convulsed in its last few moments of life.

Panting inside his helmet, Callum yelled out into the comms, "We need to cut our people out before the stomach acid burns through their suits!"

Six of the remaining team members aggressively hacked at the beast along with Callum. When they were nearly halfway through the side with their plasma swords, he gasped as he spoke, "You and I will keep digging without knives, you others keep slicing and find Juni." Callum sliced away until he felt something hard under his hand. He carefully ran the knife along the hard surface and a booted foot emerged from the cut in the peach, veiny organ. In a flurry of yanking and ripping away centipede flesh, Callum opened a big enough hole to pull Jacob through. Once he was carried away from the flayed beast, Callum pulled Jacob's helmet off and checked his breathing. His eyes fluttered open, and he gave Callum an odd look. "Open the visor," Callum instructed into his helmet and the visor slipped up. Relief washed over Jacob and he dropped his head back down onto the ground. "Are you OK?" Callum asked. Taking some slow breaths, Jacob blinked, and nodded slowly, so Callum jumped up and ran toward the team still hacking away at the flesh of the monster.

His plasma sword buzzed to life as he approached and went to work on the next segment. About a quarter of the way through the entrails, someone over the comms spoke, "I got her. No life signs." Callum ran up as Juni slid from what seemed to be the stomach of the centipede. Tossing away his helmet, Callum rushed to her side and began pulling off her helmet. He searched closely for signs of life, checking her breathing, nothing. Panic filled him as he felt her neck for a pulse, again, nothing.

"No, no!" Callum yelled as he pulled on Juni's armor around her neck to loosen it.

The rest of the team jumped into action, and one person pulled her armor off as another began chest compressions. Callum hastily yanked her armor off her arm and hand. He had to try whatever he could to save her. The idea of losing Juni was inconceivable in that moment.

Slapping his hand against hers, he initiated the connection. At first when he connected with her nerve, he found nothing, so he tried to send another signal to initiate it again. Nothing. Devastation gripped his heart as the woman doing chest compressions slowed and finally stopped. *She is gone.*

"No, she can't die! No!" Callum yelled as fury filled him.

He tried again to initiate the connection with Juni, but this time, he pushed hard. Instead of a just spark, Callum shoved his life force down the connection and into Juni. All he could think was how she deserved better than this. As his energy faded, the woman realized what he was doing and resumed chest compressions.

As Callum sacrificed his cerebral energy, he prayed and begged the creator to not let Juni die. The color in his vision dulled and slowly drained away. He kept pushing anyway, knowing he was giving her more than he could spare. He would keep pushing until he slipped into unconsciousness. As Callum's eyes shut and his strength waned, he whispered, "Please, Juni, come back. You have to come back."

He slumped over, and his hand slipped away from Juni's just as Jacob stumbled up and kneeled by Callum. Jacob reached down and took his hand and set it down gently on his chest. He knew what Callum had tried, and his heart twisted in his chest at the gesture. He wasn't sure it was of any use. She may have had internal injuries that were too great. He ran his hand down Callum's cheek and whispered, "You selfless, beautiful soul. This is why I fell in love with you."

With his eyes still shut and with what little energy he had left, Callum breathed, "She can't be gone. We've lost too many already."

After checking her pulse one last time, the chest compressions on Juni stopped, and Jacob lay his hand on her leg as he studied her face. Despair filled him, and he was overwhelmed with grief at her lifeless expression. She was so young. It wasn't fair. The rest of the team rose and walked away to salvage what was left of the camp and collect the dead.

Jacob moved closer to Juni and reached over to take her hand. When his skin touched hers, he found it still as warm as when she was alive. She was always the one person who could soften even the hardest carapace. Tears sprouted in his eyes as he held her small hand to his chest. His eyes closed, and the tears fell down his cheeks in little rivers.

Just as the sorrow filled his soul, through his tears, he swore he saw Juni's eyelash flutter. She wasn't breathing, and there was no pulse, but... Jacob began staring at her eyes an inch from her face when he saw it again. Her eyelash fluttered. *Are her nerves still active?*

Cocking his head to the side he reached his hand down against Juni's neck and felt for a pulse. Nothing. Nothing. He waited.

There it was. One, single faint beat.

Jacob threw his head up and yelled at the team, "Someone catch some big bugs, Juni's alive!" He leaned up and ripped at his armor to pull it down. Slipping his arm out, he initiated a connection with Juni. Following what he saw Callum do, he shoved his life force down the connection. As he slumped over, and his focus faded, he finally saw the glorious movement of Juni's chest as she took a shallow breath. His eyes closed just as he heard her gasp.

37

PLANET PORTUM - UTC COMMAND

"Who is going?" Amelia asked as Mercy came up behind her.

Looking down at his tablet, Carter read, "Oz, Jael, Amelia, Mercy, Zoe, Aurelia, Kagnus, Mira, and myself."

"Good. I requested some time off for Hazel. I think it's best if she returns to base. She is having a hard time coping with the loss of her brother," Amelia explained.

Carter nodded, "I think that's best."

From the opening doors of the lift, Oz walked in with Jael and Zoe and ordered, "Everyone needs to gear up. We leave in five minutes."

Turning to Zoe, he glared as he asked, "Why did you make my last name Green?"

Astounded, Zoe sharply snapped, "Are you fucking serious? Jael's last name is Green." She scoffed under her breath and snarled her lip as she asked, "What the fuck else was I going to enter in?"

"Just asking," Oz said as he threw up his hands. He

would just deal with the awkwardness. He knew Zoe prob-ably needed a break, but they didn't have time for that. She had been working around the clock and hadn't rested in days. He would mess with her later. If he kept it up now, he was bound to piss her off again.

One by one, they passed over the short walkway to the ship from the balcony in the former UTC command center. "I've been thinking, I like the last name Mills. There was a mill next door to my mother's house as a child. She worked there refining grain for the village," Amelia explained to Mercy as they stepped aboard last, intending to head to their room.

Grinning, Mercy agreed, "I love that last name."

They all filed onto the bridge of the ship. Carter, Zoe, and Amelia found a place at the control stations, and Oz made his way to the captain's seat. Amelia began sifting through the controls at the monitoring station while Zoe familiarized herself with the navigation and ship systems. They had reviewed and learned their own controls, and now that it was in front of them, they grasped the necessary procedures within minutes.

"Carter, please send a message to the lower decks that we will be leaving in less than five minutes. After that I need you to go down to the engine room. Take Mira with you. She connected with one of Jacob's team and will run engineering for this trip. When Dion and Wynn join you down there, please have them keep an eye on the coolant lines circling the radiation emitters. I heard they like to come loose, and we can't risk overheating mid jump," Oz said as he scrolled through the pre-launch checks.

Carter adjusted a few settings on his station and asked,

"If I am going to the engine room, who do you want to replace my position at weapons?"

"Is Mercy trained for the position?" Oz asked.

Carter thought and replied, "I don't think so. That's not a problem. I'll connect with her. I'll stop by deck three and have her come up to the bridge afterward."

"Send Jael and Aurelia up. I want Kagnus on the bridge when we jump in case we need navigation assistance," Oz threw over his shoulder as Carter walked out.

Within a few minutes Aurelia, Jael, Kagnus, and Mercy walked in. Kagnus, Jael, and Aurelia all stood around Oz as Mercy found her place at the weapons and tactical station. Peeking over at what Zoe was doing, Mercy asked her, "Shouldn't you be on weapons and tactical?"

Grinning with pride, she replied, "We did a little simulation test among our highest ranking officers, and I was off the charts for my spatial intelligence."

"Of course you did. I'm glad you're driving." Mercy refocused on her controls with a surprised smile.

The conversation between Oz, Jael, Kagnus, and Aurelia stopped, and Oz commanded, "Zoe, I'm sending you some coordinates. Please share your station controls with Carter's tablet. The option should be in the left corner of your control panel. I want you to use navigation control thrusters for some practice before we break the upper atmosphere."

"I see it. Coordinates have been entered, and engines are warming up. As soon as we are at altitude, I'll inform you when we are ready to jump," Zoe reported as she poked away at the controls.

Several seats rose from the floor, one for each person, right before the ship lifted from the ground. They matched the matte metallic color of the floors of the ship with a cold, dull shine. The seats produced travel harnesses from the inner corners. Surprisingly cushioned, the seat continuously adjusted with their bodies, even their tails, they shifted around. When everyone was strapped in, the green light lit up on Zoe's control panel. She pressed it, and they felt the ship heading in the direction of the jump launch coordinates. As the ship gained momentum, the seat absorbed all the gravitational forces traveling through their bodies. Before they reached the atmosphere, the ship began traveling at speeds which should have caused them to lose consciousness, but as long as they kept their limbs within the bounds of the seat, they could move freely. The moment the ship broke the atmosphere, they felt the sensation of the false gravity take hold and begin pulling them to the floor. A few of them had a small static spark shine under their boots as the connection was made.

Under his breath Oz whispered, "That was so much better than I imagined."

"What?" Jael asked next to him.

"Oh, I thought the false gravity would be uncomfortable, but it's oddly similar to real gravity. The floor pulls on us with a slight electric charge. It is fascinating how little energy it requires. Most of the time, life support will fail before gravity will, if we lose power, according to the manual," Oz explained.

"You read the manual? Who does that? It was invented over two hundred thousand years ago by accident. Someone had charged the ancient style metal magnetic floors of a ship and someone without their mag boots on hit the ground. It's common knowledge in the galactic center," Kagnus laughed in her usual gruff way after butting into Jael and Oz's discussion.

Grinning like she just discovered the taste of sugar, Jael said, "That's amazing. I can't believe no one in the known galaxy had come up with an EM engine design like mine yet."

"There was intel a while back that the Sarters had finally figured out how to jump, but there is no telling if that was true or not. It didn't come from a reliable source. There have always been rumors of the Sarters, but rarely anything comes from it. The UTC Science and Technology space station is more focused on defense and making rich people more comfortable or live longer. They don't care about true advancement. There are few massive discoveries that have been found on purpose. Society in the bigger systems runs on profit, not progress. The only central galactic empire who cares about progress is the Sarters. Their galactic kingdom is almost the size of the UTC's, but because they're not obsessed with capital, their empire is not nearly as wealthy on the surface," Kagnus explained.

"Are there other galactic kingdoms and empires besides just in the center?" Oz asked.

Kagnus considered the information for a moment before saying, "Not in the center. There are a few galactic spiral kingdoms, empires, colonies, and collectives, but most life is concentrated here. There used to be many here in the galactic center when the Sarters reigned. The Sarters still allow their remaining planets to govern themselves within reason, but they changed after the Great War and now usually require ultimate control for their protection and assistance.

"The UTC is not that way. They took over many kingdoms and governments controlling different systems, especially in the last hundred thousand years. They bled them dry. It was usually done by covertly starting interplanetary conflicts and requiring repayment contracts for aid. Usually, the aid came at the steep cost of the planet's natural resources. Over time, the UTC became so large and powerful, no one could oppose them. No one has traveled outside of the galaxy and explored other galactic centers because our wormholes don't reach that far, but for this galactic center? It's just the first human controlled empire and the Sarter's kingdom." Finding her words, she continued, "There are likely many hidden worlds and civilizations because of the First Human's and UTC's actions, but I doubt they will ever make themselves known."

Oz nodded right as Zoe announced, "We are ready to jump."

"Inform Carter and then start the countdown," Oz ordered as he reviewed the controls and familiarized himself as best as he could.

Zoe sent the update down to Carter in engineering, and when he received it, he slid his eyes down to his tablet to read off the entered coordinates. He had been studying the star charts and major commuting space highways that remained bustling. When he read the coordinates, something seemed familiar, too familiar.

The coordinates they entered would be sending them directly into the middle of one of the light speed highways. The little light in the corner was already counting down to one by the time his brain finished the calculation. His eyes went wide as his heart jumped to his throat. They were jumping directly into a lightspeed highway. It was too late.

A high pitched, blood-curdling scream left Carter as the ship blinked into nothing and re-appeared in the middle of the highway. Still mid scream, he flew to the controls at his side and typed in new coordinates as quickly as his hands could move. The ship made an emergency jump with his engine override, just as the proximity sirens began blaring overhead.

The computer announced, "Collision eminent."

They blinked out of existence and back into it in a fraction of a second, just above the highway.

Oz's face materialized over Carter's tablet with a look of terror plastered all over it. "What the fuck just happened?!" Oz screeched.

Clearing his aching throat, Carter grumbled, "We accidentally jumped into a light speed highway, so I made an emergency override."

With a stunned expression, Oz asked, "Can you, um, come back up to the bridge?"

"On my way," Carter answered as Oz's face disappeared.

Carter surveyed the engineering room, at all the blinking lights and pipes running in various directions around the freshly installed engines. Steam wafted from the engines cooling system, but the EM drive seemed to have worked perfectly.

After the short trip up the lift to the bridge, he walked in and Oz asked, "The sirens were blaring on the bridge for less than three full seconds. How did you know? How did you do it?"

"I had been studying the star charts and the light speed highways between systems. I did the calculations. I knew the moment before we jumped, so I just moved as fast as possible afterward," Carter explained as he found a place next to Zoe.

The entire room remained silent for several moments before Zoe quietly announced, "Our star charts are correctly aligned and calibrated, and we have accurate coordinates to the nearest Sarter's border port station entered."

After peering back at Carter and receiving a nod, Oz turned to face forward. "Let's go."

The countdown on the corner of the holo-screen in front of them began and when the seconds were up, the ship shot into nothingness before reappearing mere miles from the Sarter's port station. The station was the size of a moon. It was made of connected and stacked rings rotating with thousands of different sizes and shapes of ships jutting out from docking bays. Ships docked, undocked, and traveled all around them in small, organized streams.

Oz angled his head to the side and squinted his eyes trying to make sense of what he saw. Inside of the station seemed to be an oblong shaped moon, or was it a block of ice?

"What's in the center of the station?" Oz absently asked, unable to tear his eyes away as it seemed to shimmer from inside the rings.

It shone with bright stars all around, making it clear why this was a popular trading system. Several lifeless planets with no atmosphere spun around a dead star in the center of the system, and the station was halfway between two mostly baren rocky planets. Only small port buildings dotted the surface, according to the holo-map projecting from the viewscreen.

Kagnus responded, "It's water ice, and it's moon sized. They towed that big rock of ice from an asteroid belt circling this ancient trading system and made it into their perishable food market. They sealed it and installed gravity floors. It was much cheaper than building a space station freezer market.

This is one of the ways the Starter kingdom is far superior. They consider the environment and creatively design around it. I've never seen this station, but the old rumors made it seem as if it was a true wonder. By the look of it, they were right. With over ten major stars clusters in such high proximity to this area, the station glitters in all the points of light."

Confused, Oz asked, "Why would they need such a large frozen food market?"

With a sly grin, Kagnus was a little too pleased to explain. "They have some of the best meat in the galaxy. Why do you think all their creatures left behind on Emendo died off so fast? After the experiments, they would eat them."

Oz grimaced as he asked, "You mean the Sarters raise and kill the creatures on their planet and sell the meat?"

"They don't raise anything. Their world is still almost completely wild. They hunt all the meat. They are an ancient race, much older than any other. Their origin planet has a perfect yellow star and several hot gas giants orbiting near their rocky home world. They claim to have never had an extinction event because of the protection of the gas giants. They have a second sister planet of the same size which they terraformed and colonized about ten million years ago, and that's where most of their general population lives now. Both planets are equally magnificent with most of the land surface covered in dense forests. I don't know much more. I've only met one person in all my life who had visited their home world."

Leaning over to Jael, Oz said, "They are evolved from creatures like the dinosaurs on your planet. We found a few files on them."

"Oh! What?! Are we going to see real life dinosaurs?!" Jael screeched as she sat up straight in her seat.

Her brow dropped low as Kagnus scoffed, "If that's what you call them. They're scaled and feathered reptiles to us."

As they headed in toward an open dock, a warning message appeared from the station and a male voice ordered, "Your vessel is in the Sarter's kingdom territory illegally. You are violating galactic center law. Turn around, or risk being fired upon."

"Zoe, send them a visual feed of our bridge, please?" Oz asked with a smirk.

The warning alarm stopped, and the red blinking light went away before a feminine voice curiously asked, "Identify yourself at once. What is this about?"

"We are the Iungo people, and I am President Green. We request a formal audience with the Sarter's queen," Oz stated confidently.

"Hold for instructions, position." the female voice responded.

After several moments of suspense, the voice relayed, "Please dock on ring 4, bay 13-47. Your vessel will be locked into the bay, and you will require pre-authorization to leave port. Border Port Sixty Three prohibited items include: UTC issue magnetic charges, First Human implanted surveillance technology, Makro's poison ivy seeds, and any form of Iris unregistered liquor. Anyone concealing and caught with this contraband will be charged, sentenced, and subjected to legal imprisonment. If your vessel contains any prohibited items, please inform your bay manager after docking for further instruction."

Relief washed over Oz and he leaned back in his seat as he directed, "Okay, Zoe. Pull us in."

Zoe eased the ship toward the blinking red square on the screen and steered them into the bay. When the bay doors locked and the walkway connected, they rose from their seats and all filed in a line behind Oz.

The doors at the end slid open and a reptilian man in flowing, bright colored garments and a swinging tail stood at the door with a smile. "I'm afraid I am a bit speechless. Oh, who am I kidding? No, I'm not. I am dying to know why a bunch of supposed UTC manufactured insect beings, claiming to be the Iungo people, just showed up in one of the UTC's finest royal imperial ships. I would also love to know how you popped up without detection, but I'm sure that will cost a little something to learn about," the reptilian man purred, maintaining his wide smile of wonder.

The man was several inches taller than Oz. His large eyes with brilliant lemon irises and a jagged vertical pupil center shone with intrigue. His pale brown skin had a verdant undertone and seemed to be smooth, other than some scaled ridges on his brow bone. His hair was a very neutral, mid-tone brown, but seem to be iridescent in the light. He had a kind, oval face, a small nose consisting of nothing much more than two nostrils and a slightly raised area from the tip of his nostrils to his brow. He held out his four fingered hands with claws at the tips in a welcoming gesture.

Oz noticed the man's mouth full of sharp teeth and smiled back showing his own fangs as he greeted the reptilian man, "I am President Green, and we just reclaimed our planet from the UTC. We need to speak with your queen as soon as possible."

"I'm Ref. I've already sent the royal palace a message. I did it as soon as you showed up on the view screen in station security and you weren't human. I should be hearing something any moment. You look a little different than any of your kind I've ever seen before," He shook his shoulders slightly in excitement with dangling jewelry sparkling as he moved.

"We have several of the prohibited items. What do we need to do with them?" Oz asked.

"Oh, right. This situation is odd, so I am leaving that up to the palace to decide. We put shields on the station and yours were down, so we locked down your weapon systems. That ship has enough firepower to collapse six stations," Ref noted with a glimmer of stress twinkling in his eye.

Oz again saw the reptilian man's tail swinging behind him. It made a strange, twirling motion, and he wondered if it was a sign of nervousness. A loud ding sounded from his handheld device, and he read aloud, "The palace said to secure and lock down your vessel. The palace liaison will be here soon with his guard. Oh good, good. You are to be treated as special guests. How thrilling! And to think, I almost had this week off for vacation."

A relief Oz had never known blossomed in his gut. Maybe it was just the first time he felt genuine hope about their freedom, he wasn't sure. What he knew was the reptilian people had some interesting hair. Even with everything going on, his curiosity somehow still won out. Without being too obvious, he inched closer to Ref. His hair was nothing like he had ever seen, and he couldn't wait to inspect it for himself. He swore it was just brown, but every time he moved there were an array of color shining on the man's strands.

Seven reptilian people of various skin tones of green,

brown, and beige approached. The most ornately dressed of the group strode to Oz and lifted their palm to him before lowering it. They all had a wide beaming grins and nothing but fangs after their front teeth just like Ref. Their tails swayed back-and-forth leisurely behind them. The lead-person wore gold jewels on every finger and large, long golden and platinum chains with gemstones encrusted swirling designs on the pendants. Their impossibly light garments flowed as if immersed in a body of calm water. These people dripped with elegance.

In a deep gravelly voice, the lead person straightened his skirts before saying, "My name is Mr. Zillien Pinth of the third house of Nimroute. I prefer Zill. I am the Queen's liaison. I presume you are President Green?"

"Yes," Oz nodded.

"Good, follow me. You and your crew won't need anything from your ship. Everything you need will be provided. If anyone is still aboard, they will need to remain there until you gain full docking permissions from the palace," Zill explained as he turned around, and they followed him down the bustling corridor. He moved like he was flawlessly dancing on ice.

Mercy grabbed Amelia by the arm in a deathly grip and leaned over so she could excitedly whisper in her ear, "His dress is gorgeous! I am in love with all of their outfits!"

Amelia smiled, "As soon as we have some kind of currency, I'll make sure you have a closet full of new clothes."

Zill turned his head around and looked at Mercy with a dazzling grin before turning back saying, "Why, thank you. I would be happy to introduce you to my wardrobe stylist if time permits."

Mercy's grip on Amelia's arm grew much tighter as she tried to stay calm. This was a dream come true for her.

"What is the schedule for our journey?" Oz asked.

Without turning around, Zill answered, "Vistalia is a simple transport away. I love being able to say that. Transporting was just approved for higher beings a few years ago, and this one was installed recently. We will arrive on the planet's surface in a few moments."

They continued down the busy hallway until they came upon a wall of glass through which they could see a large room with a solid white oval on the stone floor and a control station at the back. A reptilian woman stood at the control panel. Her skin had a stronger, brighter lime undertone, her shoulder length hair was a saturated mustard yellow, and deep crimson eyes sparkled in her kind face.

They all filed into the room through the large sliding glass door, and Zill held out his hand for everyone to step onto the transport pad. Before his personal guards approached the pad, he stopped and surveyed all the people on the transport pad for a moment. Seeming to be satisfied with what he decided, Zill waved off his guard to their dismay, before shifting his eyes over to Oz and giving him a sly and sultry smile right before they all materialized on the landing pad.

Jael leaned over and forcefully vomited on the ground as Oz rushed to help her. "Are you okay?" Oz asked frantically, his hands gathering her loose hair.

She nodded to Oz as Zill handed her a small white towel with a cup of water. It was damp, so she cleaned the sweat from her face and was thankful for the coolness of the towel against her neck.

"That happens sometimes if you suffer from motion

sickness. I'll have someone from cleaning come take care of this. Let's move to the transport so we can start the planet tour. I'll have the medic station by the bay door give you a stomach numbing cocktail so you can tolerate the ride. Wait. Is that arm of yours healing naturally? None of that. They can wave it with the healing wand. It takes less than a second," Zill explained to Jael with a warm, compassionate smile.

"Stomach numbing? Healing my wound?" Jael asked overwhelmed, eyes blinking as she tried to process everything at once.

Zill sympathized, "Fortunately, our medical knowledge is quite proficient. We found stomach numbing is very effective and has no side effects. Your wound on the end of your arm can be healed without pain in seconds. If everyone is ready, please follow me."

As he passed by Oz, Zill smiled graciously again, and Oz was beginning to think he was being a little more than nice. He guessed Jael did too when she appeared at his side and put her hand in his.

They arrived at the transport launch pad and saw nothing but treetops blanketing the land. Jael went to the medical station for treatment, and Oz stopped stunned at edge of the platform, taking in the wonder of this new world. It was an oddly familiar sight, but at the same time quite different. The tops of the trees shook violently in various places, and he wondered what was large enough to cause them to move so drastically. Only the most giant tarantulas and centipedes could bend such a colossal tree on his world. His grip on the rail became bruising with the thought. When he scanned behind him and across to the other side of the transport pad, he held in a gasp.

The city built on top of the treetops stretched for miles. Sunlight shone on all the glass buildings blending into the skyline and twinkling with light. A mix of sharply pointed skyscrapers towered, all of them on supports lifting them far above the ground with the loftiest treetops peeking through the open spaces between the buildings. Most transportation was by air, and the transports were landing on pads jutting from the buildings. All the walkways bridging over the trees between each building were made of clear materials, allowing light to pass through so the forest flourished beneath, creating an impression of walking across the tops of the lush greenery.

A mass of giant flying feathered reptiles soared between him and the dazzling city, their feathers either an array of brilliant hues or distinctly muted browns and creams. They were simply stunning, even with their long snouts nearly the length of their lithe bodies.

Oz slowly made his way across the pad, entranced and unable to tear his eyes away from the sight. He hadn't noticed Zill coming up behind him. "The transport is ready if you are, President Green." Zill held his hand outstretched to the open door.

Trying not to act like a little child at an amusement park for the first time, Oz swallowed his awe and boarded, and the rest of the group followed. Everyone else seemed equally amazed by the brilliant, lush city. The grandeur of the architecture mixed with the respect for the natural surroundings achieved a harmonic balance. In that moment, Oz was determined to implement this practice on his own planet. He could not wait to share these memories with Jacob and Callum.

Returning to Oz's side with a newly healed arm, Jael

settled into the seat next to Oz, and he slid his arm around her whispering, "So, just to be clear. You're not ready for additional bodies in the bedroom, are you?"

"Wait. What?" Jael asked in a loud whisper, her eyes wide.

Oz slid his gaze over to Zill who was focused on explaining something to the transport pilot. He faced Jael again and quietly asked, "You are not ready to even discuss it are you?" Blinking quickly, Jael was too stunned to speak. Oz just slid his arm around her and pulled her in close.

"Ready? Is um?" Jael mumbled.

Smiling Oz leaned in and whispered, "It's okay. I should have asked you in private."

"Um. No. It's okay. I'm just not used to your people's sexual fluidity. I might be alright with it. I'm not sure. I've never openly thought about it," Jael managed to whisper back.

"We can shelf that idea until something else arises, and we can revisit it then," Oz suggested, noticing how she calmed instantly.

Jael nodded, and when he turned around, Zill gave him a kind smile. He wondered if reptilian people had keen hearing.

Zill turned to face Carter and gave him a wide grin. Oz did his best to hold in a chuckle as he thought about how it was nice to know his people weren't the only ones with a heavy sexual appetite. The Sarters and the Iungo would probably work together well, other than the meat thing, he decided.

As they traveled, Oz rose from his seat and watched the tops of the trees as they zoomed by under the transport. He noticed the trees tops nearly disappearing for a moment and bouncing back again, so he turned and asked, "Zill, do you mind explaining, why do the trees move? What is down there?"

"The largest of the creatures here on Vistalia rule the ground. Many of our people hunt the large wild reptiles of the ground, and the taxed income from the sales of the meat goes toward funding our public systems. Sarters are 80 to 90% carnivores, so we created a sustainable system which is as humane and as ecologically balanced as possible. You will learn more about the planet when we arrive at the palace," Zill explained while he adjusted his blouse.

Oz noticed the transport was turning and watched as they came around the corner of the giant city to reveal what seemed to be countless clear domes of different sizes and heights on a platform a fourth of the size of the entire city they passed. There was one giant dome in the center, and as they neared Oz realized the dome was not solid at all. It was a glass-like clear mesh around the sides, and only the top was solid.

"The domes are to keep the Alis out of the royal fruit. The Alis are an omnivorous flying reptile, with keen eyesight, and a love for sugar. Don't feed them if you see one. The center of each small dome contains a series of rooms where you will be staying. Just a warning, the grounds are confusing, even for the staff at the palace. Every wall has lights to guide you, so you just need to access the control panel and let the computer know where you need to go. We have several royal chefs on duty at all times, a full service media entertainment area, extensive medical bay with complimentary invasive and noninvasive beauty services, one of the most prestigious full body salons in the galaxy, a fitness and preventative health department, the garden lounge with open bar, and my favorite place, the private royal den," Zill elaborated with a wink while everyone climbed out of the transport and onto the royal landing pad.

"What is a den?" Mercy asked, and Amelia dropped her mouth slightly wondering how Mercy didn't know what a private royal den would imply after that wink.

Zill just smiled and answered, "It's everything sex from private rooms to large groups. Beautiful dancers from all over the Sarter's systems perform shows day and night. Anyone considered to be a consenting adult is generally welcome."

Mercy shivered with excitement about this planet, but that last statement had her about to come out of her own skin. Amelia slid her hand around Mercy's arm and squeezed it. Mercy's tail bumped into Amelia's, and they both curled up at the contact as they tried not to laugh. They were *definitely* visiting the den. Mercy turned and watched as Zill smiled at Carter, and Carter smiled back. Then Aurelia smiled. As the three discussed plans, she could hardly focus with anticipation.

Surveying the room, Mercy noticed Zoe seemed to be too busy taking in the sights to notice anything else was brewing. Kagnus and Mira were quietly content, and the sight set her at ease.

"It seems the consensus is dinner, the lounge, and we can finish the night at the den. I will send everyone the schedule for dinner and the following festivities shortly. Feel free to book any of the royal services from your rooms or call in room service for a light meal before dinner. You have several hours before food will be served. Visit the salon about thirty minutes before dinner for a particle bath and some complimentary Sarter's royal attire. Here are the guest rooms," Zill announced as he pointed to several doors around the room.

He continued, "They're all identical. Each has two bedrooms, and the galaxy center's best food generators and full service private entertainment center with all the best music and Visual-Auditory, or VA, stories in the galaxy. We even steal the Emendo and Melior VA stories for our libraries. Enjoy, and we will see you in a few hours."

Before Zill seemed to float away, he gave a little wave to Carter and Aurelia. They both grinned sheepishly with excitement and nearly tumbled into their room together. Kagnus, Mira, and Zoe all roomed together, and Jael watched as Amelia and Mercy couldn't fall through their door quickly enough. She turned to Oz and asked, "I'm the odd one, aren't I?"

"You're *my* odd one. If you're not comfortable with this, we can stay here," Oz suggested as he pressed his body against hers in reassurance.

Jael opened the door to the room and peered up, noticing the lack of ceiling.

"How the hell does that work?" she wondered aloud.

Oz jumped up and tapped the invisible ceiling, discovering it was nothing but a sound shield. The tall tree's branches and foliage spilled over the top of the walls of the rooms.

"Interesting," he muttered as he kept his eyes on the ceiling that wasn't there.

Jael released a long breath and boldly decided, "I want to take part in everything tonight."

Shooting his focus back to Jael, he asked, "Are you sure?" while pretending not to be utterly shocked, Oz's heart pounded in his body, and as Jael reconsidered and nodded affirming, he softly assured her, "You can stop at any time."

Nodding she explained, "I know. I don't want fear keeping me from experiencing something from a different culture."

With a ridiculous grin he couldn't hold back, Oz started, "We need to talk about what you're okay with and what you're okay with for me. I am open to doing anything with anyone."

Taking a slow breath, Jael smiled confidently and agreed, "That's good with me. I'm going to stay open-minded."

Astounded, he replied, "Well then, we better clean up. Do you want to use the private bathroom or book a service?"

Jael gave Oz a contemplative look and asked, "Can we do all of that here? Is there a razor?"

"I think the shower has some setting you can use to remove your hair. Look right here. Wait, what hair are you removing?" Oz asked as he shot his eyes to hers.

Holding in laugh she answered, "My legs and underarms haven't been shaved in a long time." He glared at her as she pushed by him to turn on the shower. She knew he liked her leg hair, but it was more than time to remove it. As the hot water streamed over her, it began sinking in what would be happening later. *Am I ready for this?* She could feel her face heat, and it wasn't from the steam.

38

PLANET ADURO – MINE 03

Standing guard at the end of the hall, Livia shifted her weight from side to side as she watched from the top ledge of the deep mine. It was nearly the end of the day, and she watched the clock as the hand slowly ticked away. Her heart was in a vise, she was surprised at how hard coping with the loss of Felix would be. He had been her fellow commander for years and like a brother during their time in the academy.

Even though he betrayed her, she still grieved his loss. The reason he ended up assigned to the same training level as she was because he accidentally crashed the guard transport into the side of her father's palace on Melior during practice one day and had been held back a year as punishment. Otherwise, he would not have trained with her. She forgot about his metal leg and how he always talked about his battle scar. It was really cancer, but he lied and claimed it happened in an incident that occurred when they were kids. There were often mistakes with UTC designer babies, ones that led to shame within the ranks.

He was in the second batch of soldiers ordered from the UTC genetics lab, and Livia had been in the third. The first three batches of designer children the king ordered all had to have their eyes replaced with electronic versions when they were children and teenagers. The UTC lab had not altered the optic nerve to withstand the level of radiation, so within a few years of being shipped to Aduro, they had all begun to lose their sight.

Livia had been forced to leave the palace when she was a child to join the new soldiers for training, so they had no idea she would also lose her sight until it happened along with the other soldiers. When her father chose Lucas over her as an heir, she was cast off and no longer trained in the palace. Felix sympathized with her when she first arrived. She and Felix were the only two genetically bred to be commanders at the time, so they were bunk mates as well. They even had their eyes replaced together. Guilt filled her as her mind replayed stabbing him and leaving him to die. She watched it in her mind over and over, allowing the pain to consume her.

The ringing of the bell above her head sent relief through her, breaking her memories. Her shift was finally over, and she could move on with her inspections. She just hoped August sent the message to the boy and the boy could do as he was instructed. As she went toward the hallway, she heard August whistle and knew Chris would be waiting for her in her transport. Passing through the big metal doors at the end of the hall, she spotted her new transport. She climbed in the front seat and shut the door before she started the engine. She looked outside at Felix's transport, still parked in the same place he had left it.

Charging the engine and connecting her harness, she stored away her guilt for another day. The transport began to climb, and she asked, "Chris? You can sit up front and buckle up until we come close to the next mine." She could hear rustling behind her and smiled when his little head popped up from under the box cover. He made his way up and sat down in the seat behind her. He leaned over her shoulder and was in awe of all the blinking lights and bright controls.

She saw him smile in her mirror as he said, "This is fun."

She smiled back. "Thank you for helping me. I need to deliver the staffs. I will go inside to distract the guards, and you pull one box out to hide. I don't care if it's just under some sand to the side of the landing pad, but do it quickly. I plan to move some of your people to different mines tomorrow so they will know where to look. You will have to sleep in my transport tonight. I stored everything you need in the back. Just don't make any noise and you won't get caught."

Chris nodded his head, "I got it. I can be very quiet."

In an instant, realization this child had never left the mines sank in and her heart broke. *How could the UTC have convinced so many people for so long these silent people were nothing more than brainless drones, bugs in the shape of higher beings? How did I not notice? Or, did I, and just brushed it off?*

Images of the UTC advertisements for the engineered beings would replay in her mind over and over. The commercial was of people, human people from their genetic labs, standing and discussing their abnormally undeveloped brains. They had shown a brain scan with nearly empty skulls. They showed loose brain matter with open space. She shook her head, so much conditioning, so many lies. Her focus shifted to the young boy next to her, the delight on his face as he merely gazed out of the window, made a lump form in her throat. She had to fix this. These were people, not engineered bugs. Once she took this planet, it and its resources would belong to these people, as it should be.

As they neared the landing pad, she leaned over to Chris to tell him to hide, but she found the seat already empty. *Smart kid.* Gently landing the transport, she hopped out and dust drummed up in little clouds at her feet. She was greeted by two uncomfortably shuffling guards at the door.

"Line everyone up for inspection. You have two minutes to meet me in the mine entryway," Livia commanded as she stood tall.

Their eyes widened and one woman stumbled over her words, "I, I didn't know inspection was today."

"It wasn't on the schedule," Livia explained flatly as she glared at her, noticing the woman was from the fifth group of UTC designer soldiers her father ordered. She and all of the fifth had oversized, sandy-yellow irises with a narrow pupil in the shape of an X as a result of the gene changes needed for radiation resistance. She wondered what animal the gene had been taken from or if it was an original genetic design.

Realization that it was intended as a surprise inspection fell over the guards, and they faced one another for answers with their mouths opening and closing, and their hands tapping at their sides. Scrambling up the stairs to bring the rest of the guards on duty, the two seemed to fall over one another in a panic.

She chuckled as she strolled into the mine. The emptiness of the space seemed to go on forever. This mine dropped straight down, and the sight made her cringe, so she stayed back from the ledge.

The guards filed in one by one, most seeming bored and partially unkept. Her anger rose as they sorted themselves in a line. "Is this how you roll into inspection?" Livia seethed as she took in their attitudes and appearance. They all absently shuffled around. The entitlement of these human guards would push her over the edge. "Should I send you to the wastes of Emendo for a round of re-education?" Livia asked, her tone daring them to test her. They all shook their heads no as she noticed a male at the end with an unbuckled boot.

"Never let me find this level of disarray when I call for inspection. Soldiers like your lot make my eyes itch. You have ten minutes to present yourselves and fix your stations up to basic standard," Livia glowered at them, and they scrambled after her last word.

Some ran back upstairs to the guard rest areas, and a few stayed to clean the comm stations. Livia turned and made eye contact with a deep red complected woman, one of August's people, who was peeking around the corner. She gave the curious woman a double blink and a hint of a smile. The woman returned a wide grin and disappeared behind the wall.

Once all the guards reformed in line, Livia continued her inspection. She found the comms to still have a film of dust and the weapons locker hadn't been cleaned out in months by the look of it. Relieved the inspection was going so badly, Livia hoped it gave Chris more than enough time to find a place for the stash of staffs.

When she finished with the guards, they returned to their posts and as she stalked away, she heard one say to another, "When this weekly post is over, I'm putting in for vacation time. I need to see some carnage at the games. It's the only thing that can touch this level of stress. You know?"

Livia sneered at the last comments and slammed the mine door on her way out. She climbed into her transport and huffed after the click of her seat buckle. From under the cover in the back, a kind, small voice asked, "Are you okay?"

As she lifted off, Livia answered softly, "I will be. Did you hide the staffs?"

"Yes, I found a perfect place. There was a small sand dune to the right of the door. I put them behind it and covered them with sand," Chris explained, his enormous eyes visible in her mirror.

"That's perfect. We are high enough now, so you can come back up here," Livia offered as she flipped on the interior cooling system.

Chris made his way up and buckled in. He sat quietly and looked out at the sand as the color changed with the setting sun.

Livia and Chris visited six more mines before they finished their task. As they flew to the palace, Chris seemed to grow quieter as they neared. When the palace grew large in the front window, Chris rose from his seat and hid in the back under the cover. He seemed reluctant and worry marred his face.

"I'll be here first thing in the morning to return you to the mine. We will have to sneak you back inside. I haven't come up with how I'm going to do it yet, but I'll figure something out." Livia explained in a whisper, her head pointed to the side so he could still hear her.

"Okay, be careful." Chris whispered from the back.

Livia's heart broke again. She hated the idea of leaving the boy outside, but she had no other choice. She could hear him moving and finding a comfortable place to lie down. After a long pause to be sure he wasn't going to ask for anything before she left, Livia climbed out of her transport. She hoped he liked the box of fresh fruit she had left for him. She headed straight for her rooms, but at the last moment, with her foot hovering over the trigger to open the door, she decided to pass by the king's favorite spot in the garden first.

She skirted along the short wall around the garden, then carefully navigated through the pathways between the raised beds. She spotted a place where several of the large leaves hung over the edge of the raised bed, so if the king walked by, she would still be concealed. As she neared, his voice became clearer, and she could begin to hear what he was saying.

"Alright, if that's one you want, he's yours. Livia likes to spar with him. He was going to be destroyed because he is defective, but we discovered how well he could fight. I'm sure we can come to a fair price," King Claudius explained then took a sip of an amber liquor.

Was he talking about August? Fuck!

In a hissing voice Livia recognized, Yix asked, "How is he defective? He seemed in good health to me?"

"He sleeps," King Claudius replied flatly, still irritated the Empress gifted him a defective product. He set something down, and it made a loud, dinging noise as it made contact with the glass table. Judging by his uneven exhale, it was an Iris drink. Iris liquor was some of the strongest in the galaxy center, not to mention whatever compound was in it that made the drink illegal on most worlds. She suspected some kind of undetectable psychedelic drug.

Chuckling through the hiss between her teeth, Yix asked, "He sleeps? How strange, but that won't affect what I want him for."

Laughing and grabbing his gut where he was surely having a stomach cramp from the liquor, King Claudius boomed, "I know exactly what you want him for, you sick fuck! I'll see you at the ball, old friend."

They both burst into boisterous laughter, and while Livia remained crouched, angry and nauseous at the thought of this deal. Her father was selling August to Yix as part of the deal to the Iris Queen.

That rotten parrot bitch, Livia thought as she heard her father's communicator video feed end. Another clink of his glass being sat down and the sound of his shoes being slipped off told her he would be drinking in the garden for the rest of the night. She hoped she didn't find him parading around nude, sticking his penis in random holes in the morning. He would be hung over and intensely sour after the alcohol wore off, a serious problem, but all she could think of was August. The idea he would be sold to Yix made the fire inside of her rage like their searing star.

Quietly edging away from the garden, she knew she had to warn August he was being sold. They needed to move the timing up for the plans, or she wouldn't be doing this at all. Yix could take him away at any time after the monies are exchanged, and she had no idea when that would be. Her heart strained at the thought of losing him. Entering her quarters, she raised her eyes to her mother's portrait on the wall in front of her, and the pain in her eyes all too familiar. With her eyes set on her mother's, she whispered, "I will be king. This all ends with me. I swear to you."

39

PLANET PORTUM – IUNGO BASE

Jacob had been quickly assessed by the medical team in the field and released, so they had rushed to check on Juni. She had been transported right away for care. The empty medical bay which had greeted them was to their back and most of the lights were dimmed save a small one over the empty desk near the front doors. The silence in the chilly room seemed to grow with Juni's every breath as they silently watched her, trying to remain quiet so she could rest. With no warning, startling the two, Juni asked in a cracked voice, "What are you two lurking around in my room for?"

Callum awkwardly grimaced and sighed before he whispered, "Oh, you're awake. No one was here, and we hadn't heard anything."

"It's their lunch break." The gravel in Juni's throat was no better, and her eyes didn't so much as flutter.

Juni let out a half giggle at their silence and cleared her throat. Opening her eyes, she smiled sweetly at Callum and Jacob. "Thank you. I don't know what made you try what you did, but thank you. It gave Vida and the med team a direction to go to find a synthetic way of producing the energy we need to heal. I guess heal, and now revive can be added to the list."

With relief, they each gave Juni a soft hug and repeated questions about how was she feeling. Jacob bragged about how hard Callum had fought, but Callum brushed the praise aside. When they could see she was tiring, Jacob began, "We will stop by later to visit more. When did Vida say you could go home?"

"You mean, when do I go back to full duty?" Juni asked, her lip tipped up at the corner.

One of the machines begin to beep, and Juni swung her arm backward. Her hand pressed a button, and the machine reset.

Seeming to be focused on where the sheet tucked into the mattress, Jacob asserted, "That's not what I asked."

"Give me a few days, and I'll be cleared for duty," Juni explained as she adjusted the sheets covering her.

Callum, showed off his bright, wide grin, "Then we'll see you in a few days."

Jacob and Callum left her recovery room and headed to Pike's office to discuss the new communications device they tested on the recently sent out probe. They found Pike entranced by his work. His focus seemed to almost fall into his holo-screen like light into a black hole. They stood silently next to his desk, waiting for him to notice them. He jolted as though he had an electric shock when he realized he wasn't alone in his office. "How long have you been standing there?" Pike mumbled as his flustered eyes finally met Jacob's.

His teeth white and shining, Jacob held his grin and

replied, "Long enough to know you need a door chime. Tell me about the experiment and results."

"The probe we sent out was our prototype for the quantum communicators your team just discovered. They claim it was a group effort based on one of your lessons," Pike explained with his eyebrows raised at Jacob. He turned off his holo-screen and continued, "The entangled particle was spinning in the opposite way, like you thought. We set up a binary system, and it was simple to code and program it before integrating it into the probe. All it took was turning a camera toward it then reading the direction of the radiation waves through the chamber."

Nodding, Jacob asked, "Did the new chip designs hold up?"

Grinning like a child with a sweet, Pike tripped over his words as he answered, "Y-yeah – yes. They are functioning perfectly. We are almost ready to start site to site transport testing on people. The team is already running the numbers for long distance transport, but they said it could be a month or two before they can work the math."

"You really squeezed Jael's engine design into a device the size of a wristband?" Jacob wondered aloud.

"When we discovered we could just increase the frequency by a fraction of a point and make the radiation chamber solid, it gave us the ability to shrink it down," Pike elaborated, thrilled with this progress.

"It's good to hear some substantial progress is happening with limited teams. Finally. Some kind of good news. I was thinking it would never end." Jacob rubbed his forehead as he spoke, his mind already rolling over the possibilities of what this new device could do for them and their people.

Callum nudged him with a crease in his brow, "Shh! Don't say anything else about that."

Rolling his eyes more at himself than at Callum, he really needed to stop bringing up what was going wrong and nodded agreeing.

A ding sounded on Pike's tablet with a notification from the base security surveillance team that they had an army headed toward them. Panic filled his eyes as he read the message. He read it two more times just to be sure.

"There is an army marching toward the base. I thought all the humans except our prisoners had left?" Pike asked as he turned to them for answers.

Jacob knew exactly who was approaching the base. A sour taste filled his mouth, and he began to sweat. "They did," Jacob admitted, with dread growing in his gut.

Shifting on his feet uncomfortably, Callum asked, "Um, Jacob? Who the hell would be heading toward the base?"

"I'm not going to say it," Jacob replied flatly, refusing to face Callum.

"Oh yes, you're going to say it. You had to open your mouth and talk about the good news. *The fucking cannibals are coming, Jacob*! What in the venom are we going to do?!" Callum screeched.

Pike leaned back in his seat as confusion washed over him, and he asked, "What did you just say?"

Jacob turned to look at him, "You heard him. The people in the southern town were cannibals with heads filled with brain worms."

"You can't be serious. That's where you were attacked and held right? Why did no one manage to say anything about the people in that village being cannibals until right now?" Pike's terror at the idea of being eaten coursed through his veins and reverberated in his voice.

"They were going to eat us, Pike. I don't know how it didn't end up in the mission report," Jacob grumbled as Pike rose from his seat and they all headed to the next room.

At the station where the alarm was pulled, Jacob didn't see anyone nearby, so he sat down and studied the satellite feed on the holo-screen. When he spotted the large mass of people gathering just north of them, he zoomed in. "Oh, scorpion balls, this is not good. Do we have enough sedatives? Can we gas them? What are we going to do? We can't fight them. They're just really dumb," Callum explained as he leaned in closely over Jacob's shoulder. Zooming in further, Jacob ignored Callum, absently asking, "Where is that old woman and her sister?"

"There!" Callum hissed as he pointed to a hunched over figure with a familiar falter.

Studying the three-dimensional image, assessing each figure in the picture one by one, they leaned back when they realized what she was doing. Pike raised his hand to cover his mouth in disgust. She had a wheeled butcher block on a series of stacked stones, and she was chopping some kind of meat. As they studied the picture, they discovered she had caught a giant Orb spider in the wilds and was chopping up her legs.

Pike warily asked, "Is she going to *eat* that spider?"

"Yeah. Yeah, she is." Callum answered, a look of disgust developing on his face.

"She knows those are filled with parasites, right?" Pike asked, not removing his eyes from the screen.

"I don't think she cares." Callum replied flatly.

"What's one more brain worm?" snarked Jacob.

They watched as the old woman reach down onto the block and grabbed a piece of the leg, putting it up to her mouth and taking a bite, pulling it from her teeth, tearing it in two. Disgusted, Pike let out a squeak and turned his face away then back to the screen for another look.

Pike stood still for a moment to think, "They're a few hours away. It seems like they're packing up the camp. We need to assemble our troops and equipment right now."

Over by the wall, he pulled the base's mass emergency alarm and went out into the hallway, waiting for everyone to spill out of the doors. Within moments the hall was filled, and he waited for the last few people to assemble. Memories echoed in their minds as to what occurred the last time the alarms were pulled.

"We have a large group of our own people heading this way from the north. Unfortunately, they aren't coming to join us. They are infected with parasites. We need to form a border and protect the base. They are people from the southern-most village across the mountain. When Jacob and his team visited for recruiting, things didn't go so well. The group is known to consume creatures including *our own people*. Yes, you hear that correctly. We have thirty minutes to assemble a perimeter, do it in twenty. Someone figure out a way we can subdue them without harm!" Pike barked the orders out, and people scattered. Some began to run as others frantically headed in various directions, off to complete their emergency protocols for a ground invasion.

Jacob addressed their immediate group saying, "Gear up and meet in front. Where is Vida?"

"She's visiting her parents. They had a death in the family. She won't be back until later. I'll send her a message," Pike explained as he turned to put on his armor.

Nodding, the two headed off to their apartment to prepare. As they took their armor off the new charging systems, Jacob paused a moment before slipping on his suit. Glaring at the wall as he held the top of his suit in a bruising grasp, Jacob asked, "Why did they have to come back? Why couldn't they just leave us alone? I've been having a reoccurring fear of this exact thing happening."

"Snap out of it. The nightmare is on our doorstep. Put your armor on and don't forget your plasma sword," Callum commanded.

He wasn't sure where this bold energy came from with Callum, but he had to admit he loved it. Jacob pulled his armor up as they exited their apartment, and they headed toward the front of the base where their people would be assembling the shields for the perimeter. When they reached the surface, Jacob found Pike and asked, "Are the shields up and holding?"

"Yes. I just received a report that a large group of them will be here in less than thirty minutes. They're now running through the woods, including the two old women," Pike explained with sweat dripping into his eyes causing him to blink it away.

Jacob waved Callum over. He made his way while keeping his eyes on the iridescent waves of the shield. A bright spark from a crossing insect caused his stomach to twist into a knot.

"Let me guess, I get the pleasure of talking to the old woman?" Callum asked, his eyes narrowed.

Shifting on his feet Jacob asked, "Please?"

"Of course I have to talk to the old cannibal, of course I do. Fine, but you will owe me so hard for this." Callum replied with his arms crossed and helmet dangling from his belt.

Turning, he unhooked his helmet, shoved it at Jacob, and tossed his plasma sword inside of it. Closing his eyes, he whispered to himself, "How the fuck did I end up the negotiator? I don't even work here." After pausing and taking a breath, he opened his blue eyes and glared at Jacob, "You better fucking cover me. I mean anticipate if this creepy woman looks like she's even thinking of pulling something. I am *not* getting eaten today." At that, a few gasps were heard around them.

From the satellite feed, the group was slowing down. Jacob spotted one of the old women off through the trees. "They're here." Jacob whispered to Callum.

The horde appeared from the woods and quietly moved toward the shields and a solid line of their people. Many of them appeared terribly disheveled. All of them were dirt crusted and had cracked, dried mud from their ankles to their shins. They seemed to sense the shield's energy and didn't cross it.

The old woman who had held Callum hobbled up to the barrier. When she spotted him, she seemed to boil even hotter. *Had this been a mistake? This had most definitely been a mistake. Why didn't I hide?* His mind was begging him to run as images of Jacob being cooked on an open fire ran through his spinning mind. Somewhere down in his soft heart he knew this wasn't really her fault. She was just a product of her environment and the parasites.

Callum met her at the shield and swallowed roughly before he asked gently, "What is going on? I thought we made a deal. I held up my end."

"You, your people, that *human* woman infected us with

words, and it's ruined everything!" she seethed, her hands in tight fists at her sides.

A few more of their people neared the edge of the shields. Fury burned hot in their eyes.

"What do you mean it's ruined everything?" Callum asked, genuinely confused, and starting to worry words wouldn't work this time. *What can I do then? How can I reason with the unreasonable?*

With her mouth dropped open, Callum counted she was missing another tooth before she spoke with an odd slur. "What you mean? This language made confusing and fighting among people. Some say we will all pay. They take all. North village with us. If you don't stop and let us to go to silence, we do whatever take to stop you. We are not taken because of you mistakes!" She showed off her yellow fangs and leaned forward to hiss.

Closing his eyes, Callum wondered what happened to her speech, and then it occurred to him she must have a new infection of brain worms. *What will get through to her?* He would have to just try the harsh truth and hope it worked.

"Do you know what they were doing to us? When they took us? Our enemy? Because we know," Callum asked, hoping this worked.

She shook her head *no* as her sister became visible behind her through the trees.

"First, they strap us to a table like a wild animal. Then they snip our stingers off. They take a machine and burn our fingernails to the nail bed so they won't grow anymore. After all of that, they file down our fangs. All without pain relief or sedation. Once we are made defenseless, we are sent to various planets to work until we die. Either that or we are sent to the factory planet and put to work by our enemy, also until we die. When those on the factory planet have children, the children are taken away when they're of age to work and some are given as gifts to kings.

"We are trying to search our planet for proof we were not created by our enemy. That's all we need, and we are close. We can win. The language of our people was supposed to happen many thousands of years ago. Our enemy kept us from learning. Your people will eventually learn how to live with language. I promise it will get better. We just need more time to secure the planet, and we can send more aid to your villages. Please, just give us a chance to fix this," Callum explained, beginning to truly feel sorry for these parasite ridden people. It wasn't their fault. It was an endless, destructive cycle and maybe if they kept them healthy for long enough, they could learn.

Thinking about his words, she grimaced as she replied, "The light from the colors always changes and water hits sand different always."

What? Callum thought, *what the hell does that mean?*

"You nice, kind face always. Very like. Mushrooms grow tall and die. We do too. Our octopus don't change though, sticky sticky. You like octopus," She made a slurp with her lips as she licked them.

Callum shivered with disgust, and something occurred to him. "Did you personally share the gift with your village and the whole north village?" Callum asked, swallowing down the bile rising in his throat.

She narrowed her eyes at him and sneered as she responded with a hissing, "Yes."

They had all received *the gift* from her worm-eaten brain. A whole village of their people.

He was not qualified to deal with this and turned to

signal back to Jacob for help. Jacob's smiled faded, showing Jacob's underlying thoughts about the situation. *So much for that*, Callum was on his own with this.

"Sister will talk. North village too. I see what I say," she grumbled as she teetered off.

Whispering to himself, Callum shook his head and asked, "What the fuck?"

Jacob now stood right behind him, shifting on his feet nervously, as he asked, "How did it go? We have a transport ready with a sedative. We can gas them if we need to."

"Um, Jacob, we may have made a big mistake. I don't know how to tell you this, but wormy brains spread *her* version of the gift around. She is incoherent at best," Callum explained, worry filling his eyes, trying to comprehend the situation himself as he said it.

He turned and Jacob's face showed his shock. "Stop. What did you just say?"

"You heard me correctly. This is so bad. We need to pray to the wormy brain gods these people go home!" Callum blurted out as he studied the trees to try to see where the old woman went.

When he turned, Jacob looked like he could vomit any second. "We may need a special ethics group to solve this problem. Wormy knowledge was not something we planned for. Does this mean anyone who has the gift from her will also be a cannibal? Fuck!"

"Just go sit down somewhere. I'll deal with it. I think she is trying to convince them to go home. I don't know why she likes me, but she does, and I'm not questioning it. You know this language damage is done, and we probably can't do anything about it," Callum observed as he monitored the tree line.

"I think I'm going to go over here and have a seat. Maybe die. Maybe just bang my head on the wall," Jacob whispered as he shook his head and sat down a few feet away, facing away from the shield.

Callum saw the old woman return and waited for her to shuffle back to him. She stumbled as she spoke, "The boat floats on the w-water even with big rock in. Sea-meat good, if ones are in planets not our own, bring. Where we are from wants a call. Takes six days feet." With that, she teetered into the woods, and the group began heading north.

Shaking his head with his mouth open in disbelief, Callum just stared at where she had been standing.

After a moment he frantically asked, "Can anyone explain to me what the hell that woman was saying?" Before anyone could answer, a scream erupted, and Callum turned to see the old woman's sister disagreeing and pointing toward them. The old woman Callum had just been speaking with pulled out her knife, stabbing her sister in the gut.

Callum and several people behind him let out audible gasps. They all watched as a few people leaned down to pick up the arms of the bloody and now dying sister. They dragged her behind them as the group moved off into the distance.

Pike shuffled up to Callum and with his mouth turned down in a deep frown, he cried out, "Um? Are they going to eat the sister?!" Callum slapped a hand over his mouth, and Jacob release a nauseated groan from behind them.

40

SARTER PLANET – SARTER ROYAL PALACE

When the directory and communications station by the door chimed it was time to meet the others at the salon, Jael's gaze found Oz. *Am I ready for this?*

"You don't have to do anything you don't want to," Oz leaned in, sensing her unease.

Giving him an obvious faux, strained grin, she whispered, "I know, quit reminding me."

Just hours before, Oz was deep into the spa's self-service products in the room. At one point, they each had a clay mask from some remote planet they couldn't pronounce on their faces, and Oz was painting his toenails black after he had painted hers the color of blood. She couldn't tell which one of them was having more fun, but decided it was him when he was painting his nails and started humming. Should she say claws? Filed claws? Nails, she was calling them nails.

Her freshly painted toenails gleamed in the light, drawing her eye. She wiggled her toes in the light as she explained, "I will not let the social taboos of my former world keep me from experiencing something from a culture I've never encountered. I'm not even a *normal* human. So their normal rules shouldn't matter to me. No one knows how many different human worlds my DNA came from. I was made in a damn lab. I have to stop being fearful of everything. Who knows, I might like it."

Pausing a moment as Sis crossed her mind, "One day when I find my sister, I don't want to tell her a story of reservation and fear. I want to tell her everything I dared to explore and try for myself. I am diving in headfirst. These lives we have are so short. If there is one thing I've learned from you and your people, it's no excuse exists which can hold up to regret." With his gaze affixed on his love, he marveled at her words, not at her exact words, but at the meaning. She was letting go of the box she had to force her limitless, fluid form inside, the square, punishing, iron box she was taught to build by her former world. He had simply given her a choice to take the lid off, and she had done the rest herself.

Jael slipped her arm in Oz's, and he led them down the path to the salon where they found Zoe, Amelia, Mercy, Carter, and Aurelia already deciding on their attire for the evening. It was a mix of long and short dresses, pantsuits, and navy blue robe like attire Oz seemed to love. Jael picked a simple short dress in black first. Zoe, Carter, and Aurelia all selected simple flowing pants suits in various neutral tans which matched their skin tones. Mercy picked a long dress in ruby, and Amelia put on a pantsuit, but changed her mind when she saw Oz in his robe. The Sarter's robes took on a life of their own as they glided along, seeming to float as they moved.

Once they were all dressed, they sat down in the salon

chairs for facials and make up if they chose. Mercy and Jael both enjoyed the make-up, and Oz didn't oppose when a reptilian woman with eye liner and mascara approached. After he saw himself in the mirror, he smiled, immensely pleased.

Their various braids were combed out and their hair was pulled back in simple sleek styles. Jael's curls were sprayed with product, and she watched as her hair transformed into the best hair day she had ever had. Each curl bounced without a smidge of frizz. Mercy decided on curls after she watched Jael have her hair done. Everyone enjoyed the luxurious pampering after never really experiencing such indulgences.

A scent of pine and blackberry preceded Zill as he entered the salon in a sharp black suit, He took a moment to evaluate the group and clearly approved of the changes. "Mmm - how nice! I am glad to see you are ready for dinner. Right this way."

Following Zill through winding pathways spilling over with foliage, they ended up in what Jael thought resembled a tropical patio with exquisite crystal top tables with vast slices of tree stumps for bases. The stunning rainbow array of freshly scented foliage in natural stone vases on every table combined with plush seating drew her into the lush area.

They all found seats around a long, oval-shaped table as a reptilian woman and man who resembled one another approached Zill. After Zill introduced everyone to the newcomers, he leaned in lovingly to the pair of reptilian people and nearly purred, "This is Destry and Oran. They are *siblings* from the same clutch of eggs. We consider them similar to birthed fraternal twins. They are dear friends of mine, and they are both going to be joining us tonight. They wanted to help me give you the full experience of our lovely palace."

They each nodded and found their seats. At one end of the table, Zill and Destry sat across from Oz and Jael, while Oran sat across from Zoe and Amelia. Mercy, Carter, and Aurelia all sat down at the end of the table on the other side of Amelia.

Destry was a tall woman with a soft, reddish tan skin tone and her tail swayed behind her. Her bright eyes matched her flowing crimson dress, which was elegant but simple. The sleeveless gown emphasized her toned arms while the deep V-neck showed her seemingly swollen breasts. Her cream and violet streaked hair curled down to her mid back framing her beautiful oval face, emphasizing her high cheekbones and full lips. Oran was brighter than his sister, with vibrant violet hair and shining fire-red eyes that seemed to glow under the light. His reddish toned skin was complimented by ruby scales along his brow. Both were quite alluring.

In a curious tone, Destry asked, "Oz, I heard what Zill mentioned about you taking back your planet, and I just can't wait to hear all about it, but first, Jael, what human world are you from?"

Bashfully peering at Oz first, who offered nothing, she turned and faced at Destry before admitting, "I am from a planet my people call Earth."

Blinking quickly and downing her drink at the unexpected answer, Destry chose her words carefully, "Interesting. I've never heard of it. What larger system is it near?"

"Honestly? I don't know. I accidentally transported myself with a device I made for an experiment. I ended up in Oz's woods. He found me and saved my life," she explained with a faint smile. Diplomacy was about the truth, right? She hoped they could trust these people. Their futures depended on it.

Intelligent calculation reflected in her eyes, Destry leaned closer and asked, "Tell me about your planet. Did humans originate there? What was the history of the planet?"

"Yes, humans originated there. Humans didn't split from their chimpanzee common ancestor until at least six to eight million years ago, but our modern humans didn't develop until two hundred thousand years ago. There were what my people call dinosaurs, or reptiles, which ruled the planet millions of years. We had several extinction events, and the dinosaurs ultimately died off," Jael explained, suspecting Destry had been curious about her former world's living history.

"Such an interesting time scale," Destry observed before she opened a small jar in the center of the table and pulled out a live frog with bright green skin and an orange stripe of warning down its back.

Jael stared at her wondering what she was about to do with that wriggling frog. *She's not going to eat it is she?* Holding it by the leg, Destry tossed it into her mouth and swallowed it down whole before continuing her questions. "When did your earliest humanoid ancestor evolve? Would you say about a million years ago, maybe two?"

"Yes, I think that's about right. Why do you ask?" Jael inquired, still stunned about the frog. That frog was so cute, and as she focused on Destry's bright ruby-red eyes, she realized she was becoming distracted. *How the hell am I supposed to be helpful when I can't even handle this woman eating a live frog? Okay, fine, focus. Maybe it's their version of oysters on the half shell? Maybe that wasn't so gross. Maybe it's just me* she decided but quickly revised her view when she peeked at a staring and horrified Carter, seated at the far end of the table. This reptilian woman was clearly important and something deep inside told her she needed to pay attention and not insult her with inattention. She sat her drink down and wondered if she needed to take it easy for a moment on the alcohol.

Bursting with excitement, Destry sat her drink down and adjusted her position before she explained, "I just find it interesting how a branch of chimpanzees on some worlds evolve at light speed compared to many of the other species who independently evolved on their origin worlds. Take my species for example. It took over thirty million years for our kind to develop into what we are today from our closest primitive ancestor. Our civilization has well over ten million years of historical records after the twenty million years it took for us to truly become what we are today. That's a minimum of fifty million years."

"What about other mammal species? Surely, they would evolve quicker? Maybe it's the type of creature you evolved from?" Oz asked, beginning to fear where Destry was heading with this conversation.

Shaking her head, her hair falling over her shoulders, Destry explained further, "I thought that, too. A large mammal exists, one with giant ears and an elongated nose. It took around thirty million years just to evolve the long nose it has. It is suspiciously as if evolution worked *harder* to produce humans than any other type of being on these specific planets in question. I compiled some data, and I discovered some other interesting things. I found that not only did every human origin world eventually produce only one type of human, always like you, Jael, but they also didn't produce any other type of higher-level beings.

"For example, the Makros and Parvis people both originated on the same planet, but at different times in their planet's history. All of their largest evolutionary leaps taking place around thirty to forty million years in their time scales. The Markos historical data goes back over five million years. This is reflected again in a system mere lightyear's away from Emendo, where the Corvus and the Iris both originated on the same planet. It's called Teresk, and they evolved there over sixty million years ago. It all happened in the same system the Vultus people evolved in as well. It's all just too curious when you take a step back and examine it from a bit of a distance. Listen, after the meal, when everyone goes to the lounge, follow me to the palace's animal rehabilitation facility. I want to show you one of the patients just brought in from an island on Keru. Keru is one of the many remote Sarter Kingdom planets that we received in the treaty."

"Sure," Jael and Oz agreed in unison as the server set plates of food down in front of them.

Oz's plate was filled with fruit, avocado, nuts, and fluffy steaming bread. He had never seen bread risen with yeast, and he picked it up to inspect it closely before bringing it near his face. He looked as if he feared it would bite him when he went in for a sniff. Jael's plate had what seemed to be a sandwich of some kind. She lifted it and saw everything that would be on a club sandwich, so she took a bite. Tomatoes, what tasted like bacon, lettuce, and even mayo with white meat almost identical in taste to turkey. Dumbfounded, she wondered how did they know what she'd like to eat. She then focused on Destry, and she found her also evaluating the club sandwich and seeming to watch Jael's reaction. Her pupils widening from small slits. *Was she excited just watching me eat my sandwich?* The scent of the honey and mustard in a little cup next to the sandwich wafted by her nose, and she had to swallow to keep from drooling. She bit down again. It was a real turkey sandwich. It was the best damn turkey sandwich she had ever had. She was fully aware this was all incredibly suspicious, but this meal was too good to care. The piece she held was gone in seconds, and she reached for another right away.

Jael inspected the next section, "This is just like a sandwich back on Earth. It's called a club. I used to order one like it all the time at a local deli down the road from my house. This one is much better, but it's made the *exact* same way. They didn't have the honey and mustard though, something about the scent of honey with this sandwich is heaven."

Lifting the bread, she saw the slice of cheese and peeled a piece off to taste it. A mild Swiss? *No way.* She was in a reptilian alien royal palace, and they put *Swiss* cheese on her sandwich?

"This is giving me some serious nostalgia. I didn't think I would ever eat one of these again," she said before wiping her mouth.

Destry smiled and shifted her tail before saying, "That's meat from a bird here on Vistalia. I don't know what a turkey is, but the bird the meat comes from is over four hundred pounds and has claws eight inches long. They are hunted only during a four-week season. It is a delicacy. We also have a *sandwich* as you call it that has slow cooked ground balls of seasoned meat from a more common giant bird. I love the other versions our chef makes, too. One has a fried egg with a runny yolk with a purple tomato sauce on it. The bread and meat combos are quite popular right now."

Eager to try the other foods, she asked, "Can I maybe have one of those with the sliced sausage on it, too?" Jael dove into another one and finished it. Oz watched in contentment as Jael ate her fill.

Destry seemed to be delighted. Scanning the table, Oz saw Carter and Aurelia and the star-struck glaze in their eyes over Zill. Zoe was almost stoic. He noticed her temperament had shifted when Oran sat in front of her. The two were silent, and Oz wondered if they had spoken at all the entire meal. Watching closer, he discovered they were quietly making eye contact at various intervals as they ate.

Jael squeezed Oz's leg under the table, "I know you're vegan, but I wish you could have tried those sandwiches. They were so good." Oz did his best to not seem repulsed.

With an inviting smile, Destry stood, "If you are finished eating, let's go to the sanctuary, and we can join the rest of them later."

Oz and Jael rose and followed Destry around several corners before coming to a large room with a long glass wall. There were no lights guiding her, and Jael found that interesting. *How is Destry the only one who knows where anything is in this sprawling palace?* Her long dress flowed behind her as if a light breeze blew only for her. Oz and Jael followed her as she neared the glass and put her hand on it. Searching inside the lush glass room for whatever Destry wanted to show them, Jael's heart raced. When her eyes found the upright figure walking among the trees and shrubs, she let out an audible gasp.

"I knew you would react that way," Destry declared, as Jael held her eyes on the female. She had only seen such a being in science books. It was what, or who rather, would have been the ancestor of humans over a million years ago.

She was essentially a highly advanced, hair covered, half-human, half-chimpanzee who was steady on two legs. When she saw Destry, she smiled and approached the glass. She was so very human like, her smile, her expression, her walk.

Destry softly explained, "This is Theak. She shattered her leg and needed a new leg bone. Her opposing clans have been involved in vicious war for hundreds of years. We do what we can when the innocent become critically injured, but we stay out of their way otherwise. She will have her memory cleared of her time here before we return her to the Plana."

Focusing on Jael, she continued, "The Plana's medical facilities on Keru, close to her planet, didn't have the right equipment, so they transported her here. Plus, it was their storm season. Oh, you probably don't know, I apologize. Keru is a water world where only a small percentage of the land is dry."

"Are the Plana a marine type people?" Jael asked without taking her eyes from Theak.

Smiling, Destry replied, "They evolved from an aquatic mammal. I read in my studies they went from land to sea multiple times in their planets tumultuous history, so they can now hold their breath for over five days. They have beautiful cities floating on the surface and under clear glass domes which are anchored to the sea floor. Their undersea buildings are on platforms under the domes, much like this palace. It is a breathtaking place to visit. Aside from the royal medical facilities here, they have some of the most advanced biology labs in all of the galactic center."

"How long have you worked here?" Jael asked as she looked around the large open room.

Grinning, Destry looked longingly over at Theak, "I have worked here all of my life."

"May I ask how old you are?" Jael asked, thinking about how young Destry looked.

"I'm twenty-six, but we become adults at twelve. We mature quickly and live to be around one hundred and fifty." Changing the subject, she turned to leave. "Now, we should meet everyone at the lounge. Let's hope Zill didn't start everyone on any of our local fruit liquors. They contain several chemical compounds other than alcohol. It's ironic our council outlawed Iris alcohol for the same reason, but ours is far worse," she joked with a wink.

In awe of the gardens, Oz and Jael followed Destry down a winding path to an open area with long, low cream couches covered with tasseled pillows. The other end of the room had what appeared to be a casual dance floor and some type of large scale game made of large contraptions with wooden loops and posts to toss them at as squares on the floor lit up around it. Without turning around Destry asserted, "We assumed you would enjoy the lounge and casual dining room over our formal ballroom. Were we correct in that assumption?"

Surveying the room they found their team lounging on the couches with drinks. Everyone was comfortable and seemed thoroughly intrigued with whatever the topic of discussion was.

"I would say you guessed right," Oz admitted as he leaned to Jael who was absently nodding and bobbing her eyes around awestruck.

"Have a seat and the servers will be over to take care of your order soon. I will return shortly," Destry trailed off as she glided away.

Oz and Jael found seats on the other side of Oran and Zoe on the long sofas.

"Did my sister not follow you two?" Oran asked, far too aware of his sister not being there. He whipped his head around in all directions trying to find her. His tail shifted quickly to his side and the tip began flitting back-and-forth.

Jael pointed to where she went, "She went in that direction. She said she would be right back."

"Oh, she must have gone to the restroom again. She's laying an egg in a few months and she has to go constantly. It's just one this time, but its larger than usual," he explained. Lying back in his seat, his tail went limp at his side. Jael thought back, and it did seem like Destry had a roundness to her middle.

The server approached, and the group was a whirlwind of curiosity over the menu, so Oran ordered for everyone. When the drinks arrived, they shimmered and tasted like toasted marshmallows. The ring of fruit at the top was a slice of bright yellow fruit Jael didn't recognize at first. When she took a bite, the most intense melon flavor exploded in her mouth. The texture was different than she remembered, but sure enough, there was a single white seed poking out of the side, and Jael asked, "You have melon?"

"We have many fruits and vegetables found on a variety of worlds with life. Our top scientists have thought for millions of years that all world's are seeded through icy comets with the same potential beginning proteins of life, but each world's environment dictates which plants and animal will rise to the top and how. How long it takes for the top animals to rise seems to be more constant though, being tens of millions of years, not just a few million," Destry explained as she sat down carefully next to Oz.

"That's why you mentioned the time scale for Earth's humans didn't make sense? It's happening too fast?" Oz asked as his mind working towards the *why*.

Picking up her drink, Destry grinned briefly before meeting Oz's eyes, "Precisely. That's why I showed you Theak. Her kind have developed on a planet near Keru. It is an odd world for humans. It's mostly ice, and what land is temperate is harsh at best. They have evolved very quickly, unlike all other life. Interestingly, their evolution is on a scale similar to other human origin planets. All humans seemed to be evolving much too quickly for the galaxy standard. We suspect the First Humans may be hiding something involving all human evolution."

Oran slid his arm around Destry and interrupted, "Why don't we spend tonight making our guests feel welcome and comfortable. Tonight, should be about fun. Tomorrow we can get down to business when we meet with the queen."

With an apologetic smile, Destry gave him a bashful look, relenting, "You're right. One more round of drinks, and I think it's time to visit the den."

"Wait, you can drink alcohol while pregnant?" Jael asked with her mouth dropped open.

After downing her second drink, she set it down and turned to Jael, "After the shell is fully formed, I can do whatever I want. It's the months before, waiting to see if I'm going to produce an egg and deciding if I want it fertilized. If not, it doesn't matter. Any unfertilized eggs are cooked and fed to the palace fish. Some of the Sarter people on less technologically developed worlds commonly eat their own unfertilized, cooked eggs. We see nothing wrong with it, and there is no sense in the high quality protein going to waste."

A little disturbed by that revelation, Jael gulped and

asked, "Did the Sarters people develop on more than one world?"

"No, not my species. This is a very old part of the galaxy, possibly even from an older galaxy that blended into our own. There are plenty of other reptilian beings which originated on planets within the Sarter galactic borders, but most of them haven't even formed starter civilizations yet. They originated from a variety of other types of reptilian creatures. Some of the reptilian origin planets stay to themselves by choice. We protect those planets from any outside interference, but the ones outside of our territory, those planets are still at the mercy of the UTC.

"Most of our species have settled planets which are terraformed for our overflow of the population here on Vistalia, our origin world." As a gracious host would, Destry stood encouraging the others to follow her. "Come now. Let's head over to the den before it gets too late." Jael rose with Oz, and they followed Destry as she led the way to the den. The rest of the group was not far behind, laughing and making the best of each moment.

As they rounded a corner, Mercy loudly asked, "Wait! I have a very important question! Don't egg laying reptiles only have *one* hole? How does that work exactly?"

Destry stopped and whipped her head around to look at her brother before she, Oran, and Zill all burst into a fit of raucous laughter as they grasped onto one another for support. After catching his breath, Oran elaborated, "Our reproductive organs have evolved along with us. You'll just have to find out for yourself, golden girl."

A devious smile spread across Mercy's face and Amelia nearly lost her balance as Mercy yanked her along. When they passed through the entrance of the den, Jael began to wonder what was in those drinks as a sensual warmth filled her. It moved from her throat down to her stomach and spread, swirling through her like a sweet embrace. Her skin screamed for contact, not simply sexual in nature, but one of acceptance and care. It was a euphoric experience as Oz slid his hand around her waist and placed his hand on the small of her back to guide her through the room. The glass dome above removed all light from the nearby city against the sky and showed a familiar strip of spinning stars running down the middle. She would never miss an opportunity to take in a picturesque sky of stars. Jael was having trouble taking her eyes off the magnificent sight when she felt Oz squeeze her to him again.

When she brought her eyes down, her breath caught. It was not at all the clothing optional type of dance club she had imagined. The sprawling place was filled with waterfalls and some kind of elegant, grey skinned people dancing among the streams. They didn't seem to have any hair and their fingers were webbed like delicate fans. Their noses were small mounds with one hole at the base. They all had rounded yet exceptionally trim body forms. All were draped in what appeared to be lingerie with random assortments of straps down their arms and legs in the style of a body suit.

Shifting her eyes slowly over the room, she saw a small group of humans, but other than that, all the other beings were species she didn't recognize. All of them wearing strikingly different attire. Some had large beautiful, bright feathered wings with sheer dresses while some had long winding tails and gyroscope eyes with nude skin that changed color depending on where they stood. One woman had a long white and black ringed tail matching her long white and black striped hair. She didn't know if it was makeup or not, but the black and white patterns on her face gave her the look of someone regal and fierce. Her body suit was filled with open spaces showing off her curvy figure and the black and white color patterns of her skin underneath.

Speaking over the electronic music, Zill announced, "Please make yourselves comfortable. We have a show starting in a few moments."

On one end of a large wrap around cream sofa sat Zoe, Oran, Amelia, Mercy, Zill, Carter, and Aurelia. On the other side were Oz, Jael, and Destry. Between them was a small tray with jars in various sizes. The center of the circle was a large round cushioned area filled with cream floor pillows. The couch was surrounded by a tall semi-sheer dark blue curtain.

The music changed and a darkened stage Jael had missed when they entered lit up brightly. A whoosh of wind blew all of their hair back before two people with giant iridescent, black bird wings landed on the platform. One was a tall, trim man with tan skin, dark brown hair, a square handsome face, kind eyes, and a wide smile. The other person was a lighter skinned woman with a tall, curvy form. She was stunning, with long black hair and full lips. Her face was oval, and she smoldered while she surveyed the room like a predator searching for its prey. Both were scantily dressed in strips of strategically placed cloth with gold painted skin accents emerging from beneath their minuscule garments.

The two flared open their massive wings before snapping them shut to reveal three people, one man in the middle and two women, one on either side. They were all black and white people with long ringed tails that whipped back and forth, seeming to have curious minds of their own, nothing like the Iungo or reptilian tails. They were dressed similarly to the people with wings, but their body paint came in an array of colors.

They began a show filled with dancing, tumbling, and body contortion. The people leaped through suspended hoops and did backflips, all to the beat of the music. As they show progressed, Jael realized the performers were being switched out when the bird-people would flare their enormous wings. The two could hide the entire stage, plus a vast area to either side as well. She guessed their wings would need to be expansive to hold up such large beings.

Jael turned to see how her friends were enjoying the performance but found more than she had expected. Oran and Zoe were both topless and thoroughly exploring one another as Carter, Zill, and Aurelia watched. Jael noticed Carter's hand moving inside of Aurelia's shirt while Aurelia's hand was busy undoing Carter's pants. Behind Carter was Zill who already had his hands inside of Carter's shirt, lifting it up. Mercy was topless, and Amelia was gleefully entertained by her round breasts as Jael noticed them slowly moving closer to Oran and Zoe. Oran reached his tail out and wrapped it around Mercy's thick thigh, pulling her much closer to him and Zoe. Oran quickly helped Mercy slide out of her dress and dove his face in between her thighs as Amelia kissed her neck and stroked her eager peaks. Zoe slid under Oran, pulling down his pants and slipping them off him one leg at a time. Zoe rubbed her hand down his chest and into the bulge between his legs. His length sprang free as his reptilian slit opened and Zoe gasped. It was in the shape of a corkscrew. She had never seen such a thing and could hardly tear her eyes away.

Jael felt a hand on her shoulder and Destry leaned in as she felt Oz's hands sliding down her belly, finding his way along her body. With her hair brushing against Jael's shoulder, Destry whispered in her ear, "May I touch you, Jael?"

"Yes," was all she could sigh as Oz's hands found the tips of Jael's breasts. Destry began kissing down the side of her neck. She should have known better than to be surprised, but Destry's lips felt light and warm.

Lightning went through Jael as Destry gently kissed behind her ear. Oz began pulling her dress up to take it off, and Destry took it from him and pulled it up and off her, tossing it away. Oz leaned in and kissed Jael on her lower belly and slowly descended on the center of her heat with his mouth as Destry's long ridged tongue snaked out and began roaming Jael's chest.

Spinning her tongue around Jael's peaks as Oz's tongue explored between her legs, ecstasy filled her. While enraptured by the attention of Destry and Oz, Jael looked across as Zill positioned himself to enter Carter from behind. As he did, Aurelia went to her knees and put Carter's length in her mouth. Zoe rested between Oran's legs with her back to the ground while Oran had his face between Mercy's legs. Oran was gently thrusting into Zoe's awaiting, open mouth under him. His face told the story of a gentle cry, but his lips made no sound. Following the line and expecting to see Mercy's face, she instead found Amelia sitting on Mercy's face. Amelia had her head back and her mouth open, shivering with pleasure.

It was a sensual blending of bodies and pleasures, and instead of feeling shocked, Jael found the view to be an incredible enhancement to her own pleasure.

When her own release hit, a tornado of sensations spun within Jael. Within moments of Jael's eruption of pleasure, Oz was on top of her and filling her with his length. Destry went still behind her, and she watched as Oz twirled his finger for Destry to turn around. He flicked his long tongue at her as he hooked his finger for her to back up to him. She stripped her dress off in one motion, revealing her round belly and perfectly round, taut breasts. In a deep commanding tone, Oz told Destry, "Grab the back of the seat."

In understanding, she turned around and backed up over Jael so her rear was in the air in front of Oz's face. With Oz kneeling halfway off the couch, Destry held the back of the sofa while Jael lay comfortably underneath. Oz grabbed Destry by her hips, lifting her up to his mouth and tasting her thoroughly while he thrust into Jael. Being eye level with Destry's breasts, Jael decided to return a favor and took one of Destry's swollen peaks into her mouth.

A chorus of throat clicks and beautiful singing came from the group in the middle. The sounds of synchronized releases filled the small nook. Carter could be heard throughout the den as he roared and released into Aurelia's awaiting mouth.

Destry leaned her head back and sang a beautiful sound as her release slammed into her. She shook as Oz licked her until her delicate waves stopped. Unable to hold back any longer, Oz leaned his head back and his deep clicks joined the song filling the room as he pressed into Jael. He tipped over and his mad thrusting send Jael into another precipice of pleasure. The three shook with their ecstasy as Destry languidly moved over to lie beside Jael.

Oz leaned down and kissed Jael between the breasts and angled back up to whisper over her lips, "I am going to replay this night in my mind for the rest of my life."

She responded, "I can't wait to watch with you," then closed her eyes and released a dreamy breath.

Smiling, he took her face in his hands and kissed her, "I can see how exhausted you are. Do you want to go back to our room?"

Nodding, she looked over at the rest of their group and quickly realized they had just begun round two and no intention of stopping for rest any time soon. She envied the way they didn't need sleep.

Carter had already slipped his face between Aurelia's legs as Zill held her arms down and licked her breasts. Mercy, Oran, Zoe, and Amelia were all moaning loudly. They were in a pile on the floor, and it was too jumbled to make anything out. Jael turned around to see where Destry went. She found her drinking from a tall thin glass and sitting back on the couch, a server behind her with a tray full of drinks. Her gorgeous, curvy nude body was fully on display, obviously comfortable with her sensuousness. Jael marveled at how different, but how similar, they all were.

"Water?" she asked with a contented smile.

Nodding, Jael and Oz each took one, and Jael downed hers in a matter of gulps.

"Let me slip on my dress, and I'll walk you to your room." Destry slipped her dress on, and the server took the empty glasses.

Oz held up Jael's dress for her, and he found his robe behind the couch. When they were dressed, Destry led them out of the den along the winding pathways through the never ending gardens. The flowers were lit up from underneath and glowed like nightlights. Their colors spread around the stone pathways creating a mythical, ethereal feel in the palace grounds.

"Do you have any advice for tomorrow when we meet the Queen?" Oz asked as they passed a massive palm tree leaning over the pathway. Jael couldn't help but stop for a moment and admire the absurdly tall tree bent over at an odd angle before having to jog a bit to catch up.

Clearing her throat Destry finally answered without turning around, "Just be yourselves. It's rare we have such genuine guests. Zill beamed when he told Oran and me about all of you. Zill is our kingdom's best interrogator as well as close friend, so he makes a perfect liaison. He is genetically altered to smell hormones and trained on their role in every aspect of lying. You wouldn't have come anywhere near our home world without his clearance." She finally turned around and with a wide smile assuringly continued, "You have nothing to worry about tomorrow. The queen will enjoy meeting you."

They arrived at their rooms a few moments later, and she sighed before saying, "The queen will be tired in the early morning, so expect to hear something around mid-morning. She warned us all she had anticipated a long night tonight. She said something about a crisis on a remote planet."

Nodding, Oz asked, "Will we be seeing you there as well?"

Smiling, she answered, "Yes, I will be expected."

They headed into their room and as soon as the door clicked, Oz blurted out, "I think you have cum on your face." He couldn't help it as he laughed while she shifted her eyes around and rubbed her face. She went straight to the bathroom to clean up. When she was finished, he took his turn quickly and cleaned himself off in the shower. Emerging from the bathroom, he looked over and found Jael asleep, face down on the top of the bed. He smiled and slipped her mouth guard in just as her snore began to grow in volume. He repositioned her body so that she would be comfortable and then slid in the bed next to her to rest.

It seemed like only an instant before the system star's rays spilled over the top of their rooms. Jael woke, and they ate the breakfast waiting for them at their door. It was a mix of fluffy cakes and a floral syrup to pour on top with a generous portion of sliced fruit.

When the chime on the door sounded, Oz nearly came out of his skin as he turned to glare at the door.

"Did you just panic jump? You heard Destry last night. She said don't worry," Jael asked as she shoved a slice of honeydew melon in her mouth.

Narrowing his eyes at Jael, Oz quietly huffed, "I'm not answering that question. We need to go."

She kept her mouth shut, but she knew she was right. He power walked the entire way, and she wondered if he had been stewing over what he would say to the queen all night. His boots stomped the stones as he walked down the pathway. Jael could hardly keep up. The only time Oz slowed down was to look at the lights and find the direction they were supposed to turn at an intersection of pathways. When they finally arrived at the throne room, Oz stopped in his tracks, and Jael nearly slammed into his curled up tail. He was as still as death.

Destry sat on the throne with a crown on her head and a devious smirk on her face.

Her brother, Oran, sat next to her in a lower chair, and Zill stood next to the ornate wooden dais. There was a stunning selection of flowers growing around the throne and spilling over the dais. They grew on vines with hundreds of blooms of large flopping petals in soft pinks, vibrant fuchsias, reds, yellows, and violets.

Jael peaked around Oz and gasped in shock before she grabbed him by the arm and whispered, "Oz, I think you ate out the queen last night."

"Yeah. Yeah, I did," Oz agreed, his eyes wider than Jael had ever seen them.

At the other end of the room, Destry stood and offered, "Come in. We all got to know each other well last night. There is no reason for any of that awkwardness today."

"That's easy for you to say," Oz, paused, took a deep breath then, strode toward the throne as Destry stepped down and tossed her crown on the seat behind her casually.

She padded toward them and explained, "There are very few people in this galaxy who don't know what I look like. It's not every day you have a moment in time to live as a normal person and unknown for a day. Last night was a gift I never thought I would receive and thoroughly enjoy. I'm sorry to deceive you, yet I hope you had as wonderful of time as I did."

Understanding fell over him, and he and Jael followed as she waved to them to come sit on a round couch with a small fire in the center. When they all sat down, Destry had a deep upset look to her and a dark pit grew in Jael's belly.

"Oz, President Green, the Sarters are not equipped to fight a war yet. We were decimated by the UTC when they found out Aduro was one of the richest planets in any system near the galactic center. When we lost Aduro and Emendo, we lost over twenty million soldiers. They were trapped on the planets and massacred because the UTC didn't accept their surrender. They hate the power of the Sarter's kingdom. We were the great power in the galactic center until they showed up out of nowhere and began building their territory. We never saw it coming. Aduro was so radioactive we never thought the UTC would send soldiers there, but they did. After they had acquired the resources they needed, they went for Emendo. When they took Emendo, they dropped magnetic bombs on the cities, killing millions of our people in the first bombing. The rest were trapped there when our remaining armies were ordered to abandon the battle by the Sarter king. The UTC did experiments on them, ate many of our gentle intelligent creatures, then worked the rest of our people to death. They were all dead in less than ten years. My royal council claimed they will never vote for another war against the UTC - Especially not for a world that is not part of the Sarter's kingdom."

Oz nodded solemnly and asked, "I understand. So how do we become part of the Sarter's kingdom?"

"I have already spoken to the council about that. I had my answer waiting for me in my royal rooms when I retired from the den last night. Unfortunately, you have to prove you were not created by the UTC and win your freedom first. After you prove it, we will gladly accept your planet into our kingdom. We can discuss terms later, but my brother and I agreed the Iungo and the Sarters are of a similar mindset and when we can, we will help you," Destry revealed as pain filled her eyes. "Oz, I *begged* the council. I am so sorry."

Oran walked up and put his hand on her shoulder, causing her to peer up at him. He shook his head *no* and she patted his hand, lovingly.

"My brother doesn't want me to mention something, but I've already brought it up in a way, and I think I can trust you. We are building a legal case against the First Humans. We believe they are somehow manipulating the DNA of creatures on primitive worlds."

Turning to Jael, Destry explained further, "I think I know exactly what planet you're from. There were creatures you called dinosaurs before a major extinction event, right? They were like us, reptiles? Does your planet also have a large gas planet as well as one with rings?"

Stunned, Jael nodded, and Destry continued, "I think our people may have emerged first on your planet, and I think the UTC wiped them out. I don't know how. I just know the fossil records are wrong. Something is just not adding up. We found evidence of a species of dinosaur we developed from on your planet, in an advanced level of their evolution. It pointed to an emergence of my species on your planet, far before the first lines of the primates humans evolved from originated.

"They should have been flourishing there for millions of years, but we can't find any evidence of them. According to our excavations on Earth, our species survived the asteroid extinction. We know because our species visited Earth five million years ago. Our primitive species was there. Now there is no trace on Earth we can find.

"At the same time, we have found world after world with some level of evolving human. There are over a hundred worlds where humans are evolving and all of them are far under two million years in their point of evolution. It shouldn't be possible. It's *not* possible. All the planets are within a specific galactic area as well, one that includes Jael's solar system. We believe her planet was one of the first seeded."

Oz tilted his head in thought and cleared his throat

before he asked, "Are you saying, you think the first humans are somehow trading out the species which were supposed to evolve on a world, and making the chimpanzee on the planet branch off into humans instead?"

Focusing her eyes on him, she confirmed, "That is exactly what I am saying. They claim supremacy because multiple worlds are human origin worlds. Human worlds only produce humans, but many other planets have two or more origin species. We *know* something is happening, and while we've been compiling evidence for some time, we keep hitting a wall. We believe with enough solid evidence we will even be able to convince the UTC. The galactic center planets all have representatives who will have to be presented with the evidence to force a vote. The First Humans *will* lose power if we can prove it. We have been waiting for longer than you can imagine to bring their empire of destruction to their knees."

"We have several servers from the UTC base, with full access to them on my planet. The information is yours. I'll have someone at the base start copying the data," Oz offered. It was a well of information, and it could buy them a step closer to Sarter kingdom's assistance. He knew Amelia had found some information about this in the main computers and had planned to discuss it with her first before he opened his mouth to Destry; however, this conversation changed his plan.

Destry's mouth dropped briefly, but then she swung her head around to her brother with a smile and goaded, "I told you."

He rolled his eyes, crossed his arms, and flatly said, "Fine. You get this one. I was still right about the supply issue on Keru though."

Steeling the expression on her face, she turned back to Oz and asked, "I have one more question. How did you pass through our border grid without being detected?"

"We didn't plan it. We must have jumped right through your grid, just like your transports."

"You *jumped through*?" Oran asked, his fierce eyes narrowing.

Peering over at Jael, Oz explained, "It's the same engine which sent Jael to my planet, the EM Drive. Have your engineers speak with Carter, and he will explain everything."

A beaming smile on her face, Destry slowly turned her head around to her brother as Oran spouted off, "Oh enough, I can't be a triple loser today. I have a ballgame in an hour on Keru, and I still have a *thick* hangover."

41

PLANET ADURO – CLAUDIUS ROYAL PALACE

Hours had passed as Livia prepared for the royal ball. Her face was set, lashes applied, and her lipstick was powdered and reapplied. Delicate golden highlights on the peak of her cheekbones shone in the light. Her dress, shimmering midnight blue material with straps crisscrossing her chest and wrapping around her sides and neck, converged in the back with a diamond encrusted ring in the center. The dress fit her body exquisitely and floated down to the floor where it pooled at her feet.

Lucas stood at the door with his arms crossed as she glided across the floor toward him. "What the fuck takes *three* hours? You don't even grow hair," He sneered at her as he ran his own hand through his hair.

She calmed her breath and bit her own tongue to keep her face neutral. If she so much as flinched, he would backhand her. She didn't want to have to call the beauty team back to fix her makeup, so she remained stoic. Her make-up had taken twice as long because of him in the first place.

There was damage to her skin that had to be covered. She wasn't sure how much more make-up she could stand on her face and neck and back.

"Let's go," he seethed as he began walking down the hallway toward the lift.

Livia didn't hesitate as she took the sides of her dress into her hands and lifted it to allow her to keep up with him. She walked as quickly as she could in the stilettos digging into her feet. For shoes designed around her feet, they were suspiciously uncomfortable. Lucas was much taller than she, and his stride was lengthy. She had nightmares about having to keep up with him and not being fast enough. She gulped quietly and ignored the blister already forming below her ankle. When they arrived at the lift, he grumbled something under his breath about her slowness. His ability to sour a room was uncanny. Every second with this man was torture to her soul.

She hoped the evening would move along quickly so she could retrieve August from the mine and begin their plan. All the mines were prepared with weapons, and the people knew what to do. It was just up to her and August to complete the job in the palace. For hours, her mind spun around the ways their plan could fail and what she could do to correct any possible complications. Now it was becoming hard to form a single thought. It was all she could do to just put one foot in front of another. Her body and mind felt drained, yet the night hadn't even begun.

The clicks of her heels, as if they were the clicks of a clock, ticked away as they headed down the hall to the throne room. When they crossed the threshold of the lights streaming from the open door, Lucas grabbed her arm and held it in his bruising grasp as they made their formal entrance. Livia put on her best smile, despite the deep ache in her arm. She knew she kept her face as solid as stone, but he must've known she was not smiling and dug his fingers deeper into her flesh. She cringed internally as he found a pressure point and ground his finger into it. The one lesson from the academy she was thankful for more than anything was her training to withstand torture. It was how she had won the galactic center's top warrior games on Emendo in her youth. No matter how badly she was hurt, she kept going until it was finished. Lucas, with his perfect shining hair next to her hadn't been allowed to participate, as the king's heir. *A shame,* she thought. She may have lost, but to have been able to land a few hits in on him first would have been worth the beating. Her gaze roamed the room, noting none but Melior's best.

After being announced to the room full of Melior's most affluent, Livia and Lucas found their seats. As she sat down, she noticed a familiar shade of red reflecting off a mirror within the floral centerpiece. It was a shade of red she *loved.* She felt her heart squeeze in her chest, and her vision swayed as if she had been drugged.

Not daring to move, her eyes surveyed the room. Some of the most attractive of August's people were in cages, hanging like decoration. They had been freshly washed and put in palace servant attire. Simple cream tunics with comfortable loose cream pants. Bile rose in her throat, and she fought the urge to excuse herself to the restroom. She didn't have to turn around to know August was behind her, hanging helpless in a cage like the rest of them. She should have known her father would plan something as sick as this.

They were golden bird cages. *The Iris queen must have brought them,* she thought as she fought the urge to cry at this degradation. It was becoming unbearable to hold back her emotions. *How did I let this happen? How did I fall in love with someone I could never have? How did I become so callous to the vicious treatment of a whole people?*

This barbaric decoration had ruined the entire plan and even worse, she realized this might be the last time she would ever see August. *It was over.*

She had never anticipated her father would go along with this Iris practice. Her heart hardened as she found her father, who held a wide grin on his face as he danced with one of the members of the Iris court. They were adorned in a ruby red ballgown that contrasted their bright lime wings edged with feathers of the color of flames.

"I'm going to dance with someone else if you're going to just sit here and stare off," Lucas spat after he downed his glass of wine, negating his own rudeness in not asking his spouse to dance. He acted as if Livia had a repulsive disease on a good day, so she wasn't surprised at his tone, and still grateful he hadn't asked. She needed time to think.

Without waiting for her response, he rose from his seat and approached a beautiful Iris woman with sapphire wings and royal purple hair. She was stunningly beautiful, with her big round eyes and generous lips. Her smile revealed a mouthful of bright white sharply pointed teeth. They danced off into the crowd of the royal court, spinning on the dance floor. Her wings fluttered behind her, and she threw her head back with delight.

Livia hoped that Iris woman would want to suck Lucas's dick later. "Those teeth look like they could cut it clean off with just a nip," she hoped under her breath as she ran her tongue over her own flat, blunt, useless teeth.

Searching before her, she found a small piece of mirror

that had fallen from the centerpiece. Scanning the room for anyone facing her direction, she found all attention elsewhere. Holding it up, she angled it so she could see August behind her. When she moved the mirror to find his face, she found him already focused on her. His vibrant orange eyes were filled with despair and desperation.

Livia had never felt as broken as she did in that moment. Helplessness settled in as she held her eyes to his. *How could this have happened?* First guilt and sorrow consumed her before it became rage. She had fallen for her red demon. She had fallen so *hard*. Her breath caught, and her blood boiled as she held herself still with an iron will. Her eyes remained locked with his.

The music changed, and she was snapped out of her trance by her glass being filled. When she looked up, her eyes crossed the room, and they landed on the guard from the training room, Valec Sentle. She had pulled his file after he continuously helped her without question on occasions he most certainly should have been questioning. He had been out of the academy for several years and knew much more about combat than his subdued form had implied.

She realized he might be their only chance. Their plan required two people. They had blood to spill after the ball, and she could not do it all herself. She just hoped he would be willing to help her. Even more so, she hoped he had the stomach. Moving quickly, she needed to speak to the guard before the servers made their rounds and finished setting down every plate of the main course.

Pretending to dance, she spun her way around the groups of people to the other end of the throne room and found Valec. She stood in front of him and held her glass of wine up. She held her hand out flat where she held the flute of her glass of wine for her voice to bounce off.

"I need your help," she whispered.

Keeping his soldier's focus forward, he replied, "Anything Princess." She had not been called that title in a very long time. Holding in her relief, she knew his meaning by using her former title. He saw her as the heir. Her heart beat wildly in her chest. She calmed herself as she took slow deep breaths. Despite all the training she had been through, all the beatings she had endured from Lucas, all the torture and pain from the academy, nothing prepared her for August being dangled in front of her face. She felt her heart crumble. She could hardly exist in her own skin as her eyes at the horror of seeing him in that cage. She knew exactly what they would do to him. That Iris bitch wants to drug and rape him, rip his throat out with her teeth, skin him, and then eat him. Livia would not fail tonight. The Iris were truly despicable when they wanted to be.

"I am taking my place as King. I have several targets, but my partner is strung up in gold," Livia's words spilled from her lips as she turned to face him before spinning back around pretending to dance.

Trying to hold back a bashful smile, Valec replied to her back, "I am with you, my King."

She swayed to the beat as his words found their mark, giving her a spark of hope. Shifting her gaze across the room, she saw Lucas heading toward their seats.

"I need you to free the man I train with directly after the ball is over. The palace guard station should have the code breakers. Waiting even a moment too long could endanger his life," His barely perceptible nod assured her instructions would be followed as she turned to dance back to her seat.

When she was halfway across the room, Valec cried out, "May Jupiter bless the King!"

Everyone in the room shouted in reply, "May Jupiter bless the King!" Valec stood facing Livia as she stared back at him from her place in the center of the throne room. People of all kinds danced around her, cheering and unaware. A deep sense of duty and obligation fell over her, and she gave him a slight nod. He smiled, and she went to find her seat next to Lucas for their main course. When she sat, one of the mirrors on the arrangement gave her a perfect view of August. Unable to help the smile in her eyes, he caught on and tilted his head slightly.

Livia leaned over to Lucas and just by his scent, she found him already intoxicated. He obliviously ate off the giant leg of some Vistalia game. The leg was long with white meat ending in a scaly foot and three long yellowed claws. She had the drip ready under her bracelet, but he had been guarding his glass. Lucas gulped his wine and began coughing as he choked on the liquid. He leaned over and coughed a few more times to the side of the table in an attempt to regain his breath.

She took her chance and made eye contact with August in the mirror. Giving him a brief beautiful smile, she returned to her usual stoic look. She hoped it was enough to convey the message. When she peered back over, Lucas downed the rest of his wine and waved over a server for more. The server approached on Livia's side, so when Lucas handed his glass to her to pass to the server, she slid her thumb against the edge, and a single drop of sedative squeezed out of a tiny flesh color pouch she had adhered to her skin. She watched as the drip roll down the side of the glass as the server refilled it.

She handed the drink back to Lucas, and he snatched it from her like her skin had possibly tainted the glass if it had touched the surface any longer. August watched everything from his gilded cage, and she hoped he was able to keep his calm if Lucas tried anything. As drunk as he was, if she so much as breathed wrong, he could snap and backhand her.

King Claudius strolled up to his tall throne and stood in front of it. Everyone in the room bowed their heads and awaited his words. He stood in his typical ballroom attire of what seemed to be loose sleepwear in Livia's opinion. His long flowing button down shirt was open far enough to see his entire chest. Her father disgusted her.

He signaled for everyone to be seated and began, "Welcome kings, queens, and Melior nobility. I hope your courts find this evening's ball an exciting beginning for the bidding. The sale will begin tomorrow at first light and conclude when the star sets each day. I have plenty of high quality specimens available, many personal gifts from the empress herself.

"I have displayed some selections around the room, but these are just an example of the kind of stock we have, a real show of the power of the UTC and our ability to turn even insects into formidable workers.

"If I find any of them are sent to the games, and I'm not invited, I'll expect a premium visual recording of the event with a formal apology!" King Claudius joked, followed by an eruption of forced laughter from the crowd.

Livia zeroed in on one of the members of the Iris royal court staying in the palace overnight and not returning to their ship. Yix stood in front of her father's dais, and he stepped down to meet her. After a lascivious kiss that made bile churn in her gut, the king found his seat at a table filled with the richest of all the nobility.

Livia glared down at her food and wasn't sure how she could eat at this moment. When she turned back to see what Lucas was doing, she watched as he and the Iris woman stumbled out of the main doors. He didn't care about discretion or insulting his wife, and flaunted his affairs to affront her.

She knew this could ultimately be a fatal kink in their plan, but for now, she was relieved. With Lucas gone from the room, she could focus on finding her targets and watching where they went. She should have known he would run off to fuck someone, but with the locator she planted in his suit, she knew he wouldn't be too hard to track him down at the end. If the drip she gave him worked, he would soon be asleep for hours and unable to wake up.

A shadow blocked the light and as her eyes adjusted, she found King Sarto standing before her with a look of utter sorrow on his handsome face. He swallowed, his eyes dipping for a moment, and he slowly held his hand out. "Livia, is it? May I have a dance?" He asked with such underlying sadness her breath slipped away like a chilled wind.

Nodding, she took his warm hand, and he led her to the dance floor. She gave August a peek at the first turn, and he seemed to be thoroughly content watching her dance with someone other than Lucas. A bit of relief calmed her nerves, and she fell into the dance. After a few moments, she had the overwhelming desire to inquire into his mood so she asked, "King Sarto?"

"Yes?" he asked.

"Your sadness seems to pour from you. Are you alright

this evening?" Livia asked, her eyes focused on his bright green eyes.

His chestnut hair gleamed in the lights as he shook his head, no. He asked, "Can I trust you will remain quiet?"

Nodding, Livia breathed, "Absolutely."

He spun them around before he asked, "Have you had a blue *woman* added to your mines? The Empress appeared at my palace and took one from me. I've been looking every-where for her. I was hoping she gave her to King Claudius." King Sarto's voice cracked when he said the word '*woman*' and every word he said made so much more sense. Her heart squeezed in her chest. She knew who this woman was to him. *I heard rumors for years about King Sarto and his defi-ance with the First Humans, those rumors are beginning to make a lot more sense.*

Livia shook her head, "The newest one is the man in the golden cage behind where I was sitting. Before him, we hadn't received anyone new in a long time."

Livia suddenly tensed as she reviewed her own words. She called August a man. She waited for the King to notice her slip up, but he just hung his head. "I was afraid that's what you would say," he confessed as she could see the grief creeping back into his eyes.

Livia whispered, "She must have meant a lot to you. I'm sorry she was taken from you."

He breathed roughly and his big green eyes blinked slowly as he quietly begged, "I would pay any sum for her return. I would travel anywhere, do anything. Give anything."

"If I hear or see anything about a blue woman like you said, I will send word right away," Livia assured him.

He nodded and squeezed her hand in thanks as the song

ended. After a bow to him, Livia returned to her seat. She had heard rumors of King Sarto and his relationship with his, his what? *What were August's people called?* She was sick of everyone calling them bugs. That's not what they were. They were higher sentient beings, and descendants of scorpions, or so August's people thought.

When she sat down, she found a large dessert in front of her. Digging a spoon in and bringing it to her mouth, she stopped before the tall dollop of whipped cream touched her lips. She wondered if the dessert was even safe for her to eat. She hadn't eaten anything so far and thought she better keep it that way. Her father or Lucas may have put in an order to have her drugged. It would not be the first time she had skipped a meal because she suspected it had been dripped.

Peering around the room, Livia's eyes met Valec's, and he blinked once. Sliding her eyes down to where his hand was, he revealed he had already obtained the code breaker to open the doors of the cages. As she looked at the cages one by one, something occurred to her. Her father had not ruined her plans at all. He had improved them.

42

PLANET PORTUM – IUNGO BASE

Something was bothering Callum. Jacob didn't know what it was, but something was eating at him, an idea, or fear. Jacob had no inkling what it was, this feeling of something hidden, or if he would ever come clean about it. He needed a shift in his thoughts and think about something constructive. Worrying about Callum all day never solved anything. He would talk when he was ready. This wasn't the first time a rumbling storm cloud had followed Callum around.

Lying in bed and reviewing the memories of their journey, he couldn't shake the snails out of his mind. Giant and tiny alike, all moving in a slow acidic wave over the land, sizzling organic matter in their path and leaving nothing but boiling slime, they were creatures of death in so many forms. Oz's group had encountered a mass of snails on the other side of the beach too. That was peculiar. Then there was that large monstrosity of a creature on the beach with a long segmented body and tail. He distinctly remembered the carapace plates along its back that detached and fallen into its side in its state of decay. When he had read over the report, he zoomed in on the satellite for a visual. That had been an awfully interesting creature.

In his mind, the image of the washed up creature on the beach was overlaid with a giant scorpion. They fit together so well it was like finding that one missing piece of the jigsaw puzzle needed for completion. That one piece he needed in order to move on and finish the puzzle.

He choked on his own breath with the realization. Sitting up straight in his bed as the idea struck him, Jacob leaned over and shook Callum's shoulder.

"What?" Callum grumbled, his face still deep in his pillow.

"What if we are looking at this the wrong way? What if we needed to be searching for more of our ancient genetic cousins instead of the old bones of our people? Fuck Cal, that's it! The lab said we have probably had one heavy radiation extinction event early in our genetic history. Any existing ground scorpions would have had a direct hit of radiation, warping them more than, let's say, a later wave of scorpions coming from a common genetic ancestor. This common ancestor was more protected from the radiation deep under the sea. The ones on land had their DNA too damaged and never became the higher sentient beings they were supposed to become. We have to be from a second wave. That's why we have so much unexplainable DNA like an Earth tardigrade. A horizontal gene transfer! What if the radiation we received under the surface mixed our DNA with the plants and bacteria digesting inside of us during the event?!" Leaping out of bed, his rapid-fire thoughts could not be contained. Jacob ran to his tablet and called Vida.

When her face materialized, he didn't wait for her greeting and burst out, "Vida!"

"We are looking in the wrong place! We need to find our other genetic cousins or even better, a common ancestor. A while ago I was reviewing Jael's memories, and she watched a TV show one night, something about finding humans most recent common ancestor, and I think that's what led my thoughts. Plus, did you read the labs report about the heavy radiation extinction event early in our history? It just makes sense, Vida." His face was tipped into the hologram sensor area, and his eyes were wide with exhilaration, a thrill filled every word as Jacob blurted out his expanding thoughts.

Shocked at his revelation, Vida slowly replied, "I have read the report and I get what you're saying. All scorpions we've tested just aren't close enough to prove anything. We could have been created from them with enough gene manipulation and splicing. We even have whole sections of our genetics in common with plants, too. I don't know how else to tell you, but this is not looking good."

"Not the giant ground scorpions, *other* living cousins, older cousins, we need to test *everything*," Jacob explained, his eyes wider than before though his tone began to calm.

"On what vast beach do you suggest we start the search for this mystical grain of sand? The sarcasm in Vida's tone was sharp.

Smiling and filled with pride, he replied, "That's exactly where I say we look. What about that long, segmented sea creature washed up on the beach. Cal and I can collect the samples if we don't have anyone else available."

"Speak for yourself," Callum growled, still face down in his pillow.

Vida interrupted, "It's going to take a week to test any

additional samples. I have a mountain to go through right now. If you want to take a transport and collect the samples, I will test it after I'm finished."

"You have a deal." Jacob agreed as hung up and began excitedly preparing.

Begrudgingly, Callum dressed in his armor as Jacob did the same. They headed to the transports just outside of the cave entrance and climbed in without a word.

The journey across the water was serene as they approached the giant rotting beast on the northern beach. Callum waited in the transport as Jacob ventured out. His boots crunched against the cold sand as he scooped up some rotting flesh from a crack in the creature's exoskeleton. Wondering if it was enough, he pulled out his plasma sword and cut a piece of the carapace free with some of the sticky blue-grey entrails bonded to it before heading back to the transport.

Briskly heading toward the transport to stow the carapace and flesh of the sea creature in the sample case, he peered over at the rotting carcass noticing maggots wriggling and flies swarming. Sighing, he was thankful for the CO_2 recycler in the back of the helmet. The so-called fresh air, he decided, probably smelled bad enough to kill an adult Iungo. Around the back of the transport, he pulled the case out and opened it before fitting the carapace and tissues in the freezer box.

As he scanned the beach, he saw an eclipse of moths with large beautiful blue wings and furry tan body fanning themselves in the gentle warm breeze. They were resplendent, but something inside him gave him pause. His heart sank as he recalled why they were blue, and his mind went straight to Thorn. Their wings were the exact color of his people's blood. A shiver of fright struck him, and he bolted.

Running toward his seat in the transport, he leaped inside and slammed the door. Callum cocked his head at Jacob before leaning it back on the headrest again.

"I think the big blue moths spread out everywhere on the beach are the adult stage of the type of caterpillars that killed and ate Thorn," Jacob spouted off, his words stumbling. His heart was pounding so hard in his body he could hardly form a coherent thought.

Callum's mouth dropped open as he also made the connection, and he yelped, "Let's get the hell out of here before they lay an egg on the transport!"

When Jacob believed he could not be more horrified at the situation, Callum unlocked a whole new fear.

Several of the murderous moths were now flying around the transport searching for a place to perch. A moth with footlong wings landed on their windshield and they both screamed at the top of their lungs as Jacob frantically searched the controls. Finding what he wanted, he pressed a red button, and sparks shot from the moth's needlelike feet where it was touching the glass. As it fell, a stream of electricity followed it for a few moments before finally snapping back into the transport shields.

"Did you just electrify the exterior of the transport? I didn't know it could do that," Callum asked as he steadied his breath.

"It's the rail gun defense Mercy came up with. I added it to the transport plans in case we ran into any larger railgun fire. I'm glad I over-prepared," Jacob explained, his eyes trained on the flapping wings of the moths converging outside.

"Me, too! Leave it on! Let's get the fuck out of here before we end up moth meat," Callum quipped, and Jacob started the flight engine and took off at full throttle.

Callum longingly gazed down at the turquoise waves and asked, "Why can't we fly closer to the water?"

Frustration oozing through his words, Jacob asked, "Did you not watch the video I sent you from when Oz's team crossed the water?"

"No. I'm going to be honest. I don't watch any of the videos you send me. After the first three of the stinky beetle with a horn you found, it was physically painful for me to even attempt to watch them after that, and I am not sorry. Our people need some type of man-eating predator free visual media, immediately. I'd settle for a puppet show at this point," Callum admitted defiantly.

Chuckling, Jacob grinned and replied, "First, there's no way you could have known that beetle smelled bad. Second, don't say I didn't warn you." Diving straight down toward the water, Jacob pulled up at the last second and shot straight back up to where they had been before. He tipped the transport on its side so Callum could see.

A massive rusty red tentacle with a white underside and suckers running down the length of the arm shot up from deep and slapped the surface of the water before disappearing into the depths again. The transport hovered as Callum stared blankly at the water until the ripples calmed.

"What. The. Fuck. Was. That?" Callum gasped as he turned to look at Jacob.

"The reason we are not flying close to the water. It's a very large octopus. It's a female, and we think she is around six hundred years old. We caught a glimpse of a few more in the waters of the south ocean, but they're not anywhere near her size," Jacob explained. "We think there might be an extensive underwater cave system throughout our continent, but we are not sending anyone down there anytime soon."

Staring down at the sea once again, Callum confessed, "This is why I don't like your weird videos. That was way cooler than on a screen."

Rolling his eyes, Jacob flew them back to the base and landed the transport between the trees. Callum tossed his helmet into the back seat behind Jacob's seat and paused before he unlatched the seat harness. As he released it, he turned to Jacob and placed a restraining hand on Jacob's arm.

"What's wrong?" Jacob asked.

Silence filled the transport, long enough that Jacob began looking around the clearing. The breeze was blowing, and a leaf fell from one of the trees. It floated down and landed on the ground softly - joining other leaves, soon to be dead, rotting on the ground.

Callum carefully asked, "Can we go on a walk? I need to talk to you about something."

With a bile rising in his throat from Callum's tone, Jacob managed to speak just above a whisper, "Sure. I just need to drop off the sample. I'll be right back."

As Jacob passed through the trees and down the stairs inside, Callum wondered how the hell he would tell the man he loved how he felt. The dread rolled through him with every second they didn't have an answer if they were created in a lab or not. Callum's worst fear was falling back under the UTC control and having to revert back to the eternal silence. He had too much life to share, goals to discuss, and love to express. *I could never say the words I loved you to Jacob.* To Callum, the silence was akin to returning to hell.

His eyes followed Jacob as he approached, and they burned with the promise of tears. Climbing down from his seat, Callum suggested, "Let's walk toward the silk farms. I haven't been by there in too long."

Nodding, Jacob took Callum's hand and dread filled him as he quietly asked, "What did you need to talk about?"

"Jacob, I don't know how to say this. It's going to take a few moments to find the right words. I am just afraid I won't have another opportunity if I wait too long," Callum stared off into the distance.

Not knowing what else to say, Jacob asked, "Do you want to connect and just share your feelings with me?"

Callum stopped and held Jacob's hand tighter as he finally began, "That's kind of what I want to talk about. The connection. Silence."

Jacob didn't say a word so Callum could finish his thought.

"Jacob, the reticence, I can't. I just. I wasn't doing well before. You know?" Tears began welling in Callum's eyes as he desperately tried to hold it all back.

Jacob took one step in front of him and reached for his other hand. Callum didn't dare look up.

Taking a slow breath, he started again and quietly admitted, "The inability to communicate was slowly killing me long before I ever knew what words were. Every passing moment of that time, my spirit begged me to let it free. It was withering away in the absence of expression. Now that I've had the taste of language in my mouth..." He stopped and took a few breaths before he continued, saying, "I can't go back. If we can't prove we are origin species from our planet, I can't go back to the silence and never say *I love you* again."

He stopped speaking as a lump formed in his throat and he closed his eyes waiting for Jacob's response. He could feel Jacob freeze in front of him.

The soothing movement of his hands had stopped, chilling Callum to the bone.

43

SARTER MOON MARKET

Developing a heavy scowl on her wrinkled face, Kagnus leaned toward Cinis with her prying words, "Are you *sure* you know a place we can hide the ship?"

Cinis let their head hang back as they briefly closed their eyes. They had all been over this several times. They brought their gaze back down to Kagnus as they answered again, "Yes. She said her hanger is big enough for us to jump directly into it. I already contacted her with Carter and we have the coordinates."

"President Green, is this plan really happening? I don't think you've thought this through. We are jumping millions of miles directly into a spacecraft hanger? Isn't this a new and untested length of travel?" Kagnus swung around to face Oz with her question.

Nodding he gently replied, "This time we have exact coordinates. If Carter said he can get it in there, I believe him."

Mercy slapped a hand over her mouth to hold back her

laughter, and Oz slowly turned back to face her. Shaking his head, he turned back to face the holo-screen and made some adjustments to the ship's shields before the jump. "Carter, we are ready when you are," Oz directed into the comms. A holo-screen with just Carter's head popped up at his controls, and Oz asked, "Are you sure you don't want to be on the bridge?"

Carter didn't respond at first, and stared at Oz before answering flatly, "We are ready."

"Let's go." Oz announced as he shifted his eyes over to Jael.

For the briefest moment in time, Oz felt like he had been there before. The recurrence sensation sunk into his bones as he burned it into his brain. Jael was ethereal with a halo of curls around her hairline as the light of the EM drive consumed them. She glowed from within like a spirit of light before the brightness exploded around them, engulfing them with heat and energy.

According to their brains, they had snapped out of existence. When the encompassing light and heat finally ceased, they were parked in the hanger. As tiny streams of steam wafted from various points on the bridge, Oz assessed everyone in the room before he read the readings on his display.

"That was our best jump yet. We weren't even off an inch. Amelia, what do our cellular scans look like?" Oz threw over his shoulder as he continued reading his display.

She scrolled through her tablet and answered, "The jumps are doing nothing to our bodies. We are always exactly the same on a molecular and cellular level. I think it's safe to say for now that this is an exceptional way to travel through massive distances of space."

"How long until the Sarter's call wanting this tech in exchange for their help?" Kagnus sneered with her arms crossed and an epic frown on her face. The wrinkles in her face had sunk in so deeply they seemed to be permanently set in a frown.

Oz slid his irritated gaze over to Kagnus and spouted off, "I told you we are not going to count on the Sarters. We need to focus on the mission at hand. We have to find information on the First Humans' origin world and find a hacker who has UTC network access to broadcast our message when we get word from Vida."

"You're going to be sorry for that. The Sarters are the only kingdom with a battleship fleet big enough come close to the UTC numbers. We should have stayed. A few more nights with Oz and the Queen, and he might have won us an ally," Kagnus retorted.

Jael chuckled as Oz locked his narrowed eyes on Kagnus and furrowed his brow at her as he explained, "That's a perfect example of why you're staying behind when we head to Cinis's apartment."

They filed off the bridge after gathering their things. Following Oz out of the airlock, they descended the stairs and found a pale skinned human woman in an elegant dress with long brown hair waiting for them. Her burnished copper metallic dress had brass leaves at her shoulders gathering the draping floor length dress above each arm, emphasizing her lean build. Jael looked back, and Cinis and their eyes were glazed over and a bright smile graced their face. They wrung their hands nervously as the beautiful woman glided over and gave Cinis a hug. Maybe it was a little more than just a hug as it lingered for several seconds.

"I am Rungi. Welcome to my home. I hear we have a

common enemy, and that makes us *very* good friends. You may leave your vessel in my hanger for as long as you need and access it at any time. Please follow me through the factory and out onto the street.

Don't touch *anything*," Rungi snapped as she headed toward a massive set of steel double doors. Rungi didn't simply walk - she danced and glided across a floor like she was skating over ice.

The doors swung open as she neared, and Mercy gasped at the sight inside the factory. Hundreds of people of different species were all working on various weaponry. Some were assembling massive rolling rail guns and others were building smaller, handheld shooting weapons. A group in the back was testing a type of laser by actively cutting the head off a dummy. The feathered and membranous wings, various prehensile tails, towering ears, and the arrays of colors of the people working left their group of Iungo and humans speechless.

When they reached a table at the other end of the building, Rungi turned and stared at Cinis for a moment before sensually telling the group, "Drop your tails down and put on these cloaks. Cinis, I left a bag at your apartment a few hours ago. Everything you asked for is there. It was hard to procure. You *owe* me." Cinis nodded slightly, their expression bursting with enough desire to fill the room. Rungi left the group to head up a set of stairs leading to a hallway as they finished preparing.

When they reached the street, Cinis turned to the group, "I live two blocks away. Follow me."

Keeping a fast pace, they reached a towering apartment building with balconies too small to step out onto, yet all filled with either an abundance of foliage or a pile of rusted junk. Some had both.

Inside, Jael had to leap to avoid a growling woman with a bony arm grabbing at her boot. She hissed when Jael jumped from her grasp.

"They will steal your clothes right off your body if they're not secured properly. She probably thought your boot seemed loose," Cinis explained to Jael. She peered down at her boot and shivered with the thought. This was one of the times she wished Sis was with her. She *always* knew what to do. Her heart ached with the memories. They reached a contraption that looked like an industrial elevator, and Jael cringed as the metal creaked even before any of them had stepped on.

"We need to get you dressed and ready. Rungi just sent a message to my com, and she is sending her personal transport over at eight. It's seven right now," Cinis explained as they all climbed aboard the highly questionable lift. It groaned as it rose through the floors, and it squealed like a train coming to a stop when the doors opened at Cinis's floor. They all nearly fell out into the hall trying to escape the questionable lift. Cinis led them down to the farthest apartment before scanning their key card so the door lock clicked open.

Holding the door, Cinis peeked around the corner at their grandmother, "My sister Tressa is still at a doctor's appointment, so you can use the back bathroom. I'm sorry there isn't much room." They then walked over to an old woman in a wheelchair, unaware of anything going on, and they pushed her chair over to a small window where the last of the day's light streamed through.

Mercy led Jael into the tiny back bathroom with the

dress and makeup Cinis had given her. As Jael did her makeup perched on a teeny stool, Mercy worked on her hair. Mercy had never used a hot tool before, but it was easy enough to understand. "Curl away from the face for a softer look," a kind voice offered from the dark bedroom.

The dark doorway brightened as a stunning woman with a large round belly walked into the light. "Thank you. Any other suggestions?" The question slipped into the void as Mercy took in the perfect makeup and hair of the woman standing before her. Smiling, the woman gently shoved Mercy out of the way with her pregnant belly and reached over for what appeared to be a spray bottle.

"Put your feet up," she gently directed as she spun her finger at Jael. Complying, Jael lifted her feet as she gripped the counter for balance. The woman sprayed her feet and sat the bottle down next to her.

"It's a numbing spray for my grandmother's vein connection since sometimes her skin is irritated. Your feet hurting will give you away when you walk. Fem rich live in heels, so if you're going for that, you need to perfect the look down to the walk. It's not what you're wearing, it's how you wear it. Make sure to change into the gem encrusted sandals before you dance. You will thank me later," she explained as she pointed to the sandals she had set on the bed.

"Are you Tressa?" Mercy asked softly.

With a smile, Tressa answered, "Yes," then slipped Jael's heels onto her feet for her. Tressa carefully patted Jael's leg as she spoke, "Stand up and walk."

Jael stood and her body folded, unsure of where to place her weight on her feet. Attempting to lift herself from the floor unsuccessfully, she felt like a baby gazelle.

With her eyes wide and legs braced to either side, Tressa

helped Mercy lift Jael back up onto her feet. "Pretend your ankles don't move. Now walk." Tressa directed as she kept her eyes on Jael's feet. Jael took a weary first step, but within a few more steps she was gliding. Nodding, Tressa pointed to Jael's dress as she went on, "Good. You caught on fast. Now take your clothes off. We need to get your dress on. The transport will be here in fifteen minutes."

Mercy leaned over and grabbed the sparkling dress as Jael slipped her shirt off and tossed it onto Tress' bed.

"Tressa!" The old woman screeched from the other room.

Rolling her eyes, Tressa whispered, "I'll be right back. Grumpy needs to be moved."

Jael sat on the bed and took her heels and pants off. Slipping the dress on, Jael stood up and slid the heels back on.

"Damn, Jael, you look good," Mercy stood before her with a bright smile.

Oz peeked around the doorway and when his eyes fell on Jael, he approached her purring, "I hope you can do that again because I am about to fuck it all it up."

"No! The transport is almost here. Keep it in your pants. You need to change into your guard uniform," Mercy demanded as she tossed Oz his clothes.

The wad of clothes hit him in the chest, and he caught them, both hands wrapped around the clothes, gripping them tightly. After setting them on the bed, he lifted up the blue band. He cringed as he put the band around his neck, the one that labeled him as an owned guard. Sliding his attention back to Jael, he wondered if she would be able to pull off being cold and unfeeling better than he could pretend to be on a leash.

After he finished changing, they headed to the lift and

descended to the bottom level. As they made their way out of the derelict building, several unhoused people gave them odd looks, but they were all far too stunned to grab at them. Jael was clearly out of place dressed as a rich, high-class human from Melior with two Iungo guards and a human assistant. Using Iungo for guards was not common but also not unheard of. It was a sign of ruthlessness to have Iungo people as bodyguards. Iungo were known to be formidable in physical combat when trained, but only a few were brave enough to do it, fearing the Iungo would turn on them.

A sleek black transport showed up, and Jael was shocked to see how similar it was to a limousine back on Earth, wheels and all. Several more wheels were inside each wheel-well, but they were thinner, seeming more like a wagon's wheels. The driver seemed similar to a human at first, but when she saw inside the vehicle, she realized he had bat wings and tall pointed ears. As Jael slid in the back, she studied the membranous wings. The seat was low and shaped like a V to accommodate wings or a tail. Her attention slid around the back of the vehicle noting the back was designed for human comfort only. The only seats comfortable for anyone but a human were up front. Her stomach twisted with the realization she might not be as prepared for this mission as she thought.

Oz laid his hand on Jael's leg in reassurance before he tried to find a comfortable position for his tail. Mercy gave a half eye roll when she saw the seats and didn't try and sit in the back. She made her way around the transport and sat in the passenger seat next to the winged man. The man with bat wings slowly turned to her and creased his brow, but she just shrugged to him and shut the door. Her tail fit perfectly in the center of the seat. He turned and gave Jael an inquisitive look.

"What?" Jael asked, genuinely confused.

Clearing his throat he blankly stared at Mercy as he spoke at her, "Your guards are acting *strange*."

Mercy checked the area and raised her tail in a threatening manor, the stinger section of her tail was clearly still attached.

He reared back, flashing his fangs and hissed, "*Mars spare me*. Is that a stinger? Are these guards genetically altered?"

Mercy responded by leaning in and hissing back at him, showing him all eight of her sharp fangs.

The man's gasped in fear as he leaned as far away from Mercy as he could. His head eventually bumped against his window with his wings smashed behind him. By his reaction, there was nowhere near enough room for him to move far enough away from her.

Cinis cleared their throat and nervously explained, "The guards are not clipped or declawed. They cost a fortune. Tachie is a daughter of the house of Sergii and a member of the temple of Mercury. I suggest you have us on our way before we have to teach one of the guards to drive."

Oz clamped his lips together and turned his face away from the man at the front. Jael nudged his leg and whispered, "What happened to your acting skills?" He rolled his eyes and nudged her back.

Up front, Mercy tugged at the band around her neck. As she tried to discreetly peer over at the dark haired man, she wondered what kind of being he was. He looked like a bat with those membranous wings. He had sharp ears rising above his head with horizontal ridges below the ear where it met his neck. He had similar ridges on his slightly upturned nose below his brow. *Could he fly with those wings?*

Taking in the city as they passed, Mercy found it to be a mixture of old and new minor wealth and its inevitable decay. The apartment buildings all had a similar boxy style while some of the businesses were designed with massive columns and giant ornate doors. Many of the buildings depicted great scenes of battle between the UTC and the ancient Sarter army. There were no hints of wealth on the sides of streets, which were filled with hunger and pain. The ragged tents and boxes with people huddled inside littered the sidewalks and small parks. The road, however, was filled with new, humming vehicles. They all sparkled, and their lights were bright, illuminating the dark street. Some of the older transports had all their windows down and some kind of vaporous smoke billowing from the back where the engine was.

Multicolored lights shined from advertisements, filling Mercy's eyes with dancing cartoons and regal humans speaking about the importance of their loyalty, "The UTC is helping the hungry, unhoused citizens, *caring* for them." Her eyes darkened with disgust. She knew exactly what the UTC was doing with their messages of hope and positivity. While so many were starving and sleeping on the streets, the humans on the giant screens wore clothes lined in gold with decadent jewels decorating their necks and ears. Their hair was braided in beautiful fishtail braids.

She slid her hand over her hair, her own fishtail braids, and wondered if her people's hair styles were ever theirs at all. Had they been influenced in their history by the humans even to the extent of their hair?

She slid her eyes to the street once again and bile crawled

up her throat. The fishtail braids were depicted on a statue in a small bit of greenery off the street. They came to a stop, and she read the sign, 'Venus, our lady of love.' The marble of the statue was crumbling, clearly ancient. Her eyes roamed around the small garden, and everyone was wearing *her* people's traditional clothes of a tunic and loose pants. Sweat began forming on her brow, and she searched the door for a button to roll down the window.

"Car sick?" The driver cautiously inquired as he pressed some buttons on his steering wheel.

Nodding with the back of her hand at her mouth, Mercy watched as the glass separated in the center and slid apart, giving her a slight breeze. Her stomach turned when the raw odor of the street hit her nose, but it was slightly better than the window being up. In the slight breeze, she reached up and began removing her fishtail braids. Once her hair was down and loose, she pulled it all back at her nape. In the rear mirror, she watched as Oz did the same. He had been paying attention too.

As they pulled up, Cinis seemed like they were going to leap out of the vehicle. Oz leaned forward and opened the door, watching as Cinis did just that.

"I don't like to ride in a vehicle that I'm not steering," they admitted to Jael in a whisper as she passed by.

Mercy and Oz stood at Jael's sides as she took in the massive building perched at the top of a pyramid of stairs. Spotlights shone on the building highlighting its depictions of humans dancing with joy engraved onto the walls behind a perimeter of columns casting ominously eerily tall shadows. The building seemed different than others they had passed. Older but built with more grandeur, it seemed to be a court building remodeled over time.

The beat of the electronic music pouring out of the doors only hinted at the party inside as people in line waited to be chosen. Cinis led their group past the line and to the door where a massive man with the thickest thighs Mercy had ever seen stood guard. A stocky tail whipped behind him as he put a hand up to stop the group, "Name."

Mercy stepped in front of Jael, and Oz stood behind her, as Cinis announced, "Tachie, daughter of the house of Sergii. We have private room 406 reserved on the balcony."

Checking the reservation list, the doorman's round, thick, and hairy ears twitched as he studied the brightly lit tablet in his hand. High on the sides of his head with the tips several inches above his auburn hair, that little movement gave away his only reaction to the name. Behind him strobe lights flashed as people mingled and danced.

He nodded as he met Cinis's eyes, and in a booming deep voice he instructed, "Take a right and use the lift to take you to level four. Your suite is to the left. It has access to the lounge and the private balcony's dance floor. Use the panel to the right of the door in your suite to place any orders, and that includes private dancers."

Everyone except for Cinis was having a hard time keeping up their ruse amid the chaotic dance scene. Glass furniture glowed around the edges of the dance floor, seeming to dance along with the music, varying in color and intensity. The space was grand, with a music stage in the center of the room and floor after floor of balconies, all filled with people dancing or enjoying the pandemonious view. Different species of people filled the two lower levels and main dance floor. Jael was mesmerized by all the tails and wings she could see waving and bobbing to the music.

Some tails, twisting and bobbing, were ringed in black

and fluffy fur. Other tails were bushy and brown, only twitching at the tips. A man passed by with large membranous wings like a bat, and it was hard for her to peel her eyes away. He had an aura of mystery, and she wondered if all of his species were similar. Hypnotic in his movements, the surrounding people seemed to move to his beat and not that of the music.

Jael noticed right away the beings on the upper levels were almost all humans. She slid her eyes to Oz's, and he gave her a slight smile of reassurance as they moved onto the lift pad. The floating lift rose on the magnetic tracks as soon as Cinis spoke aloud the suite number and Jael's faux name into the control panel.

The floor was quick to notice the new group enter. Many of the richest on Emendo weren't able to afford one guard of any species, much less two Iungo with a human assistant. In reality, Emendo was exquisitely poor aside from a few lingering wealthy families who hadn't moved on to Melior yet. Edible food and water were a luxury here. To visit a night club was out of the question for anyone except the richest of the population.

Cinis had never been to a club before.

When the door shut to the suite, with eyes wide, Cinis mumbled to themself as they mulled over the sparse, yet high-tech room, "We are going to owe Rungi so much for all of this."

Mercy scanned her eyes around the minimalistic sleek and tech heavy décor in the room. Not bothering to look at Cinis, she leaned in close as her eyes focused on a blinking light in the corner. Whispering, Mercy asked, "Are they listening?"

"No, the rooms are clean. The top level has a signal

blocker running through the rooms and the balcony. That's why we're here. No one can record us. The biggest crime bosses in the galaxy frequent the fourth level of the Seven to conduct business," Cinis explained, leaning back to give Mercy a little space as they spoke within a normal volume.

Swallowing roughly, Mercy asked, "Is Rungi one of those bosses?"

Cinis lowered their eyes, "She's one of the biggest weapons dealers in the galactic center. We may have a bit of a history."

Furrowing her brow, Mercy asked, "What do you mean?"

"My sister got into some trouble. They were threatening to send her to the prison planet. Rungi offered me a deal to help get her into the UTC surrogate program, and she agreed to have her record erased. I had to do some things that I'm a little ashamed of, but I didn't particularly dislike it; however, I would rather not explain," Cinis begrudgingly admitted, their pale face turning a flaming shade of red.

"What is the blood planet?" Mercy asked, her tone quiet.

Cinis shivered as they began to explain, "It's the UTC prison planet. When you get a life sentence you are sent there. We all know what really occurs on the planet and the horrors that reside there. It's full of the blood bats left behind after the great Resper war. They're blood starved and crazed. They will rip anyone apart who lands on the surface of the planet. Everyone knows it's a gruesome death sentence, and not a life sentence prison. I was raised on stories told by my grandmother, horror stories to make us behave. They were always about Resper, Blood Resper, drinking our blood in the night when we are misbehaving.

The rumors are that humans filled with fear taste better to them."

Sinking her head, Mercy admitted, "I would have done the same." Cinis gave Mercy a relieved smile.

Looking out onto the balcony with Jael at his side, Oz asked, "Who is our contact?"

Approaching his side, Cinis answered, "It's a male Haculae. He's one of the most ruthless people on the planet, but he has a soft spot for your people. His name is Qaz, and he has long believed the Iungo were intelligent beings. He technically owns many of your kind, but they all reside on his private estate far north of the great city. It's as close as it comes to a countryside on Emendo. The Haculae in the past have been exploited and enslaved by the First Humans because of their physical abilities, so I'm sure that's why Rungi thinks he will help."

Recalling what Haculae looked like from the UTC Physician's memories, Oz asked, "A Haculae has a distinct spotted hair color pattern on their heads and tails with high set, pointed ears. Did they descend from large cats?"

"Yes, their tall ears have short hair with the spotted pattern. They come from a high gravity jungle planet and are about twice as heavy as they seem," Cinis explained.

Confused, Jael asked, "What do you mean by spotted?"

With a grand smile, Cinis pointed just on the other side of the glass wall, "There he is. You can see for yourself."

When door to the suite swung open, Mercy made eye contact with Qaz, and he stopped in his tracks. He was a massive man, nearly seven feet tall with broad shoulders and a graceful yet thick, muscled body wrapped in a thin, fitted suit. The tip of his powerful spotted tail whipped back and forth behind him, curling and twisting as if it was speaking to her, along with his piercing light brown eyes. His pupils were slits running vertically in his eye, and they slowly widened into circles, perfectly round and black within his light brown iris. The sharp lines of his suit held her eye as she took him in from head to toe. He smiled slightly, revealing bright white teeth with two long thick fangs in his wide mouth. He was terrifyingly handsome.

He passed through the door without meeting the eyes of anyone else. "Well, that was easy," Cinis whispered under their breath to Mercy.

Mercy scoffed as the man made his way to her and in a quiet, growling tone he rasped, "You are simply breathtaking. Who owns you? I will pay any price. Your kind are far too perfect to have those ugly bands around your necks."

His clawed fingertip had nearly made contact with the band around Mercy's neck when he turned and found a staring room. He quickly turned back to her with a shimmer of worry in his eyes, remembering why he was meeting them.

Cinis cleared their throat and found their words, "Um, we are here to see you. Rungi sent us." Unable to break away from Mercy, his face melted into equal devastation and wonder as he demanded sharply, "Shut the door."

Oz slammed the door and locked it as Qaz finally tore his big brown eyes rimmed with thick black lashes from Mercy. He shot his bright eyes to the door and searched Oz up and down, his predatory pupils returning to tiny slits.

Unable to help himself, he turned back to Mercy and with a hand on his chest, he asked, "Your eyes still gleam with hope. Can you speak?"

Mercy purred, "I can do a lot more than speak."

His irises turned from little slits into wide black saucers inside his bright light-brown eyes as his voice turned to gravel, "Venus save me. *You still have your fangs.* What about your stinger, intact?"

Nodding, Mercy raised her tail, and it peeked over her shoulder as she shot her stinger out for him to see.

He burst with excitement and admitted, "I have been to countless worlds in and out of the galactic center, and you truly are the most stunning woman I've ever met. My wives will be filled with sorrow I didn't bring you home. May I at the least take a clip of you to show them?"

Confused but flattered, Mercy agreed, "Sure. What do you mean wives, and why would they be upset? I'm free."

Furrowing his brow, a devious smile spread on his face as he explained, "I know your kind well. My wives are all your species. I may have bought them all, but *they* are the ones who own me. Not the other way around."

With her mouth gaping open, Mercy was unable to speak as he pulled a small device from his pocket and pointed it at her for a few moments. She shut her wide mouth and tried to give him a pretty smile. *No matter what he says, this man disgusts me. I hope he buys my little show.*

Clearing his throat, Oz brought the conversation back to the topic, "We need to know where we can find a hacker willing to broadcast on the UTC network so the masses are guaranteed to see it. We need maximum exposure. That's our only chance to get in front of the council. We have to make it to the Science and Technology space station around Melior, alive, so we can make a demand to investigate our genetic origin."

Turning and straightening himself, with an eyebrow raised, Qaz asked, "And, who are you?"

"I am President Green of the Iungo people on planet Portum. You can call me Oz," he replied with pride.

After adjusting his suit, Qaz remained still and after a pause, finally asked, "You are President? You have elected officials?"

"Yes, it's a basic structure. We reclaimed our planet, and the UTC are no longer there. The UTC command vessels destroyed all the soldier transports stationed on our planet before they made it back to the UTC space station. I'm sure you can guess why."

"I am not a man easily surprised, but, I must say, I have been shocked twice since I entered this room. I am a businessperson first, and I usually demand a trade of some kind, but I admire your fight. I also have Iungo wives at home who would slowly castrate me over an open fire if I didn't give you what you need to help your people, their people. They will be delighted to learn their species has a real name and their planet has its own president. Is there anything else you require?" Qaz asked as he held his eyes on Oz.

"We need to find as much information as we can on the First Humans. Do you have anything we can work with?" Oz asked, knowing this part of the conversation could bring opposition.

Qaz stood still and shifted his eyes to the dance floor for a long pause before saying, "I had to dive into a dark place to reach where I am. More recently, I have tortured UTC commanders, in grotesque ways, for more information on the First Humans' history. The people pirates brought me have suffered in ways you can't imagine under my hand. I learned nothing from them easily because the UTC trains them so thoroughly. I would hang them from hooks through their back and slowly crush their legs with vises over months. They would eventually tell me their deepest secrets, but it was rarely anything I wanted or needed, until this one woman. She had a scar across her face. She lasted three months before she finally broke and said one single phrase I'll never forget. *You will never find Janus.* I found that interesting because the First Human's origin world is not called Janus. It's called Genus. I asked her again, and she said Genus the second time, refusing to reveal again what slipped. Even when I released my raptor on her, all she screamed was, "Jupiter bestow glory on to the First Humans," as Stars, my Vistalian raptor, disemboweled her and feasted on her entrails. I promised her a swift end, but she chose to die slowly with her secrets still hidden. You would be surprised at how long a human can live without their insides."

Peering out of the window, with a smirk on his face, Qaz turned back to Oz and continued, "If you can find a star-tographer named Baiselle at the games, she may be able to help you find the planet Janus on some of her ancient star charts. I will warn you against revealing why and what you were searching for. She is a First Human faction descendant and will not be so sympathetic."

"She's one of the investors in the grand arena and one of the richest people on Emendo and Melior. How do you expect us to just walk up to her?" Cinis asked, their hand in the air waving for attention.

"Easy. You will use my suite. It's next to hers. I don't attend the games anyway. They are barbaric, even for me. I only keep the suite for business. The great games are supposed to be entertainment, but they are effectively used to keep the people of Emendo from having any good ideas. The people with the *good* ideas are the ones who often find themselves within the walls of the arena being eaten by one of my ancestors. Here is an adequate hacker's information. I use him myself. He can do what you need. Now that business is over, let's enjoy our evening," Qaz demanded as he handed Oz a piece of paper with a moving advertisement on it.

Oz folded the piece of paper and slipped it into his pocket.

Understanding Qaz, Cinis added, "He's right. We are going to look suspicious to any UTC spies if Jael doesn't dance and enjoy herself with her guards watching."

"I have to dance in these shoes? I can't even dance in regular shoes!" Jael asked, before remembering the extra pair of shoes she brought.

Chuckling, Oz leaned on the glass wall, "Just move those hips. I know they can move."

Kicking the heels off and slipping on the sandals Tressa lent her, she peered back up at Oz with her eyes narrowed. Sticking the tip of her tongue out of the side of her mouth at Oz, she headed for the door and he leaned over to open it so she could exit first. He and Mercy followed close behind as she made her way to the private dance floor on the balcony she had not seen from the ground floor. The fast beat of the dance music vibrated through her feet and up into her body.

Turning and facing Oz she mouthed, "I wish I could dance with you." Trying to hide a smile, Oz turned his face toward her and winked. He followed as she moved toward some dancing human women. She melded into the group, and did her best to keep up with them in her gem encrusted sandals. She wasn't sure the sandals were any more comfortable than the first pair of heels, but she did her best to ignore them.

After about an hour of twirling around the dance floor in her sparkling dress, she came to a stop as her eyes landed on an Iungo woman with a bright orange band around her neck, blonde hair and lightly tanned skin.

A dream she had when they still lived at the treehouse came crashing down into her mind as she tried to pull her eyes away from the woman washing dishes through an open door. There were no Sarters like in her dream, but there *was* the barrel-chested species at the door. A sick familiarity crept inside of her like a wriggling worm. Crawling its way up her spine, she shivered in the heat of the club.

Whipping around, she found Oz standing just like he was in her dream. Peering at her stoically, with a band around his neck. It took everything she had in her to not scream in terror. Flashes of what she had seen in the dream overlaid with what was happening in reality as the strobe lights flashed above her. Haunted, empty faces filled the room as she turned around and around. As fast as the moment, began it was over, and the people around her were all dancing and smiling to the music.

Had it been a dream at all? Or a warning?

She ran to Oz and demanded, "Get me out of here. Now!"

44

PLANET ADURO - CLAUDIUS ROYAL PALACE

When the festivities wrapped up and all the most loyal of King Claudius's allies had returned to their vessels in orbit, Livia made her way to the maintenance closet where she had stashed her battle armor. Only the wealthiest of the rich had the type of metal armor she did. It kept track of her vitals, could provide a shot of adrenaline, and could administer an anticoagulant to a wound, only the best for the king's daughter. She slipped on the high tech bodysuit with the rigid plates of armor already in place on the back of the suit. She strapped her rail gun to her hip with an extra cartridge if she needed it. Once she was finished attaching the front armor plates to her shins, thighs, torso, and biceps, she was ready to move.

A noise down the hall froze her in place as two people passed by the door. She pressed her ear to the door, straining to listen. The footsteps led away, and she cracked open the door as she watched her father enter the lift. He was alone, and Livia wondered what happened to the other person he was with earlier.

Livia saw them, a guard, but he headed the opposite way. Releasing a breath and preparing herself for her first task, Livia begged Jupiter to allow this to go well. *Are the god's even listening anymore? Or had the human's disappointed their deities so thoroughly that the god's had abandoned them?* If the rumors from their religious leaders were true, there had not been so much as a half accurate prophecy from any of the great houses in over fifty thousand years. Her nerves were eating her alive. Something else was brewing aside from her little coup, and she could feel it reaching up through the ground, a new form of primal energy coursing through her. She could taste destiny on her tongue as she took a few steps down the hallway before inching up by the wall and touching the door controls, selecting a maintenance opening to avoid triggering the surveillance video.

Pushing her body through the narrow half-open door, she was unsurprised to find the palace doctor at his desk buried in his endless radiation and cancer research. Tapping the door again, it closed behind her. Straining his neck, he peered up at Livia in her battle armor and swiftly turned in his swivel chair to face her. He seemed unsurprised to see Livia in her battle gear.

Beat after beat, Livia listened to her heart pound in her ears as the doctor's warm eyes grew more solemn by the moment. Taking his eyes to the floor, he folded his hands in his lap. "I know what you are going to ask of me, and before I agree or sound the alarm, I need to know one thing," he asked without shifting his gaze from the floor at her feet.

He brought his eyes up to her and she whispered, *"Anything."*

"Do you love him?" he gently asked, his face giving no hint to whom he referred.

"Who?" Livia asked softly.

"The red one," he replied, not shifting his attention away from her.

Closing her eyes, she answered, "Yes."

Waiting for her eyes to meet his again, he turned around and pressed a few options on his screen before he turned back around and explained, "His life signs are now disconnected from the monitoring system. I have replaced them with my own. We have the same heart gene, so they beat the same."

"How did you know?" Livia breathed, so many questions burning in her mind.

He peered at her for a while, studying her face, the beautiful face he had to piece back together on too many occasions to count. For years she lay on his table as he mended the wounds from her father, from her training at the Aduro Claudius Academy, and then from her husband. This doctor before her had mended her spirit when she believed it broken beyond repair.

She had every luxury in the world, except for true freedom. She knew if she had just remained quiet, they would've rarely raised a hand to her. She would've never been stuck in the royal guard under Lucas, and she may have inherited the crown, but how could she have stayed silent about how she was treated? Why had her father ordered such a defiant soul to be his child? What did he expect if all he wanted was blind obedience and loyalty?

Before she turned to leave, she said, "I want to free them."

"I know, Livia. I know," he admitted as she headed for the door. "Be a kind leader, Livia," he added with hope in his eyes.

She turned at the door and gave him a hint of a smile before she pressed the maintenance opening options and pushed her body through. Her heart sang as she sprinted down the hall to the lift. She would make a great king. She just had to pull this off first. After entering her father's lift code, she stepped onto the pad and in seconds she was in the hallway of her father's rooms. A hissing chuckle sounded from the other side of the door, and Livia pressed her eyes shut. She had hoped he would be alone, unless of course, he was with an Iris court bitch.

With her hand on her rail gun, she entered the bypass code into his door controls and when the door slid away, she found her father nude and standing between the legs of an upside down, drunk Iris woman. The Iris woman's wings, grand and emerald with tips of crimson, spread out underneath her, fluttered with fear. The Iris had uncanny, sharp senses. The awful woman probably knew she was going to die before Livia opened the door. Livia hoped so, for every member of the ruling Iris court had committed a list of heinous crimes.

Without apprehension, she pointed and shot the nude Iris woman in the chest, killing her before raising the gun to her father. Her father saw where bullet hit his Iris partner in the chest and the red blood trickle out of the wound. He took in Livia's battle armor, and his face became a picture of horror. Frantically, he slapped above his left shoulder by his neck trying to activate his alarm.

To protect the doctor in case she failed, Livia calmly lied, "I hacked the system and deactivated it."

Focusing her eyes beyond her father, she noticed a small picture of her mother. The woman who he abused mercilessly for years, a queen forced to suffer, just like all the queens before her. I *will put an end to this family curse tonight.* She could still feel the burn of the torches on her back from when Lucas gave her the Claudius traditional wife scar.

"Why the fuck are you doing this? You never cared about my crown!" he screamed at her.

"Things change," Livia admitted as she brought the rail gun up and pointed it at her father's chest. "May Pluto consume your flesh and spit out your soul to rot for eternity. May the worms of the underworld feast on your flesh for the rest of time. You shall seek air and find none, a hunger unending. I, King Livia Claudius, in the name of Jupiter himself, condemn you to the molten lands of fire and death," Livia chanted her people's curse for traitors before firing her railgun into her father's chest.

Steam wafted up from the hole in his chest as Livia took a few steps over and looked down on her father's dead body. She removed the small pin from the side of his hair which contained his access codes.

She slipped the pin near the side of her head, and it synched with the tech embedded in her skull. During one of the doctor's many procedures to put her back together, he hid an implanted port in her skull so she could link her royal codes. That way she would need nothing on her body which could potentially be stolen. She wondered if the doctor planned for an occasion such as this.

The implant in her eye signaled when the upload was complete, the name at the top of her readings changed to King Livia Claudius. Now in order to take the palace, they would need to take her head. The entirety of the Claudius estate, on Aduro and Melior, would now recognize her as the king.

She quickly slipped the pin out of her hair and broke it in half. After tossing it in the trash incinerator, she headed for the door and didn't look back at her father or the dead Iris woman sprawled out on the floor. She couldn't imagine why she would want to fuck that old human man when she knew what being the feathered variety meant for their males. There were entire classic epics written about their screw-like penises. Royals over the centuries commonly hired Iris men to appease their wives if they were inept.

She hoped Valec was able to free August and the others by now. They needed to meet on the landing pad soon so Valec and August could start transporting the people in the closest mines to the palace while she finished the rest of the guards. They were conditioned from purchase to be loyal to the former king, so there was no sense in trying to save them. Betrayal would always be high in her periphery. She would employ an entire new guard of Iungo.

The lift carried her to the palace guard station, and she held the door open with her foot when it opened. She pulled a dual-gas bomb from her belt as she slid her armor's force-field mask up over her face. The gas was a nerve toxin that struck them dead with a mere five particles meeting the organic tissues inside their lungs. She hid behind the lift wall as she activated and tossed the bomb into the group of guards. They all stared at the bomb like they didn't know what was about to happen. *Where in Pluto's hell is their training? What useless guards*, she thought. When it went off, they all dropped to the floor. Peering around, she didn't see anyone else and wondered where the rest of the guards were as she checked the surveillance video feeds for the palace and the mines.

In the throne room, Valec and August had a pile of

guards which explained where they had all gone. As she scanned the other screens, it appeared the rest of the planet and the ships above were unaware anything was happening. When she came to the second to last screen, she stopped and stared. In the frame was Lucas and the Iris woman was on her knees sucking him off. He was slumped over from the drip she had given him, but he was not in the palace. She groaned and shook her head at her mistake. How had she not put that together? He would not have taken the Iris to *their* rooms, but to his service quarters where they conduct their military training. Livia didn't even know he had been to those rooms since they had finished training. She erected a shield to block any off-world communication. Livia didn't need her wormy cousin Weryl, one of the Claudius Kingdom council representatives, sending Lucas reinforcements from the UTC military.

It suddenly made sense why she never caught him cheating at home. He was taking them to the old royal barracks. He had covered his tracks just like they had been trained at the academy. Keeping her calm, she checked back at the throne room as August was freeing the last of his people from the cages.

Livia jumped on the lift and ran down the hall toward the throne room to meet August and Valec. As she headed for the throne room, August and Valec met her in the foyer.

"Lucas is at the academy barracks, but he's unaware of the coup. I need you to take the transports to the mines and bring your people to the palace immediately. We will meet him on the sand in battle. Livia commanded, power in her tone.

August smiled and offered, "If you connect with me, I can learn to fly the transport and so can they." He threw a thumb over his shoulder at the Iungo people crowded behind him.

Relief washed over Livia. They needed to have a trained army defending the palace before Lucas found out. He would march on them with all the remaining soldiers on Aduro, and they would surely lose with the few untrained people they had at the moment.

He took her hand, connecting with her wrist. Within moments she felt him inside her mind but couldn't tell what he was doing. After a few seconds, he tipped is head to her with a puzzled look on his face. "Good to go. You have an exceptionally organized mind. I was able to take your military training as one single unit of information. Your mind structure fascinates me. You take Valec and secure the palace while I take my people and bring the rest of us back."

Leaning up and kissing him, Livia whispered, "Hurry. We don't have much time."

August sprinted away and his people followed close behind. They spilled out onto the landing pad and lined up to connect with August to learn how to fly the transports. He passed on much more than just flying lessons from Livia. He gave them all of her tactical battle information and fighting skills. Within a few minutes everyone had the knowledge they needed to fly and each of them jumped into the cockpits and fired up their engines like they were seasoned pilots.

Arriving at the first mine, the transports landed, and August leapt out and sprinted into the doors. Running up the stairs to the guard lounge, he found two sleeping. While they slept, he broke their necks before running back down the stairs to the mine doors and peering in at where the other three would be.

The moment Dragon's eyes fell on August, she deviously grinned and leaped onto to the closest guard. She broke his neck in a matter of seconds as the other two guards ran toward her. August leaped onto the back of one of the guards as Dragon leaped onto the other. Both of the guards were down with broken necks in a matter of seconds.

August stood in front of his people and commanded, "King Claudius is dead, but *his* named successor still lives. *We have taken the palace.* We must defend the palace and gather as many of our people as we can to fight King Claudius's chosen successor Lucas. Grab your staffs from your bunks and head to the landing pad. The transports are waiting outside. We have several mines to take to the south of here. Be prepared to fight for more than just your lives!" Turning and running for the door, August could hear the bustle of his people following orders behind him.

When he returned to the transport, he contacted the palace and asked, "Did they pull the alarm?"

From the guard station, Valec checked the comm system for activity, "No, you're in the clear. The three southernmost mines are much better built, and they have integrated alarms I can't switch off. They still might have comms, so I wouldn't risk anything by freeing those mines yet. Make sure to stick to the list I gave you instead of the one you had before. Livia wasn't told about the trip alarms."

August replied, "Got it. I won't get any ideas. Has Livia finished securing the palace?"

"Yes, I have," Livia answered as she leaned over the guard station panting.

Smiling August asked, "What are our next orders, my king?"

"Return to the palace with your people from the first

mine and finish taking the mines until morning. I'm working on locking down the planet, so we don't receive any surprise transports from the guests. Valec will assemble the battle groups as your people arrive," Livia commanded with a growing pit of worry in her gut.

Lucas was still out there, and this was far from over.

45

PLANET PORTUM – IUNGO BASE

"You have to stop thinking that way, Cal. We need to have hope. We are going to be able to build our dream home soon. You are going to build all of those restaurants, businesses, and homes you have been designing on your tablet," Jacob said as he brushed his teeth in the mirror. He leaned in and stared at his bloodshot eyes, which with his blue blood made his eyes turn grey.

Clearing his throat as he leaned back raising one eyebrow, Callum asked, "How did you know I was designing on the tablet? I thought everything we did on that platform was private."

Jacob's toothbrush hung from his mouth and put his palm up, "Your tablet's remote storage is as large as mine. I know you've been using Pike's design team's software. It is the only thing that takes up that much space." He fully expected a rebuttal from Callum.

"You shouldn't have made it available for anyone to download if I wasn't supposed to be using it," Callum grumbled with snarl to his lip.

There it was.

After rinsing his mouth, he turned and explained, "I wasn't accusing. I just wanted you to know. I don't believe you entirely now when you say you're afraid we won't find proof. You know we will. Show me our house. I know you've had it finished for months."

Callum slighted his eyes before softening his glare at Jacob and retrieving his tablet off his nightstand charger. Pulling up the app, Callum selected the file, home. After selecting a few other options, he smiled to himself as he selected one last thing.

He lay the tablet flat, and the holo-image jumped from the screen. It was a natural setting home with beautiful tall arched windows and a large wrap around patio with lush vines in tall pots spilling over the edge and sprawling into the grass. The second story primary bedroom had its own private balcony overflowing with vines, greenery, and honey-suckle flowers. A natural pool in the backyard complimented the home with a bubbling brook leading to a waterfall trickling over a grotto. Steam wafted from the pool and a small stream of smoke was twirling above the rock chimney jutting from the roof.

Jacob gasped and stopped dressing as he watched the hologram slowly turn. The pants he had started to buckle slid down and he kicked them away. His gaze was trapped within the tiny simulation. It was beyond anything he had imagined his partner could create. He knew Callum was talented, but this was something out of a dream. "You are just as creatively genius as Sarah and I knew you were," he admitted quietly as he gazed at his love.

Callum's heart swelled, a compliment like that from Jacob meant so much.

A few moments of surreal silence passed before Jacob's tablet began blaring with a strange ring that sounded like the base alarms. He dove to the bed where he had left his tablet and pressed the answer button. He couldn't handle one more note of that noise. He had no idea why it sounded like that, but that setting was going to change immediately. His heart pounded from the octopamine dump in his system, and his hand shook as he held his tablet.

Vida's face materialized in the holo-screen, and her eyes were bright with excitement as she blurted out, "Get your ass to the medical lab right now!" and as she disconnected, Jacob and Callum heard she was hardly able to gasp a full breath.

Sharply staring into the blank space which used to be Vita's face, Jacob asked, "Not even a hint?"

Unsure if it was good or bad news, they dressed as swiftly as they could, and Jacob was the first to fly out of their door with Callum not far behind. Both barefoot, they sprinted across the command room, spinning and dodging anyone in their path as they continued down the long hall-way. When they arrived at the medical lab, Jacob shot through the doors, and Callum burst in less than a second later, nearly slamming into him.

Vida turned and simply demanded, "Look!"

She turned and pressed a button on her tablet, sending the image onto the large holo-screen in the center of the wall. It was the Iungo DNA and another double helix named, 'unknown specimen Mr. VP Pissy Pants decided to give me on top of my mountain of work.'

Staring at the screen guiltily, she turned contritely to Jacob and confessed, "I really hadn't planned on you seeing that." The words on the screen slowly erased letter by letter and changed to 'unknown specimen Jacob found.'

Vita had not noticed, but Jacob had barely taken a breath. He knew exactly what the screen meant, and he was far too stunned to speak. The two double helix slowly turned around one another, parts of them blinking at different times in different colors. One color in particular, blue, showed an almost complete match between the two sets of DNA.

Vida turned to them as tears poured down her face and her voice shook, "The sample you brought back, it's our direct genetic cousin. It has genetics far closer to ours than the scorpion's. It is a match. We share almost all of our DNA. I was going to put it at the end of my other work, but what you said sunk in. I had to see. These creatures are spliced up with several types of plant and animal DNA *just like we are*. We think there are two time periods where these types of creatures led to more than one emergence of scorpions on our planet. Once the ancient creature you found had been exposed to the radiation burst, the branches of scorpions were irrevocably split. Our later line of scorpions came after the creatures had been directly exposed to the radiation extinction event on our planet causing the DNA to forever be mutated in our line. The first scorpions that emerged had survived untouched as they hid in the caves, making them a close cousin, but not close enough to prove they weren't just used in part of our creation. I also discovered the giant scorpions that still prowl our planet today also have a similar genetic pathway to eventually become sentient, higher intelligence beings like us."

The silence in the room after her words could be cut

with a knife. Callum, Jacob, and Vida all just watched as the two sets of DNA slowly waltzed around one another.

With a tremble in his voice, Jacob asked, "You've confirmed with second testing?"

Nodding, with tears still streaming down her face, Vida's voice cracked, "We did it. Well, you did it. I know I said I wasn't going to test it for a week, but I couldn't get what you explained out of my mind. I tested it against five Iungo people's samples, and even one set of ancient bones before I accepted it."

Callum shook as a scream built inside. When it erupted, Jacob knew exactly what that shout meant as he threw his arms around Jacob.

No more silence, *not ever again.*

The Iungo people were going to be as loud as possible.

Vida joined in by shouting into the comms as everyone from the lab filed in and upon seeing the screen, understood.

One by one they, yelled, cried, ran, and some just stared at the screen in disbelief, too stunned to move or speak aloud. Pike walked in and carefully passed by Callum as he and Jacob embraced.

When Pike saw the holo-screen, he slapped a hand over his mouth before he turned to Jacob. "I'll make an announcement, and I'll send Oz's command ship the file. He won't receive it for a few more days, but I'm sure he will want the compressed file ready for them to send to the UTC broadcast hacker."

"Thank you, Pike. Give the medical team leave and bring in some people to cover it. Use the connection for training if necessary for everyone to have time off," Jacob was in shock and could hardly make the words.

Pike left the room right as elated chaos erupted from the

mess hall. Jacob and Callum went arm in arm down the hallway toward the increasing hollering. As they headed in the doors, they saw a room filled with hugging, crying, and smiling. Others were off to the side on their tablets calling loved ones with the news.

Risk cried out from inside the kitchen, "Line up for drinks! It's fuckin' party time!" Spotting Jacob and Callum at the door, Risk hopped over the serving counter and snagged two tall glasses filling them to the top before making his way over.

Handing Jacob the drink, he announced to the room, "Jacob gets the first drink! I was told you are the one who had the idea and insisted on it. I heard you went for the sample yourself, and you were right. Congratulations, Jacob! You just made it possible to liberate your entire species. Now we just wait for our snake to bite and set us free."

Cheers erupted, and Jacob waved to everyone bashfully. Sliding his focus back to Risk, he noted a tattoo on his forearm Jacob hadn't seen before. A green snake twisted around a ring with its head rising in the center, and its mouth open wide with ominous fangs. Jacob knew exactly who that yellow eyed snake represented.

Smiling, Jacob took the drink, downed it in a single gulp. He slammed the cup down on the counter, and squeaked through the strong taste of the liquor, "I need a vacation." The entire room erupted into laughter as everyone gathered around to snag a drink of their own. Risk leaped back over the counter and began pouring liquor like a seasoned bartender.

Once Callum finished his drink, Jacob down the second drink and blurted out, "I love you. I can't wait to spend the rest of forever with you. If they don't give me six months of vacation after this, I'm going to quit."

Laughing Callum agreed, "I would quit anyway. I hate your job."

Just as Jacob reached over to take Callum's hand, his tablet made a ringing sound and he pulled it from under his arm. A message popped up with a map. "It looks like seismic activity to the south-west. Do you..." Jacob started as Callum cut him off.

"Yes, let's go now," Callum interrupted as he grabbed Jacob's hand and dragged him through the mess hall and out of the base door.

Chuckling, Jacob asked, "Since when do you not like crowds?"

"Since five seconds ago when I needed to be alone with you," Callum explained with some added sass to his tone.

Widening his eyes, Jacob nodded to himself and put a pop in his step as they neared one of the transports. They climbed inside, dressed in freshly charged sets of armor they had pulled from the back, and secured their helmets.

Jacob wondered what the seismic movement could be. *Would there be a new landmass in the sea from a volcano awaking? Or is this from a quake deep in the ocean? Could they be looking at a tsunami?* Questions rolled through his head as he took off in the direction of the epicenter.

Arriving at a high altitude few moments later, they zoomed toward the epicenter. As they neared, they could only make out a turbulent sea near a crescent shaped island. Jacob pulled the transport back to what he thought might be a safe distance and engaged the autopilot.

"What do you think it is?" Callum asked.

Shaking his head, Jacob answered, "I honestly don't have any idea."

His tablet lit up and a red spot blinked. They both looked up and watched as a wind gusts appeared to blow the turbulent clouds away. Realizing they weren't seeing a round spot of rough sea at all, they leaned in closely to the window to see down into a deep hole in the ocean. It was as if a giant plug was pulled, and their ocean was draining into the planet's mantle. Confusion devoured Jacob as he couldn't peel his gaze from the giant hole. The blinking red light began beeping faster and faster.

Keeping their eyes on the colossal whirlpool, Jacob and Callum watched as an entire sea worth of water blasted from the center. Snapping their necks back, they both dropped their jaws as a gargantuan geyser shot sea water nearly beyond the atmosphere. Slamming the transport into drive, he ascended them into the atmosphere and lower orbit. As the transport rose, it automatically prepared for the vacuum of space, sealing off and pressurizing the cabin, as well as switching to their oxygen scrubbing technology. The windows polarized as they passed through the upper atmosphere, and when they rose above it, they could safely see, even with all the radiation bombarding the transport from the black hole.

Jacob whistled, "I bet that's where the flood in the jade forest comes from."

They watched quietly as a monstrous wave barreled across the ocean. It was heading straight toward the jade forest just as Jacob had hypothesized.

"It must happen every six months like you said. The last flood was just a few months before we launched the rockets." Callum was in awe.

When he peered over, Jacob was furiously typing on his tablet.

Leaning forward to see the ice moons above them, Jacob explained, "I bet those are comets. I also bet a large comet struck our planet and caused the geyser. It left a massive hole in the ocean floor that reached far enough into the mantle to become super-heated. I just ran it through Pike's astronomy simulator."

They both patiently awaited the results, watching the wave roll closer to the land. The program lit up when it finished and a simulation popped up on the screen showing exactly what Jacob had explained.

With a smile, he sent the file to Oz's tablet.

"Now take me home right this instant because I just saw the camera in the corner, so we can't have fun in here. You fucking asshole, why didn't you tell me they installed cameras? We need our own transport," Callum demanded as he turned and raised his middle finger to the camera.

Jacob snickered, he had forgotten all about the video cameras.

46

PLANET EMENDO – VENUS
DISTRICT 7

Jael wondered how much the dreamy dress she had on cost, but she was afraid to ask. All she heard in passing was credits were the name of the currency. She could feel a set of yellow eyes heating her skin with their hungry gaze.

The stunning gown was sleeveless, low cut and had a flowing floor-length skirt. The piercing blue-black silk with gem encrusted swirls rising from the bottom of the skirt and ending around her waist made her feel as if she were the queen of midnight. Tressa had done her hair in a swirling updo then did her make-up with smokey eyes and brilliant red lips. She had never felt more beautiful. Oz stared at her hungrily from the other end of the room, so she searched for somewhere else to sit before the man lost control and ripped the dress off.

Jael sat down on the old couch a few feet away from Cinis's grandmother, the cushion crunching under her weight. A bit of dust wafted up from the seat, and it took her back to an old dusty waiting room, one she sat in so long ago. She looked up at the window and saw tinfoil covering the sill. Memories of her childhood flooded back. Memories of a day that changed her life, the day she met Sis.

"He speaks to you, doesn't he? Shows you things," the old woman whispered, leaning in toward Jael.

Emerging from losing herself in her memories, Jael realized the old woman was speaking to her.

"What does that mean?"

With an odd smile and her eyes staring off into the distance, the old woman whispered, "The collective push for more life and progress is rooted in our lost, those from before. Their desires combine like a web of energy that spreads out much like a rumor, whispering their dreams in our ears. Those who listen to the cries of the great before, have earned the right to hear the hidden frequency."

"Grandma, I don't think that makes much sense. It's time for your bath," Tressa cut her grandmother off.

Leaning back and with an expression of utter contempt, she argued, "Fuck you. You are not laying your nasty hands on me. A baby every year with someone new it seems."

Rolling her eyes, Tressa whispered as she explained, "I'm a UTC science and technology department surrogate, and she is *not* who she used to be."

Smiling Jael held back her comment about how her grandmother's words had actually resonated within her and just nodded.

"I fucking heard that, you little bitch. I don't know why you don't take that pretty face and find a man who will actually keep you for once. I mean nine? I know we are living on your dirty money. We aren't related, are we? I would be ashamed." Grandmother's gravely voice cut the air like a chain saw as she scowled at Tressa.

Rolling her eyes again, Tressa explained, "I am your loving granddaughter. Now hush so I can give you a bath."

As Tressa pushed her chair to the back of the apartment, one last time grandmother leaned away from her and barked, "No. Fuck you." Tressa slowly loosed a breath as the bathroom door shut.

Through the thin door they all heard Tressa as she scolded, "Stop trying to kick me. Your leg is too short to reach, and you're going to fall out of your chair."

There was a growling sound that began in the bath before Cinis came in with an extra uniform for Amelia. Once she had it on, she joined the group waiting for a call from the driver that the transport had arrived. When the communicator Cinis had in their pocket chimed, they headed down to the ground floor and went through the front doors to meet the ride.

They noticed it was not the same driver, but the vehicle was identical, so Mercy did the same thing and hopped in the front seat. Her tail fit comfortably between the deep V in the worn leather seat, and she refused to be uncomfortable. Other people with tails clearly had sat in the seat. The deep spot between the V was perfectly stretched out. She needed to remember this for designing some chairs at home. The driver had a long fluffy black and white ringed tail which began flitting back and forth at the tip when Mercy sat down.

Sliding her eyes over carefully, Mercy noticed the woman's solid black hands with white palms peeking out were gripping the steering wheel like the wheel was trying to run away. Ignoring the clear annoyance of the ring-tailed woman, she stared right at her. She *needed* to know what her face looked like. Curiosity always overruled manners.

The driver was a patchwork of white and black, large-irregular spots on her arms and her wrists gradually darkened into solid black. The backs of her hands were solid black and palms were solid white. At the ends of her fingers were long, sharp, black nails. Her eyes were both ringed in what seemed like thick black makeup, but she couldn't tell if it was makeup or her skin. Her wavy hair was stripes of white and black. Mercy couldn't tear her eyes away until the woman wiggled her little nose and revealed her large canine teeth.

When everyone found a seat, the woman zoomed away without a word. Something was wrong. Heat filled Mercy's body, and her shirt felt too tight. Mercy uncomfortably reached under her breasts and tried lifting them up, as the sweat gathering under them was driving her mad. The heat kept increasing as the journey continued. They turned a sharp corner at an intersection, and that's when Mercy felt it, deep between her thick thighs.

A bubble, a large sweat bubble.

Rolling her hips, she went cross-eyed, trying to navigate it in the right direction. She would do anything to avoid the sweaty air-bubble from ending up between her front lady cheeks, but she was losing her battle. She squealed and spread her legs, yanking at her pants to release the trapped air bubble, causing her ticklish misery. The ring-tailed woman burst into laughter, and Mercy whipped around to glare at her.

"You turned the heated seat on when you plopped down. That's what you get for staring. Has nobody ever told you that was rude?" the driver asked, her big black eyes blinking innocently.

Narrowing her eyes, Mercy glared at her.

"Though I suppose your rudeness was worth it for that little show." She cajoled with a pearly white smile.

"She knows we can speak?" Amelia asked Cinis. In the backseat, Cinis grinned as they explained, "Rungi has spread the word about you winning your planet back. Pockets of resistance are popping up everywhere."

As they came to a stop, the driver held her hand out to Mercy and rattled out, "Nice to meet you, I'm Kapa, and I am an Annulos. The UTC hates my people and considers us useless. They st- stripped my planet of its resources and left us with nothing after we joined. It's been over a thousand years and our great forests st-still haven't regrown to their former overwhelming glory. Sus-still doesn't compare with what they did to your people. Only maybe the Sus-Sarters fared worse, but not by much. Have you contacted them? I bet they will help. They have a sp-space station that circles an ice moon, and they've hollowed out and made a meat market out of it. You should see that thing. It's absolutely ridiculous what those Sss-Sarter do. I mean I've never seen it, but I heard it was marvelous."

Amelia scoffed in the backseat before opening the door. Kapa chattered fast enough, it sounded as if someone had sped up a recording by the end of her impromptu speech.

"They said no," Mercy replied under her breath before she stepped out and stood in the heat of the day. The system star was bright, and it momentarily blinded her Mercy closed them. She remembered the beautiful sky back on her home planet, all the colors swirling and shining onto the land. *Where there is no bright star in the sky to sting my eyes*, she reminisced. Their home was an ethereal paradise, and all she could think about was going back there. Cinis's voice broke the brief trance, and she opened her eyes, quickly looking around and surveying the area. No one seemed suspicious, but then again, she may not even know what suspicious looks like.

"Qaz said he owns number 577 and Baiselle is in 578. Head to the left when you go up the stairs. The lifts for the upper levels are through the columns by the left corner. We have to pass through security first." Cinis faded off and became noticeably quiet as they mentioned passing through security.

Jael swung her head around and grilled Cinis, "What do you mean? Why did you trail off? Are you nervous? Are you not telling us something?"

"They might want a DNA scan. If so, we're fucked. I saw a sign outside saying DNA scanning is required for today's games due to security threats. There is no such person as Tachie who is a daughter of the house of Sergii and a member of the temple of Mercury, so say a prayer to whatever god you worship. We are going to need it. If this all goes wrong you can fight, can't you?" Cinis asked cringing with every word.

Amelia, Jael, Mercy, and Oz all took turns staring at one another as they spoke in one of their old ways, their shifting eyes all filled with trepidation. *Shit!* Are we *about to stroll straight into the blood dripping hands of the UTC?* Jael worried.

As they approached the left corner, Jael could see the UTC guard already staring at her. The long dress she wore trapped the heat of the day, and her brow began sweating, but the heat disappeared as they passed by the row of columns. It was as though the inside area of the pillars was somehow air-conditioned but the outside wasn't. Jael was full of questions about how this air conditioning technology worked as her sweat now chilled her to the bone.

Cinis approached the UTC guard and announced, "We are on a day trip from Melior. This is Tachie, a daughter of the house of Sergii and a member of the temple of Mercury. We are in suite 577. We require day passes."

"I've never heard of the house of Sergii. I am a patron of the Emendo Temple of Mercury on 17th street. Which one do you worship in?" he asked with a flair of skepticism.

Cinis fluidly answered, "She attends one in northern Melior if you must know. It's rude to ask the daughter of a major Melior house where she worships. You aren't even worthy of a day pass to visit."

Looking rather ashamed and a little astonished they didn't know that particular social rule, the guard relented, "Lifts are to the left."

Pushing by him, Oz sneered showing his fangs, and the guard reared back stammering, "M-mercury save me, that bug has fangs! Wait! Why does your bug have fangs? Please, I need to know! Is that some new kind they came out with?"

Cinis, wanting to avoid the commotion, zipped toward the lifts. Everyone piled on just as the guard neared the open door. The doors shut before he could stop the lift.

They searched the lift for surveillance and breathed to themselves, "Bio-development intel is becoming quite the business. Nothing is recording in here. The suites are also private like the top level of club Seven."

This lift was high tech and smooth, but seemed somehow outdated and aging. The scent of centuries of smoke lingered on the freshly washed walls covered in a mural of elegant ladies scantily clad in flowing gossamer gowns all dancing in a meadow, *all human women.*

"Did you have to do that?" Jael asked turning to Oz after the lift began moving slowly.

"It was necessary," he explained with a straight face.

Trying not to roll her eyes Jael asked, "Why?"

"He was a creep, and he checked out your ass after you walked by," Oz retorted, like that justified everything perfectly.

Jael shook her head and asked, "Of all things, that would make you break character?"

"I didn't break character. Qaz married a whole group of Iungo women. Why can't you be fucking your guard?" Oz replied with a wink and lifted his hands palm up.

Everyone in the elevator went silent as the doors slid open. Jael sucked her lips into her mouth to stop the bubbling laugh. A giggle slipped out, but Amelia nudged her in the rib's and she sucked it back in.

When they finally reached the suite, Jael was so over-heated she lifted her dress the second the door was shut.

"What are you doing?" Mercy asked as she tried to assess what the hell was happening.

"This dress is so hot. Everything is hot. It reminds me of home, and I do not miss home," Jael scowled as she flapped the dress, trying to circulate some air.

Cinis tapped the suites control panel a few times to turn it on, and when it lit up, they turned the air down. The room chilled too cold and after a shiver, Oz scowled before raising it a few degrees.

"How in hell do we strike up a conversation with this Baiselle woman? All Qaz said was she was next to his suite," Mercy asked the room.

They all stared at Jael as if she should know, so she nervously suggested, "Why don't I just knock on her door?"

Cinis narrowed their eyes, "And then what?"

"Ask her about her star charts? I will tell her I heard she had some ancient and interesting ones. She's old, right?" Jael asked.

Nodding, Cinis replied, "She is fairly old. She does not look old, but she is about a hundred."

After a bit of thought, Jael confidently announced, "The only people I ever talked to back on Earth were old people at the grocery store. *I have a plan.*" She held up her missing hand with a wide grin and asked, "How many rich people are missing a hand? Old people love to talk about injuries. I had to explain burned off eyebrows a few times, and they always loved hearing all about it."

Cocking their head to the side, Cinis agreed, "You may have a point. Most rich people would have had a replacement hand growing by now. They would be talking about it constantly and making a show of it. Speaking of Rungi, she said she has a bio printer and can give you a new hand. She said it's her gift."

"Throw out everything in the suite med kit and hand it to me, please," Jael instructed. "Where I come from, that sort of thing wasn't possible. Tell her to find a poor child and give them the chance instead. I have accepted my new body how it is. I may compromise for an electronic hand when it's possible, but not one of flesh and blood. Not when someone young could have it instead. I know how she is with deals."

Nodding in agreement with Jael's decision and the true comment about Rungi, Cinis headed over to the bar and opened the cabinet. Rungi would find a child in need and honor the trade. She might be a weapons dealer, but she did have a something of a heart. After opening and closing nearly every cabinet in the small kitchen area, they finally found the small white first aid kit.

When Cinis handed it to Jael, she paused a moment. That first aid kit was too familiar, the small white box. Memories of when she and Oz raided the human's camp and freed his people came rushing back. Looking up at Amelia, she remembered when she had woken up in the tent after dosing off on Oz.

Amelia had peered back at her, and Jael had been delighted to see the same kindness she had found in Oz. It was a feeling that these people had something more about them, something special, something she couldn't quite explain, but their journey could, their actions spoke volumes.

"I'm ready. I'll go take care of this one by myself," Jael insisted.

Oz and Mercy stared piercingly at one another, seeming to speak through subliminal messages as their people did before they could speak. Oz finally shrugged and relented, "If you think that's a good idea."

Jael found the trash slot and dumped the kit's contents into it as she explained, "Something tells me it is."

Cinis opened the door for her, and as she headed into the hallway, the cooled air slid across her skin. She could do this. She took a slow, deep breath before approaching the door of the next suite. With her empty white first aid box in hand, she knocked on the door.

A large man answered and asked, "What do you want? Games are starting."

"I am in the suite next door. My name is Tache. Do you have a complete med kit? Mine is missing wound wraps," Jael asked as she held her arm up.

His eyes went wide, and she heard a gasp from behind him before a loud, booming, "Move, you giant Makros. Jupiter! You sweet girl."

Shoving him out of the way was a lithe woman, tall in stature and clearly older than her face claimed she was.

"My dear, how did such a thing happen to such a beautiful, young, human-woman like yourself?" Baiselle said in a sweet tone, "Packe, go grab this poor dear our medical supply box."

"Oh, it was an accident in a lab. I blew up an experiment. Last time, all it got was my eyebrows," she explained, making sure to look the woman straight in the eye.

"You poor-poor thing. Do you have a limb specialist? I have an outstanding one. He's my neighbor on Melior. His name is Pyonte Latticus, and the limbs he grows are even exposed to system starlight radiation lamps long enough to match your current skin tone. The man is an expert at his craft. They blend seamlessly right after surgery. He uses stem cells sutures so there is no scarring," she explained with a smile that was a little too perfect, a little too pearly white.

Smiling wide, Jael replied, "Thank you, I would love his information."

Just then screams erupted in the stands, and Jael made her way to peak over the edge at the center of the arena. A line of various people, including a few Iungo, were forced out of a door on one side as some kind of massive cat she thought belonged in the Ice Age on Earth began to prowl around the edge. When it leaned its head back and roared, dread wriggled through her like worms. If she didn't back away, she would witness something deeply disturbing, and it was the last thing on her agenda today.

As she backed away, Baiselle came up behind her and

kept her from retreating. Putting her hand on Jael's back, she gently guided her back to the window. "This is the best part. You must not miss the opening battle. Those fools, they were picked because they're criminals. I come every month to watch the games. I loathe anything with wings or a tail, but especially bugs. One smothered my baby. I know it was her, that nasty insect. The baby was a special designer model from the UTC's best geneticists. There could not have been anything wrong with my little child. They were perfect. I shouldn't have ever trusted her." Baiselle seethed, baiting her to ask questions.

She was not falling for it. She's been around people like this woman at the college she worked for. She was just like the rich doners who funded their research. Jael wasn't sure how she could watch the carnage unfold and keep her last meal, but she did her best to stand tall. Baiselle still had her hand on her back, and Jael knew this was somehow a test.

"Watch, one of them will be brave and try to save the rest. They always die first. It's spectacular," she whispered, grinning over Jael's shoulder as she stared down into the arena.

A lump rose in Jael's throat as she focused on keeping her breaths even, trying to hide the deep dread of what she was about to witness. She hoped Oz, Mercy, and Amelia were not watching.

The beast was freed of his invisible perimeter, and it pounced on a woman with a fluffy brown tail, ripping her throat out and spraying a fan of red blood across the dirt. One of the larger Iungo men leapt onto its back and tried to wrap his legs around the cat's thick neck.

The creature simply shook him off and ripped into his

back like he was made of paper. Blue blood pooled as the beast tore into the man's flesh. Jael fought for breath as she watched the horror unfold. How were Oz, Amelia, and Mercy dealing with this? She pleaded inside hoping they weren't watching this macabre injustice.

With more willpower than she ever believed she possessed, she sighed, "This is fun, it really is the same every time. My real love is deep space travel and visiting ancient, abandoned worlds. As soon as my hand is grown, I'm going to travel to the farthest place I can find. I've heard there is a particularly old planet named Janus. Have you heard of it? I can't seem to find it on any star charts, but I've been hearing rumors here and there and I've asked around, but no one knows. I want to go somewhere no one else has gone."

With a look of delight, Baiselle remove her hand from Jael's back and grinned as she spoke, "Well, you were simply asking the wrong people, dear. I have some of the oldest star charts known to the First Humans. You can search them if you like. The database is wirelessly connected to my console here. I love showing them to fellow star travelers."

She led Jael to a computer with some type of UTC hologram technology, though it wasn't nearly as advanced as the Iungo holo-tech. Sitting down at the table, Jael studied the keyboard and prayed she had the Latin spelling correct. She eventually found the letters she needed and when she typed in Janus, a star chart popped up with a blinking light in the center.

"Oh, look. It is right there. Wow, that one is at a tremendous distance from here. You might be traveling for a while. It might take ten wormholes or more in a smaller vessel. Normally I charge for these, but I'll let you have this one on me since you lost your hand. The next search will be twenty thousand credit," Baiselle offered as she slid some kind of small drive into the computer.

It took a few moments, and she handed Jael the small drive. Jael slipped it into her pocket and cringed when she heard screams from the arena. The mixed screams of horror and delight would haunt her forever. Packe handed Jael the refilled medical kit.

"You can let yourself out, I don't want to miss this. The next show will start any minute," she said as she glided across the floor to the window.

"Thank you for your generosity. I hope to see you again." Jael rose from her seat, and tried not to run from the suite but didn't hesitate for a moment. When she arrived at Qaz's suite, she slammed the door behind her, pulled out the trashcan from its slot in the wall next to her and vomited up everything in her stomach. When she turned back, she found Oz, Mercy, and Amelia all with their backs turned to the carnage below. All eyes were on her.

Holding up the disk as Basille's med kit dangling from her arm, Jael croaked, "I got it. She had the star chart, and I found Janus. Cinis, did you say your sister is taking care of the broadcast?"

Nodding, Cinis replied, "Yes, she said she recorded it this morning, and the hacker is broadcasting it along with an unopened file transfer that came from Carter being sent tomorrow morning. They are unraveling the data now, but they are fairly sure your people on Portum found proof the Iungo are an origin species."

Jael gave a half-hearted smile and wheezed, "Great. Let's get the fuck out of here before the next round of these fucked up games starts."

Screams erupted below, indicating they were too late for escaping the sounds of round two. She bent back over and continued to throw up into the trashcan.

Oz approached and handed her a water and breathed, "Let's get the hell out of here so we can stop this forever."

47

PLANET ADURO - CLAUDIUS ROYAL PALACE

Turning the palace into a makeshift military base had shown August what Livia could do. She embodied the king he knew she could be, but he knew his turn to fulfill his role was coming. His title may have been general back on his home planet, but he didn't lead any armies into battle back home. He and Oz practiced fighting one another as broody teens, and it may have paid off, but he hoped the knowledge he had taken from Livia about warfare and strategy would be enough for actual warfare. He was decades of training behind Lucas, except for one-on-one combat skill. They may be more equally matched than Lucas could ever guess. He planned on using every angle, including his own perceived deficits in Lucas's eyes. He would feign weakness and strike when he least expected.

Their surveillance showed Lucas assembling the remaining guards and his battle fleet of soldiers and pilots at the barracks. August's stomach turned as he watched the screen. Lucas was a gifted commander, one of the best in the galaxy according to Livia. His strategic prowess was built over many years of space battles with the royal family's fleet of breakaway battleships. The ships travel to location as one and then break into multiple pieces each commanded by individual pilot, each equipped so heavily it could face targets sixty times their size.

Lucas had begun his time as commander at twenty-two, and during his years in the service, he claimed six pirate ships and managed to disarm and take down one pirate hub. The hub had been responsible for human, drug, and animal trafficking, as well as medical facilities for distributing pirated pharmaceuticals.

Flashes of August at nineteen flew through his mind, times of joy undermined with silent fear. He had been running through the woods, crying over the loss of Oz, and Mazarine had been there to comfort him. His upbringing was nothing like these Aduro, Melior, or even Emendo humans. He wasn't sure they had much of a choice in their career path from what he learned from Livia's memories, but it didn't change what he had to do now. *Does that make me just as bad as Lucas?*

Livia placed her hand on his shoulder before assuring, "We can beat him. Your people are capable. They've assembled themselves and are preparing for battle on the sand at dusk. Chris is in my royal rooms with the doctor and his daughter like you wanted. He understands his instructions to flee with them in an escape ship and to find your home planet."

Shifting his tail behind him, August asked, "We have ten minutes before we start transporting our people to the sand on the mountain lifts. Has anyone ever crossed the dunes?"

"No, we have never had a reason to venture into the sands," she explained, her gaze distant.

With a rough exhale, August shuddered, shoving away the thought of what his mind saw slithering under the surface of the sand.

Watching Lucas and his forces draw closer on the screen he acknowledged, "It's time."

Livia studied the screen and saw Lucas and his assembled army beginning to transport their troops to the side of the nearest massive sand dune. They switched to the satellite feed as a team of soldiers built a platform on the sand from what must be broken down wooden bunks. There was nothing else made of wood on the planet she knew of. Without the rest of the transports from the palace, the soldiers were forced into the open and vulnerable in the middle of the sands. She made sure the southern mine transports all had maintenance scheduled for the same time knowing once the process started it took four full days of work to finish. There were no shortcuts. Lucas likely knew this was pre-planned when he discovered them all taken apart as scheduled earlier that morning. That would have been right before he realized the palace wasn't responding.

Livia took a step back, and August pushed back the chair he was sitting in. When he stood, he brushed his hands down his chest and wished he had the armor designed by Mercy. The king's old armor Livia had found fit well, but it wasn't the same. He missed his friends and his people.

He wondered how his connection trained people would fair against Lucas and his army of exceedingly trained genetically engineered soldiers, and hoped a desire for freedom and revenge for years of injustice would tilt the balance of the scales in their favor. His heart squeezed, and he begged the creator to hear his pleas of help. They were minutes away from fighting an almost impossible battle.

The lift carried them to the main floor, and when it opened, Livia could see Valec at the other end of the hallway. When he saw August and Livia, he lit up and made his way over to them.

"Everyone heading out to fight has been outfitted with armor, electric staffs, and two rail guns each. We managed to make around fifty shields, but we haven't been able to test them. I hope the tech you explained works," Valec reported as he shifted on his feet.

August explained, "As long as you set the shield current to the same frequency as the rail guns, we are good to go."

"Yes, and the current is set to aim the deflected round into the sand just like you said," Valec replied in awe at the idea behind the shields.

The three headed out onto the landing pad and watched as four transports landed to take the remaining people down to the guard towers on the edge of the sand, just down the mountain from the palace. Watching his people, August turned back to Livia and reminded her, "I know you want to join us, but this battle is not for the king."

With anger in her eyes, she knew exactly why August had demanded she stay behind. Aside from her need to survive to hold the title of king, she was a liability on the battlefield. The enemy was too close to her. She would be too predictable after years of training with the same people she was going to battle against. She was easily the best they had aside from August, but she knew he was right even if being sidelined flamed fury inside of her. She would watch and wait, and the moment the battle turned, she would swoop in, promises be damned.

Without waiting on an answer, August followed Valec onto the last transport. When he brought his gaze back at Livia, he found her stoic and except for her fierce eyes. The transport lifted off, and she sprinted inside to monitor the satellite feed.

Valec flew the transport down to the main tower, touching down on the landing pad behind the tall fortress. After landing, Valec waited for August to pass so he could enter the room first. August stopped in front of Valec and surveyed the room. He looked around the massive space filled with his people, now dressed and ready for battle. He smiled a bit when he saw the holes they had torn in the uniforms for their tails.

With a shaking voice, August turned, "Valec, I wanted to..."

"We can celebrate, together, after the battle, if you wish," he replied with a grin, cutting off August's nervous words.

Smiling August softly added, "Yeah, that's what we'll do."

Valec put his hand on August's arm and assured, "We are going to beat him. I've seen you fight. I watched you and Livia spar. I know what you can do."

"But what about them?" August asked as he gestured to his people.

Valec slid his hand down and grabbed August's hand as he leaned in and affirmed, "You are their liberator and their hope. Your people have been docile to a fault for thousands of years. You stand out from that mold. They would all gladly hand over their lives for this chance of autonomy you've offered them. They appear to worship you like my people worship Mars. Lead them and they will follow through whatever fire you may pass."

When August looked beyond Valec and at his people again, they were all standing with their eyes trained on him. One by one they began to nod.

A voice came from the room directly below them announcing, "Commander Lucas and his soldiers are marching over the dune. Prepare the first wave."

Just like highly skilled, trained soldiers, August's people exited out of the tower's side door and onto the lift outside. After the platform filled with their soldiers, it sent them to the ground in groups of fifteen, and in a matter of seconds, their first wave spread across the sand behind August. There were two hundred of them, roughly double their enemy's numbers.

With their large flat sand shoes, they marched quickly up the first small dune and down the other side. If August timed it correctly, they would be meeting Lucas as he headed up the last of the small sand dunes in between them.

As August approached the top, he held his hand up for his soldiers to halt behind him. The system star was burning above them and shining into August 's orange eyes.

He stopped and reached down to the sand. Sticking his hands into the hot grains and closing his eyes, he felt for the vibrations of their enemy's feet. The moment he picked it up, his eyes flew open, and he looked around to his line of soldiers, crouched and ready. All of their eyes were focused on him, waiting for the command to advance.

It was time to *become* the demon they all called him.

He nodded once and held his hand up, pulling his rail gun from its place on his side. He scowled at the weapon and decided they would rid this planet of these vile weapons the moment this battle was finished.

With the rail gun raised, feeling foreign in his hand,

August tipped it once and like a boom of thunder; they struck. Crested in a wave over the top of the dune, August's soldiers landed in front of the unsuspecting human soldiers.

Shifting his attention back-and-forth down his line of soldiers, Lucas ordered, "Attack!"

August's soldiers were already firing, some foregoing the rail guns and using their electrified staffs. Lucas's soldiers dropped all around. The enemy wasn't taken by surprise for long as battle cries rang out. His people were able to adapt to the sand and sand shoes quickly, but it made minor difference to soldiers hardened in the sand. Lucas's soldiers moved like the ground was solid under their feet.

August raised his gun and fired at the first soldier he faced and was filled with disgust as he watched him fall over dead in an instant. He pressed the self-destruct key and pulled the trigger to activate it before he tossed away the gun. He pulled the electrified staff from its place on his back as he scoured the desert for Lucas.

When he spotted a high-ranking Claudius Royal Commander through the swinging staffs and electrified screams of death, August charged for him. Lucas turned and saw August dredging through the sand, wearing the former king's armor. Rage boiled within him as he screeched, "That's *my* armor you vile insect! I am the chosen Claudius King!" With his words, his soldiers all released battle cries and seemed to be renewed with strength.

Fighting the sand and heat as he approached his enemy, August flared his eyes wide and commanded, "Come and take it from me you little bitch!"

When the two charging men slammed into one another, they collided with such a force, August felt a rib snap and puncture his lung. Breath was slipping away, and he fought to suck in air. The pain from his pierced lung left him struggling to pull in enough oxygen.

Using an opening, he dodged a fist and leaned back before slamming his own fist into Lucas's nose, causing bright red blood to spray onto the sand. Lucas's head snapped back, and he lost his grip on August's shoulder, sending him careening backward.

As Lucas's body hit the sand, August sucked in a desperate, gurgling breath and pulled a knife from his belt as he tackled Lucas. In a flash, August embedded the knife into the top of Lucas's chest, aiming the tip downward into his heart. He slammed the palm of his hand over the hilt and shoved it further into Lucas's chest. He heard a crunch and met Lucas's gaze. Lucas spit blood out of his mouth before grabbing August's neck and pulling him close as he whispered, "May we meet again in the underworld, you gods forsaken demon."

August rolled from Lucas's body, and he fought for another breath. More blood poured into his lung. He was suffocating, drowning in his own blood.

He looked back and found his soldiers had turned the battle in their favor when a different kind of scream rang out, one of horror and warning. August's soldiers wildly search the sand as they jumped away one by one. One of August's larger soldiers spotted him leaned over Lucas' dying body and helped him to his feet. "I am injured," was all August could quietly utter as the massively built woman slid her arm under his.

She warned in her deep voice, "Those creatures in the sand are close! We have to get off the dunes!"

August shot his gaze behind him, and his heart burst with panic when he saw Valec, alone at the top of the dune, battling one of Lucas' soldiers. Two men a few yards away from them were being eaten alive by the silver, scaled creatures August thought he had imagined when he was chained to the pole.

They were real! "No!" August shoved away from the woman and used the last of his strength to leap.

August landed next to Valec, and in one motion slit the soldier's throat and pushed him toward the slithering monsters. Outraged at August's deteriorating condition and what had just occurred, Valec finally turned and noticed the silver creatures diving into the writhing flesh of the man August had just killed.

Arm in arm, August and Valec slid down the dune then wearily climbed the next. When they reached the top, August fell to his knees as stars filled his vision and demanded, "Go, run. I am moments from death. Please just run."

"I would rather be eaten alive by the sand snakes than leave you to their mercy," Valec vowed. In front of them, he could see the large woman approaching to once again save him.

Mercy, his heart broke at the thought of her name. He deserved this end.

He prayed Livia and Valec forgave him. He was glad they still had one another.

He looked over at Valec, who was tugging on August's arm and begging him to rise. With love swelling inside of him, August pushed Valec down the dune. As Valec fell uncontrollably, he screamed in frustration. He picked up speed as he rolled and caught the woman on his way down. Both of them careened down the dune and onto the safety of the hard ground around the tower.

August turned and watched the sand, his eyes followed the movement under the surface as the sand serpents headed his way from the top of the previous dune. His head pounded and his lungs burned for oxygen as he peered back and saw Valec being carried by the woman as he kicked and screamed. From the way Valec's arm dangled at his side, August was sure his elbow was dislocated.

After inhaling one last pained breath, his lungs gurgled as they finished filling with blood, and the darkness creeping in overtook him.

48

PLANET ADURO - CLAUDIUS ROYAL PALACE

Leaning up from the mattress she had pushed to the window in her rooms, Livia blinked away the sleep from her eyes as she looked out onto the sand dunes. A storm had just rolled in and sprouted tornadoes, twirling around one another over the dunes, spinning and dancing. The sand at the twisters' bases formed little cones in the air and left deep trails of missing sand in their path. The sky was painted with greens, blues, and deep gray reflecting the intensity of the storm.

A groan next to her sent her head whipping around to see if August had woken up yet. His procedure had been quick and easy the doctor had explained. A broken rib had punctured his lung, and it had fully collapsed by the time Livia had pulled him from the sand dune. She had seen the blow and knew he would need a transport out before the king's suit alerted her of a fatal strike. If she had only known about the silver sand worms, she would never have sent August or his people out there.

She would have still tricked Lucas into meeting them on

the sand though; she's not all good inside after all. Her father made sure of that. She was just ruthless enough to be a proper king, despite her good heart. Lucas being eating alive by silver flesh-boring worms *was* a fitting end.

As his hand landed on her ankle, August groaned, "What happened?"

"I had Dragon hover in a transport so I could climb down and pluck you up before the silver worms ate to you. Valec is furious with you. Your ribs are bonded, and we used tissue growth enhancing sutures so you're over half healed. I am sure you still feel like hell, but you're doing exceptionally well. You've been asleep for a day and a half." Livia explained as she looked down at him.

"We discovered the sand serpents are a flesh-boring, carnivore flat worm related to parasitic liver fluke. Lucas wasn't dead when the worms reached him; I thought you should know," Livia explained with a smirk.

As she knelt by him, he pulled her shoulder strap down, gently caressing her shoulder as he did. She leaned over, their mouths meeting in a deep kiss. As they kissed, August pulled her silk dress down and slid his hands over her breasts. She moved to straddle him, and as she did, she pulled the sheet off him.

Livia leaned her head back as he lined himself up to her entrance. When she slid down onto him, she moaned as she fully seated herself on his length. She rolled her hips as her eyes followed the tornados ripping across the land outside of the window.

"Where's Valec?" August whispered as he reached up and gently dragged his fingers down her jawline.

Stopping her movements, she leaned over to face her

second bedroom and slightly raised her voice to call out, "Valec?"

He emerged in the light of the doorway and relief fell over him. He was wearing grey lose sleep pants and no shirt, his pants set low on his hips. August had never seen him like this. He was lean but packed with muscle. He approached the bed and as he reached the edge, August waved his hand for him to join them. Valec's pants fell to the floor at his feet, and he crawled onto the bedding.

When Valec moved over to him, August grabbed his face and kissed him. Livia rolled her hips as August reached between Valec's legs and gently gripped his length. His body shuddered as August stroked him. Valec kissed down the center of August's neck, and he leaned back, sounding the clicks of pleasure in his throat. Livia sighed as she tipped over into bliss and her waves crested; August was not far behind and spilled into her with his body rocking back and forth.

As August pumped into Livia, he rubbed Valec's length in a smooth rhythm, and Valec spilled over next with a heavy groan. The stress and fear of the previous days released with their joint pleasure. The three spread out onto the bed and didn't wake until the star's light brightened the horizon the following day.

Valec was the first to rise, and after he showered and dressed, he woke Livia and August. "I'll cook breakfast. You two stay there." Valec offered, but Livia rose and joined him in the kitchen, anyway.

"My king, you don't need to help with breakfast," Valec explained with a nervous laugh.

Smiling, she hooked her arm in with his and replied, "We all shared a bed last night and you're welcome in it with us whenever you please. My name is Livia to you, not King."

Valec grinned and spoke a little louder as he said, "I was hoping you would say that. I am still upset with you, August."

From the bed, still sprawled out in his spot, August offered, "I would expect nothing less. We can spar after I'm healed, or we could fuck it out."

With his eyes wide, Valec coughed, cleared his throat, and retorted, "Yes, or we could do both."

Livia smiled to herself as she pulled the dough and fruit out of the icebox. Valec and Livia worked in tandem and quietly made August the pastries he had told her about.

When they were finished, Valec showed August the steaming pastries. He leaned up and inspected them before his mouth opened slightly.

"Are those what I think they are? I was wondering what that scent was," August asked, his face hopeful.

Nodding, Valec set the plate down on a tray and helped August sit up, sliding a pillow behind him. He reached over for a pastry and tore one in half to let it cool. The steam wafted out, and he couldn't help leaning in for the scent. It was a mix of berries, and he was nearly drooling on himself. He blew on it a few times before daring a bite. It was still too hot, but he didn't care. It tasted like his home, and he was overwhelmed with joy, hissing around the heat as he chewed. They must have been speaking with some of his people from the mines.

After he chewed a few bites, he asked, "They are perfect. Have you had any luck setting up a communication line with my people yet?"

"I have no news. Over half of my field scouts quit when they found out Lucas was dead. The other half had nothing to report, but I'm not sure if I could trust it. I already have some of your people in training to take over the jobs of the lost guards, and we will need to find some rebellious souls to fill in for the lost scouts. I've passed on my space flight training to Dragon, and she took over readying several groups of your people for space." Livia updated him as she reached over and wiped a bit of fruit from the corner of August's mouth.

"Our people. It's our people. They want to stay here. They know exactly how much the ore in those mines is worth and a few of them had some excellent ideas for robotics to take over the mining work. They know the surface radiation doesn't hurt us, but it is a turn off to beings who can't withstand it for long. My people are docile, and they want solitude. It seems like a perfect place for my kind if we can set up true settlements and a nice place for them to live. We could do some additional terraforming and build greenhouses. We could eventually turn you the Claudius pace station in orbit into a trading hub," August explained as he munched on the pastry in his hand.

Valec just stood by the window and watched the bright star rise before he admitted, "Our only issue would be pirates, but I think your plan is sound otherwise. If that's really what your people want Livia, you were always better than Lucas in space tactical class. I'm not sure why your father always had him go deal with the pirates. I would have thought he would want his best there."

"All my father saw in Lucas was himself. He was too blind to see any talent I ever had. I was always the star in the academy space battles, but I was docked for every mistake in grading. Did you even take that class?"

"Yes, I took it a few months later. You're two years ahead of me on academics though," he explained.

"How many times did you get whipped by Super Tilcos? I received thirteen whippings." Livia cringed as she asked. She could hear the cracks of the whip from her father which always followed the brutal whippings from the academy superintendent.

"Sixteen times." Valec winced with the memory.

Leaning on the wall by the window, Livia peered out in the direction of the academy building and casually offered, "Let's burn it down."

49

PLANET EMENDO – VENUS DISTRICT 7 – RUNGI'S SHIP HANGER

After the UTC emergency broadcasting tone filled the hanger, an artificially generated figure appeared on a viewing screen at the other end of the large space, "This is an announcement from the office of the Premiere of the First Humans and The United Trusts and Colonies Empress. The United Trusts and Colonies many departments, as well as many of the ruling powers of the worlds belonging to the UTC, and the good citizens of our empire have received a profoundly disturbing transmission this morning. A rebel faction of new, more intelligent insects who call themselves Iungo, have taken over a UTC owned planet used as a growth and development factory. This is planetary theft, and severe repercussions will follow. They have committed a massacre of the soldiers sent to eliminate the uprising. All one thousand of the UTC soldiers were lost to enemy sabotage. They rigged our own bombs to detonate the transports the moment they reached orbit around Emendo. We are unsure at this time if any of the people from the facility survived. The First Humans have a message for the leaders of the rebel Iungo faction. You are not an original species and any proof you have is fabricated. We have officially declared war and filed the declaration with the UTC. The declaration went uncontested after your sabotage. Any attempt to approach the UTC Science and Technology Department will be met with a swift and deadly response by the First Humans. Every UTC ship has an immediate destroy order for any stolen vessels they identify from the captured planet. The Iungo have elected a leader with the name of Ozias Green. He is dangerous, and he is now the galactic center's most wanted individual. He is wanted alive, and the reward is a new one hundred mile estate along the equator of Melior as well as a cash reward of up to one billion in First Human credits, transferable to any currency. If he is recovered dead, the reward is one hundred thousand untransferable FH credits. In addition, any wanted individual, wanted for any reason, who produces this dangerous creature will receive a full pardon from the Empress herself."

Standing in the hanger, Rungi, Oz, and Jael watched the broadcast the First Humans had just released with their mouths flapping like fish out of water. A picture of Oz had been converted into a 3-D rendering and slowly turned on the screen. Alarm spread through them like wildfire. They had no idea what the response would be. There is a law that says any origin species has protection. Was this their loophole? All because the proof had not been delivered yet? How can they claim evidence is fabricated if they haven't received it yet?

"Run. Get in your ship and fly as fast as you can back to your planet. Get the samples to the UTC science and tech lab station around Melior by any means necessary. I have a lot of your people in the underground liberation circuit who are counting on you. I'll evacuate the factory, and we will go in hiding until the smoke clears. May Jupiter himself bless your journey," Rungi fired off before she abruptly turned and left.

Oz and Jael ran up the stairs and boarded the ship, and in less than a minute, Oz was in the captain's seat and punching in commands to the main computer.

"Let's go. I have a heavy warrant for my live capture. We need to get home, pick up the samples, and go back to the UTC science station before they catch up and collapse the ship into a ball of metal with us inside," Oz explained once Carter's face materialized on the view screen.

Carter already had a look of distress before he began, "Bad news, I just took sensor readings from the planet's atmosphere. We have to make two jumps. One to put us in orbit and the second to take us home. The UTC put transport blockers in their satellites, so we will have to shoot one of them down to make a hole in the network to jump through."

"Fuck. Let's make it fast. We have to reach Portum and make it back before the First Humans catch up." Oz was speaking so quickly his words began to run together, his heart was lodged in his throat.

Scratching her chin, Kagnus asked, "So the UTC hasn't declared war yet, just the First Humans? I guess that's not the worst news."

Ignoring and not correcting Kagnus, Oz demanded, "Carter, anytime now. We need to get the fuck out of here. Mercy, load weapons and have them hot. Shields are going up now."

"Jumping now." was all Oz heard from Carter before the ship blinked out of existence.

It materialized just under a satellite, and Mercy locked on to fire just as another ship pulled out of light speed and opened fire.

"Mercy, fire! Everyone hang on we are going to have direct hits!" Oz yelled as the computer blared a signal of warning along with red lights blinking on the bridge.

The ship shook as they took hits to the shields as Mercy fired, hitting the satellite, and causing a small explosion. Fire and debris spread out into the atmosphere, the pieces of metal twinkled in the sunlight as they fell. A stream of missiles burst through the debris, and the ship responded in warning.

"Get us out of here, Carter!" Oz screamed right as the ship disappeared.

The ship jumped into orbit around Portum, and everyone on the bridge took a deep breath of relief. Blinking red lights all-round the interior of the bridge indicated the damage from the impacts.

On the view screen, the Sagittarius A* black hole was spinning in the distance, and a bright star was being sucked inside from far above. The star was not visible from under the auras on the main continent of Portum.

"What's the damage?" Oz asked Carter's holo-graphic head.

"Just shields, we made it out without any severe damage. Those were cannon guns that struck us. I can have the shields back up in ten minutes. We will eventually need to do some additional repairs to the hull, but we have functioning patches in place now," Carter explained, but his voice was somewhat uncertain.

"Jacob and Callum will be here with the samples soon. After they dock and send the transport back to base, we are jumping directly to the coordinates of the UTC Science and Technology Department in orbit around Melior. Get the coordinates and video feed off the probe we had follow the First Human's and make sure we have the video the hacker broadcast loaded onto the ship's drive. I want a merged backup added to the travel drive Jacob will have in hand when he boards. Any questions?" Oz asked as he looked around the room, his eyes meeting all of theirs.

Several *no*'s sounded across the room, and everyone hustled as panic spread through Oz. *Could they make it in time? Would the UTC use one of their magnetic charges to take their ship out before they could make it and have a chance to present their case to the science chancellor? From the sound of the UTC broadcast, all they really want is me, but would they stop with just me? What would they do to our people??*

"Carter, can you somehow change the resonate signature of the ship so they can't detect us so quickly? Maybe change the frequency of the shields?" Oz asked, desperation in his tone.

Narrowing his eyes Carter admitted, "That's a brilliant idea. I will mask us with a space rock signature. With the new shields that mimic our armor tech, we can easily change the resonate waves on the hull to any frequency. I'll have several other frequencies lined up to roll out when they decode the first. The computer should learn by then, and the shields will begin to adapt."

Nodding, Oz heard a whoosh behind him and turned to see Jacob and Callum pulling their helmets off. Jacob spoke with a trembling voice as he handed Oz a metal case. "Our people's salvation is in that box. Let's go."

"You heard him, Carter. Let's go. You and Callum hang

on. This might get rough." Oz adjusted himself in his seat to make his tail more comfortable.

Two seats behind Oz grew from the floor so that Jacob and Callum could sit down. They buckled themselves in nervously staring at one another, still uncertain about the future, but well aware of one fact. This is one journey they knew they had to take, no matter how risky it was, no matter how much their hearts were screaming at them to go back home.

Carter's face materialized as he reported, "We just finished with the shields. It was much easier to repair than we originally believed. We are ready to jump."

As the ship disappeared, Oz begged the creator to spare them.

50

PLANET MELIOR – UTC SCIENCE AND TECHNOLOGY SPACE STATION

Materializing at the space dock of the UTC Science and Technology Department on the massive space station lab circling Melior, they all stood frozen with fear that they would be blown up on the spot. Instead of in instant death, the airlock sounded on the other side of the door of the ship, and the S & T station guards stormed in the ship with rail guns drawn.

Kagnus cleared her throat, through her hands into the air, and cried out, "We evoke the law of origin! We plead the 2-4-57 article of the 6th revision of the United Trusts and Colonies that no suspected origin species be harmed while their planetary origin is under investigation! You may not open fire or risk violating galactic center law! Now move out of the way while we plead the case."

The armed guards froze in place until a short, light brown skinned human man with white curly hair emerged from the ship's hallway with another guard hovering behind him. "Your citation of the law is accurate. We will accept your plea," he rasped with a deep sigh and a frown on his face. Turning to the guards in the room with a scowl he calmly announced, "Put those damned things away before you do something you regret." When they all dropped their weapons, he faced Oz and spoke with power, "If this evidence of yours is tampered with, we will know. If I find that you are not an original species from your planet, I will have my sons personally hunt you and your crew down. They are twins and are by far the most feared pirate hunters in the galactic center. Don't confuse my compliance of the law with mercy. I loathe your kind, but I will follow galactic procedure. The results will be ready in seven days."

51

PLANET PORTUM – IUNGO BASE

Days of silence. No one dared to say more than necessary at the base. Spoken words were said in hushed tones. Anyone who knew what they were waiting on was gripped with worry. It was as if the cave walls were holding their breath as well. They seemed to swell and fill the cavern, daring to swallow and devour them at a moment's notice.

They had not formally announced why they were waiting on the seal to the public or anyone other than the command personnel to prevent the same weighted worry among all their people. The base felt it anyway. The silence spoke the truth. There could be nothing else that would drive them back to near silence.

Jael stood at the doorway of their apartment in the base and watched Oz as he stared at the large holo-screen with the base updates streaming across it.

One of the updates read: Base security teams 1, 3, and 7 are scheduled to deliver holo-screens to every citizen along with communications tablets. All security teams report to

Pike at the end of work shifts for altered assignment schedules.

She wondered if Oz was reading any of the updates, or if he was just blankly staring at the screen while waiting for some kind of news. He had hardly left that spot since they had arrived back home. Jael came up behind him, wrapping her arms around his waist. He leaned into her and rubbed her forearm with his hand. "They will find the truth. I know it," Jael whispered into the back of his shirt the heat of her breath lingering on his skin.

Oz questioned, "What if we are sabotaged at the lab? What if they lie about the results? So much can still go wrong. The empress could show up and kill us all anyway, and there is no one to stop her."

"I don't think that old man is a liar or cheater. They won't kill us all. Your people are too valuable to her. She wouldn't kill anyone but us, and maybe Jacob," Jael offered, unsure of if her words were true or not.

Sighing, Oz admitted, "That doesn't exactly make me feel better. You're probably right though."

That part, *she wouldn't kill anyone but us.* That's the part he thought about constantly. He could hardly look at Jael. *What if we are taken? What if I can't protect her?* He shoved those thoughts away and did his best to keep his mind on the treehouse in the near future. Those few months they had together, back at the treehouse, were the best of his life. He begged with all of his being he would have those moments again, with her, the woman he loved, the woman who gave him and his people opportunity, the woman who saved his life.

As they stood in silence, Jael noticed a small red light blinking on Oz's tablet a few feet away. She stopped and stared at it for moment. Remembering the red blinking warning lights on the ship, the distress and adrenaline pumping through her veins overtook her senses. Bringing herself back to the now, she began wondering why there was a blinking red light on his tablet. *Is that a message?*

"What's that?" Jael asked, her eyes burning holes in the tablet.

"What's what?" Oz asked as he turned and faced her.

Staring at his tablet, she whispered, "I think you have a message."

Whipping around, he made a line straight for his tablet and grabbed it off the table. His heart pounding in his body, he knew the red blinking light was not a message from the intranet at the base and was coming from an exterior source. Clicking on the message with a shaking hand, Oz saw it was from the UTC Science and Technology Department Chancellor. Giving Jael a look of hope, he opened the message and held it so they could both read.

Chancellor Tarks:

> Your results are complete. Your DNA matches the sample as claimed. Report to the UTC Science and Technology Space Station to receive your official origin species digital seal deeming you the owners of your planet. The First Humans have been ordered to abandon any planets in use for the sole purpose of the biological manufacturing of your kind.

In accordance with United Trusts and Colonies law, the exploitation of an origin species results in the automatic loss and surrender of any planet and facilities used in such exploits of the origin species in question.

The law does not extend to the lungo under current ownership. Their ownership remains legal under the law.

Oz faced Jael and gave her a half smile before saying, "It's a start." He flipped through his tablet and found Jacob's number. Jacob's face materialized, and Oz explained, "I just received word that we are officially our own species, but the war is not over. Our people are not automatically freed either. We need to learn galactic center law as soon as we can. It doesn't look like we're going to have any protection."

"Our people who have been sold are not freed? Only those of us who hadn't been sold yet? Are you sure that's right? How could that be?" Jacob asked his brow furrowed and fury flooded over his face.

"We keep the two planets they used to farm us, I guess, as a form of instant reparation. We also have to risk our lives again and go claim our digital seal or whatever that means."

"We have to go back?!" Jacob asked in a panic.

With his hand on Jacob's shoulder, Callum reassured him, "Jacob, we can do this. We have to see this through. It's almost over. I can't believe I'm actually saying any of this, but we have to go. This is important."

Nodding to him Jacob turned back to his tablet and relented, "OK. Let's go. We'll meet you at the transport. I'll call everyone else."

Giving him a half smile, Oz ended the call and turned to

Jael with unease in his eyes. "Don't you dare. I am coming," Jael asserted, glaring at him.

Smiling, yet with grief in his gaze, he accepted her declaration quietly, "I would expect nothing less from you. Let's go."

Making their way to the transport, Oz called his mother.

"We are going off planet again We will have incredible news when we return," Oz anxiously hoped she could not detect the anxiety under his words.

Smiling as Rew chirped behind her, she was convincingly cheery, "OK. I love you. Please be careful."

"I will. I love you, too," Oz spoke boldly while the vines of dread squeezed his heart. This could be the last time he spoke to his mother.

When he hung up, he slipped his tablet under his arm, "When we finish all of this, we are going back to the treehouse. I think about it all the time."

"I can't wait," Jael's voice shook, alarm still coursing through her, but with a little flicker of hope, too.

Oz opened the inside door to the base to let Jael through. The large faux rock entrance they had created to hide the base in the beginning had been torn down and a thick metal blast door was built in its place. Jael did nothing but walk as they headed toward the stairs at the end of the lava tube. There were hidden cameras everywhere. After finding out what Iungo venom does, there would be no sudden moves from her in this tunnel. She knew the base security had the entire way rigged with venom laced projectiles.

A slight breeze blew through the tall trees, rustling leaves high above. The air was crisp, and the leaves on the ground crunched under her feet. She breathed deep and took in the fresh air. Someone has been planting pink, red, and violet flowers in the woods all around the base, and she admired them as she passed by. Despite the beauty all around, all she could comprehend was fear.

When they reached the transport, Jael dropped her clothes and began dressing in her armor. Jacob and Callum walked up, but she didn't seem to worry about her nudity as she pulled the suit out and began sticking her feet inside the legs. Oz knew Jael had previously been modest. The changes in her made him smile to himself. She was never meant to be the meek woman he found in the woods. She was meant to be the bold and powerful woman he had before him. He finished dressing and climbed in the pilot seat before sliding on his helmet.

Jael and Callum climbed in the back as Jacob sat up front. Amelia, Mercy, Zoe, Carter, and Aurelia all arrived dressed in their armor. Once everyone was seated and strapped in with their helmets on, Oz fired up the engine, and the transport climbed through the trees. There wasn't a cloud in the sky, and the auras shone brightly. Their colors blanketed the ground in shifting colors of green, purple, pink, and yellow, adding to the beauty of their home planet.

"As you know, we are going to the science space station orbiting Melior. The UTC is not offering us protection from the First Humans. We know they've had plenty of time to add anti-transport buoys around all the First Humans and UTC owned planets and stations by now. We will have to fly in, so I have the crew on board installing new tech for the magnetic charge shields that Pike designed and Carter perfected. Since the charges have rotating frequencies, we first had to match the frequency before we could flip it within a fraction of a second. The shields should repel any of the First Humans' missiles, but we didn't have time to test it. We should have some protection, but that doesn't mean much. I just want everyone aware of the danger we are heading into before we dock. If you want to return to the base, that will be your opportunity," Oz explained waiting for some type of response from someone. No one seemed surprised or phased by the news, so Oz focused on his flying. He had a great deal to worry about, but the people he loved having his back was not one of them.

When they docked and the airlock whooshed with the pressure changing, everyone rose from their seats and floated through the transport then planted their feet on the floor of the ship. The artificial gravity holding them down was just enough to be able to move quickly on the ground, but not quite as sturdy as a planet's gravity. They all found their places as Oz sat in the captain's seat, Jael next to him. Within a few moments, Carter was now a full holo-gram standing next to Oz on the bridge. He still wouldn't leave the engine room after the first mishap.

"Put us in the high upper atmosphere of the gas giant so we can take readings on where the First Humans' ships are before they detect us," Oz commanded, his eyes on the controls.

"Entering coordinates now. Ready to jump," Carter relayed.

"You heard him. Let's go," Oz's own voice seemed to come from somewhere far away as anxiety roiled in his gut.

When they materialized, they were hidden in a cloud in the atmosphere of the gas giant. "Where are they?" Oz asked, his muscle in his jaw tensing. A hologram of the region popped up in the space in front of them, and Oz peered over at Carter's hologram and admitted, "Nice."

He gave Oz a half smile and reported, "Looks like just two First Humans ships are docked. They have transport blocker buoys positioned where you see the blinking red dots. We have a few moments to reach an area close enough to the space dock where we know they can't fire on us. That area is now lit in violet. Our target is here on the dock, lit up in green."

Oz nodded and asked, "Where is our best transport point?"

"Looks like it's right here, where I've added a blue dot," the hologram of Carter explained as he seemed to be looking down at his computer which no one else could see.

As he lifted his eyes, Oz saw just how far the transport point was from the space dock and his heart sunk to his feet. He closed his eyes and took a deep breath trying to calm himself. *This was suicide.* "Fuck it. Everyone strap in. This is going to get rough. Looks like we are testing the new shields. I want everyone with helmets on and shields synced to our suits so if we are hit and the main shields fail, we may have a chance to be repelled away if a magnetic charge opens the hull. If we do lose the ship, we can signal for help and have the base jump in with our emergency transport," Oz commanded and everyone reached down for their helmets secured next to their seats and slid them on.

"Jacob, send Pike a message at the base informing him of the plan. Carter, take us in."

Within seconds they materialized at the edge of the no transport zone. Two FH command vessels were barreling toward them while prepping weapons, according to the ship's warning system. "Brace yourselves. The first missile is coming," Oz warned as he turned to the right and took them straight up for a moment before shooting them forward and back down, desperately trying to run from the guided missile.

He managed to avoid it for a few moments, but as it inevitably neared, everyone held onto their seat straps in preparation to either die, or hopefully, have the missile bounce off the hull. They had no idea what would happen. They all watched the holo-screen as the missile shot toward them then finally struck the hull, shaking the ship.

The impact was minimal, but Oz didn't take his eyes off his target for anything. He swung them down and to the left, then back around to the right and straight for the space dock.

Calculating their trajectory in his mind, Carter warned, "We're coming in too fast! We're going to hit!"

"We have to get closer or they'll blow us up! Reverse thrusters when I say!" Oz cried out to Carter through the comms just as the ship's warning system blared an alert of another set of guided missiles had locked on.

Terror exploded in Carter as Oz's plan fully materialized in his mind, and he couldn't help it as he screeched, "Fucking scorpion tits! What the venom are you thinking?!"

Oz slammed on the forward thrusters and sent them accelerating toward the dock, the people inside scrambling away from the gate.

Carter released a blood curdling scream as Oz demanded, "NOW!"

Throwing the ship into full reverse sent anything not attached flying toward the front of the ship. The ship groaned with the force, and Oz felt himself slipping out of consciousness. As the darkness overtook him, in his mind he prayed they would wake and find themselves parked at the space dock.

A knock sounded on his helmet, and the imperceptible hum in the back of his helmet from the CO_2 scrubbers nearly lulled him back into the darkness. The bright light shining in his eyes brought him back to consciousness. Squinting, he shook his head and leaned up, the bright light backing away, and his eyes opened and closed trying to adjust to the brightness of the room. He took a slow deep breath trying to regain his wits. His eyelids fluttered as he decided if his body was in one piece and his mind was still sound.

Slipping his helmet off, he searched the bridge and found everyone slumped over.

He leaned his face up to the chancellor and slurred as he spoke. "Did we make it? S-s-s everyone alive?"

"I should have you arrested for that stunt. You're lucky my daughter loves her nanny of your kind. You crushed the station's space dock, and it took the guards twenty minutes to break through. You've been registered in the galactic center as a new species, and your plaque has a signal unique to your people for identifying your vessels. Take your records and don't ever come back."

Something told Oz it was not the *child* who had their eyes on the Iungo nanny. The chancellor dropped a metal plaque at Oz's feet that simply stated, "Official seal of the United Trust and Colonies, the Iungo origin species is now formally recognized."

Without giving the unfalteringly sour man acknowledgment, Oz slipped back on his helmet just as Carter's hologram rose from the ground. "Carter, as soon as the Chancellor is off the ship and their emergency shields are back up, bring our shields back online. Hide our weapons signature. I'm blowing up the closest buoy from right here, and we are transporting out," Oz commanded, knowing that would seal the UTC's animosity toward them and possibly bring legal charges. *Fuck it, bring it on.*

Carter, still slightly dazed, shrugged before doing just that. As weapons went live, Oz locked onto the transport blocker and fired. The blast caused alarms to blare behind them. Through the space station window, he could see a stream of UTC soldiers running for their ship.

"Take us into orbit around Portum," Oz commanded as a smirk of victory grew on his face. However, the moment before the ship blinked out of existence, dread filled Oz. Terror wrapped its bony, icy fingers around his throat. Something was wrong, but it was too late. They were already in pre-jump. When the ship arrived in orbit above Portum, they were frozen in place. No one breathed a word. The door of hell had been opened above their planet, and through it had come an empire of death.

Through the view screen, they found themselves staring out at the majority of the FH space fleet with the Empress's ship at the head. The flagship stared them down as the last few of her fleet dropped out of a wormhole behind them. Bay doors along the hull of the ships began opening in tandem, and missile cannons emerged.

The empress had brought her war to Portum.

52

PLANET PORTUM

"Amelia, draft a distress message the Sarters. Send it directly to the Queen," Oz commanded quietly before he turned to Jael and slipped his helmet off.

The rest of them took their helmets off while their silent eyes searched for answers, a plan, *anything*. Hovering above the planet were over forty bulky, aging battleships besides the Empress's massive, sleek command ship. They only had the mid-level command ship they were in. The Iungo's second equipped command ship wasn't in orbit, since it was still in the maintenance bay having upgrades added.

The empress sent one single blaring auditory message to the Iungo ship, "Surrender and send your leader to the imperial command flag ship or face the destruction of your world. You have twenty minutes."

A warning message popped up on the bridge view screen, one that simply read, "transporting blocked." The blinking light on the diagram showed the signal came from the depths of the command ship. According to the image, the device was mid-level next to a central open corridor stretching from the top to the bottom of the ship. A glass dome capped either end of the corridor.

The type of stillness only found in moments of crisis when time stops for the mind, fell over the bridge. It was a quiet so deep, when everything in existence halts and all thoughts, wants, and needs cease. The bridge filled with something other than air, and it held them all in place.

No one moved their eyes from the message on the screen.

Pike's hologram materialized next to Carter's on the bridge as he started, "We have everything we've got locked on every ship, ready to jump. We just have to knock out their transport blocker."

Carter and Oz both faced one another, each silently urging to the other to break the news. Still unable to find their words, they both simultaneously turned to Pike. The fight written on Pike's face was erased in the matter of an instant. The hopeless despair painted on Carter and Oz's was unmistakable.

A few moments passed by before Carter was able to find the words to say. "Pike, I'm sorry. They have found a way to amplify the signal from inside the empress's ship," Carter softly explained.

A small red light blinked in the corner of Amelia's tablet sitting on her station, her hand shook as she placed her finger on the notification.

When it opened, she let out a soft gasp as she read the message aloud, "It's the Sarters. It says, stall them. Do anything you can. We are coming."

Oz turned his head around to face Amelia as the rest of

the room followed suit. He focused his eyes on her as a plan began to form in his mind. He had to buy them time.

He turned back to face Carter and commanded, "Prep a transport now."

Jael reached her hand over and put it on Oz's arm, but he didn't turn to her. He couldn't face her yet.

With his eyes now on Pike, he ordered, "Evacuate the village and send everyone inside the base. Warn the other towns and villages. I'm going to the Empress's ship with a magnetic missile. When they open the airlock, I am going to force my way inside the ship. If I can make it to the center of the ship with the missile, I can knock it out with the blast."

Turning back to Carter he instructed, "Take the engine off another missile and put it in a travel pack. Upload the guidance software into my helmet. Sync my armor with the shields resonance frequency program, and when the missile goes off, the blast will repel me, and I'll be able to transport out."

Carter and Pike both yelled in unison, "What?!" They knew what he was saying was not possible. He would never be able to transport out in time. The glass domes at the ends of the corridors were shielded. They also knew they could not argue with him. They didn't have the luxury of time.

"You heard me! Move! We don't have time!" Oz shouted at them.

Jael sat frozen behind Oz with tears in her eyes, not daring to say a word. There was nothing she could say to change Oz's mind, and she understood. With a deep breath, she turned quickly and took his helmet into her hands. When he finally turned and reached for his helmet, meeting Jael's eyes as he did, they didn't say a word, they just stared at one another in silence, both holding onto either side of the helmet. After a drawn out moment, Jael finally gave him a faint smile and let go of her side of the helmet, and Oz stayed frozen in place, still unable to move. Jael knew she had to say something, but all that came to her lips was a whispered, "Come back to me."

She knew his plan was suicide, but something deep inside told her to trust him, to have faith in his judgement, and in his risky plan. She knew more was at work than she understood, yet she could hear her heart pounding in her ears. *How can I continue without him?*

A heavy weight fell over the bridge as they all moved to carry out Oz's orders.

Amelia felt Mercy's hand slip into her own. They connected, and Mercy asked, "His plan doesn't sound possible. He's not coming back is he?"

"No," Amelia responded, severing the connection with Mercy before she could ask any more questions. There was nothing either of them could do or say. He made his choice.

Within a few minutes, Carter was standing with the small missile and pack in his outstretched hands facing Oz on the bridge.

No one had spoken much since Oz had barked out the order, and Carter found himself void of words as Oz took the pack and slipped it on. Jael reached out and put her arm on Oz's. He leaned over and kissed her sweetly, just once, and whispered, "I'll be right back, Spots."

LIAR! Her heart screamed in her mind, but she quietly slipped his helmet over his head, and he stepped into the airlock and into the transport. After he boarded and secured the door, he gently set the missile down in his lap and strapped himself in. Checking the time, he saw it had been almost nineteen minutes, and he had a little over one minute to make it to the empress's airlock. That was all he needed as he pulled away from the Iungo's command ship.

What he didn't tell anyone was that his command seat had access to more readings and biometric scans from the ship's sensors. He knew the device causing the transport block was deep inside the ship, sandwiched between two decks of soldiers. The transport engine from the missile was just for show. If he had told them he wasn't coming back, they would've never let him go.

The smell of her, the way her little spots were flush against her skin. The breeze bouncing her little curls. The cool air rushing against his skin as he chased her through the woods. One last time, he wanted to hear her squeal as her small legs moved as quickly as they could, feel the way her body melted into his when they fell to the ground, the way she tasted. His heart wrenched in his body, and he felt as if it may crack in half. He was going to save his people and the woman he loved, no matter the cost.

This was precisely what he had been afraid of all along. The moment he was elected president, he knew it was going to be his head on the end of the pike. Here, and now, he was heading toward the tip of the spear. With his hand on the missile in his lap, he just hoped he could protect it until he could move far enough inside the empress's ship.

As he approached the ship and the airlock began to open, he scrambled to unbuckle himself. In zero G, he prepared to face off with the guards who were surely waiting to pour in any moment. Pulling his plasma sword from his back, he braced his feet under the support of the back seat as the door opened.

A shocked FH guard only had enough time for recognition before Oz skewered him between the eyes. Simultaneously shutting off his sword and pulling the guard into the cabin of the transport, he used the added weight transfer to launch his own body into the hallway where his form felt the sensation of artificial gravity increasing as his sword handle found the awaiting faces several soldiers.

Just before gravity took hold, he pushed off and flipped his feet forward to slam them into their approaching soldiers, causing them to fall backward into a heap. Lifting his plasma sword, it buzzed back to life.

The dead guard he took down first floated in the zero g behind him as he found his footing and cut three of the remaining standing soldiers down. As the heap of soldiers began untangling themselves, he dashed down the hall.

Turning as he followed the map in his helmet, Oz sprinted down another hallway and found himself in a large room with several pathways suspended across an open area which, from the echo, seemed to reach all the way to the bottom of the ship. Hurtling down the path, he heard shouts behind him but didn't stop.

Rail gun shots landed all around him as he ran. When he reached the point where he knew he was close to the center of the ship, he leapt over the edge of one of the bridges and into the open space. The massive glass dome at the bottom shone brightly, causing him to squint.

As he fell, he counted, level one, two, three, four. He pressed the engagement code in the side of the missile and tossed it onto the fifth level as he shot by it on his way down. He could hear it attach, and that little click gave him great solace. A stream of gunfire went by him as he plummeted, but stopped when the angle neared the trajectory of the glass dome. He fell toward the transparent glass below him, through which glowed the planet he was trying to save. With the black hole in the distance and Planet Portum, as well as the red giant behind it in his view, he wished he could've taken a snapshot and saved it forever. It was beautiful. The delicate balance of the planets, forever spinning around a galactic monster.

One of the bullets struck his suit, he spun it and it slammed against the railing of the corridor.

When he peered over at his plasma sword, it flickered like he was falling faster than he anticipated. The gravity must be higher in the center, he thought as he smiled. The UTC soldiers and guards couldn't shoot worth a damn and wouldn't risk hitting the dome.

He knew it would be another few seconds before the bomb went off. His heart exploded with hope. He tapped his visor and took a sharp breath before studying the glass below him.

Another plan formed in his head as he neared the glass below. He flipped his body around and pointed his plasma sword down toward the dome. There was something not quite right about it. When he finally made contact, the tip of his plasma sword touched down on the glass before his feet did, and it slipped through. His knees landed on the glass, and he could already hear the hiss of the seal breaking. The glass was thinner than he expected, and as he cut through, he saw sparks of an electric current. The plasma sword was slicing right through their dome's shield, which clearly wasn't designed to withstand plasma level heat.

Checking the corner of the display inside his helmet, the detonator read five more seconds. He pulled his legs in and crouched before dragging the sword around him in a circle on the dome's surface. As Oz leaned forward, the pressure cracked the glass. He shut off his plasma sword and slammed it down onto the glass to break through. He shot through the hole he made in the dome and the immense pressure sent Oz hurdling away from the ship. As he spun through space, he laughed uncontrollably. With the tears of his belly laugh still floating away from his eyes, he frantically hoped he could make it far enough away before the ship exploded. As the timer hit two seconds, he saw a twinkle in the corner of his eye and shifted his focus to it. He watched a small pod shoot from the top of the ship and head toward the next ship.

The empress.

That had to have been her. She knew it was a trap and, like a weak coward, left her crew behind to die. The empress distracting him may have cost him his life as he checked the timer and it was already up. The blast was blinding as it lit up the darkness of space. Oz knew he had seconds to act before he would be crushed by debris, so he cried out into his helmet comms, "Lock me onto the command ship and jump!"

One... He could see a chunk of the hull barreling toward him. Two... It was so close he could see his tiny reflection in the polished metal hull. Three... Bracing for impact, Oz closed his eyes and curled his body. He felt warm, but the deadly crash hadn't happened.

He slowly opened his eyes and looked around. He was facing the window behind the view screen of his own ship, and Jael was standing on the bridge with a look of desperation he had never seen on her before.

In an instant, her face changed, her eyes went wide, and her hand slammed against the glass of the bridge's view screen window. She was frenzied as she pointed and shouted something. Oz locked his eyes on the emergency airlock as it opened on the side of the ship. A large battleship dropped out of a wormhole on the other side of the ship, followed by another, and another.

Oz recognized the ships right away. It was the Sarters, and they brought over twenty ships. Once they had all come to a stop and the wormhole had closed, Oz felt arms wrap around him, and he turned to find Zoe's scratched helmet at eye level as they were pulled toward the airlock of the ship.

The transmission came through the ship and Oz's comms. It was Queen Destry speaking, "President Green? I called a special session after you and your people left. We convinced the council to allow us to show up when you inevitably called. We are here until the end."

The moment his feet touched the airlock, Oz spoke as he ran toward his captain's seat with gravel in his throat, "I'm glad you could make it. I just took out the Empresses ship with the transport blocker though she has evacuated onto another FH Imperial ship. They will be opening fire at any moment. Carter is sending you the magnetic shield frequencies."

As Oz jumped into the seat, Carter was already sending the frequencies. Oz brought his eyes up just as the first magnetic missile was shot from one of the FH battleships.

Like a wave, the little satellite missiles around the planet disappeared and reappeared next to the FH ships. Explosions erupted all around as the battle broke out, and Oz's hands fumbled as he struggled to buckle himself into his seat. He wasn't even supposed to be alive right now. He hadn't thought this far ahead. Everyone was already strapped in as the first missiles rattled the ship, but shields held.

Two Sarter ships collided and burst into flames before abruptly extinguishing just as quickly as the oxygen was incinerated. Cringing, he swung his eyes back to the FH vessels as they broke formation and began attacking the Sarters.

After scanning the area, he finally located the ship where he saw the empress's transport head and locked weapons.

"Got you," Oz whispered as he fired four missiles at the locked target. Another ship passed in the way, and the missiles hit it instead. Oz swore, "Damn!" Behind him, Amelia and Mercy worked together as they hit ship after ship with magnetic charges.

As the conflict progressed, some of the FH battleships were destroyed or severely damaged and dead in the water. The Sarters were taking heavy damage from the magnetic charges, and their ships' computers couldn't keep up with the rotating frequencies. One by one, the ships were being hit and sustaining massive damage. Six were completely destroyed and only ten were still in the battle against the FH fleet, which was now at thirty.

They were losing by a landslide. It was about to be a massacre if something didn't give. So many had already been lost. Guilt pounded inside of Oz as his eyes found Jael. The death count would be too high. Just then, another of the Sarter ships imploded. Destry's words rang in his head, *We are here until the end.*

This had to stop. This was all over his surrender, and he could end this. She was going to destroy everything. It wasn't worth just him. He couldn't let anyone else die. Oz held his eyes on Jael, and with a broken heart, commanded, "This has to stop."

She didn't respond; she couldn't. She just watched as her worst nightmare came true. Oz commanded a cease fire through his captain's seat and sent a message that he was surrendering. No games this time. It was over.

The empress immediately requested an open line to the ship's bridge and he accepted, unbuckling himself from the seat and standing tall to face her. He flipped his visor up, and everyone in the room followed suit.

The empress materialized in front of them. She stood with a dark grey pant suit, tall heels, and a sash around her with something Jael couldn't read written on it.

"Your surrender is not enough. What else do you offer?" she demanded, her eyes stern.

Oz held her gaze knowing full and well he would not give up the people he loved.

"All of us," Amelia offered from behind him. "We would all give our lives to end this. If it means you leave our people alone, we accept."

The empress laughed like the maniacal dictator she was and crooned, "Oh, you naïve child. Do you really think you get to negotiate? Whatever made you think that? I asked, what can you offer? I didn't mean your lives. I meant your planet. You die, your beloved people here die, we take this planet back, and we will abandon Sclavus six as ordered, with stipulations of course. We demand mining rights on Sclavus Six as well as one generation of servitude from the living people on the planet. The next generation born will be free of the debt. I won't consider any other offer. The alternative is total annihilation. You have three minutes to make your choice."

The transmission ended, and Oz asked, "Is she gone?"

Amelia answered, "Yes, the comm connection is closed."

Oz paused and quietly asked, "What the fuck do we do now?"

Silence spread through the bridge and seeped into as their overwhelmed hearts as ideas spun in their minds trying to figure out what to do. Jael took her helmet off, then reached over and put her hand on Oz's forearm.

Oz pulled his helmet off and turned to her.

"I'm so sorry, for everything. We should've said no. We should've stayed back at the treehouse," Oz's voice cracked, and his resolve finally fell apart. Regret rushed in as he knew there was nothing he could do to save this woman he loved so dearly.

A serene smile spread on Jael's face as her eyes went to her missing hand. Her gaze slid around the room to her friends, and then back up to Oz before she admitted, "I don't regret anything. I would do it all again. A hundred times, I would do it over. It was worth every second. This was a life I am proud of. I finally became the person I dreamed of as a child, and I found love, real, all-consuming love."

He reached over and pulled her close to him. He shook his head as he solemnly contested, "This can't be it. There has to be a way."

He turned back to Carter as he insisted again, this time more loudly and pleading, "This can't be it. There has to be something we can do!"

Oz turned to Jael and whispered, "It wasn't supposed to end like this."

Oz ordered, "Amelia, send her a *yes*." After sending the message to the empress, Amelia leaned over and slid her hand into Mercy's. They all stayed silent, no one knowing what to do or say. All their options had been used up. Their missile stores were desperately low.

Oz frantically turned back to Jael with devastation

consuming him. "This can't be all of it. There has to be more." Checking the clock, they only had thirty seconds left.

Carter tapped his chest a few times and took his helmet off before saying, "I feel odd."

Checking the controls on his seat, Oz noticed a red warning light with a reading that said, "Singularity detected."

With his heart threatening to beat out of his chest, he lifted his aching eyes up to the viewscreen. He watched the timer end at zero and missiles launch from all the FH ships at once. Terror exploded inside of him as a massive bright light filled the bridge and everyone shielded their eyes, bracing for the impact of the missiles. Oz held Jael to him, pressing her head against his chest. The ship shook with the shockwaves from hundreds of missiles exploding at once. The gravity held them to the floor as the ship rolled backward. Grabbing onto the captain's seat in the chaos, Oz initiated the stabilizers to right them again. Once they were stable, he couldn't take his eyes from the viewscreen.

Blinding explosions rocked their view and Oz wildly searched the view screen around as he cried out, "What the fuck is going on?!" *How are they still alive? Why is the ship holding together? How is this possible?*

Jael grinned wider than she had ever before as she pointed to the screen and yelled, "There! Little ships!"

A grand fleet of small, impossibly fast fighter ships soared around the FH battleships and causing massive amounts of damage with their smaller sizes of magnetic charges, standard explosive missiles, and oversized rail guns. The fleet of ships rapidly overtook and shifted the entire course of the battle.

One of the unidentified ships headed toward them and Oz demanded, "What level are shields at?!"

Panic filled him as he realized he did not know whose destructive fleet this was. Will they attack his ship and people as well? In that moment, he felt impossibly small in the galaxy's vastness, vulnerable and at their most helpless.

"They want to open a comm connection," Amelia offered behind Oz.

Her voice shaking, Mercy reported, "Shields are at a third and dropping."

"Fuck. Open the comm," Oz instructed, apprehension making his chest tight. Every breath was a battle.

A ruddy haired humanoid's holo-form materialized on the bridge in front of them and a familiar deep voice joked, "You owe me so fucking hard for this one."

"What the fuck are you doing here?!" Oz cried out in a delighted panic, his hands splayed and his arms wide.

Smiling and laughing, August checked behind him at the raging battle before he admitted, "I have so much to tell you. I'm docking. Prep your airlock."

With his mouth hanging open, Oz watched August's form disappear, and his eyes shifted back to the battle outside. The FH already had a wormhole open and were in full retreat. His only question was, had the empress escaped?

The sounds of elated cheers from Jael and the rest of the crew drowned out his thoughts before August slammed into Oz's seat from behind. August reached over him and popped the buckle on Oz's seat to haul him over the back of the seat. They both hit the ground and August cried out in pure joy as he wrapped his arms around Oz and held him in a crushing embrace.

The sound of a communication trying to come through rang on Oz's seat so Jael leaned over and pressed the button.

Livia's hologram materialized on the bridge, and everyone became quiet before she asked, "August?"

He popped his head up behind the seat, and Oz followed, causing her to break her regal stoicism and grin. Mercy shifted her gaze between the two and smiled as Amelia peered over at her.

Amelia wondered how this reunion would end up. Reunions were something her people were not accustomed to.

Livia disappeared as August and Oz stood up. "How did you know?" Oz asked as he was trying to catch his breath. One of his hands, still gripping the back of the captain's seat.

Shaking his head, August shifted his feet as he admitted, "We didn't. Livia was just holding up her end of our bargain."

The airlock sounded, and Livia strolled down the hallway and onto the bridge. Her presence dripped of royalty, filling the room with her power and grace.

Mercy gasped with a smile, and her eyes went wide as Livia approached August and stood intimately close to him. Amelia felt a sliver of relief at Mercy's reaction and held her hand tighter as they stood and watched. Mercy internally giggled at Amelia's hand squeeze and wondered if she had forgotten their own people's customs. Mercy would be lying if she said she didn't miss August, but what she and Amelia had now, she would never give up. Amelia gave her the kind of unconditional love she knew she deserved.

Livia turned to Oz and announced, "I am King Livia Claudius of Aduro. August was instrumental when I usurped my father and in exchange, I was to assist with your rebellion. What is the current status?"

Clearing his throat, Oz shifted awkwardly then explained, "Well, you just swooped in and won the battle for us. We had just arrived back from the UTC Science and Technology space station with our official origin species seal, but the Empress was already here. She was one step ahead, and we didn't see it coming. We are now officially the Iungo people. We own our planet and Sclavus Six, which needs a new name as soon as possible."

Livia began to speak, but August cut in and asked, "Wait, what? You did *what* already? How?"

Smiling Oz pointed to Jacob and praised him, "It was him again. He is now two for two on saving all of us. He found a recent ancestor of ours rotting next to the northern sea. We were just up the beach from the creature when we crossed the sand on our way toward the mountains."

August turned and saw Jacob sitting there unbuckling himself and jumped onto him. Jacob yelped as August landed in his lap with his arms out, ready to wrap around him. Crushing him with a hug, August yelled, "I missed all of you so much!"

So happy she was overwhelmed, Mercy's joyous laugh could be heard over everyone else's and August froze. He slowly turned and saw Mercy across the room, arm in arm with Amelia.

Her bright smile brought more emotion spinning inside than he was prepared for- love, regret, repentance. He slowly approached, and the room went silent as he faced her.

"It's good to see you," August choked out as tears welled up in his eyes. Mercy threw her arms around him as she let out a sob.

August's eyes met Amelia's before he pulled back, and spoke with gravel in his throat, "Mercy, I'm so sorry."

"We can talk later. We're okay." Mercy replied, letting August go.

While August and Mercy were talking, Livia updated Oz on the current situation. "This is not over. Amelia, call Destry's ship and get her on the comms." Oz commanded sharply.

Destry's hologram appeared, and relief shone in her eyes as she reported, "We were able to save a vast number of our people from the destroyed ships. Your shield rotation worked better than we could've ever imagined. It bought our people valuable time for the emergency exits and into the escape pods. Is the battle going to continue, or are we discussing a new tactic?"

Oz deviously grinned, "We are going to Genus. It was called Janus before they changed the history books to hide it right under everyone's noses. We need to find out what the First Humans don't want anyone to know. They buried their origin planet for a reason, and we need to find out why."

53

PLANET PORTUM

"We've never jumped anywhere close to this far. If anyone wants to head to the surface, now is your last chance," Oz announced as he faced everyone on the small bridge.

No one moved.

"We will stay here with both fleets in case the empress returns," Destry reassured him.

Turning to face Destry, Livia agreed, "I will inform my ships. They are virtually all Iungo."

Oz's eyes widened and turned to face August as he admitted, "You're right. We have a lot to catch up on."

August nodded, "After we find some dirt on those slimy fucks. Let's go."

Tucking a bit of loose hair behind his ear, Oz sat down in the captain's seat and the ship floor moved. The metallic floor shifted and molded itself, creating several seats with harnesses to accommodate everyone on the bridge. Heading down the center walkway, Destry found her way back to her transport, and the airlock sealed just as they all finished finding their seats.

"Mercy, enter the coordinates and pull up the jump trajectory on the bridge's main holoscreen," Oz ordered as he checked the power reserves and began locking down the ship's systems to prepare for the expansive jump.

Within a few moments, the ship's location was in red and the location of Janus was blinking on the holo-screen in green. There was a yellow arrow protruding from their location, showing the direction of the jump.

With her mouth in a snarl, Livia addressed the room, "That's over half of the galaxy away and in one of the oldest sections. The First Human's claimed that Genus's star started to burn out millions of years ago, but it's showing a small yellow star still active in that system. Even at this distance, I estimate right now the star should be just beginning its growth into its red giant phase. Where the planet is in the system, they would still have millions of years of viable sunlight. The history we were taught and what is before me is not adding up." Livia paused before asking the computer, "Highlight the location of planet 08342, and our former Genil home world, Monex." The three planets blinked on the holo-display, with Janus positioned in the center. Livia smirked, "Planet 08342 is Earth. The Genil home world and Earth both are less than 60 light years from Janus."

"Are you not part of the First Humans?" Zoe asked, softly as not to offend. *Just in case,* she thought as she admired Livia's regal posture. She was one woman Zoe would not piss off if she could help it.

Livia turned to her and replied, "Their genetics were added to mine because I was engineered by them, but my kingdom was originally from the second human origin planet, or rather, we found them after they resettled in a system close to ours."

"What happened to those worlds?" Mercy asked, distressed as she thought of all the worlds the FH had conquered.

"The humans depleted their natural resources until there was nothing left. The planets were mass evacuated and picked clean by scavenger teams. They left mining bots to strip the core of its valuable minerals and all metallic elements. They eventually moved on leaving a rocky shell of a planet to collapse in on itself or remain hollowed out," Livia explained, her own words filling her with disgust.

The room fell silent for a few, long seconds before Carter announced, "We are ready to jump."

"Alright, let's go." Oz's knuckles ached from the grip he held on to the seat straps. Releasing his iron grip, he flexed his hands a few times before he reached down to his controls and pressed JUMP.

A stunning flash of light filled the bridge, entering inside of their bodies, engulfing every atomic particle aboard the ship with its luminosity. The ethereal sensation of flowing along a heated wave finally passed and the walls and floor seemed to warp before their eyes with the mirages of residual heat. The ship's air circulation ramped up, swirling cool air through the bridge.

Still dazed, Oz wiped the sweat from his brow with his hand and turned to Amelia, "Report?"

"No health issues on the scans. The transporting seems to be benign. The readings show we even passed through the edge of a gas giant and directly through the center of a massive ice planet. I'll send the data to Pike when we return," she explained as she studied the holo-screen readings. Mercy peered over her shoulder and seemed pleasantly surprised at the anatomical scan results.

"Carter, please interpret the molecular scan results for us," Oz asked as he unfastened his seat harness.

"Other than the hull and interior of the ship reaching a temperature of three hundred twenty-five degrees kelvin, everything is as it was down to the exact atomic particles. We used next to no relative energy. We could jump for another ten years with the fuel we have now if life support didn't use it in an Earth year. They must be filling their ships with condensed radioactive ore every few months for their worm-hole generators to have enough power," Carter reported.

"Consume, pollute, and ditch it when you're finished. What a profoundly vile philosophy to embody. They'll decimate the galaxy if we don't stop them," Amelia ranted with a look of revulsion on her face.

At the controls, Oz opened the view screen, "Let's see what's outside." The view screen lightened and became clear as the bridge dimmed. Before them was a large tangerine star and a primarily bleak brown planet with a few green patches in mountainous regions at the highest elevations. The clouds seemed to be an ocher hue and any bodies of water were murky grey or solid black. The bones of ancient cities were visible from their altitude. Their derelict skyscrapers looming shadows over the land were ghostly reminders of what once was. Not one satellite was in orbit, nor were any hint of metallic debris.

"Scan the ground for life," Oz ordered as he searched the view screen. Amelia performed the scans and reported, "Only minimal plant life and some flying insects, nothing harmful. The air is high in carbon dioxide and several other toxic chemicals, so we need to wear our helmets."

"Any sea life?" Oz asked as he slid his eyes to Jael, waiting for Amelia to respond. She faintly smiled as she met his eyes.

The moment stretched on, and Oz unable to take his eyes from his spotted alien. He never wanted to miss an opportunity to make a memory of her he could always revisit. He was compelled to savor every moment with her like it was the most divine treasure in the universe. He could hear someone begin to speak, and he forced himself to turn and pay attention.

"The only water bound life on the whole planet are some patches of algae and a very prolific water beetle. Their ice caps melted long ago and several smaller coastline cities appear half submerged," Amelia answered as she focused on the data before her.

"Find the capital or what looks to be the largest city," Oz directed, stealing another glance at his love before refocusing on the view screen.

A few moments passed, and the planet appeared as a holo-gram on the bridge with a blinking light in two places.

"Let's send a probe down to each city to look around before we land," Mercy suggested.

Raising her eyebrows, Zoe agreed, "Good idea. I'm deploying the probes now."

The screen split into two, displaying both probe's journeys jumping down to the planet and into each of the cities. They searched for several minutes finding one of the great cities was in deep decay, but the other seemed to still have sealed buildings.

Noticing a few buildings looked promising, Oz ordered, "Take us down and land just north of the city to the east."

"I'm deploying landing gear and jumping now," Carter replied.

The ship landed on the ground without so much as a vibration. They all slid their helmets on and headed for the airlock at the end of the hallway. One by one they passed through and headed down the stairs emerging from the airlock.

Once they were all on the ground, Oz turned around, "I spotted what looks to be a few sealed buildings about half a mile north. They look promising."

"Are you speaking of the building with the columns?" Livia asked as she took the last few steps.

"Yes, why?" Oz asked.

"It is a typical building design the First Humans used for their courts and councils. It will be a logical place to start our search."

"Then it's settled. Let's head out," August agreed as he began heading south toward the center of the city.

Mercy was glad her visor was dark because her face would surely be giving away her thoughts of the change in August. It made her happier than she could put into words to see him shining with such certainty.

As they made their way through the ancient city, the style of architecture was filled with arches, columned entry-ways, and worn etched art in the walls of many of the build-ings. Much of the art depicted the purpose of the building or a scenic view, but some of it seemed to show the spirit of conquest. Others seemed to describe a great battle which was won, a freedom of some kind earned through bloodshed. The eerily familiar buildings had Jael questioning the ancient history of Earth. Latin? The Roman architecture? It was all too similar to be coincidence, but how could it be?

When they finally reached the colossal building, August stopped abruptly and spun around. Approaching Oz, he leaned in and muttered, "I had a disturbing dream about this place."

"Wait, did you just say you had a dream?" Oz asked, confusion filling his tone.

Still confused himself, he peered around at the group and explained the best he could, "I don't know, I can't remember. Something happened right before I was taken, and now, I sleep at night like a baby."

"I turned on your sleeping gene so you would stay out. You inhaled a toxic pollen with a hallucinogen in it when you were with Mercy in the woods," Amelia had intended to say, *on a date in the woods* but changed her mind at the last moment. The last thing she needed right now was to bring up their relationship, even if Mercy was taking it well.

Finally understanding, August explained, "I dream often, but I had a nightmare about this place. There were fluid filled tanks enclosing human babies in a back room. There was a baby I tried to save. It desiccated in front of my eyes and died screaming. It disturbed me for days."

Feeling dread snake inside his gut, Oz cringed as he offered, "Let's get this over with. I didn't really want to go inside at all, and now I feel like we're making a mistake. Are we walking into a trap?"

"No, we have to find out what the First Humans are hiding. The empress will nurse her battle wounds in one of her infamous orgies, but it won't last long. Once she's all sexed out, she will thirst for blood once again. We need to hurry before she tracks our transport signatures," Livia explained as she pushed by everyone.

As she walked closer to the door, everyone followed, one by one, they halted near the door. Oz had a disturbed feeling deep inside. He nearly turned back after she opened the door and went inside first. Jael waited for Oz to proceed, unsure of what he and the others were feeling. She was not thrilled about going in, but didn't see it as the worst thing they'd done.

Amelia, threw her hands up and asked, "Who else feels like walking through that door into the dark abandoned building that will lead to eminent death?"

"We watched Livia walk-through, so we know we can do it without dying." Mercy stepped forward and stood next to Amelia but didn't move any further.

With his hand pressing in on the profound sense of malaise in his gut, Oz leaned forward and took a step across the threshold. As he stepped inside, the feeling of impending doom evaporated into nothing.

He turned on his heels as he reassured the group, "The rotten sensation ends when you walk inside."

In a burst, August groaned before he ran through the door trying to get it over with as quickly as possible. Everyone else followed suit quickly making their way through. On the opposite side of the door, Amelia seemed perplexed at what could cause such a thing as Mercy ended up next to her doubled over trying to catch her breath. Mercy grabbed her belly and admitted, "That was the worst I've ever felt."

"It must be a way to keep out anything non-human," August explained as he watched Livia glide through the center of the giant building. As his eyes surveyed the room, a new kind of discomfort filled his gut. One that echoed inside, *you're in grave danger here.*

Jael stood next to Oz, too interested in the buildings familiar architecture to pay attention to what was happening. She felt as though she had been transported through space and time to be back on Earth when the Roman Empire ruled. A chill flowed down her spine like an icy river. The ominous statue in the center of the great room seemed to emit a darkness, creating a thick cloud of uncertainty and dread fell over the room.

The room was filled with giant columns and the remnants of massive ruddy curtains lying in piles on the ground. The curtains remaining on the wall draped over tall stick like protrusions, and Jael wondered what was underneath, not quite curious enough to look though. They seemed haphazardly covered, as if it was all done in a rush. An odd computer structure stood to one side of the room near a massive statue.

Livia stood, scrolling through options on the screen, in front of the massive statue of a human with robes draped over one side of their body. They had long curled hair with a crown of laurel leaves around their head. Something about the statue seemed odd, as if it had been altered or changed somehow. The bottom half of it seemed to have an older finish to the stone. The top was a slightly lighter color stone and subtly different texture. The artist who constructed this piece initially had been a much more talented sculptor.

"Can anybody else tell that statue had been altered at some point? The top was clearly created by a different artist than the rest," Jael asked, her eyes locked on the statues cold and hollow face.

Feeling normal again, Oz approached Livia who was still poking away at the odd computer, and asked, "Are you finding anything worthwhile?"

Everyone gathered around her, and she replied, "The erasure of a previous people's culture and society is likely. Humans are notorious for it. That might mean this is not the actual human origin planet, but we shall find out soon." Jael was not at all surprised by that answer.

Leaning close to Livia in order to see what she was doing on the screen, Oz watched her entering line of code after code. Softly, Oz offered, "My sisters code, we should try it-- 299 792 458." She did not respond, but he watched as she entered the code he had given her. The screen went blank, and he heard a slight gasp from Amelia watching on the other side of Livia.

The eerily modern computer dinged as it allowed Livia to access the files.

Even with Mazarin being brought up, August couldn't keep his eyes off the door in the back. She flitted through his mind like the butterfly she was named after, unable to take his attention away from the memory of the night terror.

"This computer is filled with information. Give me just a few minutes, and I can find what we need," Livia reported as she unclipped a device from her forearm and slid it up and down the computer screen until a green light shone from the device. Within a few moments, the pinpoint light turned red, and she slid it off the screen and back in its place on her forearm. Whistling, she admitted, "That didn't take long."

Oz asked, "What did you find?"

Livia pointed to the screen, "I just downloaded all of the encrypted data with the code you gave me. The drive I used automatically discovers hidden files and reveals them in order of the depth in which they are hidden within the system. It is a spy drive designed to reveal people's dirtiest secrets first."

Livia stood back, and they all watched as the video played and an asteroid struck the planet. It was the same video he had seen back on Portum at the old UTC command center. Amelia had found it when she was searching for the files. After the clip they had already seen, they watched as the video sped up. It flew through what seemed to be a time lapse of millions of years and when it was finished, the video zoomed in to show human cities. It looked like it was a presentation video simulation made to show how something works.

"What the fuck?" Oz whispered.

"Keep watching. This is our evidence. We must bear witness," Livia demanded, as dread filled her. She had an idea what the video was going to show next. The screen flipped imperceptibly, and her heart broke. It was recorded footage from a probe.

This time it showed a missile heading for a populated planet, and Amelia gasped and quietly asked, "No. This can't be right. How could they?"

The missile on the video seemed to stop mid-air over an area of open sky with what appeared to be giant butterflies flying underneath. The video zoomed in to show they were actually higher level beings seemingly evolved from butterflies. Their beautiful wings flapped, sending them soaring through the sky. Some hovered and spoke to one another as others seemed to hover in an embrace. Their clothing was ornate and flowed with the circulating wind from their giant, colorful wings. All of them were enjoying their day, unaware of the doom device that just found their way into the atmosphere of their planet.

A gas seemed to spill from the inside of the missile as the video reverted to its previous angle. Once the tank was emptied, the missile lifted above the atmosphere, and the video increased in speed once again.

Jael, in disgust whispered, "They left the probe in orbit just to document this species' annihilation?"

What seemed to be hundreds of thousands of years passed, and the video feed glided down into the atmosphere to check on the progress of what had been done. As it flew over the cities, Jael had to turn and walk away. Slowly, each one of them turned away, too heartbroken to keep watching.

The cities were filled with *humans*.

Livia kept her eyes on the screen until the end and read off what the scrolling credits explained.

"We are the First Humans. This memorial is for any human who stumbles upon our once great origin world so you can appreciate the efforts of your ancestors. After we conquered and took our planet, we knew there were still more threats to the human species out there. We knew we had to create a safe place for our future generations so that humans may flourish in the galaxy. That is when we created the Life Virus. It reprograms developing worlds to exclusively evolve the human species and rid them of destructive, invasive lower creatures. Soon, the human species will be safe by becoming the dominate higher being in the galaxy. May the First Humans live on into eternity."

54

PLANET JANUS

The silence in the room fell over them like a frozen wave, chilling them all to the bone.

Swallowing her fury, Livia dredged up her regal prowess as she stared at the obvious boundary line between the two artists who constructed the statue before her and asked, "What punishment could ever fit this crime of evolutionary annihilation? What other extinction crimes did these First Humans commit? And from whom did they conquer their world?"

Oz faced Livia and asked, "Where could we find evidence of that?"

Heading toward the back, August huffed, "I'm tired of waiting. I'm going to search the back. There was some type of lab back there in my dream. I have to know."

The group followed and when August swung the door open, he could hear several gasps through the comms. There was a room full of large round metal stands with tall glass chambers on top of them. August walked over to the first one and looked down into it. It was nothing but dust and some tubes, otherwise it was almost identical to his dream. As he turned, he peered down at the display. It was cracked and didn't work.

With large strides, Amelia stalked to the other end of the room heading toward a curious computer in the corner. The screen lit up in seconds after she placed a magnetic charger against the base attached to the panel below the screen. As she scrolled, she turned saying, "The code for the previous computer works here too. Come and look at this. I've found the Life Virus file. The Latin written translation software in the helmet works perfectly." As everyone gathered around, Amelia scrolled through the information, "This virus was reprogramed from another one." Livia approached, parting the group as she walked through and removed the spy drive from her forearm to collect the data from the computer as she had done with the previous one. She reached around Amelia and connected the spy drive. With her brow furrowed in concentration, Amelia clicked on the Life Virus file and it opened. Amelia finished reading the information then turned to find Oz behind her with Jael next to him. The original virus had been made to force chimpanzees to evolve into humans in only a few hundred thousand years.

With a lump in her throat, she turned back to the screen and announced, "Humans were not an original species at all. They had been created." Amelia further explained, "Humans were created, they're not a naturally occurring higher being. I guess this explains something I've been meaning to discuss with you and Oz."

"It's your immune system. It's flawed, and it routinely attacks healthy tissues. Aurelia has the same problem, and I haven't found one of our people who has the same thing occurring. Humans sleep so much more than many other species. Their lifespan is short compared to all other higher beings. The amounts of cancer, and even reproductive problems, are disproportionate as well. Human genetics are fragile and faulty at best."

Livia nodded as she offered, "That's why the UTC has such a large genetic engineering department. I only sleep a few hours a night, and I don't have the immune system problems. Those were all deleted out and replaced with other being's DNA. I will live to be the higher being standard one hundred and fifty. Most humans are dead, on average, by fifty to sixty years old. They have DNA editing procedures on Melior I can purchase for Jael and Aurelia. When this is over, I will speak to my physicians. My personal physicians can work on the genetic implantation, and I can have the treatment sent directly to you. Any quick ideas on how to find the original species on the planet who made the First Humans?"

After a few moments of silence Mercy asked, "Why don't we go look at the other city? It looked like it had been abandoned, too."

"The First Humans reprogrammed the virus which created them to kill off the original species on the planet first while forcing the mammals on the planet to evolve into chimpanzees that eventually became humans. They deployed it on planets all over the galaxy. This explains why there are so many human origin planets. If we can find proof of a true origin species who created the humans, on top of this virus file, we can end this. We *need* to find biological proof." Amelia explained, her eyes filled with hope.

Holding his shoulders in tight as he peered around the room, August asked, "So, let's go back to the ship?"

"Yeah, this place gives me the creeps," Oz agreed as he made his way toward the door.

Not risking anything, they all sprinted through the front door of the building. A quiet, eerie walk back to the ship through the decaying city followed.

When they reached the ship, Livia quickly uploaded the file to the computer before Amelia took over the station. Once Amelia was back at her position, she began scanning the planet for large natural mammalian protein deposits. A few places highlighted on the screen, and she noticed one outside of the city they had not yet explored. She sent coordinates, and the ship transported to a field close to the readings.

From the captain's seat, Oz commanded, "Scan the ground. This is a suspiciously large and flat area compared to the terrain around."

Nodding, Amelia did just that and within a few moments, she gasped, "Oz, this is a mass grave."

Sinking his head, he asked, "Are they close enough to exhume?"

"No. They're under a million years of thick sediment, but I can run a thorough scan of the genetic material, enough the computer can create the life form from it," Amelia explained as she pecked away at the computer.

"I want to see these beings. Maybe the computer can decipher what they developed from," Oz suggested.

A moment later Amelia said, "Got it."

The hologram of the creature materialized in front of them. They were short and round, with little round ears. They had short brown hair on their arms and legs and wide noses that weren't much more than a small mound with slits. Two buck teeth came from their mouths and they had small, beady, black eyes. They seemed to be kind and gentle-looking creatures, thoroughly defenseless, as if they had evolved from teddy bears.

"The computer says they developed from a large species of rodent widely considered a mild and helpful creature. It also says they had exceptionally large brains with elevated levels of emotion. Their limbic system makes up over half of their brain matter. Their diets were strictly vegetarian. I think they are similar to what is called capybaras on Jael's world," Amelia explained.

"Upload the scans and save all the information on the file to give to the UTC. I think we're finished here," Oz directed as he reviewed the readings on his controls.

Carter replied, "I'll jump to Melior."

Feeling a strong need to move on, Oz commanded, "Let's head out. Everyone strap in. It's going to get messy." As the ship prepared its jump, a stone formed in Oz's gut as a cloud of distress fell over him.

55

PLANET JANUS

Overwhelmed with fear, Oz reached down and activated the shields as static spread across on the screen, caused by a wormhole opening. He knew they had company even before the massive ship visualized on their scans.

"Carter, take us out of here now!" Oz demanded, as the crew struggled to absorb this newest disaster.

The Empress's new ship revealed itself as the static on the screen dissolved.

With a high-pitched wheeze from Carter, "On it!" he moved his hands over the controls faster than he had ever moved. A stream of magnetic missiles emerged from the First Humans command ship as the ship prepared to jump.

"Anytime now!" Oz cried out, watching the missiles close in, "Fuck! Hold on!" Taking the helm from navigation, Oz careened high left and back to the right. Dipping low and pushing the thrusters to maximum output, it wasn't enough. The ship shook with a hit to the hull, but fortunately the rotating shields did their job, though just barely.

"They've found a way to make their missiles detect the shield resonance frequency. We don't have long before it learns the pattern, and one of those magnetic missiles smashes the ship into the size of a transport! Carter!" Oz screamed as he took the ship in an arc, only to be struck again.

The ship shuddered violently as the shields fought the frequency multiplying the magnetism. The metal groaned as the missile lifted its powerful pull and lost power.

"We're stuck. They have a transport blocker. We are opening a wormhole now. Everyone needs to hold on. If those charges follow us in, we might end up in the wrong place and time!" Carter shouted out in warning. They all slipped on their helmets as quickly as possible as the ship was struck again. The projectile carbon-starter ejected into the open space, and the ship sent a concentrated beam of EM ultra-gamma radiation directly into the collapsing singularity. A warning of exceeding heat limits chimed just before the high Kelvin heat shield blanketed the ship. Carter finished entering the coordinates, and the ship turned to face the wormhole.

A churning, steaming-edged void opened as if they just burned a hole through space-time.

Frantically searching his captain's seat controls, Oz could find none of the missiles. There was something much bigger behind them. Instead of the magnetic charges following them, it was the Empress's ship.

Through the helmet comms, Oz cussed, "Damnit! She followed us in! Where the fuck did the charges go? Carter, can we jump from the wormhole?"

"Fuck no! It would take me an entire day of creating new math to even begin to answer the question of jumping from the wormhole! What do you mean where are the missiles? She probably recalled them back to her ships so she could shoot them at us again!" Carter shouted.

"Well, what the venom do we do?"

"How the fuck should I know? I just started flying through space a week ago!" Carter screamed.

The Empress ship hit them with a different kind of missile, shaking the ship and everyone inside. A warning came on the screen, shield disrupter attached.

"Shields are dropping fast. We need to send a charge through the hull and knock that thing off!" Mercy yelled. Not waiting for the order, she sent a bolt of electricity through a sensor circuit behind the hull at the point of contact. The sensor circuit exploded sending a bolt of electricity into the device. When it popped off the ship, the warning disappeared.

"Are you sure we can't shoot a magnetic charge at them?" Oz asked.

"Do you want to die a thousand years ago or what?!" Carter snapped, "I'm trying to re-route the wormhole, but every correction I make, she follows! She has to be tracking us somehow. I'm going to send a reverse polarization wave across the hull to see if I can detach anything else." Carter explained, hoping the transport blocker didn't work in the wormhole. They couldn't send a polarization wave of any kind without the transport technology.

As the ship shook violently, Oz added, "Look, I know you're working fast, but we need faster. We don't want to die, Carter."

The view screen showed the hull illuminate from underneath as the hidden tracking device detonated and vaporized.

"Got ya!" Carter yelped as he entered in the coordinates they used to place them in the atmosphere of the gas giant which Melior circles. When the wormhole spit them out in the dense gaseous clouds, the debris from their mid-journey battle dumped as well. The debris began its decent into the gas giant as the stabilizing thrusters kicked in, and the ship settled. The alarms blared when the empress was detected just on the other side of the planet, nearing the UTC science and technology space station.

"Someone send out a probe. We need more than just her location," Oz ordered.

Amelia sent the probe and a few minutes passed as it made its way across the planet. When it arrived in position, the view-screen synced to show the other side of the planet. Oz watched her ship as it pulled into a defensive position in front of the science and technology space station. She knew they found something on Janus, something damning.

"She's preparing to defend her lies. How typical of her! Can you transport me to your planet?" Livia asked.

Oz shook his head and explained, "They have transport blockers everywhere. I know where you're headed with that, but we are limited to wormholes which we can't do again without being detected. You going alone may start a galactic center civil war if one hasn't already begun after your coup." After the push of a button on his controls, they all lit up in red on the holo-screen rotating at the front of the bridge indicating where all the enemy ships were located.

A devious smile fell over Mercy's face as she studied the formation of the enemy ships. "They think we want to go to the Science and Technology space station, right? But, we don't really *need* to go there. What if we went straight to the UTC Council meeting on Melior instead?" Mercy pulled up the route she had quickly planned and put it on the holo-screen.

With an agreeable grin, Zoe acknowledged, "This can work. We would need to set off bright charges with our ship's signature to distract them."

"On it." Carters hologram flickered as he went work below deck.

Unflinching, Livia regally ordered, "I will lead you into the chamber. The Claudius seats are weighted."

Oz freed a shaking breath as he turned to Mercy and agreed, "OK. It's settled. We're crash landing on Melior in the UTC Council Chamber gardens. Why does this near-impossible plan sound like something I would come up with?"

Mercy laughed, "It's worth it. Plus, how else are we going to do it?"

He shook his head before turning to Jael. She just reached her arm over, and Oz wrapped his hand around her forearm. They didn't say anything. They didn't need to.

"I have the magnetic missiles reprogrammed to become visible light charges. They will glow bright enough to knock out all their view screens. It's considered night on Melior where we are landing, but I'm showing Council is in a late session, almost every seat is filled," Carter reported with a growing grin.

"A special session was called over the laws regarding genetic ownership. This is the perfect time to interrupt mid-session with some relevant evidence about their own empress and the First Humans. They will finally be unseated as the power in the galactic center," Livia sneered as she slid her eyes to August. A growing smirk on her face stated exactly how much joy she was finding in this.

As they all faced forward to the view screen and the gathering First Human vessels around the space station, a collective calm fell over the bridge. They were staring at the path to their end, or the beginning of the collapse of the First Humans' domination, maybe both.

"Take us in, Mr. President," Livia commanded as she turned to Oz.

Nodding once, Oz took the ship's controls and re-routed power to their small maneuverability thrusters as well as to shields. When he was finished, he slowly pulled them out of the atmosphere of the gas giant. Taking off, he noticed Carter rotating their signal as a space rock so the ships couldn't detect them by sensors.

Checking back up to the view screen, he waited until he was in the right position and punched it. The ships around the space station powered up their weapons. The station was just on the edge of the planet's horizon, and their landing destination was almost directly underneath. Night had just fallen, but the moon was lit by the sprawling rings of orbiting cities high above the surface.

The ship barreled toward the space station while Mercy and Zoe shot the electric light charges toward the enemy ships. Too small to detect, the enemy ships were unable to lock on and shoot them. The charges flashed their lights randomly at half power; meanwhile, the empire's ship's tracking signal bounced between the charges. In the chaos, the Iungo ship slipped through the center.

Right before Oz took the nosedive down to the planet surface, he yelled, "Now!"

All the charges blasted flashes of light at once, blinding the area and illuminating the ground like daylight. They held their luminosity just long enough for Oz to dive down and break the atmosphere's surface before the FH battleships could react. The ship was entering the upper atmosphere and lighting up the sky once again.

After a few last laser hits to the hull caused some vibrations, Amelia reported, "Minimal damage and laser shots have ended. They won't risk the council chamber building. Take it down with a little more finesse than we planned. No reason to slam us into the ground."

The empress's ship followed them down to the planet surface, and as they landed softly, the empress's ship was also dropping its landing gear.

Zoe, Mercy, and Amelia stayed and defended the ship as Livia, Oz, Jael, August, Jacob, and Callum ran for the council chamber building. Amelia stood at the base of the ship's stairs and held up a large rail gun braced against her shoulder, aimed right at the empress's ship. Behind her, Mercy and Zoe both stood with hand railguns of their own.

The massive bay doors opened, and the empress emerged with a large number of guards surrounding her. The guards glared at the three Iungo as they passed by their ship, but the empress didn't so much as glance their way. The fury on her face burned into Amelia's mind forever; it was the look of defeat hidden under a burning fury. Something occurred to her as the Empress passed by - she looked strikingly similar to the icy receptionist who worked at the same college as Jael. *Could that receptionist have been one of the engineered children like me? Had the empress put her own DNA into that project?* Those were questions for another day. Only taking her eyes from the Empress's group for a moment, Amelia checked to see if her friends made it inside yet. Just as Livia reached the doors, they slammed shut.

With the ferocity of a hurricane, Livia empowered her voice and commanded, "I am King of Aduro. You will open these doors *now,* or you risk your death." With her multi-frequency detecting eyes, she saw the waves of the scanners register the royal seal codes synced to the implant in her skull. Within a heartbeat, the doors were opening, and two stunned UTC guards on the other side stared back in disbelief.

Livia reared back and knocked one of them out with her fist as the other dropped to his knees, trembling with fear. She didn't have time to explain anything; it was better if they were subdued. She pointed to the guard on his knees, and his eyes went wide in fear. Livia's reputation for being the most proficient fighter in the galactic center preceded her wherever she went. He immediately dropped face down, begging for mercy. She stepped over him.

"This way. Civil war be damned. I'm taking the stage," Livia announced as she raced forward, leading them toward two colossal metal filigree etched doors.

As they neared, Livia lifted her eyes to a scanner and after a beep, the doors slowly slid into the wall. On the other side of the doors, they found the chamber floor and a podium with the First Human's speaker standing at it. They squeezed through the opening before it finished opening, disrupting the gathered assembly. Livia took large powerful strides as she headed toward the speaker in the center.

"Stop. Princess Livia, you were not scheduled for today. You must follow protocol and file your grievance first," the robed, stomping human council member argued as she took her last few steps up to him.

Shoving him from his place, the rather robust man fell with a grunt on his well –cushioned behind next to the podium as Livia climbed to face the microphone. She turned back one last time before speaking, spotting the empress herself standing in the open doorway of the chamber floor. The vitriol in the Empress's gaze made Livia gleeful.

"My father and his chosen heir Lucas are both dead. I am now *King* Livia Claudius of Aduro. Council Members of the UTC Chamber, I have urgent, sorrowful news. Life in the galaxy has been a victim of a crime I can only describe as a viral manipulation of evolution resulting in the calculated annihilation of a planet's intended origin species. We discovered proof that the First Humans spread a virus throughout life producing planets in the galaxy programed to wipe out the original higher species in any stage of development. Instead of the intended species coming to fruition as the higher being for the planet, the virus triggers the evolution of the human species. The Iungo President, Ozias Green will detail the rest of the findings." Uneasy murmurs rippled across the chamber.

Oz swapped places with Livia, winking at her on his way up. He approached the podium and noticed how many of the numerous council members shifted uncomfortably in their seats. Good. He hoped they were sweating.

"Council members of the UTC Chamber, I am Ozias Green, President of the Iungo people. My people's injustices only make up a fraction of the horrors inflicted upon the countless victims of the First Humans. They have committed the crime of evolutionary annihilation against a known one hundred and eight worlds with each planet's respective origin species falling victim to a total genocide of their kind. The leaders of the First Humans and the Empress knew all of this and have fought to keep it a secret. Their battle was not simply with my people, the Iungo. They waged war on truth, and we simply chose to fight back. We found the abandoned planet of Janus, which proved to be the lost planet of Genus. The system star was just beginning its red giant phase, and nowhere near the total darkness they claim. What we discovered there was a shattering truth begging to be found. Not only are the First Humans *not* an origin species, but they also committed a total species extermination against their own creators."

Standing and shouting, the members of the council broke into an uproar as Oz turned to search the doorway of the chamber. The place where the empress and her guard of First Human soldiers stood was now empty. When he turned back, the chamber leader was banging his gavel for quiet, and the chamber calmed. One of the balconies was shining brightly.

"Do you have unyielding testable evidence to prove all these preposterous claims?" the human man asked from the microphone in the illuminated suite.

With a broad smile brightening his face, Oz asserted, "We have all the evidence you need as well as the location of the source. That is if your empress didn't just take off to destroy the rest of the evidence. You may want to track her down. I believe she has fled during my speech."

Frantically searching the chamber, the council members exploded in another tempest before one of Livia's Aduro representatives stood up and yelled a masculine voice, "Order!"

A woman on the same balcony approached the microphone and a smooth feminine voice demanded, "Order! You will calm yourselves. We will evaluate the evidence for authenticity and reconvene shortly."

Oz stepped down from the podium as someone in a hooded cloak materialized seemingly out of nowhere to collect their evidence files. Jacob handed over the drive, and the lithe, cloaked person scurried off into a dark doorway. The door descended, camouflaging the passageway.

Livia wedged her way into the huddled group and whispered, "This might take a while. If they wish, we could be stalled here for up to three days while they deliberate. If they are feeling kind or particularly afraid, we may have an answer in a few hours. Let's move to my suite for some rest."

They followed Livia up to the fifth floor where her senators lived. When she approached, the door slid away and a thin man with deep set green eyes and pointed face stood in the doorway and sharply asked, "Do you want to explain what the fuck is going on *King Claudius*?"

"Move over, Weryl. I don't owe you an explanation, and you know it." Livia replied as she pushed her way past him. "You may want to remember your place."

He dramatically backed against the wall, as if she had shoved him with force.

Behind Weryl, a beautiful woman with a kind face stood in the entryway. She was tall with blonde hair and blue eyes. Livia hugged the woman standing in the foyer, "It's good to see you. How is Weryl acting? Have you had to drop him on his head yet?"

Smiling, she beamed, "He behaves most days, but forget about that. We just received word the evidence has been accepted. We are just waiting on the vote of warrant."

Turning swiftly, Livia introduced her saying to the others, "This is my cousin Halkie."

"I am your cousin, too," Weryl whined wearily with irritation under each word.

Scowling at him, Livia seethed, "You helped talk my father into my marriage to Lucas. I will never forgive you for that."

"If you hadn't married him, he would have killed you before now! Don't you understand I did that to save your fucking life? Did you forget our mothers were best friends?" Weryl's eyes were begging Livia to hear his intent and extend leniency.

"Don't remind me. Shut your gaping hole before I have you re-assigned. You should know, my father was mid fuck with an Iris when I shot him. I *told* you he fucked Irises at the last harvest festival I attended, and you told me I must be seeing things." Livia's gaze remained locked with Weryl's, and she revealed no emotion.

Clearing her throat Halkie interrupted, "We need to review the information and give our vote. What are we voting, King?"

Livia stood regally as she addressed the room, "We are voting for criminal charges to be brought on our current empress and the complicit heads of the First Humans. I am formally nominating myself for empress of the UTC."

Halkie gasped and grinned as wide as she could before she giddily squeaked, "Of course, my King. I just love saying that. Empress sounds even better."

Rolling his eyes Weryl muttered, "Your great grandfather only lost by a few votes the election he ran in when he was *seventy*. He was the closest anyone got to removing a First Human from the empire's top seat. Do you really think they will elect you, a brand new king?"

"Fuck off to somewhere before I feed you to the silver sand worms on Aduro. The way Lucas cried out as he was eaten alive by them will live in my mind as a bittersweet tune of triumph," Livia retorted, a satisfied smirk on her face growing as Weryl's wavering demeanor melted before her eyes.

His brow beginning to sweat in the chilly suite, Weryl sputtered, "Who-o did what to him? Wh-what is a sand worm?!"

"A silver worm that sucks your insides out, or something equally awful, from a bite they make in your skin. I didn't know what was going on exactly, but they thrashed as they were eaten alive," August nonchalantly chimed in as he studiously inspected the tall, open chamber from the balcony.

Weryl turned a paler shade of beige and sat quickly, hanging his head between his legs.

Time crawled as they rested around the room until a chime sounded breaking their uneasy silence. They all turned to look at the blue light now shining on their suite. Everyone rapidly piled onto the balcony, and Halkie took the microphone.

A display shone brightly from the edge of the balcony with the results they had been waiting for.

"Council members of the UTC Chamber, I have received results of the vote. A warrant with reward is now in effect for the capture of our current empress, Fausta Ursus III of the House of Venus, and her immediate council. This is a living warrant only. If she is found dead or killed, the body should be delivered promptly for verification. No reward will be given unless she is breathing and can answer questions. The First Humans will stand trial for their crimes.

"A vote will be conducted to choose the new UTC Emporix. The candidates have been sent to your voting modules. The vote is due in seventy-two hours as is law. Once votes are reviewed and authenticated, the seat will be announced.

"As for the resolution to the evolutionary manipulation

virus and its resulting annihilation of the various primitive stages of animals specifically with the pathways to evolve into higher beings, the science committee chamber chair has decided on a course of action. The UTC will release altered versions of the original viruses that will allow the original species to evolve naturally as was intended on any primitive planets which have not yet developed any stage of humans. These viruses will be programmed to simultaneously halt the manipulation of the evolution of the chimpanzee's development, and they will restart the natural course of evolution toward the respective planet's intended origin species. The science and technology labs now have the files and claim they can synthesize the new virus within three weeks. It can be deployed within six.

"We will reconvene over the implications of the currently developing human planets when a strain of the virus can be created which simultaneously allows the evolution of the intended origin species of the planets in question."

56

PLANET MELIOR – UTC COUNCIL

O z rushed back into the suite from the crowded balcony and braced himself on the wall. It was *over*. They had done it. Stars pranced in his vision as he shut his eyes, squeezing them tight. After a few deep breaths, he felt her presence before him, before his vision cleared.

Jael slid herself under his arm and announced, "I think it's time to celebrate."

All eyes were on him as he faced the quiet room and grinned as he agreed, "Let's get the hell off this miserable planet. The Sarters are expecting us."

"I'll make sure the UTC security teams receive the orders that transport blockers are all deactivated permanently as a gesture of goodwill to begin the process of possible UTC-Iungo treaty negotiations. After what has been uncovered, I doubt it will take more than a request to the security committee," Halkie proposed in her honied voice as they all filed out of the suite and toward the ship. This time they knew they could move leisurely.

As they approached the ship, Amelia and Mercy stood at the end of the stairs, both wearing bright grins. "I'm assuming the Empress is now wanted? You should have seen them running. The empress didn't even look at us as they ran by to reach to their ship. Mercy took a shot on a hunch, but they had some kind of shielding, and it diverted the molten round. Carter said all the top FH command ships have abandoned the UTC command stations and soldier fleets," Mercy gleefully reported as she began climbing the stairs of the ship.

One by one they climbed into the ship, and Oz took his place at the Captain's seat. Signaling to Amelia, he smiled and offered, "I think it's your turn to sit here."

She nodded acceptance and sat down in the captain's seat as he moved next to Jael.

"Carter, take us directly to the Sarter's trading station. It looks like Halkie already lifted the transport block. I've alerted them we are jumping directly into the spaceport," the command burst from Amelia's lips as if she had been waiting her whole life for her moment to lead.

"We will jump in three, two, one." Carter announced, and in seconds they were materializing and attached to the dock of the spaceport.

The airlock door lifted and Destry and Oran stepped foot inside, meeting Oz and Jael.

"If you don't mind, we would love a ride," Destry inquired with a smile.

"No secret transport to the planet this time?" Oz asked, a thrill running through him, one of trust and alliance.

Shaking her head, she explained, "No. You more than earned the right to visit our home world on your own ship.

Are you here to solidify your people joining the Sarter Kingdom? "

He turned to Amelia, giving her the lead, and she answered, "Yes, that's exactly why we are here."

Nodding as she held back her excitement, Destry asserted, "Well, then, I'm sure you don't need to inquire about what our terms will be. Let's jump to Vistalia and draw up a contract. The coordinates have been sent to your ship from the port."

Smiling Amelia replied, "Anything for the friends who have our back."

Having received the information, Carter announced, "Coordinates are entered. Jumping in three, two, one."

Below them Vistalia shined like a verdant jewel placed among a sea of tiny diamonds. The stars were more concentrated here, giving space there an ethereal glow. Destry peered down on her planet from their place suspended in orbit and didn't look away as she speculated, "This could change everything for the galactic center, not just for the Sarter Kingdom. Your transport technology will do more than you have any idea. We will share how ours works in return, but I suspect your design has the power transfers we have been missing for larger scale movement.

"The leaders from all of the Sarter Kingdom planets will be present for the celebration tomorrow night. A few trusted leaders from UTC planets have inquired about the celebration as well. Rest tonight, and then please enjoy yourselves at the salon before the festivities begin tomorrow."

57

SARTER PLANET – SARTER ROYAL PALACE

The drums beat and the melodies of the music resounded through the ballroom occupied with various different species of dancing people. Oz stood next to the glass dome facing the vast forest surrounding the palace. The trees below rustled with building sized reptilian creatures, slowly moving along the ground. One of the massive animals stuck its head up and seemed to peer over at him. It leaned over and began munching on the top of a tree. He was told the brain of the creature was no bigger than a walnut, but he wondered if that was true as he stared into its circular black eyes. It tracked his every move without shifting its head.

Feeling a light tap on his shoulder, he looked behind him to find a human man adorned in regal robes had approached. He abruptly spoke and stumbled over his words, "I-I am King Turius Sarto. I h-had an Iungo, one of your people, who was dearer to me than my own life. I cared for her immensely. I would do anything to have her back. I will pay whatever your price for information about her. She was blue, a sapphire hue. S-She didn't want to leave me. She fought alongside me. The empress took her by force, and I've been searching for her ever since. I'll give you anything to trade, or pay any price, for information about her, or-r even where she could be found. I'll do *anything*."

Oz faced King Sarto solemnly and softly sympathized, "I know the woman you're speaking of. She was my sister. I'm so sorry to have to tell you, but she's gone. She died helping give us the code to the computer on Janus. It was the computer which had information we used to convince the UTC to file the warrant for the empress's arrest. She has potentially saved countless lives. She helped change the entire course of the galactic center. She died a hero."

A ghostly pale fell over King Turius before he whispered, "T-Thank you." Turning, he briskly cut through the crowd, running the last few yards to the door. He burst through the opening of the automatic doors and disappeared from sight.

As Oz peered at the doors slowly closing, he remembered the empress saying something about his sister and the compromised condition she was in when they found her. The empress had been suggesting his sister had been abused. It had *all* been lies. That man had lost a great love. His sister had been cared for, not harmed. It was the last piece, the one unknown he found himself revisiting. This information would to be saved for a conversation with August on a different day. He hoped it would bring him peace, too.

He searched the crowd and spotted Jael, so he joined her as she watched Jacob and Zoe climb onto some kind of flying feathered reptiles just outside. "This is a trip back in time. I saw variations of these creatures in natural science books and in movies. They didn't usually show them with feathers, but nearly all the reptiles I've seen here have them. I guess feathers wouldn't hold up well in fossil records. Sarter's people have long tiny feathers for hair. Have you found one and looked at it?" Jael asked, her eyes filled with wonder.

Oz teased, "Do you always walk around picking up other people's hair off the ground to look at it? That sounds a little creepy-stalker-ish."

With a pointed look, Jael replied, "No, it was scientific observation. I'm not the one who kidnaped an alien in the woods."

He tucked a lock of hair behind his ear and asked, "Do you remember when you made me open my mouth on the deck? I think you looked in my ear, too."

Jael threw up her hands laughing, "I can't help it! I was curious!"

"I can't lie I was pretty obsessed with the fact you didn't have a tail," Oz admitted.

She peered at him curiously and made a point to ask him about that later.

Destry approached with a frown, "We just received word from Portum, Cinis and Tressa have been reported missing. Pike said a woman helped them on Planet Emendo contacted the Iungo base asking for help. Rungi? She said she found their grandmother dead in their apartment when they were all scheduled for pickup. The old woman died from having her throat slit. Rungi suspects they were taken by a group of First Humans who are enacting revenge."

"Talk to Amelia. She will put our best people on it," Oz directed, deciding it was time to begin deferring responsibility.

Destry leaned her head to the side questioningly, and,

with her sparkling reptilian eyes shining in the light, she asked, "Are you stepping down, Mr. President?"

Smirking, Oz scoffed as he replied, "We have been dreaming of going home, to the treehouse, for what feels like an eternity."

As Jacob and Zoe flew overhead, Jacob could be heard screaming with delight. Oz was fairly sure he had had a little too much of a mood elixir to drink, but he more than earned a wild night of letting loose.

They all laughed at Jacob before Oz continued, "There were a few months at the treehouse that were the happiest of my life. The thought of returning to our home with her, to live out our life. It is a dream come true."

With a kind smile, Destry reached over to lay a hand on the side of his shoulder. "You are an exceptional person. Will we ever see you again?"

"I'm sure we will make our way out of the jade woods, eventually," Oz answered as Jael smiled in agreement.

August threw his arm around Oz as he reminded him, "You better make your way out. We have planets to explore with our mothers. We made promises." Oz nodded in agreement, then August moved along to find Mercy. They had some things to discuss, or rather, he had some apologies to make.

He found Mercy speaking to Oran and asked, "Can I speak to you?"

Smiling, she shifted to face him, "Sure. Oran, will you excuse us please?"

She followed August to a bench at the edge of the dome. They sat down between a pair of trees bent over to accommodate the curve of the dome.

"I'm sorry," August offered, trying to find his words, but as usual, they were failing him.

Mercy stopped him before he could say anything more. "Vida found your tablet. They had to search through it for your work notes. She told Amelia what she found in your notes. Amelia eventually told me during our journey through the mountains. I was angry at first, at everyone, but I understand. I also know our people don't wait for someone to come back. That's not how we survived as a species. We survived because we are resilient. We survived because we never waited for lost love. We moved on and found new love. It's engrained in who we are, just like the connection. "Don't apologize for your honest feelings. You and Livia seem much more compatible than you and I ever were."

August smiled bashfully, "Thank you. It meant the world to see you on the bridge, to see what you had done. You did everything you thought you were afraid of."

"I knew Amelia loved you long before I was taken. I saw how she looked at you and responded to you, and only you. You deserve to be loved the way she loves. I want an invitation if you two marry. Don't think those little wishes didn't sneak through the connection. I know you want a big wedding with a fancy dress like the humans have on Earth."

Mercy slid a hand over her mouth, half-embarrassed, before she admitted, "That worked?!"

They both laughed and watched the landing pad next to the ballroom where Jacob was finally climbing off the flying reptile.

They could hear as Callum stood under him yelling something about him being "Too drunk to keep flying that overgrown lizard!"

PLANET PORTUM

"I want the patio grill here, and the table will go here, so the porch needs to extend at least twenty feet this way," Callum explained as he pointed to various places in the dirt.

Jacob watched intently yet didn't respond.

"Are you even listening? Your mind is back on that damn breakaway-battleship you're building, isn't it? Mother spare me," Callum mumbled to himself as he narrowed his eyes at the area he was pointing at.

"Look, just do exactly what you want, and I will be more than happy with it. I promise. You are an inspired architect, and I know it will be stunning. I saw the original plans for our house, and I know you've changed it over twenty times, but the point remains. I saw the plans for the restaurant with the gardens, and if it's anywhere near as beautiful as that building, I know I will love our home. It's going to be you. I love anything that has your heart in it," he warmly replied.

Callum turned to face him and sought reassurance. "Do you mean that?"

Reaching up and putting his hands on either side of Callum's arms, Jacob admitted, "I should complement you more. I'm sorry. You're one of the most creative, and brightest people I know. I may have been drawn to your unforgiving boldness initially, but your soft heart is what I fell in love with. Long before we could speak you made me realize it was okay to allow myself some piece of goodness. I just now understand that even if we had been separated from one another, our love would have still been worth it. Not a regret, *never a regret*, but a new reason to live and not just exist. Our love is something I could hold onto forever, no matter what happened next. I shouldn't have waited so long to kiss you. I'll never wait that long again." Jacob leaned in and pulled Callum close as he passionately kissed him.

Callum rested his head on Jacob's shoulder as he sighed, "We still have work to do." Furrowing his brow, Callum continued by saying, "You can go to your lab and work on your battleship. I love you, too."

"I'll go back later. I've been meaning to talk to you about something important," Jacob explained, his body stiffening.

Pulling back, Callum worried, "That doesn't sound good."

Smiling and scoffing bashfully at himself, Jacob corrected, "No, it's not anything bad. I just needed an opportunity where I could catch you alone and have your full attention." Peering around the small clearing, he started again, "I guess the middle of the woods where we're building our home is the best place... I wanted to ask you about children. Do you really want to have kids with me?"

Tears already threatened to spill over as Callum squeaked, "Of course I want to have kids with you."

"Good because I already asked Juni, and she said she

would love to be our surrogate. She screamed yes," Jacob beamed with a glowing smile.

With a tear finally streaming down his cheek, he threw his arms around Jacob and cried, "I love you so much. I want little Jacobs so bad!"

After a long embrace, Jacob whispered, "Let's get to town. Sarah is announcing the results of the election."

Throwing his head back to look at Jacob, Callum blurted, "I forgot all about it!"

Rushing through the trees on foot, they made their way to the hover-bikes and climbed on. Once their helmets were in place, they took off for the now bustling town. Some of their people from the UTC Iungo factory planet had moved back, mostly those who were more recently taken. They came to a stop at Sarah's house and both waltzed inside as they had for years.

Sarah and August's father Jay were already sitting on the couch while August was a holo-gram standing in the corner. He was looking exceptionally regal, right down to a sash across his chest. In Latin, it read Claudius. Beside him, a young Iungo dressed in a similar fashion. He stood proud and his sash read, Heir of the Claudius Kingdom. He must be the boy August spoke of, the one who helped them with their coup, Jacob thought.

For this election, there had been candidates from all participating villages and towns. The holo-screen was shining brightly in the small home. The results were being tallied on the screen. Jacob's heart seemed to try to keep up with the racing numbers, no matter how much he told himself he would be happy either way. He had good competition, and he would accept defeat with grace. Okay, now he was just lying to himself. He wanted to win so much it hurt.

"I'm glad you went for VP again. President is too much heat and responsibility," Callum admitted as he wrapped his arm around Jacob's.

The scoring slowly crawled to a stop, but Jacob's heart was still busy mimicking the racing numbers. The suspense was gutting him.

The numbers on the screen awarded Zoe as General, Jacob was re-elected Vice President, and Amelia was the new Iungo President. A glimmer of hope blossomed, for he had done it. He had been rightfully elected.

Sarah and Callum both yelled in unison, wrapping their arms around Jacob as his mind calculated away.

PLANET PORTUM – IUNGO BASE

After reading the results on the screen, Amelia turned to Mercy and leaned her back and met her lips. The lab technicians all quietly filed out to give Mercy and Amelia privacy after her win.

There had been presidential competition from a village on the other side of the mountain, the one she had been from, but she had been elected president by a ten percent margin. Her heart was still racing from the results. Since Livia was elected Empress, the future seemed infinitely brighter.

"I knew you would win," Mercy insisted, just as confidently as she had before the results were revealed.

"The construction crew is almost finished with the Iungo Presidential house. Let's go see how much they have left. If they are staying on schedule, we should probably start packing soon," Amelia explained as she leaned Mercy upright.

Alight with joy, Mercy replied, "I would love to."

They strolled out of the base arm in arm, and Mercy

turned to look back at the massive building being constructed on top of the cave. The Sarters' reptilian people, a horned reptilian people she hadn't seen before, along with some of the Plana people, could be seen working alongside their own Iungo people. People from all over the Sarters' kingdom had found out about what their people had done, and the response was overwhelming. When news spread, many of their individual governments sent aid or volunteers. They had even received a drone transport from a K'hornibus warlord on the planet K'hurian. The frame was almost completed, and Mercy could see the geometric shape taking form. It would be a stunning design, made to catch the light of the auras and promote the growth of indoor plants. After all, it was Callum's design, so she wasn't surprised it fit well in the natural environment, yet remained grand, like a raw diamond, unrefined, yet glorious in its own right.

A cargo transport pulled up and materials were unloaded to pack up the caves. They had discovered the positive polar charge on the surface gave anything below the surface a negative charge. This was what had been draining their seemingly limitless energy H-cell batteries. When the science team discovered it, they named it the Luna phenomenon, and the decision was made to permanently shut down the base. The former base would become a cold storage facility for their new Science and Technology Lab.

A transport lifted off with an uprooted tree, large metal claws holding the trunk below the craft. Any trees in the way of the project were all to be replanted in sparse areas. She watched as the transport flew away as if the massive tree was weightless. Loose leaves floated to the ground as it disappeared in the distance.

Climbing on their hover-bikes, they slid their helmets on

and took off for their soon-to-be home. The hover-tech was light years better than those awful foul, wheeled vehicles on Emendo. They were like the trucks and cars on Jael's world, repulsive things. Emendo was one place Mercy never wanted to see again, once was too much. "I am so glad we joined the Sarter Kingdom. I would hate to have to go back to Emendo. Any time soon, anyway," Mercy admitted as she waited on Amelia to catch up on her bike.

"Speaking of the UTC, Livia's legal counsel found a loophole in their ancient UTC contract. They are still a UTC planet until the contract dissolves in another few thousand years, but they are no longer bound to sell their ore at the previously negotiated rate and only to the UTC. Livia's line just became the richest human royal line in the galactic center, and she has named a young Iungo boy as her heir. She successfully shifted power directly to herself and the Iungo in a single, brilliant move. The shift in power has already affected votes in the UTC council. We are planning on visiting them on a diplomatic trip. We need to establish a strong relationship with the new UTC Empress. I am still not surprised she won by a such a spread. We could really use a friend like her to help mend the divide in the galactic center," Amelia explained, as they weaved through a thick section of trees along a marked path.

"Oh, Amelia! Look!" Mercy pointed ahead of them as they slowed.

In a small clearing, surrounded by tall oak trees was an inviting, natural setting home. The winding pathway interweaved the sprawling foliage creating a picturesque garden, filled with colorful flowers from the woods, except for those little yellow ones, she noticed.

Mercy pulled to a stop, and it struck her that the house

was finished. She tossed her helmet onto her hover-bike as she pounced onto the path. She had no patience to wait for Amelia. When she reached to the front door, it opened on its own, sliding into the walls on either side. The entryway had several large potted plants and colorful, abstract art on the walls. As Mercy found her way into the living room, she tilted her head up and found a glass ceiling revealing a breathtaking scene of the auras which lit their planet. Her unbound, straight hair slid from her shoulders. Awestruck by the view, she hadn't noticed when Amelia came up behind her. Turning around, she found Amelia standing with something in between her fingers.

"Mercy, I fell in love with you so easily, and I have wanted to ask you this for so long. Will you be my wife?" she asked with love burning in her eyes.

In true Mercy fashion, she squealed at the top of her lungs with her tail straight out behind her. Amelia braced herself, but still had to take a few steps back when Mercy leapt onto her. The simple silver filigree ring went flying as Mercy crashed her lips onto Amelia's. She kissed Amelia until both were breathless.

Leaning her head back, Mercy cried out, "Yes! More than anything, yes! I want a big wedding!"

Amelia leaned Mercy back and smiled against her lips, "Anything for you."

60

PLANET ADURO – CLAUDIUS ROYAL PALACE

Running down the open walkway, August was on his third lap of the palace, and he was sure it was more than the mere mile Livia *swore* it was. He would see if the doctor had at a distance tracker in all the little gadgets kept in the back of his medical office. Sweat dripped down his face and into his eyes as he looked around the gardens. He was still in disbelief they had overthrown the former Claudius line and Livia was now Empress.

Chris walked up justifying August stopping his run, and reported, "Construction on the city is ahead of schedule. The sand piers are already poured and set. They are dropping the foundations later today. You have a training session with the guard recruits tomorrow morning.

"Also, the doctor said he spoke to Amelia and can have your sleep gene switched back off. He has tail reconstructive surgery all day today, so he said come by tomorrow after your morning training."

"Thanks, kid. You sound more like Livia every day.

Don't you want to go to Portum and stay with my parents for a while? Somewhere there are other kids your age. You could just be a normal kid before more of our people move here," August suggested, feeling sorrow churn over the boy and how his life started.

Chris had never been given the chance to run freely, and that was all August could think about. His time with his friends in the woods of Portum were still some of his favorite memories.

"The day I saw you, I thought you were my dad. I knew deep down you weren't, but you look so much like him I just decided it was the truth. I don't want to go yet. I do want to visit, but I want to stay with you for now. When I go, it will be like parents bringing their kids to see their grandparents," Chris admitted a smile growing on his face as he thought about the many stories about Sarah. His favorite story was when she burned down that mean man's garden. She had found fresh fruit at her door for months.

Trying to dam the tears threatening to spill over, August relented, "I guess Livia and I will just have to provide a place in the palace for children needing homes so you can have some company."

"You mean steal back the exploited group of non-human UTC genetically engineered children from those pirate traffickers Livia found out about last week?" Chris asked, a look of skepticism on his face.

August protested, "I didn't say that, and you sound far too grown-up. We need more kids for you to play with."

Smiling, Chris left August to turn and watch the construction outside. Losing track of time, he intently watched as one of the freshly delivered, Iungo built hover-transports stopped over the pier and slid the long metal support into the polymer filled hole. Bedrock was found a few miles down under the dunes, so the city would rest on a sea of piers anchored to a single massive support.

A hand slid up his back, a hand he knew, a hand he loved. Turning and facing Livia, he smiled at her. Her presence thrilled him like nothing he had ever experienced. "The council decided on wages and a structure for the economy, as well as sorted out their own government. After I told them they have free reign to figure it out and present it to us, they took off with it. They're holding an election next week. Only ten people want to return to Portum, but around a hundred thousand want to move here from Sclavus Six. We will have a bustling planet with a booming economy by the end of this year. The allure of wanting to live in a new settlement on Aduro was too enticing for some, I guess. I heard Sclavus Six is a lush planet with immense natural resources. Your people are quite wealthy now," Livia updated as she slid her hand up and down August's back.

"My people were held back for so long, this feels like the rubber band has finally snapped back, and we are being catapulted into our future," August admitted, his eyes fixed on the horizon.

With her hand on his shoulder, she guided August to face her and insisted, "I need you to sign the royal consort papers."

"Are you afraid I'm going to get into trouble and need Claudius Royal immunity?" August asked.

"Yes, no question," Livia firmly stated, deviously smiling at him as he finally met her eyes.

He took her face into his hands and as their lips met, a

thrill slithered down his spine at the adventures he would have with this glorious woman, and oh, the way his heart sung when she was near. This was everything he could have ever wished for.

61

PLANET PORTUM

The lift was silent as Jael rose to the first floor of the treehouse. The door opened, and she stepped out, catching her toe on the seam. It was still taking some adjusting. It was a nice convenience, but she would have been fine with it the way it had been before. Their home had been upgraded over the last few months they had been home. It was now four stories and had a wrap-around porch on every level.

The new high-tech kitchen gleamed as she lay her bag of freshly picked fruit from the orchard on the counter. The fire was burning steadily in the fireplace, and she smiled at the little divot in the wood with a bit of sap slowly dripping down the wall. A moment frozen in time, one she refused to let Oz fix. Her electronic hand whirred as she unlocked it and set it on its charging port. She blew on her wrist where the implanted prosthetic had been connected. Severing the nerve connection always sent an odd sensation up her arm. She wasn't sure why she blew on it, but it seemed to help.

Wondering where Oz was, she used the lift and searched

the second level where their new office was. Oz had been working on a project with the Sarters' kingdom to share the seeds from their planet with some of the dimly lit star systems. Portum's plants seemed to grow in nearly any low light and high radiation environments, making it possible to grow food even in the most inhospitable places. His work also encompassed Aduro's need. They had just received a handsome bio-terraforming grant from the Claudius Kingdom. Peering around the corner, she noticed the paper cabinet stood cracked open. She inspected the cabinet closer and found Oz's notebook and one of his ink wells missing.

Being back at their treehouse, after everything they had been through, was something like a dream, and Jael found herself waiting to wake up. The scent of the air, the taste of the fruit, and the warmth of their home was enough to over-whelm her with joy. The nightmares still woke her occasion-ally, but Oz always held her until she went back to sleep. They had fought for this, all of it, their freedom and their lives. She took in her beautiful home and smiled. It had all been worth it.

A cooler than normal breeze through the window had her padding over to shut it then went to check the weather on the communication panel mounted on the wall. A small rainstorm was approaching and would be there in an hour. She still had plenty of time.

She paused at their portrait hanging on the wall. Oz had insisted they take portraits for their home as soon as they arrived on Portum from Vistalia. He always knew the best ways to make her feel loved. She had always wanted a family portrait to hang up, but never thought she would have a family. Now that she did, her heart sang with joy. The sweet scent of her home filled her lungs, and she sighed, filled with a sense of comfort.

Rew scurried down the hallway, a strip of silk stuck to one of her back legs causing her to wiggle it in the air as she ran. Little chirps of glee told Jael she was headed for her fruit bowl as she flew by and halted abruptly in the lift for a ride down. As it turned out, teaching a tarantula how to use a lift wasn't all that difficult. Rew always took the shortest path to food, so it only took showing her once.

Hearing a creak in the wood from far above, Jael headed over to the lift after Rew had descended. Bypassing all the bedrooms on the third and fourth floor, she knew where he was. As the lift took her to the roof deck, she wondered what Oz was working on. He had taken up writing and was documenting the last few wild years of their life. Instead of using all the high-tech computers and software they had, he chose to continue using his pens and inks. They had paper delivered by drones every week to keep up with his writing. There was no way Rew could keep up with his demand for silk stiffened by sap, especially with Mercy always needing her specific tan color for clothing projects.

Seeing him sitting with his back to her at the table across the deck, Jael made her way over. Per his new usual, he was hard at work, writing away as the breeze whistled through the trees. He bat away a fly, but didn't look over as she approached with near silent footsteps. Laying her hand on his shoulder, she read his words. He was detailing their first few months at the treehouse, specifically when Jael thought Rew was attacking Oz. He was laughing even as he wrote, and she would never forget the sound of his laugh that day.

Her right hand slid down his bare, muscled arm and he leaned into her touch. Peering down at the little squeeze bottle he had been using to refill his pen reservoir, Jael had one of her brilliant ideas. Nonchalantly taking the little squirt bottle in her hand, she headed to the edge of the deck. They had just installed an angled ladder for her to be able to climb to the treetops as easily she used to. She held up the little bottle to the auras to see the level of the ink. It was full, *perfect*, she thought.

Turning and watching Oz, she counted to three before squirting him in the face with ink before flying up the angled ladder. Grunting, Oz had to wipe his face before he could run, and it had bought Jael just enough time to reach the top of the ladder. Not daring to peek behind her, she sprinted across the treetops as swiftly as her legs would carry her. Only a few moments passed before she could hear his pounding, heavy steps behind her, the thrill of the chase pumping through her veins like a raging fire.

The first rumbles of thunder in the distance had Jael turning her head to see the rolling clouds light up. In her moment of distraction, Oz made his move. He slammed into her. Taking her to the ground. The oxygen left her lungs as they rolled several feet in a heap of arms and legs. The sound of her clothes, being ripped off her body was music to her ears.

Oz had her bare body flipped over in less than a second and was already spreading her thighs. Licking her from under her knees to her neck, Oz growled softly in her ear when he reached her face. His fangs grazed her jaw line as his hot breath searing her neck made her toes curl. Tilting her head back in an invitation, his hand slid up her side to cup her full breast. Leaning down, Oz took her nipple into his mouth and rolled his tongue, pulling a whimper of delight from Jael. Her heart raced as he moved down her body and settled his face between her legs. His twirling, sucking, and nipping at her bud had her arching her back and pulling at her loose curls. He shoved her down with his hand around her neck to keep her still. As the waves of pleasure neared, a moan stuck in her throat and a gasp barely escaped. As she shattered into a million jagged pieces, her body shook.

Oz moved to settle over her, pulling her under him and spreading her thighs. Entering her in one thrust, he groaned as he leaned his head back. Her heat was his paradise, and he wanted to bury himself there forever. Moving in her feverishly, he knew it wasn't going to be long when the clicks bubbled up in his throat and their song flew from his mouth.

Looking into his eyes as he exploded within her, Jael knew she had found her little slice of heaven.

With greying hair and fine lines beginning around her eyes, Jael squinted as she peered up at the sun. A bright, yellow star she had not seen in over thirty years. It was more orange now from the haze. The sky was dingier than she remembered, and the people grim.

Earth had changed substantially. Global warming had killed off many of the animals she remembered, but it was still essentially the same place. A third world war had devastated the planet, and it was still recovering. Oz had made Jael take some radiation medication before they transported down because the levels in the area they were visiting were hot spots. The genetic enhancements Livia had given her were enough to extend her life by many years, but not nearly enough to make her resistant to radiation.

She knew the reprogrammed UTC virus had been deployed in the atmosphere over twenty-five years prior. It had begun the process of allowing the origin creature, suspected to be a Sarter species to develop a branch from a living genetic relative and follow its intended path.

The human worlds with modern humans were given viruses to only affect the natural origin species growth halting the living human's progress. The line had to be drawn somewhere, and the council didn't feel it was ethical to reverse any modern human's course. *Typical for the UTC to still vote in favor of the humans, even after all the harm they had done.*

Oz wiggled his leg trying to keep his tail straight and hoped his coat was long enough to hide the obvious bulge running down his pant leg.

"The building is around the corner. You can let your tail out when we go in her room." Jael offered as she gave Oz a sly smile.

"That would require me taking my pants off. I'll pass," Oz replied. He was wearing tan flesh-colored makeup on his face making him look like a human man. Jael hated it and couldn't wait to see his green skin again. She genuinely thought it was going to be a fun experience seeing him human, but it was honestly unnerving.

By 2053 Earth had not developed space travel technology, nor had they made contact with any alien species. Jael had long wondered if the grant program to develop a space travel engine had worked, but it was clear to her it had not.

They continued around the corner and approached double doors with a sign above that read, "Yancey's Assistive Care Center."

"Do you think she will remember you?" Oz asked, trying not to open his mouth wide enough to show his fangs.

Without turning around, Jael answered, "Of course. She would never forget me."

A man in a black trench coat pushed between them, and Oz narrowed his eyes at him. The man turned around and hissed at Oz, showing a set of vampire teeth in his mouth. He scoffed at the man's fake fangs and loosened up a bit. He guessed no one would believe his teeth were real anyway. Shifting his focus back to Jael, he reached over and opened the door to the building for her.

At the front desk, Jael smiled at the woman who was clearly not the receptionist and asked, "Hello. Can you tell me where room 42 is?"

A young woman with deep-tan skin and a tag that read, "Resi Mikeler, MD" looked up from shuffling through papers and she answered, "Take a left, and it's on your right at the end of the hallway. Visiting hours are not over until seven, but she does have her transfusion scheduled at five."

"We won't be staying long, just passing through to say hello," Jael replied as she pulled her coat closed in the chilly facility.

The lady grinned kindly as she replied, "Have a nice visit."

Making their way down the hallway, Oz curiously asked, "Do all humans dump their elderly off for other people to care for them?"

"A lot of them do. You have those meds Amelia gave us in your pocket, right?" Jael asked as she eyed him over her shoulder.

Oz nodded he had them as he spotted room 42, "There it is."

The name on the door read, Penelope Orvite.

Peering in the window on the door, Jael saw the lightly aging, grey-haired woman sitting in the hospital bed with several monitors hooked up to her. The beeps from the machines didn't seem to bother her as she contently read from her book.

Jael almost laughed aloud when she read the name of the book, *The Cute Alien in Apartment 7*.

Knocking first, she opened the door, and the woman dropped her book. Her big brown eyes widened as her mouth dropped open in shock.

"Sis," was all she could mutter as Jael and Oz came in and shut the door.

As Jael approached the bed and sat down in the chair next to her old friend, she grinned, "You are *never* going to believe what happened."

Hours passed as the three discussed Jael and Oz's journey before Jael revealed, "It turns out you are my sister after all. Amelia ordered an investigation into the remaining children from the group I was created alongside, and I saw your picture in the list of children. It took many years to find you, but I am so glad we did. We brought a treatment for your blood disorder."

"What do you plan on doing next?" Penelope asked as she squeezed Jael's hand.

Jael met her eyes and asked, "That depends. Are you up for a little space travel, and possibly some galactic adventures? Age appropriate, of course."

Penelope laughed and tossed her covers away as she asked, "Can I have a hot alien boyfriend too? Where is that treatment? Let's get out of here!"

ABOUT THE AUTHOR

Lauren Logan is a neurodivergent, disabled science fiction romance author from North Texas. After high school and junior college, she attended the University of North Texas and studied Psychology and History. She met her husband in 2008, married in 2010, and they now have two little boys. They all enjoy watching science programs about astronomy as well as staying caught up on the latest Star Trek episodes.

In 2015 Lauren developed a passion for hair and began a journey that would lead her to hair school in her thirties. She specialized in vivid color and within a year and a half she had been nominated as a top 100 pastel colorist in the Behind

The Chair global hair awards. Unfortunately, the ultimate hair honor had come too late. A few months before her nomination was announced, Lauren had been forced to quit her dream career as a vivid hair colorist. The loss was devastating and she fell into a dark place.

November of 2020, Lauren was formally diagnosed with an autoimmune disease, Rheumatoid Arthritis. The disease course is aggressive and effects nearly all of her major joints, as well as both hands and feet. She has developed deformities in her fingers, making any chance of regaining her former hair career impossible. On rainy days you can often see her walking with a cane because the changing weather can bring on a flare. Since her diagnosis, she spends much of her time unable to leave her bed due to the constant pain and fatigue. The medication she is prescribed leaves her immunocompromised as well as having many difficult side effects.

Refusing to let her disability steal her ambition and kill her determination, Lauren began writing at the beginning of April, 2022. Over the course of one year, she completed two full length Sci-fi novels. Since the completion of the Reticere Series, she is now working on several stand alone novels in the same universe. Writing gives her hope and being an author gives her a future. She pours everything she is into her stories and she hopes you love them as much as she does.

For more information visit:
www.AuthorLaurenLogan.com

facebook.com/authorlaurenlogan
instagram.com/LaurenLoganArt
tiktok.com/@lauren.logan